EOS

DAWN OF THE ATLANTIS GRAIL

BOOK 1

VERA NAZARIAN

COPYRIGHT PAGE

EOS
(Dawn of the Atlantis Grail, Book One)
Vera Nazarian

Cover Design (created in 2020) by James, GoOnWrite.com
Original Logo created by Vera Nazarian incorporated in design.
No AI software was used in the creation of this cover or book.

August 5, 2025
FIRST EDITION

Trade Hardcover - ISBN: 978-1-60762-198-0
Trade Paperback - ISBN: 978-1-60762-199-7

Published by Norilana Books
P. O. Box 209, Highgate Center, VT 05459-0209, USA
https://www.norilana.com/

Printed and bound by Ingram Lightning Source LLC.

Australia: Ingram Content Group AU Pty Ltd, Melbourne, Victoria. US: Lightning Source LLC, La Vergne, Tennessee / Allentown, Pennsylvania / Jackson, Tennessee, United States. UK: Lightning Source UK Ltd, Milton Keynes, United Kingdom. Europe: Lightning Source UK Ltd, with facilities in Germany, France, and Spain.

The authorized representative in the European Economic Area is Lightning Source France, 1 Av. Johannes Gutenberg, 78310 Maurepas, France. compliance@lightningsource.fr

EOS

DAWN OF THE
ATLANTIS GRAIL

Book One

VERA NAZARIAN

For Susan Franzblau

With love, gratitude, friendship,
and immense appreciation, always.

AUTHOR'S NOTE

The following terms for time and temporal intervals are used in the series *Dawn of the Atlantis Grail*:

"of Ra" is equivalent to AM.
"of Khe" is equivalent to PM.

"Daydream" is equivalent to minute.
"Heartbeat" is equivalent to second.

CHAPTER
ONE

Earth, 10,504 B.C.E.

January / Month of Setaet, 14th Day.
98 days until Impact.

Before the world falls apart, before the gods send us death and destruction, it all begins quietly . . . with mushrooms.

I chop mushrooms.

I have only one accursed job, and it is dreary, monotonous, and without end.

It's not even dawn when my daily shift begins in the warehouse district of Poseidon—great City of Sacred Circles, Imperial Seat of all power of Atlantis—in one of the immense, climate-controlled kitchen pantries of Chiprahat Exquisite Foods.

From the dismal darkness of fourth hour of Ra until noon, I stand leaning over a long work table. It is lined with industrial cutting boards, racks of cook knives of all sizes, and enormous wooden bowls filled with different fungi varieties.

The mushrooms range from the cheapest, commonplace round buttons and many-headed wild bunches, to the ones with slim stalks and wide-brimmed hats, and everything in between.

Some mushrooms are formed in elegant, tiled colonies. Others exhibit patterns of divine symmetry found in sacred temple architecture—so we're told. And yet, it's the most ugly and misshapen ones, resembling earthy lumps, that are priceless. And my duty is to handle all of them accordingly, in their own particular ways.

On both sides of me are other workers, mostly women, girls, and underage boys. And we constantly elbow each other by accident, since we're packed together like locusts, with little room to move. Minor accidents happen but, because we deal with sharp knives, everyone soon learns to handle their cutters with skill.

You either learn precision and dexterity or lose this job. That's because the workroom is *sterile* (something akin to being thoroughly cleansed by the gods) and there are strict rules. Cool, moist air, of a precise temperature conducive to mushroom well-being (and fortunately, ours) is pumped into the room. We all have to be cleansed at the entrance and wear uniform aprons and hair caps of strange, fancy linen.

Anyone who cuts themselves enough to draw blood has to abandon their cutting board and contaminated batch of mushrooms, leave the shift, and lose the remaining day's pay. Yes, you can come back the next day with a proper sterile bandage, but you've just earned your first reprimand. Each worker only gets three before they're dismissed permanently.

The pantry is brightly lit with overhead orb lights. A few hovering orbs can be called at need to provide focused, bright illumination during particularly delicate tasks. However, they are annoying, since they tend to float near your face and bump the top of your head like low-hanging fruit, so I don't bother.

The thick smell of loamy, pungent earth, rich with mycelium spores, fills my nostrils every time I enter the pantry. Overseers stroll through the room every so often, observing us work, and needlessly reminding us to pick up the speed, to meet our quotas.

Upon the hour, every hour (announced loudly by the overseers), delivery workers arrive from the specialty mushroom farms and grow-houses with fresh new containers to refill the dwindling contents of our bowls. They remove our finished chopped batches.

Accursed, never-ending mountains of mushrooms. . . . Bastet, forgive me for thinking ill of my blessed source of livelihood.

Blessed mushrooms. (Is that better, Holy Bast?)

Once sorted, a few remain here on the storage shelves for aging and drying. The rest are taken away from the facility. Some will go to the local exclusive, high-end eateries to be prepared into artisanal delicacies for the wealthy restaurant and grocery patrons. Others end up in the industrial kitchens next door for the mass production stage. Of their final fates, I am not quite certain. . . .

By the end of my shift, not only are my wrists and fingers in pain, my back aching, but my lungs are choked with the pungent mushroom miasma which fills the room. Why don't they use automated machinery to cut these precious and accursed things, one wonders? Because human labor is cheaper than the proper upkeep of industrial tech.

And so, the girls and women around me moan with weariness as we clean up for the day, put away our knives, and prepare the work surfaces for the second shift that will arrive here at first hour of Khe and stay until the night darkness of ninth hour.

That darkness is inevitable. Whichever shift you get, you either arrive with it or depart into it. Often, we curse our fates that we must work the darkness shifts, just as much as we thank the gods for giving us free employment in an air-conditioned room, as opposed to serfdom or slavery.

In addition, many of us curse the enforcement of the new Rules of Humane Consumption that require the whole of Poseidon's Sacred Circles and indeed, the whole mortal world, to only consume plants—fruits and vegetables, fungi, legumes, grains, and the seeds of the earth.

Humanity is no longer permitted to eat meat.

Hence, the mushrooms, a rich source of flavorful *protein* to substitute the flesh of beasts and cover our *nutritional needs.* What is "protein?" What are "nutritional needs?" Supposedly, it's what alleviates hunger and keeps us alive.

I know little about it, only what we've been told by the learned ones—the singing voice techs who run all the machines and technology of *Atlantida* on behalf of the noble elites and the Imperial Kassiopei Dynasty. I often wish I knew more, but then, as Grandmother says, with most things in this world, I would probably end up knowing just enough to regret it. Besides, schools are not for the likes of us.

And neither are mushrooms.

EVERYTHING STARTED JUST a few years ago when *they* arrived—the gods.

And by "gods" I don't mean our current divine rulers, the Imperial Kassiopei (may their ancient Dynasty Name be Eternally Blessed, as far back and forward as it goes, unto the Ages), but the *others.*

From the sky. . . .

These nameless others, golden gods made of pure light, dropped from the vault of Ra's heaven like flaming stars and taught us the true ways—the standards of goodness and virtue.

"Taught" is the wrong word. They forcefully insisted we

make the changes in our lives and *return to infinite clarity* (whatever that means), upon pain of punishment and destruction. Which they swiftly demonstrated when anyone disobeyed.

Explosions . . . screams of agony . . . people incinerated . . . buildings turned to dust. . . .

Even our divine Imperial rulers had to pay heed to them, since they too are only mortal men like the rest of us, regardless of what the priests teach.

Holy Bast, was it only four years ago?

Feels like it's been a lifetime since the last time I ate a proper bite of goat meat stew or skewered and charred pieces of lamb. Not even rabbit or rodent flesh is allowed. No fish from the ocean, no insects, nothing that moves of its own accord or visibly suffers when killed or harvested. And least of all, bulls or cows. Those were already half-sacred, and the occasional partaking of their flesh was reserved for the rich and noble, even before the golden gods upturned our world.

Amurabia, my Grandmother, insists it has indeed been one fourth of my lifetime since the golden gods came. I can only count on my fingers and toes, so I'm not quite sure what that means as far as my own age.

I might be seventeen winters but only sixteen summers, because I was born soon after harvest time, at the end of the month of Hekaet—which, according to Amurabia, makes me sixteen years old (ten fingers and six toes; that much is certain).

All I know is that I may already be of an age to marry, which sickens me. I dread the thought of leaving our poor but familiar home. I would be leaving Amurabia and little Urumer, my seven-year-old baby brother, and the stupid, useless Guzum, our misfortunate Father whose name I prefer to say as few times as possible.

As a married woman, I would be going with some smelly goat of a man to live in a strange hovel with his family and clean up his filth after him . . . in addition to letting him rut inside me and fill me with pitiful children.

So instead, I choose to chop (and carve, and grate, and eviscerate) mushrooms—for which I thank Bast and praise Bast (and occasionally misuse her name during cursing; forgive me, Holy Bastet, Thou Whose Glory Shines Brightly).

And I remind myself of my fortune every time I wake up in the abysmal pre-morning darkness and hurry through the treacherous streets in the outermost Circles of Poseidon, traveling inward to Circle Eight and the sprawling Chiprahat building. The alternative to chopping mushrooms would be a much darker fate.

I know it will catch up with me at some point. Yes, I will be sold to a smelly man-goat or boy-goat . . . but not just yet.

Amurabia is still *mam-ra*, still the mistress of our household, no matter that it's tiny and impoverished, and my pathetic Father must listen to her or be denied the sharing of our home.

Since my Mother, Eigeti, became deathly ill and boarded the Depet of Eternity during last year's great plague, he has no claims left upon us. As a provider he is sadly lacking, and his random work in the markets is as unreliable as the weather outside Poseidon's outer Circle boundary. We're lucky if he brings in a single metal coin every three days.

Amurabia would have to choose to sell me herself, and she would not do so, I'm certain, since she cherishes us dearly. My little brother and myself are all that remains of Eigeti—beloved Eige, her departed daughter.

And besides, both Urumer and I work well, and we bring in metal coins every day. I do the mushrooms while Uru runs errands around the marketplace districts on foot or using his cheap hoverboard. Amurabia would be an old fool to dismiss either of us for a one-time lump sum. And if she is gone, and it remains up to my no-good Father, he might still choose to rely on my steady earnings.

Why do I dwell on all this? Am I worried? Not in the least . . . at least for now. I trust the secure household of my Grandmother (may she live longer than the Imperator—Holy Bastet, hear me; I spit three times upon the ground to distract the evil *sha* eye). And I am confident of the solid meal we have every day as a family.

All things considered, the mushroom work is tolerable. Admittedly, at some point, I hope to actually *taste* for myself the miraculous *mushroom meat* they make for the noble and rich. Sadly, I've never eaten mushrooms, despite knowing every fungus variety and precisely how to handle each kind.

Furthermore, I've never stolen a single mushroom, even though some girls who work my shift have done so, I'm certain (such as Jigudin or the shameless Labaat who has a hidden pouch sewn in her skirt) because I cannot risk this job. And because . . . I don't steal. It's a matter of pride in my family; Grandmother taught me and Uru well. We may be poor, but we never stoop to the dishonor.

Thus, our own protein needs are met by commonplace beans, peas, lentils, and grains. And our honor remains intact.

Until today.

Today is when everything changes.

And it's all my fault.

ACTUALLY, the fault lies in my propensity to daydream and make up stupid stories in my head, even as I work, which distracts me.

I'm conscientious and quick with my fingers, but the monotony of moving the knife puts me in a stupid daze.

Luckily, the knife motions have become second-nature, and I've never cut myself. But I spend most of my shift chopping in a dream.

Such as now. . . .

Sometimes, I pretend I'm a skilled warrior, going to battle with supernatural enemies whose flesh is formed of mushrooms, so I can defeat them with a few carefully placed slices. I focus on each mushroom I'm handling and visualize each as a tiny soldier in miniature armies.

Die, you filthy, mangy minion of shaitunaat!

The many-headed, tiny mushroom clusters become military divisions of hovering chariots out of ancient legend. Carefully, I chop off each limb, separating them from the great mycelium network that connects them all beneath the earth. And that's how I defeat the monstrous *sha* from the underworld.

Die, you who are most foul, with the unholy breath of jackals!

These pieces I arrange in funeral pyres (storage containers), and pretend they must face the death gods in the subterranean infernos (kitchens).

And when I work with the precious and expensive misshapen lumps of the black *turufili* mushrooms, I imagine frightful and yet sorrowful *nefi* giants who once walked the earth, and how they are turned into running sand by my all-powerful hand (*turufili* must be finely grated, not chopped).

It's what I'm doing right now, this very heartbeat: story-dreaming while awake, barely an hour into my work shift. . . .

Suddenly, I start.

I am pulled out from my nonsense reveries.

My name is being called.

"Semmi!"

I blink and look up, but don't stop moving the *turufili* chunk back and forth against the blade of the grater.

"Semmi, you're bleeding!"

The loud whisperer is Odira, the older woman working directly to my right, whose deep brown skin is several shades darker than my own light brown.

At once I pause. I stare at my fingers, examine the black

lump of fungus (which is worth more than our entire house), the sharp grating surface. "Huh? No, I'm not."

"Yes, you are," Odira continues whispering. She motions with her head to my back.

"Huh? What?" I frown.

"Your moon flow! Check the back of your garments!"

"My *what?* Oh. . . ." At once I twist my waist, turning around in my cramped spot, and glare at the part of my skirt behind me. I see a small red spot forming in the old sackcloth fabric.

Ah, Bast! No, no, not now!

My body has chosen to enact its female function, and somehow I didn't even feel it starting. . . . (In fact, I still don't feel it—*what is happening, Bast?*) At what time during this ungodly morning did I even have time to *sit down* long enough to stain the skirt? Was it when I gulped water and stuffed dried chunks of yesterday's lentil pottage in my mouth?

Regardless, I forgot to note the moon cycle days (because I can't count properly and, to be honest, I can't be bothered to) and haven't worn the bunched rags between my legs as I normally would. What a sorry mess I made! *Bastet!*

Just then, I hear the voice of the shift overseer approaching. "You!" he says. "Stop all work! You are contaminated! Go home and come back next week when the moon flow is over."

"But—" I begin to retort.

This particular overseer is a small, hard-faced man, with a shadow of a sneer around his mouth as he speaks. He's definitely not one of my favorites, and not someone to argue with.

"You are fortunate that we allow common, unskilled girls such as yourself to work here," he reminds me. "You now have one reprimand—your first, as I recall the work records. Remember your great fortune to be employed in this establishment, and go home. If I have to repeat myself, I will give you a second reprimand."

Silently I nod, lower my gaze, and step away from the work table, while the women on both sides give me pitying stares. I've just lost a week's worth of pay due to my own carelessness, and exposed myself to disdain. Women's flow time is considered an unclean time, and any opportunity to remind the men of its existence does not serve any of us well.

Disdain I can live with, but lack of coins?

Ah, Bastet help me!

I LEAVE my industrial apron and hair covering at the doors and exit the sprawling building into the pre-dawn darkness. I spit several times at the dust on the ground of the industrial street, to ward off any evil *sha* spirits that might have decided to attach themselves to me since I'm bleeding.

A cool night wind blows in my face and tugs at my tight curls of hair. Soon, Ra's sacred disk will breach the horizon with light, but the orb lights and occasional live torches still glow—the former with artificial gold, and the latter with living orange flame—in the posts lining the street.

Other large buildings and warehouses make up this lonely industrial row on the outer edge of Sacred Circle Eight, and now I must walk in the dawn twilight, all the way home. No one is out, not even the hovering billboards that begin making their slow sailing passes through the City streets at dawn. For the most part, this area is not on their automated itineraries.

The cheap transport carts don't show up in this district until next hour, and I can't afford fare for a fancy hovering bus without getting paid at the end of my shift. I don't often bother with public transportation, since coins don't come easy. Besides, I love brisk walking, even though it's a long way, and I have to cross a residential Circle and two canal bridges to get to the outskirts where we live—Sacred Circle Ten, also known as Denwen's Pit. We locals refer to our portion of the Circle as the

Armpit. (There's also the Crotch, located directly on the opposite side, but we don't talk about it).

Amurabia is going to be so disappointed in me today.

Not as much as I am with myself.

I HURRY along the mostly lonely street. It's almost dawn now, sometime between shifts, and those who work in this district are either already at their worksites, or else they haven't begun to arrive yet. Fortunately, it's not too dangerous to be out and about here and besides, I can run like the wind, and I dare anyone to catch me.

As I'm about to pass one alley, however, I hear uncommon noise up ahead. It's particularly dark here, midway between two distant light posts illuminating this street. And there it comes—a sharp cry, then several voices raised, and the sounds of a rough struggle.

"Let go of me!" A young boy or a girl yells.

"Not until the old man pays!" An older male voice sounds in reply.

I slow down my fast pace. Then I freeze, considering my next course of action. . . . Whatever filthy *transaction* is happening in that alley, it is none of my business. Not that I would attempt to intervene or help anyone; no, that would be insanity. I'll leave that to the City Guard—though they rarely patrol here, and won't bother to show up promptly unless called by warehouse management.

Instead, I focus on what would be my best way of going around this unfortunate incident without being noticed. *Bast help me!*

If I back-track halfway between these two buildings, I can try diving into that other alley I just passed earlier. Or maybe I can just cross the street here, and then creep along the perimeter of the buildings and run across this alley, but on the opposite side?

If a hard crime is being committed, they might still see me, and naturally they can't have a witness. . . .

Just as all manner of violent images fill my stupid head, I see a dark streak flying past me down the street, in the same direction as I'm going. The hover-rider, cloak flapping behind him, turns directly into the alley. I barely see a flash of orichalcum metal along the long edge of the board . . . a form-fitting suit of iridescent, glimmering black . . . the streamlined shape of the rider almost lying flat, parallel to the board's length, controlling it skillfully with the lower body. The man or boy leans sharply into the corner, one foot anchored in the hoverboard stirrup, as he disappears down the alley.

Three heartbeats later I hear fighting noises—men landing blows, objects striking—possibly fighting sticks, sounds of a tussle, more yells. Then I see a small, wiry boy and two girls come pounding out of the alley, closely followed by an older man who has a bloodied face and what looks to be a broken nose. I don't think he was the one threatening a child; rather, he must be with them, the one who was referred to as "old man." Their father, maybe?

All I know is, these people are running like all the underworld's *shaitunaat* is after them, while I remain frozen a few steps away, and the fighting is still going on in the alley. No one else is on this stretch of street with us, no one to offer additional help.

I tell myself, *no, Semmi, no.* I'm prudent enough not to interfere even now. . . . And yet, curiosity pulls at me. And so, I sneak the few steps forward and plaster myself against the limestone wall of the building at the corner. Very carefully I peek inside the alley. . . .

And observe an amazing sight. The man in shimmering black (or boy, or *sha* in human form) on the hoverboard, straddling it with practiced, military ease, is single-handedly fighting five people.

A mix of men and boys, rough and dirty, strike at him with sticks and long knives, even as he maneuvers easily out of the way, making short whistling tones to direct his hoverboard a few feet off the ground. And then he lashes out at them with his black-gloved hands and a three-tiered short metal staff that he spins before him, around him, over and under—so fast that it blurs in motion, like a wind farm propeller.

It occurs to me that his sparkling black cloak should get in his way at some point, as it sweeps around him in dramatic fashion. But then I see that it also *hovers*, acting like an armor layer of sorts, an additional barrier between him and the opponents. Must be lined on the underside with orichalcum fabric.

Whoever this person is, they must be rich. I stare, mesmerized, at the hover-rider's fluid movements, deadly and skilled in combat. Why does this individual seem so familiar? Where have I seen this type of sleek black outfit—dark as *niktos*, yet alive with the sparkle of stars—and that shoulder-length mane of equally dark hair?

No, it can't be. . . .

I've seen him on the video screen. On our old media-box. To be precise, there's this popular story-feed drama that Amurabia and her neighbor women friends, and even Uru, love to watch mid-week, or on replay every Ra-Day evening.

The Love Life of the Man in the Niktos Cloak.

That's the ridiculous title of the rogue, network-independent show that half of Poseidon raves over, now in its third season. And the popularity is only growing. Supposedly it's some anonymous individual funding the whole thing out of his own money bag, as he himself plays the romantic hero, with a very small cast of play-actors, in a short, weekly episode.

Normally I avoid it because of the stupidity of the premise— it's always the Man in the Niktos Cloak caught in bed with a new woman or man every night, and he has to fend off the husband or wife, or other lover without *ever getting out of bed* to do it.

Yes, *that's* the gimmick. I roll my eyes violently, trying not to wrench them from my sockets, just thinking about it.

The Man in the Niktos Cloak never quite shows his full face to the camera. But apparently, he is young and quite handsome, judging from the brief flash-glimpses of his beautiful features that the audience gets every week. Trying to get a new glimpse of his face when he is not masked—even just a new angle on his features—is part of the challenge and appeal of this show. That, and the passionate lovemaking in the first portion of each episode, during which there are frequent glimpses of his perfectly chiseled abs and chest, his toned shoulders, muscular arms, and so much more. . . .

Ah, the moans, the steamy sighs, the barely-stifled cries of desire—and that's just the women in our living room, watching the hot action.

In all that, the Man in the Niktos Cloak always wears clothing made of the same shimmery, reflective, black fabric, while the garment itself changes slightly. . . . Even if he disrobes, there's always his elegant, black cloak. It is cast aside nearby, so that he appears completely unclothed under the silken sheets, with nothing but his lustrous black hair to cover him and his lover of the moment (usually a new female play-actor in every episode).

Amurabia and the women *adore* him—his mysterious looks, his cleverness, his honey-smooth, low voice. . . . In fact, I'm quite certain that the *voice* alone makes up the bulk of the attraction. It definitely makes all of them melt, as they stare and whisper and giggle when he utters sweet and *very dirty* words to his partner.

I have to endure this nonsense every week, under my own roof, for a quarter of an hour. . . . *Ugh.* Why must we be among the few in this part of hovel town with a working media-box and screen? Amurabia is far too indulgent of our neighbors; she should be charging them per viewing, I tell her often. Or they can go watch the newer and better media-box unit, three hovels down, over at Bayadi's place.

And then, there's the other thing. A much more interesting thing.

The Man in the Niktos Cloak *fights*. He always pulls out some incredible, clever weapon and uses it to vanquish or beat off the jealous attacker who comes to interrupt his love tryst.

From his bed. Without getting up.

I admit, I turn to watch those final few moments, when the rutting ends and the fighting happens—just for the clever moves, just to see what he would do and how he would escape possible death, or at least a whole lot of pain and a beating.

When it's all over, and the enemy has either fled or lies knocked-out nearby, the Man in the Niktos Cloak kisses his amazed (and duly impressed) lover farewell, then summons an expensive hoverboard to the bedside. We never see him actually get on it, because the screen darkens as the episode ends. It is followed by some stupid commercial from that week's sponsor.

And that's *The Love Life of the Man in the Niktos Cloak*, summed up.

That same exact hoverboard, that garment fabric, those martial arts moves—I recognize all of it now, as I find myself peeking inside the alley. . . .

No, I've not gone mad.

This is happening. This is *real*.

WITH A POUNDING PULSE, tense and ready to flee in a heartbeat, I watch the action in the alley. Just a few intense moments pass, and the hover-rider in black dispatches all five of his opponents. Two of the biggest men lie motionless on the ground, while the other three, younger boys, take off running and scatter deeper into the alley.

The hover-rider whistles a tone sequence, and his hoverboard obeys, turning him around smoothly and tilting him nearly upright. Simultaneously, he flips and folds his tri-segment weapon in on itself, using just one hand, and hides it in the folds of his clothing.

He then flies in my direction, one foot in the stirrup, cloak flapping behind him.

Immediately, I shrink back against the wall of the corner building, trying to make myself small, coiled like a spring in anticipation of running. If I'm lucky, he might just pass by without noticing me at all, so if I *don't* run it might be better. . . .

But no, too late; he's seen me.

The hover-rider reaches the mouth of the alley and turns his head to look directly at *me*. He wears no mask, and his features are visible in their entirety—lucky me (I offer up an eyeroll heavenward to any deities who might be watching). Not sure what I expected, but I see the lean face of an undeniably good-looking young man, framed by longish, dark hair.

His sharp gaze strikes me with a focused scrutiny. In the near-darkness, far from the streetlights, I barely catch the liquid flash and color of his eyes. They're neither black, nor brown, nor blue. Some kind of lighter shade, possibly tawny-green, possibly off-grey—hard to tell in the pre-dawn dusk. Whatever it is, these eyes are not the kind I expect to forget. . . . And not only because of their color.

Arrogant, supremely confident, mocking. . . .

"*Nefero eos,* you saw nothing," he tells me in passing, even as I stare like a dumb-struck fool. "You should get lost, before the Guard arrives." And he flashes me a grin full of healthy white teeth.

Ah, Bastet, that voice! Now I recognize it without a doubt. Yes, it's him . . . he is the Man in the Niktos Cloak, the play-actor, play-idiot, whoever—he *has* to be.

"*Nefero eos,*" I reply stupidly.

But the Man in the Niktos Cloak is already many paces away and leaning into the wind, as his hoverboard now rises above street level. In moments he disappears out of sight into the rosy dawn-lightening sky.

I stand gawking in his wake.

Then I head home.

Grandmother is not going to believe this!

CHAPTER
TWO

W hen I finally turn at my narrow street in our dirt-packed slum, lined with squat, ugly hovels of baked clay and limestone, and arrive at the fifth hovel on the left, it is full morning.

The sky is bright blue and Ra's disk is beginning its vaulted journey toward noon's zenith. Probably a mild day is coming, since it's Setaet, the first month, after all, and the winter is almost behind us. Here, on the outskirts of Poseidon —great and glorious Capital of Imperial *Atlantida*, Eternal Atlantis, greatest empire on earth, so on and so forth (Bast forgive me if I begin to gag at the usual accolades when so little of the bounty actually falls upon us)—the effects of weather control are less noticeable than in the City center. So yes, we get more chills in the winter and more heat in the summer than the far more fortunate residents of the inner Circles, especially the elites at the Imperial Heart of All Things.

I pause briefly outside the wooden door of our crumbling home, and wave to a neighbor woman who is hanging up laundry on her roof.

"Aren't you back early today?" she yells down at me, snapping and flapping some ragged linen sheets.

"Yes, they made me go home," I yell back. "Moon flow."

"Ah," the woman says with immediate sympathy. "May the gods take pity and may it end soon."

"*Chuvu*, Babi," I say, nodding. "From your mouth to divine ears. Hope you're right. I need the coins."

"Don't we all," Babi finishes, and goes back to drying her laundry.

I start to fiddle with the door latch when I hear Amurabia's ringing voice from indoors.

"Semmi? Is that you, girl?"

"Yes, *Mei-Ma!*" I holler back, fighting with the stuck latch. Old junk metal has rusted and is also bent; we need to get it fixed. "It's me, I'm coming in!"

But Amurabia is hard of hearing, so she yells again. "Semmi? Uru? Who is it? Who's at the door, I'm coming now! I have a poker stick, straight from the coals!"

"*Mei-Ma*, it's Semmi!" I cry, rattling the door now.

"Who is it?"

"Ah, crap of a goat, *Mei-Ma!* Come to the door and help me open this thing! It's Semmi! *Semirameos*, your *granddaughter! Did you latch the door again from the inside?*"

At this point I am yelling at the top of my lungs, and I can hear the neighbor laughing on the roof.

Seriously, how many times do I have to tell Grandmother not to latch the door from the inside before noon? Both Uru and I need it to be open since we come and go at all hours, especially Uru.

Finally, the door opens, and Amurabia—old, skinny, and short, with dark brown, wrinkled skin and a rag kerchief around her gray head of frizzy hair—looks up at me with startled reproach.

"Oh—Semmi. . . . Why aren't you at work?"

I walk past her inside our murky living room, and then twist and lift the fabric at the back of my skirt to show her the red spot.

Amurabia squints and shakes her head. "Did you wear a linen sheath under that?" she asks curtly.

I frown with annoyance. "Of course. I always wear the underskirt, just in case. I just forgot the rags."

But Amurabia shakes her head again. "Let me see." She leans closer, lifts up my coarse skirt fabric, and sure enough, I have my linen liner shift underneath.

"No blood," she says. "No moon flow."

My mouth falls open. "But—"

"Child. You've been made a fool," my sharp-thinking grandmother says, raising her warm brown eyes at me with pity. "Someone used your skirt as a towel. The *outer* skirt. Probably cut themselves, then quickly covered it up, but first had to clean up in a hurry."

"Bastet!" I curse loudly. "No wonder I didn't feel anything! Must be one of the whore-bitches who work next to me, wonder which one—"

"Don't invoke Bast's holy name in vain," Amurabia tells me patiently and not for the first time, since I tend to run hot, with a foul mouth. "And don't insult hard-working whores. Their job is harder than yours and mine."

"I lost a week of pay because of some lying, mangy, she-goat!" I continue. "I'm going back there, I will tell the overseer, have him check all the bitches' fingers! Those on both sides of me, and the ones next to them too!"

Amurabia nods. "You do that. But, tomorrow. It's too late now—by the time you return to Chiprahat, the shift will be over. But you go in early tomorrow and explain."

"I bet it's Odira," I continue fuming. "She's the one who pointed it out to me, told me I'm bleeding. Or it could be that green-haired red-ass baboon Labaat, or Jigudin. . . ."

"Don't waste your breath," Amurabia says, patting my arm. "Come, girl, I'll find something for you to do here, you can help me wind the yarn."

Grandmother is a skilled seamstress and works from home, so her work room corner is always overflowing with fabrics and hemp yarn from neighborhood clients.

I nod and we go through the front living room into the smaller of the two rooms in the back, where Amurabia works and sleeps. Our house only has three rooms. The low-ceilinged living room is the largest, with the long sitting bench from which we watch the story-feeds (and where our Father sleeps at night), the infamous media-box on the opposite wall, and the table in the corner. The other two rooms are Amurabia's tiny bedroom and workroom, and my and Uru's bedroom.

Behind the house, under an overhang, we have our outdoor kitchen with a fire pit and an ancient blackened grill grate that Amurabia inherited from her own mother's household. Beyond it, our small enclosed yard is crammed with tiers and rows of growing pots filled with earth and vegetables. No mushrooms, of course, since that requires a permit and a specialty grower's license—not to mention, we don't have the proper soil or the humidity-controlled enclosure.

Meanwhile, our roof is a large flat area which has even more planters full of growing herbs and more vegetables, and can be used as an additional open-air room when the weather permits. Up there's also a narrow, enclosed cabin stall where we shower under running water, wash our laundry, and use the drain as an elimination latrine.

The water is a true luxury here in the slum, piped by means of an old high-tech pump from the common well that reaches this blessed row of hovels. Not everyone is near a well, especially equipped with a pump. The long drain pipe runs down from the roof into the ground underneath the house and then ends up in the public sewer that serves our street. An additional sewer drain is in the corner of the yard on ground level, with a hollow toilet seat on top.

To get up onto the roof, we use a ladder from the back yard. It's secured between the small apricot tree and the wall, for safety. We have a second fruit tree, but it grows sour lemons, so it might as well be a useless shrub, as far as I'm concerned. I yell at it often as I walk past its useless trunk. Why couldn't it be an olive or a fig? Thank Bast we have the apricot, at least. . . .

Just as Amurabia and I disappear into her workroom, we hear the front door rattle once again. Then, Uru's boyish voice calls out.

"*Mei-Ma! Mei-Ma*, are you home?" my young brother Urumer yells urgently. There's a world of excitement in his voice.

Amurabia pauses her slightly limping walk and gathers a deep breath. She then hollers past me, loud enough to blow my ears off. "Since when am I not home at this hour? Open the door, boy! It's open! It's *open*, I said!"

"He heard you, *Mei-Ma*," I say, tapping her on the shoulder.

Moments later, Urumer rattles the door open, slams it behind him, and rushes into the workroom, panting and out of breath. My little brother Uru is annoying and adorable at the same time, with his wild, curly waves of dark brown hair that he always forgets to tie up in a proper tail, his big brown eyes, perfect falcon-wing brows, and pretty, long lashes. He still has a long way to grow before he comes close to my height (yes, I'm a little taller than the average girl, Bast be praised—I can reach tall shelves). But at some point, he will pass me, and then the girls will start swooning after him.

Thankfully, that's a long way off, and he is still a skinny, wiry child who can run very fast and who likes to climb everything—trees, ladders, rooftops, City posts.

Uru also likes to bring everyone the latest news (which

makes sense for his job as messenger and courier) and is often the first to spread gossip all over the street.

Such as now.

"Semmi—how come you're home?" he mumbles, noticing me, then immediately forgets and turns to Amurabia. "*Mei-Ma!* I have big news! So bad, so bad!"

"What is it, child? What's so bad?" Amurabia asks blandly, humoring him, as she turns away and begins to open her fabric boxes on the work table.

But Uru glances from me to her, with wide eyes. He begins to tug my shirt in excitement, then rattles off: "Just came back from the Old Fish Market, and there was this huge digital billboard flying in. Big as a wall! Looked like it came from the Circle Interior, from some rich Circles, not our kind. It stopped in the middle clearing . . . and then it turned on to an Imperial channel, I'm talking full Announcement mode!"

Amurabia briefly glances at him. "Is that so?"

"Go on," I add.

"It started to play the Imperial Hymn, so loud that everyone in the market shut up and stopped what they were doing. Even Makar's pie stall got quiet, you know that's crazy, right, anyway—"

I shake my head slightly and chuckle. "Yes, go on."

"Yeah . . . and so," Uru stumbles and picks up his story. "So then, there was Blessed Churu. His face, big as a wall, his crown shining, with all the gold around him. And he said that the other gods are angry at us. Four years ago, they warned us to obey, and now they are coming back to punish us because we didn't. They are sending a giant Sky Rock ahead of them. The Sky Rock is going to fall on us and there will be death and pain and tears —so many tears that they will turn to rivers and the rivers will turn to mountains, and flood us—"

"All right, what nonsense now, child?" Amurabia interrupts. "I really doubt the Blessed Imperator said anything of the sort.

What was the real message? And before you exaggerate, think what I told you about making up pointless lies—"

But Uru's face gets a hurt look, and he wails, "No, *Mei-Ma!* He really said that, mountains of tears and big water like a mountain! And—and—"

"Come on, Uru," I speak up. "Okay, whatever. What else did he say?"

My little brother scrunches up his face and frowns, quieting stubbornly.

"Urumer!" Grandmother says loudly. "Enough! If the Imperator chose to speak to us in the marketplace in the middle of day, then it must've been important. So now, out with it! What did he actually say?"

"You don't believe me, just turn on the box and watch!" Uru says sullenly, pointing to our media-box.

"Urumer!" This time Grandmother yells his name like she means business. We both know she wouldn't waste precious digital energy to run the box this early in the day. She even yells at our Father if she sees him watching before our evening mealtime.

"All right, you don't believe me," Uru resumes talking. "But Churu did speak about the Sky Rock and the water, and how everyone will die—except the few fortunate ones here in Poseidon and a rare few from outside. He said they will be choosing among us."

"Choosing how? They who?" Amurabia asks with guarded weariness.

"They, the Kassiopei gods, not the golden sky gods," Uru elaborates. "And the nobles. They will be choosing among us— picking the best people in Poseidon to serve them, as they escape the death and the Sky Rock and the water."

"Escape? Where? How do they escape all this supposed misfortune?" I ask, to humor him.

"They're building ships. The kind that fly. But not just

ordinary ones that can only rise over rooftops or go over a mountain. These ships will fly so high up into the sky that they reach the stars! And the Kassiopei, together with the nobles, will go inside these great flying star ships, and escape! And if we get picked, we escape too!"

"Oh, Bast . . ." I mutter, rubbing my forehead and nose, even as I shake my head at Uru's crazy story. "You are being useless right now, Uru. This is *shar-ta-haak* nonsense. If even a tiny grain of this is real, it's bad. And it *can't* be that bad."

"Yes, it can! I tell you, it's real, and really bad." Uru nods. "Also, there's more . . . bad."

He pauses slightly, narrows his eyes in fearful anticipation, then rattles off: "You know that data pole on our corner? The one that's hard to see when you're coming from the other street? Okay, on the way back here, I was *thinking so hard* about the bad news that I forgot and crashed into it with my hoverboard. Leveled it flat."

Both Amurabia and I exclaim simultaneously. "*Again?* Oh no, not again, Uru!"

"Crap of a goat," I add angrily. "So much babbling, when you should've led with that!"

CHAPTER
THREE

"My hoverboard is okay," my idiot brother tells us with a tiny smile, as if that will excuse everything. "Not even a dent. I'm okay too. Didn't fall off this time, I jumped, and saw it coming at the last moment—"

"Wait, you *saw* it and still crashed?" I interrupt, advancing threateningly to loom over him. "Or you didn't see—which is it? How could you be such a *hoohvak?*"

The traffic and data pole on our street corner is not a joke. It's a public utility, used by the City to transmit our media feeds, and all the information to all the tech in the area, in addition to setting traffic patterns and other important comms stuff. If it goes down, we all lose reception and lose half of our tech. And the City Guard will come and make arrests!

"Well, never mind, it doesn't matter," Amurabia says loudly, interrupting both of us. "Is the pole still down? Right now?"

"Yeah."

"Ah, gods preserve us!" With determination, Amurabia heads back to the living room and then the outside door. On the way she grabs her cane, adjusts her kerchief, and motions to both of us to follow.

I'm already right behind her, allowing her to hobble forward quickly, while Uru lags after us with a guilty expression. I notice the offending hoverboard of his is leaning against the wall where he dragged it in and left it, right near the door.

The moment we're outside in the morning sunshine, Amurabia begins to yell in her mightiest voice. "*Ei, ei, ei*, we need help! Help! Pedros! Someone get Pedros!"

She looks around, sees our neighbor Babi with her laundry on her roof.

Babi pauses her work and stares down at our Grandmother.

"Stop gawking, Babi!" Amurabia yells at her, shielding her eyes from the sun with her palm. "Come help, the data pole is down again! The blasted child ran into it, and we need to raise it up right now! Quickly now, call everyone you can see!"

"Oh, no, Uru! What did you do?" Babi calls down at my brother. And then she puts her hands together over her mouth to amplify her voice, and starts yelling too.

"Pedros! Come help! Gaitahat! Maitu, call your husband here! Maitu-u-u-u!"

"Pedros, wake up! *Pedros*, son of Faduia!" Amurabia yells even louder, and uses her cane to strike the ground, as if that would help. Maybe the *shaitunaat* underground need to know our business too.

One by one, the neighbors around us come out—those who are home, that is, since this is a workday. Doors open, and a few old women or old men peek outside.

"The pole is down! Come help us raise it up!" I call out also.

We all begin walking quickly down the street, and people start joining us. Babi gets down from her roof, and a big man called Pedros finally shows up. Pedros works the night shift, so we woke him up, unfortunately.

By the time we get to the corner with its downed pole, we're a small crowd.

The pole is not too thick, the girth of a young tree. But it has a metal core, and it is sufficiently tall—two people stacked on top of each other, that's how tall (like when Pedros's wife climbs on his shoulders to reach the upper branches of their fig tree)—so it requires at least three people to even move it. Together, fifteen people manage to hold it up immediately and lower it back into its proper hole.

"Are the City Guard coming?" people ask nervously as we work.

"No, not yet! Quickly now, quickly!"

We pile earth at the base of the pole, stomp it down, someone slaps it with a shovel, someone else hauls clay bricks to pile around it for reinforcement, in a retaining circle.

"Amurabia, you need to whip that boy!" a neighbor woman says angrily, and gives an incinerating look to my poor, fool brother.

"Thank you, Chiuga, yes, I'll handle him," Amurabia says with a grim expression, observing from the sidelines, while big Pedros grunts and moves the pole yet again a tiny bit, to make sure it's at a perfect vertical alignment.

"Make sure this doesn't happen again," another man says, holding a tech gadget to the pole, as he calibrates the computer inside. "It's working now, all okay. But next time it falls, we may not be able to reset. The inner circuitry can fry and we won't be able to avoid a visit from the authorities. They can still show up today—"

"They won't." Amurabia exhales a tense breath. "For once I praise Bast, and Denwen, and all the gods of *Atlantida*, that we live in Denwen's Pit. Thank you, all of you, *sen-i-senet* for your blessed assistance!"

"Yes, the Armpit takes care of its own," Babi adds.

AFTER ALL THAT EXCITEMENT, Amurabia promises the neighbors some of her delicious *eos* pies, next time the apricots ripen on our tree. And then we all head back to our respective hovels.

"Anyone know anything about some big Sky Rock sent by the golden gods to drop on our heads?" Amurabia asks people in general as we walk.

The neighbors all plead ignorance, and some offer very confused replies.

"You're the one with the media-box," Maitu, wife of Pedros, says to Amurabia.

"I will turn it on in the evening," Grandmother replies firmly. "Just wondering if anyone heard anything, or if my boy-child here is just spreading more nonsense gossip. City is full of it."

"Well, he *has* been all over, as usual," remarks Pedros thoughtfully, following with a huge yawn. "Gods alone know the truth of all things. If the Imperator spoke in the marketplace, it must be important."

"Get back to sleep, Pedros," we tell him, since the man is now yawning profusely, and has a whole work night shift ahead of him.

"I suppose if it matters, we will all find out," a different neighbor concludes wisely, waving to us before heading for her own door.

And on that note, we part.

Once back in our home, Amurabia turns to Uru and gives him a harangue. "I really need to pull your ears and slap your backside for all this trouble you've caused." She sets her cane against the wall and then lowers herself tiredly on our long bench.

"I'm sorry, *Mei-Ma*, I won't do it again, I promise, please don't hurt me," Uru whines, knowing full well that she would do nothing of the sort. Grandmother almost never raises her hand at us, and all her threats are verbal.

"Don't make promises you can't keep, Urumer, son of my daughter. At least don't do it again for a long time, child."

"It's almost noon, should I boil some hot tea?" I say mildly.

"I could use some tea," Amurabia says after a long breath, forgetting her aggravation.

And so, I make us all some tea from the dried herbs we have in the back of the house. And while the fire pit boils the pot outside, I tell Amurabia and Uru about what happened to me on the way home, how I saw the Man in the Niktos Cloak.

"No, you didn't!" Uru exclaims in minor awe.

"Yes, *hoohvak*, I did. Who's the one who doesn't believe me now? It was the Man in the Niktos Cloak, in his shiny suit and on his hoverboard, and he was fighting, except this time it was in a dark alley full of murderous *chazufs*, and he saved all these people—"

"How do you know it was him, and not some strange guy dressed up like him?" Uru persists.

"I just do. Too many familiar details to be a coincidence. I know how he fights."

"You know his naked backside, you mean!" Uru giggles.

I snort. "Naked backsides are all alike. But fighting styles are unique."

"Says who?"

"Says I."

"Hah!" Uru slaps his leg. "You don't even know how to fight, Semmi-moo!"

I shrug. "I know enough."

"Both my *mei-saai* are making up all kinds of stories today," Amurabia says with a martyr-like glance to the ceiling (where the gods dwell supposedly; why is it always the ceiling or sky?), but there's a smile on her lips as she sips tea from her clay grail.

"You may not believe me," I say, with a similar little smile, taking a seat on the bench next to her, "but I saw his face. I saw the *face* of the Man in the Niktos Cloak."

Amurabia lifts one brow and her relaxed, sleepy-eyed

expression perks up. "Is that so, girl? And was this supposed Man in the Niktos Cloak as handsome as we all think he is?"

I pause for a moment, thinking how to reply, and for some reason feel a little wave of heat in my neck. I really hate it when Grandmother pushes these uncomfortable subjects with me. But what can I do now? I did begin to tell them this story, so now I must finish it, and expect the natural questions. "I guess he is," I reply. "Handsome enough, I guess."

"Ooh, you guess, you guess!" Uru exclaims. "So he really must be, since you never admit that anyone is handsome!"

"Hush, Urumer!" I say sternly. "Few people are truly handsome. I only say it like it is."

"Interesting." Amurabia offers up her empty grail for a refill of tea. "I rather think most people are very handsome, even the ones sometimes called ugly. It's all about the expression in their eyes, not the features. Features are an empty framework granted us by the gods. Meanwhile, the way we permit our eyes to express our soul's true visage in its sacred three parts, is all our doing."

"Maybe." I pour myself another cup also. "Anyway, I think the Man in the Niktos Cloak is a wealthy fool, actually—handsome or not. That story-feed on the media-box is proof enough. Either he's a vain *hoohvak* who likes to show himself off, or he is doing it for even more money from the show sponsors. Besides, what's he doing, flying around before dawn in an industrial area?"

"Sounds like he's saving people." Uru taps my arm for his own tea refill.

"If you truly saw him," Amurabia ponders with a light smile of appreciation, "what a wonder it must be!"

I say nothing and stick my nose deeper in my cup to smell the pungent herbal steam full of honey clover and citrus (all right, the lemons do have some use after all).

"Hey, maybe you can try to see him again tomorrow, and

then find out who he is! If you could find out, we can make the social news all over the Windnet, and even make some good coins—" Uru starts to babble, and I shake my head.

Pondering the true identity of the Man in the Niktos Cloak is the most pointless thing of all.

So, who is he? There are infinite speculations. There is also plentiful betting, and coins exchange hands, all around the City, as my brother just reminded us.

First, everyone concurs that the Man in the Niktos Cloak must be independently wealthy to be able to fund the show—hence, he's a powerful merchant or landowner's son, in the very least. His chiseled body is perfection. Therefore, he must be the product of noble breeding, the son of a Great Family. He fights like the *sha*, so there's military training—or else he's a murderous criminal rogue who's living on stolen riches. . . .

Some fools even wonder if he's related to the divine Imperial Kassiopei Dynasty, and is secretly one of the Princes of *Atlantida* or a bastard son of Blessed Churu Himself. So many *hoohvak* rumors, one more stupid than the other.

My annoyed thoughts are interrupted by the sound at the door. It opens, and in comes Guzum, our Father, walking unsteadily because as usual he is likely semi-drunk and in need of a shave. Our Father is a thin man, with medium-brown hair consisting of very fine strands, and somewhat lighter skin than the rest of us, light tan instead of light brown. He has a permanent dazed look on his face, and under his thick eyebrows, his hazel eyes are heavy-lidded from need of sleep.

What's he doing here? it immediately occurs to me. It's only noon, and he isn't even attempting to work today.

Before Amurabia can make her own reprimand, Father lifts one hand to us, with one finger pointing up.

And then he says, "Don't . . . don't say nothing, Amurabia. . . . There's a Sky Rock. Up there . . . with the gods. . . . It's coming for us, and we're all going to die."

"*Nefero dea*, Guzum," Grandmother says after a very long pause. "So, it's true?"

My Father slowly pulls up his eyebrows and stares at all of us. "Hm . . . I see you've heard already." And then he continues into the living room and plops down on the other side of the bench next to her, while Uru makes room and slides over to sit on the very end.

There's another long pause as we all stare at Father.

"So, what exactly is this Sky Rock business?" Amurabia asks. "Your son tried to explain what was said in the market but he made very little sense. Are you sober enough to do a better job?"

"I could use some of that." Father points to the pot of tea.

I stand up and get his old wooden mug from the shelf in the corner, then fill it from the clay pot. Watching the steam rise from the tea, I carry it to my Father who receives it with somewhat unsteady fingers.

"Drink, then talk," Amurabia commands.

Father buries his face in the mug and takes deep gulps, while we wait.

And then he tells us a truly startling story.

Apparently, Uru was mostly accurate in what he managed to convey to us. The Imperator did make a serious Announcement in the middle of the marketplace. The golden gods are angry at what little progress we have made over the past four years since they taught us the true sacred ways. They are returning, and this time they will punish us. They are indeed sending a giant flying Sky Rock, the size of a mountain, that will crash into the heart of *Atlantida*—in other words, right here, in Poseidon.

And it will make a hole in the earth, in the very same place where this City stands. Fires will come pouring from the underworld, while great waters from the ocean will rise into great waves, and will wash away all that's left.

"In short, we will be dead before summer," Father concludes wearily. "The technicians who examine the sky for such things as falling rocks are still determining the exact day it will strike, but it is within about three months, no more. Either the month of Osiriet or Thotaet."

Amurabia lets out a held breath. "If we travel far enough away, maybe across this land to the other side in the north, or even across the ocean, can we escape it?"

"Not according to the Imperator," Father replies.

"Those underground fires, that great wave, how bad can it be? Can we climb tall trees? It can wash over us, and if we borrow a boat, such as the one that glides from the canals to the ocean and carries cargo—?"

At that, Guzum shakes his head and laughs tiredly. "Amurabia, have you ever been in an ocean storm? No? Well, this is supposed to bring waves that are like mountains, greater than any storm. Greater than *actual mountains*."

Grandmother's expression is strained to the utmost. Her wrinkles are stretched tight across her forehead, and it's as if she is trying to comprehend. . . . And failing.

"No," she says finally, shaking her head. "I don't believe it.

That kind of wave, it would destroy all living things, all of us, the animals, the *world* itself!"

Our Father bites his lip and nods. "Exactly so."

"Stop scaring the child!" Amurabia says gruffly, noticing Uru's frightened expression.

The irony is, Uru was the one who first spread this news to us, likely without any true understanding. And now it is starting to sink in.

We're all going to die.

"There has to be something that can be done!" Grandmother persists. "Not for me—I'm too old and bear no grudge against the gods if they choose to send my soul onward on board the Depet of Eternity. But the children, even you, Guzum. There's still much life to be lived for all of you. . . ."

A long pause.

Then, Father clears his throat loudly with a harsh rasping noise. "Speak truly. I'm not worth much in this life," he says. "But the boy and the girl, they should live."

"So then, what can be done?" she asks.

"The Blessed Imperator spoke of preparations being made for an escape up into the skies and to the stars." Father says after another long pause. "Not very clear what it means, but they will be choosing among the general population. Ordinary people to serve the nobles and the Imperial Family in their journey."

"What manner of skills do they want?"

Father shrugs. "They're going to tell us in the coming days, I suppose. Not much more was said during this Announcement."

"Guzum!" Amurabia says harshly. "Use your head, what exactly did Blessed Churu say?"

"Using my head or not using my head, it's all he said. Why don't we turn on the feeds and see what's on the news?"

"What time is it?" Grandmother glances at the distant lit timepiece on the wall which is embedded in the frame of the media-box. It's showing three long lines and one shorter, partial one, which I know means "after third hour of Khe." It's the only thing using constant energy day and night that she allows in our house. "Not sixth hour yet, so no feeds!"

"Ah, in the name of Khonsu and Ra!" Father mutters. "Make an exception this once, will you, woman? With only a few months remaining to us, the energy bill will not matter."

"It will matter to me!" our very stubborn Grandmother retorts. "Even as I'm gurgling my last breath underwater, I will go with a clear conscience that I've not accumulated debts that will further burden the Scales that weigh my mortal soul!"

"Ei. . . ." Father waves his hand at her and makes a sound of disgust.

AND SO, we wait, nervously, and not very patiently. Only a few hours to go before evening and the time of media-box usage.

Amurabia busies herself with getting our meal going in the back yard, and I go to help her, while Uru runs outside, claiming he can collect more news. Our Father, meanwhile, stretches out on the bench, puts his feet up, and closes his eyes. Soon, those of us in the kitchen outside can hear his rasping snores.

Our meal today (as it happens to be nearly every day) is roasted vegetables over bulghur grain pottage. The type of grains varies depending on what was found cheap in the marketplace this week, and the vegetables vary depending on what's ripe in our yard and ready to harvest.

While Amurabia stirs the large pot filled with grains and water, I go around the yard and look at the various grow pots, both on the ground and on the roof, to see what's come up. Looks like we have a few carrots, onions, turnips, leeks, garlic, and cabbage, plus a multitude of herbs: coriander, rosemary, dill, tarragon.

I dig up the vegetables and rinse them in a large wooden

bowl, then help with the flatbread that's popping on the hot stones. Then I return and start cutting up the produce with our one and only, less-than-effective, always-dull old knife. No matter how many times I sharpen it, it never reaches the sharpness of the ones I use at my workplace. But since this is the *one thing* I'm really good at, the task falls to me to cut and chop.

"Sorry that it's more of your usual work, girl," Grandmother says guiltily, as she does every day, looking up from her other meal prep tasks. "But you do it so much better than any one of us."

"I know, *Mei-Ma*, I know," I mutter, shaking my head slightly, but not displeased at this regular compliment to my skills. And it's true, I cut quickly and precisely, even with this lousy knife, finishing the job in half the time it would take the old woman or anyone else on our street.

As the bulghur softens and cooks, we start tossing in some of the vegetables and herbs, while others we coat in olive oil and set out on the metal grill for a nice char.

I also add beans to a second pot of water to soak overnight for tomorrow's meal or another one later in the week. Uru comes running back in the yard just then, says "Poot, poot!" at the beans, and makes a farting noise, then runs off again.

I shake my head at him, but cannot help holding back a giggle at the little *chazuf*. Amurabia simply raises her wooden stirrer and brandishes it in his wake. She keeps her wrinkled mouth in a very straight line, and yet a tiny smile is straining to break out at the boy's antics.

By now, a delicious aroma wafts from the grill and the pot, filling the air with mouth-watering spice and pungency. Soon our neighbors will smell our supper, while we in turn will smell theirs, drifting on the breeze from all around hovel town. Another hour, and it will be overwhelming—the smells, the smoke, the voices, and the living noise of laborers returning from work, or simply coming outside to cook.

In other words, the best time of the day is almost here.

WHEN THE WESTERN sky starts turning warm peach colors, and Ra's golden boat skims the horizon, our meal is ready. We fill four wooden bowls, carry them and the basket with the loaves of flatbread indoors, and set everything on the table near the wall. Then Amurabia raises the beer jug on a rope from inside a deep storage hole in the ground that keeps things cold.

Everyone gets one mug of the pale, watery beer to have with supper, and back down the jug goes. Father is forbidden to retrieve it on his own, as are we. Although Amurabia covers the hole with a wide plank of wood and sets something heavy on top, I know for a fact that it doesn't always prevent our Father from getting to it in the darkness of night.

But now, it's time to eat, and not a moment late. The media-box timepiece shows six long lines (I think of all fingers on my one hand, plus one finger on the other hand, which constitutes six), so evening is officially here, and with it, our digital entertainment.

With our bowls and bread, we take our seats on the long bench and Amurabia does the honors. She sings a few carefully memorized and now very familiar notes in a slightly shaking voice, and the media-box comes alive. It unfurls from the wall, taking on a larger screen configuration, and it lights up to show a selection of smaller windows, each one with a different video feed. The networks take turns every day to get premier placement on this starting board, but the main choices are usually the same.

Not sure why I feel a sudden hard twist of nerves in my gut when I first glance at the feeds. . . . Actually, I'm sure. I know *exactly* why—it's the anticipation of the grim news from the Imperator, the news gnawing in the back of our minds all day.

Sky Rock. . . . We're all going to die.

Even though my Father and Uru both confirmed the details of the deadly misfortune coming to us, my mind refuses to grasp it even now. I need the hard evidence of this new reality to be *shown* to me; I need to hear it for myself.

All of it. Everything.

Uru gets up from his spot on the bench and looks at us. "Which window?"

"Go, touch the Imperial channel," Grandmother replies, pointing to the central feed.

My brother runs up to the screen and taps the central window with his fingers, then returns to his place. The window immediately takes up the entirety of the screen, and the broadcast noise hits us at high volume.

A glorious image of the Center Circle of Poseidon fills the screen. The Center Circle is a lush garden island containing the Imperial Palace and the grand temples of all the greater gods. In the heart of the Circle is the new *Kassiopeion*, the Temple of the Imperial Dynasty, erected only a few years before the coming of the golden gods, by Imperial Decree, in place where the old *Kassiopeion* temple stood (ordinary and boring, in comparison).

The new *Kassiopeion* is a truly strange building that always makes me wonder how in Bast's name is it even standing. A transparent glass dome sits on top of four grand columns, and within it is another structure, made of gold and shaped like a four-point star, the sacred *astroctadra* shape.

The bottom point of the star shape touches the ground, and the top point touches the center of the dome like the tip of a pyramid. And within the *astroctadra* is yet another sphere—a great orb of pure energy which contains the blazing power of Atlantis, full of moving rainbow light.

Often, jets of plasma are ejected from the orb in bursts of iridescent brilliance, and supposedly they are living creatures, beasts from another world or universe coming into our own.

Our singing techs can harness them and use them for all kinds of unspeakable wonders. The name for them is *pegasei*, and they are truly prized by the elites.

Right now, I can see at least two such *pegasei* energy forms burst forth and escape the orb, then immediately get captured by the surrounding circle of priests who guard the sanctum. Meanwhile the grandiose voice of the news announcer narrates that preparations are being made by the divine Imperial Family for the "ordeals that await all of us."

In just moments, we're told, the Imperator's address to the nation this morning will be replayed. Meanwhile, rows of squiggles that are hieroglyphics and letters scroll by the frame of the screen on all four sides, going around in an endless loop, but none of us can read them, of course, so we must rely on the spoken words of the announcers.

"Aha!" Amurabia says, raising her hand for silence. "Finally, we will hear it for ourselves."

Just as the screen changes to the Imperial Palace Throne Chamber and the magnificent figure of the Imperator, we hear polite but insistent knocking from outside our house.

Grandmother makes a sound of frustration, and points at Uru, who immediately jumps up to open the front door.

At least six of our neighbors are here, peeking in at the entrance to be let in to watch our media-box. Babi, Maitu, and Gaitahat are among them, with their children.

"*Atlantida!* Attend me—to what I must relate to all of you, my people," Churu Kassiopei speaks, as the camera moves in closer, enlarging his glorious, stern features.

Amurabia gestures quickly with her hand, and the neighbors crowd tight into our small living room, surrounding our bench, perching everywhere. Two little girls pull themselves up, and end up on my lap, while I make a face at them and tell them to hush.

And so, we listen.

. . .

THE IMPERATOR SPEAKS SLOWLY in general terms, using big words. He describes the Sky Rock—its deadly velocity, its mountainous dimensions, the explosive contact it will make with the ground—in impersonal terms, as if it were an ordinary weather pattern. His divine voice is deep and resonant as usual, echoing in the grand room, and pouring into our tiny room with sufficient force to send chills up and down my spine. He does not attempt to explain or excuse the golden gods and their motives. Instead, there is a hint of contained anger in his carefully measured tone.

" . . . the Sky Rock is intended as punishment. It is the retaliation for our rejection of *their* impossible mandates," Churu says. "*Atlantida* has made every effort to follow the strict . . . 'guidelines' set by *them*. And now, we are told, it is not sufficient. We have strayed. We have been found lacking—according to their unspeakable standards. And we are to pay for it, to forfeit our lives. I will not have our ancient Dynasty end due to alien mandates from alien gods. We are *Atlantida*. We are Forever!"

In uttering that sentence full of disdain, his *voice* rings with such power that all of us, so far away, huddled in our distant City Circle Ten, shiver and cringe and pull ourselves closer to one another.

One of the little girls on my lap digs her skinny fingers into my arm and starts to wail without knowing the meaning of the Imperator's words, only their dire *sound*, their living crawling power.

"We shall not perish," Churu continues. "We shall depart, and we shall continue *elsewhere*. Kassiopei blood will persist onward unto the ages, and those of you who *serve us* will be graced by our protection. I hereby give my Imperial Word to that effect."

"That's great," my Father mumbles softly. "But what about the rest of us?"

Neighbors sigh and shake their heads.

The Imperator finally gets to the specifics. "Even now, work has started on the preparations. A great Imperial ship is being built, and many lesser ships, to take as many of those who serve us as possible—in the time frame presented to us. We shall rise up to Ra's heavens and we shall continue even higher into the dark Vastness of Eternity that lies beyond.

"To be permitted on board the Vastness ships, you must have the abilities and spirit required. I would take all of you—all those who serve me and the noble families loyally, all of you, ancient Poseidon, great City, and the surrounding regions and provinces—but there is only so much room on the vessels and only so much time and labor allotted for our departure. You will learn what you must do to *qualify* for Imperial service. Remain ready and listen carefully, for these requirements and categories of skills will be given to you later today and in the days following. And we shall choose amongst you for the best and most worthy."

He pauses, and the camera moves even closer to focus on his eyes.

"As for the rest of you—I weep for you, my *Atlantida*. My blood is divine, and yet not even my Kassiopei power can protect all of you from what is coming. Stay strong and do not give up your soul's triumvirate to the encroaching dark. Live until your last moment with honor, and die bravely, as befitting the greatest people of this earth."

When the recorded speech of the Imperator ends, the network announcers begin reading a list of initial broad categories of service eligible for the Imperial service—and hence, for rescue.

The people in our living room grow even quieter and listen.

"Military service category," reads the announcer, and

squiggles appear on the screen. "Domestic service category. Technical service category. Food and resources category. Artisan skills and crafts category. Medical category. Entertainment category. Education, training, and knowledge preservation category. Legal and priestly category. Hard labor category. More details will be given soon, including the process of how to apply for this special service. . . . And now, we present to you the hymnal prayer for the infinite souls of *Atlantida*—"

The scene switches to a different familiar temple structure, and the sound of a stringed *zaurhi* and drums, while acolytes dressed in white robes trimmed with golden lace begin to sing in pure young voices—and everyone here in our room seems to exhale a held breath. The familiar song and prayer service will be long and no need to pay much attention to it.

"Well," Amurabia breaks the silence, turning to the neighbors. "Gives us something to consider now. It's better than nothing, see? We have skills here, all of us. So there is a solid chance we can work our way onto those sky ships. For example, you, Maitu, you've a way with making those little wooden beads and painting them so pretty with the flowers—"

Oh, Mei-Ma, *if only. Poor people's beadmaking is not the fancy skill the Imperator is looking for,* I think sadly.

But the neighbors seem reassured by my Grandmother's positivity.

"That's right," Maitu says, nodding. "I can cook better than most, do all manner of domestic work. And Pedros can lift four sacks at once! They can use a strong man on the ships, can't they?"

"Sure, they can!"

"And you, Amurabia, can mend linen with the tiniest fine threads," Gaitahat adds. "While your girl there can chop those fancy mushrooms! While I make the best hair braids and twists and can do a fine lady's hair in half the time those lazy servants of theirs can manage—"

As they continue dwelling on their various talents with enthusiasm, I turn my attention to the muffled sound behind me, and see that one of the neighbor women is weeping.

"Oh . . . Jahai," I say her name awkwardly. Many of us turn to look at this older woman with a bad leg who leans against the wall, tears running down her thin, weathered face.

"I—I don't have the strength to do anything," she says softly to us, between breaths. "Never learned fine skills. And now . . . I'm too ill to do solid work, not even to scrub, or even carry a sack, and can only manage simple cooking. The house of whores around these parts won't take me, unless it's for cleaning work —I've tried—and as for cleaning, I can't bend easily these days. . . ."

Jahai pauses, and in the new silence, she looks around at us. "I'm going to die, aren't I?"

"No, no, no. . . . No one's dying," Amurabia rushes to speak, in her most stubborn, convincing tone.

But for once, underneath all her usual mannerisms, I hear a subtle, dissonant note of uncertainty in her voice.

And I feel a profound stab of fear.

CHAPTER
FIVE

E ventually, we all tire of our own chatter, of watching the various feeds where wildly uncertain information is being ridiculously analyzed and gossiped over by panels of experts and entertainers. Without more facts from the Imperial channel, there's no point in speculation. That will come tomorrow and in the coming days, no one has any doubt. . . .

But the nerves remain. Everyone is now worried, afraid, confused.

The new reality is so overwhelming that it's almost *too much to grasp*.

It's getting late, much later than everyone's usual bedtime, and the conversation in our living room peters out into yawns. The neighbors leave one by one, while Amurabia nods to each and gives an encouraging smile.

"Go on, Babi," Grandmother says to the last of them, our immediate next-door neighbor. "Rest and worry tomorrow. For now, we must all sleep."

"Maybe in dreams we'll see something useful," I mumble.

"I hope so. *Nefero niktos*," says Babi, giving me a tired look as she pushes her little boy out the door and closes it behind them.

Amurabia clears her throat and sings the media-box to shut down for the night. Immediately our living room is plunged into darkness, since the screen serves as the main source of light for our evening activities. Only the timepiece display on the frame remains on—showing five, and another five, and one short partial line, indicating tenth hour of Khe—and its faint amber glow is hardly enough to illuminate anything.

I light a small, squat beeswax candle that we always use for brief moments at night, and by its flickering light start cleaning up after our meal. I carry the dirty bowls outside in the back, to soak them overnight in a bucket of washing water. Meanwhile Grandmother and Uru move the big covered pot filled with leftovers from the fire pit outside to a corner indoors, so that no wild critters get to our food. We take turns using the backyard latrine—but first checking the wooden seat for any crawling insects which come out in the dark . . . ugh, I always hate that part.

Time to get ready for bed. Uru goes to lock the front door, while I bolt the back one leading into the yard. The night wind sweeps my face just then in strong gusts before I shut us in (as always, spitting three times into the ground for protection, to prevent the evil *sha* eye), and I briefly glimpse the thick, familiar darkness of hovel town all around, and the glitter of stars overhead, filling the *niktos* sky.

When I return, Father has already retrieved his blanket from the storage chest underneath the media-box and is now stretched out on the long bench. He's been more quiet than usual for most of the evening, and has his eyes closed, ignoring everyone, indicating sleep. But since he's not drunken-snoring, I know he is unable to sleep also, so he must be thinking about everything.

Amurabia nods to me and hobbles to her own room in the back, pushing Uru into the other tiny room where our two cots stand against the walls.

And now, I too have to get some rest. All of us have tarried too long this night because of the bad news. Yes, my mind is racing, but I absolutely must lie down in my own bed and attempt to sleep, if I am to get up in the middle of the pre-dawn darkness in time for my usual work shift. I recall my plan to attempt to convince the overseer that I'm clean enough to work and the whole thing with the blood stain was a big misunderstanding.

Ah . . . such minor problems of the normal times, before all this befell us.

Before we learned about the Sky Rock.

Before we learned that—

I force my racing thoughts to stop, and quickly blow out the candle. It smokes, fading, but gives me one last glimpse of the room, just enough to orient me in the darkness. I quietly step into my bedroom, feeling along the wall. Uru is already in his bed because I can hear his quiet sniffling as he shifts in the cot.

I find my own cot by feel, remove my outer clothing, and lower myself, pulling the thin blanket over me, and resting my head on the thin-as-flatbread, under-stuffed pillow.

Sleep absolutely must come. *Bast, help me,* I pray, exhaling a tired breath, letting myself relax.

At some point, the needed peace finds me.

I WAKE up much too soon, not trusting my body to be up in time, and hence not sleeping properly. I get dressed quickly, moving softly so as not to wake the household as I stumble around in the pitch black and pull on my clothing and walking sandals, then comb my curling hair into a semblance of decency. In the living room, I move past the sleeping form of my Father and glance at the faintly glowing timepiece on the media-box to see two long lines and an almost fully formed third, to indicate the last moments of second hour of Ra.

Blessed Bast, I did it, just barely!

Normally I have to be ready and out of the house by third hour of Ra to make the hour-long journey on foot. It's just enough time for me to get out of hovel town and make it all the way to Circle Eight in time for my shift. I tiptoe outside into a moonless, star-lit night, close the front door behind me, and then start running.

By the time I arrive at Chiprahat Exquisite Foods, I'm more out of breath than usual, my blood pounding in my temples. Keeping my head down, I get in line with the other workers who are filing in at the main warehouse entrance in the rear where we must pass a sterilization booth and then receive our aprons and headgear. I hear more anxious line talk than usual, as the sleepy women whisper about the Imperial Announcement from yesterday. Phrases such as "the end of the world" and "divine punishment" move in hushed waves down the long queue.

When it's my turn at the front of the line, the uniformed guard at the doors watches indifferently as I place my hand over the fingerprint scanning device. Bracing myself with anxiety, I sing my identification tone and touch the smooth surface. Just as expected, instead of the usual blue color light to admit me, the scanner pulses a sickly yellow.

Ah, crap of a goat. Yesterday's overseer, the accursed *chazuf*, recorded me as unfit for duty. "Yellow" means I am temporarily restricted.

The guard comes partially alive and puts up his hand before me to prevent me from coming any closer.

I open my mouth, ready for the confrontation, prepared to argue my way in. "I can explain. I must talk to the overseer," I say firmly.

"You, no," the guard says in a dull voice. "Return another day. Now, stand aside, and let the others in line approach. Next!"

I take a deep breath and raise my voice. "I need to speak with the supervising overseer right now!"

"I said, step aside," the guard says.

I note that the women in line behind me start to grumble, and give me dirty looks, since I'm making them late. Meanwhile, the ones already admitted within and dealing with the sterilization booth, are glancing back at me with curiosity and disapproval.

It's not customary to argue with the guard. "Yellow" means what it means—come back another day. It could be worse, could be "red," which means no admittance due to termination of employment—or otherwise unauthorized.

But I'm in a particularly foul mood—lack of sleep exacerbating the injustice of what happened to me yesterday.

. . . and the shadow of what's hanging over our heads. . . .

"All right, listen to me," I say, taking a step forward and feeling my pulse start to race yet again. "I was falsely dismissed yesterday. There was blood on my clothing—it was *not* my own. Someone else wiped their hands on my skirt!"

"I don't care," the guard says. "Begone, girl. You don't want me to escort you off the property."

With one rational part of my brain, I'm fully aware that the guard is being polite right now. He could very easily give me a hard shove and physically lift and carry me out of here. He's a brute, more than a head taller than me, and while I'm tall and strong for a girl, my muscles are no match for this *hoohvak*.

But there's a stubborn mule inside me. There's always been one and, not sure which of the blessed gods put it there, but I feel that mule stir regularly, so I feed it and allow it to come out.

Such as now.

"The overseer," I say, my voice becoming very hard . . . bright and resonant. "Call the overseer right now. I *know* my employee rights. I *invoke* my employee rights!"

"Ah, come on," a woman speaks up behind me. "Give it up, fool, just go home. We're all going to be late!"

I ignore her, and stare at the guard, looking up directly into his black eyes, never blinking my own.

A long pause. And then the guard makes a snort of disgust. He lifts his wrist to his mouth and speaks into the communication unit encircling his thick limb. "This is entry one. I need supervisor assistance at the gate," he says in a bored tone. And then he adds to me: "Now, step aside, while the overseer arrives."

"Thank you," I reply in a stilted but now polite manner, and move to stand next to him, while the line of workers resumes moving. Women pass me and give varying looks—irritation, disgust, curiosity, pity, even outright approval.

"Gods give you luck," one of them whispers with a smile.

It doesn't take too long for the supervising overseer to approach us. It's not the same man as yesterday, but I know him. Unfortunately, he is even less pleasant than the *chazuf* who sent me home the previous morning. And he also happens to be the head overseer of all the shifts, a thick man with a fancy wig and excessive kohl around his eyes, as if he aspires to nobility. . . . Right now, as he walks swiftly toward us, his deep mahogany-colored upper management robe flapping over his uniform trousers, he appears highly irritated, and carries his scheduling tablet in his hand.

Ah! Bastet . . . Not a good sign. . . .

I stand firm, closing my fingers over the folds of my skirt and grasping the fabric for inner strength.

"What's the problem here?" the head overseer asks the guard in a condescending tone.

The guard merely points at me.

The overseer gives me a cold, scathing look. "Name?" he asks, swiping his tablet.

"Semirameos," I say, "Circle Ten, Denwen's Pit."

"Put out your hand. First finger and thumb."

I comply.

He passes the tablet underneath my fingers to scan, then reads my employment record. "It says here, you were dismissed yesterday for bleeding, and to return next week. Why are you here now?"

I explain, the words rushing out of me in an emotional river. "It wasn't my blood!" I conclude. "Someone else wiped their hands on me and made it look like it was mine, but it's not! I can prove it! Check my body if you have to, check the hands and fingers of those others who work right next to me in my row! It was most likely Odira, or Jigudin, or Labaat, check them—"

But the head overseer's expression is hard and merciless as he cuts me off. "Silence, girl. Chiprahat doesn't have time to check filthy bodies of all of you who make such claims. I see that you have one reprimand on your record. I give you a second reprimand for wasting my valuable time. Now, get out of here, and don't come back until the first day of next week."

And he starts to turn around, dismissing me with his gaze.

My jaw falls open. "But—" I say. "This is—this is absolutely *unfair!* All because of some lying bitch who set me up! Please, I need the work! Listen to me, please! I really need this shift, I can't go half a week without coins—"

The overseer pauses. His corpulent face tightens in thought, and his features twitch with what has to be pure malice. He lifts his tablet again, and looks at me with an incinerating expression of finality. "Third reprimand," he says with a sneer, and marks the tablet.

"What?" A gasp comes out of my mouth before I can control myself.

Shut your mouth, Semmi, just shut your mouth, girl. . . . my thoughts race, even as I force myself to not say another word.

But it's too late.

At my outburst, the overseer smiles, showing his *sha* teeth, almost gleefully. "What was that you said?" And with a hard swipe he marks the tablet yet again. "You are now permanently dismissed."

And with a motion to the guard, the overseer says, "We have a trespasser. Have her removed from the Chiprahat property at once."

Out of nowhere—no, out of the depths of my soul—a sudden swell of anger at the injustice rises in my blood, making it boil . . . rises to set me on fire. My head and neck, my chest—all of me—I am burning.

"You—you *terminated* me?" I exclaim, a song of a thousand stomping mules singing in my temples. "You are letting me go *for nothing?* I've done nothing wrong! Nothing to deserve this! What kind of evil, heartless *chazuf* are you? I'm a first-rate worker, I chop faster than anyone in my row! Check my record for months! I've never cut myself, never bled on the job! Never stolen anything, never complained! I've worked with all my heart for the prosperity of Chiprahat Exquisite Foods, the ungrateful *bakris* lot of you—"Exquisite Foods" my ass! You are not even fit for goats, you and your accursed *shar-ta-haak* mushrooms—"

As my voice rises to the level of yelling, workers nearby pause to watch in a kind of fascinated horror, and there are mutterings in the line.

The head overseer stares at me in genuine shock. His own jaw has dropped in outrage, and he lifts one trembling finger to the guard. "Out!" he yells in a high voice. "Get her out of here!"

The guard grunts, almost with regret at having to bestir himself and do his job. Suddenly I feel his thick muscular arms lifting me off my feet.

Did I mention, in addition to mules, I have other beastly things living inside me? The gods chose to fill me with a herd of horned bulls and rabid monkeys, several herons and wild geese, ducks and roosters, slippery water snakes . . . and deep inside there's probably at least one monstrous crocodile. . . .

I begin to struggle like a pack of *sha*. As the guard attempts to carry me, I squirm and kick and punch him with both my fists, flailing around and landing blows—not only on the brute carrying me but at everyone and everything within reach.

The women all around us start to scream, while the head overseer screams also, his high voice going even higher still, as he calls for reinforcements.

"You have no power to hold me! Now that I no longer work for Chiprahat and your hairy baboon-ass, I can speak my mind! You think you took away my job? What does anything matter anyway? The Sky Rock is coming to smash us, and we're all going to die, and that includes you and your rotten mushrooms!" I yell, kicking and scratching, and hear the guard cry out in pain—I must've twisted precisely right and landed my knee directly in his privates.

Serves the shar-ta-haak *right!* He was starting to choke me, close to cracking my ribs in his brutal hold.

"I request correctional assistance!" the overseer yells into the tablet. "I request City Guard at Chiprahat Exquisite Foods immediately! We have a madwoman assaulting me and my employees!"

Before he finishes, I strike out in his direction. Twisting wildly, I squirm like a snake, both my legs kicking upward, and the balls of my feet somehow end up in his face.

There is a crunch . . . and there's a gush of blood and undoubtedly a broken nose.

As the head overseer of all shifts at Chiprahat Exquisite Foods drops his tablet and wails in agony, holding his bloodied face, my mind starts to spin out. The profound realization of what just happened sinks in, and with it the cold, implacable reality.

What have I done?

Everything has become so sharp, rendered in such intense focus. . . . The night sky overhead is full of stars, and the artificial light orbs cast a golden glow and shadows at the warehouse building all around.

Just then, the guard gives me a hard blow on the head which stuns me enough to make me stop moving. And now as I hang limp, I feel like I'm floating, a disembodied entity watching myself peacefully from a remote, safe distance.

Except, now I hear the screeching sirens of the approaching City Guard.

Grandmother, forgive me . . .

Bast, most Holy, o Bastet, Thou Whose Glory Shines Brightly . . . what have I done?

CHAPTER
SIX

B y the time the City Guard arrives—in not one but three polished metal hover cars, apparently dispatched to overcome not merely one scrawny girl but an entire warehouse uprising—I've stopped struggling and have fallen into a stupor. There are several painful bruises on my neck and head from the guard's meaty fists. My ribs ache, and I can barely breathe while I continue to hang limp in his merciless hold. It's amazing that my worn sandals are somehow still attached to my feet, their rope ties cutting into my ankles.

The shift overseer waits for the City Guard, even as he's being cared for by several warehouse med techs right outside. As soon as the officers emerge from the cars, wearing their distinctive gray uniforms, he eagerly points me out to them.

"Take her! Take this crazy *sha* away and lock her up!" he cries thickly, while a medic works on resetting his nose. "She deserves to lose a limb or worse!"

The Chiprahat guard transfers me over to the CG custody. I feel the new rough and impersonal hold of their gloved hands, the cold metal of the vice restraints placed around my wrists. Then, I'm dragged by my arms, two men walking on both sides of me. Their impassive faces are partially obscured by helmeted visors.

They push me inside, deep into the back of one hover car, and I am plunged in windowless darkness and absolute silence as the door shuts on me. I sprawl on the floor since there's no seat, only floor, ceiling, and walls of this movable holding cell. There's a musty, disgusting smell of vomit and alcohol and human body rot and filth. Add to that a salty, metallic tang of blood. No one apparently cleans the back area of this hover car. It could be intentional.

I am going to prison.

And that's just the beginning. I will be charged with multiple crimes. I might be mutilated. I might even be sold into indentured labor to pay off the damage and injuries I've caused.

THE HOVER CAR JERKS ONCE, reorients smoothly, and then starts moving. Desperate thoughts swirl inside me as I sit with my feet awkwardly stretched out on the filthy floor, with my wrists bound in front of me. I must let Grandmother know what happened. Somehow, I must let her know.

As I shift and stretch out my legs again, there's something that feels like a sack on the other side of the holding cell. A lump against the soles of my sandals. And then I hear moans. . . .

Gods help me, I'm not alone.

I try not to move any more, because whoever it is, they could be more dangerous—genuinely dangerous, unlike me. Or it could just be a pitiful drunk the CG picked up on their rounds.

At once, thoughts of my Father come to me, and I try to imagine what Amurabia and he will do, now that I'm gone (*because I'm not coming back from this incident, I am well and done*). They'll just have to manage somehow. . . . Uru will continue to run errands, maybe double up on his time in the markets and work late afternoons and well into the evenings. . . .

. . . Until the Sky Rock comes and brings death and destruction to all.

My biggest regret now is, I won't be with my family when it happens. I've hoped to be with them at the end—

A QUARTER of an hour passes and the hover car stops with another jolt. Then the door opens, and bright light shines in my eyes, making me squint and blink.

An officer reaches in and pulls me up on my feet, while another one goes to pull out the sack-like human behind me. I see it's a filthy older man in torn clothing, with filmy, dazed eyes —just as I thought, some kind of pitiful homeless or drunk. Whatever he's done, it's most likely desperate—petty theft or trespassing. Poor *chazuf.*

Without any explanation, we are shoved forward and made to walk along a featureless walkway between two tall buildings and past a gate into a fortified jail yard, artificially illuminated by orb light and surrounded by tall walls of mauve and black stone. There are sharp metallic lance points bristling with spikes embedded all along the top of the walls to deter escape. The sky is starting to lighten slightly, with a faint blue at the eastern horizon.

Despite my mental haze, I now recognize this place. I've seen those imposing walls on the news feeds and crime show feeds. This is the Poseidon Municipal Correctional in Circle Six.

The largest prison complex in the City.

I've never been near it, but then, I've never had any business in Circle Six. Indeed, I can count on one hand the number of times I've ventured this far into the heart of the City.

Why am I here? Why not some small local jail in Circle Eight? How much trouble am I in?

The dull stupor of despair rises in my gut. My freedom is

gone. The one and only thing I've had going for me as a free-born resident of this greatest City of *Atlantida*.

I've lost it, all of it now. I'm never coming out of here, except to be sold as an indentured laborer or even slave. . . . And the best-case scenario is, they let me keep my limbs so that I can perform the work. An indentured laborer is no good without hands or feet.

Think positive, Semmi. . . . Imagine what Grandmother would tell you to think under the circumstances.

Ah, my Grandmother. *I'm so sorry*, Mei-Ma! *So sorry. . . .*

A gushing flood of guilt and remorse comes over me. I mentally scream at myself, rant in my vast echoing head at my own stupidity and hotheadedness.

We arrive inside the building, stepping past the imposing entrance into the compact admittance chamber. Beyond it is a large area behind transparent, clear material that I know is marvelous, reinforced glass. So much of it, all in one place! The guards communicate with their wrist bands to the clerks and officers in the brightly lit chamber on the other side, and then the glass is parted via floor-to-ceiling sliding doors.

"Book her for primary assault, bodily injury, and trespassing," the arresting officer pushing me tells the seated officers. "Chiprahat Exquisite Foods warehouse in Eight called it in. And this one—" He points to the stumbling, tattered man behind me. "This one just needs to be locked up overnight. Let him out tomorrow, this time. Dump him back in Ten, Denwen's Pit; don't want him wandering here in restricted, *clean* areas."

I'm then directed to step into what looks like a large sterilization booth, and the man is pushed in right behind me. I know how this works, so I close my eyes as the sharp stinging spray of antiseptic mist fills the chamber, and try to hold my breath and ignore the pain in my various bruises and open wounds. Meanwhile, the poor drunk has no idea how to act. I hear his pitiful moans and cries of pain as he gets his eyes full of the cleansing spray, then stumbles, nearly falling on me.

Next, we are released through heavy, secure doors into another large room with long benches circling each of the four walls and a large upraised desk in the center, behind more reinforced glass. Two scribe clerks occupy the desk enclosure. Meanwhile, a number of bedraggled, grim, scary, or otherwise despair-filled men, women—and quite a few children—fill the benches around the perimeter. Everyone's hands are restrained in metal cuffs before them, just as my own are, and some have additional ankle cuffs with thick chains.

Sticking out among them, like garish roses among weeds, are three extremely well-dressed youths—two young men and a young girl, all of them my age or slightly older. They appear noble, rich, privileged.

The two young men wear their shining black and brown hair long and loose, over fine embroidered fabric jackets and pants in warm earthy colors of the latest style seen on the feeds. The female's braided human hair wig is painted *niktos* blue, garlanded in pearls. Her flowing black tunic spills like the evening sky over layered pants of diaphanous, sheer gold mesh fabric with a velvety plum underlayer, while her high platform shoes are trimmed in gold. All three have exquisite kohl around their eyes, and rich color gloss on their lips, and are laden with expensive jewelry. They could be newly arrived from an elite house party. . . .

And although their hands are similarly restrained with metal cuffs, these three are lounging casually on the bench, whispering among themselves—entirely unlike the rest of the pitiful denizens of this chamber. There are even occasional stifled sounds of laughter.

The officers at the enclosed desk are apparently resolved to pay little attention to them, but occasionally cast stern glances in their direction when the giggling becomes too loud. The other detainees in the chamber, however, ogle them with varying degrees of curiosity and resentment. Especially their jewelry.

I am directed to approach one of the clerks at the desk, while the pitiful drunk behind me is merely told to sit down—which he does, staggering and landing hard in a small free spot on the bench between two other arrestees who barely glance at him, their expressions equally dull.

"Your name," the officer clerk, a pale, dark-haired woman, asks me, barely looking up from her small screen.

"Semirameos," I say, without adding anything else. The less said to the City Guard, the better. Or, so popular wisdom goes.

"Show your hands—palms down, on this spot."

I lift my bound hands and awkwardly place them on the small flat surface near the glass, marked by an outline of two human hands.

As the device scans me, the officer checks the screen. She then looks up and gives me a withering look. "Violent assault of a superior at Chiprahat, resulting in significant injury. Disruptive behavior, trespassing. Surprisingly, no priors. Hard to believe such a skinny thing as you can cause so much trouble."

"I was unjustly dismissed from my job, for absolutely nothing," I respond suddenly, without thinking.

The officer's unblinking gaze is fixed upon me. "And what was your job?"

"Same as everyone else," I say. "Chopping mushrooms."

At that, there's a stifled burst of laughter behind me. I turn around and see the well-dressed trio watching me. The girl holds her restrained hands over her mouth, and is rocking back and forth, her jewelry tinkling with motion, while the black-haired youth spits out a choking sound, and the brown-haired one has his head down and is shaking in hilarity.

"Quiet, all of you!" the officer states loudly. "Another outburst and your bail price doubles."

She then turns back to me. "Based on your multiple serious charges, this magistrate office determines you will be confined to this prison until further punishment is ruled by the court and your final sentence is issued to you."

"Confined . . . for how long?" I look her in the eyes as I speak.

The officer makes a sarcastic sound. "You dare to ask? Three weeks until court, then you get ten years at a minimum, with additional labor to work off the price of the injuries incurred upon Chiprahat's management. Specifics to be requested by their arbiter, later in the proceeding. For now, sit down over there and wait to be processed for incarceration."

Ten years!

"May I—may I send a message to my family?" I ask. "My Grandmother—she'll be worried, and my Father—"

"Sit *down*." The officer replies, her voice slamming into me.

I comply, and cast my gaze around the room to find the nearest empty seat along the bench. There's one near the corner, next to a man who appears to be asleep against the wall, and I head for it, passing the three well-dressed detainees who whisper and stifle laughter once again as I move past them and their expensive footwear.

I sit on the hard bench and exhale. Moments later, I begin to tremble.

AT LEAST AN HOUR PASSES, maybe longer. The room is poorly ventilated and is starting to feel airless and hot. It's mostly quiet, with low whispers and periodic creepy stares or sneers from hardened faces. The officers at the desk continue to work, ignoring us, and process occasional newcomers who are told to sit on the overcrowded benches.

Boredom, anxiety, and despair. . . . A dire mix of dissonant emotions boils inside me. The *chazuf* next to me, seemingly asleep or passed out at the wall, does not move. For all I know, he could be dead.

Officers come and go, and some of the detainees are removed from the room and taken elsewhere in the facility through a different set of doors. No doubt, taken to be incarcerated.

To be incarcerated, I think. *Any moment, someone will come for me, to take me away.*

And I will disappear for a minimum of ten years . . . but, in reality, for the rest of my life.

At some point, the officers at the desk receive a call that, for whatever reason, causes them to become more alert and animated. I look up from my neurotic fidgeting; cease clutching my skirt and tapping my fingers over my thigh to keep the trembling down. And I watch the heavy entrance doors opened solicitously by two officers. An elegant man enters after them.

He is definitely not a detainee.

The officers hold the doors and bow before him, and the two at the glass enclosure rise from their desk seats.

The newcomer is a young man. He is on the tall side, of a lean but sufficiently muscular build. He has long black hair that falls behind him, loose and unfettered, over a dark olive outfit—an expensive jacket trimmed with fine gold mesh and similar pants, fine suede boots with sharp, fashionable toes. Long-fingered, strong hands clad with glittering rings, catch the light.

His skin is golden tan, lighter than mine. A coldly handsome face.

Underneath dark, proudly arched brows, eyelids highlighted with kohl, his eyes are a murky, *indeterminate* color. . . .

Oh, no. . . . Crap of a goat.

I know those eyes. Yes, the illumination here is wrong, but now the details are brought into focus, made clear in this bright, artificial light.

Once again, impossibly, it's the Man in the Niktos Cloak.

Stunned, doubting myself for an instant, I freeze.

"Welcome, *Ter* Bisfuri," the woman officer at the glass enclosure says with a nod that is almost a bow. "It is a profound honor. You grace us with your—"

"Where are they?" he interrupts bluntly in a deep, rich voice (it serves as a confirmation; I recognize it immediately). And he looks around the room.

"Regrettably, they are here, ready for you—" the second officer at the desk begins to speak, and points in the direction of the three young nobles on the bench.

But the Man in the Niktos Cloak, who has been addressed with the gentleman honorific *Ter*, has already seen them.

Bisfuri, Bisfuri, my mind races, as I try to recall what noble Family that is, *Bisfuri.* . . . Compared to most people, I know so little about the elites, only what we're shown on the social feeds —which I tend to ignore.

At the same time, the blue-wigged girl exclaims, "Benaten! Thank the gods, there you are!"

She attempts to wave cheerfully with her shackled hands, then starts to get up. But the brown-haired young man pulls her back down by the arm, with a meaningful look at the officers in the enclosure.

The Man in the Niktos Cloak, *Ter* Bisfuri . . . Benaten.

Slowly he saunters toward the three. And he stops over them, ignoring the girl and staring directly at the young man with black hair. Black hair that's very similar to his own.

For that matter, it occurs to me, there is additional resemblance between the seated youth and this *Ter*. Something in their lean, well-formed features. The seated young man's face is slightly more rounded, softer, younger.

A relative, maybe?

"Took you a while, Aten," the youth says, looking up with a bland expression.

Benaten, *Ter* Bisfuri merely stands over him, saying nothing.

Several excruciating moments pass. Everyone in the chamber is staring—detainees, officers.

"I took my time," he replies at last, in a hard tone. "What stupidity did you do now? What am I paying for?"

"Nothing," the seated one says carefully, after the tiniest pause. "Nothing—much."

"We were just driving around, looking for some late-night fun, no harm intended," the brown-haired youth inserts. "Sorry that it got out of hand. Something's wrong with my hover car, so we took Eham's—"

Ter Bisfuri looks around at the officers. "What's the damage?" he asks loudly.

The officers glance down at their screens. "*Im Ter*, there are three crashed vehicles, two ruined storefronts, a smashed temple delivery cart, various merchandize petty damages, removal fee for vehicles structurally embedded in an upper floor, a minor injury to one of the drivers—"

"And who is being charged in the incident?"

"It's regrettable to say, once again, it is your brother. Behamenut Bisfuri is the primary perpetrator, driving the vehicle at fault," one officer recites. "The *Taq*—the female perpetrator, Shebaat Eliafu, gets secondary charges, for throwing objects from the upper floors and vandalism of property after the initial air collision. Finally, third to be charged is Naviur Danai—"

"All right," *Ter* Bisfuri, says coldly, stepping away from his brother and beginning to pace. "What is their bail amount, plus all . . . incurred consequences?"

"For all three of them? Just a moment, *im Ter*, allow us to tally. Unless you'd prefer to simply cover the bail amount now and, for your convenience, receive a bill at your residence for the final settlements at a later date?"

"No bill," he says. "We settle it all here and be done with it, on behalf of all three *hoohvaks*. None of the Families are to be informed."

"Of course, *im Ter*, understood. A few moments, then."

Still frozen, hardly breathing, I watch as *Ter* Bisfuri waits, pacing a few steps away from me—not looking at his brother or his friends, but glancing instead around the room. Underneath the bright lights overhead, his long, glossy black hair is slightly wavy at the ends, with a ruddy-violet sheen. I watch it cascade down his strong back, stirring with each step. Images of him fighting suddenly come to me . . . muscular limbs moving very, very fast in the darkness of the street. . . .

At some point his wandering gaze falls upon me.

The moment is fleeting as he glances at me, does not stop, does not seem to remember or recognize me.

Nor should he, I think. We interacted only for a few brief moments yesterday, in the dark, and so far away from here. There is no context for him to place me. Besides, my face is now bruised and ugly with dirt and some blood smeared in my hair where the Chiprahat guard mauled me; I could be developing a black eye. . . .

"How much longer?" he asks eventually, stopping to look at the desk officers.

"Almost done, *im Ter*, just working on the third perpetrator's tally."

Bisfuri shakes his head slightly and resumes pacing. This time I see him cast a very dark look at his brother.

"Just another few moments, *Ter* Bisfuri, our apologies," the male officer says hastily, a few heartbeats later. He continues doing something on his screen, then calls the female officer to look at it.

"No," she explains in a hissing whisper. "That's the departmental total. You need to add these: bail plus charges, *then* round down, and subtract from the booking room total—

see this big, auto-generated number here is the room—just run that routine against the offense code—"

"*Enough,*" Bisfuri says suddenly, in a cutting voice. He stops and motions with one hand, palm up. "How much for the room?"

The two clerk officers look up. "Begging pardon, *Ter?*" one of them asks.

"The room," Bisfuri repeats with a shadow of sarcasm. "The 'auto-generated number.' What's the bail for everyone in this room?"

There is stunned silence.

My breath catches. In my temples the pulse starts to race. . . . Everyone else around me also seems to stop breathing as we all freeze and *stare.*

What is happening?

The officers' expressions are incoherent. "What?" the female asks.

"Do you mean, *Ter* Bisfuri," the male clerk echoes stupidly, "that is, are you saying you want to pay the bail for *everyone* in this room? You can't mean—"

"Yes," *Ter* Bisfuri replies, looking directly at the speaker. "That is what I'm saying. What is the total?"

The officer's jaw has dropped. The detainees in the room begin stirring, life coming to deadened eyes.

Even the three young nobles are impressed, watching Bisfuri with amused surprise. The female, Shebaat, snorts and giggles without restraint, and opens her mouth wide to share an expression of disbelief with brown-haired Naviur who wiggles his eyebrows.

Meanwhile, the brother, Behamenut, runs one hand through his silky dark hair and shakes his head, then sucks in a deep breath.

"*Ter* Bisfuri! It is impossibly generous of you," the woman officer intones. "If you are very certain, then—the total bail for the present detainees is—" and she reads off a number that I literally cannot even comprehend.

Bisfuri doesn't even blink. "Very well," he says, and approaches the glass enclosure, reaching out with his wrist which has a bracelet device. Then he stops and says, "Hold it— what about the rest of the settlement charges for the room? Whatever else—name the amount enough to cover the court expenditures and projected labor debt for all the convicts. Let's go ahead and *double that*. It should cover their unencumbered freedom."

"What? *Ter* Bisfuri!" both the officers exclaim. "Your generosity towards Poseidon Municipal Correctional continues to be astounding! We will inform the Warden immediately, and there will be a new wing named after the Family Bisfuri, in addition to the South Wing structure which was so kindly donated by your esteemed Father, the Lord Bisfuri—"

"Aten . . . seriously? Are you sure?" Behamenut speaks up just then. "That's crazy even for you. You're gonna pay for all these dirty *bakris*?"

His brother barely glances in his direction. "Shut your *bakris* mouth, Eham," he says coldly. "I'll deal with you later." And turning back to the officers, he taps on his wrist with one long finger and says, "Scan it."

My mind is reeling. *I'm going to be free!*

And my second thought is, *just how much insane money does this Bisfuri have?*

Bastet knows, it's a sorry fact that no one ever pays their bail. Most of the arrested detainees don't have anywhere near the funds required to cover their release. Except for the wealthy, the outrageous bail fee is a legal formality. Instead, everyone just goes to prison and does time—usually for most of the rest of their lives.

And yet, somehow, Bastet the Holy and Merciful heard my unworthy pleas—all our pleas—and a miracle has occurred!

The detainees in the chamber start making noise. People are getting up, clutching each other in case of families, disbelief and joy and *life* coming to some faces, hard suspicion flickering in others.

As the officer scans Bisfuri's wrist device, she adds quietly, "Now, *Ter* Bisfuri, are you certain you want the worst of the criminals to be released? Most of the rabble is relatively harmless but there are also murderers here, rapists—"

Bisfuri pauses for an instant, then nods with a cruel smirk. "Why not?" he says in his deep, dark voice, as his piercing gaze scans the room. "Let them all out. You know that in about three months from now, none of it will matter? Not for any of them—or you."

"Oh—yes, the Sky Rock," the female officer says with new anxiety.

"Divine retribution." *Ter* Bisfuri nods at the room. "They won't have time to do much of anything in the coming days, and some of the better souls will even spend it with their families. I'd say that's more *amusing* in the greater scheme of things than having another building named after us."

His immense monetary transaction is completed, and now additional officers arrive in the room. They start going around and removing restraining cuffs and shackles, beginning with the three nobles.

As they move about the chamber, people come alive. "Go, thank the generous *Ter*," the officers say to each, as cuffs are removed. "Get out of here! But first, go thank him for your worthless lives and your freedom—it's a miracle granted to you by the gods!"

And the arrested detainees all surge toward the man who just gave them their freedom. There are gestures of gratitude from some, exclamations and even weeping; simple curt nods of respect from others. Only a few sullen ones show no reaction at all, simply hurry out of the room through the now wide-open doors.

When it's my turn and the handcuffs are removed, I spring up from my seat and start to move toward Bisfuri, my heart beating so hard that it's ready to jump out of my chest.

But by the time I make it past the pressing line of others, he and his liberated brother and companions have moved away and exited the holding room.

I follow.

To maintain a semblance of order in the unexpected chaos, the CG officer guards vaguely enact crowd control in the exterior chamber. I see Benaten Bisfuri's striking profile as he negligently nods to the poor, bedraggled men and women pushing and shoving all around him—barely acknowledging their flood of thanks, it seems. He then walks quickly, with the young nobles following close at his side and chatting lightheartedly.

When I reach the main exit outside, they are still visible in the distance, and then they're gone.

Meanwhile, the freed detainees rush the walkway between prison buildings, a sea of humanity, and I am pushed along with them into the bright sunshine and cool air of full morning.

Outside the mauve-and-black stone prison walls, I pause, flexing my painfully bruised wrists. For a heartbeat I stand like a *hoohvak*, my fingers tugging uselessly at the folds of my skirt. . . . I wipe my forehead, my nose, squint my eyes from the sun, as the wind fills my face with curling wisps of my dirty, messy hair.

Where is this? Where am I? Ah, yes, somewhere in the middle of Circle Six. Beyond the sterile and imposing stretch of the prison complex lie manicured streets and high-tech industrial facilities, judging by the level of airborne traffic glittering with colorful metal against the blue sky.

I didn't get the chance to thank him.

And yet, unbelievably . . . I'm free.

CHAPTER
SEVEN

W alking briskly, stunned and still in disbelief, it takes me several hours to make it back to Circle Ten's hovel town and the street of my home.

As I walk, it feels like someone gave me a deafening blow on the head and knocked the *thinking part* out of me. It's like a boiling soup in there, everything churning. . . . All these strange, confusing events, good and bad.

Just to think—I've broken the nose of the management *chazuf* at Chiprahat . . . and got arrested. I got mauled. I lost my job. . . . But miraculously, I'm not going to prison.

The latter, thanks to the insanely rich and strangely generous Man in the Niktos Cloak . . . whose name is Benaten Bisfuri.

Persistent, nagging guilt rises in the back of my head— *Mother of shibet, I didn't thank him.*

At last, I turn at the familiar street corner, past the data pole (safe and upright), and hurry to our hovel.

It's definitely later than noon, and the door is not locked. I pause, as now the shame and all the repercussions slam into me, full force. Quietly, I enter our empty living room.

"Mei-Ma . . ." I call out, my throat hoarse and dry after hours without water, and my voice uncertain.

"Is that you, Semmi?" Amurabia responds from her room.

I walk in, and she sees me—all of me, covered with bruises and filth, looking like *bakris* fallen out of the sky.

"Semmi! No! What happened?" Grandmother says, pausing her work and reaching for me.

"I'm so sorry, *Mei-Ma,*" I whisper as, out of nowhere, tears rise to blind my eyes. "I—did something stupidly awful and lost my job."

And then I tell her everything.

WHEN I'M DONE EXPLAINING, Grandmother takes a deep breath then places her hands around my cheeks, cupping my face. She stares into my eyes with her warm, dark brown ones. And then she pulls my head down, and her wrinkled lips press tightly against my forehead with a loud smack.

She kisses me several times, and spits on the floor between each kiss to ward away the evil *sha* eye.

"Child," she says. "It's all right."

"I lost my job, *Mei-Ma!*" I repeat, sniffling my nose.

Amurabia exhales loudly. "We'll manage."

"But—"

Grandmother raises one finger and shakes it at me. "Not another word! You'll find new work. Instead, tell me more about this amazing *Ter* Bisfuri! Are you quite certain he is the Man in the Niktos Cloak?"

"Well," I begin. "His eyes . . . and his voice—"

"Ah, Denwen and Bast help us!" Amurabia exclaims suddenly. "We cannot be indebted to him! You must thank him! We must *all* thank him! You must go and find him immediately!"

I watch as Grandmother goes into a frenzy, hobbling around

her tiny room, lifting objects as though trying to assess their value, looking around her as she rubs her hands.

"You and I will both go," she mutters. "But first, I will make *eos* pies! Yes, I must make my *eos* pies for him! But the apricots are not ripe yet! Oh, gods—"

"*Mei-Ma*, I really don't think he needs our *eos* pies," I say gently, blinking away the remainder of my tears. "He can probably buy a whole bakery of them. And—yes, I really want to thank him myself, I really do—I just don't know how. How to even find him?"

"Not want my *eos* pies? Nonsense!" she contradicts. "I make the best *eos* pies in all of Poseidon! I challenge any baker, even those at the Imperator's Palace, to make a better one! He shall have my *eos* pies!"

"But *Mei-Ma*—"

"*Fruit!*" Amurabia exclaims. "I must find other fruit at the markets! We'll go right now, and we'll find whatever is in season —pears are ripe now, and apples—"

"I need to get cleaned up," I say, trying to change the subject. "Right now, *Mei-Ma*. I'm filthy and the bruises are hurting with the dirt."

"Yes, go wash up! You must apply some honey paste on those scratches! And put your clothes in the basket for now, I'll take care of them, you need to rest and heal, and look your best when we visit *Ter* Bisfuri!"

"Oh, *Mei-Ma*. . . . We really shouldn't bother him." I shake my head in resignation, then wince as something stings and hurts at the back of my neck with my movement.

But Amurabia shoos me away with her hand. "Just go, wash! Then, honey paste, and find some nice clothes to wear, girl!"

AND SO, I take out my one and only so-called "nice" tunic and skirt from our clothes storage chest, grab a length of old linen for drying myself off, and tiredly climb the ladder to our roof. There, in the little shower cabin, I discard my fouled clothing and drop it right outside in a pile on the rooftop, just next to the folded clean clothes. Then I shut myself inside the stall.

Naked and feeling all the bruises, I pump the little water tank until it's full and ready, then steel myself for a cold jolt and open the water nozzle. The chilly water hits me with the usual shock, and this time there's the added pain of open cuts and sores.

I endure and let it wash the grime and blood away, working my hands carefully through my kinky hair (which unfortunately must be washed to remove this filth) and elsewhere to rid myself of the ugliness of this morning. Pausing the water, I use the good bar of soap to lather the rest of me, then re-open the rusty shower nozzle.

Quickly, quickly, before the water runs out. . . . Moments later I'm decently clean, and the water nozzle dribbles away into nothing. The used water around my feet runs down the drain into the sewer pipe. I stand on the stones for a few moments and let my hair drip—it's turned into a mop of unruly curls, and needs to be oiled promptly—then use the linen rag to dry myself.

Finally, I peek outside the cabin and scan the area of surrounding rooftops for any nosy neighbors (such as Sargon from two houses down who thinks he's an irresistible rooster for the girls, who likes to peep, and always ogles me). Fortunately, it's all clear. So, I sneak out naked on the roof, where all of hovel town can potentially see me, and quickly pull on my fresh clothing.

When I come down the ladder and back indoors, Amurabia is fussing in the living room, and Uru has returned from his latest errand. "Semmi, your face is all messed up," Uru says matter-of-factly, with a silly grin. "*Mei-Ma* says you beat up the overseer!"

"You think that's funny?" I crane my neck at him, but the ridiculousness of my otherwise pathetic situation and my little brother's tendency to tease, causes me to smile a little back at him. Just a tiny little, not too much; don't want to encourage the little *chazuf*.

"Yeah, it's funny, you broke his nose! Serves him right!" Uru says.

"Well, I did lose my job, so we'll see how funny you find things when we don't have enough coins to buy food."

"Maybe the Man in the Niktos Cloak can buy us food!" Uru exclaims. "He is richer than the Imperator!"

"Urumer!" both Grandmother and I cry out in horror.

"Don't say such shameful things, boy," Amurabia says, stopping to glare at him. She offers me the jar of our medicinal honey ointment, obtained recently from the local apothecary and still fresh with healing powers.

"I already owe him for paying my bail," I add, taking some of the honey to dab at my worst scratches. "This is not funny, little *sha*. Need to figure out a way to pay him back—not that I can see how."

"First, we need to find out where he lives," Grandmother says sternly, as she moves aside a decorative rug hanging on the wall that covers up the concealed cubby hole in the limestone where she keeps her money purse. The money purse is just a small cloth bag with a handful of coins the family has saved up. They're not the high-value gold ones etched with Imperial heads but the small, cheap bronze pieces—the only kind we ever earn. It's about enough to last us for two months going forward, but that's it.

Again, horrible guilt scrapes at my insides. *How will we make do until I find new work?*

And then I remember the Sky Rock. . . .

Grandmother takes out three coins then replaces the bag in the wall and covers it up. "This," she says, "should be enough for pears and quality honey, a jug of the best olive oil there is, and a few spices for my special recipe. We already have the flour. . . ."

"Are you really going to make *eos* pies?" I say, feeling a stab of embarrassment.

But Amurabia's one hard look silences me. "I will make them tonight—will stay up all night if needed. Then, first thing tomorrow, you and I will put on these same nice clothes and take a hover bus to wherever that good man lives—probably in one of the inner Circles."

"Where *does* he live?" I muse, frowning.

"Enough chattering," Grandmother retorts. "We're going to the market, this instant! Come along now, you'll help me carry things. You too, Uru—while we shop, you'll run around and find out where *Ter* Bisfuri lives!"

"Yeah, I can do that," my little brother says proudly.

"I know you can." Grandmother nods at him. And then she reaches for her cane.

AND SO, we head for the market—not the nearest local one in our own Circle, but the big one in Circle Nine, also known as the Old Fish Market, the same one where Uru does most of his errand work.

Amurabia hobbles along as quickly as she can, with determination, but still moves slowly compared to our usual gait. Normally she visits the big market maybe once a month, making a big deal out of it, because of the better-quality produce and goods overall. But today, we're all in a confused hurry.

"Run ahead, Uru, start asking questions about the Family Bisfuri," she tells him as we walk along the wide, mauve cobblestone-paved bridge over the black water canal connecting Circles Ten and Nine, passing mostly rolling carts and pedestrians.

The canal water sparkles like polished metal in the sunlight, under the brilliant blue sky. There's very little hover traffic in these parts, mostly small quick boards like Uru's for messenger and delivery workers. They whoosh past us, usually at street level or slightly above, as couriers deliver small packages or messages.

"Okay, I'm going!" my brother says. "You're so slo-o-ow, slow pokes."

"Bastet's kittens, Uru, just go." And then I add, "But don't you *dare* mention the connection to the Man in the Niktos Cloak."

The little *chazuf* whirls around. "Huh? Why not?"

"Because it's his secret, obviously!" I shake my head and frown at him. "We owe him so much, and the least we can do is keep it safe!"

"Your sister is right, boy," Grandmother nods, as she huffs slightly from exertion. "Speak nothing of it. You are looking for Bisfuri, nothing more. You understand? Tell me you got that!"

"Yeah, okay, got it." And my brother bursts forward at his normal, swift pace. Light as a baby goat, that boy, even without his board.

WHEN WE GET to the market, it's crowded as usual, filled with tantalizing smells of spices and smoke, fragrant flowers, freshly cut greens and hay, and sweet fruit . . . but today there's an added level of anxiety. Everywhere we turn among the stalls, people talk about the big Sky Rock, argue about what it means, what can be done.

"It's all a lie," one large woman pushing an onion cart yells loudly to her customer. "Buy the onions, stock up as usual, be smart. Don't believe the lies the fancy *shar-ta-haaks* tell us!"

The customer, a woman with three little boys, holding sacks

ready to be filled, makes a gasp. "Are you calling Blessed Churu a *shar-ta-haak?*"

"So what if I am?" the onion seller yells back angrily. "It's enough that times are tough, sales are slow, and now he's spreading this fake news of some made up Sky Rock. He thinks we're children to believe that? Where is this so-called rock, up there in the sky? How did it get there? Why didn't it fall on us sooner?"

"Don't question the gods, woman," another passerby retorts. "The gods keep the rocks where they like, and if they choose to throw them at us, we can't do much about it."

"Ah, *varqood* you, mind your own business!" says the onion vendor, with angry hand gestures at the man. "When was the last time anyone saw a rock falling from above, huh? Unless some *hoohvak* tossed one from a flying machine?"

"Water falls from the sky, and frozen hail, so why not rocks. . . ."

We pass beyond reach of that pointless conversation, as Grandmother hunts for whatever items she has in mind.

We get to the fresh fruit and produce stalls, and Amurabia steps forward and starts touch-testing the fruit while the vendors watch her—some closely, others with feigned indifference.

Finally, the best pears and apples are selected as the base for the *eos* pie filling. Amurabia also picks two over-ripe bananas for binding the dough, one perfectly ripe mango for flavor balance, and two fancy little fruits for which I don't have names but recall tasting them once or twice in my life—tart, juicy, and amazing—to liven up the filling. Such is my Grandmother's amazing secret recipe.

Amurabia haggles, then pays, and the vendors drop the purchases in the sack I'm holding ready.

Next, we head to the sweets, spices, then oils, and obtain the items needed. My arms are loaded with two sacks now, and the medium sized jar of olive oil bundled in netting swings on a rope across my shoulder.

"Almost done," Amurabia tells me. "I just need better cinnamon than this, and a bit of saffron—"

"You can't find better cinnamon," the vendor says with loud annoyance. "This is the highest quality, suitable for the Imperator's table."

"Then let the blessed Imperator have it," Grandmother retorts, turning her back on the vendor.

A few more stalls, and she finds what she's looking for. She sniffs, buys, while I stand next to her, overloaded, and listen to two vendors discuss the possibility of being chosen to serve the Imperator and the elites and go on the space ships.

"Where are they building them anyway?" one asks. "Can't be anywhere in this City, or we'd know. Did you see the early billboards that were here this morning? The Imperial news feed didn't say anything about the location—not that they would, probably making them all in secret somewhere far away in the outer provinces, to keep them safe from crazy *chazufs*."

"Who knows? Those ships must be immense. Should be easily seen from a great distance, like tall buildings," the other vendor replies.

"So how many do they expect to have all together?"

The first vendor shrugs. "Heh . . . not enough to fit all of us. But they did say the biggest ship will bear the Imperator and the noble Families and all who serve them. All that rich food and priceless belongings. So much wealth in one place. Imagine being hired by them, one would need Ra and Hathor's blessing. . . ."

Amurabia hands me the last of the purchases, and I make room in one of the sacks. "We have what we need, let's go home," she tells me, adjusting my load for better comfort, with additional rope around my back. "Now, where's that boy? Never mind, he'll have enough sense to return home on his own."

Just then, there's a change in general market noise. People look up, as a large hovering billboard approaches from on-high, a rectangle silhouetted against the bright daylight. When it gets close enough, like a flying wall, it begins displaying moving images. It descends to street level and pauses to levitate not far from where we are. Network commentator voices blast forth loudly, reading the latest news—something about Heru wanting to cooperate with the Imperial Kassiopei in regard to common resource logistics in the building of space ships. They're sending a new batch of experts and negotiators to Poseidon, all while there's general unrest in the Deshret Province.

I try to listen, but Grandmother shakes her head in disgust and tugs my arm.

We start back, moving in a hurry past the circulating crowds and staying vigilant of pickpockets. I glance around a few times, also watching for any sign of Uru.

By the time we get to the bridge, my hands are sore, plus Grandmother can barely walk, so we take a short break. I set down the sacks and the jug of oil on the cobblestones, and Amurabia collapses to sit on a low step border that runs along the bottom of the railing. She perches tiredly, cradling her walking cane in her gnarled fingers.

I remain standing. Resting my elbows on the railing, I lean forward and stare at the black canal water rushing below and the occasional hover riders streaking in the air like bird-specks in the sunlight.

The canal water is inky, its oily, iridescent surface casting indigo and rust shadows, even though it sparkles metallic in the light. Compared to other canals closer to the wealthy interior of Poseidon, this one is filthy and stagnant, overgrown with algae and polluted with garbage from the two Circles it divides. If I look closely, I can see disgusting things floating in it.

"*Mei-Ma!* Semmi!" Uru calls out, and comes bounding up to us. "I found out where he lives!"

"Good!" Amurabia shades her eyes from the sun with one hand as she looks up at him. "Where?"

Uru scrunches up his nose and his mischievous face appears extremely pleased. "In Circle Two!" he exclaims after a tiny dramatic pause. "Bisfuri is so rich and fancy, they are High Court!"

"Ah, crap of a goat." I exhale and make a sound combination of resignation and disgust. "That means we'll have to take the most *expensive* hover bus."

And that's the least of it, I think, as my stomach sinks with renewed anxiety. Circle Two is the most exclusive region of the City after the Center Circle that holds the Imperial Palace and Seat of *Atlantida*. To get there we would need to traverse half of Poseidon. Very likely, once there, we wouldn't even be permitted anywhere near their residence.

I tell this to Grandmother but she shrugs me off, and we continue home.

WE ARRIVE HOME HALF an hour later, moving as fast as Amurabia's pace permits. All along the way I offer numerous solid arguments to convince her that we should just give up on this insane idea of visiting Bisfuri. And bringing him our *eos* pies (ugh, I shudder with embarrassment).

Meanwhile, Uru tells us what he learned about the Bisfuri Family.

"They're as rich as the Imperials!" he starts off. "They own all these buildings everywhere, and I mean all over the City, and all these other lands outside! So much land, it's crazy! There's even a province named after them!"

"Ah! That does sound familiar . . . Bisfuri Province, yes, now I recall. So that's the same Bisfuri? Oh, my. . . . Go on," Amurabia says, as we unload our purchases. Next, she immediately goes to stoke the fire in the cooking pit outside, and only then returns indoors to sit down and rest before beginning her monumental baking project.

"Yeah, so the Bisfuri land is all over, far beyond the City, where the wild people live, and much of that land has riches you can dig out from underground," Uru continues. "Precious gems and metals—which includes the stuff that makes things fly —you know, oricook'em!"

"Orichalcum," I correct him.

"Yeah, that!" My little brother repeats, pronouncing the word slowly. "They have all the *ori-chal-cum!*"

"Well, that explains it," Amurabia says. "That stuff is priceless."

"And Bisfuri Family controls most of it," Uru says. "Lord Muutat Bisfuri is friends with the Imperator, and he has two or maybe three sons, and too many daughters, or maybe none. The Man in the Niktos Cloak—I mean, *Ter* Benaten—is the oldest of the sons. Or maybe the youngest? I forgot, sorry. Anyway, also found out that they live in the biggest high-security estate in Circle Two, and we might have to go past all these walls and guards to get inside."

"Well, so much for that," I say with some genuine relief. "We're not going, *Mei-Ma*. It's simple, they won't let us in."

"All the gods willing, they *will* let us in!" Grandmother exclaims stubbornly as she puts on her flour apron. "Enough! I'll begin my baking now, and you two keep out of my way, and don't even think to touch the fruit! And same goes for your Father when he gets home—tell him not to touch anything!"

It should be clear by now that when Grandmother sets her mind on something, there is nothing anyone can do to stop her. Probably not even the divine Imperator himself.

And so, while Grandmother goes into a baking frenzy, I make the supper tea and heat the pot with yesterday's leftovers.

Holy Bast help us, it's going to be a long evening, followed by a late night for her—and hence, for all of us.

Of course, the most terrifying things will happen tomorrow morning.

CHAPTER
EIGHT

True to her word, Grandmother stays up baking for most of the night. Only when the perfectly crispy, crusty, deliciously aromatic *eos* pies are cooling on the tabletop—and it's the second hour of Ra—does she collapse in bed, and so do the rest of us. Father, of course, falls asleep early, at his usual time, unhindered by the baking tumult in the living room around him. Father can sleep through anything, with the help of strong drink.

Despite the lateness of the hour, I have trouble falling asleep. I lie on my cot in the dark, listening to my little brother occasionally wheeze and mumble in his sleep. Anxiety runs wild in my head like a flapping goose, images of tomorrow's ordeal tumbling, stifling me. . . .

I don't recall falling asleep, but I certainly feel the sickening stab of nausea when I wake up with a start from a stupid dream of chopping mushrooms in prison while *Ter* Bisfuri watches me with reproach. That's what I get after a short night, even though I've officially "slept in," compared to my usual middle-of-the-night work schedule. *Bastet, yes* . . . I no longer have a work schedule.

It's barely dawn outside, a faint glimmer seeping through the thick rug hanging over our tiny bedroom window. Feels like somewhere around sixth hour of Ra. I creep past Uru, curled up on his cot and fast asleep, and into the living room and check the timepiece on the media-box to confirm my guess.

The room still smells fragrant and mouth-watering, full of the rich scent of the *eos* pies. They lie in perfect stacks on the table, ready to be placed in our nicest basket and covered with pristine linen.

As I contemplate them, Amurabia's tired face peeks into the living room. I note she is already fully dressed.

"Good, you're ready," she whispers, seeing me, and beckons with her finger. "Come. Let me see your clothes and hair, girl."

I follow Grandmother quietly into her room, so as not to wake up the sleeping lump on the bench that is my Father. There she straightens my skirt and pulls the tunic neatly around my slim frame, adjusting the folds at the top. Then she pats down and unsnags my curls with her large-toothed comb, so that they assume a more controlled way of framing my face. And she dabs a bit of olive oil throughout my hair.

"Ow." I wince a few times at the worst snags.

"Your bruises are not too bad. I was afraid the one around the eye was going to darken but it actually faded."

"Thank you . . . that's enough, *Mei-Ma*," I say, when she searches through her sewing box looking for a decorative ribbon to tie around my head.

"Hush, girl, we're going to a very fine place—you need to look your best!" Amurabia insists. And so, I end up with a band of silky fabric tying back my hair and opening up my forehead.

"There—with all that hair out of the way, now they'll see your pretty face," she adds with a satisfied grunt.

"Why?" I ask with an immediate self-conscious frown as I look in my grandmother's wrinkled face, her warm brown eyes. "What does it matter what they see?"

"It does matter to some people," she replies with a little sigh. "Such as noble House servants and guards at the doors, so that they see you looking presentable when they let us in."

"Huh. . . ." I make a meaningless sound.

"And it wouldn't hurt for *Ter* Bisfuri to see you looking nice either!" my ridiculous Grandmother adds smartly, even as I exclaim in outraged protest.

ONCE THE *EOS* pies are carefully packed in the basket for travel, we gulp down a few hurried bites of what's left of the leftovers and wash it down with plain water. No time to make tea. . . . Then, in the pale bluish twilight of dawn, Grandmother and I set out on our long and possibly futile journey.

Grandmother is wearing her best dress, her embroidered kerchief over her head, and has attached a special decorative handle to the top of her cane. It is polished wood with fine carvings of jackals and cranes interspersed by lotus blooms, and is only to be used for holidays and special occasions—such as now.

I walk at her side, carrying the basket entrusted to me with utmost care. And now we have to walk to Circle Nine once again just to reach the closest stop for the type of hover bus that goes to the City interior. Once we cross the canal bridge, the stop is not too far away.

As we walk, I cast concerned glances at my poor exhausted Grandmother, who hobbles along with steely willpower alone.

At the bus stop we wait for a quarter of an hour and the hover bus finally shows up, descending from the dawn-colored sky as a dark metallic speck. It approaches swiftly, taking on its usual elongated shape, then comes to a stop before us and hovers at ankle height above the ground. The door slides open and Grandmother steps on board, with me following, and drops her coins into the slot at the entrance. It's the poor people's option, next to a digital currency scanner for the wealthy patrons. I do the same thing with my own coin fare, and then we find our seats.

The interior of the bus is mostly empty, except for a few early shift workers. The only sound comes from the animated media walls where various feeds and sponsored commercials play.

"Attention, patron! Specify your destination now," our seats sound underneath us, playing the instructions in an annoying repeating loop. A row of ten circles lights up on the arm rests.

"What? Which one do I choose?" Grandmother asks hurriedly, fumbling at the armrest. She doesn't use public transport much, if ever, so I have to explain it to her . . . yet again.

"See this blue one, *Mei-Ma?*" I point. "It indicates where we are now. It's the second circle from the end, Circle Nine. We are going to Two. So press that one—" And I point to a different circle, also second-to-last, but on the opposite end of the row.

Grandmother and I select our destination, and the new circles light up gold. The seats underneath us shut up immediately—thank merciful Bast.

The bus waits a while longer, while another passenger gets on. At last, the door slides closed, and with a soft lurch, the vehicle lifts up into the sky.

WE STARE through the windows at the amazing sight of Poseidon below us, bathed in rosy morning light. The Circles and the canals, and the various distinct regions take on their true form, and the perfection of the City's circular geometric design is astounding.

Twinkling golden lights from residences and street lamps still sparkle among the ocean of indigo blue shadows of the retreating night. Directly below us, we see the familiar black canal and parts of hovel town with many tiny plots, closely packed alleys and streets, and cluttered rooftops—all of it swiftly receding as we advance onward. At the same time, more and more gilded rooftops and large structures of fine marble take shape in the distance, in the direction of the interior.

Amurabia sits stiff-backed and motionless, her fingers digging into the arm rests, as the unfamiliar sense of flying overtakes us. Not that my Grandmother is afraid, but she is cautious about being so high up, with the birds. . . .

The hover bus moves quickly, but it also makes frequent stops along its smart-programmed itinerary. It swoops down multiple times along various Circles, letting passengers out at the stops and picking up new ones.

The closer we get to the heart of the City, the more my gut feels like a bunch of knives are stabbing me. I look down at the canals, noting how they gradually lighten in color, fading from polluted black to cleaner brown, then green, then almost sky blue. The closer we get to the interior, the cleaner the water. Finally, recreational traffic becomes visible as small private boats and mini barges float upon the clear, nearly transparent surface of the innermost canals—between Three and Two and between Two and One, looming in the distance before us.

And the Circles themselves—they get smaller in diameter but become lush and green, with spacious residences and vast estates visible among verdant parks, instead of the multi-story urban clutter of low budget housing among narrow streets (such as what you see in Circles Ten through Seven).

By this point, we are the most bedraggled-looking passengers on this bus. Well-dressed wealthy people surround us, wearing fine fabrics and shining jewelry—business owners and high-end merchants, skilled tech professionals. They occasionally deign to cast disdainful glances in our direction.

I'm somewhat used to this kind of public transport discrimination, though maybe not to such an extent—but not my Grandmother. Amurabia's wrinkled face grows more and more somber as moments pass. She either stares out the window or occasionally looks at the nearest media wall playing a feed.

I also try to ignore the elite passengers around us and turn my attention to the closest wall that happens to be streaming the Imperial feed. On the screen are images of some kind of Court Assembly from the night before, with the Imperator and the Imperatris and all their children in attendance.

There are panoramic shots of the grand Assembly chamber, with the golden sunburst wall of the Thrones, the splendor of the Court, then closeups of our sacred rulers, their magnificent attire and perfect, immobile faces that we know so well. . . .

Framed by the tall-backed Imperial Throne in the middle, there's Blessed Churu with his divine Kassiopei features— beatific and benevolent as always, and yet with a new undercurrent of solemnity. The Imperator seems to barely repress grim weariness in his lapis lazuli-blue *wedjat* eyes naturally outlined in black, underneath raven-dark brows, while tension carves hollows in the deep bronze of his skin. He is wearing the golden Khepresh headdress with the Uraeus serpent rising from his forehead, which together constitute the Imperial Crown of *Atlantida*. His mane of long, Kassiopei-gold hair falls like glowing silk upon his shoulders. . . . That sacred hair of his Dynasty is impossible, true gold, purer even than the golden metal threads embroidering his *niktos* purple robes.

Next to him, on the Consort Throne, is his Imperial Wife and Consort, the imposing Imperatris Merneit whose stunning lavender-blue eyes and dignified beauty befits her position, and whose hair, the color of warm cinnamon, is bound and hidden by layers of shimmering veils. Then, on both sides of them, upon the lower Seats, the camera shows us the Imperial Princes. . . .

Prince Oron and Crown Prince Narmeradat sit on the Imperator's right hand, while Princess Arlenari sits on the other side, in the Seat next to the Imperatris. The camera floats to linger upon each one of them, the layers of gold, cascading jewels, their expressions fixed in empty regal masks. They might as well be wearing actual golden masks, so motionless they are, as they look out upon the Court.

The Crown Prince Narmeradat is young, striking, and handsome as his Imperial Father, but with a more menacing, hard expression in his eyes. His golden Kassiopei hair falls around him in waves, and he wears the Lesser Uraeus Crown on his forehead, with the serpent coiled in repose. The color of his jacket is scarlet. As Heir, he sits directly next to the Imperator.

On the other side of Narmeradat, his slightly younger brother, Prince Oron, shares the Kassiopei physical traits and benevolent expression of his Father, but with an additional current of brightness, a glimmer of hopeful energy in his eyes. He is the only one of the Imperials whose face does not seem imposing, but candid and almost childlike. And his jacket is of a muted, nondescript shade, as if he is trying to disappear into the background.

Last of all is Oron's twin sister, the Princess Arlenari—a pale pink lotus blossom of sparkling veils. She is possibly my own age, delicate and lovely, with the same Kassiopei gold hair and Dynastic features, lapis-blue *wedjat* eyes, perfect midnight-dark brows and light bronze skin. But her face has the strangest, most distant, most *vacant* expression of all.

I pause, staring at her in all that fragile, shimmering pink, and recall that the Imperial twins, Oron and Arlenari, are said to have been born moments apart. Oron came out first, with his infant sister literally clutching his feet, not willing to be separated from him even for a moment. . . . Bastet knows, that has to be nonsense, but it does make for a fine story.

Rumor also has it that Arlenari is *touched* by the gods, and not in a good way. Her mind is not quite right, they say. Or maybe, she is merely haughty and proud, so far above the rest of us mortals that she almost never deigns to speak or use her voice in public.

"The Princess is just crazy. Her servants say, when she's alone, she talks to herself," Uru has informed us on more than one occasion, bringing us the latest rumors from the markets, or else pointing at her when we watch the Imperial feeds at home on the media-box. "Look at her, she is so weird. . . ."

Even now, watching the obligatory close-up of the Imperial Princess Arlenari—she's hardly blinking, hardly breathing, wrapped in veils like her Mother and fixed in the same rigid pose, but without any sign of awareness—I must admit that the rumors must have some basis in reality. She *looks* strange. She resembles a fragile golden doll, not a living girl.

It's also possible that it's all an act, and she just genuinely doesn't want to be here. If that's the case, I briefly pity her.

OUR BUS RIDE lasts almost two hours, because of the interminable stops at all the Circles, but at last it is our turn. The hover bus descends low over the clear-water canal between Three and Two, and almost skims the sparkling water as it approaches for a landing on the bank of Circle Two, at a perfectly manicured stop among lush greenery and gravel paths.

Grandmother and I stand up and make our way past elegantly dressed passengers to exit the bus. The moment we step outside upon the marble-paved landing, the cool breeze hits us with a sweet perfume of blooming flowers. Honeysuckle bushes and shade-bearing trees rise in clusters of artful symmetry, casting dappled sunlight upon the ground. Flowerbeds full of greenery and bursts of colors form step-pyramids upon gentle hillsides, and everywhere, climbing vines of roses wind around latticework trellises.

Even the air is different here. . . .

We stand, somewhat stupefied, squinting in the sun. Both of

us have never stepped foot in Circle Two . . . at least I haven't. And I highly doubt that Grandmother ever wasted good coins to venture so far into the heart of Poseidon for no good reason, considering how everything is so outrageously expensive in the interior.

"Where to . . . now?" I mutter, looking around us, while the hover bus behind us rises swiftly and becomes another great bird in the sky, leaving us stranded in a pristine paradise.

"Do they have street signs here?" Amurabia asks, shaking her head. The bus stop area seems to be the only thing resembling a traffic landmark. There's a decorative pedestal, marked with the oval-and-wing symbol of the hover vehicle—its only identifying feature. There isn't even a bench.

"I don't see any." I shift the weight of the *eos* pie basket from one arm to the other. "Not even sure if they have streets."

"Nonsense," Grandmother says, striking the ground with her cane. "Let's go! We'll ask someone along the way."

And we set off walking along the path that meanders gently. For a quarter of an hour, we appear to be quite alone, no other passerby, and no dwellings, only an endless park.

"Must be nice to live like this," Grandmother mutters every time her gaze falls upon a statue, a small pedestal shrine, a pond with a sculpted fountain, or some other fine landscaping feature. It's hard to miss them, and we both involuntarily pause to gape every few paces, until she resumes hobbling forward with determination.

"*Mei-Ma*," I say, glancing at her with worry. "Before we go too far and get too lost, let's stop and maybe try to figure out where we are and what this is. . . . Why don't you go sit down on this stone bench here? Rest a little, while I'll run ahead and try to find someone to ask for directions—"

Before Amurabia can protest, we see an older man walking our way, with a small hovering platform sailing behind him. It is loaded with gardening implements, and the man wears a neat uniform and a wide-brimmed sun hat.

"Ah, blessed Bastet!" I exclaim, and immediately move toward him. "*Nefero eos, Ter*, we are somewhat lost! Would you please kindly direct us to the Estate of Bisfuri?"

The man sees us, glances from me to my Grandmother, and considers us for a moment. His expression is bland but not unfriendly. "I'm a gardener," he says with amusement, "not a *Ter*. But you are on Bisfuri land. Most of this side of the Circle is Bisfuri. The main House is over there." And he points behind him. "Keep to the left when you reach the first split in the path. Pass the gates and tell them you need the small deliveries entrance—it's in the rear, next to the airfield."

He sees the eos *pie basket and assumes we're making a delivery*, I think. And, I suppose, in some way, we *are. . . .*

"Thank you, good man," Grandmother responds.

"Thank you so much," I echo her.

The gardener nods politely and keeps going.

GRANDMOTHER AND I CONTINUE WALKING, this time, equipped with directions. A few daydreams later, the path splits in two. We follow the left one and then eventually arrive at a grand wall of sculpted bricks of a sun-bleached color of cream and honey. The path ends before gates of ornate, gilded metal. They are shut, and two black-uniformed guards armed with short staffs stroll lazily before them.

Before Amurabia has the chance to say something to ruin our luck, I get in front of her. "We need the small deliveries entrance," I tell the guards, holding up the basket.

"What is it?" one of them asks, nodding at the basket and examining us closely.

"*Eos* pies," Amurabia says, stepping past me.

The second guard approaches closer and reaches for the linen covering the pies.

Immediately, Amurabia slaps his hand away. "Don't even think to touch—these are for *Ter* Bisfuri, not the likes of you!"

Oh, Bast help us! My heart starts to pound at my Grandmother's daring.

But the guard merely chuckles and moves to open the gate.

"Which *Ter?*" the other, more cautious guard persists.

"*Ter* Benaten, of course," says my insanely fearless Grandmother.

"The deliveries entrance is in the back."

And just like that, they let us pass.

We could be carrying rocks, or knives, or fancy contraband firearms, I muse, my thoughts still whirling in residual anxiety. *Don't they care? Shouldn't they double-check?*

But then all such nonsense thoughts slip away, as the gates open and we see what's on the other side. . . .

THE HOUSE OF BISFURI is a palace. It is a many-tiered sprawling building of pale marble with gilded reliefs and moldings framing the roofs, sparkling glass windows reflecting the sunlight, with balconies and overhangs . . . and is at least five stories high. The façade in the front is carved with stone garlands of wheat and celestial objects worthy of temples, underneath a colonnade, with a flight of stairs leading to the grand entrance.

Both Grandmother and I stand gaping at it. I even make a little panicked sound.

Dear, glorious Bast the Holy and Sacred. . . . We should turn back.

But Grandmother tugs my arm, and we bravely head to the back, to the deliveries entrance. And yes, by the time we find it, we see the airfield with parked rows of elegant, metallic, latest-model hover-vehicles of all sizes and colors. Beyond the airfield is a hillside with stepped tiers of swimming pools and waterfalls cascading into the others, culminating in a large pond—all of it paved with exquisite mosaic stones, and then more gardens and parkland. . . .

I tear myself from the sight of it all, shut my mouth, and walk in front of my Grandmother to the first smaller side door we can find in this spectacular building.

It's unguarded, but appears to be locked.

We knock.

That is, I begin to knock, rather *politely*, but then Amurabia once again steps in front of me and uses the wooden handle of her cane to rap loudly on the elegant wood of the door.

I cringe involuntarily.

A few moments later, the door opens, and a man in a pristine uniform of a household servant looks out at us. "What do you have for me?" he says, looking at once at the basket in my arms.

"The best *eos* pies in all of Poseidon," Amurabia says confidently. "But not for you—for *Ter* Bisfuri. We must hand deliver them directly."

The servant lifts one brow. "When was this order placed? By whom?"

Amurabia takes a deep breath and straightens herself as much as she can. "This is not an order. This is a gift. We are here to see *Ter* Bisfuri—*Ter* Benaten Bisfuri."

The servant immediately assumes a stern expression. "What? What is this? Who are you?"

Now I take a deep breath—while my heart pounds like crazy —and I take a step forward, ahead of my Grandmother. "I need to see *Ter* Benaten Bisfuri in order to thank him," I say. "Right now. Just a few moments of his time. Please let us in!"

The servant makes a haughty snort. "This is a joke. Who sent you?" And then he glances back indoors and calls out loudly but using polite, schooled language. "Kitchen staff—who's responsible for these questionable *persons* showing up here with *eos* pies? How many times must I tell you not to call in personal meal delivery orders from outside venues without express permission—"

Whoever is behind him has no chance to reply, because in that moment I clutch the basket tightly and then shove my way inside, past him . . . with Grandmother following directly behind me.

The servant stands back in stunned outrage, inadvertently allowing us in. We find ourselves in a spacious admittance room, with a long corridor running beyond it, and various kitchens and supply rooms clearly visible. A wonderful aroma of cooking food, oven steam, and spices envelops us. Uniformed staff are visible everywhere, and some of them glance at us in brief curiosity, then continue their tasks.

"Stop, you cannot be here!" the servant at the doors exclaims, and moves to block me.

But I continue moving, racing quickly into the corridor, with Grandmother behind me, tapping the floor rapidly with her cane.

"Guard! Stop them! Someone, alert the guard! We have trespassers coming inside—" the servant is yelling in a high-pitched voice at our back. I notice he doesn't bother to lay his hands upon us himself, which is a good sign—gives us a few moments.

Just enough time to figure things out. . . .

I admit, sometimes I don't think things through very well, don't really plan ahead before plunging into action. Bastet knows, I might be imbued by divine luck, or possibly, the gods take pity on my rashness as they laugh at me from their divine seats in some unearthly realm. . . .

Such as right now—I have no idea where I'm going. However, some fortunate turn of events allows me to make my way—past *all those people* in the staff areas who have no time, or are simply not bothered enough to step forward and block me—through the long corridor and out into a large grand hall.

It opens up suddenly before me, and around me, and over me—stunning splendor of marble and gold and deep wood inlay, walls of plum wine, marble cornices and niches with pedestals, decorative urns and orb lanterns, and a grand staircase in the middle leading up to a gallery on the next level. . . . Overhead, a cupola ceiling with several skylights, each one casting rays of brilliant sunshine upon a polished mosaic floor. . . .

Holy Nyx, Mother of earth and sky. My mind spins, and I stop, while Grandmother runs into me, so that we're both hugging each other.

Moments later, several servants corner us—including the one who opened the door. And yet, our luck holds.

"You cannot be here," a burly uniformed man says calmly (he must be the guard), and he moves toward me, taking me by the arm, but not with violence.

"I just need to thank *Ter* Bisfuri," I say in a firm tone, trying to keep my voice steady. And then I hasten to speak, "Please, be so kind as to call him here! I only need to see him for a few moments and then we'll leave! Please, I cannot be so indebted to him. He did a great kindness, paid for my bail yesterday at the prison—"

As I speak, I notice two people coming into the hall toward us, emerging from a small hallway entrance similar to the one where we arrived, but on the opposite side.

The first man is another of the uniformed service staff, and he's carrying a large case. Walking behind him is a familiar young man clad in an elegant sleeveless jacket over a short sports tunic, with sandals laced around muscular calves. He turns his face at the sound of my voice, and I recognize him and his long black hair, which today is gathered in a segmented tail.

He's Behamenut Bisfuri, Benaten's younger brother. The one

who was bailed out alongside me and all the others. He sees me, and his expression suddenly becomes circumspect.

But I turn toward him, even while the guard holds me, and exclaim, "Oh, it's you!—*Ter* Bisfuri, you were there yesterday when your brother, *Ter* Benaten, paid the prison bail for all of us! Please tell them I only want to see your gracious brother and thank him with all my heart! Please, if you can only allow me to speak my gratitude, and give him this—"

"Enough, quiet!" Behamenut says, putting up his hand to silence me, and walks quickly toward us. "Release her, at once— yes, both of them. . . . Yes, of course."

He stops before us, only a little taller than me, and I see his expression full of suddenly leashed energy, his dark eyes showing alarm, while his mouth curves into a shallow smile. "Meuri, go get my brother, right *now*," he says quietly to the man carrying the case next to him.

"Yes, *Ter*."

The man called Meuri obeys, leaving the case on the floor. Meanwhile, the guard lets me go and steps back politely. At once, Grandmother surges forward at my side, takes my arm, and clanks her cane on the marble floor.

Behamenut examines both of us, then says to the curious staff gathering from the hallways, "It's all right, all of you can go —I'll deal with this."

When a few hesitate, he commands them in a louder, more petulant tone. "I said, leave us!"

The servants bow and disappear back into the hallways.

Only the three of us remain in the grand hall.

AS SOON AS everyone is gone, Behamenut rubs his hands together, then folds them at his chest, cranes his neck, and continues watching us with narrowed eyes.

Then he says, "How much do you want?"

My lips part. I find myself at a stupid loss for words.

Grandmother doesn't have the same issue. "Begging pardon, young *Ter*?"

Behamenut makes a mocking sound, and glances at my basket. Then he says, "Come now, I know why you're here. You're not the first extortioners to attempt to blackmail me or my brother, knowing how well funded we are."

"Oh, no! *No!*" I say with confusion, followed by a strong surge of emotion. "No, you misunderstand completely!"

"Young *Ter!*" Grandmother says, her voice rising in outrage. "How can you think—what in Bastet's holy name? We're not here to ask for anything!"

"Ah, but of course not," Behamenut says mockingly.

"It's true! I want nothing but to thank him!" I exclaim. "Not only do I want *nothing* from him but I owe him everything! He gave me back my freedom! He paid for all of us in that prison, a price that may mean little to you, considering your own bail amount—"

"Hush!" the youth interrupts me at once. "Say nothing about *me*, you hear? My brother is coming, he will pay whatever you need, and the servants should hear nothing of this—so be *quiet!*"

"But I don't want—"

"*Quiet!*" Behamenut leans closer into my face, then whispers. "The more you speak, the less he'll pay you! Do you understand? Stop talking! *Stop!*"

Just then we hear solitary footfalls on the marble.

Next, comes a deep, rich, familiar voice.

His voice.

The Man in the Niktos Cloak.

It sends a strange chill through me. At the same time, an unexpected sense of relief enters my gut, giving me strength.

"What's going on here?" *Ter* Benaten Bisfuri asks loudly, approaching us.

• • •

BENATEN IS DRESSED SIMPLY TODAY, in a short, sleeveless tunic tucked into long pants over boots. His black hair is loosely tied behind him in a segmented tail, with messy wisps escaping, sticking to his neck and chiseled jawline. He wears no rings, no jewelry of any kind, and appears to have come from working outside, because there is dust on his boots and spots of dirt on his shirt, and a sheen of sweat on his powerful tanned shoulders and gorgeous muscular arms. His striking face is relaxed and almost bored as he glances at us.

And yet, dusty and sweaty, I have to admit, he is spectacular.

Crap of a goat. . . . Did I just think that?

Grandmother and I both freeze, seeing him.

I can only imagine what Amurabia must be thinking, seeing the Man in the Niktos Cloak in person. *In the flesh.* Because, yeah, I can tell she is very *impressed.*

"*Ter* Bisfuri!" I say, and nearly drop the basket of *eos* pies. Thankfully, Grandmother catches the handle before things go terribly wrong.

"You wanted to see me?" he asks simply, stopping before us. And he looks directly in my eyes.

Does he recognize me?

"I—I want to thank you, *Ter* Benaten," I say in a faint voice that has become a squeak, as I look up at him. "You paid my prison bail yesterday, and—and I'm so much in your debt. . . . I have no means of paying you back the full amount, but—but my Grandmother made these for you—" I take the basket of *eos* pies and hold it up before me, offering it to him. "And these are the best—she makes the best *eos* pies—"

"It's true, *Ter* Bisfuri, I make the best pies in all of Denwen's Pit, and no doubt all of Poseidon!" My Grandmother interrupts, smiling and nodding at him.

"Is that so?" Benaten says, glancing down at the tiny old woman before him, and suddenly smiling.

That smile, it is brilliant. . . .

I blink, trying to keep my composure.

Meanwhile, the brother, Behamenut, clears his throat.

Benaten glances at him, then back at us. "So," he says, and his expression closes up, becoming bland. "How much do you need to remain discreet?"

He asks us this question tiredly.

My jaw drops, and a surge of bitter emotion returns. "*Ter* Bisfuri, no! I *don't* want anything! That's not why I'm here. I just wanted to come and thank you in person for your generosity because it's all I can do to live with myself while being so indebted to you. My Grandmother and I are here to pay our respects! I've no doubt you've had many other detainees from that prison coming by to thank you—"

"Actually, you're the first," Benaten replies with faint sarcasm, shaking his head slightly.

"What? I can't believe it!" Grandmother says. "Well then, they're not worthy of your kindness, shame to them!"

"Please, please just take these silly *eos* pies, *Ter*," I say, stupidly trying to shove the basket at him. "We must be on our way now, and you can be sure that your secret is safe with us— all of your secrets!"

"So, you're certain you don't want anything . . . in recompense?" Benaten says gently, looking from me to Grandmother and back. He still doesn't accept the basket.

"Oh, for Ra's sake, just pay them something, Aten!" Behamenut mutters. "You know there will be no end to it unless you do."

"Young *Ter*," Grandmother turns sharply to Behamenut, taking the basket from me and shoving it unexpectedly into his hands. "I repeat, we want nothing, and we would be worse than rotting *bakris* if we did. Now, receive this as a poor but honest gift from our meager family, and be done with us."

Then she glances up at Benaten, with a completely different, benevolent smile. "We'll have all the recompense we need when we watch you every week as the Man in the Niktos Cloak."

"Mei-Ma!" I exclaim in horror. "Hush! No!"

What if the younger brother doesn't know? Benaten might be keeping it hidden from everyone, the fact that he's the Man in the Niktos Cloak. Amurabia has just effectively revealed his big secret.

Benaten and his brother grow still, exchange meaningful glances. Behamenut's eyes narrow and then he cusses and snorts with laughter. *"Shebet* . . . it's worse than I thought, Aten!"

But Benaten ignores his outburst and slowly turns his face to look at my Grandmother and then briefly at me. "I've no idea what you mean," he tells Amurabia in a cool tone. His expression is so bland that it hurts.

I sigh, then say, "I'm so sorry. . . . She didn't mean to say anything . . . it's nothing, we won't tell anyone."

"Tell what?" Benaten continues, his gaze cutting through me with intensity.

I take a deep breath. "I *know* you're the Man in the Niktos Cloak. I saw you, two days ago. . . . You were in Circle Eight, fighting a gang in an alley. I was walking on Bohwa Street there, saw you wearing the costume. Saw you on the hover board. We even spoke briefly—"

"You are quite confused, girl." Benaten shakes his head and continues to look at me with unblinking eyes. "Clearly you've mistaken me for someone else."

"Ah, give it up, Aten, she knows," Behamenut says, and lifts the linen over the basket to reveal the beautifully crispy *eos* pies. He then selects one and takes a bite. "Hm, this *is* good."

"You're not helping, *hoohvak*," Benaten replies without pulling his gaze away from mine. And then he also takes a deep breath and exhales. "All right, so you *know*."

"We won't say anything to anyone, ever—I promise." I bite my lip with anxiety.

Grandmother nods vigorously in my support. "Not a word, only infinite blessings upon your head."

"Yes, thank you again for all you've done, *Ter* Bisfuri," I say, with a bow of gratitude. "We're going now, we're going. . . . Many blessings upon your—"

"Not so fast," Benaten interrupts me, as a curious, amused expression comes to him. "Very well, yes. I do remember you, girl, wandering alone near dawn, as you came around the corner, and then yesterday, at the prison. But now, unfortunately, I can't permit you to leave just yet. It appears we have some things to discuss."

He pauses and points a finger at his brother. "Whatever plans you had for the afternoon, they're cancelled. Now, Eham —back to my quarters."

He returns his attention to Grandmother and me. "Both of you, follow."

CHAPTER
NINE

Benaten takes us out of the grand hall into the same doorway from whence he arrived earlier. It connects with a long corridor that takes several turns past other doorways, other halls, other grand chambers and small niches, past occasional uniformed service staff who bow before Bisfuri. Then, unexpectedly, we end up outside, moving into a verdant walkway, underneath an arching trellis full of dappled sunlight, headed toward another grand structure adjacent to the first.

We walk behind the two brothers, Grandmother hobbling along quickly, with renewed energy, and I bring up the rear, while my temples pound with anxiety.

Once indoors again, we end up within another large hall—this one on a somewhat more antique scale, with an abundance of wood paneling lining the walls in exquisite carved lace. The hall is deep brown with ivory and mahogany embellishments near the lofty ceiling. A torch-filled ancient-style light fixture is suspended overhead from bronze chains, and the slim torches are lit with real flames, not modern orb lights. Columns covered with reliefs and carved from grand logs of thick tree trunks line the rear wall in a massive colonnade.

This is old . . . so old.

Everything here evokes ageless wealth, going back untold generations. But not merely wealth. . . . A sense of deep history overcomes me, and my breath stills in awe.

I know close to nothing of history or any other scholarly subjects. But from what little I do know (learned by watching media story feeds and magical dramas set in old times), this hall is genuinely *ancient*, phantasmagorical even. My mouth falls open and my imagination starts to soar with scenarios from myths and legends of the past. I can't help myself as I stare upward at the light fixture full of flickering firelight.

But we're not done walking. At one wall, a discreet elevator awaits. I recognize it for what it is because of the few times I had to ride such contraptions at the Chiprahat factory when summoned to the upper floors by management (such as during my hiring interview). Benaten swipes his hand over a modern wall panel which opens the elevator door and permits us to enter.

"Come inside, now." Benaten motions with his hand, seeing Grandmother hesitate.

It occurs to me, Grandmother may not have been inside an elevator before. As far as she's concerned, it's a tiny room with no means of escape.

"Go in, *Mei-Ma* . . ." I prod her gently. "It's okay, this room is a machine to go up and down."

"Perfectly safe," Behamenut adds with a full mouth, chewing his second *eos* pie.

"Oh," she says, then firmly steps inside, and I follow.

The doors close behind us, the elevator lurches gently, and my poor Grandmother briefly closes her eyes, apparently praying. Not sure why, maybe because it's such a tiny room and there are four of us crowding it, but it seems to make her more uncomfortable than riding in a big hover bus high in the air over the City.

A few heartbeats later, the elevator opens again, and we emerge in a sunlit open-air balcony terrace with curving arch doorways lining the outer wall. We're almost at the top floor and below us is a view of magnificent gardens and the surrounding park beyond the estate walls.

Benaten walks quickly ahead and then opens one of the doors, entering a spacious chamber full of luxurious furnishings the likes of which I've only ever seen on the popular dramas on the media feeds. We're greeted by divans and chairs strewn with pillows, elegant hangings of fine fabric, side tables with marble tops and gold inlay, and so much fancy expensive stuff for which I have no name. . . .

The two Bisfuri brothers sit down nonchalantly on the nearest chairs, pushing aside the pillows to sink back in heedless comfort, and Benaten points to the divan before him, indicating for us to sit.

Holy Bast, the fabric of this divan, it is so fine. . . . Both Grandmother and I hesitate momentarily, staring at it. What if we make it dirty? There's a lot of road dust on our clothes. . . .

"Sit, please," Benaten says.

Grandmother smooths her skirt, then lowers herself with some relief on the soft, pristine seat cushion. She remains stiff-backed. I follow suit, sitting directly next to her, equally fixed.

There is a moment or two of silence. We all stare at each other.

"Now," Benaten Bisfuri says. "I want you to tell me how exactly you figured out my identity. You, girl—your name?"

"Oh," I say. "Semmi. . . . I mean, my name is Semirameos. Daughter of Eigeti. From Denwen's Pit." I glance at Grandmother. "And this is my Grandmother, Amurabia."

"Also from Denwen's Pit," Grandmother confirms, as if that's not a given.

"Semmi—Semirameos," Benaten repeats. For some reason,

hearing him say my name in that bone-deep, honey-rich voice of his, sends a weird shiver down my spine.

The Man in the Niktos Cloak knows my name . . . how strange. How terribly awesome and strange.

"Just Semmi," I echo awkwardly.

"So—tell me." He nods, looking directly at me, fixing me with his eyes.

In the light of day, and close enough now that I can see the irises, his eyes are grey . . . like warm smoke. Like orichalcum—when the sun falls upon it at that precise angle when the golden flecks begin to sparkle. . . .

"Well—I—" My lips part in a kind of stupor. How to even begin?

Grandmother watches me, even slightly widens her wrinkle-lined eyes. She's communicating *something*, but for the life of me I don't know what it is. And then she speaks up.

"My Granddaughter notices things. She is very clever that way, *im Ter*. You should see how well she works! That knife—she can chop vegetables faster than you can blink—"

"*Mei-Ma*, stop," I say firmly, silencing her, even as I recover my senses well enough to speak for myself. "*Ter* Bisfuri . . ." I take a deep breath and meet his gaze. "I always watch certain parts of the show *The Love Life of the Man in the Niktos Cloak*."

Behamenut snorts crudely, glancing at me then at his brother. "I bet she does. You put on a great performance, Aten. Especially with your naked *puzukaat*."

"I watch," I continue, looking directly at Benaten, "only the part where you *fight*."

Benaten observes me without blinking, completely discounting Behamenut's commentary and giving me his full attention. "So, you don't watch the part where I *varqood?*" he asks bluntly, but there's a trace of amusement or curiosity, or something else unreadable in his expression.

At once I feel a flush of heat envelop me. *Merciful gods!*

Grandmother is watching and listening! What is he doing, speaking so outrageously to me in front of her? Bastet, strike me, now!

Forcing myself to remain dead-still so as not to reveal the extent of my mortification, I draw in a slow breath and shake my head. "No, I don't," I reply, making my tone as cool and calm as possible. "I only care to see the fighting moves, the combat techniques. The—*other* stuff is boring and annoying."

"Oh, ho-ho!" This time Behamenut laughs outright. "A miracle, Aten! We've discovered the one girl in all of Poseidon who finds your lovemaking boring!"

My head absolutely ignites with embarrassment. "Oh, I didn't mean—*no!* Please forgive me, *Ter* Bisfuri!" I put one hand over my mouth at what I've actually said and how it came out. I think there's already a foot in there somewhere.

I continue, in a pitiful attempt to remedy my blunder. "I don't mean that yours is boring—not at all, I mean, I find all romantic stuff boring. I'm so sorry! My—my worthless words are so awful, especially after you've done so much for me . . . so sorry to offend—"

"No offense taken," Benaten replies calmly. "Go on, finish your point."

"My point is, I've watched you fight so many times," I say awkwardly. "I know your fighting moves. And not just your actual moves but the *way* you move. The manner in which your hands strike and flow. That's what I recognized first in that alley. Then I saw the costume, and it just all came together. And when I heard your *voice*—that was when I became certain."

A pause of silence. Benaten nods. "Your Grandmother is right. You do have a good eye for detail. And for making connections."

"I—thank you," I say.

There is a brief pause, during which, apparently, my Grandmother takes matters into her own hands. "*Ter* Bisfuri, as you can see, she's a smart girl! Clever, perceptive, diligent, a great worker, and it would be in your best interest to take her into your service, immediately! But, no sex work, she's a decent girl!"

"*Mei-Ma*—what?" I exclaim, widening my eyes at her. And just like that, Grandmother's sneaky motivations become clear. *Did the old woman really have this in mind when she told me to dress in my best clothes? Holy Bastet!* My lungs collapse as though someone punched me, and suddenly I can't breathe. . . .

But Amurabia ignores me and continues firmly, addressing Benaten. "She can do so much for you, *im Ter!* Anything you need to get done, quickly and discreetly, she's at your disposal!"

Benaten watches my Grandmother carry on, and one of his brows rises. "So, that's what you're after," he says with sarcasm, leaning forward slightly, and begins to laugh. "I understand now. This—all of *this*. You want me to give her a job. Except, why in the name of all the gods would I bother hiring an urchin from Denwen's Pit when I already have hundreds of highly-trained servants at my disposal?"

"Because my Granddaughter is better than any of them! Fie to your servants!" Grandmother says, lifting her cane slightly to tap it on the polished marble floor in emphasis.

"Well, they certainly thought this through," his brother puts in, nodding his head in dark amusement. "My guess is, you hire her or else—they reveal the secrets. And the Windnet rumor mill churns, starting to sing a song of Bisfuri. Ah, I can almost hear it now." He sets down the basket of *eos* pies on a side table wistfully, but not before taking a third one, and crunches on it loudly, heedless of crumbs falling on the fine floor.

"No, of course not, *Ter!*" I look up fiercely. "No one's revealing anything, you can be sure." All the while, my mind is swirling with an overload of embarrassment coupled with sudden possibilities.

I do need a job, desperately.

And so, I take a deep breath, lift up my chin even higher, and speak quickly before the crazy, dauntless *sha* in my head changes her mind and retreats back to cower.

"*Ter* Bisfuri, my apologies for my Grandmother speaking up like this, and really I did not plan this at all, but . . . if you have work for me, I would be glad to take it."

"And there it is," Benaten says, turning his full attention to me. He cranes his neck slightly, examining me, as if for the first time. "So, what can you do for me that my army of servants cannot? Speak, girl! I grow weary of this."

"I—I can chop mushrooms . . . and other vegetables in the kitchen—very quickly, which I'm sure is not a big deal, considering all your kitchen staff," I reply in haste, sounding pitiful and foolish even to myself. "But—I can also run, very fast. I can deliver messages for you. I can be a lookout. . . ." My forehead tenses up in effort as I try to think, *think*.

And then it comes to me. "I can *spy* for you. And I can fight!"

Behamenut snorts, choking on his *eos* pie. Crumbs go flying in all directions as he coughs and laughs simultaneously.

But Benaten's expression remains compelling. "Spy for me?" he repeats. "Why would I need a spy, girl?"

"You need a spy because you have a fortune," Grandmother interrupts, speaking in her smartest tone. "In fact, you need more than one, as I'm sure you understand."

"And what makes you think I don't have . . . spies already?" Benaten glances from Amurabia to me and back again.

"You need spies to spy on your other spies," I reply with sudden intensity. "I can be that for you. I will be quiet and invisible. You can rely on me; I will swear before gods—"

Benaten puts up his hand to slow down my torrent of words. "Can you read?" he asks.

Just like that, the world that had infinite possibilities moments ago, comes crashing down. My breath halts once more. I take a moment then reply softly, "No, *im Ter*. I'm sorry. I have no such . . . schooling."

There are no schools for the likes of us, I want to add.

But he merely nods. "I didn't think so."

"I can learn," I say, inspired out of nowhere. "I mean—I can learn whatever you need me to learn—or know. I can do whatever tasks you assign."

"You can learn to read, true." Bisfuri nods. "But—" he exhales loudly. "Not in the time that we have left to us. Not with the world about to end."

Benaten Bisfuri looks at me with what I suddenly recognize to be genuine pity. "Look," he says gently. "I can hire you for the kitchens, or as a menial servant for the estate—in exchange for you remaining discreet about my . . . secrets. But you need to understand that I cannot hire you *permanently*. I can't hire you as part of the specially selected elite group of service staff that will go in the space ships with us in a few months from now."

He's talking about the Sky Rock.

Somehow, I'd forgotten all about it for the last hour, and now it comes back to me, hard. Suddenly, all of my Grandmother's planned machinations on my behalf, her eager attempt to get me a job, take on even more significance.

Amurabia intended and hoped that I might be taken into service by the noble House Bisfuri in order to save my life. So that I could escape to the stars alongside the elites.

Oh, Mei-Ma. . . .

My chest begins to hurt, drowning in a bittersweet swell of emotion. *Don't you know I would never leave you or Uru behind?*

I face *Ter* Bisfuri and nod. "I understand. You—will not hire me for *that*."

"I may not," he repeats. "There is limited space on the ships. Limited numbers of personnel allowed—for all of us. Bisfuri is indeed more fortunate than many other noble families, in that we can take more than so many of the others. But even we are only permitted to take five hundred people to serve us—and no more. Only the Imperial Kassiopei will have more."

"I see," I say.

I glance at my Grandmother and notice her *eyes*—tragic, stricken.

For the first time there is little hope in them.

But something crazy and wild surges within me—that same untamed *sha*—and it makes me glance at her with perverse energy, with a reassuring expression. I'm very likely lying to her now, lying blatantly with my gaze, but I am willing with all my heart for Grandmother to think that *not all is lost*.

Benaten interrupts our silent communion. "Now that you understand," he says, "it's settled. I'll give you work for the next few weeks, while we're still here, on earth. Because—why not?"

"Oh, thank you, kind *Ter!*" Grandmother exclaims, while I lower my head in a demure bow.

"Thank you profoundly, *im Ter*," I say, with a solemn face. "I will serve you well—however brief it might be. And I will be discreet with all your secrets, taking them to my grave. Thank you."

Behamenut, the younger brother, makes an incomprehensible sound. Not sure what it's supposed to be, sarcasm, mockery, but it interrupts my earnest mood, and from that moment on I admit to myself that he's highly irritating. But then he says something that changes everything, in a blink.

"You can always enter our Service Competition, girl," he says to me. "Pass the qualifications, and you can be one of the lucky five hundred. Right, Aten?" and he glances over at his brother.

Benaten does not answer immediately, and starts to frown. "Don't be cruel, Eham," he says at last. "You're giving her pointless hope."

"Huh?" Behamenut says. "Am I not right?"

Benaten shakes his head slowly. "Yes, that's technically correct. But the Competition is going to be fierce. Most applicants will be denied. And those who are least qualified—" he glances at me— "will be the first to be dismissed."

A sudden spark of anger ignites deep within me. *Just because I'm poor and uneducated, he assumes that I'm least qualified.*

My pulse begins to pound in my temples. "How do I enter this competition, *Ter?*" I ask daringly. "Am I permitted to enter?"

"Everyone is permitted," Behamenut replies in his brother's stead.

Benaten curses softly then exhales in frustration. "Yes, you may enter," he says with a brief, blank look at me, and then a hard glare at his brother. "The Service Competition terms will be formally posted soon . . . a day from now. And yes, anyone is permitted to enter. You may do so along with everyone else. But —expect nothing to come of it."

"Very well, *im Ter,*" I say softly, with another small bow. "But hope is a powerful force, and it's all we've got these days, those of us from Denwen's Pit. So, I hope you don't mind but I *will* be entering this Service Competition. In fact, my little brother, Urumer, will be too. He's small but he's the fastest messenger in all the markets."

"That he is indeed," Grandmother echoes, nodding wisely. "Well said, Semmi, well said."

Benaten observes me, then my Grandmother, glancing back and forth at the two of us, almost incredulously.

"Okay, are we done now? Blackmail averted? Windnet plugged?" Behamenut says loudly, standing up, and tapping his wrist device. "Enhuvarat is on his way here, and he tells me we have *new* plans for the day, followed by even better plans for the evening."

"Yes, you're free, get out of here, *shar-ta.*" Benaten lifts his finger to show his brother to the door. And then he glances back at Grandmother and me. "As for you—arrangements will be made for the girl's employment. But first, we'll have tea."

"Tea is not necessary," I mumble, watching the younger Bisfuri brother hasten out of the room.

"Tea will be good," Grandmother contradicts in her usual way. "Employment terms can be finalized over tea, perfectly lovely of you, *im Ter*."

And as Benaten rings for service, my ridiculous Grandmother suddenly adds, "But, as I said, no sex! She's not to be touched that way, and not made to act the whore on your show—"

"Crap of a goat! Shut up, *Mei-Ma!*" I cry out, turning completely red with the crazy flush that's covering my neck and head.

Ter Benaten Bisfuri tactfully ignores both of us. He stands up and goes over to the basket of *eos* pies. Picking up a pie, he examines it then takes a large bite, chews, swallows. One of his brows goes up. "You're right. This really *is* good *eos* pie," he says with an amused glance at Amurabia.

"The best in all of Poseidon." My Grandmother smiles at him confidently.

As for me, I sit straight-backed, overwhelmed with all of this. My mind is in a turmoil of too many emotions all at once, excitement, and angry, fledgling, *real* hope.

Suddenly there's hope—yes, hope, for all of us.

The tea service arrives in just a few daydreams. Almost as soon as Benaten finishes speaking into his wrist device and then sits back to silently examine my Grandmother and me, there is a polite knock on the door. Uniformed servants arrive with a serving table and several trays full of aromatic luxury food and steaming-hot glass carafes of the deep amber liquid.

Grandmother and I stare at the delicacies being set out before us. It occurs to me to wonder, how typical is it with the wealthy nobles to show this kind of generosity to low-class guests? Does *Ter* Bisfuri treat other impoverished strangers with this kind of polite hospitality, or is it just because we're a special case and happen to know his secrets?

I can almost see the same kind of suspicions and questions arise in my Grandmother's astute gaze. At the same time, a sudden crazy thought strikes me.

Oh, Bastet! What if we're being poisoned?

I suppose that would be one quick way of getting rid of both of us, without having to give me a job in exchange for our silence.

But for some reason, the notion of Benaten Bisfuri stooping

to this kind of heinous act feels really out of character for him—at least from what I've seen of him so far. Indeed, if he really wanted to get rid of us, he could have set his servants upon us, or sent some murderous guards to deal with us afterwards when we left to return home. . . . Of course, that might still happen.

I continue to think these dark thoughts, watching the polite servants move around, paying no direct attention to us, as they pour aromatic tea into three delicate glass goblets on the center tray for *Ter* Bisfuri's approval. Benaten picks up a goblet and, with one finger, directs Grandmother and me toward the other two.

"Go on, drink," he says to us. "The day is hot, and you have a long ride before you, back to Circle Ten." And then seeing our continued hesitation, his expression turns to amusement.

"It's not poisoned," he says, tilting his own goblet to sip the tea with nonchalance. "Or it could be? But, no, it's not. There are much easier ways to get rid of unwanted guests, and if I wanted to do so, you wouldn't have made it up here to my private residence."

Holy Bastet, did he read my mind? Or is it merely so obvious, on both our faces?

"Oh, no, of course not . . . great apologies," I mumble with a pang of new shame, and pick up my goblet as if it were a precious thing, raising it to my lips. I haven't handled a drinking vessel made of glass before, and it's slightly terrifying.

But then I forget the vessel itself as the first taste of the fragrant brew surprises my mouth. . . . It's a shock of perfection. I've never drunk anything like it in my life; surely this is an elixir of the gods, poisoned or not.

Grandmother hesitates a moment longer before taking the remaining goblet. She handles the fragile glass with similar care and then imbibes from it with weary resignation.

"Don't apologize. The fact that you might think the worst of me, gives you a certain kind of credit," he says, watching us drink. "Suspicion is prudent, and I would rather have my spies be careful and clever than instantly dead."

I glance up from taking another sip, and see that *Ter* Bisfuri is laughing. "Oh," I say. "So, I *am* to be a spy, then?"

He continues to chuckle, then lets out a relaxed breath. "Honestly? I haven't yet decided what, in the name of all the gods of *Atlantida*, I'm going to do with you. The easiest thing is to simply send you to the kitchens. But for some reason, I hesitate. I find you—*both* of you—very curious. I sense a potential of some kind, something, *something*. . . ."

I'm unsure how to respond to that.

Instead, Amurabia makes a little sound. "It's clear you don't know too many people from Denwen's Pit, *im Ter*," she says as she drinks her tea.

"No, I don't. You're right." He glances at my Grandmother. Unexpectedly, his expression turns serious. "And now I won't have the opportunity to remedy it. Maybe that's why I'm having tea with you. . . ."

The way he says the last part is surprising—it's genuinely sad.

Again, I think of the accursed Sky Rock.

In that moment there's a knock on the door. A loud, insistent, older female voice sounds outside.

"Benaten! Are you within? Are you decent? I need to speak with you now!"

Ter Bisfuri stills momentarily, then lets out a breath that doesn't bother to hide his immediate exasperation. He sets down his goblet of tea and leans back against the cushions. "Yes! Come in," he replies loudly. His face takes on a bland, almost bored expression.

Grandmother and I freeze also and exchange glances.

The door opens, and a tall, bony, middle-aged woman enters like a queen. She is dressed in fine persimmon-colored silks, with a long veil trimmed in pearls and gold wrapped around her shoulders. Her dark hair is swept up in a braided twist, with pearl-studded pins. The look on her hollow-cheeked face radiates both haughtiness and anxiety.

Benaten follows her approach with his overly relaxed gaze. "Aunt Ishtaz—to what do I owe the pleasure?"

The lady thus addressed continues into the room and then stops before the divan and the seats. She casts a dismissive gaze at all of us, including the servants.

"What is this, Benaten? I'm well aware you're always entertaining whores. But—these?" She points one painted claw-nailed finger at Grandmother and me with disdain. "They don't look like your usual *amretene*. What's going on?"

"Have a seat, My Lady," he replies, continuing to recline in casual fashion. "I'm conducting business."

"What manner of business?" Aunt Ishtaz ignores the invitation, and glances at us with reproach. "Sit? Where shall I sit? I see only commoners besmirching your furniture. Command them to move and depart!"

I make a motion to rise, and Amurabia grunts, taking hold of her cane.

"No, remain seated." Benaten puts up one hand, halting us.

"I will *not* share a seat with whores!" the lady exclaims.

Grandmother makes a small sound of outrage, and prepares to rise from her seat on the roomy divan.

"My apologies, but you are mistaken, My Lady," I speak up. "We are merely interviewing for decent service work for *Ter Bisfuri*. He required . . . um . . . workers for a . . . special event."

"What kind of workers? What event?" The aunt turns her pinched face and her full displeasure upon me.

"I am—I'm an entertainer—" I begin, as my thoughts race wildly. "That is, I'm a *storyteller*!"

Oh, crap of a goat. . . . What in Bast's Holy Name am I saying now?

"A Storyteller?" The lady's dark eyed gaze incinerates me.

"Yes!" I continue quickly, and sit up straight. Then I lean forward and raise one hand in a dramatic gesture—the kind I've seen on the media feeds. "I tell the most pleasing stories, and—and I can bring much wondrous entertainment to your evening."

At this point, even Grandmother is staring at me in disbelief. As for Benaten, his eyes have widened slightly . . . and now his raven brows have lifted also. But he says nothing.

"So, you tell stories—what of this old one? Is she a Storyteller also?" The lady points at Amurabia (whose jaw is about to drop).

"Oh, no," I respond in a hurry. "I tell the story. Grandmother uses her cane to strike the floor—for timing, during the exciting parts!"

"Hm. Very unusual." Bisfuri's aunt turns to her nephew. "Is that correct?"

"Yes, apparently, it is," he replies, with a shadow of wicked fascination, and looks at me, then sensually moves one hand to stroke the fabric of the nearest cushion. "In fact, the girl was about to demonstrate telling me one of her stories, just as you arrived."

Oh, no! What is he doing?

My heart . . . it is now racing with anxiety.

"Very well." The aunt says, turning slightly to survey the room, with barely a glance at the servants. "For what occasion is this, exactly, Benaten? Another useless party? I was not informed—"

"Something like that—a little surprise party for my brother. Please do take that lovely seat, Aunt Ishtaz, I insist." Benaten interrupts her, and points firmly to the nearest empty chair.

"Very well, I do begin to tire from standing," she says sharply, and sails over, rustling her silks and veils, to occupy the comfortable seat. She makes a long, drawn-out sigh that manages to convey woefulness and disapproval.

"The Lady Ishtaz will have tea," Benaten motions to the servants. Then, continuing to lean back against the cushions, he returns his gaze upon me and watches me through narrowed eyes. "You, girl—you may proceed."

I stand up, my mind wildly spinning.

What unholy sha *possessed me to speak? How did I get myself into this mad predicament?*

I find that I'm shaking slightly. I turn awkwardly so that I'm facing everyone, then force myself to begin. "Um—what kind of story would you like to hear? A funny story or a tragic story? Or —or a clever story, or maybe a romantic story? How about a magical tale? Or one filled with wisdom—?"

Benaten looks at me with his deceptively heavy-lidded eyes. "Surprise me."

Crap of a goat. . . .

"Yes, *im Ter*," I say with a small bow to cover up my panic-filled expression. Meanwhile, my heart pounds like mad, and my thoughts scramble for purchase in a slippery well of sudden *emptiness* that is my mind. For some stupid reason all I can think of are piles of stupid mushrooms at the Chiprahat warehouse.

What do I do, what do I say? I need to come up with a story, on the spot!

Help me, Bast!

Maybe the great goddess indeed hears my plea, right then. *Did I just hear the divine mewling of cats?* Because, it occurs to me, I need to let my mind go blank and open up to the dreamlike wonders, and then pretend I am telling this story, this adventure, to *myself.*

The way I always do.

After all, I've spent so many hours of drudgery and boredom dreaming of battling mushroom armies. The images that came to me every time my knife cut down the endless fungi of all shapes and sizes—I need to summon them!

My voice starts out breathless as I begin to speak.

"A long time ago, *ter-i-taq*, there lived a great and powerful *sha* king. He ruled all of the underworld, and all the *sha* of darkness trembled before him. He—he sent out his armies to conquer all worlds below, all levels of immortality. And then, once there was nothing else for him to do, he decided to—to find a—a queen to rule at his side. . . ."

I pause, my mind grabbing at images, most of which are again, ridiculous mushrooms.

Everyone watches me silently. Even the servants have stilled.

"And so," I continue, "the *sha* king ordered all the unmarried women in the lands below to be brought before him so that he could choose his glorious wife. It must be said that the *sha* women were all beautiful, wicked, and terribly clever, just as the *sha* men. When they lined up before the palace doors, they all started to trick each other in devious ways in order to get ahead and be the first in line. They secretly pinched and tripped each other, stuck those closest with hair pins, plucked out individual strands of hair, unraveled sandal ties, even resorted to pouring perfumed oil bottles on top of their rivals' heads from behind. It didn't help that the line stretched far to the horizon of the underworld—first going around the palace many, many times, in endless widening circles, since there were so many of them."

I pause again, as my mind gathers more images out of nowhere, each one stranger than the other. Where's all this stuff coming from? I must have a giant soup cauldron of nonsense inside my head!

Momentarily, I permit myself to notice that everyone, especially *Ter* Bisfuri, is listening to me very attentively.

Is that a good sign? Right now, it doesn't matter. . . . I need to focus on the story, on what happens next!

"The beautiful, and clever, and very wicked *sha* women grew tired of cunning tricks and eventually fought and argued outright. That is, all except one. There was one *sha* woman who did nothing, simply stood in line, waiting her turn to be seen by the king—"

"So obviously the king noticed her," Benaten interrupts me suddenly, tapping one index finger in boredom against the cushion. "And he chose her for his queen. The usual kind of thing that happens in such stories—I've heard enough."

I'm silenced momentarily. Maybe he's trying to help me here, extricate me from this *hoohvak* storytelling nightmare?

But out of nowhere, new images flood my imagination . . . and I interrupt him in turn, "Oh, no, *im Ter!* The king did not notice her at all. In fact, she was so still and quiet that everyone passed her by, and then she ended up being the last in line." Saying this, I experience a surge of perverse pleasure at my unexpected opportunity to surprise him and be contrary.

Benaten raises one brow. "Fine. Go on."

"Yes," I continue. "The *sha* king was so overwhelmed with having to interview so many women that he ordered the palace doors to be shut. Bolted too, because some of the *sha* women were throwing themselves at the gates of black metal like wine sacks, and making them quake and shudder from the relentless impacts. And since so many of those women still remained outside, including the one that was still and quiet and last in line—"

"What was her name? This still and quiet woman?" Lady Ishtaz asks.

"Her name? Her name was—" I force down renewed panic at the unanticipated question, as my mind flounders for a quick answer. "Her name was *sha*—Sharzaad," I end in a ridiculous manner, making up a stupid name on the spot.

And then, with an intake of breath, I continue. "So, this Sharzaad—because she was left outside, and it was getting late, she simply turned around and went home."

"Is that it? What kind of dull story is that?" Benaten speaks again.

"Oh, but the story is not over, *im Ter*," I retort with a little crafty edge to my voice. "Because after Sharzaad went home, it turned out that the *sha* king was so angry at all the fighting happening in and around his palace, and the damage to his black metal gates, that he ordered many of those women to be punished, and the rest to be cast out of the palace and never to come back."

I raise one hand in dramatic fashion, and point to my Grandmother, hoping she would get the hint and strike the floor with her cane for dramatic emphasis. But Amurabia merely stares at me with bewildered eyes.

Crap of a goat. . . .

So, I continue, unassisted.

"And so, the next morning, the *sha* king ordered all the remaining unwed *sha* women who never had a chance to be seen, to line up outside the palace and wait. This time he himself would come out to examine them—and avoid any more damage to the ancient palace gates."

I raise my voice, and simultaneously raise one finger in semblance of a sage elder imparting wisdom, as seen on a media-box drama. "Those gates! They remained intact for centuries, indeed since the dawn of time, and withstood the onslaught of tremendously large armies and powerful foreign magic. But for some reason they were very vulnerable to *sha* women looking for a royal husband. It must be said that the *sha* women, clever and wicked and beautiful, were also magically strong—as strong as a herd of bulls—and even more dangerous when provoked, such as when hungry baboons want to graze on the same grass and shrubbery as the cattle, because baboons can't find ripe fruit which aren't in season, but the grass is there, and so are the cows, and the bulls let them graze first because they're lady cows—"

A quickly suppressed snicker comes from the direction of the servants. I pause my rambling, glad for the interruption.

Honestly, just now, I've gotten myself into an unspeakably *hoohvak* plot tangent with no hope of a clean escape.

Fortunately for me, Lady Ishtaz glances in the direction of the servant noise with reproach. "Go on, continue this story," she says to me archly, motioning with her hand.

"Yes, well—the *sha* women," I say, relieved to pick up the main story thread and leave the cows and baboons behind. "The remaining women lined up for the *sha* king, including Sharzaad, and he came out and started to walk the line. He stopped before each *sha* woman and asked them a single question."

"What question?" Benaten asks.

I take a deep breath. "The question he asked was: 'What is the one thing you can do for me better than anyone else?'"

Benaten nods slowly, his gaze never wavering from me.

"And so, the *sha* women gave him all kinds of grand answers: 'I can cook you the best meal and the sweetest dessert!' 'I will make you a magnificent outfit like no other!' 'I can give you beautiful *sha* children!' 'I will please you with my body more than any other lover!' 'I will dance for you like a goddess!' 'I will sing to you the most glorious song!' 'I can offer you my family's most precious riches in dowry!'

"There were also a few less attractive offers: 'I will pluck a chicken faster than anyone in your kitchen.' 'I will stroke the spot in the back of your head most pleasantly, in a way no one else can!' 'I will make sure your bed is always warm because I never have cold feet!'

"All these answers, even the less attractive ones, the *sha* king considered carefully, until he arrived in line before Sharzaad. When she was asked the question, Sharzaad said: 'I will tell you the best story in the world. But only if you promise *not* to choose me as your queen.' And the *sha* king immediately made his decision."

"Huh? What was his decision?" Lady Ishtaz murmurs. "Did he pick this strange *sha* woman?"

"Or did he not?" Benaten says thoughtfully, with a shadow of a smile.

"Hah!" I exclaim with sudden inspiration. "The *sha* king's decision regarding Sharzaad will be continued in the next story, to be told at another time!"

And then, turning my gaze directly at Benaten Bisfuri, I ask brazenly. "So, *im Ter*, having now been interviewed as your Storyteller, am I hired?"

Before Bisfuri can answer, his aunt says, "If you don't hire this one, *I* will. I absolutely must hear the end of this asinine tale! It is ridiculous, yet strangely compelling . . . not sure why. Regardless—hire the girl this instant! Inform me when she is to perform for your party, and I will certainly attend."

In that moment, as though finally waking up from her stupefaction, my Grandmother lifts her cane and strikes the floor loudly, in emphasis.

CHAPTER
ELEVEN

"Very well. I make my decision based on your wise advice, Aunt Ishtaz," Benaten Bisfuri says with a hint of sarcasm that his aunt misses. And then he turns to me and, with a perfectly straight face, says: "Storyteller, it was inevitable. You're hired."

I feel a wild surge of disbelief and joy at such a favorable resolution to my insane ramblings, but hide it by keeping my expression as calm and bland as I can. "Thank you, *im Ter*," I say carefully, bowing my head to express appropriate gratitude. "You will not regret it. . . . I promise, the ending of my story will bring you—and your most noble guests—much delight." From the corner of my eye, I notice that my Grandmother's face is flooded with relief.

"Good. I don't like regrets. As far as the specifics of your employ, we'll settle that after I converse with my esteemed Aunt. For now, sit. You may finish your tea," he adds in a tone of careless benevolence.

I nod and return to my former spot on the sofa next to Amurabia. My hand trembles when I pick up my glass goblet, and I barely avoid clanking it against the silver tray. Stiff-backed, I raise it to my lips.

"With that out of the way. . . ." Benaten gives me a single glance, then turns his attention to Lady Ishtaz and gives me no further notice. "My dear Aunt, you are gracing me with your presence for a reason. How may I be of service?"

Lady Ishtaz pauses for a moment. She briefly looks at me and Amurabia, then apparently decides that we've earned our invisibility as domestic servants and may be ignored from here on.

"Benaten, I must speak with you in regard to a certain delicate matter we've discussed before. Now that your Father has returned from the provinces, he will likely have you join him at his next meal some time tonight. It's the perfect opportunity to bring to his attention that I'm more than ready to assume the role of First Lady of this great House."

Bisfuri makes a weary sound. "Ah, yes. . . . I recall we've had this conversation."

"Quite a few times." Lady Ishtaz sighs and assumes a martyr expression. "And now, there has been some additional unpleasant talk at Court—foul rumor mongering shamelessly done within earshot of the Imperatris herself. This time, it cannot be put off or ignored."

Benaten's expression remains unmoved.

His aunt continues in a carefully reproachful tone. "In short, unless your blessed Father remarries—which we both know is highly unlikely at this point—there is a natural imbalance in the way we formally present ourselves. The Family needs a woman's firm hand, and a matriarch is required for the dignity of the Bisfuri reputation."

Benaten does not answer immediately. He leans forward to pick up his glass of tea which is immediately refilled by an attentive servant. The golden amber liquid poured from the decanter sparkles in the sunbeams coming from the nearest windows.

The lady attempts a different tactic. "Think of Aymira, your saintly Mother! Her departed soul gazes down at this Family even now, from her blessed journey on board the Depet of Eternity. . . . Oh, how she grieves your circumstances! When we meet in the *niktos* skies, how will I face her, knowing I did not assume her duty to guide and watch over you—her sons, and her *amrevu* husband, my own blood?"

Lady Ishtaz studies her nephew's reaction (or lack thereof), running her polished and painted claws over her chair armrest in anxiety.

My Grandmother and I stare in rapt curiosity.

I can't believe they're talking about such matters in front of us! And not just us, but all of the other servants present in the room. . . .

Seriously, neither I nor Amurabia could ever imagine that we might one day end up seated in the living room of the highest nobles in the land and be privy to their conversation, much less be invited to drink their extraordinary tea!

While such dizzying thoughts assail me, giving me an outside-of-my-body sensation of continuous disbelief, *Ter* Bisfuri finally speaks—after taking a long drink from his goblet. "I've considered what you ask."

"And?"

"He is *your* brother, My Lady. It would seem to me that your concerns would be better addressed if you speak to him directly, not use me as a pointless proxy."

"But it would be highly inappropriate, Benaten!" his aunt exclaims, clutching at her veils. "As the Heir, you alone must speak of such matters! A proper lady does *not* conduct such business on her *own* behalf! What would people say if they knew that I dared express my aspirations so candidly to the Lord of the House? Fie, such crassness! It is bad enough they already gossip at Court how Lord Bisfuri allows his household to run wild in his absence. . . . His sons always unsupervised, constantly carousing with whores, throwing exorbitant parties—gods only know what else is going on around here—while the estate is left to be plundered by devious stewards and shameless servants!"

Benaten makes a sound of annoyance. "Nothing is being plundered. My dear Aunt, you know this household is run as well as any other, if not better. Let the Court gossip in these final days of *Atlantida* if they have nothing better to do—such as working on their means of escape to the stars. It makes no difference to any of us, especially not now. We'll be long gone from this miserable planet, and the estate can supervise itself. Or it can *varqood* itself beneath the flood waters."

"*Ah . . . Benaten!*" Lady Ishtaz gasps, and puts a hand over her mouth.

"Apologies for the *crassness*," he says, emphasizing that last word. But he doesn't appear to be remorseful in the least. Rather, his eyes reveal mocking sarcasm.

"Will you speak to Lord Bisfuri then?" his aunt persists, this time bluntly, dropping the artful double-speak. Her voice ends on a petulant rising note. "Or will you not?"

"Most likely I will speak to him, yes. Our conversation will be about the spice level of the dishes served at our meal and the business of his latest trip. But it will not be about this subject." Benaten takes another sip of tea, while looking directly in her eyes. "Though, I might change my mind. Or—maybe not. No—definitely not. Or, maybe I will?"

"Enough! I will not suffer such discourteous behavior from you, Nephew!" Lady Ishtaz tries to retain a semblance of composure, as her face takes on a succession of unpleasant expressions.

Benaten's subtly mocking tone continues. "May the gods of courtesy be merciful then, for I will not suffer either. I admit, my manners have abandoned me, Aunt. But I see no recourse. It's just more convenient for all of us to have things remain precisely the way they are. Why would I—indeed, any of us—want them to change?"

"Fie! You're in dire need of a matronly figure such as myself to correct you!"

"Being corrected is not something I seek. Even if I *am*, as you say, unsupervised," Benaten replies with a shadow smile. "Feel free to complain to my Father—at once. And then, take the opportunity to conduct your own business with him directly."

"Unbelievable!" The lady gasps again, this time in full outrage. "You think I will not speak to Muutat? And when I do, I will tell him his sons must be curbed and disciplined! In fact, I take leave of you now, and proceed to speak with him immediately!"

"My dear Aunt, at last, we are in complete accord," Benaten says, watching Lady Ishtaz rise and head to the door. "Don't forget, you are cordially invited to our next party."

AS SOON AS the door shuts behind his aunt, *Ter* Bisfuri visibly eases and returns his attention to Grandmother and me. "And—the blessed woman is gone," he says with sarcastic amusement, and his gaze sweeps over me. "So, Storyteller? Shall I make it your formal job description? Why not, it just might work—at least for now. You did make an impression on my Aunt, and she is not easily entertained."

"Thank you, *im Ter*," I say.

Did I make an impression on him?

He examines me, and now the relentless gaze of his unusual grey eyes makes me somewhat uneasy, in an inexplicable way.

"Did you really come up with that cleverly insane story yourself?" he asks suddenly. "Or was that some kind of local drunken fairytale from Denwen's Pit?"

"If it is, I've never heard of it," Grandmother speaks up.

"No—" I hasten to reply. "I mean, yes, *im Ter*, I made up that story just now. It came from inside my head—which is full of all kinds of things."

"An interesting head."

"Thank you, *im Ter*. It is a little weird." A strange surge of heat rises to warm my cheeks.

He continues watching me. "Also, the way you *told* that tale —your *voice*, its modulation. Something about it—it begs attention, evokes curiosity. . . . Almost, a compulsion to listen, even to the *hoohvak* part about the cows. You must practice a lot, telling your stories."

I bite my lip. "Actually—this is the first time I've told a story from inside my head to anyone. When I chop mushrooms—I mean, when I used to—during my shifts I would tell myself all kinds of tales, silently. Now I keep them all in here, as I work." And I lift a finger to point to my temple.

"Is that so?" He widens his eyes in curiosity. "You have an unexpected skill. In fact, I might *actually* have you entertain my guests at the next social event. Be sure to come up with a clever ending to that story."

"Oh, I will," I say, starting to smile at the immediate surge of mental images.

"Just don't mention plucked chickens again, since any talk of meat is no longer appropriate or legal."

I nod, but press my lips together tightly to hold back that smile. It has nothing to do with the plucked chickens I inadvertently brought up earlier when describing the *sha* women. (That happens to me occasionally when I get hungry. I think of chicken, a rare bird delicacy we've only had on special occasions—and now will never eat again, because of the golden gods and their infernal decree.)

"Something funny?" He cranes his neck slightly.

"The *sha* king is!" I reply—and at once I become aware that my voice indeed *flows* in the manner of a yarn being spun, as soon as I speak of it, or merely visualize the characters.

"And Sharzaad, too," I add. "They're both clamoring to come out now and tell me their fates, so that I can, in turn, tell you."

"Hmm. . . . And what exactly do they say to you?" Bisfuri asks, meanwhile motioning to a servant to bring him a small business tablet lying on a side table—the kind of tablet I've seen used at the work offices of Chiprahat overseers. "Tell me now how the story ends."

"Oh, I can't do that," I reply, watching him key in something on the digital surface.

"Why not?" He looks up at me from his task.

I feel an instant of panic. But then I decide to speak the truth. "Because, *im Ter*, I don't *know* the end just yet. It's not how it works. The story is a ball of rope. It unrolls itself more and more while the characters speak and act. The unraveled pile grows bigger and more twisty with each new revelation, until the final resolution becomes visible. Rest assured, the end will come eventually, but—only *at the end*."

Benaten chuckles. "Very well. . . ." And he resumes keying in something, then looks up again. "Semirameos, I've entered your name in my employment record. Now I need your address."

I feel a warm wave of relief yet again. He is not angry at me for holding back the story. So, I give him the name of our little street, and the house number. "We live on Pit Row Twenty-Three—"

Two hands, two feet, and three fingers. . . . I pause momentarily to ascertain that I have it memorized correctly, the way Grandmother had drilled it into me. "And the house is number five on the left side."

Amurabia nods at me in confirmation.

Ter Bisfuri enters the things I said into his device, and finally hands me the tablet so that I can put my thumb print on it to sign and confirm.

The tablet makes a satisfying tone to indicate I am now officially employed once again. Granted, it's a really strange job, and I'm not even entirely certain what it will be like, but who cares?

"Storyteller, messenger, general duty household staff. Irregular hours. Standard level one compensation."

That's what, Bisfuri tells me, is indicated as my formal job description.

In that moment I notice my Grandmother's eyes, and they're sparkling with enthusiasm.

WE FINISH OUR TEA QUICKLY, so as not to inconvenience *Ter* Bisfuri any longer. And then, to our surprise, he assigns a staff driver to take us back home to Circle Ten, in a private car. Which means we don't have to walk so far and wait for the public transport.

"A household driver will take you, just this one time, on account of your Grandmother, so she can avoid the heat and rest her feet," he tells me, as we rise and head for the door. "Naturally, I expect you to find your own transportation when you come to work."

"Oh, of course, *Ter!* And when should I come to work?" I ask, pausing shyly.

In answer he calls another servant who returns with a box and hands me a metallic object that looks like a large round button pin with some kind of embossed pattern on its surface. It fits in the palm of my hand. In awe, I recognize it as one of the latest tech communication devices I've seen in commercials on the media-box.

"All Bisfuri employees are issued a badge comm," Benaten explains while I carefully turn the thing over in my hands.

"Keep it on you at all times. When you're summoned, it will blink and play a tone. There's also a voice call option. Ask the staff to show you how to use it. For now, simply get here as soon as it lights up. Should be some time tomorrow morning."

And that's how Grandmother and I end up sitting in the back of a luxury hover car upon soft velvet cushions, with tinted windows and cooling air circulating around us, while the soft-spoken uniformed driver skillfully flies us across Poseidon. He finally lands us, not merely at the closest bus stop, but directly on our street, *in front* of our hovel.

Neighbors on Pit Row Twenty-Three come out from other dilapidated hovels of limestone and baked clay to gawk and stare in wonder as we climb out of the fancy hover car that levitates a foot off the ground and sends up clouds of fine dust. As soon as we're deposited on the street, the car takes off once more, rising swiftly until it becomes a silvery bird speck in the sunny sky.

"Well, that was quite a day," Grandmother says casually, adjusting her skirt, and turns to all our neighbors. "What are you all looking at? Get back inside, nothing to see here! Just a tired old woman who for once decided to splurge for a ride from the markets!"

"Heh, that's some splurge," our closest neighbor Babi says, wiping flour-covered hands on her apron. "Are you sure you're well, Amurabia? Don't see you carrying any packages."

"Did I *say* I was well?" Grandmother strikes her cane on the ground in a flare of annoyance.

"Bastet help you! Considering all that's happening, all right. . . ." Babi widens her eyes and shrugs, heading back inside her home.

As our nosy neighbors begin to disperse, the front door of our house opens and Uru peers out. "*Mei-Ma!* Semmi! So, how'd it go? Where you been all this time? Did you hear?"

"Hear what?" I follow Grandmother, who hobbles tiredly

with the help of her cane inside our poor home and starts taking off her street shoes—oh how the contrast strikes me in that moment, the difference between the grand estate we've just visited and this tiny, dirty hole where we live. . . .

"The Imperial Kassiopei and a bunch of other noble Houses have already posted their Service Competitions! They're starting *today!*" Uru exclaims. "And I already signed up for one!"

I halt in my tracks. Amurabia drops her cane against the closest wall.

"Shut the door, child," she says quietly. "So that we can speak freely."

And as Uru runs to slam and bolt our front door, I say fiercely, "Only one? You sighed up for only one? Crap of a goat, you and I are going to sign up for *all* of them!"

"What do you mean?" Uru asks. "All of them? Huh?"

"Yes, all of them," I repeat in a firm voice, as I head for our living room bench and sit down next to Amurabia to deal with my own footwear. "We have to assume the worst each time, that we won't make it. The more places we try our luck, the better our chances at winning a service spot in these *chazuf* contests."

"Oh, okay." Uru wipes his nose with the back of his hand and makes a loud, nostril-clearing slurp.

"Now tell me exactly what happened in the markets today, and what you signed up for," I command my little brother.

And Uru starts blabbing in his usual unbridled manner.

"Slow down, child, slow down," Grandmother says, as Uru rattles off the noble Families and the specific Competitions and Categories.

"Sorry, yeah." He takes a breath. "I got there real early, before most of the billboards arrived, but House Ideva and Qurvamsur already posted the first of theirs, and it's Combat Competitions, under Category One, Military. They're being held in the Circle Three Arena tomorrow, using multiple weapons. Swords, daggers, knives. Any kind of bladed weapons. Also, stuff you shoot or throw. Other mixed weapons. And hand-to-hand combat."

"Fine," I say. "I hope you didn't sign up for any of that."

Uru wrinkles his forehead. "Huh? But I thought you said we must sign up for all of them? Didn't you just say, we sign up for all—"

"Not that one!" I interrupt, feeling my heart begin pounding with stress. "Uru, *chubrui* little goat, tell me you did not sign up for Combat!"

He shakes his head, "I didn't, and you're the one who's *chubrui*. I told you—"

"Bah! You didn't tell us anything yet! Keep talking!" I exclaim, feeling a pang of minor relief that my fool of a brother didn't commit himself to a certain death situation. That kind of Competition would mean going up against fully-grown, trained warriors who probably weigh five times more than him and would crush him like a booger with one finger. Just thinking about it makes me queasy with terror on his behalf.

Uru must survive this somehow . . . of any of us in this godsforsaken family, my little brother must make it and live. . . .

"*Ra and Bastet!* All right!" Uru frowns fiercely at me but continues. "Then there was—let's see—there were—House Vamsu, and also Ximunat and Sumerad. They were all posting delivery type stuff, messengers and running errands, speed and obstacle courses. I think that goes under Category Two, Domestic Service."

"There! That's it," Amurabia interrupts, lifting a finger. "That's more in line with what you do, Uru."

"Yes," I nod. "Did you enter one of those?"

"Yeah, Vamsu. I signed up with Vamsu . . . I think."

"You *think?*" I glare at the silly boy. "Where's your great memory that you can't remember the most important thing ever?"

"No, I remember!" Uru wails at me, his own voice rising to match my own. "I signed up for the Vamsu Competition! There's a race or something. Supposed to be tomorrow morning. Rules say we have to run around an entire Circle and find these special tokens and bring it back to them. Whoever finds and returns them to their overseers the fastest gets the win."

"Good, and what about the other two Houses? You must enter their Competition races also—"

"Okay. But those two are held almost at the same time, two days from now. I just picked one with a registration site closest to Circle Ten—that was Vamsu, in Circle Seven. Line started getting long, soon after I got there, and I was one of the first in line. No way would I make it to the others today. Bet you three *eos* pies and goat crap, theirs are just as bad."

I sigh in exasperation. The sudden urgency that has taken over me is making me push my little brother much harder in this than I normally would.

He must live . . . Uru must survive this nightmare . . . and the end of the world.

"Hey, *you* should sign up for those," Uru says, watching my sour expression which is probably showing a horrible frown. "While I do Vamsu, you can run for Ximunat and Sumerad. They're both next to each other in Circle Five. Or maybe Six?"

"I can't," I say. "I have a job now, starting tomorrow morning, so I'll just have to figure out how to fit in all of this later."

"What? You do?" Uru widens his eyes, then glances from me to Grandmother and back and starts to smile. "She really got a job, *Mei-Ma*?"

"Yup. With Bisfuri," I say, and Grandmother nods. "That's why it took us all day to get back home."

And then we quickly tell Uru what happened at the Bisfuri estate, without going into too many grownup details.

"Ooh, you get to work for the Man in the Niktos Cloak!" Uru exclaims with a laugh.

"Well, yes, but only temporarily—for now," I clarify. "It's not the same thing as being officially chosen in their Service Competition."

"Which they will be posting tomorrow, didn't the *Ter* say?" Amurabia reminds me. "You should find out more and sign up immediately when you get there."

"I will," I say, with an instant flutter of nerves in my gut as I think of going back *there*, going to Bisfuri. . . . Then I return my attention to Uru. "What else got posted? Which noble Families?"

My brother finishes telling us the news, the best he can. In short, there are ten Categories of Service, as previously announced by the Imperator, and the different Great Families will hold Competitions in each of the ten areas, in whatever random order they choose, in the coming days—up to and until the moment of departure from Earth, or for as long as it takes to assemble the perfect service staff for each of the noble Houses.

We learn that, as of today, Houses Urartumi and Tlactlu have announced artisan and skilled craftsman Competitions, under Category Five. Houses Shanguo and Baichizar posted a call for cooks and kitchen staff Competitions—which is Category Four, Food and Resources. House Egemavda, for some odd reason, is starting with the frivolous Competitions under Category Seven, Entertainment—singers, dancers, musicians, actors, and even courtesans (very likely, it occurs to me, this includes storytellers). Meanwhile, Kinakra and Giparu opened their Competitions with the practical Category Two, general domestic servants and Category Ten, muscle labor.

"Oh, wait—I just remembered, House Hekufati will be announcing tomorrow, and Nasrudi too," Uru mumbles, pressing the top of his head with his fingers, as if to help him recall all these endless noble Family names. And then he proclaims, carefully pronouncing everything, "Theirs is going to be Category Three, Technology. They're looking for brains, high-level techs to run the machines. Also, the scribes and number counters, which is, um—Category Eight, Education, Training, and Knowledge Preservation."

"See, you can remember the hard words, Uru," I say, reaching out fondly to tug his ear. "Good boy!"

"Eeow, stop!" he wails, moving out of my grasp like a slippery garden worm.

"What about the Imperial postings?" Amurabia asks. "Did you say the Kassiopei already announced theirs, child?"

"Oh yeah! They're holding *all* of them nearly at once! All the different Competitions! The first one starts today and then something else every day, for ten days, one for each Category. Like, a giant, stinky *ehoo*-pot of different contests and jobs!" Uru giggles until I start to reach for his ear again. "The first Imperial Competition begins this evening in front of the Palace—I think? But it's a stupid one, in Category Ten, for weightlifting and hard labor, so I didn't pay attention. Big, strong *chazufs* only, like porters to carry heavy stuff and big muscle to do construction."

"Yes, that won't work for us," I say, raising brows in wry amusement.

"It would work for Maitu's big man, Pedros," Grandmother says, thinking of our neighbors.

"Oh! Oh!" Uru recalls again. "House Heru, too! They didn't announce yet, but supposedly they will also hold every type of Competition at the same time as Kassiopei."

"Ah, well. Makes it harder for you, *im saai*, to enter multiple ones," Grandmother says. Wish they would spread them out more. It's not like the Sky Rock will hit tomorrow."

"I bet it's intentional," I say, standing up to put away my nice shoes in the corner basket. "They all create a rush to get the best people in each area of work. So there's no time for us to pick and choose where to apply, at a time when we're all so desperate."

"Yes, the nobles get to pick, as they always do."

Grandmother exhales a long sigh. "Well, then, let's make an exception today and see what the media-box has to say about all this."

I'm amazed. *It's not even the third hour of Khe, the sun is high up in the sky, and Grandmother says it's okay to watch the media-box?* Things are dire indeed.

Amurabia carefully sings the necessary notes in her unsteady, tired voice, to call and wake up the wall screen. The thing expands and lights up with a crackle, loading a familiar selection of smaller windows, for us to choose a specific video feed.

Grandmother points her finger at the portion of the screen with the Imperial City News and Uru runs up to tap the surface and enlarge, making the news feed the dominant window. At once, there's a blast of noise.

". . . The registration lines are similar everywhere, stretching endlessly along the streets, and have been like this since morning! Just look at these crowds! The position-seeking applicants from all around Poseidon are here to try their fortune with the noble Great Families of this fair nation . . ."

The voice of the commentator bursts in, while the screen shows a panoramic drone view from above an industrial district block in Circle Eight—familiar to me since I used to work not too far from there at the Chiprahat warehouse. A huge line— several people deep, more like a crowd—goes around the block, with no end in sight. City Guard officers attired in riot gear patrol the perimeter, their reinforced armor shining metallic-gold in the sunshine.

The crowd is boisterous, full of visibly stressed men and women of all ages, including many youngsters, shifting in place, arguing, voices raised. Among them, billboards of all sizes hover, passing barely overhead and at street level, displaying live announcements, instructions, media feeds, and more.

At the head of this unruly line, rows of officials stand in

House-specific sections holding registration tablets. One by one, people approach, offer their thumbs to be scanned, receive entrant tokens. . . . Billboards keep running tallies, and the squiggles that I assume are numbers, move in an endless scroll.

Oversized logos and symbols of various noble Families dominate the smart displays. I'm ashamed to admit that I neither know nor recognize any of them, except maybe the one that looks like a half-circle with warrior arrows and wavy lines inside it, supposedly belonging to House Qurvamsur. It stands for the mountain lakes in their province, and I only know this from watching some documentary program about them.

"Behold, Poseidon," the dramatic voice of the commentator continues, "this is what the viewers at home must brave if any of you decide to vie for a coveted spot with—"

A knock sounds on our front door just then.

"Guzum? Is that you? Come in!" Grandmother hollers, without taking her gaze off the mayhem on the screen. "Uru, let your Father in."

Uru runs to unbolt the door, and Father enters, looking somewhat more cheerful than usual. "Found work this morning," he says at once, wiping his dusty brow then taking out and shaking a small coin pouch from his pocket. "Wasn't much competition in the usual hiring lines today."

"How much?" Amurabia asks, again without turning to look.

"Three gold pieces for digging shallow trenches."

"Wonderful! Should pay for this week's grain and olive oil, and the energy bill to run this box. Now take those dirty shoes off, then come and watch."

"You have the media-box on, Amurabia? What miracle is this?"

"The end of the world indeed, that's the kind of miracle," Grandmother replies. "We must watch and listen carefully so that the children can learn what best to do, starting tomorrow.

And you, too, if you're up to it. Oh, and Guzum, your daughter has a job again. With none other than the Great House Bisfuri, over at Circle Two!"

AFTER FATHER COLLECTS his jaw from the floor of our hovel, we explain to him what happened today. Relating our adventure yet again, this time to an adult, Grandmother gives more details than she did with little Uru.

"And I told him, 'No sex!'" she concludes (*I roll my eyes at her*). "So, rest assured, Semmi will not be treated like a whore by these fancy nobles. This young *Ter* Bisfuri seems very reasonable, and was quite respectful toward me. Your daughter will remain a decent girl, and perform honest work for them, for as long as she is able—until we can get her permanently attached there, somehow."

"But . . . a Storyteller? I thought she chops mushrooms," my Father muses.

"That was yesterday." Amurabia shakes her head slowly, as though she herself hardly believes it, then lets out a confident breath. "Today, she has revealed a new talent, something unexpected. Sacred Bast herself must've inspired her efforts and gilded her tongue, for she told a fine story! Didn't finish it, stopping at just the right spot to make them beg for more!"

"Wish I'd been there to hear," Guzum says.

"Reminds me of my Eige. . . ." Grandmother suddenly says softly. "Eigeti had a way with words too, do you remember? Ah, my Eige. . . . How is it that she's gone and I'm still here?"

Father doesn't reply at all, only lowers his head to stare at the packed dirt floor. *He must miss our Mother, even a little*, it occurs to me. In between all his drinking, he must think of her sometimes.

After a few moments of unspoken thoughts and wistful silence—with only the media screen blaring noise and announcer voices at us—we return to paying attention to the news.

They show us more similar scenes all around the City, in different settings, depending on the nature of each specific Competition. Registrations are held at the various sites and, we're told, those stations will remain open day and night for as long as the Competitions continue to run, in order to accommodate late and last-moment entrants, people who can't get away from their regular jobs during normal hours.

Good, I think. *That would be me.* I'll need those late hours if I am to sign up for any of this.

Just then, something starts to *vibrate* at my waist. Then comes a soft, machine-sounding buzz, which turns into a delicate bell tone.

Like a slow-witted fool I realize it's coming from the expensive, latest model comm badge that I've carefully wrapped and hidden in my pocket. It's demonstrating a luxury high-tech function I've never had the opportunity to experience for myself, having only seen it on the media-box commercials with actors portraying beautiful rich people.

Holy Bast! Now?

Why is Bisfuri calling me already?

Everyone turns to stare at me as I reach in my pocket, fumble with the pouch, then look at the badge.

"Semmi?" Grandmother asks. "What is it? Is that—"

I turn the thing over and see a blinking amber spot at the center of the comm badge. I know enough from the commercials that you're supposed to press it. So, I do.

The buzzing and ringing ends. The amber light goes steady, and then I hear a familiar deep voice, rich like honey, needing no introduction.

From now on, I will recognize it always. . . .

"This is Benaten Bisfuri. I am summoning all household staff to be present at the main estate hall tomorrow, the seventeenth day of Setaet, seventh hour of Ra. House Bisfuri will be making an announcement concerning all of you. Arrive promptly."

"Oh!" I exclaim. "Yes, *Ter* Bisfuri, I will be there, thank you!"

There is silence.

"*Ter* Bisfuri," I repeat. "This is Semmi—Semirameos, yes I will be there—"

"Push the light . . ." Uru whispers, pointing at the amber spot that remains lit up. "Push . . . push there—"

"Okay, yes!" I whisper back. Then I press the light spot and say, "*Ter* Bisfuri, this is Semirameos—"

At once his voice interrupts me with the exact same words: "This is Benaten Bisfuri. I am summoning all household staff to be present . . ."

Apparently, it's a recorded message. I really need to learn how to use this thing.

"Is that . . . him?" Father asks.

I nod.

"Hm . . . sounds familiar. Where have I heard that voice before?"

"Nowhere," Amurabia says at once, quickly changing the subject. "Well, at least now you know what time to be there tomorrow, girl."

I recall, Father is the only one of us who doesn't know about the identity of the Man in the Niktos Cloak. Grandmother must realize that even Uru can keep this secret better than Father after he's full of beer. And we owe Bisfuri that much.

"Yes," I say. "And now that I know, I can have some blessed peace this evening. Should we start making the supper, *Mei-Ma?* I'll go stoke the fire pit and cut the onions and carrots."

"You do that, child. Also check the soaking peas, they should be softened enough. Leave the beans for another day." Meaningfully, she nods at me, and gives a sharp glance to Uru who appears aware enough to get the hint. "Might as well get cooking, before the neighbors start to come over to watch this accursed thing."

I get up, still holding on to the comm badge in my hands. And then I notice the amber light in the center is blinking again, at a slightly different rate. At least there's no buzzing noise this time.

"What now? What's it doing?" Uru notices the steady blinking and points.

I crease my forehead, feeling my heartbeat pick up, and take a deep breath, then press the amber light button again.

This time, my own voice comes out, loudly. I hear myself saying, "*Ter* Bisfuri, this is Semirameos—"

And then, to my horror—as my entire family stares at this accursed, *hoohvak, shar-ta-haak,* expensive, blinking *shebet* piece of technology—we get to hear most of our recent conversation repeated back at us, all the way up to the moment I pressed the button just now.

Holy Goddess Bastet, Mother of cats and *sha* women! Did I just record and transmit *all* of this goat crap to Bisfuri?

It's clear. Right now, I need to die.

CHAPTER
THIRTEEN

For the next quarter of an hour, I cuss my head off in bursts of self-fury, stopping and resuming, every few moments or so. Pausing frequently, even as I prep the vegetables and cook the supper along with Grandmother, I continue to curse and exclaim, and even stomp my feet. I call myself every slur imaginable for being an absolute *hoohvak* and sending that embarrassing recording to my new employer.

Not sure how many daydreams it takes, but I don't appear to be able to calm down. I periodically recall what I've done, and the anger starts over again. Uru giggles whenever I start exclaiming and spitting and huffing again, and slamming my fist against the knife-marked wooden surface of the old cutting table.

Eventually Amurabia says, "That's enough, girl. At least put the knife down before you hurt yourself—or someone else. What happened, happened. Nothing you can do about it. Bisfuri will understand an honest mistake. He has better things to do than be offended by such nonsense. You'll see, all will be well tomorrow."

What will he think of me for being so stupid?

What have I done?

Eventually, by the time our supper is ready to eat, my temper has cooled down somewhat. Grandmother and I carry our bowls filled with fried vegetables and pea pottage, and take our usual spots on the bench next to Father who's already filled his own bowl and is slurping hungrily. Uru gets his dish last, and perches next to Grandmother on the other side.

We eat and watch the news feeds showing crazy lines of people all over the City and the relentless action on the mediabox, until there's the usual knock on the door. Our neighbors start arriving, as expected. On such an important day, everyone wants to see the news. And today, Amurabia lets them, without a grumble.

Eventually, it gets dark, and people leave our hovel and us in peace.

"Feeling better, Semmi?" Grandmother asks me as we step outside into the cooking area of our yard to stow away the last of the dishes and cover up the kettle with the remains of our tea.

"Hmm." I make an unintelligible grunt in reply, as I quench the fire in the pit, and the smoke starts rising against the indigo sky. I must still look very grim and surly, otherwise she wouldn't have asked me outright.

"Don't over-worry," she says, looking at me with her warm eyes. "All will be well tomorrow."

I only shake my head in disgust at my own self. Thank Bast, it is time for bed, and I can go to sleep and forget briefly what's going to happen to me tomorrow.

APPARENTLY, the events of the day have tired me out more than I expected, because I fall asleep at once, sleep like the dead, and wake up with a start, well before dawn. A surge of reality strikes me, and knives of anxiety immediately twist my gut. I tiptoe quietly in the dark past sleeping Uru, past my Father on his bench out in the living room. First, just in case I overslept, I check the media-box timepiece display, and it is barely four and a half notches, the fourth hour of Ra. Plenty of time for me to get to Circle Two by seventh hour.

And so, I make myself presentable, splash my face with cold water from the small wash basin outside and get dressed in my regular clean work clothes. I use a small amount of olive oil on Amurabia's large-toothed comb to untangle my unruly hair, consider tying it with a ribbon again, then decide to just wear it loose as usual. I also make sure that horrible comm badge is safely stowed in my pocket.

I gulp down some leftover cold tea and eat a few lumps of pea pottage from the big pot. Then, I put on my sturdier pair of shoes (of the two that I have), and head out into the dark street.

Here's my plan. I need to get to the closest bus stop—the one on Circle Nine, just past the canal bridge—to catch the very first hover bus of the day that goes to Circle Eight and the warehouse district.

Normally this bus alone would suffice to get you to the heart of the City (such as yesterday with my Grandmother), but it takes forever, making endless stops along the way. Therefore, once on Circle Eight, I must get off and immediately rush to another stop, several blocks away, to transfer to the more expensive express transport line that goes directly into the City interior, including my destination, Circle Two.

I start running.

I CATCH the usual first bus just in time, heartbeats before its doors glide shut, and it takes off into the pre-dawn sky. The bus is busier than normal, with passengers who look like they might be heading not to work but to the various Service Competitions being held around the City. Even the animated media walls inside the bus play last night's registration footage in between commercials, and show huge lines forming again, everywhere.

Once we arrive on Circle Eight (which is such well-known territory to me) I get off, and begin running at breakneck speed along the familiar industrial streets lined with lampposts, past quite an unusual number of other pedestrians, on my way toward the other bus stop that may or may not require a long wait for the next transport. I can't afford to wait at that second stop for too long if I expect to make it to the Bisfuri estate in any semblance of a timely manner—especially today of all days.

Normally there are only a few people out at this hour— workers returning from their *niktos* shift or heading to work. All these extra people must be out early to get to the Competitions all over Poseidon.

Fortunately, the fancy bus arrives soon after I get to the stop. I board it, together with a small crowd of other people already gathered in the waiting area and generally better-dressed than the denizens of the first bus.

Off we go, soaring into the sky which is now the color of bluish dusk turning to rose with the coming dawn.

This hover bus still makes too many stops for my comfort along our route, and I perch in my seat, tapping my fingers with impatience, while my stomach feels like it's being knifed with nervous anxiety. It takes at least an hour to fly the course, and when I am finally deposited on the green shores of Circle Two, it is almost full morning, and probably after sixth hour of Ra.

Holy Bast, help me be on time!

I start to run again, making my way through the fragrant, sunlit greenery, along the gravel path that leads to the House Bisfuri. This morning, I am not alone in the park, because a number of uniformed staff are also hurrying, likely to obey the same summons I received last night.

When I get to the familiar high wall of sun-bleached stone and gilded metal gates, I see that they stand wide open, while the guards in black uniforms have moved aside to allow in a steady stream of people.

I join them and enter past the gates along with the household staff, continuing on toward the rear of the grand building to the service and delivery entrances. As we walk, I catch shreds of uneasy conversation. People speak in subdued voices, wondering which of the Service Competitions the Bisfuri will announce first, and if anyone has heard anything in advance.

A few of the staff give me suspicious, close looks, probably seeing that I'm not wearing a uniform. However, no one stops me at the doors as I enter the building. Taking a deep breath, I follow everyone through the many corridors, past the pantries and kitchens, and into the same magnificent hall from yesterday, splendid with marble and gold, wine-colored walls, mosaic and precious wood, and a central grand staircase leading up to a gallery on the upper floor.

Here, a crowd has already formed.

I push my way from the back, and press forward politely, as close as I can, making myself as small as possible, which is not difficult since I'm like a twig and barely take up space. The two women standing next to me, wearing tidy uniform skirts, kitchen aprons, and carefully pinned up hair, give me brief looks, then choose to ignore me.

More servants continue to arrive and crowd in behind me, so we're packed in, and the hall is overflowing with people. There has to be at least several hundred of us here.

Everyone stares up at the top of the staircase landing where a gallery runs along the hall perimeter.

"What time is it?" someone asks right behind me, breathing at my neck. I glance back in the direction of the breather and see a slender young man of my height, wearing a red messenger tassel near the collar of his uniform. He could be addressing me, so I open my mouth to whisper, "I don't know."

"It's almost seventh hour," one of the women standing in

front of me replies, turning her head quickly, and her dark, frizzy hair, gathered in a thick bun, swipes at my nose—so closely packed together we are. "Only about ten daydreams left before the hour. You barely made it, Girsul. Next time, you may not be so lucky. He catches you missing and will dismiss you."

"Heh," the young man called Girsul retorts with an awkward grimace and shakes his head. "I'm here now, that's what matters." And his gaze briefly meets mine. He then winks at me.

I don't react, holding back a little smile.

We continue waiting. Low-voiced conversations and whispers move around in waves. Some people take out their badge comms, and I can see illuminated displays coming on, with what looks like timepiece notches. *Interesting, I had no idea those accursed things also showed the time. . . .*

I glance up and see the distant cupola ceiling overhead, with its skylights casting brilliant morning sunshine upon us. . . .

In that same moment I notice movement on the upper terrace balcony. Three elegantly dressed figures emerge from the upper quarters and step forward onto the balcony, to survey all of us below.

With a lurch of nerves, I recognize Benaten Bisfuri. He is wearing a light jacket and no shirt underneath, while golden chains glint against his sun-bronzed bare chest. Next to him is a stylish, older man dressed in a more conservative jacket and shirt, with similar handsome features but a lesser build, who must be his father, Lord Muutat Bisfuri. The man's hair is not black but dark brown, a few shades lighter than his son's raven mane. On the other side of the Lord stands the other son, Behamenut, with the same black hair as his brother—which must come from their mother's side. He too wears a casual shirtless jacket like Benaten. It must be the latest fashion among the nobility, I recall, having seen this look on the media feeds.

At once, the crowd falls into silence. A few coughs are heard.

"*Nefero eos*, all of you who serve Bisfuri," says the older man next to Benaten after a dramatic pause. His voice carries well and resonates throughout the hall. I note, however, it is missing the silky rich intensity of his oldest son's deeper timbre.

"*Nefero eos*, Lord!" many in the crowd reply.

"You're aware, I have been absent these past few days," Lord Bisfuri continues. "I have been conducting important business in the outer provinces, on behalf of the Imperial Dynasty, pertaining to the critical circumstances in which we find ourselves. And now, complying with the Imperial Decree, House Bisfuri announces the Service Competitions for five hundred select positions in our household.

"These five hundred exemplary individuals who earn their place with House Bisfuri, will accompany us on the great journey into the black skies of eternal night and distant stars that lie beyond this earth, to escape these *circumstances*. It is very regrettable that we cannot take all of you, who have served us loyally, but the sky ships have limited room, as you've been told already."

Lord Bisfuri pauses, as small waves of whispers sound throughout the hall. "Let me make it clear, your loyalty and—in many cases—long years of service, are fully noted and profoundly appreciated. It devastates my soul to tell any of you that you must remain behind to face whatever . . . *sorrow* the gods have intended for this world—"

"Sorrow? Eh, I think he means death," whispers the young man behind me with a tiny huff of disgust, and his breath again stirs my hair at the nape.

I glance backward at him, but don't reply.

"—and it grieves me further to say that the winners of the Competitions will not be able to take any members of their families with them. It is a lone honor."

Again, more whispers, rising tones of discontent, as the deeper realization of what is happening starts to sink it.

My own gut wrenches with despair, thinking about my little brother Uru, my Grandmother, my Father. *None of them can come with me, even if I win this thing. . . . Uru, Father, they would have to win spots for themselves, wherever and however they may. As for my poor elderly Grandmother—*

I force myself to not think and focus on the present.

Meanwhile, Lord Bisfuri continues talking, probably aware that the faster he finishes telling us all these ugly details, the sooner he would no longer have to face a room full of desperate people.

"There are ten Service Categories in general, but we don't necessarily require every kind," Bisfuri continues. "We will be quite frugal in our needs, I emphasize. Quite frugal. . . . Indeed, all of you who do not qualify and must stay behind will be given handsome additional *compensation* to help you with the—um—difficult times ahead. For your final month of service, we will pay each and every one of you *five times* your monthly income—to do with as you please."

Muutat Bisfuri pauses, to gauge the reaction, and to be fair, there are many gasps and positive reactions at his words.

Merciful Gods! I think. In the worst case, if I don't win a spot, at least I will take home five months of pay—for whatever good it will do us in these final bitter days.

"And thus, we now open the Competition with a search for the best armed security and bodyguards," Lord Bisfuri pronounces forcefully. "One hundred spots! Our first Service Competition will offer one hundred of the best warriors a coveted place with Bisfuri. The details of the contest, including the registration location, types of weapons and combat knowledge required will be displayed on the public billboards around Poseidon in the next hour. But you—all of you—get to hear it first. As current employees, I promise to give you the first opportunity to register for this and each subsequent Competition before it is made public." He turns suddenly to his oldest son. "Benaten, will you address this? Cover the rest of this—"

"Yes, of course, my Lord," Benaten replies, and I momentarily start at the sound of his smooth, deep, utterly confident voice. He then picks up where his sire left off. "Our in-house registration station, intended for our current staff only, is being set up as I speak, right outside the building, near the employee entrance. A permanent board will display all the details and the results, daily, as they happen, including advance notice of each upcoming Competition.

"Furthermore, this board will include not only House Bisfuri postings but all the Competitions posted by all the other Houses and Families. By Imperial Decree, you are also permitted to take time off work to register and participate elsewhere in Poseidon. We may not forbid you this opportunity, as long as you give your supervisors advance notice and find suitable replacements for your work on the days you will be absent. You may now go and register, if you so choose!"

The crowd around me surges. "Well, so much for that." The nearest women in kitchen aprons look at each other and shake their heads.

"Military category, ugh, definitely not for me," many other people mutter.

"When is the domestic servant Competition?" some people cry out loudly. "Lord Bisfuri, please, when is the one for general domestics?"

But Muutat Bisfuri has already turned away and can be seen walking along the balcony toward the private living quarters.

"*Ter* Bisfuri?"

Benaten and Behamenut linger on the balcony, near the

balustrade. The younger brother mills about awkwardly, but Benaten once again speaks up in response to the asked question, pointing with one hand. "You! You wanted to know? The Domestic Service Competition is in five days, I believe. It's the next one. Check the board outside later today."

"Thank you, *Ter* Bisfuri!" several servants call out.

Benaten nods, and remains standing on the landing, surveying all of us below, probably in anticipation of more questions.

I stand, stupidly unsure of what to do with myself, and stare up at him. A sudden terror grips me. . . . He's going to see me now, having received that *hoohvak* recording from me. . . .

Oh, holy Bast!

"Move along, girl," a stern, middle-aged woman says to me. "Don't just stand there—"

"Why not?" another younger woman says bitterly. "It's not like she needs to rush to sign up to be a bodyguard—"

"Because there's work to be done!" the woman cuts her off. "And you too, Noor, get back to the laundry, now. Unless you plan to compete for a guard position yourself."

I look at the one called Noor, and see she is a girl my age, with light, freckled skin and wisps of honey-colored hair escaping from her linen-wrapped head. There's a green tassel at her uniform collar.

Noor gives me an amused and annoyed look then makes a face at the older woman who has already turned away. "Don't listen to her," she whispers to me. "Failah is a bitter hag. The gods made her barren, so she likes to order everyone around."

"Oh," I say. "How do you know that she is—"

In that moment, I happen to glance up again and see that Benaten Bisfuri is looking directly at me. He points a finger in *my* direction. And then, with that same finger, he beckons me.

I freeze.

"Go!" Noor nudges me at once, seeing Bisfuri's gaze. "The *Ter* himself is calling you now, go!"

I nod, with a bewildered expression, and then rush through the thinning crowd toward the fancy staircase, elbowing my way. Then I take the stairs two at a time and fly up to the landing in a matter of heartbeats. Once there, it occurs to me suddenly that maybe I should've gone up a bit more slowly, with a tiny amount of decorum, instead of bouncing from stair to stair like a monkey. Well, too late now. . . .

Slightly out of breath from my panicked climb, I stop directly before Benaten Bisfuri, who is looking at me closely, and whose brows have risen in apparent surprise.

"*Ter* Bisfuri!" I gasp out. "I—I'm here."

Holy gods! Will he now admonish me for my horrible, foolish recording from last night? That evil sha *recording! What if he hasn't received it yet? What if it sits inside his comm badge, still unplayed, what if—*

"Yes, you're clearly here. Good, Semmi." He interrupts my panic thoughts by speaking with such calm that he almost sounds bored. And his expression is not reproachful at all, almost amused—but no, that can't be.

"Come," he says, then turns away and heads along the terrace to the inner quarters, obviously expecting me to follow. Behamenut is already walking ahead of us, along with several uniformed servants whom I notice only now. They must've come upstairs by some other means than the grand staircase.

He said nothing about the recording! Nothing! Oh, Bast you are merciful indeed! Thank you, thank you, thank you. . . .

My pounding heartbeat settles down somewhat as I follow Bisfuri, his younger brother, and whoever else is ahead of us, into a chamber that connects to a very large suite of rooms by means of several twisting narrow corridors.

There is no sign of Lord Bisfuri. Only the two brothers and

us, the staff. One of them I recognize as the young man who stood right behind me downstairs, the one called Girsul.

Benaten follows his younger brother into yet another chamber, brightly lit from overhead with orbs. I notice it is decorated in light, airy, pastel colors, with a ceiling-high curtained off area in the center. Various incomprehensible tech devices are stacked on side tables all around the wall perimeter, interspersed with wooden chests and boxes, and several chairs and divans. The room and its furnishings look somehow peculiar, even to my own untrained eyes—I've seen enough dramas on the feeds to know a little about how nobles live. This place looks more like a workroom.

"So, what did you want me to do?" Behamenut asks, plopping down on the nearest sofa and putting his feet up on a low serving table. "Remember, I'm heading out to the Palace in an hour. Narmeradat will not like me being late."

"In a moment," Benaten replies, lifting his finger up, and then heads to a side table where I see a console screen. Could be a media-box? Or a tech controller of some kind?

Standing before it, he hums a series of tones in his beautiful, deep voice, and the screen comes alive with what I now recognize as the House Bisfuri logo, an intricate circular design. There's some kind of keypad directly below, and I watch his fingers move skillfully over the illuminated surface.

The several servants in the room move in closer, and watch their employer enter something, while the screen comes alive with scrolling rows and columns of flowing symbols that I vaguely recognize as writing. They are interspersed with occasional squiggles that could be numbers. I wish I knew how to read!

Benaten continues fingering the keypad, and then pauses to take out a small, metallic, coin-shaped device from a tiny drawer. He places the coin over the keypad, and suddenly it animates, popping upward, of its own accord. The thing hovers just above the surface then lights up like a comm badge, flickering briefly with gold and blue lights, then eventually glowing a steady green. As soon as that happens, he taps it with a finger, and the coin darkens again.

"This," Benaten says, plucking the coin from mid-air and handing it to his brother. "I need you to give this to Oron."

"Okay." Behamenut stares at it and flips the coin between his fingers.

"Discreetly. Place it in his hands only and don't let anyone else see you do it, especially not the other Kassiopei. Do you understand?"

Behamenut nods, then flips the coin one more time before putting it in the inner pocket of his jacket. "Yeah, got it. Any message along with it?"

"Only that it's from me, and we'll talk during my Father's formal evening event, here on the estate, the day after tomorrow. Everything he needs is inscribed on this Thoth-pin."

"What, exactly?"

"Not now, Eham. Now, go."

"Fine." Eham scrambles up from his seat and heads for the exit corridor.

Benaten turns to the serving staff. Three men, two women, and me.

"The rest of you, I have your *confidential* assignments," he says, glancing around at each one of us.

We all wait, standing. I nervously clutch at my skirt with one hand behind my back.

Benaten moves toward a large cushioned chair and sits down, leaning back and resting one booted foot over his knee in a relaxed, confident pose. He addresses the tall, muscular man with dark brown skin, dressed in a black security uniform, similar to that of the guards at the gates. "Vakrem, you'll visit Hathor's House. Get me a couple of *amretene* females for tomorrow's performance."

"Just two? Not the usual three, *im Ter?*" Vakrem asks with a slow nod.

"Not this time. We're only recording for three weeks in advance, and I already have Almahara lined up."

"The redhead? She's a real beauty."

"Ah, yes . . . Almahara and her perfect hips." Benaten raises one brow and pauses, as if contemplating, while a faint smile of wicked amusement curves his lips.

For some *hoohvak* reason, a surge of heat floods my face. *Good thing no one is looking at me.*

Vakrem clears his throat politely. "What are your preferences for the other two? Age, body type?"

"Let's have one young matron, and the other can be middle-aged. Brunette and blonde. One slim, the other voluptuous. As for the rest of their charms—surprise me."

"Understood, *im Ter.*"

"Then, find matching actors to play the husbands. I don't care what age or appearance. They just have to be able to fight with flair, or at least look like they know what they're doing. Hire all of them for both the morning and afternoon. It will be a long shoot." Benaten tosses a small pouch to the man who intercepts it deftly in mid-air. "That's for any personal extras incurred. Put the rest on my line of credit. Go."

The security man bows and exits the chamber.

Benaten turns his attention to the two women, one around my age, the other slightly older, both with orange tassels on their uniforms. "Dunea and Menahit, I want three designs from you by tomorrow. First, make me an Imperial golden bedroom. Airy fabrics, in sun colors. The second, a deep *niktos* indigo, bed draped in velvet layers, for a moonlit night, large crimson pillows for contrast. The last one, in garden greenery—green of all shades from light to dark, to offset Almahara's stunning red mane. Use white roses for spot contrast."

"Yes, of course, *im Ter,*" says Dunea, the older woman with deep brown skin, a fine-woven black wig, and a delicate smile. She makes quick notes on a digital tablet with a stylus.

"What about the music?" Menahit, the younger woman with elegantly tinted purple hair and light brown skin of the same shade as my own, asks. "Should I have Erevi and his band play live, or just use recorded sound?"

"Recorded is sufficient, this time," Benaten says quickly. "My Father expects perfection at the evening party, so Erevi and the others will be busy practicing for their live performance, with no other distractions. Now get started, go."

The two women curtsey and hurry away.

Only Girsul, I, and another tall young man remain.

"Chifuz, do you have a report for me?" Bisfuri asks the young man who has pale wheat-colored hair, very pale pinkish skin, and a grey tassel on his uniform collar.

"Yes, *im Ter*." Chifuz bows and hands Benaten a similar metallic "coin" device called a Thoth-pin. "My notes on the entire journey with your Father are encrypted for your eyes only."

"Including that detailed incident report on what happened during the flight malfunction over the Far Eastern continent—specifically, the Middle Territory?" Benaten watches him closely.

"Yes, all of it is there. The *shamshir* vessel plasma cloak failure, and how the primitives saw us from the ground. Your Lord Father was extremely displeased."

"I can imagine. He complained enough about it last night, at our evening meal." Benaten turns the Thoth-pin in his fingers. "I'll take a look and call you back if I have further questions. Now, dismissed."

"Thank you, *im Ter*." Chifuz bows with military precision and leaves.

Benaten looks at Girsul and me silently for several long moments.

"Im Ter," Girsul speaks up first. "I—obtained three, as you asked."

"You did? Good." Benaten leans forward in his seat. "Where are they?"

"Right now? They—um—they are at the stables. I retrofitted a special *shielded* room—" Girsul pauses and glances at me awkwardly. "What about her? May I speak?"

"She is Semmi, a new hire," Benaten says, noticing his hesitation. "Yes, you are permitted to speak freely before her. She's already heard everything in this meeting, and is in our confidential circle."

And then Benaten turns to me. His unusually colored, grey eyes meet mine, and just for a moment I feel a strange pang of additional nerves.

"Semmi, this is Girsul. You will be working with him this morning."

"Yes, *im Ter,*" I say, standing with as much poise as possible, frozen with anxiety. "What must I do?"

"First thing, you'll have Girsul show you the proper use of your comm badge." Benaten's expression remains bland, but I see his lips start to quiver at the corners. "For some unknown reason I've been made aware, in excruciating detail, that your family had pea pottage last night for supper—"

Oh, holy Bast! No!

I turn as red as a baboon's ass. My face, my head, my neck, all the upper parts of me are burning. I raise my hand to my mouth and press the back of my hand against my teeth.

"Oh . . . I'm so terribly sorry, *im Ter!* That stupid message—I didn't know it was recording, I am so sorry!" My voice turns into a whisper and cracks, as I lose the ability to inhale. . . .

"It's good that you're sorry," he responds sternly—or mockingly. His deep, rich voice has gained volume. "Being sorry indicates that you're aware of your transgression. However—it is but your first step to technological enlightenment. Today you'll learn every possible function of the comm badge. And now, let's move on to the real work at hand."

"Yes . . . *im Ter*," I mumble, continuing to cringe and die on the inside.

But apparently all is forgotten. Because Benaten motions to Girsul, who in turn looks at me.

"So, yeah, hey," Girsul says to me. "How much do you know about *pegasei?*"

"**W**hat?" For a moment I'm unsure if I've heard Girsul correctly. So, I stare hard at his angular, light-brown-skinned face and look for any sign of mockery or humor in his dark eyes. "Did you say . . . *pegasei?*"

"Yes. Have you heard the term? Do you know what they are?" The young man watches me quite seriously. In fact, right now, he's the one who appears uncertain of my reaction.

"Um," I say, tensing my brows. "Are they the rainbow cloud spirits that the Kassiopei priests catch? The ones that come out of the Imperial Temple orb?"

"Yes and no," Girsul replies. "They're not really spirits—not in the sense of departed ghosts of our ancestors. But yeah, the priests capture and harness them for various purposes."

"Not spirits?" My eyes widen with strain. "Then what?"

"You'll learn soon enough," Benaten replies in Girsul's stead. He gives me a single penetrating glance that seems to reach all the way through my most vulnerable layers of worry and self-doubt—that frightened part of me that is once again plunged into silent panic at the thought of what I'm about to deal with—then motions to Girsul. "Go and teach her, so that she can assist you with their handling. And don't forget the comm badge. By the end of today, she should be well versed in both."

"Yes, *im Ter*," Girsul says with a short bow. But Benaten is already looking away, having picked up a nearby digital tablet.

I FOLLOW Girsul out of the fancy quarters into a network of corridors and then into morning sunlight. We end up on an exterior balcony terrace that runs along the perimeter of the building several stories above ground, and finally get downstairs via a small corkscrew staircase at one corner of the grand building.

Once on the ground, we walk quickly, surrounded by manicured greenery, toward a nearby grouping of other lesser buildings. There are few people out because most of the staff is still out in the front area, dealing with the Service Competition registration.

Girsul throws me occasional amused glances and periodically comments with: "This way," and "Almost there." He also points out the layout of the estate, saying things like "That's an old residential building, now used by staff," and "Those are additional storage buildings."

"You're not going to register for the first Bisfuri Competition?" I ask.

"You think I should?" Girsul raises one brow sarcastically, pointing to the red messenger tassel attached at the collar of his uniform. "I'm just an errand boy . . . with a few additional duties known only to *Ter* Aten, *Ter* Eham, and a few of their *discreet* staff. I'll wait for the next one, thanks. Unless you want to go and register as a guard yourself? You look like you have muscles —somewhere."

"Oh, no," I retort with a small laugh. "That would be a joke of the gods. Though my Grandmother says I have a loud mouth, so my tongue might be muscular."

"Good to know." Girsul winks at me.

In that moment I realize that could be taken wrong, so of course my face immediately flushes with heat. *Holy Bast, please, oh please, curb my big mouth! And . . . "muscular" tongue? What kind of* garooi *idiocy did I just spew?*

Thankfully the young man does not pursue that turn of conversation. "Don't worry, you're not missing anything," he says calmly. "Let the crowds go first. We can check the board later in the day, and register for any other Competitions around the City. First, we have to get our work done."

"All right," I respond with some relief as my cheeks cool down. "As long as we don't miss out on any important opportunity."

Finally, we arrive at a long, narrow structure that has a low, flat roof, for the most part. It encloses, on three sides, a very large open yard which continues into some kind of grassy clearing. Beyond it, I notice various fences splitting it into smaller parts, probably to separate the animals.

"Here we are, the Bisfuri stables," Girsul says. "They keep the *sesemet*, the *camral*, and over there, with the high roof, the *bau-ehl*."

"Horses, camels, elephants?" I echo, barely recognizing the upper-class terminology for the beasts. The nobles breed the creatures to be strongest and most beautiful, and once they reach certain top traits, the breeds are formally distinguished from the ordinary beasts of their species.

"Yeah, but don't let them catch you using the poor people's terms around here," Girsul says with a short laugh. "There are only *sesemet*, *camral*, and *bau-ehl* on this estate. Seriously, we have the finest *sesemet* anywhere. And now we have *pegasei*."

"All right," I say, and my curiosity is at its highest.

"This way," Girsul says again, pointing with one hand, and opens an unusually small narrow door leading inside the short end of the building housing the stables. "Watch your head and feet, really low door jamb here, and a raised threshold," he warns me. "Supposedly so that beasts won't be able to escape easily."

"Really?" I say, ducking my head as we enter, and narrowly missing the threshold with my toes.

"Mostly it trips up people," Girsul says with disgust. "All the stable hands hate it, and whoever built it was a carpentry fool. But it's been like this forever, and you get used to it."

"Why not just change it?" I whisper with care, breathing the sudden pungent animal smell that assails us here indoors. "The Lords have so much money, they can afford to fix this door?"

Girsul laughs again. "Nah, the chief stables overseer likes it. He's the *hoohvak* in charge and thinks it serves its purpose as intended. And none of the grooms would go over his head to complain. Not that it would matter now anyway. . . ."

We both pause, momentarily reminded of the grim doom in the form of the Sky Rock coming to get all of us.

"All right, this way." Girsul points ahead of us.

I take a good look at the long space stretching far before us, in the dimmed light of a single orb installed in the wall. Immediately ahead is a small front area with several stools, work tables lining the walls, shelving full of straps, tools, rope, assorted bridles and ties, and various footwear suitable for mucking the mess. And then the actual stables begin.

Animal enclosures and stalls run in endless rows along one limestone wall, and I notice equine heads poking out over short barred gates, or occasional swishing tails. Quiet sniffing noises fill the great space, as the beasts appear to be asleep for the most part, likely having been fed and exercised already, before dawn. Overhead, wooden beams stretch, with utilities such as retaining hooks and suspension chains installed at various lengths. No one else is here, but us.

"Let's move quickly, while the others are still out there checking the Competition boards." Girsul correctly notes the nature of my curious glances. "*Ter* Aten prefers to keep the presence and the location of the *pegasei* discreet for now."

I nod.

"But, before we continue, he did say to show you how to use your comm badge," Girsul says, pulling up two stools. He pats one, and I sit down next to him. "All right, let's see it."

I pause, then pull out of my pocket the carefully wrapped round object that has caused me such embarrassment.

Girsul takes it, then starts tapping and running fingers over its surface at various points. The badge lights up, and I notice several screens on it, including a time display that I recognize. "That's the main menu," he tells me, showing the largest screen and the different tiny symbols on it. "Here is the call function, the record function, the alarm, the calculator, the music player—"

"The what?"

"Music player," the young man says with amusement.

"It can play music too?"

Girsul simply taps the symbol, and at once a soft pounding beat fills the air, a swell of pipes and a woman's voice singing a popular song. "There's a whole music feeds sub-menu."

My mouth falls open in wonder.

He taps the symbol again, which silences the music at once. I stare in such shock that he probably thinks something's wrong with me. Honestly, I've seen some devices that play music and voice recordings, such as our media-box at home, but we've never actually used that capability because it costs additional money each month to enable it. And, of course, there are the commercials for luxury technology shown during the various feeds and dramas I watch. But I've *never* seen anything like this little round device! And in truth, I don't think I've ever properly understood the true functionality of those high-end items the commercials advertise.

And now . . . I know. This thing is almost like a digital tablet!

A quarter of an hour later, and still no other stable workers have returned. Meanwhile, we've gone through the whole comm badge menu, one item at a time. Girsul has me repeating endless finger-tap sequences to call up the various sub-menus and functions. "Like this?" I ask.

"No, this," he corrects me, repeating a tap sequence. "Now you do it. No, not that! Unless you want to disturb Lord Bisfuri himself—don't *ever* touch that button, not ever, not unless you absolutely have permission. It's for supervisors and overseers reporting to him mostly, we never use it."

"Got it." I nod. And then I practice calling up the employee directory (useless to me since I can't read the squiggly letters that encode people's names) and then entering Girsul's employee number that I've memorized, and calling his own comm badge. The small ring tones echo through the stables, until a horse snorts and starts to neigh.

"You don't know how to read, huh?" He ignores the horse and cranes his neck sideways, looking at me with a flip of his dark hair, right in my face. We sit, heads leaning forward over the device, close enough that our foreheads and knees nearly bump.

"No," I admit with shame.

"It's okay," he says. "I can't read the letters very well either, just barely enough to get work done. Numbers, I'm good with."

"I'm okay with numbers," I half-lie. In fact, I'm barely able to keep track of my fingers, thanks to Amurabia's schooling. "But I can memorize well."

"That's all that matters," he says with a crooked grin. "As long as you memorize your own employee code and mine, and of course *Ter* Aten's code, you should be fine. Later, you might need to know the codes to reach Vakrem, Chifuz, Menahit, Dunea, and a few others, but this is enough for now."

I exhale. "Thank you so much. At least now I know how *not*

to record nonsense and send it to *Ter* Bisfuri's device in the middle of the night."

"Did you seriously do that?" Girsul laughs.

"Yeah. And I almost died, thinking about *Ter* Bisfuri being so angry upon receiving it."

"Angry? Nah." Girsul snorts, then shakes his head. "*Ter* Aten probably laughed his ass off."

"Oh. . . ." I exhale in sudden relief.

"All right, so we're done here? Think you know how to use this thing properly now?"

"More or less. . . . Yes."

Girsul springs up from his stool. "Great! Now let's go meet the *pegasei*."

WE WALK a long way past the many horse—pardon me, *sesemet*—enclosures, and reach a corner where the stables continue in another direction. As we turn the corner, immediately there's a small caged-off section, stretching from floor to low ceiling. There is no actual wall divider, only a metallic fence formed of evenly spaced chain links, and beyond it, a heavy blackout curtain covering something in the center.

Girsul quickly unlocks the metal cage enclosure, looks warily in both directions, and beckons me to follow him.

I hesitate momentarily, then take a step forward, from the beaten clay floor of the main stables onto the metallic slab that constitutes the floor of this enclosure.

Once we're inside the cage, he shuts the gate behind us. And then he carefully pulls back the curtain that comes down from the nearest wooden beam overhead.

Inside that hidden area, a curious sight greets me. I'm not sure what I was expecting, but certainly not these three medium-sized orbs full of swirling multi-color lights, all three suspended on chains from that same beam in the ceiling. There is no other light source in this immediate area, and as a result the orbs are the focal point, as they pulse and flicker with faint rainbow light.

"Here you are, my beauties!" Girsul exclaims in a whisper, as he steps closer to the orbs which hang low enough to reach chest level.

I stand, petrified, staring at them. "They look like weird light orbs," I say. "What exactly are these? Some kind of *pegasei* eggs?"

Girsul smirks and shakes his head. "Go ahead, touch it."

"Okay. . . ." I slowly reach out and poke the nearest orb with my index finger. It feels solid and slightly warm to the touch, with a glassy surface and a faint pearly sheen, like the strange expensive stuff inside sea shells, called mother-of-pearl. "Is that a shell?"

"In a sense. . . ." Girsul leans closer to the orb, and it illuminates him in profile. "It's a *quantum containment field*."

I stare at him without comprehension. Those words, they could be dog barks, for all the sense they make to me. "A *field*, I understand," I say carefully. "A field of grass, or wheat, or barley? The rest, not so much."

"It took me a while too," he replies, glancing up at me. "But —it's *energy*, manipulated on the smallest, tiniest level."

"Huh? Like sunlight? Or, whatever powers the lights and the media-box?" I try very hard to make sense of this.

"Yes, that's all energy. But this—just think of it as energy that's stuck in a kind of weird, temporary solid form."

"How is energy solid?"

He bites his lip, after a pause. "I don't know. And seriously, it doesn't matter. All you need to know is that it just *is*. This solid energy is a barrier that surrounds and contains the rainbow cloud creatures. Because *they*'re energy too. That's what I was told. They can't escape it. It's the only way to hold them. Energy on energy. And the only thing that can break this solid energy barrier is a *sound command*."

I run one hand through my tightly curling hair and scratch my scalp.

This is just too much. . . .

"So . . . the rainbow clouds are inside," I restate, mostly for myself.

"Yes."

"And how did they get in there?"

"The priests and the sound techs sang the commands while they baited the *pegasei* with light."

"Huh?"

"Light, the *pegasei* eat *light*. Sunlight is their favorite. So while they were loose in the Temple, they harnessed them quickly with the solid energy. And now they're trapped."

I furrow my brow. "Isn't that kind of awful? That they're trapped, I mean? Are they—suffering?"

Girsul pauses to consider, then shrugs. "Maybe. Probably not. We're not really sure about anything when it comes to these things, only that they have certain uses. Anyway, we'll talk about it later. Now we need to feed the *pegasei*. And then we'll practice releasing them and taming them."

"Seriously?" My mouth parts again. "Feed them?"

"Yeah. And you're going to help me."

Girsul bends down and picks up a folded sheet of black cloth from a stack in the corner of the cage, same material as the curtains, and tucks it around his uniform belt. Then he reaches up and disconnects the chain of one orb from the wooden beam overhead, and gently lowers it so that the orb swings near the ground. He hands me the chain end. "Hold this, carefully."

Silently I accept the metal chain and feel the light weight dangling in my hands, a slightly moving, pulsing thing that feels like I've caught a fish.

"Try not to swing it too much and don't drop it," he tells me, while reaching to unhook the other two suspended orbs. "Follow me."

Balancing the two chains, one in each hand, as if he's carrying buckets of water, Girsul turns around, then pauses once again, and offers me one of his two orbs. "Hold this one too, for a moment."

I take the second chain, so that now I'm the one balancing two orbs, while the young man unlocks the cage containment gate and steps outside into the main stables hallway area.

"Very, very careful, now," he says softly, again looking around to make sure we're still alone. "We're outside the *shielded cage*, which means that if the quantum containment fields break, they will escape completely, and *Ter* Aten will kill me . . . and you."

"Where are we going?" I step outside the cage, careful not to swing my *pegasus* orbs.

"Just here, through this door." Girsul motions with his head in the direction that continues deeper into the stables, where I see a slightly elevated roof and the beginning row of camel enclosures. And in one wall, just before the camel area, is a narrow, unobtrusive doorway.

Girsul walks before me and opens the door with his free hand. Bright sunlight immediately hits us, followed by a warm breeze and wonderful fresh air.

We go outside, and the moment we step past the threshold into the inner exercise yard, I feel a small tug at my fingers—there's a subtle shifting of weight at the ends of both chains I still hold. I glance down, and *O, holy Bastet help me!*

The rainbow-filled orbs are flaring and pulsing with fierce brightness! They look like they're on fire!

"What's happening?" I ask breathlessly.

Girsul's single orb is similarly burning-bright now, scalding, incandescent near-white, and he grins at me. "They're feeding!"

We take a few steps into the otherwise empty yard, and

Girsul tells me to just stand there and let the sun bathe over the orbs. "They only need about half an hour to fully feed for the day. As long as the sun is out, they get their full meal. On overcast days, they need longer, at least two hours in the daylight."

"Oh," I say. "What happens if they don't get the light?"

"I'm told, they fade away. . . . Die, I suppose. They shouldn't be kept in the dark too long."

"Like in that dark cage, behind the curtains?"

Girsul bites his lip. "Yeah, that's just temporary. Once we tame them, we will have them at our disposal and will be able to keep them in the main stables—I think."

"You think?" I say with a tone of minor accusation, continuing to clutch the two chains.

"Well, they didn't tell me much at the place I procured these. Just enough to keep them alive and tame them."

I shake my head. "I don't suppose you bought these directly from the priests of Kassiopei?"

He snorts. "The *Kassiopeion* temple charges too much. I saved *Ter* Aten some money and got these beauties from a—let's just say, a third party."

"All right, whatever," I say. "I don't need to know."

"That's correct, you don't," he retorts with a wink.

I roll my eyes.

We stand, milling about in the sunshine, while the *pegasei* inside seem to grow brighter and brighter with each daydream, if that's even possible—the pulsing sensation increases, and I can feel it all the way along the chains.

A sensation of dancing at my fingertips. . . .

Meanwhile, the rainbow lights blink and flux, running faster and faster to circle the interior diameter of each orb, in what seems to be wild ecstasy. I'm guessing, after being for so long in the dark behind black curtains, they are gorging to relieve their hunger . . . *poor things.*

Girsul keeps glancing around to make sure no one is coming. "If anyone shows up, we'll just put the black sheets over these, and say we're carrying light orbs. Got it?"

"Yeah." I nod, feeling a slight sheen of sweat on my forehead, despite the pleasant breeze, since the sun is very hot right now, and we're far from any shade. "How do we know when they're—full?"

"Like I said, half an hour is enough. We're almost there. Another way to tell is when those rainbow lights start to move so quickly that the motion blends the colors, and they appear almost white. Kind of like that one—" and he points to the *pegasus* orb hanging from my right hand.

"So, what now?" I ask.

"We need to go back indoors, out of the sun," Girsul replies. "Otherwise, they might 'overcharge,' become too strong, and can even break out of the quantum containment field."

"What about these other two?" I motion with my head. "They don't appear white, so are they still feeding?"

"Good enough," he says, taking the black sheet from his belt and wrapping it around his *pegasus* orb, then hands me the other sheet. "Cover up yours, and let's head back in."

WE GO BACK inside the stables through the same door and end up a few steps away from the special shielded cage. Just then we hear voices coming from the end of the stables. Looks like we got back just in time.

"Quickly. . . ." Girsul fiddles one-handed with the enclosure lock.

Once we're back in the metal cage, he exhales a long breath and then quickly pulls the black curtain around us. It occurs to me he's been nervous this whole time. I don't blame him.

"All right, now," he says in a loud whisper. "Let's first hang them back up."

One by one, he hooks the chains up to the wooden beam, as I hand him my two. The three orbs are bright as daylight, super-charged to the point of casting a very powerful radiance in a nimbus around them.

"I hope that black curtain is enough to keep their light from shining through," I whisper back.

"Sh-h-h-h!" Girsul hisses, putting one finger over his lips, as we hear the sound of several footfalls approaching, and the conversation of grooms talking about the Service Competitions and gossiping about the Bisfuri.

We freeze in silence, until the stable workers pass by us, heading deeper into the stables.

"Okay, they're gone," he says at last. "We can get back to work."

"What now?" I ask, continuing to stare at the bright orbs.

"Now we try to tame them," he replies with a mischievous smile. "First, you should know that if they manage to escape these energy orbs here in the enclosure, they won't be able to get out entirely. They'll simply float around the shielded cage. So, keep the gate closed all the way—to complete the energy circuit."

I wrinkle my brow. "But they're like vapor clouds—won't they simply get out through the holes between the chain links? I used to have a mouse at home that I put in this small basket cage to see if I could make it a pet, but it just got out after it chewed through the straw. . . ."

Girsul makes a short sound of laughter. "Yeah, I bet it got out. But this is not a mouse. And this cage is quantum-shielded. Each chain link is made with special orichalcum-coated metal that reacts to sound commands, and the commands have been issued by a skilled tech. So, it acts like a magnet that makes energy *stick* to it. And the *pegasei* will stick to it too. Holes and small openings don't matter, as long as the orichalcum carries a charge—or so the tech has told me. Do you understand?"

I nod, even though I don't completely know what he's talking about. I only have very vague knowledge of what orichalcum can do besides making things levitate if the right sound tone is sung. I mean, I *do* know how to make the media-box start up and shut down. . . .

"All right," Girsul continues, as he goes to open a small wooden box in the enclosure corner underneath the stack of black sheets. "First, we need to voice-key the energy spheres to ourselves and these metal cords." Rummaging through the box, he pulls out what looks like coils of metal rope or wire, of a slate grey color with small gold flecks shining in it, similar to the chain link fencing of the enclosure around us. I recognize the sheen of orichalcum. . . . It's like fool's gold.

Very expensive hoohvak's *gold.*

"You know how to *voice-key*, right? Here, catch." He tosses one coil to me, and I grab it.

"Um," I say. "Sort of, I guess."

I don't mention the fact that I've only seen Grandmother do that with our media-box when it was brand new. You have to initialize them before first use, and that involves voice-keying of each new device by the customer. I've never done it myself.

"Good. It's pretty straightforward. You tie the cord around it then sing the keying command—while you hold on to both. And, while you do it, you also have to *think* of whatever shape you want the *pegasus* to take on."

"What do you mean?" I ask. "What shape? Huh?"

Girsul smiles. "This creature is a *shapeshifter*. And, it can *read* your mind. It will see whatever animal you imagine, and it will take on that physical form!"

My jaw drops, and I am absolutely stunned.

He sees my shock and smirks again with amusement. "Yeah, I bet you didn't know that. Now you do. These things are so prized, partly because they can shapeshift!"

I put my hand over my mouth.

"As you key the orb to yourself, the solid energy collapses, releasing the *pegasus*. That same energy then immediately adheres to the new harness cord which becomes the creature's new restraint. Now the *pegasus* is loose, out of containment, but cannot escape. The harness puts you in direct control, giving you the chance to train it—and even ride it!"

"But—" I attempt to speak.

"Just follow my lead and sing these three notes exactly. But, not just yet. First, we have to have all three of them rigged up with those harnesses. Each one of them gets its own harness. Like this—"

Girsul turns his attention to the *pegasei*. He supports one of the orbs on the palm of his hand, while he unhooks the encircling chain, so that the orb is freed and rolls loosely on his palm. Next, he takes the coiled metal cord and starts wrapping it around the sphere—once, and then a second time so that it's perpendicular and forms a very basic metal "cage" around the orb. He ties it off in a simple knot, and holds on to the remaining length of cord like a thin bridle, while continuing to support the orb in the palm of his other hand.

"Ready?" He throws me a meaningful glance. "Watch me!"

I'm staring so hard my eyes are about to fly out of my head.

But he hesitates again, then pronounces, almost with pride: "This is what, supposedly, the original *pegasei* looked like when the priests first figured out how to make them shift form. Here we go, imagining it now . . . *watch!* And stand back to make room!"

He takes three steps backward away from me, and sings three notes, the first one long, the other two short, and repeats the sequence several times, focusing his attention on the orb in his hand. His voice is a clean tenor, and he hits the notes accurately.

On the fourth repetition there is a loud pop sound, followed by a searing flash. The flash is so bright it blinds me momentarily, and flares like a crack of lightning against the black curtains around us.

The orb in Girsul's hand deflates like a burst wine sack. But, unlike a wine sack, it *disappears* in thin air. In its place, a cloud of rainbow light explodes into the small space around us.

With a stifled scream, I jump backward, so that I'm pushing and slapping at the curtains in panic, in an attempt to get away. . . .

Only now I'm surrounded completely by a vaporous *thing* of multi-colored light. Except . . . I see that this blob of rainbow vapor is pulsing like a beating heart and struggling.

A portion of it—a tangible limb, maybe, a neck—appears to be mysteriously *contained* between the coiled loops of the metal cord in Girsul's hand. It throbs and pulls at the cord violently, while the young man holds on with both hands, showing visible effort, and continuing to sing the three notes. . . .

And then a miracle takes place before me. The shapeless mass of colored light fluctuates wildly a few more times, and starts to coalesce into some kind of physical form.

"Get back, back!" Girsul yells at me, having stopped singing. He wrangles the blob of light which distends and reforms with each heartbeat, growing and retracting multiple limbs, and suddenly it is no longer mere light.

It is something else.

The limbs lengthen, and there is a wide barrel torso and a long equine head. Filaments of radiance form into a mane and a tail, streaming like flames, until they fade, turning pearlescent white. And from the back of the torso, enormous pale wings erupt, covered in impossible feathers—as if a giant eagle bird decided to gift its flying appendages and feathers to a horse!

"Crap of a goat!" I exclaim in a combination of absolute awe and absolute terror. "Crap, crap, crap! What is that?"

The winged horse suddenly rears up on its powerful equine legs, so that it literally hits the wooden beams on the ceiling, and has to fold its wings somewhat, short of tearing them. It then stomps the ground of the metal enclosure, making the floor *ring. . . .*

As we stare, it swings its head and neck from side to side, baring perfect white teeth at us. And its wide, rolling eyes are an impossible lavender violet as it glances back and forth from me to Girsul.

No neighing, no snorting sounds of a true horse or *sesemet* come from it. . . . Even as it struggles, its jaw contorts and *screams*—all in terrible, perfect silence.

Worst of all, there is no comprehension in its gaze, only *alien* wilderness.

"This—this is a *pegasus!*" Girsul exclaims to me in proud exultation, even as he continues to clutch the orichalcum cord with both hands.

And then he sings a long single note, the kind used to train herd animals.

The *pegasus* creature stops struggling.

Just like that, it stands frozen, listening to the long sound, as though mesmerized.

I don't blame it, I'm mesmerized too.

Though, I think I almost crapped my undergarments.

G irsul holds on to the end of the harness that's tied in a loop and then steps closer to the motionless *pegasus*. Carefully he reaches up to run his fingers over the mane, then touches the skin of the neck. The creature does not respond, only periodically rolls its lavender eyes in senseless random motion.

"Whoa, my beautiful one!" Girsul begins to repeat in a singsong whisper and rhythmically caresses the neck. Not sure why he's saying "whoa" since the creature is not exactly moving or responding in any way. And then he looks over at me and nods meaningfully in the direction of the two remaining *pegasei* orbs. "Go on, your turn."

"Me?" I say with wide eyes. "What? Are you sure?"

"Of course. You need to be able to do this and handle them. Just do exactly what I did. Tie the harness around the orb, then sing the three keying notes, then visualize the *pegasus* shape in your mind and sing a single herding note."

"Crap . . ." I mutter. Clenching the folds of my skirt with one hand to wipe sweat from my cold fingers, I reach out and take the nearest of the two remaining orbs suspended from the wooden beam, trying to keep my hands from shaking too much.

I unhook the lower end of the chain and unravel it, releasing the orb into my palm. It's the size of a melon, but feels incredibly lighter, almost buoyant with some kind of leashed energy.

Warm and slightly heavy, and pulsing with life. . . .

"Now the harness." Girsul nods to the box in the corner where the orichalcum coils are stored. Continuing to stroke the neck and mane of his *pegasus*, he stares at me.

"Okay." I hold on to the orb in my hands, resting it partially against my chest for leverage, then pick up a cord and start winding it around the spherical living object.

"Now, back up," Girsul says. "You're going to need to make more room for your new horse with wings to stand next to mine, so step back even more."

I back away toward the other end of the curtained area and stop. Pressing the orb with the cord around it with my left hand against my chest, I make sure I'm gripping the loop end tightly with my right. *Did I do it correctly? Is it tied properly? Is it too loose? Is it—*

"Go on, now. Keying command."

Silently I nod. Then I clear my throat and start to sing the same notes that I'd heard him make earlier. My voice starts out a little shaky, but I have a decent control of the notes.

"Don't forget, imagine the *pegasus* in your mind!"

I hear Girsul's voice but don't shift my visual focus away from the thing of swirling colors in my left hand—the orb is so warm now, so radiant. I continue singing as I try to *see* in my mind's eye this unnatural shape, this *pegasus* creature with a horse body and crazy bird wings. . . . With each note I make, the sensation of weight and pulsing *agitation* in my hands increases —almost as if it echoes each of the sounds I make with a sympathetic twinge of energies colliding.

Holy Bast, but it's going to be huge! How will I hold on to it? Will it escape? No! I must hold on!

Just as panic starts rising from the pit of my stomach, an

explosion comes in a blinding flash. Impossible radiance strikes my face . . . and then I feel nothing in my hands, only a brief shock of residual energy.

Crap, it's gone!

And then. . . .

A rainbow cloud of light fills the air, engulfing me with tiny embers of living flame. These living dust motes of every color swirl around me in a violent swarm. In a matter of heartbeats, the cloud begins to coalesce into a moving blob—a thing, a *being* that still has no definite shape but a unified direction. And now it's like a wild *sha*, pulling and tugging hard at the end of the harness that I clutch desperately. And it's reforming before my eyes, shifting into *something* for one heartbeat then shifting again. . . .

Okay, now what? Think, think, think. . . .

I falter only briefly then sing the single herding note.

This is it! This is the moment.

I try to imagine the noble great *sesemet*, its tall, imposing shape, its huge wings, maybe a similar pale shade of skin and mane to the one that Girsul has made—almost white, or maybe slightly grey, maybe even with patterns like splotches of black and brown. . . .

Out of nowhere, a spinning cascade of childhood memories and images floods my mind, and suddenly I recall all kinds of animals from our street in Denwen's Pit, from the time before the golden aliens arrived and made us stop eating meat.

Back in those days, everyone in the neighborhood had some kind of animal living in their yards. Sheep, cows, donkeys, chickens, ducks, geese, dogs, and cats. . . . Several hovels down the row from us, this man called Judhu and his daughter kept these little goats. . . . I was much younger then, a little girl who played with the goats sometimes, petted their rough, curly fur. . . . *No!*

In my hands, the struggling light blob of orange and green

and red and violet stabilizes its wild motion. At the same time, its overall shape feels more compact now—instead of growing in size it is deflating, falling inward on itself. And just like that, it starts to take on a definite physical form.

Bastet! Mother of all that's holy, all-powerful goddess, no, no, no!

I look at the small four-legged beast materialized before me —two little horns, two pointed ears, spindly legs and all. Residual sparks of color and energy erupt from the tips of its horns and fall like sparkling dust into thin air, before coalescing finally.

Not tall and majestic—its back barely reaches my waist. No glorious feathered wings. Just little cloven hooves. Not silvery white. Kind of earthy-mushroom-colored with dark brown splotches.

I've just created a *pegasus* goat.

GIRSUL CUSSES AND NEARLY SHOUTS, "Oh, come on! What did you do? That's a *hoohvak* goat!"

"I know, I'm sorry!" I exclaim, putting one hand over my mouth, while still holding on to the harness with the other. Not that the goat is even bothering to struggle in my grasp. It just stands there, stock still, head partially turned, watching me with one beady, unnatural *orange* eye. Or maybe watching the black curtains behind me—hard to tell. And, just like the first *pegasus*, it is completely silent—no bleating.

"*Varqood* me!" Girsul continues cussing. Almost dropping his own *pegasus's* harness, he leans forward to examine my creation, his expression full of disbelief. "What kind of *shar-ta-haak* thing did you make? A goat? *Varqood!* You have to change it right now!"

"How? How do I do that?" I cry, while my pulse pounds in my temples. "I told you I have no *varqood* idea what I'm doing here! I tried to imagine, I tried! But all I know is goats and cows and ducks! There was a donkey down the street, but his owner never let anyone get close for fear of stealing, and I've seen some bulls up-close a few times, but mostly goats and—"

"Shut your mouth! Just. Shut. Up!" Holding his forehead with one hand, Girsul shakes his head in disgust. However, I realize his expression is genuinely anxious now, almost panicked. "Let me think, let me think . . ." he mutters, "I need to remember what needs to be done to make the *pegasei* switch form . . . Sacred Mother of gods, let me think—"

"Is there another voice command?"

The young man frowns, his forehead straining. "Probably— but I don't know it, don't remember! This was never supposed to happen, so the tech didn't really give me any more commands, just the basics. What are we going to do now? What will I report to *Ter* Aten? He's not going to like what he sees. He'll expect us to parade noble beasts before him—"

I let him ramble on for a few heartbeats, then interrupt in turn. "So maybe we can try different herding notes, try to imagine this flying horse thing you made. Or better yet, we can just—"

"Just what? And not we—*you!*"

"All right, *me*. Yes, me. I screwed up!" I bite my lip and start to raise my voice. "But—it's a shapeshifter, isn't it? So, *not* a problem. And that's the whole point of it, isn't it? It can be changed any time to be anything. We—I will figure it out. Maybe, you can call your tech and ask? Besides, what's so bad about goats?"

I take a step forward and rest my hand lightly on the fur of the unnatural goat. It feels very normal, far less coarse than I recall, even silky-smooth to the touch. I pet it carefully a few times—with no reaction from the goat whatsoever.

Because it's not. It's something else altogether. Holy Mother Goddess. . . .

Girsul watches me tensely, still frowning. "I can't call the tech. He was a one-time deal. . . . He's gone now, so that's out of the question."

Possibly, he expects me to say something, to come up with a solution.

An interesting thought comes to me.

"You have these curtains in this already small cage," I say, glancing around us. "You do realize that if there were *three* large *pegasei* horses with wings here—like the one you made—they might not fit in this enclosure?"

Girsul looks around also. "They should fit—I measured it beforehand."

"Maybe, just barely," I say. "They would have to stand close together, and never take a step, else they push open the curtain."

"So, what's your point?"

"My point is, if you want to keep them hidden, they should *all* be little goats. All three of them. They would fit nicely in this area, and be inconspicuous if someone came in here to look."

"Huh? Hm. . . ." But Girsul's expression is lightening.

"I can turn the third *pegasus* into another goat," I say in a reasonable tone, feeling a swell of enthusiasm and a kind of stupid relief. "And then we can figure out how to turn your crazy horse with wings into a goat also!"

"Hm-m-m," Girsul makes a thoughtful noise, but I can tell he is giving in. "That might indeed make everything simple. But— let me first check with Bisfuri."

I STAND HOLDING the harness of my *pegasus* goat and listen to Girsul call *Ter* Bisfuri on his comm badge. He explains our situation and then presents the three-goat solution.

I'm likely mistaken, but I can just hear the crackle of *Ter* Bisfuri's deep baritone voice emanating from the badge, and then something that sounds almost like laughter.

". . . Yes, goats," Girsul is saying, holding the badge close to the side of his face near his ear. "All three of them, *im Ter*. No, her idea. Yeah, I'm sure no one saw us."

Bisfuri's voice sounds again, but I can't quite make out what he's saying. At least his tone doesn't sound angry.

"Very well, *im Ter*, understood. We'll proceed as you instruct. Thank you." And then he taps the badge to end the conversation and looks at me, exhaling loudly.

I widen my eyes at him. "So? What did he say?"

"You're lucky. *Ter* Aten agreed with your *hoohvak* idea of keeping the *pegasei* in the shape of goats. He thinks this will make it easier to keep them secretly in the stables and raise fewer questions."

I exhale also, in relief. "There, see! I knew it was going to be for the best!"

Girsul shakes his head but his dark brown eyes crinkle at the corners with humor. "Let's hope it will be. Meanwhile, the good news is, *Ter* Aten told me how to make the *pegasei* change shape again. It's very simple, fortunately for us. You simply need to choose another note—any note, sing and hold it while imagining the creature transforming in your mind. You can even think the word 'transform' so that it gets used to reading your mind properly and obeying your commands."

"All right," I say, nodding. "I still can't get used to the idea of these *pegasei* reading minds, but, sure. . . ."

Girsul turns away from me and focuses his attention on his large and handsome *sesemet* with wings. "Sorry, my beauty, looks like you'll have to transform again, this time into something less noticeable. Okay, I'm trying to imagine a goat now," he announces, then begins to sing and hold a random note.

It takes a few heartbeats, then the glorious great horse starts to lose cohesiveness. It becomes momentarily transparent, then literally falls apart into a blob of rainbow colors. The bright dust motes start to swirl once again in a cloud, and then reform into a much more compact shape.

Girsul's goat is admittedly funny looking, with a brown back and white underbelly—which is fine—but it has strange, oversized ears. Meanwhile, its horns are set too close together and not quite right.

"That's a crap-looking goat . . ." I remark, watching the pitiful transformation. "Why don't you let me try?"

Girsul makes a sound of exasperation then hands me the end of the harness. "Fine, whatever. I don't remember what those beasts look like exactly, especially considering that I've only practiced imagining the *pegasus* horse with wings shape in my mind, not other cattle. It's been a while."

"Don't worry," I say, taking over the harness of the newly forged misshapen goat. "You hold my goat."

And we trade our *pegasei*.

I closely examine the monstrous and pathetic thing before me, then sing another note in a strong, steady voice. *Transform*, I think at it. And then I visualize slightly corrected features, better aligned horns, a nice tuft of fur on its chin, more natural ears. . . .

As I sing this new note, I briefly feel a strange tingling sensation in my head—starting as a vibration at the bridge of my nose, almost a kind of buzzing. This annoying, itchy tingle travels up toward my forehead, then disappears. *Ugh.* . . . I feel a sudden need to sneeze.

I ignore it, and continue singing and visualizing a proper goat. The *pegasus* before me coalesces into its improved shape. I go silent, and check it over in satisfaction.

"Yeah, that's better," Girsul admits. "Not perfect, of course, but much better."

"Not perfect? Harumph," I say. "Hold this goat too."

While Girsul takes the harness leash of the second *pegasus*— which now looks very similar to my first creation, only a darker shade of brown—I turn to the last remaining orb suspended from the ceiling. "I'll make this one black with a white belly."

Now that I've gotten the hang of this process, it occurs to me that dealing with *pegasei* is not that difficult at all, and my confidence has been restored.

Ah, the confidence of a fool!

MOMENTS LATER, WE HAVE THREE "GOATS" in the enclosure, two brown, one black. They all stand motionless and don't even look at us as we tie their harnesses to the metal anchors at the back wall of the cage, where the black curtain does not reach.

"Definitely more manageable," Girsul admits, as we push the goats closer together, letting them stand side by side, with plenty of room to spare in the curtained area of the enclosure.

"So, how come they don't make noise?" I ask. "And why so stiff?"

"Crap if I know." Girsul shrugs. "Maybe because they don't know how—how to *be* these animals they resemble."

"Makes sense, I suppose." I wipe the bridge of my nose with the back of my hand, feeling a sheen of sweat there, from all that stressful effort. "So, what now?"

Girsul starts drawing the black curtains around the three *pegasei*. "Done here, for the moment," he says. "We'll start their training tomorrow. But now we need to head back. *Ter* Aten has other work for us to do. Oh, and we have to secure this enclosure. Remember what I said earlier about how keyed orichalcum works to trap and contain their energy. We *always* have to keep the cage door closed. And locked—in case some *chazuf* decides to go in and mess with the goats."

"Understood," I say.

The young man pauses, and his eyes meet mine with a meaningful expression. "If anyone ever asks about these—since the Bisfuri don't normally keep such lowly beasts in the stables —we say they are *Ter* Aten's personal, special breeding project, and that's all we know."

"Got it."

And then we head out.

WE LEAVE the stables and pass several other staff (whom Girsul casually acknowledges) working in the sun-filled courtyard with three huge, beautiful *sesemet* stallions who need exercise.

And then we walk back to the main building. But first, a detour to look at the Service Competition board and registration station just outside.

When we get to the side of the building near the employee and deliveries entrance, there are only a handful of people there. Two women stand staring at the Competition board, and one man is bent over the registration table, entering his information into a digital tablet while three registration staffers watch him.

"We got here at the best time," I say to Girsul. "The crowds have dispersed, so we can get a good look."

"Yes, but quickly." He glances at me then approaches the huge, industrial billboard-sized smart board. It hovers, flush against the wall of the building, with its bottom frame at waist level. Its screen is covered with running amber-yellow squiggles that are written text, various logo images which I recognize to be symbols of the noble Houses and, interspersed with the squiggles, some numbers.

With a sinking feeling in the pit of my stomach, it occurs to me that this board with all its postings, is pretty much useless to me, since I can't read it.

I can't read.

I frown, as my pulse pounds again, in a kind of familiar despair, and look at Girsul—who appears to be straining to read whatever is up there—then again at the board, then at the few people nearby.

Of the two women who also examine the board, chatting quietly among themselves, one notices me staring. She is young, maybe slightly older than me, with neatly pinned black hair in a tight knot on top of her head, light brown skin, warm hazel-green eyes, and a rose-colored high-end domestic service tassel at the collar of her impeccable uniform.

"Do you need help reading the postings?" she offers in a mild voice.

I take a breath, and nod. Next to me, Girsul also immediately looks at the girl, and his expression appears momentarily awkward, even shy. "Yeah, Hageet, we can use some help."

The young woman called Hageet gives him a little smile, then turns to the smart screen and starts to recite quickly. "That big text on the very top line says 'Upcoming Events.' Starting from the top left, it has the Houses in that first column, the Categories of Service in the second, followed by day, time, and location of the Competition event. Finally, on the right—see those two numbers? First one indicates the number of Service positions that have been won and filled. Last one is the total number of positions still available."

Girsul stares closely while I nod.

"The House in the first row—in prominent, big text—is Bisfuri, with zero won and five hundred open. Immediately below is the Imperial Kassiopei in the second row. Then, all the rest of the Houses are listed underneath, one per line, with their own events. It might be easier if you memorize their emblem images inside those circles, or at least remember the ones that interest you most. . . ."

"Or you can simply tap the circle at the beginning of each row, and the text in that line will be read to you by the machine," says a sarcastic male voice.

The speaker stands behind us, and I half-turn to see a young man, dressed in a similar crisp uniform, with a collar tassel that's dark blue to indicate a technician. He is well built, handsome and confident in the arrogant way of upper-class servants, and has dark brown hair gathered in a long, segmented tail behind him. Underneath heavy, straight brows that contrast with his light, sandy-tan skin, his eyes are a cool, sharp blue.

I stare at this young man, momentarily fascinated by his confident swagger and sense of know-it-all that emanates from him.

Hageet sees him and smiles wider, her expression almost melting. "*Nefero eos*, Mihravat. Of course, you're right! I forgot."

Mihravat barely nods at her, then steps past me and approaches the board. He taps the lowest circle logo within reach, and a loud androgynous voice issues from the board surface, starting to recite: "House Urartumi. Artisan and Skilled Craftsman Competition. Tomorrow, eighteenth day of Setaet, ninth hour of Ra, Tiamat Pavilion, Circle Seven. . . ."

He taps the House Urartumi emblem again and the mechanical voice is cut off mid-speech.

"Oh," I say in amazement. And then I glance up at the tall board and raise my hand to reach for the other circles. "What if it's on the very top?" I ask. "Should I get a stick so that I can reach it? It's too high up—"

"A stick?" The young man called Mihravat turns to me with almost incredulous disdain, then starts to laugh. "No, you simply swipe the screen and it will scroll up and down or side to side, for that matter. Don't you know how to use a digital display?"

"I—" I start to reply then close my mouth, while my cheeks are on fire in frustrated embarrassment.

"Hey, she's new," Girsul says, breaking the awkward moment of silence. "Lay off her, Mihr. Not everyone knows the fancy tech as well as you do."

"Apparently not." Mihravat raises one brow then uses his right hand to quickly swipe downward in a well-practiced motion, and the screen starts to roll.

In that same exact moment, a loud alarm begins to wail, echoing throughout the courtyard.

Everyone pauses whatever they're doing.

For a moment I'm disoriented, trying to grasp the source of the ear-splitting sound. Then I realize it's coming from the smart board itself.

"What in Bast's name is happening?" I ask.

And then I glance up at the board and notice that the Imperial Kassiopei circle is illuminated and blinking rapidly.

"Means that the Imperial Kassiopei has an important announcement," Mihravat replies. "Could be one of their Competition results, a score update, major news, or something else. Let's find out."

Reaching up, he swipes the screen again, moving the Imperial emblem closer, and taps the circle with the Ra sunburst, the symbol of the Kassiopei Dynasty.

CHAPTER
SIXTEEN

At once the entire smart board clears away all the information about the competitions, and the display is replaced by an Imperial *steleon*—text enclosed and framed by the oval cartouche of the Kassiopei Dynasty. I know it without having to read, since it incorporates the familiar design of the sunburst along the border. The *steleon*, and the message it encloses, are immense and take up the entirety of the smart board.

At the same time, an automated voice issues from the board, reciting the announcement.

"Attention, citizens of Poseidon and residents of all the provinces of Atlantis! In addition to the Service Competitions specific to the Noble Houses and the Imperial Dynasty, the Imperial Kassiopei announce a new Category of Service that crosses all boundaries and serves *Atlantida* itself. Atlantis is looking for skilled Pilots!

"Atlantis requires individuals of great talent and precision able to pilot flying vehicles that will exit the atmosphere and traverse the space beyond, as we travel the vastness between the stars. Pilots must demonstrate their ability to fly and maneuver in the air and in the dark empty spaces where the air ends and the void begins. Once selected for Pilot Service, Pilots will be trained further to fly our great starships on which we shall depart the earth into the dark vastness.

"Pilots who compete must provide their own vessels capable of flight, such as standard air transports, *depets*, buses, and other means, as long as they are air-borne for the duration of the Competition. The Pilot Competition will be in the form of an extended, multi-stage Race, and will take place in the coming days, with the exact time and starting location to be announced shortly. You have at least a week to prepare yourselves, and to procure and equip your appropriate vehicles.

"You may begin to register for the Pilot Competition in three days from now, this coming Six-Day, the twentieth day of Setaet. Plan accordingly! This has been an Imperial Announcement."

The automated voice goes silent.

There is a long pause, as we all consider this new information.

Mihravat is the first of us to break the silence. "Very interesting." The young man appears thoughtful as he taps the smart board surface, bringing back the normal display with all the Competitions and Houses.

"Really? Will you compete as a Pilot?" Hageet asks him. "Do you think that's something you might be interested in?"

"Very likely." Mihravat doesn't bother to look at her and continues to study the board. "It's certainly within my area of expertise. Because it ultimately involves technology. Maneuvering and precision can be trained."

"It takes time to develop quick reflexes," Girsul says. "Driving a bus is harder than it looks. I know a guy who drives freight, and he—"

"You always know a guy who does something or other," Mihravat interrupts him mockingly. "What you don't seem to know is that the Pilots who fly military transports must be proficient in sound tech *and* be able to maneuver. Ask me which is hardest."

"No need," Girsul says with a frown. "You always have an answer for everything."

Laughing, Mihravat tears himself away from perusing the board and glances at Girsul then the rest of us. "And that is the truth." He then quickly turns away from all of us and heads into the main building.

GIRSUL and I spend a few more awkward moments staring at the list of Competitions. We take turns tapping the House emblem circles to make the machine voice read the text. Some of the Competitions sound more promising than others. But for the most part, I realize with a sinking feeling, they're beyond my specific abilities or skills.

I need to aim for domestic service, kitchen staff, or messenger. Anything else is mostly out of my reach and beyond my station. Even the kitchen, unless it involves basic cleaning and chopping of vegetables, is not my strongest point—in our house, Grandmother is the best cook, while I merely try to emulate her.

"Scroll up," Girsul tells me at some point as my fingers fumble on the screen. "Hit that one—what's that, House Kinakra? The one with the feather and flower? I think they're domestic service?"

"Yes, Kinakra says general domestic," Hageet remarks softly. "I already registered for theirs. You should too."

I nod, and then press the circle so that we can all hear the details.

"House Kinakra. General Domestic Service Competition. Nineteenth day of Setaet, seventh hour of Ra, Luamat Marketplace, Circle Five. Hard Labor Competition. Twenty-first day of Setaet, first hour of Khe, Ariet Warehouse, Circle Eight. . . ."

"That first one, yes. Sounds good to me," Girsul mutters. "I'm signing up."

"Me too." And then I recall what Uru told me earlier about Houses Ximunat and Sumerad, both holding domestic service Competitions the day after tomorrow, something involving running and delivery. So, I play their emblem circles.

"House Sumerad. General Domestic Service Competition. Nineteenth day of Setaet, ninth hour of Ra, Raivaal Way, Circle Five."

And then:

"House Ximunat. General Domestic Service Competition. Nineteenth day of Setaet, tenth hour of Ra, Denderaat, Circle Five."

"Bastet's breath!" I exclaim with frustration. "That's one right after the other!"

"Yes, not possible to do both," Hageet remarks with a sigh. "I already considered it, and chose not to worry about those two, and registered only for Kinakra, at seventh hour of Ra."

Girsul scratches his forehead and rumples the back of his dark head of hair. "Depending on how long the Kinakra one goes, you could possibly pick one of those two and fit it in after Kinakra, on the same day. Probably pick Ximunat since they are later, to have more time to arrive there."

"At least they're all on Circle Five," I say, frowning with effort, as I think hard. "Any idea how long each of these things will take?"

"Why, are you thinking of trying for all of them?" Girsul glances at me sharply, raising one brow. "That's impossible. Just pick Kinakra and one of the other two."

"Did you know that Luamat Marketplace is on the opposite side of Circle Five from Raivaal Way? It's quite a hassle getting from one to the other." Hageet looks at me with what might be pity. "And as for Denderaat—"

"I don't even know what Denderaat is," Girsul says. "Never heard of it."

Hageet looks at him. "Some kind of industrial building?"

"Not on Five. They don't have industrial areas there, it's too fine," says the other woman next to Hageet who has been silent all this time. She is short but seems older than all of us, with hair hidden by a brown-blue-and-gold braided wig, reddish brown skin, and black eyes. She also has a rose-colored domestic service tassel at the collar of her sharp uniform.

"Oh, that's true, Kaerah." Hageet nods to the other woman. "I tend to forget that Circle Five is residential. I haven't been there that often. So then, what is Denderaat?"

"Checking now." Girsul takes out his comm badge and taps it skillfully to bring up what I now know is a search menu. "Find Denderaat, Circle Five," he says to the device.

"Denderaat is a bridge connecting Circle Five and Circle Six," a soft automated voice replies immediately. "It is City Bridge number 552 out of one thousand capital bridges, and is located in the Southern Quadrant of Poseidon."

"A bridge . . . I suppose that makes sense," Hageet says. "If the Competition involves a race and it starts on a bridge."

"Let me pull up a map." Girsul taps the comm badge and a tiny amazing *hologram* pops up. A translucent, miniature replica of the City, barely the size of my palm, hangs in the air over Girsul's comm badge.

Oh, this thing is amazing!

I barely know what a hologram is (only because I watch commercials that are played between media feeds, and I've seen some fancy products). But I've never expected to see our comm badges have this capability. My mouth hangs open—so wide that I could be inviting flies and honeybees inside. . . .

Meanwhile, Girsul sings a brief tone and then does

something with his fingers in the air. It looks like he is stretching the intangible map with his fingertips, and I involuntarily draw closer, gaping at his movements.

"Display Circle Five only," Girsul commands. "Show Luamat Marketplace, Raivaal Way, and Denderaat Bridge. Include proportional distances."

At once the other City Circles disappear, and the disembodied image of Circle Five without its surrounding canals, hangs in the air, a hollow gold disk. Three red location dots materialize. Two of them are indeed across from each other, north and south, on the opposite sides of the Circle. The third is right between the two, placed on the left, the western side.

"Okay, so they are moderately accessible," Girsul mumbles. "If you start north, with Kinakra at Luamat Marketplace at seventh hour, you can take your time and pick the next closest one which is House Ximunat on Denderaat Bridge at tenth hour. Or, if you like to run through a nice neighborhood full of trees, shrines full of cooing doves, and marble temples, then keep going south and pick the distant Sumerad on Raivaal Way at ninth hour. And *then*, assuming the Sumerad Competition is over in under an hour, double back to Denderaat Bridge and hope you make it in time."

"No one is going to attempt to do all of this in one day, this is ridiculous," Kaerah says quietly, with annoyance.

But I lift my head, while a strange swell of energy fills my chest. "I'm doing all of them," I say.

And then, before anyone tells me otherwise, I walk toward the registration station.

AFTER I'M DONE REGISTERING—BASICALLY informing the registration staff which Houses and what Competitions I want, followed by thumbprints for each of my selections on their master tablets—I stand back, and wait for Girsul, while he and a few others register.

Girsul finishes, having picked the more reasonable Kinakra and Ximunat combination. He raises one brow at me and shakes his head, but says nothing. I bet he thinks I'm crazy, and so does Hageet who is still studying the board, together with Kaerah.

"All done. Now, enough wasting work time, let's go, before *Ter* Aten starts looking for us." Girsul moves away from the registration, and we head back inside the grand estate building.

As we walk, blinking in the sunlight, I get weird random thoughts plaguing me.

Those little pegasei *goats . . . poor things, are they still standing motionless in their enclosure, behind those black curtains? What if they suffer and starve overnight without sunlight? What if. . . .*

Meanwhile, Girsul glances at me occasionally and continues to shake his head every time. Not sure if I read amusement or annoyance in his expression.

"What?" I finally ask, as we climb the corkscrew outer stairs to reach the upper terraces.

"Nothing," he retorts, moving ahead of me. "It's your business, signing up for three Competitions in one day. I just think you're mad."

I shrug. "Probably. But I'm still doing it."

And we arrive back at *Ter* Bisfuri's work quarters.

WHEN WE ENTER the brightly lit chamber, Benaten stands talking with an expensively dressed, elegant young woman.

She has a classic figure (a palm frond and its upside-down reflection mirrored in a pond), milk-pale skin, a lovely face, and a stunning mane of bright-red hair bound in a top knot, with a thick, long tail cascading loosely around her creamy shoulders (barely concealed by a diaphanous shawl) and down to her lower back.

The hair has a rare golden sheen that has turned to flame in the sun streaming from the windows. I can only imagine what it might look like without the knot, falling completely loose around her.

The young woman stands very close to Bisfuri, conversing in a soft, musical voice. Her slender arms and wrists are embraced by stacked gold bracelets, and delicate gold chains dangle from her earlobes and around the swanlike column of her neck. She has graceful poise, and looks up at him with a flirtatious smile and familiarity. There's an immediate sensation of intimacy between them as *Ter* Bisfuri looks down at her, leaning forward warmly. I can just imagine him reaching out to touch her cheek or her brilliant silk hair.

Holy Bastet . . . are they lovers?

The thought strikes me with a strange pang that cuts at my gut. And then I frown inwardly at myself. *What would it matter if they were? Seriously. . . .* The Man in the Niktos Cloak has hundreds of lovers on the show! He *varqoods* someone new in every episode. It would make sense that he takes some of them to his bed in real life.

It doesn't matter. . . . None of my business.

In that moment, Benaten sees us come in and waves casually with one hand. "Finally, you're here—come," he tells Girsul while briefly glancing at me.

Then he turns to the redhead. "Almahara, you already know Girsul. Meet Semmi. She's newly hired to do a number of jobs in various capacities. Semmi, Almahara is an *amretene* from Hathor's House, hired as an entertainer to perform on my show. You will be working with her tomorrow."

"Yes, *im Ter*." Standing tensely next to Girsul, I look at Benaten Bisfuri. Out of nowhere, for some inexplicable reason, I feel awkward as I nod at the redhead. "*Nefero dea*. What will I be doing?"

No sex. . . .

A silly thought comes as I recall my Grandmother's stern words to Bisfuri.

"Nothing on camera, fear not," Benaten says, suddenly looking directly at me with his penetrating gaze. It's as if he's read my mind!

"Oh. . . ." At once my face floods with heat.

"You will help me say my lines." Almahara glances at me with a friendly expression.

Crap of a goat, but she really is beautiful! Soft brown eyes, delicate smile, just a nice, lovely person. And it makes absolutely no sense at all that in this moment I am extremely annoyed by her.

"All right," I say, meeting her friendly gaze with a somewhat cocky look. "But I don't know how to read. Will that be a problem?"

I can just feel the attitude rising inside me, and it must show. Because she blinks once, and then blinks a few more times. "Oh, you don't really need to read. I don't know how to read either, I memorize. You just have to remember the lines well enough to help me during each scene. The lines are recorded and numbered, and you can play them back to yourself quietly, and prompt me if I forget. I—sometimes forget."

"There aren't many spoken lines, mostly action," Benaten adds. "She'll show them to you, and you can practice with her later."

And then *Ter* Bisfuri looks from me to Girsul. "Now, the more pressing question is, how are my . . . *goats?*"

Girsul clears his throat and glances at Almahara. She's a hired *amretene* after all, not a staff employee, so it's possible that *Ter* Bisfuri has not confided to her about the *pegasei*.

On the other hand, if they *are* lovers. . . . Men are known to unburden themselves to sex workers, in more ways than one, relieving both mind and body. . . .

"The goats are doing very well, *im Ter*," Girsul replies, deciding to speak with caution. "We fed them and housed them in their proper stalls. Will proceed with more—um—work tomorrow."

"Very well. And I assume you've both had time to peruse the schedule and register for the Service Competitions?"

"Oh yes," I say. "Thank you for the opportunity and time off work, *im Ter*."

"You can thank the Imperial Kassiopei. It is their decree, and all must follow the rules for these things," he says. "If it were up to me, I'd make you work a full, hard day shoveling *sesemet* crap and herding *goats* before permitting you to indulge in this lax behavior."

I pause with surprise at such hard words coming from him—not at all typical of what I know this generous man to be—but I notice Bisfuri is holding back a sarcastic smile.

AFTER TALKING some more with Bisfuri, Girsul leaves on another errand while I'm directed to stay. For the remainder of the work afternoon, I remain in the suite, perched on some chairs in a corner with Almahara, paying close attention as she holds a digital tablet and scrolls though squiggles of text. She plays then recites her lines of dialogue from the upcoming episode in a slightly meek voice, blatantly overacting in some instances. She then plays the dialogue again for me and shows me how to manipulate the screen.

Eventually I take over and help her recite. Memorizing lines seems rather easy, and I find myself needing no prompter—while the *amretene* is a bit slower. Not that it should matter as much, I remind myself. She wasn't hired for her poetic acting abilities, but for her looks and erotic charms.

Bisfuri did say there will be *mostly action* . . . of the intimate kind, followed by fighting.

I know this show, I know how it goes—*everyone* does.

It's popular smut of the best kind.

Meanwhile, people come and go around us, and *Ter* Bisfuri himself is busy directing various staff in his employ.

I'm not entirely sure what he's doing or what else is happening in these big, brightly lit chambers, but I realize that only some of it has to do with tomorrow's recording of the episode of *The Love Life of the Man in the Niktos Cloak*. The rest is . . . complicated and somewhat mysterious. Some is related to the fancy evening party being held at the Bisfuri estate the day after tomorrow. Many noble guests are expected to make an appearance, including members of the Imperial Kassiopei.

And I am supposed to be there too, along with many other Bisfuri staff. Will I have to recite my ridiculous story and pretend to be a Storyteller before a room full of the highest nobles and even royals?

Bastet help me. . . .

BY THE TIME I'm dismissed and take the multiple buses to get home, it is early evening. There are grey smoke stacks of cooking fires rising into the orange sunset all around Denwen's Pit when the hover bus finally lands me on a street nearby. In our hovel, Amurabia, Uru, and Father are finishing up eating our evening meal. With a pang of guilt, I think how I wasn't even there to help cook it. Is this going to be a daily occurrence now, me being so late coming home?

"Long day, child?" Grandmother asks me casually, pretending not to care too much. I fully know how much curiosity she's holding back about my first day at work.

Briefly, I let my tired mind think back on the churning soup pot of today's events, the almost unbelievable images of people, things, and even . . . *pegasei*!

And then I simply mumble that everything was fine, and I'm too tired to talk.

I am also starving, not having eaten all day. How did that even happen?

"Eat. You can talk later." Amurabia hands me a bowl of fragrant vegetable stew with onion and herbs, and I settle down next to them to watch the media-box feeds. Today it means watching the lines of commoners registering for Service Competitions, and the strange sights of people taking part in some of them already, all around the great City of Poseidon.

"Uru, how was your Competition this morning at House Vamsu?" I ask, getting some of my mind restored along with the warm chunks of food in my belly.

Uru barely glances at me. "It was all right. I didn't win or even advance past the first round."

"What?" I say, pausing my chewing. "How come?"

Uru shrugs, sullenly. "I should've won. I ran very fast and almost caught the ribbon, but two *chazufs* held me back. They cheated! One grabbed me and the other stepped on my foot, hard, coming from the back."

"Oh no," I say. "But yeah, cheating is to be expected. People are desperate right now. Next time, you'll be ready for anything."

"Whatever." Uru looks grim.

"There will be other Competitions, *im saai*," Amurabia remarks.

"That's right," I say. "This was just the first of many. Think of it as practice. I signed up for three of them, all on the same morning, the day after tomorrow. Kinakra, Ximunat, and Sumerad. All on Circle Five."

"Good," Grandmother says.

"Uru, you should sign up for those too; they are all Domestic Service. We can run together. Or do whatever it is they tell us to do to compete."

Uru glances at me. "Yeah, okay. Will go register tomorrow."

And then he turns back to the news feeds where they're showing a big muscled man pull a huge weight on a rope during a Hard Labor Competition, coming in first for House Giparu.

Suddenly it occurs to me, as I watch the weightlifter pull the rope, that the three Competitions I signed up for are happening on the same day as the Bisfuri evening party.

Crap of a pegasus goat! That day is going to be insane.

I stuff food in my mouth mindlessly, and soon find myself full of warm stew but physically and emotionally exhausted like I've never been in my entire life. And so, off I go to collapse in my cot early, while my family remains in our living room, watching. Even Uru gives me a curious look.

But at this point I care about nothing but sleep.

THE NEXT MORNING, in the silvery darkness before dawn, I wake up with a head full of *sha*. Everything from the day before slams into me. . . . *Everything*.

Fears and doubts and a gnawing terror stifle me, pull at my gut and my heart, even more so than usual. Yes, today is particularly bad, but a variation of it happens every morning, and I force myself to remember why.

Grandmother says that *everyone* wakes up with fear and despair, especially in the first few moments.

Everyone. . . .

From the poorest drunken *chazuf* in Denwen's Pit to the Imperial Kassiopei.

And we need to remember this, because Uru and I (and she, and Father, and each one of our neighbors) are no different.

That's because, every night, the evil *sha* gather around us with their dark leeching forces, like mosquitoes, to feed on our weakness. It's especially strong with adults and elders who have lived a longer life with a greater number of difficult experiences that can be used against them to create self-doubt. They provide the best feast for the forces of darkness.

Meanwhile, children are still fresh and strong and *simple* with the life force, their soul triumvirate perfectly balanced, the *ka* pure and unblemished—as yet. They are recently arrived from the eternal *other side* into this mortal world, guided and led by the hand of the blessed goddess Hekatri. Their life energy is strongest—*unburdened* by the events of this life—and therefore least susceptible to the *sha*.

In addition, all the loving spirits of the universe and our ancestors guard the children overnight—more so than they do the adults—to make sure their *ka* thrives, taking root in this world properly. It's what gives the young a fighting chance in this life.

As we grow older, Grandmother says, the guarding spirits stand back, allowing us to make life choices on our own. It doesn't mean they've abandoned us (*Never! Fear not, child!*), but they are acknowledging that we're capable of carrying on our own fight. Besides, they need to prioritize their own supernatural and benevolent resources to guard the young.

Ah, Grandmother, I think, *why does it have to be so bad every morning? So, so bad . . . in those first few moments . . . sometimes even that first quarter-hour? As I wake up, I have no will to live. . . .*

"Because the *sha* can only affect you in that transition between sleep and wakefulness. That's when they attack!" Grandmother pronounces every time, with a smile (and occasionally with a snort of annoyance that I have to be told this same thing over and over).

"Furthermore, the onslaught doesn't last all night, as some foolish people believe, but in the *transition* between wakefulness and sleep. When you're truly asleep, you're good and *gone*. Swallowed by the great eternity, communing with the divine, completely safe from the *sha's* evil meddling and influence.

"But when your *ka* returns through the opening in your

forehead, the third eye, and settles back in your chest, it's the only time it is vulnerable to true attack. Because the journey back makes it briefly *disoriented*, especially as it passes the doorway between *here* and *there*."

"But aren't the *sha* strongest at night? And what about bad dreams?" Uru or I usually ask at that point, again and again, just to be reassured.

"The *sha* can do nothing to your body or to *you* all night, *hoohvak* child. Even though they sit around you in a dark cloud, they are powerless. They're only waiting for your *ka* to return. Each one of your brief wakings throughout the night, each moment of *transition*, each *opening* from the other side into this one, invites their attention. . . . The immortal doorway opens and closes but they may not pass, only try to influence the *ka* at the threshold," Grandmother elaborates.

"Torment, temptation, guilt, despair—these things erode the integrity of the *ka*, scraping away at its pristine energy form, making it unstable and causing it to vent precious energy which the *sha* hungrily consume.

"The night affords them the most opportunities to feed on *ka* energy, that's why they are active at night. Indeed, they often begin to torment the vulnerable adults early in the evening, with an inability to sleep. As soon as we relax, lower our defenses, and start to drift away toward the tunnel into eternity, that's when they throw our own guilt and responsibilities at us. But it's all an illusion.

"Dreams are *not* their playground, it is *ours*—if we let our waking concerns come along with our *ka*, burdening it like a sack of turnips. The *sha* can do nothing, only lie to us and deceive, plague us with our own troubled thoughts, until we give in to the *shar-ta-haak* complexity of our lives. Remember, we are safe in dreams! Safe at night! Safe all around. Fie to the *sha*! The great goddess Hekatri protects us from them, always. She brings clarity, the morning in our heads."

Hekatri . . . she who rules doorways and boundaries, the endings and beginnings. . . .

And it has nothing to do with Bisfuri, or my new circumstances, or even the Sky Rock coming to end the world.

It all comes down to an active choice I make for myself.

I can have *sha* in my head, or I can have the bright clarity of morning.

And this morning in particular, I cannot afford to be bogged down by self-doubt or fear.

Today I go to assist the Man in the Niktos Cloak in whatever way he needs me.

Morning in my head, O Bright Hekatri. . . . Morning in my head!

CHAPTER
SEVENTEEN

After overcoming my morning *sha* onslaught, I brave the long, multi-bus commute and the uncustomary pre-dawn crowds of people heading to the various early Competitions around Poseidon.

When I get to the Bisfuri estate, I head directly upstairs to the noble Family's living quarters.

I've been told to be in *Ter* Benaten Bisfuri's work suite (the one accessible from the main building, from the grand staircase terrace, as opposed to the more personal one in the older building in the rear where Benaten took Grandmother and me on that first day) to work with Almahara and her lines of dialogue once again, this time during the recording of the episode. And then, I'm to assist others.

Taking a big breath, I tap on the suite doors. At once a staff member opens the door, gives me a sharp, suspicious look, but lets me in. And I'm immediately blinded by strong illumination. The whole suite is lit up with directed projection lights in addition to numerous regular small ambiance orbs floating in the air all around us.

There's so much impossible light that, after the grey dawn

outside, I squint and blink, taking in the sight of the front parlor and then the source of the greatest brightness, a room toward the back and down the inner hall.

The suite is already full of people. I recognize a few familiar faces from the day before, including Vakrem, the tall, dark brown-skinned security guy in charge of actor procurement, Chifuz, the very pale-skinned young man with wheat-colored hair who reported on Lord Bisfuri's recent trip, and the two decorator women—younger Menahit with purple hair and light brown skin, and the older one, Dunea, with deeper brown skin and an elegant black wig.

Several staff I've not previously met are busy with what appears to be technical devices including the special projector lights. Others are moving around with pieces of décor, carrying and arranging flowing fabrics, shiny objects, and pieces of art. Most of the activity is inside the brightest room in the back. That's where the acting and the video recording will take place.

"Semmi! Over here!"

Someone calls my name and I see Almahara, the beautiful *amretene* redhead. She's seated on one of the sofas next to two other women and three men, who must be the actors, and probably *amretene* also. How do I know? They are all exceptionally good looking—the women being a voluptuous older blonde and a slim younger brunette, and the three men ranging from early to late middle age, with impressive physiques. All of them are clad in plain white sheets covering them like cloaks and apparently little else underneath, while their hair is wrapped in towels, and skin appears flushed from bathing.

"Semmi, you'll help me with my lines while they do my Face Art and style my hair," Almahara tells me in a friendly tone as I approach. She adjusts her white cloak-wrap around her, and her freshly bathed skin has the matte glow of rose petals. "Should be very soon now when the hair dressers and costumers work on me."

"*Nefero eos,*" I say somewhat awkwardly. "Or course. Sorry—am I late? Seems like everyone else is already here."

"It's episode recording day," one of the seated male actors on the sofa mutters, giving me a disdainful glance. He's a handsome bearded man with glistening bronze-brown skin, and nothing but a fabric wrap around his middle. "We start before dawn."

"Don't worry, you're not late." At the sound of a familiar voice, I turn around and see Girsul entering the suite behind me, with sleep-reddened eyes and a yawn. "They're on an earlier schedule than normal today."

"And for once you're early, Girsul," Vakrem says with a wink, strolling by us.

Girsul makes a mocking sound and shows the older man a crude finger gesture.

"Oh," I say with relief. "Glad to know."

"I'm just dropping in from the stables," Girsul adds with a meaningful glance. "The *goats* are fine. Had to check up on them first thing."

"Oh yes, of course," I mumble, while the actors give us superior looks then mostly ignore us and occupy themselves with their digital tablets. "Do you need me for the *goats* later?"

"Not until midday," he says. "We'll take them for a walk when the sun is brightest."

"Understood." I nod.

Girsul takes a step closer to me and leans forward near my ear. "It's also when they take a recording break to eat, so you won't be missed from your primary duties here."

"Got it."

In that moment, Benaten Bisfuri himself arrives, emerging from the interior of the suite. He enters from a different part of the hallway that's least illuminated, which I am guessing is his private quarters, probably his dressing room.

And the moment I see him, I freeze in a kind of awe-struck amazement.

Benaten is attired as the Man in the Niktos Cloak. Not sure what I was expecting to see this morning, but for some reason, not *this*. Not the legendary costume itself, *up close*. . . .

Seriously? You're a hoohvak, *Semmi!* I tell myself, even as my heart begins to pound in my chest. . . . (Why exactly is it doing that? What did I think was going to happen? Am I actually experiencing celebrity worship like some fool from Denwen's Pit who's never seen anything?)

Holy Bast help me, but he is spectacular. All black, glittering, shimmering, primal night itself. . . .

In the fierce lights of the chamber, the midnight fabric of his famous cloak dances with oil-slick rainbow colors, shifting and sparkling along the folds with every tiny movement he makes.

Underneath the cloak, *Ter* Bisfuri wears a black silk shirt, and skin-tight black leather pants, with matching tall boots, polished to a radiant sheen.

Meanwhile, his long, naturally black hair falls in thick, raven-wing darkness about him. He has no mask, nothing to obscure his face, because he will use *motion itself* to hide his features from the curious camera as soon as the episode video recording commences.

I also realize, somewhat stupidly, that he wears no makeup. Unlike the rest of the actors in the episode, the face of the Man in the Niktos Cloak will never be shown directly, so he can do—or *not* do—whatever he pleases with his skin and eyes and lips. . . .

Not that his features or piercing smoky eyes need any enhancement.

I stare at Bisfuri for several long moments, mesmerized, as he walks across the chamber with surprisingly silent steps full of grace, cloak swirling around him. His gaze passes over all of us, but he only nods at the actors without stopping, then beckons a technician who immediately follows Bisfuri into the brightly lit inner chamber.

As soon as he disappears, it's as if a temporary lull has come over us, and now we're permitted to resume *being*.

I hear one of the actresses exhale loudly, while one of the actors whispers, "What a magnificent man. . . ."

"Hush!" Almahara replies, elbowing him. "Don't let *Ter* Bisfuri hear your insolent comments."

"Well, he *is* rather delicious," the older blonde actress whispers back with a suppressed giggle. "I can't believe I've been finally picked to work on this show. . . . I watch it every week, you know. So sweet to finally know what a fine-looking, high-ranked aristocrat is behind this—"

"Yes, now be quiet, before you're dismissed," another actor says sternly. "I will not lose this opportunity because of anyone's inability to remain discreet. Not after so much secrecy and the non-disclosure agreement, not to mention, such amazing pay."

Girsul and I exchange glances, then the young man moves away to join other staff to handle the tech equipment. Meanwhile several additional servants arrive, carrying boxes of cosmetics, brushes, and other tools for working with hair and skin.

Almahara and the other actors are made to sit on tall stools, while surrounded by the Face Artists. I stand up also, and take Almahara's digital tablet while she begins to recite her brief set of lines to me, in between having to pucker her lips, close her eyes, and endure her beauty treatments.

"Our episode is recorded first," she says (as if I don't know this already) while motioning to one of the male actors, a fair-haired muscular specimen by the name of Hulag who is to play her husband. "Are you ready with the cues?"

"All memorized." He doesn't even bother to look in her

direction while an attendant paints his brows. "I have only three lines and the rest is knife combat."

"Hey, girl—yes, you—come here and help me read my lines," the dark brunette actress waves at me, and I step toward her, leaving Almahara for now.

ABOUT HALF AN HOUR LATER, Almahara's fiery red hair is pinned up in an intricate masterpiece and threaded with pearls and small white roses, and her Face Art is complete, enhancing her already lovely features. Then, a seamstress arrives with a gorgeous green dress of a translucent fabric, and Almahara casts down her white cloak and stands confident and absolutely naked, while her body is draped by the exquisite garment.

I try to pay attention to the brunette actress I'm presently working with, and not to gape too much as the seamstress adjusts the diaphanous dress around the redhead *amretene's* flaring hips and perfect breasts. Then Almahara practices removing it with one elegant motion—over, and over, and over again, until it is seamless and very artful.

While this is happening, I turn around and watch Hulag, the male actor who's cast in the same episode as Almahara. He has gotten a large prop knife, and is swinging it over and under.

"Line!" the brunette actress calls me, so I snap back and pay attention.

"Oh, yes! Right there, touch me! I am so happy to be with you tonight, my mysterious stranger!" I recite the stupid dialogue for her, and she echoes it back to me in an exaggerated manner. By this point, I can barely contain myself from rolling my eyes.

ANOTHER HALF HOUR, and everyone is in costume and wearing full makeup. The brunette *amretene* has practiced putting on and seductively taking off a crimson outfit of similar, very nearly transparent fabric that flows like water over her slim limbs and boyish torso.

Meanwhile, the older curvy blonde is attired in a skin-tight dress of sparkling gold that hugs her massive chest and hips. This outfit is intended to be ripped off her body in a skillful move by the Man in the Niktos Cloak himself—so she cannot practice disrobing on her own.

The male actors rattle their weapons, including an axe and a long sword, making dramatic lunges and exclamations.

"Time to record the first episode!" announces a servant, emerging from the brightly lit room. "You and you!" he points to Almahara and Hulag. "Are you ready? Come! The set is prepared for you and *Ter* Bisfuri is waiting!"

Almahara throws me a suddenly anxious glance, and hands off to me her digital tablet. Silently I follow her and Hulag into the recording chamber and the blinding light.

THE ROOM IS SURROUNDED by light projectors, and the actual set is in the middle. It consists of a great bed draped in green fabric, layers upon layers, and tossed with pillows. The bed is raised on a dais, and behind it is a large hovering smart board that displays the scene backdrop—a realistic image of a wall, flowing verdigris curtains, and a sunlit window.

As we enter, servants are scattering handfuls of white roses all over the coverlet. Benaten stands toward the back, near an actual wall, and watches the finishing touches. He practice-flips a slim metallic rod back and forth between his fingers, and I suddenly recognize it as the handle of his famous whip. . . . It's one of his favorite weapons on the show, used interchangeably with his three-tiered short metal staff which I'd seen him use in actual life, in that alley on Circle Eight. The whip or the three-piece staff appear in random episodes, and I feel a chill of awe seeing this classic prop just a few feet away from me.

And then I see his hoverboard.

The hoverboard stands upright, leaning against the same real wall next to him. Its stirrup end is on the bottom.

My mouth involuntarily opens in awed amazement as I see that board, fiercely lit up by the projection lights, the dull gleam of orichalcum along its edge.

This is real.

In that same moment I notice that *Ter* Bisfuri is looking directly at me—looking and seeing me gape like a *hoohvak*.

I snap my mouth shut and gulp, and allow the actors to step forward, passing me.

"Prompter!" a technician addresses me. "You stand here. See the yellow lines on the floor? That's out of camera view. Do not under any circumstances step past the lines during video recording."

I nod.

Then I watch as Benaten and another staff member—who appears to be the scene director—consult briefly. Next, the director takes over, pointing at various spots around the set, and explains the exact positions and spot cues to the actors. Almahara and Hulag listen and nod.

Then, the three of them briefly practice entry cues. Almahara and the Man in the Niktos Cloak exchange certain lines, then Hulag bursts in from the sidelines, establishing the start of the fight action scene. He drops his prop knife, picks it up again. . . .

Two light technicians run out and do a last-moment illumination alignment, repositioning a few projector angles and hovering light orbs. A sound tech sings tone sequences to turn on and off a background soundtrack. I recognize the familiar musical motif, and once again experience a moment of thrill and goosebumps. . . .

Finally, a camera technician opens a container, releasing a

dozen small hovering video cameras, and manually sets them in the air in certain key locations around the set. The tiny units, each one no larger than my pinkie finger, hover in the air exactly where they were placed, like obedient metallic hummingbirds.

"All clear now? Are we ready?" the director asks.

The camera, sound, and lighting crew retreat out of sight to the back, to attend to various computer monitors.

Benaten glances around at all of us present, his expression revealing something that could almost be sarcastic amusement and barely leashed, excited energy. He then raises one brow. "Very well. Let's begin."

THE FIRST THING that happens surprises me, because no musical theme plays to open the episode.

Hah! That gets added in later, I realize, marveling at my own denseness.

Instead, the action starts right away.

Almahara, the Lady of the House, lies in bed, wearing her green dress. She is artfully draped on top of the covers, pretending to be asleep. She stretches and yawns, then opens her eyes, looks up. And stifles an exclamation.

A delicate, very soft background track of stringed music starts to play.

A dark Man steps forward into view, his shimmering Niktos Cloak covering his back, and raises one black-gloved hand, finger pointing up, to indicate silence.

In heartbeats, he removes his gloves. Then, the shirt. Finally, the leather pants, which miraculously occurs out of sight of the camera. As it's happening, the camera view sees only the back of his head, his shimmering cloak unfurling like immense bat wings, and none of the disrobing. However, the audience gets the full view of the Lady's initial look of surprise transforming into a smiling, sensual expression of lust.

Then they start to exchange inane lines of flirtatious dialogue —he speaking in his unforgettable, honey-deep voice, and she in a squeaky breathless soprano—while the Man, covered by his voluminous cloak, circles the bed. At last, he dives at the Lady, and they pretend to tussle.

She resists him for about an instant, then casts off her translucent green dress with one well-practiced move and passionately embraces him. In fact, she's the one who turns up the aggression, so that for a moment, humorously, the Man is the one who is taken aback slightly.

This is where the crude audience laughter gets inserted during the episode, I realize.

"Take me now, stranger from my darkest dreams!" the Lady exclaims, pulling the Man by the roots of his long, gorgeous, *niktos*-dark hair, drawing him closer to her—and still he's shown only from the back.

"It will be my greatest pleasure, *im nefira!*" the Man replies, and skillfully lifts the bedcovers, moving them both underneath, and then drawing his Niktos Cloak around them for good measure. "I will give you even greater pleasure now. Open yourself up to me!"

"Ah! I'm yours!" the Lady cries.

They tussle some more.

The Man tosses off his Niktos Cloak at last. And his naked muscular body is revealed to the camera from the back in all its glory—wide shoulders, powerful curve of lower back, tight buttocks, sun-bronzed skin. . . . The bedding only covers his legs from the knees down. Did he even bother taking off his boots?

Wait, how did he remove those tight pants without taking off the boots?

My mind, growing more and more uncomfortable by the moment, goes into a random thought tailspin. Then I realize his pants too are specially designed props that can be torn off with one tug.

Meanwhile, the Lady's slender long legs come around him, her skin lighter in contrast against his deeper shade, her curled toes. . . .

Oh no, Bastet help me. . . .

Unable to close my eyes, I look away, and focus on the edge of the bed *(so much green fabric!)* so as not to see them rhythmically *moving. . . .* Not even with the edge of my vision.

Just, no.

But I can't avoid hearing their moans, interspersed with the stupidest dialogue ever.

The lines are fake, absolute *shar-ta-haak* nonsense, but the moans. . . . *Crap of a goat.*

The *moans* are real.

WHEN IT'S OVER, the Man barely turns his head so that you can see the side of his lean cheek and some of his nose—almost, but not really!—and reaches with one hand to draw his shimmering Niktos Cloak back around them. They settle in comfortably, pretending to cuddle and fall asleep.

"I never want you to leave me, handsome stranger!" the Lady mumbles.

"Impossible to leave such a sweet beauty as yourself," the Man replies in a low baritone purr, stroking her mane of red hair. "Well, only for a few daydreams, maybe. . . ."

"But you must know one thing—I'm a married noblewoman. We must keep our affair a secret."

And that's the cue for the jilted Husband to arrive.

I release a breath of relief, a breath that I haven't even realized I was holding. The smut portion of the episode is over; it's now time for the good stuff, the fighting to begin!

The Husband barges in with a violent roar.

"What's this? You whoring *slut!*" he cries, waving his hands about. "And you! I will kill you, foul stranger! Argh!"

I try not to giggle at the dialogue. In that same instant the Man once again half-turns so that you can *almost* see his face (but once again, not quite), and he whistles a tone sequence. Immediately, his hoverboard jumps and flies toward him. He catches it artfully with one hand, then wraps his cloak around himself and it.

At the same time, the soundtrack changes over to a drumbeat—fast, energetic music to indicate the action sequence.

This portion is where I definitely pay attention, watching the whole thing with an amplified admiration because it's seamlessly choreographed and is happening right before my eyes in a *single* take.

The Husband pulls out the large knife and lunges forward. The Man evades him effortlessly, and ends up lying on the hoverboard, then rolls back on the bed, ending up under the covers . . . while the Lady screams.

The fight is a ridiculously fun and acrobatic affair.

The Man in the Niktos Cloak cracks his whip, and the weapon unfurls, striking various portions of the Husband's attire—clasps, belt, pants—without actually causing any physical injury (which is a marvelous feat in itself, and a testament to the skill of the whip wielder).

"Aw! Aww!" the actor cries with exaggerated drama, attempting to twist away, then attacks again, finding the Man casually reclining on a different spot of the bed.

Hulag, as the Husband, is quite an effective fighter. I realize he's been picked for this role because of his skill in this, so it's not too surprising. His lines are short and simple, "For this, I disembowel you!" and "Die now!" Mostly, he focuses on brandishing his blade and lunging in every direction.

But the Man in the Niktos Cloak is so skillful that he literally has to hold himself back somewhat just to give the opponent time to make his countermoves and extend the scene.

It occurs to me that, in real life, this fight would be over in a few heartbeats.

But for the sake of the show, we get acrobatics and exaggerated motions.

"Apologies, but I have no plans to die today," the Man finally says, speaking with sarcasm in the Husband's ear, almost leaning in for a kiss, as they're struggling close. He then flexes his whip one more time and snaps it lightly across the Husband's cheek and throat until the rope portion curls, winding around the actor's neck.

The Husband pretends to be choking, flails his limbs, and then falls backwards, crashing on the floor (and out of camera view).

The Lady, in a moment of regret, puts her hands up to her cheeks and turns with great tragic eyes to the Man. "Please don't murder him, marvelous stranger! I might be in love with you, but I do value my marriage and my position."

"May I hurt him just a little? No?" the Man teases. "His neglect toward your charms is obvious, my Lady! Do the gods themselves not whisper that he deserves some pain? A pin prick?"

"Oh, he does, he does! But I beg you do not! He is rich and titled, and thus I must endure my burden!"

"Very well, then we must part—keep your wealthy husband and fare well!" the Man says, raising himself up to lie flat on the hoverboard, then lifts his cloak to obscure the camera. "I'll never see you again, and my heart might never recover, but it's been a brief pleasure!"

The theme music swells, as it always does in those final moments, as the shimmering fabric of the Niktos Cloak is the last thing the audience sees, and the Man's deep honey baritone is the last thing they hear.

"End scene!" the director cries.

The episode is over.

. . .

AT ONCE THE chamber comes alive. The actors rise from their spots, while technicians and staff move about. I back away in haste so as not to be run over by people. Even as I do so, I see that Benaten stands up, naked but for his black polished boots, and then casually wraps a white cloth over his middle. The Niktos Cloak has been cast off to lie on the bed.

"Well done, everyone," he says calmly, smiling at Almahara then glancing at Hulag who stands scratching a small welt on his neck where the whip rope has grazed him just a tiny bit. "You, okay?"

"Or course, *im Ter*," the actor says politely. "Not a problem. All good."

"You—" Benaten points to a random servant. "Call the medic and have this man checked to make sure nothing is damaged." And then he adds to Hulag. "You'll be compensated additionally for your trouble."

Hulag bows, appearing pleased. "Thank you, *im Ter*."

But Bisfuri has already turned away.

"Take a break, everyone!" the director exclaims. "Next episode recording will begin in exactly one hour. Now, set change! I want to see the dark blues and indigos, and this bed draped in moonlight—"

Girsul comes up to me in that moment. "Ready for some *goats?* It's only tenth hour, but the sun is sufficiently high up. We may not get a chance at noon, so might as well go now."

"Sure," I say. "They didn't even need my prompting services this time."

Girsul makes a small sound of disdain. "Ah, but they will at some point. Trust me, these actors always forget their lines."

And then he adds, "But never *Ter* Aten."

"Does he come up with all the dialogue for the episodes?" I

ask, as we hurry quietly out of the suite, making ourselves as inconspicuous as possible.

"Usually, yes." Girsul moves ahead of me along the upper-level hallway of the Bisfuri Quarters, then down the grand staircase. "Though, he improvises much of it during the scenes. At least his own parts."

"I see." I take quick steps to keep up. "Is that why so much of it is so bad and utterly ridiculous?"

Girsul bursts out laughing.

"What?" I say. "It's absolute crap."

"It is, isn't it . . ." Girsul agrees, shaking his head helplessly. "The only reason people love this show is because of the Man in the Niktos Cloak, the *character*, not the fine words spoken. It's about what he does and how he does it."

"In other words, it's his story," I say.

We exit the main estate building into morning sunlight.

CHAPTER
EIGHTEEN

W hen we get to the stables, there are a number of other staff working with the animals or cleaning the enclosures, so the place is considerably busier than I'd seen it the first time yesterday. The animals are also more agitated. I hear the snorting of *camral* and the neighs and sputters of *sesemet* coming from every stall, and up ahead from the section with the high roof, the deep trumpeting of the *bau-ehl*. Must be close to feeding time.

Girsul continues to lead the way, exchanging brief greetings and commentary with various stable hands while I just nod and say nothing.

We arrive at the cage enclosure with the black curtains on the inside covering our *pegasei*, and here we have a small problem. Two stable workers are mucking the floor nearby, so Girsul has to make a point of explaining what it is we're doing here.

"That's new. What do you have in there?" a boy asks, pointing to the orichalcum reinforced cage.

"Those are *Ter* Aten's fancy new goats," Girsul replies. "They're a fine rare breed, but a little too skittish, so Bisfuri ordered me to keep them in the dark."

"Oh yeah?" the second stable hand, an older youth says, pausing his sweeping. "Let's see them. I used to own a couple of prize goats myself, raised them from birth. . . ."

Girsul and I exchange quick glances. Of the two of us, I definitely know more about goats, so I take over. "You don't want to disturb them," I say, stepping forward. "They bite and they spit—right in your face, if you get close. And they don't look like much of anything, just your typical *hoohvak* goats. Kind of ugly, actually. Don't know why *Ter* Bisfuri even bothered to acquire them."

"Yeah, I think it's just for their value as breeding stock," Girsul picks up, echoing me.

"Anyway, if you want to waste time looking at them, be my guests," I continue. "In fact, we could use your help picking up their crap—"

"Nah, I don't think so," the older youth says at once. He then wipes the back of his forehead with one hand, and looks away with waning interest.

I shrug, making a point of expressing utter boredom.

The other boy lingers a moment longer then also shakes his head and gets back to work.

Which, for a moment, makes me wonder—*do* pegasei *even produce poo? And if so, would it be something shiny on the floor around them? Or would it just disappear like light into darkness . . . into thin air?*

While I entertain such absolutely *hoohvak* thoughts, Girsul turns to the lock on the cage and opens it carefully. We both go inside, past the black curtains.

The three *pegasei* goats stand exactly as we left them the day before. And I mean, *exactly*.

They are lined up next to each other, spaced the same way as we positioned them, and I could swear they haven't shifted their feet even once overnight. There is something terribly creepy about their fixed, inanimate forms and complete lack of living movement. No stir of breath makes their backs rise and fall. And yet, as soon as we arrive, their eyes seem to focus slightly—not on us exactly, but just overall . . . somehow.

I have no words to describe the weird sense I get staring at them.

And then something else occurs to me. The sun brightness that had emanated from these three figures yesterday has faded overnight.

They need to be fed. . . . Immediately.

"They're no longer glowing," I remark.

Girsul nods. "Yes, I noticed how dull they looked when I checked in on them earlier this morning. We need to take them outside in the sun, right now."

"How exactly? With all those people working out there? Won't they see?"

Girsul points to the stacks of black fabric in the corner. "Grab that black cloth. We'll drape them like blankets. It won't be a big deal when we go out, but on the way back, when they're all well-fed and shining brightly, this will help cover them. . . ."

"Got it."

I pick up several pieces of the black fabric, and Girsul and I get to work covering the three small creatures as well as possible. Then we take their orichalcum leads, sing the tones, and focus on imagining how they need to *move* because we're all going for a nice walk in the sun.

The goats come "awake" stiffly like mechanical dolls. They take a few awkward steps before their gait improves to seem more natural.

Girsul draws the curtain, opens the cage—while I hold on to all three goats on their leads—and we go out into the hallway, past stable hands who barely glance at us and our blanket-covered charges, down to the small door near the camel—pardon me, *camral*—enclosure, and out into the sunlight.

• • •

WE WALK AS FAR AWAY from any other stable workers as we can in the courtyard, toward a small, isolated wall nook that has several tall trees shielding it from sight.

"They use this place for cornering wild *sesemet*, I think," Girsul tells me. "Good place to take their blankets off and let them feed. No prying eyes here."

I am already pulling back the black cloth from the *pegasei*. And oh, the immediate sparkle that comes to their black and brown fur as soon as sunlight strikes it! At first it seems the fur is merely unusually glossy. But in a few heartbeats the fur itself takes on light and transforms. Black and brown bristles fade into filaments of vaporous pallor which practically float in the air and pulse with rainbow radiance. The glamor swirls and spins along their surfaces, faster and faster. . . .

The *pegasei* goats no longer exhibit the coloration we originally assigned to them. . . . Now they are incandescent, blinding white.

We stand, letting them soak in the light. And for once the *pegasei* seem to breathe as if they have actual lungs. White backs move up and down slightly, unfurling rhythmically in the sun. They expand more and more—reminding me of dry sea sponges soaking up water—so that the goat shapes have swelled to almost two thirds their original size.

"That's going to be hard to explain," Girsul mutters with sarcasm, switching the end of the orichalcum harness lead of one *pegasus* from one hand to another.

I hold on to the other two. "We'll need to spread out the blankets to cover more. Good thing I doubled the fabric up so it can be unrolled."

"This whole thing is just so strange." Girsul shakes his head, as we examine the overall lengths of the blankets at our disposal. "So, I'm thinking, now we might postpone any kind of special training until another day, when it's less busy. Also, all those Service Competitions tomorrow—"

Out of the corner of my eye I suddenly see someone standing right against the wall of the courtyard nook in which we're in.

"*Bastet!*" I exclaim, nearly jumping in reflex, and stare at the hooded figure covered from head to toe in a dark brown cloak, its fabric stirred by the breeze. In the next heartbeat, I try to block the view, and grab a blanket to quickly toss over the backs of the shining *pegasei* goats. Not that it would help anything; the person has already seen their *hoohvak* shining fur. . . .

"Eh? What?" Girsul turns around sharply at the sound of my voice and glances at the wall behind me.

But when I turn back also, preparing to glare at the figure of the newcomer, and ready to make up some nonsense excuse, suddenly *no one* is there.

"Okay, what?" I mutter, as my jaw drops. "Where did he go?"

"Who?" Now Girsul is staring at me as if I've lost my mind.

"Someone was just here! Some guy in a brown cloak!"

Girsul narrows his eyes at me. "I didn't see anyone come in or leave. There's no passage back there, just a stone wall. No one's here."

"Okay," I say, "But what—"

"What are you talking about?"

"I just saw *some guy* in a brown cloak!" I exclaim, pointing at the wall. "Right over there! I know there's no one there *now*, but there was someone a moment ago!"

I feel stupidly agitated, because I can still picture the way the folds of the long brown cloak flapped lightly, the figure completely covered, the wide hood. . . .

"Like I said, there's no place to go there around the corner—"

"He could be hiding again!"

"Fine, let me go check." Girsul hands me the lead in his hands and goes to look around the corner. He steps back out a moment later and shrugs. "No one there. Seriously."

"Then I must've had a goat kick me in the head," I mutter, frowning stubbornly, absolutely confused.

"Well, it is remotely possible some *chazuf* snuck out and around us when we were both turned, though very unlikely," Girsul responds in a placating tone, but I can tell he is merely trying to humor me. "It doesn't matter now, let's head back inside. I think these things have had enough sunlight. If they get any more bloated, we won't be able to cover them. And we'll attempt training another day."

I nod, still frowning, still angry, this time at myself. I must be more tired than I thought, if I'm hallucinating weird crap in the middle of day.

Only one explanation. The morning sha *in my head must still be screwing with me.*

WE SWADDLE the three *pegasei* goats in as much black cloth as possible and head back. Walking carefully past any stable staff in our way in the huge courtyard, we narrowly avoid two large rearing *sesemet* who are being barely controlled by five workers at once. One is a beautiful glossy cream color with a sheen of true gold. The other, rearing and neighing in frenzy, is a silver-white with an amazing long mane. . . .

"Semmi! Move back!" Girsul yells out at me, and I barely have time to pull my goat away from the rearing *sesemet* hooves.

A stable hand cusses at us for getting in the way, and we make haste, finally reaching the door leading inside the stables.

Here, in the dimly illuminated interior, lies the most difficult part. Our accursed goats are fully charged and glowing like *hoohvak* light orbs. You can see their brightness seeping through the black cloth and unavoidably coming from their feet.

Bastet, let no one see us, I pray. *Just a few steps more. . . .*

Carefully leading the *pegasei*, we walk up to the cage, and Girsul rushes to undo the lock.

Then, we're back inside, behind the black curtain.

Both Girsul and I exhale in relief. Then we "arrange" our *pegasei* goats like shiny dolls in a row, and tie their leads to the enclosure walls.

They stand motionless once more, no longer responsive to us. The only difference is, now they're swollen with light.

WITH BASIC *PEGASEI* chores done for the day, it's time to return to the main building and assist *Ter* Bisfuri.

When we get back to the private Quarters, the second episode of *The Love Life of the Man in the Niktos Cloak* is being prepped for recording. The actors in this one are the boyishly slim brunette *amretene* attired in her fiery crimson outfit, and the bearded actor (slightly smaller in stature than Hulag but with well-defined muscles).

The bedroom set has also been transformed with fabrics of dark blue and indigo colors, and the backdrop smart wall shows a realistic image of a moonlit night.

To my surprise, there is a third actor in the scene who wasn't there earlier this morning. The individual is somehow even more elegant than the three *amretene* actresses—extravagantly dressed in a gold wig, endless sparkling veils in shades of lavender and ripe persimmon, and very expensive looking jewelry. This new *amretene* reposes on the nearest sofa seat in a posture that is very fluid, very supple, and yet manages to convey a sense of superiority and boredom.

But when they turn around, I see an androgynous beautiful face with angular features and a possible shadow of a beard along the cheeks and jawline. Or is it there? I strain to understand if the person is a man dressed as a woman, or a woman who is masculine. Must be a bluish trick of the light on this person's very pale, rosy skin. Especially since the glossy, blood-black *noohd* lip color they're wearing makes such a contrast with the delicate mauve pallor of their skin tone. . . .

"Who's that?" I ask the brunette female actress in confusion, taking the digital pad with the lines of dialogue.

"*Ter* Bisfuri rewrote the script just now and sent for an additional *amretene* for this episode," she tells me in minor annoyance. "More lines! I have more lines now, and must accommodate this expensive *chimeratene* into our love scene!"

"*Chimeratene?* What's that?"

"Oh, Hathor strike me!" the brunette replies, almost snarling. "I have no time to explain the fine specialties of our trade just now—ask someone else!"

I frown at her. "Sorry!"

"Play back the new lines, now! Then recite them back to me!"

"All right, all right," I retort, barely holding myself back from making a rude rejoinder at her whiny, demanding tone, and begin tapping the tablet to listen to the new dialogue. In that moment the new actor turns again, and gives me a slow, languorous glance of amusement.

Bastet, those long, dark lashes are amazing!

I am briefly distracted from my task and can't help staring at the impossibly androgynous *amretene*—man or woman—and especially the delicate cluster of wire-thin sparkling bracelets around their wrists. Unlike the brunette before me, this person doesn't bother with a tablet. Either they have an amazing recall, or they have no lines to memorize?

Meanwhile, the other staff rush around us for a few moments longer, as the sets are finalized, and the dark blue and violet spot-lighting is arranged by the light orb technicians. Girsul is assisting with some of it, I notice.

Finally, *Ter* Bisfuri emerges from his own quarters, once again attired in his full black costume and Niktos Cloak. For some inexplicable reason, yet again, I feel a weird stab of anxiety in my gut, at the sight of him. . . . As if a little bit of wind has been knocked out of me. He looks directly at the new *amretene* with a lively smile that lights up his features.

"So delightful to see you, Ixenoel. I appreciate you making yourself available on such short notice."

"It is always my pleasure to please you, *im Ter*." Without leaving their seat, the *amretene* named Ixenoel nods gracefully, metallic jewelry tinkling with the slightest motion of their graceful head, and replies in a sonorous, honey voice—either an alto or a tenor, I'm not quite certain. "Fortunately, I was able to move several appointments from this afternoon, and I'm completely at your disposal."

Male or female? Bastet have mercy, but now I'm consumed with curiosity. *And oh, those elegant nails, shaped into perfect, gilded claws. . . .*

Ter Bisfuri then turns to the brunette actress who is pouting on a sofa seat next to me. "And you, my dear Yokreoh, I hope you've had the time to study the minor changes to the script. You only have two additional lines, and you'll need to make room in bed for Ixenoel."

"Oh, I'm perfectly ready, you can be certain, *im Ter*," Yokreoh replies in a completely different tone of voice, and gives Bisfuri a giddy smile that turns sensuous. "And it's a privilege to be working with the magnificent Ixenoel!"

Ixenoel lifts a hand and blows an artful kiss in the other's direction. She—or he—makes me think of a temple lotus blossom at the perfect moment of its bloom.

"Very well." Benaten smiles back at both *amretene* in a faintly sarcastic manner. "In the new version of our script the scene opens rather wickedly with the two of you enjoying each other's company. Are you ready?"

"Oh, yes!" Yokreoh gets up from her seat and slinks elegantly toward the bed. She waves one beckoning hand toward Ixenoel.

"Of course," Ixenoel's glorious voice teases. And then

Ixenoel moves with feline grace to join the other one on the large bed. "The question, *im Ter* is, are you ready for the two of us?"

In reply, Bisfuri laughs. "Have I ever disappointed you?"

While the two *amretene* take their positions on top of the bedcovers, still fully clothed, and start making exaggerated noises of carnal delight, he steps back out of camera view and joins the bearded actor who is playing the spouse as they wait for their entrance cues.

I take hold of the tablet nervously, ready to cue the lines if needed. At the same time, I notice the hoverboard propped against the back wall and the infamous whip appearing out of nowhere in Bisfuri's fingers. Both are ready to be utilized in the scene.

The director calls out for the action to start.

Once again, I feel my breath catch in my throat. . . .

AND SO, this *garooi* episode is performed and recorded. I really don't want to dwell on the details of what happens because it is both embarrassing and ridiculous.

What can I say? It's the same *hoohvak* story as nearly every other episode, except with an additional surprise. A moonlit night. The faithless Lady and her unknown Lover are rolling around in bed, embracing but still clothed in their shiny garments and veils. The Man in the Niktos Cloak appears and joins them, under the flimsiest pretenses. Much giggling and moaning occurs, as the Man skillfully divests the two of their attire until everyone is mostly naked, but skillfully covered by blankets except for the occasional special closeups.

Once again, I try not to stare too closely at *that* action. Except, this time I find myself peeking in curiosity at Ixenoel who seems to have rather tiny breasts, so I'm still uncertain if they are male or female. . . . *Nearly flat-chested, but maybe not quite?*

For once in my life, I'm actually hoping for a glimpse of

whatever it is they might have *down below*, in the front. *Bastet, what have I become? It shouldn't matter, and it's highly stupid.*

Furthermore, I inadvertently caught a glimpse of Bisfuri's tight ass.

Did. Not. Plan. That.

Crap of a goat. . . .

At last, it's over and the Husband appears. The twist in this episode is that not only does the Husband catch the Wife in the act with the Man in the Niktos Cloak *and* another Lover, but it also turns out that the Wife's Lover is also the Husband's secret Lover. So, there's dramatic screaming and brandishing of fists on all sides (while the laughing audience sound is inserted), as the Wife finds out her Husband has been faithless too and starts pummeling him. Meanwhile, the Lover slinks away, cleverly wrapping their lower body in veils (so it's still unresolved if they are a woman or a man), pretends to climb out of the fake backdrop window, and ends up off camera next to me.

I glance somewhat awkwardly at all that linen-pale skin up close, catch a whiff of expensive floral perfume, as the *amretene* continues standing right next to me and casually adjusts the veil over their middle. I see very elegant, very androgynous limbs, torso, shoulders, and have to look up a bit since Ixenoel is taller than me, and their magnificent gold wig is perfectly intact despite all that erotic tussle on-camera. Our gazes meet, and Ixenoel winks at me with mischievous green eyes underneath finely shaped dark brows.

I find that the tablet is slightly shaking in my hands. . . .

As far as what's happening on camera—at last, the weapons come out. The Husband and the Man fight. The Lady screams. The whip snaps through the air, many clever times. I hold my hand over my mouth to stifle giggles. Whenever I occasionally glance at Ixenoel throughout this, the *amretene* is watching the fight scene and shaking with silent laughter.

• • •

WHEN THE EPISODE ends and the Niktos Cloak is tossed to cover the main camera, the director calls the end of scene. The decorating staff gets to work transforming the set for the third time, while we get another small break before the third and final episode for the day is filmed.

The bearded actor who played the Husband is fortunately unhurt in the stage fighting. He stands flexing his impressive biceps and rubbing his forearms. Both he and the brunette Yokreoh appear visibly relaxed now that their work is done, and dress themselves.

Meanwhile, Benaten sets down his own props and approaches Ixenoel casually. He is naked to the waist, with only a bit of linen cloth over his lean middle, his long raven hair loose and tousled from all the action, and on his feet, his glossy black boots which, again, he doesn't bother to take off.

I stand nearby, still holding the tablet, and try not to stare, or listen in, but it's impossible.

"Thank you again for today. And I must have you at the evening party here tomorrow night," Bisfuri tells Ixenoel. "We expect an Imperial presence and much of High Court, so your *chimeratene* charms are going to be needed."

"Of course, *im Ter*," the other responds with a deep nod and a knowing smile.

That term again, *chimeratene*. I really need to ask someone what it means.

In that moment, Benaten suddenly glances at me. "And you —will you have your clever story ready in its entirety for my guests tomorrow?"

"Story? Oh—oh, yes, *im Ter*," I reply, with a surge of alarm coming over me, as I recall that dratted storyteller task still hanging over my head like a rusty pail of dirty water.

The *chimeratene* Ixenoel turns in my direction, examining me closer. "You're a storyteller? So, you do more than merely cue our lines? Do you also write this script?"

"Oh no," I say at once. "That script is entirely *Ter* Bisfuri's work. I would never come up with something so—so—"

I clamp my mouth shut, realizing that I was going to say something I would regret.

Suddenly, Benaten Bisfuri's grey eyes pierce me as he focuses on me entirely. "What? Were you going to say so—brilliant? Or so abysmally *daft?*"

There's a terrifying heartbeat of silence.

And now, I can't breathe. . . . Bastet has taken away my tongue for once, and the evil *sha* are laughing in the back of my mind.

"Well?" Bisfuri repeats, staring at me.

"Please . . . don't dismiss me, *im Ter*," I barely manage to utter, feeling a rush of heat interspersed with cold.

Please, don't force me to speak the truth. . . .

Another terrible pause.

Then, Benaten smiles. "Dismiss you? To the contrary. It's unfortunate that you don't know how to read or write, Semmi, or I would immediately assign this task to you. The Man in the Niktos Cloak would benefit from a confrontation with cows and baboons."

CHAPTER
NINETEEN

earing Benaten Bisfuri's words, I feel an instant wash of relief. He's not angry at me! And neither does he mind criticism of his scriptwriting. What an amazing thing!

If only I could read and write!

I mutter something semi-coherent in reply, but *Ter* Bisfuri has already turned his attention elsewhere. I watch him flash a smile at Ixenoel then head out to get dressed again for the third episode.

"And so, it's been a fabulous delight." Ixenoel turns to me, smiling also. "Enjoy the rest of the show, my dear. My task here is done. Until tomorrow night, then, when the aristocrats converge and the entertaining stories must flow. . . . *Nefero dea.*" And the *amretene* gracefully moves away, departing.

I nod and step back, making room for more activity, as staff and techs begin to transform the set one final time, and there is only one female *amretene* and male actor left.

THE THIRD EPISODE is acted and recorded without any significant disruptions or surprises. For once, I actually get to cue a line (in a slightly nervous whisper) to the voluptuous older blonde *amretene* in her skin-tight, golden dress.

She gets flustered and forgets a simple sentence: "I must be dreaming, for it's my dream to be disrobed by a dark mystery man such as you."

The Man in the Niktos Cloak swirls his Cloak with an additional set of flourishes to help us cover up her mistake, then rips the gold outfit off her body in one very skillful move, and pounces. . . . There are the usual giggles and noises of delight. Then the Husband walks in to interrupt the fun, and so on and so forth.

I stand off camera, trying not to roll my eyes and not to look at any naked stuff, but pay attention once the good, acrobatic fighting starts. And when the whole thing is over, Girsul and I help with the general room cleanup.

The episodes will now be processed and cut, the theme music and other fun effects added, and the first of the three episodes will be played for the public in just a few days from now.

Suddenly I get a weird, uncomfortable image of these episodes airing everywhere around Poseidon, including our own living room, with Grandmother, Uru, and Father there, watching the usual show. . . . Except this time, I would be right *there*, barely off camera, a witness to the performance. *So weird.*

As I allow myself to contemplate these strange visions of what's to come, *Ter* Bisfuri has long since disappeared in his quarters, and as far as I understand, my day of service here is done.

"Enough now, go home, Semmi," Vakrem, the security guard, tells me. "You too, *chazuf*." And he motions at Girsul. "A very long day, tomorrow. You have the morning Competitions to worry about. *Ter* Bisfuri expects all of you Domestic Service applicants employed by this House to do your best. But when that's over, be *here* promptly at seventh hour of Khe for the

Bisfuri evening party! You might have the day off work, but not the night! So go, get out of here, and rest well before morning."

"Yeah, going," Girsul replies, stacking the last heavy box of technical equipment on top of several others in one corner.

"May the Gods give us all Fortune," Dunea, the set design mistress says, rolling the last of the bales of silk fabric and handing it to Menahit for storage.

"You signed up for tomorrow, too?" I ask.

"Of course," Menahit speaks up tiredly. "Most everyone in this House will be trying for some spot tomorrow. I signed up for Kinakra at seventh hour."

"House Sumerad at ninth hour," Dunea says.

"I'll see you there," I say with a wry twist of my lips. And then I head home.

MY BUS RIDE IS UNEVENTFUL, except for navigating the crowds. The sky is indigo, filled with evening dusk again when I get home to Denwen's Pit. I'm so tired that I can't think clearly. Once again, I haven't eaten since morning, and my empty stomach is rumbling in fury. What kind of *garooi* existence is this? My second day working for Bisfuri was even longer than my first.

"Did you register for the Competitions tomorrow?" I say to Uru, as soon as I walk in and see everyone eating.

Uru looks up from his bowl and nods wordlessly, continuing to slurp and chew.

"All three?" I ask, filling my own bowl with barley and aromatic turnips from the large pot which Grandmother has cooked all alone, without my help yet again.

"Yeah, all of them," Uru replies. "Barely made it to Sumerad. They almost closed registration by the time I got there."

I frown at my silly little brother. "Why didn't you sign up for all three in one place?"

"Huh?" Uru furrows his forehead back at me.

"You can sign up for all the different Competitions at any valid registration site. You don't have to run to each different House if you know ahead which ones you want."

"I didn't know." Uru looks angry and embarrassed. "I thought—oh, man, I flew on my hoverboard all over Circle Five!"

Grandmother reaches over across the bench and ruffles Uru's dark head of hair.

Father merely grunts and gnaws at a stale chunk of flatbread with the side of his mouth which has the fewest teeth missing.

"You know they have those big smart boards, right? They have sound and can speak the recorded stuff to you," I continue, taking a huge bite of food. "Next time, you arrive at the closest site, check that board first, find out all the details, and then go register right there."

"All right." Uru stares down at his bowl sullenly and resumes eating.

I shake my head and make some kind of mumbling noise. Amurabia's amused gaze meets mine and we exchange glances of understanding.

"*Mei-Ma,*" I begin a few moments later, having finally gathered the courage to say this to her. "Tomorrow, I will be gone for most of the day—*and* night. So sorry, but I won't be able to help you cook supper again. . . ."

At the sound of my serious tone, she looks away from the media-box screen and gives me her full attention. "Why's that?"

"Remember how, when we were there that first time, I told a story to *Ter* Bisfuri? So now tomorrow night they're having that party, and—and I'm supposed to work as a Storyteller before their guests. They told me to be there at seventh hour of Khe."

Grandmother thinks for a moment, then nods. "Do your work as obligated, but don't stay too late. The night buses are unreliable."

"Okay," I whisper, then scoop the barley and turnips in my bowl with a chunk of bread, and put some in my mouth. To be honest, I expected more of a negative reaction, but this is good. Grandmother obviously understands how important all of this is.

"Eat well, everyone. Then, bed, early." Grandmother tells us. Soon afterwards, she turns off the media-box.

THE MORNING of the nineteenth day of *Setaet* arrives much too soon. I wake up from a stressful *hoohvak* nightmare in which I'm running barefoot in a crowd of other people, along a gravel path surrounded by greenery in a fancy park. For some reason I'm moving weirdly slow, and my feet feel thick and heavy as though they're sinking in mud with every step, while everyone else is passing me. . . .

Definitely stupid, a typical worry dream.

I blink in the pre-dawn darkness, yawning. And then all the morning *sha* strike me hard with their combined terrors. Suddenly, my heartbeat races in anticipation of what's to come, and I bolt up in my cot. I can vaguely make out Uru's shape, as he stirs in his own bed. The boy likely didn't sleep well either. And now both of us will be heading to the same place.

"Uru!" I whisper. "Are you awake? Time to get up!"

"I know," he responds, then sits up. "What time is it?"

"Doesn't matter. Probably around fifth hour of Ra. We've got to get ready and go. Quickly, now!"

We put on our work clothing and try to tiptoe as quietly as possible around Father sleeping in the living room without tripping over anything.

"Hey! Sturdy shoes . . ." I whisper to Uru as he heads outside to use the latrine seat. "Put on your good pair after you poo. . . ."

"Okay," my little brother says.

We both take turns with the latrine, put on our best shoes,

shove leftover food in our mouths, and are ready to face the crazy day.

"Should I bring my board?" Uru glances wistfully at the hoverboard propped up against the wall near the door.

I consider, briefly. "Good question. Did you bring it the last time?"

"No."

"What if, at the start of the Competition, they make you leave it behind and you lose it?"

"Then I won't, I guess."

"All right, then. Let's go!"

In the silvery blue darkness of earliest dawn, we rush to the bus stop.

WE BOARD the bus to Circle Five together with a small crowd of anxious, simply dressed people—working men, women, children of all ages, on their way to the Competitions. Where did all these people come from, to end up on our remote stop? Must be from all over Denwen's Pit and Circle Nine.

And then, after the bus takes off, we gain more passengers at every stop. Most newcomers are better dressed than any of us from the outer Circles, as we get closer inward to City center. By the time we arrive at our destination the bus is so full that all of Poseidon must be crammed in there with us.

"Is this the stop for Kinakra?" several people call out. "House Kinakra, Domestic Service Competition?"

"Yes! Get off here . . . *Kinakra!*" others reply.

And the stampede begins.

I grab Uru's hand and press on toward the exit. Most of us in this group of passengers need to get off right here, and so we shove our way past smelly bodies and out into the open air. Meanwhile, another wave of passengers takes our place, to head deeper into the City for other Competitions. Apparently quite a few are happening today, in multiple categories.

Once off the bus, Uru and I pause, and let go of each other's hands. Both of us must experience a brief instant of uncertainty, as we try to get our bearings, without getting knocked off our feet by passersby pouring off the bus and onto it.

It's still bluish dusk, and the sun hasn't risen yet. Fixed street lamps repose on tall posts with ornate metalwork, and occasional hovering orbs glow with warm golden light. They are the only source of illumination against the gradually brightening sky. I glance at my brother who knows parts of the City somewhat better than I do, since he does all the messenger work. However, this isn't one of those parts.

"So, this is Circle Five," I state the obvious, glancing around awkwardly at the shadowy, tree-lined street, the well-kept houses of clay brick, limestone, granite, and the occasional stone walls enclosing more well-off residences where I get glimpses of fine veined marble and roofs with gold trim, gleaming in the artificial lamplight.

"I guess," he mumbles. "Don't know this area that well. Got lost a few times yesterday. . . ."

Looking in Uru's dark eyes, I find a corresponding sense of momentary doubt.

"I didn't take this bus," he continues defensively. "Flew there on the hoverboard from Circle Three, so not sure about this bus stop and where it's at, and Luamat Marketplace . . . I think it's that way. . . ."

Uru glances around and orients toward where the majority of people who got off the bus are heading. "See, a bunch of them are all going that way—"

While he does that, I notice a peacock strutting along the grass in the yard nearby.

Bastet help us, this is a fine neighborhood. . . .

"All right," I muse out loud, starting to walk away from the bus stop in the general direction of everyone else. Uru follows me. "Let's think. House Kinakra. General Domestic Service Competition. Luamat Marketplace, Circle Five. Which way do we go?"

"Follow the crowd?" Uru repeats.

"We're not going to follow random, confused strangers to *sha* knows where," I retort. "At least not until we have a better idea." Then I reach inside my pocket for my Bisfuri employee comm badge. "We need a map."

I tap the badge a few times, trying to remember how to bring up the hologram map. Nothing happens. And then I tap another sequence that I definitely recall. It is used to call up a program called Journey Guide. "How do I get to Luamat Marketplace from here?" I ask it, speaking into the badge while holding the middle button spot.

"Continue directly ahead along this route for five hundred and seventy-nine paces. Then turn right on Avenue of Olives," says a mechanical voice. And a tiny hologram pops up, displaying the street as a line on a map, and the cross-streets ahead.

"Ooooh," Uru says, impressed.

"See this dot on the map? That's us," I say. And we keep walking.

SOON ENOUGH, we arrive at a large clearing full of vendor stalls, which must be Luamat Marketplace. By now, the sun has barely risen, filling the eastern edge of the sky with pink light. I check my comm badge and it informs us that it's twenty daydreams before seventh hour. Just enough time to find the Competition area.

We don't have to look far because there's a huge line forming, many people deep, near a wooden raised platform with a standard bearing the Kinakra House symbol. Several officials stand on the platform, and right below are rows of tables full of chests and baskets.

"What's that?" Uru rushes ahead and asks some women in the back of the line, while I approach more slowly, trying to look in all directions. They shrug, knowing as little as we do.

So, we wait in line. It occurs to me to wonder if any of my fellow Bisfuri employees are here, such as Girsul or Menahit. I glance around, but don't recognize anyone.

At the same time, more people arrive behind us. The crowd is ridiculously big, and everyone is whispering and pointing, straining to look over their neighbors.

"What kind of Competition, did they say? What are we supposed to do?" is a question asked over and over.

"Attention!" One of the Kinakra officials standing on the platform finally speaks, his amplified voice carrying over the crowd. At once the waves of whispers quiet down.

"You are all here because you want to take part in the Service Competition sponsored by the noblest of Houses, Kinakra!" the man continues. "You will form proper queues before these tables. Do it now! Each one of you will be identified against the list of registered participants and given your first task."

At once we all shove forward, and attempt to stand single-file. Uru and I find ourselves in two different but adjacent lines, which is fine, because we can watch each other if needed.

We still don't know what we're supposed to do at the tables once we get there.

I offer up a quick prayer to Bastet and whatever gods might be listening.

Please, blessed Bast, let Uru do well. Let it be something he and I can do easily. . . . Please.

"Once you complete the task," the Kinakra official continues, "you will either advance to the next task or be told to go home. Pay attention to the instructions, and do your best, as quickly as you can!"

The line starts moving. We can't see clearly what is happening up front at the tables, but it doesn't seem to matter. We see people step forward, do something at that table . . . then, moments later, most of them return and walk past those of us still in the line, their faces showing disappointment and confusion. Only a few are told to walk in a different direction, onward.

Uru and I arrive at the head of our respective lines simultaneously, as we hoped. "Go!" I whisper loudly, seeing my little brother hesitate briefly and stare at me. "Go on!"

And then Uru and I both step forward.

Women wearing Kinakra symbols and various-colored employee tassels on their uniforms stand on the other side of the long tables, opposite from us, one person per line. Each holds a digital tablet. On the tables before us are endless rows of small boxes and lidded baskets.

"Name?" says the stern-faced woman across from me, assigned to my line.

"Semirameos," I reply, "From Circle Ten, Denwen's Pit." At the same time, to my right, I hear Uru give his own reply in his childish voice to the woman in charge of his own line.

"Put your thumb here." My woman extends the tablet toward me.

I press my thumb on the spot as instructed.

"Confirmed," the woman says. She then launches into a weary, memorized speech that she's given too many times already. "These are your instructions. First, you must listen to these instructions to the very end and do exactly as told. Second, open the container before you. Third, take out the fabric inside and fold it neatly into a small square no larger than your hand. Fourth, hand me the folded fabric. Fifth, you must never touch the container, simply stand before me. Begin now!"

Huh? Crap of the gods!

Instead of moving quickly, for some reason, I'm thrown into

doubt and confusion. *Those weird instructions—did I hear them right? What—what?* My heartbeat pounds, because in that moment I am unsure. And so, I freeze.

I don't know what to do.

Wait, I think. *Did she say to open the box?* But . . . she also said to *listen* to the instructions all the way to the end . . . and that's when she said I must *never touch* the container! *What to do?*

Meanwhile, I hear, to the left of me, the man in line quickly open his container and grab the fabric. The same thing is happening in multiple lines on either side of me—bursts of activity, people furiously folding their bits of fabric. . . .

I throw a quick glance at Uru and notice he too is stalled, giving me a panicked look with his huge black eyes. Obviously, our minds work alike, both questioning those instructions.

And then it strikes me.

If I'm to follow the instructions exactly, it means *listening* to them to the very *end*, as per the very *first* instruction. Which also means, as per *last* instruction, I must *not* touch the box.

At once I glance at Uru again and widen my eyes like crazy, and then barely shake my head, "no."

Don't do it, Uru, I will him to understand. *Don't touch it.*

And then I remain standing very still, doing nothing.

Uru momentarily extends his hand, but then drops it back at his side, and also stands still. He never touches his box.

A few madness-filled moments later, while most people in the various queues around us rush to fold their fabric, the Kinakra woman nods at me. "Well done," she says. "You advance to the second task. Proceed to your right and to the back of the platform."

And then the woman taps her tablet.

I look at Uru and see that he is smiling and has advanced also.

Thank you, o holy Bast!

M y brother and I, along with a very few others, walk in the direction of the wooden platform, while the majority heads away, disqualified.

"That was wild!" Uru whispers loudly to me as we approach the scaffolding and go around the back. "I was so scared to do nothing, but the instructions didn't make sense."

"They didn't," I agree. "They were probably meant to be tricky like that, to see if we could pay attention."

"Correct," says the nearest woman in a Kinakra uniform waiting for us at another, smaller grouping of tables. "The first test was to see if you could follow instructions properly. Such skill is highly valued by the noble Family of the House Kinakra. Congratulations, you passed. Now, see if you can pass this second task."

Uru and I end up in a much smaller crowd, as we wait for our next instructions. The tables before us contain various, seemingly random objects, arranged in piles next to empty boxes and baskets with their lids open. Once again, a Kinakra staff worker stands behind every table.

We're told to form single-file queues in front of each

container. As Uru and I get in line, we again choose to stand next to each other in adjacent lines, so that we can do this together. I throw quick glances at my nearest competitors and see other very serious, very determined-looking people in this group. They had to have been sufficiently attentive and sharp, to have passed the first test, and so, our competition has self-selected to be a certain type of individual.

I suppose, my brother and I both fall into this category, unexpectedly.

How strange, I think, *I never considered myself particularly clever or observant.*

"Attention!" a Kinakra representative from the platform speaks loudly. "We congratulate all of you for having passed our first portion of the Service Competition. However, it only gets harder from this point forward. House Kinakra expects accuracy and impeccable attention to detail in their service staff. This second task before you will test your ability to work with precision."

I glance briefly at Uru and give him an encouraging nod and blink.

"Your instructions are—" the Kinakra official continues, "You must carefully transfer every single item in each of these piles into the container on the table before you, arranging them so that *everything* fits inside with the lid properly closed. You must not damage any of these items. And most important, you must do this as *quietly* as possible—so as not to disturb a sleeping child or noble lord in their bedchamber where you might be working. There is a device on the table next to each of you that measures the amount of noise you make during your performance of the task—every clink and clatter and shuffle and crinkle and random knock. If you exceed the noise level designation, you will fail the task. You will also be timed. If you exceed ten daydreams, you will fail the task."

Another quick glance sideways at Uru, and I see my brother

making huge terrified eyes at me. Uru is not particularly good with this manner of careful busy-work. . . .

Bast, I pray once more, *Please help him!*

I notice that my assigned Kinakra staff worker, standing across the table from me, has her fingers resting on top of some kind of small lumpy gadget, probably a sound measuring machine or timer.

The main Kinakra representative continues: "At the count of three, begin your task. One . . . two . . . three!"

The woman overseer across from me quickly taps the gadget which responds by flashing with colored lights. Once engaged, the lights continue to blink to the rhythm of heartbeats, counting. . . .

We all spring into frenzied action.

I try not to think of Uru, but focus my attention on the box before me, the lid, and the pile of things I need to organize. There are hairpins, spools of fine yarn, bits of lace, metal brooches, rings, combs, amulets, and other potentially clanky cheap jewelry with thin, dangly chains . . . sewing needles, wooden spoons, little trinket boxes filled with tiny noisy beads that rustle like sand *(crap of a goat!)* which I discover too late as I pick up one.

As I stare at all this *hoohvak* junk, my mind immediately forms a plan.

Pick one hard object, and one soft object, and start layering them.

And so, I begin stacking, carefully and methodically. My hands are steady, so this is not a big deal for me. Now and then, I glance at Uru and see that he is doing something similar, except his expression is strained and his forehead is tightened in a frown. And then I glance around at the others, and everyone seems to have figured this out too.

Moments race away, and the pile of objects outside my box grows smaller as I fill the container. Finally, everything is inside. Now, the big test is to put the lid on and see if it closes, without

crunching the more fragile objects within. I lower the lid, and—
no. Something is sticking out too much. *Bastet, take me! Argh!*

I start removing and rearranging a few things. Then I try the
lid again. *Varqood* this crap!

Still, no luck. . . .

My pulse speeds up. Anxious heartbeats measure time flying
by. I've no idea how many daydreams remain, but I can't risk
slowing down. So, I rearrange the contents of the box again and
again (while the Kinakra woman stands across from me
impassively and pretends not to look at the blinking lights of the
sound recording device, every few breaths). Finally, I manage to
get everything inside, and shut the box with a gentle click.

I stand back, then look at Uru and see he is already done,
with the lid closed over his box. And on the other side of me, the
woman is still finishing up. Our time is called just as she lowers
the lid over her container.

"Stop!" the Kinakra representative says loudly from the
platform. "Your time is up. Stop what you're doing and be
evaluated."

The Kinakra assigned to me taps the gadget before us and
glances at its light readout, which is blue. "You pass the noise
test," she says. "Now, let's look inside." She opens the container,
and overturns it, dumping the contents unceremoniously on the
table. "Looks fine, nothing damaged," she says, after checking a
few of the more delicate items. "You pass the second task. Now,
wait here for the next instructions."

I nod in relief. Then I look at Uru, and he appears to have
passed also—and so has the woman next to me. Uru and I
exchange smiles of relief.

This particular task wasn't too bad at all. Rather easy,
actually.

I look around and see that most of the people at the tables
have also passed, and only a few are sent away for being too

noisy (according to the light indicators on the gadgets glowing red) or too careless.

"Congratulations to all of you who have completed the second task," the Kinakra official announces from the platform. "Now, the third and final task. You will line up at the entrance of that tent with the Kinakra symbol and go inside to be interviewed individually."

And the official points to a spot about a hundred paces beyond the platform where a large light-colored fabric tent has been set up with the House logo over the entrance.

All of us immediately head toward it. We arrive as a small crowd at the entrance, then form a long, snaking line. Once more, we stand single-file. And the first person goes inside, quickly followed by two others—as instructed by the Kinakra workers at the entrance.

Just in case, I push Uru behind me in line, telling him quietly to do his best and watch my facial expression if I come out ahead of him, so that he can learn something useful from my look.

Moments later, another batch of three people is told to come in, while the first three must've exited from the back of the tent, unseen. . . .

Eventually, I get near the front of the line. I throw one glance of encouragement at Uru, then go inside, in a batch with two other people.

An interesting thing greets us within the large tent. There is a privacy kiosk set up with three adjacent metal room compartments and each one is a narrow cubicle with a door. It appears similar to the sound-proof interview booths I've dealt with at the Chiprahat warehouse and elsewhere.

"Go in, one person per room," a Kinakra worker tells us.

I step to the nearest booth and open the door.

• • •

INSIDE, there's only room for a tiny table and two chairs. A light orb floats overhead, providing harsh illumination. A man in a Kinakra uniform occupies one of the chairs, and a digital tablet rests before him. Wordlessly, he points to the empty chair, and I sit down across from him, hands nervously hiding in my lap.

"Name?" he asks in a dull tone, without even glancing at me.

"Semirameos, Circle Ten," I say.

There is a long moment of silence as the official examines the tablet. I stare at his stern face, waiting. . . .

He finally looks up at me. "It says here, you passed both tasks one and two. However, it also says under the advanced analysis results—visible only to a higher supervisor such as myself—that the sensor device registered a mismatch in weight for the container and the objects inside."

"What?" I lean closer, confused.

"In other words," the man says, "The total item weight has been pre-measured with a highly sensitive instrument, and when you closed the lid, you did not include all the items."

"Huh? What?" I repeat, like a *hoohvak*. "I'm sorry, I don't understand."

The Kinakra glares at me.

"You *did not* include all the required items that had been presented to you on that table. Each time the container was filled during the Competition, the total item weight was registered with perfect accuracy. You withheld back one or more of the items so that you could close the lid. It is clear you stole something from your allotted pile. Or you threw something under the table, to gain an advantage. In either case, you *cheated*."

My jaw drops with indignation. "But—no!" I say, "I did not! I swear!"

The man watches my reaction impassively.

"Maybe—maybe it was the person before me? Maybe they

did something? Here—look, I don't have anything!" I stand up in the tiny cubicle and empty the one pocket in the front of my skirt. "See, I have nothing, just my current employer comm badge!"

The Kinakra official barely looks at my pocket contents and does not blink. "The participant before you registered the correct total weight. Which means that *you* did something to your container or to the items inside."

"But—but—" I stand shaking my head, starting to tremble with outrage, and think very hard. I try to remember if indeed I somehow screwed up, maybe dropped something by accident. . . . But, no. The memory image of that table surface and my careful movements comes to me, and I'm certain I did nothing wrong.

"I am telling you, I didn't cheat. I didn't hide anything! Your gadget is broken!"

"You cheated, and you are disqualified from the Competition."

My temples start to ring with furious energy.

"I do *not* cheat!" I exclaim. "I have *never* cheated in my life!"

The man stares at me coldly. "Are you willing to undergo a full body search?"

"You know what?" I retort passionately, "*varqood* this *garooi* Competition! I've had enough!"

And I turn to leave.

"Stop," the official says, putting his hand up.

I pause, frowning in confusion.

"You are right. You did not cheat, and the weight of the container was correct and unchanged," the Kinakra man says tiredly, his icy expression loosening. "However, you just failed the third and final task. This was a test of character. House Kinakra requires meek compliance and polite, deferential, and submissive behavior in all their staff, before superiors and management. And your demeanor when confronted was excessively defensive, rude, and non-compliant. Had you obediently agreed to a full body search, I would have passed you, but you lashed out instead. You are therefore *incompatible* with our service code of conduct."

I let out a tense breath, my anger deflated and replaced by disgust. "Why even bother telling me this?"

"Because House Kinakra is just. In all fairness to you, you have come this far and are owed an explanation."

"Well, thank you, *ter*," I say, moving to the door. "And in case I wasn't compliant enough just now, *varqood* House Kinakra."

I STEP out from the booth, and am told by the workers to exit the tent in the opposite direction. Once outside, I see a few other grim-faced participants leaving in equal disgust.

Here I pause to wait for Uru.

My little brother joins me in a few daydreams. He looks ready to cry. "Semmi!" he calls me. "Did you pass? They told me I didn't, because I argued when they accused me of stealing!"

"I know," I say softly, hugging Uru, and he doesn't even protest. "I didn't pass their evil test either. House Kinakra is looking for desperate, pitiful *hoohvaks* to serve them, not regular people. They want slaves not servants! Who in their right mind wouldn't defend themselves when unjustly accused? And they expect us to work quietly and achieve perfection while taking all this abuse! You and me, we can do better!"

"Yeah!" Uru says, looking up from the hug, sniffling somewhat and turning his little dirt-smudged face toward me. "I bet they won't find anyone like that! They'll end up without any servants at all on those flying space ships!"

"At least not any self-respecting servants." I ruffle his hair, and we begin walking away from the Kinakra area of Luamat

Marketplace. "Let's see what time it is and where we need to go next."

I check my comm badge and call up the little map. Apparently, we only have half an hour to make it to our next Competition at ninth hour, House Sumerad on Raivaal Way which is far south along Circle Five.

"Crap of a goat, Uru! I hoped we'd get more time, but we have to go!"

And we take off running.

CHAPTER
TWENTY-ONE

We race south along the streets of Circle Five, and by now the sun has risen completely. In the light of morning this wealthy neighborhood reveals itself, and I'm reminded of what Girsul had said the other day, about "trees, shrines full of cooing doves, and marble temples."

Apparently, it's not an exaggeration. Aged green trees with leaves like fine maiden hair and thick, noble trunks line the avenues on both sides and cast delicate shade on the stone sidewalks and the ancient cobbles of the streets.

We pass fine residences, garden statuary, occasional fancy hover cars of gleaming polished metal (landing or taking off, but never spending too long at street level), and leisurely pedestrians. Not a single ground-bound wagon or vendor cart here, such as we're used to seeing at home in Circle Ten, Denwen's Pit.

I notice, we're not the only ones running. A few other brave souls must've left the Kinakra Service Competition to get to the next one being held today, Sumerad. I see determined people rushing in the same direction along our route. Some of them might even look familiar from the crowd at Luamat Marketplace, though I can't be entirely certain.

"How much longer?" Uru keeps nagging me, as he runs lightly at my side.

"Two more streets . . . then we turn right," I manage to reply between gasps, feeling the strain in my breathing. I might be an excellent runner, but it's been a long route at a hard pace. Uru, on the other hand, is an even better runner—the boy is effortless, and not even a little out of breath after all that.

We make a right turn into a wider avenue, a cardinal route— one of those major streets, curving gently along with the Circle— and then, just ahead of us, I note another wide street that bisects this one at an angle. Recalling the map, I believe this is Raivaal Way.

"This is it," I say to Uru as we come to a stop at the street corner full of people.

Here, everyone has gathered, and we and the rest of the latecomers get to stand at the edges of the crowd.

We mill around the front lawn area of a large corner property, an estate by the size of it, surrounded by a metallic trellis-like fence covered in climbing vines and roses. The front lawn is considerable, and I see the insignia markings of the noble House Sumerad on each of the gates and smaller insignias topping the fence posts at regular intervals.

Several tables are set up, staffed by uniformed workers, and a man is already speaking and giving instructions in a loud, amplified voice by the time we arrive within hearing range.

". . . you will demonstrate sufficient speed, which is the primary quality House Sumerad is looking for in its service staff. Approach the tables and verify your identity, then receive your tassel. You will take this tassel with you as you run around the perimeter of this property fence and pick up as many small stones as you are able along the way. The stones are specially marked and painted red. Those red stones are the only ones you may take. You will see them on the ground very near the fence walls."

The Sumerad official pauses to point at the fence, where we notice a sprinkling of red on the ground. "Once you can no longer carry any more, you must return to these tables. Your time will be noted and the stones will be counted. Those of you with the fastest times and the most stones will advance to the next round of our Service Competition. Now, come up to receive your participant tassels, then line up over there!"

Everyone surges forward, including my little brother and I. There are no orderly single-file lines here, just all of us pushing and shoving to get ahead.

In this utter chaos, I hear my name being called.

"Semmi! Ei!"

I turn around and see my Bisfuri coworker Dunea, the older of the two women who were handling the set decoration and design for the episodes of the show. She's not wearing her formal black wig today, but a simple white cotton kerchief over her shortly cropped hair, in stark contrast to her dark brown skin.

"*Nefero eos*, Dunea!" I call back, waving, then make my way closer to her, with Uru following. "Are you ready for this?"

Dunea looks anxious and tired. "I'm not sure I can do this," she tells me, tapping my arm with her bony hand, as we continue to shove our way forward. "You on the other hand, are young, and can run, and this youngster looks spry—"

"This is my brother Urumer." I pat Uru's shoulder. "He can definitely run!"

Dunea nods, smiling at him.

". . . *Eos*," Uru mumbles a greeting to my coworker.

And then we're at the front, before the tables.

The Sumerad representatives quickly accept our thumb prints and names, verify identities, and give us bright pink tassels. Heartbeats later, we are on the vast lawn, spread out in a wide horizontal line of people poised like runners. We stand shoulder to shoulder, Uru on my right, Dunea on my left, with endlessly more people beyond us in either direction.

A gong is struck, its low sound echoing deeply.

And we're off.

I SPRINT FORWARD, toward the closest portion of the fence, my focus on the red stones scattered sparsely on the ground. The first arrivals there are already grabbing the stones, stuffing them in pockets, in aprons made of their clothing, and other places on their persons. And then they run forward a few more steps, and pick up more. . . .

The unforeseen result is, as the fastest people get to the stones ahead of others, there are fewer and fewer red stones left to pick. The only thing left to do is to run ahead of them and start picking up further along the perimeter of the fence.

Which is what Uru and I end up doing, along with many others. We might as well be playing a variation of the game of leap-over-*chazuf* just to get to the next spot with any red stones still available.

I step, bend down, and stuff the stones in the big pocket of my skirt, then run a few paces to the next red stone and repeat. . . . The process is stupidly tedious, and involves constant bending and straightening at a rapid tempo.

Soon, my skirt pocket is bulging with rocks, and I see the same thing happening with Uru's pants on both sides where his deep pockets are sewn.

Any more rocks, and we're going to overflow.

Checking our competition, I see most people are in the same predicament. Many of the women are using their skirts as aprons, and I do the same thing, pulling up the edges by the hems and continuing to throw in red stones. . . .

At the same time, we persist forward, moving quickly along

the perimeter of the property fence, which is huge and endless. At this point, I note that many of the participants have given up on grabbing any more rocks and are simply running ahead, as instructed, following the metallic fencing, burdened by as much as they can carry.

I see a big guy waddling ahead of me with overflowing shirt pockets and a hat filled like a sack . . . Several kids, Uru's age, have their shirts completely off, using them as bags . . . a woman nearly stumbles, with her skirt carefully tied in multiple knots, and each section completely full of red stones. All of them are having trouble running now.

Dunea is far behind us now, overburdened and barely able to drag along her rock-filled skirt just to walk, much less sprint.

"Enough stones, Uru . . ." I call out. "Let's just go, or we won't be able to make it in time."

"Yeah, okay," he gasps out, struggling with his load.

"You have too much. . . . Just throw some of them away, or you won't run fast enough."

He nods, and lets go of several handfuls.

We start to run along the fence, passing many others ahead of us. Even loaded with stones, we still run well.

By the time we go around the whole estate, we're struggling and out of breath, but we're some of the earliest arrivals at the finish line, back to where we started, near the tables.

Here, we show our tassels, give our names to register our time, and then unload our red stones.

Panting, I stand in a spot next to Uru at the tables and wipe sweat off my forehead, while a Sumerad official counts my pile of rocks. Same thing is happening with Uru.

We exchange tired smiles, and watch others arrive far behind us.

"You have one hundred-nineteen stones," the Sumerad worker before me announces after counting everything. "It's sufficient to pass. Your time is also sufficient to pass. Advance to the second round. Next!"

"You have one hundred-and-eight stones," a different worker tells Uru. "You pass the count limit. And your time is sufficient, so you pass. Advance to the next round."

The Sumerad officials direct us to a different section of the lawn, this time away from the fence. Here, a wide stone-rimmed fountain pulses with water sparkling in the sun.

Uru and I walk toward it, while we see many other people being dismissed from the Competition. They trudge away in disappointment, and Dunea is among them. She waves at me sadly and shakes her head to indicate failure.

"What now?" Uru mumbles, as we stand with a much smaller group of contenders, waiting for our next set of instructions.

Not too far from us, no more than fifty paces from the fountain, is some kind of weird contraption and several Sumerad workers. A small wooden tub sits on top of what must be a weighing platform. One end of a long pole with a shallow groove cut in it, rests over the tub at a slight downward angle. The other end of the pole is suspended from an upright wooden post—erected near the rim of the fountain—which keeps it higher up, creating a gradual incline.

Several small wooden pails and buckets are stacked on the ground, halfway between the fountain and the tub contraption.

Now, a Sumerad official speaks, addressing us: "Your next task is to use those small pails to fill that tub with water from the fountain. You must do it as quickly as possible, and you will be timed. However, you may only fill your pails five times."

"Easy!" my brother Uru whispers loudly, glancing at me with excitement.

"Be aware, all the pails have holes in them, so you will lose water," the official continues. "Therefore, you have a choice. You can either run very quickly carrying your pail directly to the tub, and hoping that enough water remains. Or you can stand next to the fountain and use your pail to carefully pour the water into the gulley of that long beam, hoping that it makes it into the tub."

"Crap of a goat. . . ." I shake my head at Uru.

"At the end of your attempt, the tub will be weighed," the official concludes. "If there is sufficient water for our purposes, you will pass. Otherwise, you will be disqualified. The tub will be drained for the next person. And now, line up, one at a time, and begin!"

People around us make grumbling noises, but we all line up. Uru and I are not too far from the front of the queue, so we get the opportunity to watch other people try this task first and hopefully learn from them.

The first man in line is given a bucket, and the timer is set. He chooses to run quickly back and forth from the fountain, five times. Each time we see him leave a wet trail on the grass as he spills most of the water through the holes in the bucket before reaching the tub.

When it's time for weighing, the tub is woefully short of being full. And the man is disqualified and dismissed. Several of the Sumerad workers step forward and upturn the tub, so that it's empty again. And the next person is called.

A woman decides to use the other technique. Standing near the fountain, she fills her leaky pail with water and carefully attempts to pour it on the wooden pole. Most of the water spills over the sides of the pole and only a small trickle runs along the long groove in the center and reaches the tub many paces away. While all of this is happening, her pail continues to leak.

The tub is weighed once again, and the result is even worse. The woman is disqualified. She sobs quietly as she walks away, while the Sumerad workers again overturn the tub.

The next few people in line try different things. One man tries plugging the holes in the pail with his arms and torso, as he runs awkwardly, splashing water all over himself. He manages to get more water in the tub, but his time is too slow, so he is disqualified on that basis. The man curses loudly as he walks away.

Several people try to pour their water over the lip of the long pole while hugging their pails. One *chazuf* takes off his shirt and wraps it around the pail, and still the water leaks through and he gets dismissed. A small skinny girl runs fast but drops her pail twice which gets her dismissed. An older woman cleverly grabs a few rocks and drops them inside her bucket to line the bottom and minimize the holes. Unfortunately, there are more holes all along the sides too, so this does very little to help retain water, and in addition, she runs quite slow.

Since this particular Competition process happens very quickly, our turns come sooner than expected.

Uru goes first. He gives me one determined nod, and I whisper, "Run!"

Uru grabs his pail and sprints to the fountain. He fills the bucket with water, then sprints to the tub. My little brother is quick as a darting baby goat. Unfortunately, five buckets later, the tub does not contain sufficient water. "Almost, but not enough water. You fail. Dismissed!" says a bored Sumerad official, checking the weight.

Uru grimaces and frowns, then starts walking away, to wait for me on the fringes.

I nod at him in sympathetic disgust at his results.

It's my turn. There's no way I can run faster than Uru, so I pick up a pail and hurry to stand by the pole near the fountain. Quickly, I dip my pail in the water. As I bring it up, heavy in those initial moments, I observe with despair a cascade of liquid escaping from the sides and bottom out of numerous holes.

I balance the pail in my hands and raise it to the lip of the pole, the best I can, then start tipping it to pour. . . .

This is ridiculous. Water splashes uselessly on both sides,

and hardly any of it runs along the groove toward the distant tub. I try four more times, and overall it's a *hoohvak* exercise in uselessness.

I abandon the leaky pail, approach the tub, and stand sullenly as they weigh it. "Not enough water, and your time is slow. You fail. Dismissed!"

I snort, and don't bother to give the Sumerad *chazufs* even a single curse as I walk toward Uru.

WE LEAVE HOUSE SUMERAD BEHIND, with its manicured lawn, rose-covered fence, and *garooi* rocks and water, and sprint toward our third and final Competition for the day. Good thing we were done early, because we have even less time to get to our destination. We need to make it to Denderaat Bridge—which is halfway back to our original location on Circle Five—where House Ximunat is holding their Competition at tenth hour of Ra.

"Time? How . . . much . . . longer?" Uru asks me, panting, as we run. Even he's out of breath and energy by this point. I barely manage to glance at the map hologram on the comm badge, to note our tiny location dot and the destination marker dot.

"Almost . . . there," I reply, gasping for air. Our shoes slap hard against the cobbles, and the morning sun is starting to roast us from overhead. Lucky for us, it's still the cool season, else we'd be completely overheated by now.

As we approach the location of that bridge, there are fewer trees, and the houses and streets are more spare in their architecture and layout. In passing, we get only rare flashes of gold from the roofs, and only a few large estates. Still, it's a beautiful neighborhood.

As we come upon Denderaat Bridge, we see a crowd in the distance and the sparkle of canal waters in the sun. Once again, we're latecomers, and the formal instructions are already being proclaimed by the House Ximunat representatives with amplified voices. Three officials stand on top of a wide hovering platform that levitates at least the height of a tall man over street level. I don't see anything on the ground of the street or the surface of the bridge itself. No tables, no tents, only the Competition participants, their mass and numbers overloading the bridge.

"Everyone, clear the bridge!" the main Ximunat official calls out in a commanding tone. "Make room, immediately! Move this way, onto the street and line up! Line up! Line up, at the beginning of the bridge on this side, Circle Five!"

As he speaks, the crowd surges in our direction, and since Uru and I are already at the edge, we get pushed back and further down the street.

"What are we supposed to do?" I desperately ask the nearest people in front of me.

"Don't know," a man responds with a quick glance back at me, as he pushes forward ahead of us.

"Aww! *Man!*" Uru exclaims, as someone strikes him on the head with an elbow.

"Watch it!" I cry out angrily at the individual, at the same time as I press my brother closer to me and rub his head.

"Stop!" Uru whines at me, moving from my grasp, "I'm okay!"

"All right." I release Uru, letting him keep his pride.

"Attention, everyone!" The amplified voice of the Ximunat official breaks through the noisy chaos of the crowd. "Each one of you will receive a token and be scanned. Take it with you as you cross the bridge to the Circle Six side. Once you arrive at Circle Six, you will be scanned again. House Ximunat is looking for the fastest and smartest among you!"

"What's the task?" several people call out. "What must we do?"

"Your task," the Ximunat worker replies, "is to make it across the bridge, as fast as you can, using only *one foot*. You may *not* have both feet touching the ground at any time."

At once the crowd noise swells, full of exclamations of displeasure.

"What?"

"Are you crazy?"

"What kind of *hoohvak* task is this—"

I curse soundly, invoking many, many goats and their excrement. Uru does too, and so do most people around us.

"Be warned!" the Ximunat official continues. "Your tokens are specially calibrated with sensors that will determine if you attempt to cheat and put both feet on the surface of the bridge simultaneously. If that happens, your token will emit a tone. And you will be disqualified!"

"Bastet take you, *chazuf* . . ." I mutter.

"So, what—are we supposed to hop on one foot all the way across the bridge?" a woman behind me speaks angrily. "Who comes up with these things?"

"*Line up!* Line up to get your tokens now!" the Ximunat man continues.

And the rush toward the front resumes.

AFTER PUSHING AND SHOVING, we arrive at the entrance point to the bridge where we finally see several Ximunat workers holding containers filled with small red tokens. They don't even bother asking us for names or identity verification.

Uru and I grab our tokens, and stand as close to the front as we can—which is not that close, because the crowd is very thick here.

"So do we hop on one foot?" Uru asks me as we wait for the call to start.

I scratch my head and pull at my curly hair in anxiety and frustration. Crazy ideas tumble.

"We could, but that's so far to go, Uru. I don't know that anyone can hop for so long. Look how far the bridge goes over the canal!"

"Yeah. You can barely see Circle Six where the *garooi* bridge ends." Uru scrunches his forehead and looks angry. I don't blame him.

"One thing we can do is hold hands when we hop," I say. "For better balance."

"Yeah, we could."

Poor Uru. For him to consent to holding hands like a baby with his big sister is a *significant matter*. But—I'm glad he knows how serious this is.

"All right," I say, looking around at all the people around us and trying to see what they're doing or seem to be planning to do. "Let's think, let's think. . . ."

"I'm thinking!"

"I know. . . ." I exhale loudly, and then my anxious gaze falls on a familiar face, not too far ahead of us, maybe three people deep in the crowd.

"Girsul!" I exclaim. "Ei! Girsul!"

The young man turns his head, and I raise my hand to wave.

The moment he recognizes me, his cautious, tense expression loosens up a bit. "Semmi!" he calls back. But because we're so tightly packed, he can't exactly turn around or approach us. "May the gods smile on you!" he says.

"Luck and fortune to you too!" I call back.

In that moment, the Ximunat official calls out the start of the race. And the hovering platform on which he and the other officials stand, rises, speeding away ahead of us to the opposite end of the bridge.

Immediately, I grab Uru's hand, and it's a good thing too,

because the crowd surges forward like a wave and it's all we can do to keep our footing.

We watch the first competitors cross the line separating the street and Denderaat Bridge. Most of them begin hopping awkwardly forward on one foot, and in heartbeats many of them are pushed from behind and thrown off balance by the rest of the surging crowd. They flounder, their other feet come down, and their tokens go off with a small shrill alarm.

Disqualified.

People are being disqualified after just a few paces. . . . This is seriously bad.

We use the few moments remaining to us to observe what our predecessors are doing on the bridge. A few of the clever ones hop close to the fence along the sides which serves as the pedestrian walkway, and they hold on to the railing as they hop. Very soon, both sides of the bridge are full of people holding on to the railing.

And now it's our turn. . . .

"Let's go!" I exclaim, holding Uru's hand in a death grip.

And we hop forward onto the bridge.

One hop . . . two hop . . . three hop.

We're both pretty strong on our feet, but after about twenty hops, and trying to keep out of the way of others, and not get knocked down, we start panting hard. . . .

"Don't let go . . . of my hand . . ." I say, as Uru tugs at me with every hop. He is already doing better than I am, hopping a little farther each time, and I find it hard to keep up with his rhythm.

Meanwhile, people are dropping out all around us. Some are just old and in worse shape. I see older men and women putting both feet on the ground, and bending over, clutching their abdomens in exhaustion. . . . *Giving up.*

Alarms are going off everywhere.

Well, at least that's one good thing—the crowd is being thinned out, the farther we move along.

We start counting. "One . . . hop. Two . . . hop."

And again. "One . . . hop. Two . . . hop."

We've gone maybe one tenth the distance along the bridge.

And then, just as we pause briefly to catch our breaths, holding on to each other as we fight to keep our balance, a strange idea comes to me.

Prancing.

Goats don't prance, but fancy *sesemet* do.

It's a strange decorative gait where the animals literally hop from one foot to the other, quickly. And one foot is always held high off the ground, upraised, and then they switch. . . .

"Uru!" I say, "I have an idea! We don't hop, we prance like *sesemet*! Take big springing steps, shift from one foot to the other! We can do this!"

"Huh?" Teetering on one foot, Uru looks at me with weary resignation.

"Keep holding my hand, and I'll show you as I prance in place!"

And I demonstrate, doing the silly high steps, quickly switching from one foot to the other. And my token alarm does *not* go off!

Uru's expression brightens and he starts to grin. "Oh, yeah! I can do that!"

"Yeah!" I say, grinning back. "But keep holding hands, just in case!"

In reply, my brother prances in place, faster than any *sesemet* I know.

And laughing, we set off at a fine pace, prancing along toward the opposite side of the bridge.

Bastet help us!

. . .

IT TAKES us only a few daydreams to race to the end of Denderaat Bridge and arrive at Circle Six. We've literally left everyone else in the dust, far behind us, and we just might be the first ones to cross the finish line!

We stop prancing and stand, panting heavily, before the Ximunat officials. Two of them descend from the hovering platform and greet us with bland expressions. "Well done. You pass," the worker who scans my token says. "Your name?"

"Semmi—Semirameos, from Circle Ten, Denwen's Pit. And this is my brother Urumer."

"Very well." The same worker encodes my identity and then scans and encodes Uru's token. "Both of you stand over here, and wait for the final selection."

I nod, still breathing fast, and put my hands on Uru's shoulders, guiding him along. We move away a few steps as instructed, and stand awkwardly near the corner post of the bridge railing, waiting. The canal water sparkles cerulean blue and sun-white below. Uru looks up at me, grinning, and I smile back at him, feeling *good*, for once.

We don't have to wait long, as more competitors start coming in. People have seen us prancing and figured it out, so now everyone's doing it. Girsul is one of them, and I smile at him as he comes in, prancing from one foot to the other, and shows me a hand sign of approval. He gets scanned, then comes up to join us.

In moments, a much smaller crowd, but a crowd nevertheless, has gathered on this side of the bridge. At last, the main Ximunat official up on the platform calls out time and formally closes the race.

"Congratulations, all of you who completed the task. Now you will be observed by the Lady of this Great House, who will choose among you."

In that same moment, an expensive hover car approaches, shining polished metal, fierce, bright red like a crimson sunset.

It's been hovering nearby, and now that the race is over, it floats closer and stops near the platform.

The door opens, parting like a folded wing, and a fine Lady emerges. She is tall and stately, with up-swept dark brown hair covered in a golden net, salt-white skin, and she wears a sleek, shimmering dress of expensive silvery-rose fabric. The dress hugs her elegant curves, and the wide collar around her neck is studded with gems that turn to rainbow fire in the sun. Similar bright gems sparkle at her earlobes, and bands of fine gold wrap along her pale wrists and arms like serpents. Her shoes are gilded platforms with razor pointed toes. And her nails are sharp claws painted *niktos* blue and studded with tiny pearls.

The Lady's shadowed dark eyes are cold and impassive in a beautiful oval face with crimson painted lips that do not smile.

As soon as the Ximunat officials see her, they all bow deeply in obeisance.

The Lady flicks one clawed finger at them, and says in a bored, sensual voice, "Proceed."

"At once, My Lady!" the main official exclaims in a different voice of servility, straightening. And he turns to the crowd and again addresses us in the booming manner.

"This is the First Lady of House Ximunat—line up before the great Lady Ashura!"

And the official points toward the area where we must stand.

We all push forward, then line up in a long queue. Girsul and I exchange glances, while Uru looks happy and excited, while we all stand as straight as we can.

"Stand up proudly and show yourselves before First Lady Ashura! Only *twenty-five* of you will be chosen!"

My heart begins to race. . . .

First Lady Ashura Ximunat begins strolling along our line. She is followed by a servant holding a bowl of rose-colored tassels. Apparently, there are twenty-five.

The Lady stops before a muscular, well-built young man and

looks him over with her hidden gaze. Almost carelessly, she stretches her hand to the servant behind her, who immediately bows and hands her a tassel.

"You," she says, and hands him the tassel.

The chosen young man smiles, and then bows curtly before her, receiving his tassel of Service.

Lucky *chazuf*! He's just gotten himself a place on the ships!

Before he straightens, the Lady has already passed, moving on to the next person in line.

Uru suddenly clutches my hand nervously, as she draws nearer and nearer to us. I give him a reassuring squeeze and nod.

The tassels are given out sparingly. It is likely that the Lady wants to observe all of us first, then make her final selections. Because she picks up her pace, barely glancing at the finalist competitors as they stand before her.

When she approaches Girsul, both Uru and I hold our breaths.

We're next.

Lady Ashura's musky perfume precedes her, carried by the breeze. And then she stops before me.

I feel an icy stab of nerves as her sharp gaze lands very briefly on me. And then she continues on to Uru . . . and then the next person in line.

Then, Lady Ashura Ximunat heads back, for a second pass.

We all exhale then hold our breaths again.

But, with a sinking feeling, I watch the Lady pass Uru without even looking at him again, and the same thing for me, and Girsul. Not a glance at any of us.

She stops a few more times further down the line, and during this second pass she hands out all the remaining tassels. Most of the choices are handsome, well-built young men, with just a few of the prettiest girls thrown in.

"You, and you," she concludes. Then, without another word, she turns her back on the rest of us and gets inside her hover car.

"Congratulations to those fortunate twenty-five of you who have been chosen to join the service staff of House Ximunat on the great sky journey!" the official cries loudly. "Stay here for your formal employment registration and further instructions. The rest of you—we regret, but you are dismissed!"

I stand, my heart quietly breaking, squeezing my little brother's hand.

"But . . ." Uru looks at me with confusion. "But *we won*! We made it across the bridge, we were the *first*! Why didn't she pick us, Semmi?"

"I know, Uru," I whisper. "And I *don't* know. I'm so sorry."

Seeing as I'm this close to crying, and Uru is a confounded mess, Girsul turns to my brother and gives him a light slap on the shoulder. "Hey, little *chazuf*, we don't need House Ximunat anyway. There are many more Competitions still to come. Cheer up! Your sister—that's your sister, right? Your sister, and you, and I—we will make it somewhere!"

"Thanks, Girsul," I say, regaining my breathing and swallowing back the lump in my throat. "Uru, this is my Bisfuri coworker, Girsul. He and I have to get back to work now. But you—I want you to run home and tell *Mei-Ma* that all will be well!"

D espite my confident words, Uru still appears dejected. But seeing my forced smile, he takes a deep breath, tosses his head defiantly in the direction of the Ximunat officials, then speeds away in the direction of the nearest bus stop.

"See you really late tonight!" I call out in my brother's wake. "Remind *Mei-Ma* I'm working late—"

Girsul and I watch my little brother break into a run across Denderaat Bridge, while the Service Competition crowd disperses around us. Most people also head back across the Bridge toward Circle Five, while a few remain here on Six and move onward, disappearing along the streets of this Circle.

"I suppose we need to hurry to work," I say, milling from foot to foot in restless anxiety, while Girsul checks messages on his comm badge.

"No rush," he says, looking up. "They don't officially expect us until seventh hour of Khe. They know everybody's at the Service Competitions today, all over the City. Not just Domestic, but many other kinds too, held later in the afternoon. So, we're blessedly spared from going in immediately. Praise to all the gods of Poseidon."

"Oh," I say. "All right."

"We have some time to waste, and I'm hungry," he continues, rubbing his sweaty forehead with the back of his hand. Indeed, the heat from the blazing sun is relentless, and it's now late in the eleventh hour of Ra, very close to noon.

"Want to go find some food stalls?" I ask. "I haven't even been paid yet, so I don't have many coins, but—"

"Oh yeah, that's right." Girsul casts a concerned gaze of his dark eyes on me. "You're so new at Bisfuri, that it's only been what, two days now?"

"Three. I mean, this is my third."

"Right. You'll definitely get paid tonight after the Bisfuri party. They're good about that kind of thing, and after late evening work they usually give us additional coins."

"Good to know." I scratch the top of my bare arm where some kind of annoying black insect has landed, so I swat it away.

"You know, we're at Six now, and we're not far from my home."

"Really? You live here on Six?" I crane my neck to stare at Girsul sideways, giving him a semi-serious appraising look. "Fancy neighborhood."

The young man wrinkles his forehead and gives me a lopsided smile. "Yeah, not what you think. Come along, and I'll show you where I live. My brother and I have a secret hiding hole in the back of a rich *ter's* storage building. Well, not that secret really—the old man knows we're there. But he's decent, and he tolerates us, and a few other souls, as long as we're quiet and don't make a mess. We also clean his back yard regularly, and cut the grass, in exchange for a place to sleep."

"I see."

"So, let's go. I've got to check up on my brother anyway."

And we start walking.

. . .

AFTER HALF AN HOUR of navigating shady, tree-lined streets interspersed with long stretches of storefronts, we turn a corner into another smaller street with three large two-story buildings surrounded by greenery. They look semi-industrial, and the nearest one appears to be partially abandoned, or at least in minor disrepair, and attached to some kind of vast property surrounded by a tall metal fence.

The fence has sturdy wrought iron gates, but they are missing a lock. And the cobbles past the gates are overgrown with grass between each paver stone.

There are more tall trees farther in the back, and I can see the glint of an ornate gilded roof—part of a formal estate structure built in the old style, probably in the past century. The estate building lies beyond an additional inner fence with properly locked gates, and a cleared driveway, so it is better maintained.

"The old *ter* lives in that one." Girsul points at the gilded roof. "We're in the storage house, right here. Follow me."

I hurry after Girsul as he walks briskly along the grassy cobblestones and opens a weathered side-door of the storage house.

The interior is dim, and somehow cluttered with junk—an old abandoned warehouse with a high ceiling, filled with covered broken furniture, wooden crates, and some kind of ancient parts and mechanical equipment. Along the perimeter of the walls, I notice tents—that is, random pieces of board and wood and sackcloth tarp clobbered together into makeshift shelters. And scattered randomly are several small firepits built out of piled limestone bricks. One or two are smoking with low flames.

Three plainly dressed figures emerge, two middle aged women and an old man leaning on a stick. They give Girsul and me curious glances. One of the women hobbles crookedly, lame in one foot.

"Home early?" the old man says in a grouchy voice. "What

happened? Lose your fancy job, boy? What did I tell you? I said, they'll eventually get rid of you for being late—"

"*Nefero dea*, Muz," Girsul says to the lame woman, ignoring the old *chazuf*. "How's Jema?"

"Jema is sleeping," the woman replies. "I gave 'im breakfast, he calmed down, and now you owe me two more turnips."

"Will get you the turnips and more tomorrow," Girsul says. "We get paid tonight. The nobles at my fancy job are having a big party."

"Who's that?" The other woman squints suspiciously and points at me.

"I'm Semmi," I reply. "I work with him."

"Yeah, she works with me; she's safe, don't worry. Nobody's taking your spot or your tent." Girsul chuckles, then throws me a mischievous glance. "They don't like it when strangers show up here, since this is a prime spot, a well-kept secret in this neighborhood. A nice building, with good walls and roof and no drafts, even a shower stall in that booth in the corner. Usually, I don't bring anyone to our camp. But I figured, you're okay."

"Oh, *sha* knows, I'm okay," I say with a little pride in my voice. "I have a home in Denwen's Pit, so not going to take anyone's room."

"Good," the woman called Muz says. "We don't want any more people squatting here. We're full as it is."

"Why aren't you at work?" the old man persists. "Everyone else is at work except us old ones. What's happening with the youth of this forsaken City?"

"Remember—Service Competitions happening, all over Poseidon." Girsul says to him with annoyance. "I explained to you already—how many times, now, Neno? About the Sky Rock falling and the noble Houses hiring servants to fly away into the sky with them before the world ends. Today many of them will be choosing servants. They gave many people the morning off, so that we can participate in the Competitions. We must return to work later tonight."

The old man called Neno shakes his head and makes a crude gesture. "Eh, there's no Sky Rock. Who heard of such a thing? Don't know what kind of *shar-ta-haak* lies they tell you. The world's not ending. No one's going to die. It's all lies. We drop dead when the gods call us, that's all. No sooner, no later."

"Whatever, *garooi*. . . ." Girsul frowns in increasing annoyance. "I have to go see Jema now, and then we'll be on our way back to work. Go sit on your sack and mind your own business."

The old man growls in reply, then turns around and shambles away, clacking with his stick to support his uneven gait.

"Come, Semmi, my hiding hole is that way," Girsul says, moving casually past the two women.

We walk to the back, past several tents, and Girsul stops before one of them. He pushes aside the tarp fabric, bends his head at the low entrance, and steps inside.

I follow him.

The tent is not large, barely the size of my small bedroom back home in Denwen's Pit. There are two low cots, a few sacks, and three crates, serving as table and two chairs. In one of the chairs, padded with a blanket and propped against a tall wooden board for a back, sits a young, skinny child with dark, longish hair similar in coloration to Girsul's own. The boy is slumped over, head lolling to the side, eyes closed. He is drooling slightly, and appears to be fast asleep. His breath comes in occasional moans. He appears to be no older than my own brother Uru.

"Is he sick?" I ask.

But Girsul puts a finger up to his lips to silence me.

Too late. The child hears my voice, and starts awake. His brown eyes open wide with alarm. And immediately his little face contorts with pain and he begins to whine in a high voice, pausing only to breathe in ragged gasps.

"Ah, crap," Girsul whispers, shaking his head at me. Then he turns his attention to the boy and pats him on his head, then uses a small rag to wipe his mouth and cheeks. "Hey, now, I'm back, Jema! See, here I am! Hey, look what we have here! Your little *mamai*!"

Girsul picks up a little fabric pillow doll that's been lying in Jema's lap. He shakes it and then offers it to Jema, who pauses moaning for a moment, mesmerized, then resumes.

"Bastet, I'm sorry . . ." I whisper. "I didn't mean to wake him."

"It's all right. Jema is easily disturbed by most people, strangers especially. Needs me there to calm down, and tolerates Muz, for feedings. Everyone else, not so much. And yeah, she's sick. . . ." Girsul pauses abruptly, then quickly corrects himself. "I mean, *he's* sick."

I widen my eyes, and give Jema a closer look. "Wait, that's a girl?"

"Sh-h-h-h! *Quiet!*" Girsul's expression is suddenly alarmed. He pushes himself close to me and raises his hand to hover near my mouth, almost touching but not quite. His head is shaking back and forth as if to negate whatever is happening. And then he continues in a hurried whisper. "Ah, *varqood* me. . . . Okay, yes, *she*—but you cannot tell anyone! *No one here knows!* Except for Muz, no one."

"Oh . . ." I say, in a similar whisper. "So, she's your sister?"

"Exactly. But they have to think it's a boy, else I can't leave her alone here. The camp's generally safe, but a few *chazufs* here can't be fully trusted. Easier to overlook a pitiful boy than a girl. Jema is left all alone most of the day, with only a small, lame woman to protect her, until I return from work."

"I understand."

Girsul continues shaking his head. "At least Jema is still

young, only eight. But soon it will be more difficult to hide who she is. It's why I keep on checking up on her throughout the day."

I nod. "And why you're late to work in the morning."

Girsul snorts. "So—you've heard them all complain about me at Bisfuri, and even old Neno here. Yeah. She wakes in panic from pain or from choking, and it takes longer, most mornings, to calm her down. Plus, she has breathing trouble, so her wheezing fits take a while, until I give her the herb tea."

"How did the two of you end up living in this camp?" I ask, while Girsul turns momentarily to again distract Jema with her doll, which the child clutches then drops again in her lap. "You don't have any other family?"

"Not anymore. Father died long before the golden gods' arrival." Girsul speaks blandly and doesn't look at me. "And Mother and uncle died last year from the great plague. We used to live in our own home, but I couldn't keep paying the rent on three rooms, since there were only two of us left. Jema was born slow in her head and sickly, so not much help from her. We got evicted, but I soon met a kind old *chazuf* who brought us here to this camp. He's no longer here, the gods have taken him, but I remember and pray for him every week."

"So, you've been living here a year?" I pick up the fabric doll and start moving it in funny circles before Jema's anxious face, while crossing my eyes briefly to make a silly face. "What about your job at Bisfuri?"

"Yeah, almost a year living here—a good deal, with no rent to pay. And ten months working for Bisfuri. Another fortunate thing." Girsul turns and looks hard at me, his gaze becoming intense. "Listen, Semmi. Don't tell *Ter* Aten where I live, all right? He doesn't need to know I'm squatting. Had I told him, he mightn't have hired me."

"Really? You think he's like that?" I ask.

Girsul sighs then shrugs. "Probably not. But—I don't know. I can't risk finding out. *Ter* Aten is a fair man, a good man, but he's a nobleman of the highest sort. If he suddenly decides that he can't have that kind of staff around him—"

"Well, it might still be better for you if you tell him eventually—about your sister, at least—rather than just letting him think you're late for *hoohvak* reasons."

"Maybe. Yeah. But—never mind now." Girsul looks at me steadily. "Promise me you won't say anything."

"I won't, don't worry."

Girsul exhales in relief, then smiles at me. "Thanks, Semmi. I knew I could count on you."

WE SPEND about a quarter of an hour sitting on crates and entertaining Jema by shaking her doll. With each passing moment her face grows calmer. Eventually she looks directly at me without fear and makes a semi-intelligible sound, smacks her lips, and finally smiles widely.

"Hey, look at you!" I smile back at her, and then stab a finger at my own chest, saying "I'm Semmi!"

"Shem. . . . Shem." Jema echoes me, and gurgles. Apparently, she doesn't speak much or very well.

Meanwhile, Girsul grins at his sister and clears her mess of tangled curling hair around her forehead with a few strokes of a comb. "Jema likes you, Semmi. That's good, she doesn't like many people."

"I have a funny face," I say, and stick out my tongue, then raise my hands over my ears and pant like a dog, which makes Jema laugh even more.

"Jema! We have to go now, but I'll be back soon," he finally says. "Here, give the little *mamai* a combing, her hair needs it!" And he places the comb in Jema's fingers.

Immediately, the girl starts running the comb over the fabric doll which has strands of string for hair.

We get up, and quietly exit the tent.

GIRSUL and I catch a bus that goes directly to Circle Two, and
arrive at the Bisfuri estate within the hour. We still haven't eaten,
but Girsul tells me that he usually gets fed at the estate kitchens
—as do many of the other serving staff.

"What? Free of charge?" I exclaim, stopping in place, when
he reveals this amazing information.

"Free of charge. It's part of your employment benefit."

"Bastet! I didn't know," I say, as we walk past the fancy
grand gates and enter the main building from the delivery
entrance, then proceed directly into the hallway leading to the
kitchens. At this hour, the place is unusually busy, with kitchen
and other staff running everywhere, shoving past us with boxes
and crates, and fresh produce and decorations deliveries being
unloaded. The household is already getting ready for this
evening's major festive event.

"Oh, did no one tell you about meals?" Girsul makes a
laughing sound.

"No! And I've starved during the day these past two days,
not knowing what to do!"

Girsul chuckles. "Well, now you know. And so, we eat. *First*,
we eat. Then, we go feed the *goats*."

"Ah . . . yes." I recall the *pegasei* who haven't been cared for
since yesterday. "Are they okay, you think? Should we maybe go
feed them first?"

"Nah, they'll be fine." Girsul walks ahead of me into the heat
of the largest estate kitchen—a bright room filled with clanking
dishes and rapidly moving servants.

The warm aromatic air assails me, bursting with wonderful
food smells. They're baking something sweet, and frying
something savory. And, oh, sacred Bastet strike me, they even
have bowls of mushrooms! Huge piles of them, all fancy, all

different kinds (with which I am direly familiar). Before my disbelieving eyes, cooks grab handfuls of mushrooms, tossing them nonchalantly into different steaming pots, and onto various sizzling griddles, grills, and pans.

"Wait," I say, pausing tentatively. "Are you sure we're allowed here?"

Girsul curls his lip in amused mockery, then points to a long table in the back, away from the fierce heat of the ovens, where at least ten people wearing staff uniforms and different service tassels are seated, eating. I recognize some familiar faces among them, including the good-looking and arrogant technician Mihravat with his sharp blue eyes, who glances up from his plate to observe us with subtle disdain and pointed superiority.

I really wonder what that *chazuf's* problem is. . . .

But it doesn't matter.

I timidly follow Girsul to a serving station, follow his lead and pick up a big, shiny, metallic plate (the like of which I've never touched before) from a tall stack. When it's my turn, the server fills my plate with hearty portions of different amazing foods from a variety of dishes.

It smells like a feast of the gods, oh gracious Bast!

For the first time in my life, I'm about to taste *mushrooms*.

CHAPTER
TWENTY-THREE

I sit down on the long bench seat next to Girsul, with my immense plate loaded with food. *"Nefero dea,"* Girsul says to everyone, and I repeat the greeting.

The nearest people across the table from us stop chatting and look at us, and several others farther down the table (and in a foul mood) barely acknowledge us, while the middle-aged woman next to Girsul nods and then pats him on the shoulder. Then everyone resumes their meal and conversation, which is all about the Service Competitions and the various dire outcomes. Turns out, Girsul, Uru, and I were not the only ones treated awfully—so far, everyone has been dismissed from the various Competitions they entered all over the City.

"Kinakra has no honor," a man says, taking a deep swallow from a beer mug. "After all the *shar-ta* little tasks we had to perform, they accused me of stealing, as a test of my compliance." He spits over his shoulder.

"No, Sumerad was much worse." A younger man waves his eating utensil with angry passion. "Impossible *shebet*. Buckets full of holes in which you had to carry water. *Varqood* that. . . ."

I take a deep breath, pick up my shiny metallic spoon, and

dig into my plate. The first dollop of food is loaded with well-browned mushroom pieces in a thick sauce, and I carefully put one mushroom chunk in my mouth, tasting it almost fearfully.

A juicy, savory, *earthy* burst of unbelievable *flavor* hits me.

Holy Mother Bast! This tastes like chicken! Or goat! Or at least what I remember of meat, having last eaten it several years ago. Even the texture is resilient and reminiscent of very good cuts—the best cuts of meat! No wonder the wealthy elites make such a big deal of these strange earth fungi.

I chew, swallow with a hungry gulp, and make an inadvertent sound of pleased surprise. "This—this mushroom is *good*!" I announce, like a *hoohvak*.

"Oh yeah?" Girsul pauses tearing a piece of flatbread and glances at me. "You like it? Or just that one mushroom in particular?"

"*Shaitunaat*, yes!" I continue, ignoring his minor tease, and then take another spoonful, this time heaping. "I didn't know!"

"You didn't know what?" asks a dark-skinned young woman across from me with a rose-colored domestic service tassel.

"I didn't know what they were like," I elaborate. "Haven't eaten mushrooms before. Worked with them at my previous job, but never tasted them."

"She is new, just started here," someone down the table whispers with a chuckle, and I feel the sudden heat of self-awareness rising in my head.

"So new she forgot to wear her tassel. What is your line of service, girl?" a neatly dressed, thin-lipped older woman asks with a stern look. She, too, has the rose tassel of a general domestic on her impeccable unform collar.

"Her name is Semmi," Girsul says to the speaker. "And she works with me for *Ter* Aten directly."

"So, she's what, a messenger like you?" The woman gestures to Girsul's red tassel.

"I—I wasn't given a tassel," I say, straining my forehead with a mixture of continued shame and rising anxiety, not to mention irritation at some of these people. "And *Ter* Bisfuri has assigned me various tasks. We look after some of his prize animals. Also, I'll be working as a Storyteller tonight, at the party."

A few people raise eyebrows and give me evaluating stares.

"She'll probably get her tassel tomorrow," Girsul adds.

"Better make sure she dresses appropriately, if she is to entertain the noble guests and not be an embarrassment to the noble Bisfuri. That thing she has on is unacceptable," the same stern, older woman says to the room in general, then again narrows in on me. "Where's your uniform?"

My mouth parts. "I don't have one. They only gave me the badge—badge comm—when I started. It was late in the day—"

"Someone in Staff Services did a very poor job of registering your hire." The woman frowns with a world-weary sound of disgust.

"It was *Ter* Bisfuri himself who registered me," I say.

The older woman appears impressed enough to momentarily go silent. "Well! Then you need to talk to the Steward in charge of employment—that will be Steward Hekadut. He will provide you with all the rest of the necessities, including a proper uniform and tassel."

"I will, thank you," I respond politely. And then I look down at my food and resume eating the amazing savory mushrooms, the very excellent turnips, and other vegetables and grains on my plate.

And the servants get back to their complaining.

AFTER THE MEAL IS OVER, Girsul and I hurry to the stables to take care of the *pegasei*. When we step behind the black curtain, the three motionless goats are all very *dim*. Dangerously dim. Their rainbow light is barely present, and only a faint radiance swirls just underneath the surface of their unnatural fur. Their strange eyes don't even focus on us as we approach.

Ah, Bast! A jolt of worry runs through me.

Girsul also looks somewhat troubled at our obvious neglect.

"We took too long . . ." he mutters. "Let's hurry and feed them before they dissolve completely."

"Next time, we feed them first! Didn't I say to feed them first?"

"Yeah, yeah," Girsul says, grabbing their harness leads. Quickly, we drape them in black fabric, and rush outside into the afternoon sunshine. In our usual hidden spot in the yard, we let the *pegasei* feed to their content, and then some, until the poor things resume their brilliant shine.

By the time we return them to the stables, the sun has moved far in the sky, and soon it will be sunset. Fortunately, the estate is in such a hectic state of preparation for the evening festivities that no one gets in our way, and the stables are mostly empty.

"All right, what now?" I ask, as Girsul and I make our way back to the main building past rushing servants.

"I need to go up to *Ter* Aten's Quarters and move decoration sets and then set up music equipment in the great hall." Girsul rubs the back of his head. "And you—I suppose you need to go see the Steward about a uniform or whatever they might want you to wear."

"You mean Steward Hekadut? The one that woman mentioned?"

He nods. "Old Bairama is sharp as a *bakris* vulture, but she's right. Just get the uniform and the tassel and then come back upstairs to help out."

"Where is he?"

Girsul takes me down the hallway, past the stretch of multiple kitchens—but just before it opens into the grand front hall area—and shows me a door with a black tassel hanging on it, to indicate management.

I take a deep breath and knock on the door, while Girsul runs off.

JUST AS I KNOCK, the door opens on its own. Two maidservants emerge, carrying large bundles of fabric. They push past me, and I try to step aside, barely getting out of their way.

I find myself inside a front office alcove with a desk in the front. Beyond it is a very long room that resembles a closet, with wardrobes running against both walls, full of hanging clothing and stacks of more fabric atop chests and boxes.

A large middle-aged man with olive skin, thick black eyebrows, and a black curled wig sits behind the desk. He wears a trim, well-fitted uniform and a black tassel at the collar. A digital tablet rests on the desk before him and he taps its surface with his fingers. I note the gleam of his well-polished nails and several gold seal rings.

There are additional seals and formal legal papyrus scrolls stacked all around him, taking up most of the table surface. Seeing me stumble into the room, he looks up.

"Yes?"

"*Nefero dea*—" I begin.

"Name?" His tone of voice is authoritative and cool.

"Semirameos."

Sharp black eyes stare at me. "Family Name?"

I open my mouth. "It's just Semirameos. Or Semmi. I'm from Denwen's Pit. *Ter* Bisfuri hired me three days ago. I was told to come here and—"

"I see." The man looks down at his digital tablet and enters something then peruses the results. "You are registered by *Ter* Benaten Bisfuri as a general domestic. And—a few other things."

"I'm supposed to be a Storyteller today, during the party." I bite my lip anxiously. "I'm not sure if I'm supposed to wear a uniform. Also, I don't have a tassel—"

"Three days. Why didn't you come by earlier?"

"I don't—I mean, I didn't know. So very sorry, *Ter*—"

"You may address me as Steward Hekadut," he interrupts.

"Yes, Steward Hekadut, *Ter*—" I shut up, and put one hand over my *garooi* mouth.

"*Just*—Steward Hekadut."

Wordlessly, I nod.

"Very well." The Steward stands up, pushes back his chair, and beckons me closer with one manicured finger. "Stand up straight, and turn."

I do as he says, lifting my shoulders and then turn around, feeling awkward.

"You're a skinny girl, fortunately, so not much fabric required." Steward Hekadut examines me up and down. "However, you're possibly too tall for the standard cut. It will need to be a slightly longer skirt—we'll have to check inventory. How old are you?"

"Sixteen," I reply after a tiniest pause, to make sure in my mind.

The Steward meanwhile takes out a fancy measuring device from his desk drawer, the kind of gadget that I've seen people in the marketplace use to measure length of fabric and depth of sacks. He points it at me, then checks something in his tablet.

"Follow me." And he starts walking past the front office section into the long wardrobe area.

I stare with curiosity, and see endless rows of men's and women's uniform components, top and bottom, then more dresses and pants and jackets of other kinds, including items in much more expensive and glittering fabric. There are also rows of various shoes, work boots, and other specialized footwear on the lowest shelf running along the wall perimeter. Meanwhile, wigs, hats, scarves, and other headgear fill the upper shelves stretching above the clothing.

"So much stuff!" I whisper. "Like a marketplace. A really big stall. . . ."

The Steward ignores my nervous mumbles, and comes to a stop before some pristine uniforms hanging in a row. He selects a shirt, a skirt, and a belt, and hands them to me. "Try these on —*not* here, over there, behind the screen. Meanwhile I'll look in our entertainment section for something more suitable for your Storyteller work this evening. Uniforms are strictly for food servers tonight, so this will not do."

I look around and see a small niche nearby, with a privacy screen. Glad to *not* have to strip down to my poverty underwear in front of this upper-rank supervisor, I hurry to the cubicle. No doubt, the Steward is glad for the privacy screen too, considering how many people in questionable underclothing he might have to observe on a daily basis.

Behind the screen, I shed my clothes with the speed and agility of a monkey, then put on the fine uniform shirt and skirt, which fits somewhat loosely. Finally, I tie the belt around my waist, not quite sure what to do with the ends—I've seen how all the servants have their belts seamlessly folded away in some mysterious fashion.

There's a tall, floor-length mirror propped up against the wall, so that for once in my life I can actually see what I look like. . . . I can't think of a time I've been in the presence of such a luxury item of vanity, except for seeing them from a distance in the more expensive marketplace clothing stalls (which I've never dared approach), and on some media-box dramas populated by rich people.

When I emerge, Steward Hekadut takes one look at me and shakes his head. "Too loose. You'll need to be fitted by a seamstress, and that hem needs to be adjusted. But it will have to wait until tomorrow, after the staff's evening ordeal is over.

No seamstresses are currently available; they have higher priority work to do. Instead, put this on."

And Hekadut hands me what appears to be a flimsy length of glittering lavender fabric.

Hesitating, I open my mouth in amazement.

"Go on, take it. The Great House Bisfuri is *quite* generous with their employees in every way, including presentation. And a Bisfuri Storyteller needs to be exquisitely dressed for the elite audience. However—I expect you to take extreme care as you wear it. Any stains or rips in the fabric will be deducted from your pay. And trust me, you do *not* want to be paying for *this* level of outfit."

In silence, I take the impossible, expensive piece of fabric, and slink away to disappear again behind the screen. Here I divest myself of the new uniform, and then carefully examine the fancy costume that I must wear.

It appears to be a floor length one-piece dress with long sleeves and a high collar that has exquisite golden trim. Furthermore, the color is not merely lavender (which I thought at first glance), but a strange pearly rainbow of many hues, all fighting each other in the light, becoming dominant or receding, depending on how much shadow there is. . . .

It reminds me, in a way, of the iridescent colors of the *pegasei*.

My mouth remains open and my breath comes in shuddering gasps of wonder that I try to hold back so as not to make ridiculous noises—as I soon realize that I simply cannot fit this incredible, color-shifting dress over my old underclothing.

I must first strip naked . . . and wear it directly against my skin.

Holy gods of Poseidon! What is happening to me? Is this real?

With trembling fingers, I remove my plain undershirt, feeling sudden cool air against my body, and then pull down the bulky linen wrap-strip that I wear over my privates.

Dropping them both on the floor, I begin to carefully slide on the sparkling dress, starting with trying to get the collar over my big head with its curly mess of hair. It turns out, the collar is snapped together with some kind of complicated sewn-in pin and needs to be undone first.

What in all unholy shaitunaat *is this thing? Argh!*

It takes me long, terrifying moments to work on that collar. . . . Finally, it comes open. I slip the dress past my head and this time succeed. Then I attempt to thread my skinny arms through the sleeves.

The delicate fabric falls around me like spiderwebs, gently wrapping around my body, but not too tightly, while cascading below my hips and just past my ankles into a loose, swirling cloud. Despite being flimsy, it is not see-though (which I feared), and is demure around the neck.

The person I see in the long mirror is a strange young woman who has my face and head of hair but . . . she is *someone* else.

Bast, who sees all and knows all, help me. . . .

I step around the privacy screen, with the long fabric swishing softly around my feet in a luxurious manner which I've never experienced.

And then I approach the Steward.

He gives me a sharp, appraising glance and nods. "Fortunately, this dress fits you well. Be careful of the somewhat loose sleeves as you move, else they might snag on things around you. Fasten your collar. And put on this tassel—purple, for your role of entertainer, just for this evening." He hands me a purple tassel. "Tomorrow you'll wear the red messenger tassel— not general domestic pink—since *Ter* Bisfuri expects you to do much outside work that defies the usual category."

Awkwardly I fasten the pin at my throat, then attach the tassel to the center front of my gold collar. It contrasts beautifully with the gold and subtly matches the iridescent lavender fabric of the dress.

"Now, your shoes, and your face and hair," Hekadut says in a businesslike tone. "Your sandals are filthy, and your head a mess. Since you'll be entertaining under a bright light, you will need a professional stylist. I'll call Ribaheit to deal with you, since I'm no expert in the finer detail of latest fashion, and the noble guests will require it. Meanwhile, I'll pick out some suitable footwear for you. Wait here. Use the time to practice your Storytelling in your head."

And so, I stand in place, like a stupefied goat, while the Steward makes a call on his badge device. Afterwards, he goes down the length of the wardrobe area and returns with a few pairs of delicate gilded sandals.

"Try these on for size."

I pull off my dingy shoes and start trying on these expensive metallic things. The first pair hurts my feet, but the second feels fine. I take a few careful steps, feeling the gold ties wrapped around my ankles barely dig into my skin.

"These will work," Steward Hekadut says, handing me a sackcloth bag. "Now, pick up your own clothing and shoes and store them in here for tonight. Your new uniform too. Return to this room to pick them up before you go home tonight. Remember, tomorrow you must get the uniform adjusted. In the morning, talk to Seamstress Vilras."

"Yes, Steward Hekadut." I take the sack filled with my things and deposit it where he tells me, at the front of the wardrobe section, on one of the storage shelves full of employee belongings.

"Very well, we are concluded here. Return to your duties, and be sure to maintain your costume in clean, impeccable form until this evening. But first—go to see Stylist Ribaheit. She has been informed about you, and will complete your appearance for the evening."

"Yes, Steward Hekadut. Where do I go to see her?"

VERA NAZARIAN

"Return down the corridor in the direction of the kitchens and knock on the door with the purple tassel."

And I am dismissed.

I CAREFULLY LIFT the hem of my skirt so as not to sweep it along the floor, and then practically tiptoe down the hallway, taking careful steps in my gilded sandals that make delicate clanking noises with every stride.

Three doors down, I find the one with the purple tassel, and knock politely.

"Come in!" a woman's sonorous voice calls out loudly, rising against the noisy clamor coming from within.

I open the door and find myself in another office chamber, except this one is more brightly lit and even more visually chaotic. The longer portion of the room beyond the front section is filled with floor-to-ceiling shelves containing inexplicable garish objects, including decorative actor masks, musical instruments, boxes of colorful face paints, hair combs and brushes of every kind, jewelry boxes, jars of unguents, and bottles of various perfume—the blended aroma of which hits me with a powerful floral blast of earthy musk and blooming garden.

Several people are inside, mostly women, seated behind small tables with mirrors. They are chatting loudly, singing, and humming, while busy applying makeup and other cosmetics, and in many cases doing each other's hair. All of them wear a variety of incredible, sparkling or colorful costumes, and I realize that I, in my glittering dress, fit right in.

At the front desk sits a voluptuous middle-aged woman with a crimson wig and pale rosy skin. Her eyes are outlined in very dark kohl, and her lips are almost the same deep crimson as her wig. Her plump shoulders are covered by a black shimmering veil worn over a similar *niktos* dress.

"Nefero dea," I say. "I'm looking for Ribaheit."

"'Dea," the woman replies with a good-natured expression. "That would be me. Are you Semirameos?"

"Yes, just Semmi. Steward Hekadut sent me. He says my hair and face need to be—"

"Yes, I can see you need some work," Ribaheit interrupts me kindly with the lift of a rounded hand, while examining me. "Don't worry, I'll take care of you. So, a Storyteller, eh?"

"Yes . . ." I reply, feeling awkward to hear this role applied to me, since even now I can hardly believe it.

Ribaheit meanwhile stands up and comes to me. She lifts my shoulder-length curly locks of hair and starts fidgeting with them, pulling this and that way.

"All right," she eventually mutters. "Let's get you over to a mirror table and I will have one of the girls do your hair and Face Art."

"Face Art?" I echo her faintly.

"Why, yes." Ribaheit chuckles. "You can't simply wear your little girl face unadorned to a noble party. That would be very unprofessional. Come along now."

We move down the room to the closest unoccupied table and chair with a mirror.

"Sit," the stylist tells me, and I comply, still holding up the delicate skirts of my dress as I lower myself in the chair.

"Ulaite, come here," Ribaheit calls over a young dark-haired woman with almost-black lacquered lips that glisten like ripe plums. "I want you to put up her hair—pull it back, hard, and then twist into a lotus up on top. Then apply sparkle dust."

"Of course," Ulaite replies, coming to stand directly behind me, and picking up my loose strands.

"And then—" Ribaheit taps my left cheek lightly—"Do her skin. Very lightly, she doesn't need much, it's generally clear as is. As for her eyes, apply dramatic colors that will do well under strong lighting, since she will be Storytelling solo."

I listen to them discuss me, with rising pangs of anxiety. Suddenly, the terrifying reality of me having to repeat that *hoohvak* story I made up, in a big room of high-ranking people, hits me hard. All this while, I was able to repress this inevitable fact—more or less—while overwhelmed with everything else . . . but not anymore.

I have to tell a great story tonight.

As if reading my mind, Ulaite nudges me lightly on my neck, as she moves around my hair. "So, let's hear your Storytelling, girl! Now's a fine time for you to practice, along with the rest of us."

And only then do I realize that all that chatter and singing and humming around me—that's not mere conversation, but entertainers warming up their voices for the performances to come.

CHAPTER
TWENTY-FOUR

I clear my throat once—just once, for courage—and then begin reciting my ridiculous story about the *sha* king.

"Be sure you speak much louder during the actual performance," Ulaite interrupts me immediately, even as she pulls my hair back and up, combing and smoothing it.

"That's right," Ribaheit calls out over her shoulder, as she moves away from us, returning to her desk up in front. "I want to hear you from where I sit, child. Speak up!"

"Very well," I reply, and continue in a more aggressive, strong voice. I struggle a little to remember the story I made up, but soon enough it comes easily to mind, and so I just open my mouth and let it flow, before all these other, far more experienced entertainers.

Just a few sentences in, and for some reason, it's gotten very quiet in the room around me. Everyone else has ceased talking and humming, and only my voice is heard, modulating between each phrase and section of the story.

It's gotten so silent that I pause, feeling uncertain, all of a sudden.

But the moment I stop, the women around me, and a few young men, all seem to regain held breaths.

"Blessed Hathor, you're not half bad! Indeed, you're quite good!"

"Unexpectedly good," someone else says. "You had me listening instead of working!"

"Oh," I say, feeling an instant flush of heat around my cheeks. "Thank you."

"Go on now, don't stop," a young woman says.

"Or maybe she *should*," another one says, tapping her fingers in annoyance. "Her piercing tone of voice is distracting me from my own practice."

"Eh, yes, the voice definitely gets your attention. I wouldn't call it piercing, but there's something uncanny about it—"

"Right, because the story itself is worthy of Hathor's buttocks, but the way she tells it is compelling—"

"Very well—*everyone*, hush now!" Ribaheit interrupts with her own rich voice. "Enough! All of you, practice in silence! Giving me a headache, the whole lot of you."

And so, I keep quiet, continuing the telling of the rest of the story entirely in my mind, while Ulaite picks up loose strands and resumes working with my hair.

When she's done, she rotates me half-way by the shoulders until I am facing the table directly, and forces me to look in the mirror before me, head-on.

"What do you think, girl?"

"Oh. . . ." I breathe.

What has she done with my head? Holy Bast! I can *see* the actual shape of my head because she pulled my curls so smooth and tight, and gathered them on top! The bunch of hair up there looks like a big open flower, and there are fancy pieces of ribbon wound into coils and flower petals. . . . Even all the shorter curly locks are under control, and—

I look amazing! Like royalty! My head!

I sit with my mouth open in amazement.

"I assume from your silly look that you like it," Ulaite says, teasing.

"Oh, yes!"

"Good." Ulaite pats me on my cheek.

"How—how did you do that?" I manage to say. "I could never pull my hair back so well—"

But Ulaite just laughs and then calls out to Ribaheit. "Hair's done on this one!"

"Now do her face!" Ribaheit replies without looking up from whatever she is doing at her desk. "But wash it first!"

"Wash?" I ask.

"That's right." While I observe in curiosity, Ulaite goes to a nearby large communal basin of water reposing on one of the tables and picks up a fresh towel from a stack. She dips it in the water to soak, wrings it out, then returns to me. "Must wash all that sweat and dust from your skin, or the makeup will not adhere properly."

"All right."

"Close your eyes."

I do as she says, and feel her wipe my face, neck, forehead, and even scrub my ears thoroughly with the cool wet cloth.

"Now we can do the Face Art properly," Ulaite says, then turns me around again and gets to work.

For several long daydreams, Ulaite issues funny commands regarding my face—close my eyes then open them, suck in my cheeks or puff out my cheeks, pout my lips, tense my forehead, don't move, don't blink, look up, look down, hold my breath. . . . All this, while she applies endless dust powders, creams, and various unknown gooey stuff to my skin, cheeks, eyelids, lips, and everywhere imaginable, by means of cotton balls and fine brushes. Those itchy *hoohvak* things tickle me so much that I constantly squirm and giggle when the bristles touch my skin.

"There, all done," she announces at last, in a proud tone. "You appear nicely dramatic."

"Can I look?" I ask awkwardly.

"You certainly can."

And Ulaite turns me toward the mirror.

I look in the mirror and my breath stops.

Bastet and Hathor and every great god of Atlantis! Who is that?

"Well?" Ulaite asks with a smile.

I gulp air, staring at an impossible, glamorous, alluring, fiercely *beautiful* stranger. This stranger is not me. *No, Bast, no, it cannot be me. . . .*

"Is that . . . do I . . .?"

The fierce, haughty female in the mirror moves her glossy, wine-dark lips, echoing my movements as I speak, so it must be a true reflection. *But, no.* Even her neck appears more elegant, and is held differently, proudly. And her eyes—her immense eyes surrounded by *niktos*-black glittering kohl—are those *my* eyes?

I literally *cannot believe* this is myself.

"Do I really have big eyes like that?" I finally manage to ask in a stiff, wooden voice of mortification. For some reason I am ashamed, embarrassed, stunned to appear like that.

"The dark eyelid highlights usually make everyone's eyes a little bigger," Ulaite says, noticing my shock. "Haven't you ever worn any cosmetics before?"

"No . . ." I reply after a tiny pause. And I briefly think of the several working whores who live in my neighborhood, and whose tawdry, cheap paints are *nothing* like what I see here today. This—this is *amretene* level Face Art, or even higher, worthy of nobility! I continue to stare at the stranger in the mirror.

"Ah." Ulaite smiles, patting me on the shoulders. Then she leans close to my ear and says, "In that case, let me give you some advice. While you wear cosmetics, avoid touching your face, scratching your nose, or rubbing your eyes. You must remind yourself constantly, because you'll be tempted to scratch something—just don't. At least not until your performance is over."

I nod, and she continues: "And remember that with the Face Art on, we all look the same—elite nobles and common folk alike. Yes, working folk like ourselves. It's an opportunity for us to live in *their* world, no matter how briefly, for as long as we entertain them. So use the time to your advantage. Don't just *look* like them but *be* them. It's quite fun!"

"Really?" I ask.

"Yes, really." And then Ulaite makes a little sound of delight. "Almost forgot! I need to dust you with sparkle! It will make the light truly dance in your hair tonight."

I'm too afraid to even ask what that means, so I just sit very still while Ulaite picks out a glass jar from a tray of others like it, glittering in all different colors. This one is full of shiny stuff in a deep purple hue.

She opens the jar, takes out a pinch of purple sparkling powder, and tosses some of it over the top of my head. "There— let's dust the lotus of your hair, to match the color of your dress," she says playfully. A delicate cloud of sparkling dust motes lands on me, turning faint lavender where it touches my light brown skin.

"Close your eyes for a moment, one more time," Ulaite says, taking another pinch of sparkle dust.

I do, and feel something over my eyelids and cheeks and forehead.

"Now, you're ready to be a Storyteller at the Court of Bisfuri!"

HAVING THANKED THE STYLISTS, I leave the chamber in a daze of amazement. Once I'm out in the hallway, I pause to catch my breath, and to allow multiple servants to hurry past me in both directions. I realize I'm still clutching the folds of my dress skirt, as I begin to walk in the direction of the grand hall near the front entrance—as quickly and carefully as I'm able, in my fancy new golden sandals.

Is everyone looking at me? People must be staring. . . . No, that's ridiculous, why would they?

I go up the main staircase to the upper level where the noble family Quarters are located, trying to keep out of the way of crowds of estate staff moving around me on the stairs in both directions, many of them carrying all kinds of incomprehensible items including big, bulky furniture pieces. As I navigate my way, I see several large hovering freight platforms rising and descending to and from the top gallery, with even more items loaded on them—including the more fragile kind such as crystal and glass.

The self-conscious intrusive thoughts continue nagging at me, making me wonder painfully at every turn if someone is staring at my new appearance. *Hoohvak* thoughts!

When I arrive at the entrance to Benaten Bisfuri's work Quarters, I find the doors wide open, the interior brightly lit, and servants bustling around with trays and boxes. I recognize big Vakrem, the guard, and ask him if he's seen Girsul.

Vakrem is also dressed up tonight, in a crisp new uniform with a shining gilded collar. He pauses momentarily, narrowing his eyes at me without recognition. And then he lets out a breath and a chuckle. "Semmi? Is that you? Well, well . . . they certainly transformed you for the evening."

I blush underneath all my layers of makeup at the sudden evaluating look in the man's eyes. All my self-conscious anxiety slams back at me. "Yeah, that's me, *chazuf.* And what are you looking at?" I say sharply. "This is my costume for tonight, for the fancy nobles. You can keep your stare to yourself or I'll transform your nose!"

My bluster has a different effect than I expected, because Vakrem starts laughing. "Oh, don't worry, girl, you're safe from me. And no one here will even think of harming you, else I'll personally harm *them*. House Bisfuri takes good care of all employees and shows proper respect to the female serving staff. I just didn't recognize you there with your new sparkly appearance. Girsul is in the other room."

"Harumph. Fine," I say. And, glittering fiercely, I sail past him in my shimmering costume, in search of Girsul.

I FIND Girsul unpacking a box of tech equipment, and loading a small two-tier hovering freight platform with unfamiliar spheres which, I'm guessing, are related to sound amplification. The moment he sees me, his brows go up. He stops working and lets out a whistle. "Oh man, now *that's* a fancy costume, Semmi! You look good! Like some kind of noble lady!"

"Shut up! Not you too!" I start to blush again. "Vakrem stared at me rotten, and now you whistle. Don't get any ideas or I'll kick your—"

"Hey! Hey!" Girsul lets out a laugh and puts both hands up. "Just acknowledging that you're well dressed and look ready to do your job tonight. No crap intended."

"All right." I exhale loudly, while my fingers continue to clutch the folds of my airy skirt. "I'm here now, so what can I do to help?"

"To be honest, not much," Girsul replies, giving me another up-and-down long stare. "At least not in that attire. I was going to have you help me take these sound spheres downstairs and place them around the main hall, but you might ruin your dress—"

"Ah, crap of a goat . . ." I say. "You're right. I didn't even think about it. I wasn't expecting to have to wear this kind of expensive costume. Honestly, it didn't even occur to me."

Girsul makes a small grimace and shrugs. "You're lucky. Just hang around here, but stay out of people's way, and practice your Storytelling quietly."

"I can tell you what she *can* do," interrupts Menahit, the set designer for Ter Bisfuri's show, moving toward us from the back of the room. She is also wearing a pristine uniform with a similar gold collar as Vakrem. Her wig is persimmon, sprinkled with gold sparkle dust, matching her orange tassel, and she wears subtle cosmetics on her pretty oval face. "Come with me downstairs and help with the arriving guests. They'll start showing up in about half an hour, and they'll need to be told where to go, and be pleased in whatever way possible, with smiles and compliments."

"There's an actual job like that?" I ask in surprise. "Just smiling and complimenting guests?"

"Oh yes." Another uniformed servant whom I don't know, with a weary face and carrying a decorative vase, pauses his task to join our conversation. "To mingle with the guests and greet them at these events is a job everyone on staff wants to do. It's easy—you just need to look good and smile and show them where to go. But you have to earn the privilege. Usually, it's a reward for good work and a long period of service. *Usually.*" And he gives me a severe look, then picks up the large vase and heads out of the room.

"Ignore him," Menahit tells me. "He's just sore that he never gets asked to do it."

"Yeah, well, he's often a clumsy *chazuf*, not surprising," Girsul mutters.

"So, are you coming?" Menahit asks me. "Dressed like that you'll fit right in."

"I guess so. Since I look—"

"Not bad. Not bad at all. . . ."

I hear the words of appraisal spoken in a honey-deep voice

behind me, and whirl around instinctively, exclaiming, "Oh yeah? Watch it, *shibet*, or I'll kick your *oruhu*!"

And then I gasp and almost put my hands over my big *garooi* mouth . . . but stop, short of smearing the glossy layer of *noohd* paint on my lips.

Benaten Bisfuri stands behind me, looking at me closely. This evening, he is magnificent in a dark crimson jacket worn directly over his bare chest in the latest style, and a tight pair of black pants and boots underneath, trimmed in fine etchings of gold. His raven mane of hair, brushed to a high gloss, falls loosely around his wide shoulders, and I can almost see the muscular structure of his upper arms underneath. . . .

In that first instant as I turn and catch his gaze, there is something somber and serious in his grey eyes . . . then his eyes widen slightly, and the unreadable look of intensity is replaced with a mixture of surprise and amusement.

"Aiee! I'm so sorry, *im Ter*!" My words spill forth in a cascade of anxiety and shame at what I've just said to my noble employer. "I didn't mean—that is, I didn't know it was *you*—so *sorry*!"

"You do look fine tonight, Semmi," he says, continuing to look at me steadily, analyzing and measuring me with his gaze. "But spare my *oruhu*, by all the gods. My obligation to this noble House is to perpetuate the line, so I'll need my *oruhu* intact."

"I'm so terribly sorry!" I continue talking, very, very quickly.

"Shush," he says calmly, while a corner of his mouth twitches with laughter. "Now, go on, and make yourself useful downstairs. I expect your Storytelling act in a few hours, when you are called to it. Until then, contain yourself and your kicking impulse. You may kick all you want during your performance." And then, winking at me, he walks past us nonchalantly—so close that I catch a whiff of his expensive musky scent.

For a few long moments, with a clenched jaw, I stare in Benaten's wake as he chats briefly with some of the staff, giving

last-moment orders, then disappears in the depths of his private
suite. And then I leave Girsul with his sound equipment and
follow Menahit outside the Quarters and down the stairs, past
harried crowds of serving staff.

AS WE ARRIVE on the ground floor in the grand hall,
Menahit turns to face me and puts one hand on my shoulder,
halting me. Then she says quietly, "That was extremely
unacceptable what you did upstairs, Semmi. You were rude to
Ter Aten. I certainly hope you know better than to be so rude
and outspoken to the guests."

Sudden, infernal heat rises inside me. Once again, I feel the
overwhelming burden of embarrassment. "I know . . . I was very
wrong!" I say haltingly, "I apologized to him, and I'm so sorry,
truly I am, I was—I was startled, that's all—"

Menahit watches me seriously and shakes her head. "Look—
you need to understand that *Ter* Aten is very forgiving, and
finds many things amusing. But he's also quite different from
most other nobles."

"I understand."

"Do you? Because he gave you a chance—as he did for all of
us—and you should be very careful to remember your place and
show your gratitude."

"Yes, of course! I—"

"I know how overwhelming this is for you right now, girl."
Menahit's stern expression softens. "I was in your place once, a
new servant of Bisfuri. It was terrifying. But you just keep your
mouth shut and do nothing—and I mean *nothing*—to call
undue attention to yourself. You'll learn your way soon
enough. But for now—just control your impulses. And, for the
love of Bast and Hathor, *no kicking*, if a guest is rude to *you*.
They're permitted to be so. You are not. You say and do
nothing."

I nod, avoiding her eyes and looking down at the polished marble floor.

"But—if someone, if any one of the guests tries to grope you—"

I look up, my eyes coming alive with outrage.

"There—this is what I mean." Menahit raises one finger to point at my face. "You're very transparent. Your emotions are immediate. You *cannot* do that in the service of the elites. So, if someone makes a sleazy, ugly comment or tries to grope you, which is possible—you extricate yourself politely, make some excuse, and then go find Vakrem, or another one of us, and let us know. If needed, *Ter* Aten himself will be notified, and he will handle it."

I stare at her, biting my lips in frustration.

Menahit pats me on the shoulder. "It's a big party, and there will be many drunks before the night is over. Most incidents are going to be forgotten. But anything serious—Bisfuri will protect you. You got that?"

"Yes. . . ."

"Good. Then we're ready to get to work." Menahit smiles.

I take a big breath and smile back.

But Menahit is not done. She points to the lower parts of my dress. "You really don't need to be hitching up your skirt hem so much all the time," she says. "These are not the stables. The floors around here are polished clean, and your dress is intended to sweep along the ground. Let it be."

"Oh, okay," I say, letting go of my skirts. I find that my fingers are shaking slightly with nerves and the tension of what we've just discussed. In addition, there's the incredible panorama of sights and sounds and smells. And suddenly my head is spinning. . . .

It's no wonder. The immense hall all around us has been transformed into a glamorous place of splendor for which I have no words.

I'm not just exaggerating. I literally have trouble describing what it is I'm seeing, because there are now small *trees* growing indoors—trees covered in fruit, planted in giant vases, draped in garlands of gold . . . and there is a multi-tiered fountain in the center, spurting dark liquid that glitters with overtones of gold and plum, and could be some kind of beverage. . . .

Sacred Bast, what has been done here?

I recall my original amazement at this hall of marble and gold, the deep wood inlay, plum-colored walls with marble cornices and niches . . . that same grand staircase from which we just descended . . . the cupola ceiling with skylights . . . a polished mosaic floor. . . .

And now—now it's a hundred times more magnificent.

In addition to the potted fruit trees, there are flower vases everywhere, and tiny orbs of golden light float among the branches.

An arch trellis of flowers has been erected over the grand main entrance, which is where the guests will be arriving, I assume. Servants are putting the finishing touches on it, hanging and winding more garlands of gold.

"Watch out," Menahit says, putting out one hand before me to pull me back out of the way of a long hovering platform filled with tiers of empty crystal glasses, dishes, and plates, with two servants accompanying it as it sails slowly through the hall. "Stop staring now, we have no time to waste."

"Sorry, yes," I reply in haste. "Where will the guests sit? Are they going to be placed around that fountain?"

"What?" Menahit narrows her dark eyes and smirks. "This is just the front entrance, no one will be sitting here."

"Huh?" My mouth parts.

Menahit continues looking at me with sarcasm and shakes her head. "Did you think this is where the main party happens?"

"Well, where else?" I ask, starting to get a little annoyed by her superior airs, especially after that long lecture. She's not much older than me, after all. "This is the hall, isn't it?"

"Semmi, this is the antechamber." Menahit points around us. "It might appear grand to someone such as you or me. But see that large door on the other side of the staircase? See the direction in which all the servants are going? That leads to the actual assembly hall. That's where *everything* will be happening tonight."

"Really?" I ask like a *hoohvak*. "But this room is so huge!"

"I know." Menahit nods patiently. "It seems that way. Until you go inside and see the real venue. Fear not, I'll show you around, since you will need to know where to go during the party. Let's go, quickly! Go!"

CHAPTER
TWENTY-FIVE

A nd so, in the next few moments, Menahit gives me a quick tour of the premises, walking briskly ahead of me, past endless serving staff, and explaining things along the way. I can barely keep up, because my fancy shoes feel strange on my feet, and I'm extremely wary of slipping in my new golden sandals on the polished marble floor.

She explains to me that the guests will enter this antechamber from the main entrance and pass underneath the arch trellis, where they will be greeted on both sides by several servants—including us—and given flowers to carry or attach onto their outfits or hair.

"The guests are going to be immediately dropping those flowers, or tossing them after just a few steps, since this is merely a welcome gesture. Some of us will have to be there to pick them up to keep the floor clean—"

I widen my eyes, just imagining this.

"Then, they will stop by the fountain, and receive goblets with honey wine from the servants at the fountain, to refresh them before they enter the main hall—"

As she speaks, Menahit reaches the large wooden carved

doors to the right of the staircase, that stand open, blazing with light . . . and we enter. . . .

Mother of all the gods!

We're suddenly inside an immense rectangular hall that's possibly three times as large as the antechamber.

There's a vaulted ceiling overhead, but it's much taller than the other chamber, with multiple antique chandelier light fixtures suspended via elegant sculpted rope of braided gold from very high above. In addition to these, endless light orbs of all sizes fill the expanse, floating high overhead and low near floor level, casting a brilliant warm glow.

I crane my neck and stare upward . . . and start to imagine a bunch of grapes escaping from the vine while being set on fire from within, or an army of soap bubbles. . . . *Forgive me, Bast, for having such nonsense thoughts even now.*

I stop gawking at the wonders overhead and glance down, noticing the same mirror-polished floor continuing here from the antechamber. It is slippery under our feet, formed with cream marble inlay, and its veiny seams are filled with true gold.

The immense open floor space in the center of the hall is bare of furnishings or set piece decorations. Menahit tells me it is left that way for dancing, and for the performances—such as my own, possibly. "They'll bring in a raised dais for you to stand on —and for the singers, acrobats, and other entertainers."

I gulp in terror, and continue to follow her as she rushes through the grand hall.

The perimeter of the room is lined with rows of comfortable chairs and cushioned sofas. There are many arched niches interspersed with colonnades along the walls, each niche leading into smaller adjacent rooms that offer the attendees relative privacy, and allow for smaller gatherings. It occurs to me, this place is like a beehive, a grand hall connected to endless small chambers.

Menahit quickly takes me through some of those rooms,

letting me peek past the niche doorways inside the richly dark, wood-trimmed interiors—all to give me an idea of their size and function. Some contain libraries of antique scrolls, art, and statuary, or rooms filled with instruments dedicated to music. Others are equipped with built-in hearths or free-hovering metal basin firepits around which gently swinging chairs are suspended from the ceiling. A few are toilet and wash rooms for the Ladies and Lords—which is important to know if I'm faced with needing to direct one of the guests to such a toiletry chamber. And several rooms contain divans and resting couches strewn with pillows for a more intimate kind of entertainment and trysts, if the guests so choose. . . .

"Maybe they'll have you perform in one of these small rooms, before a limited audience," Menahit says, to calm me, and then we continue traversing the main assembly hall.

In the very back, against the rear wall, is a narrow, raised dais and a row of carved high chairs resembling thrones. Indeed, the entire wall is covered with a symmetrical gold relief of curling vines around a central shape which is the House Symbol of Bisfuri—an intricate circular design which I've now seen enough times to recognize.

"That's where the Bisfuri and the Imperials might sit during more formal occasions." Menahit points to the back of the grand hall. "But not today. They will most likely lounge on any of the reclining sofas and be served their food there. It all depends on what manner of entertainment *Ter* Aten will offer them. It is, after all, *his* party, even though he says it's being held on behalf of Behamenut, his brother."

"What about the Lord himself—their Father, Lord Bisfuri?" I ask, as we approach the high seats to admire their exquisite carved wood and gold relief in detail, and then pass them, continuing along the perimeter. "Is he not considered the Host?"

"Not this time. The Lord has been traveling, so he's likely too tired to take on this responsibility so soon after his return home.

Besides, *Ter* Aten is known for throwing the best parties among the elites. Lord Bisfuri will simply relax with the guests. Rumor has it, he has been looking around High Court for a suitable First Lady. He is said to be highly fastidious and overly discriminating when it comes to female companionship, but he might use the opportunity to observe the high-born female guests, and possibly even find his future bride at tonight's event—"

Menahit pauses talking because a loud pounding of drums begins up ahead, echoing in the distance. Then, in just a few heartbeats, string and wind instruments join them in a cacophony, as musicians tune everything for their live performances.

"That's Erevi and his troupe of players." Menahit points to the nearest corner of the assembly hall where the musical band is setting up, consisting of several energetic and elegantly dressed men and women. "They're the Lord's personal favorite musicians, expected to play at every Bisfuri gathering of this size." And then she casually waves in their direction. Several of the younger musicians see her and wave back. I note that they are all wearing glittering outfits not much different from my own, instead of staff uniforms. Erevi must be the gaunt older man in the center of the group directing everyone and waving around a short stick.

"See that small door behind the musicians?" Menahit points to a recessed wall niche directly behind the band. Several people with purple tassels are milling around the entrance.

I nod.

"Make note of it. That's the dressing room and entertainer preparation area—including service staff toilets, if you need to go. Be sure to check in there frequently to see when your performance is required. There will be a supervisor in charge of the entertainment program. He'll tell you the time of your performance. After we're done with receiving the guests, head there directly!"

"I will."

We keep walking and approach the corner area with the musicians—so that I have a moment to peek inside the niche with the dressing room—but don't stop, and continue onward, returning to the front of the hall. Along the way, I manage to wave to Girsul who runs past us, skillfully dodging other bustling staff, while carrying a large handful of sound spheres. He stops repeatedly to place them in various discreet spots along the wall perimeter to establish an acoustical frame. I watch Girsul rush about, fleet-footed, barely acknowledging my greeting since his arms are so full.

Meanwhile, many tables are being readied along the walls. Menahit tells me those will be food stations where the servers will bring out the dishes freshly made in the kitchens. It will all be arranged beautifully here, before being offered to the noble guests.

"Now you've seen the main hall," Menahit says. "They're still far from finished decorating it. Much of what's been done in the antechamber will continue here. But come along, we need to line up near the flower arch and be ready to greet the guests and hand out flowers."

A QUARTER OF AN HOUR LATER, Menahit and I stand in one of two rows of servants along each side of the flower arch. Most are wearing formal uniforms, but several are dressed in glittering entertainer dresses, with purple tassels, such as myself. Large bowls filled with cut flowers of every kind repose on tripods behind us. We've been instructed by a staff supervisor—a short, uniformed man with a tall golden wig, an anxious expression, and a powerful, ringing voice—to offer flowers and compliment our guests as they walk past us.

"Do what I do," Menahit whispers to me. "The less you say, the better. Just smile and hand out a flower to the nearest person who walks by. That man who just spoke, that's Steward Kidu, in charge of Ceremonies. He will proclaim the names and noble ranks of all guests as they arrive, so that we'll know how to address them."

"What do you mean?" I stare at her in rising worry.

"You do not want to insult a Lord and call him an ordinary *Ter*. When in doubt, address everyone as 'My Lord' or 'My Lady.' Or better yet, say nothing at all, smile, give them a big flower—"

"Bastet help me. . ." I whisper.

And that's when the courtesans and the *amretene* begin to arrive.

They enter in small, glittering flocks, wafting perfume and ethereal veils, tinkling with bells, chains, and slim metallic bracelets, laughing and giggling among themselves in soft, enticing, specially trained voices. . . . Courtesans of all ranks pass by us—female and male, impossibly beautiful, some slim, others voluptuous, others yet athletic and muscular, but all with perfect bodies barely covered by expensive, delicate fabrics.

The highest ranking among them are the *amretene* from Hathor's House, distinguished by their proud bearing, superior beauty, and teardrop-shaped gems of the color of blood, suspended on chains over the middle of their foreheads. I recognize several familiar faces among them—they are the same *amretene* who participated in *Ter* Bisfuri's episodes, including Almahara with her blazing red hair, slim brunette Yokreoh, and the mysterious *chimeratene* Ixenoel.

"They're supposed to fill the hall before the guests do, ready to mingle as soon as the nobles arrive," Menahit says near my ear, noticing my amazement. "We do not give them flowers."

I nod silently, and look with wonder at the gorgeously attired arrivals. "They are dressed so beautifully. They look like nobles."

Menahit merely smiles at me. "Don't forget, so do *you*."

My mouth falls open. But I clamp it shut, because now the first of the actual guests arrive.

POSITIONED at the front doors of the main entrance before the arch trellis, Steward Kidu, the Steward of Ceremonies, loudly calls out the first noble newcomer's name. His voice is artificially amplified, so that it resounds with dramatic clarity from *everywhere* at once—all over this antechamber, and it can be heard equally well in the distance of the interior, where it apparently echoes in the grand hall.

Thanks to Girsul and his sound gadgets, it occurs to me.

"Lord Neid Tlactlu of the Great House Tlactlu and First Lady Miqara!"

Those of us in the servant receiving lines turn our attention, as one, toward the middle-aged man and woman who walk in with heads held rigid and high, likely due to the immense gold wigs atop their heads woven with garlands of sparkling precious stones. Their clothing is deceptively simple. The Lord wears a jacket over pants, the color of wheat, while the First Lady has an olive and plum dress of several fabric layers, with strange, segmented long sleeves that cover her plump arms in horizontal bands of fabric attached via fine gold chains. And then, as the bright illumination of the antechamber falls upon them, the fabric begins to glow and emanate its own impossible light. . . .

The first two servants in line on both sides step forward, bowing, and offer the Lord and Lady flowers. "A glorious night, My Lord!" one servant says, presenting a great lotus blossom to Lord Tlactlu, while the other servant hands another immense lotus to the First Lady, saying, "My Lady, your light eclipses all!"

The rest of us in line remain with our heads inclined, while the Lord and Lady accept their flowers without saying a word, sniff them with light disdain, then walk a few steps and let the flowers fall on the marble floor. Meanwhile, they proceed toward the drink fountain and the entrance to the main hall.

Immediately, one of the servants in the back of the line steps forward and picks up the fallen flowers, then moves out of the way to discard them in a special receptacle.

I frown in confusion and then lean slightly toward Menahit. "He just threw them away? Why waste them? Just give those same flowers to the next guests!"

At my side, Menahit's eyes widen as though I've just said something incredibly *garooi*.

"No! You can't do that!" she hisses. "That would be terrible, disrespectful! Just—no!"

I shrug slightly. "Too bad, such a waste."

But the Steward of Ceremonies is already announcing the next noble arrivals.

We all stiffen in place, ready to perform our ridiculous service.

"Lord Ferim Baichizar of the Great House Baichizar, First Lady Chigaid, and their daughters, Lady Ramira and Lady Ogdara!"

Four nobles pass the arches, to my mind, dressed like peacocks. Lord Ferim wears a robe of so many colorful layers of fine fabric, that he shimmers like a rainbow. And so does the First Lady Chigaid with her effervescent dress, while the daughters appear to be puffs of cloud cotton, wearing flimsy veil-dresses that barely cover their flawless lily-gold skin.

They receive their flowers from the nearest servants, and cast them aside almost immediately, except for one of the daughters. Lady Ogdara decides to keep her blossom, twirls its pink head between manicured fingers, then stuffs it in one of the wide, golden serpent bracelets hugging her upper arm.

"Lord Keodris Egemavda of the Great House Egemavda, his son *Ter* Daevat and daughter Lady Nanivel!"

I stare discreetly at the handsome middle-aged Lord in a simple black jacket who wears no wig, only a slim circlet of metal around his forehead. However, his short, dark brown hair and neatly trimmed beard sparkle with *niktos*-blue glitter. I assume it's similar to the dust that has been sprinkled over my own hair.

Meanwhile, his son and daughter walk quietly behind him, also modestly dressed, compared to the previous arrivals. The young *Ter* Daevat, probably the same age as Benaten's younger brother, has long hair of a much lighter shade of sun-kissed brown. He negligently wears the recent fashion, with only a pale linen outer jacket over his tanned bare chest, and sleek, muscle hugging pants. Lady Nanivel is clad in a long silver dress with a fine single veil layer over her bare arms and coiled, sculptured hair of a similar light brown hue.

As we all move in with our offerings of flowers, ready to present in case they turn in our direction, I notice that Lord Keodris takes the offered flower and does not throw it away. Instead, he turns a rather kind face in our direction and gives us a faint smile, then places the flower in the folds of his jacket, where it sits, pale and lovely against the black.

The same happens when *Ter* Daevat takes the flower from Menahit, tucking it in his jacket. Meanwhile, Lady Nanivel pauses before me, and her sky-blue eyes are full of energy as she looks at the lotus I hold out in my hand. "How lovely," she says in a soft voice, and takes the blossom from my palm.

"As lovely as you, My Lady," I mutter, inclining my head, and watch the Lady regard me with a serene gaze and continue moving past me, with the flower now attached to the front of her bodice.

Menahit gives me a barely perceptible nod of approval.

• • •

THE NOBLE GUESTS continue to arrive, more and more frequently, for an interminable hour, while we in the receiving line are presented—for the most part—with an overwhelming, stunning, glittering sight of insane wealth and splendor and incomprehensibly expensive outfits.

"Lord this-and-that, Lady so-and-so. . . ."

The names and ranks all blur into one messy sound and impression. I watch the other servants around me, and note their subtle reactions to specific arriving guests. Some are greeted warmly, others, less so, but never enough to make it obvious.

On the other hand, I barely understand what I see, as far as their fashions. There's just so much glittering color and metallic shine, expensive fabrics, and endless, precious, faceted gems that reflect the light with fierce beauty. . . .

In addition to the more conservative outfits, some of the more daring nobles arrive nearly naked. I look away in embarrassment from the jacketless bared male chests clad in nothing but golden chains and wrist-and-arm braces over sculpted muscles, with short tunics and sandals covering their lower regions. As for the females, some are only covered in veils and sparkling jewelry, showing off the groomed perfection of their skin, from the palest cream to the darkest ebony.

Eventually, I feel numb and lightheaded from staring at all of them, and from trying to keep track of Family names and ranks and noble Houses. Mostly, I bow my head, and occasionally get the chance to present a flower to someone if they happen to glance at me. I hand out the flowers the best I can, voice some kind of vacant compliment, and watch how, within moments, most of the blossoms end up on the floor.

What a hoohvak *waste. . . .*

At one point, I look up briefly, and notice that Benaten Bisfuri and his brother Behamenut both stand on the gallery at the top of the grand staircase, elbows resting over the railing, and watch the arriving guests. They are clad in elegant jackets over sleek pants, both bare-chested underneath, with subtle threads of golden jewelry sparkling against their beautifully tanned skin.

Understated elegance. . . .

Benaten's midnight hair is a striking contrast against his blood-crimson jacket (I've seen it up close, earlier in his Quarters, when I nearly kicked him in reflex . . . *Bastet forgive me!*), while Behamenut wears a deep green.

It occurs to me to wonder why they're not coming down to mingle with the guests.

Just then, a minor stirring of servant whispers reaches Menahit and me in our spots in line.

"What?" I mouth my question as Menahit leans close to the person on the other side of her.

"They're coming!" she whispers, finally turning to me. "The most important guests! And the Lord himself is finally here, Lord Bisfuri!"

The noise level rises around us, and quite a few passing guests pause to look back.

Meanwhile, up on the gallery above, the Bisfuri brothers begin to descend the staircase.

BENATEN AND BEHAMENUT reach the ground floor just as the first of the prominent guests enter the antechamber.

"The Most Venerable Vardavar Urartumi, Born of the Great House Urartumi and First Priest of the Imperial Order of Kassiopei! The Most Venerable Tuataan Madru, First Priestess of the Sacred Order of Amrevet-Ra!" Steward Kidu cries, his voice thundering with additional emphasis.

A man and woman in long dark robes walk from the entrance past the arch trellis. The woman is young, tall, and hard, without any spare flesh on her bones. She is dark brown-skinned like my Grandmother, with an elegant neck and a stern, angular face of grim beauty. Her floor-length *niktos*-black garment is trimmed with white, and her black hair is gathered in a sculpted bun on top of her head. A veil of fine gold mesh covers her head and sweeps down her back, to indicate her priestly rank.

Meanwhile, the man is short and heavy-set, middle-aged, with skin the color of desert sand and a clean-shaven head except for a small gilded forelock coiled like a serpent in a spiral on top of his head. His long black robes are more intricate, multi-layered, and trimmed in gold. His face is unreadable, like a mask of serenity.

As soon as they approach, all of us assembled in service rows, bow our heads deeply, and I do the same. We stand offering flowers while the lofty priests sail past us. And now, all I can see is the moving fabric of their black robes at waist level, and the gold or white trim at the hems near the floor. Far too afraid to raise my gaze any higher while they are directly nearby, I nevertheless see, very soon, two beautiful flower blossoms fall discarded at their feet. . . .

I look up moments later, as the Steward of Ceremonies announces very enthusiastically, "Our Most Gracious Lord Muutat Bisfuri! First Lady Ashura Ximunat of the Great House Ximunat, and her son Lord Enhuvarat!"

Everything is happening too fast, vying for our attention all at once. I'm unsure whose arrival to watch, where to turn my anxious, scattered gaze. . . . The Bisfuri brothers intercept the priests, while their father, Lord Bisfuri arrives from the other direction—

"Welcome, Most Venerable Tuataan, and Most Venerable Vardavar, to our—that is, to *my* festivities," says Behamenut loudly, stepping ahead of his older brother, after only a moment of awkward hesitation. I watch Benaten stand directly behind him, and notice the discreet placement of his hand as he pushes Eham forward, since it is officially his party to host.

First Priestess Tuataan stops and gives Behamenut the faintest of nods. "It is a pleasure, as always, to be received in the House of Bisfuri," she says in a deceptively bland voice that manages to ring with power. "Young Eham, your festivities are charming. Do we owe this to your older brother, or your own efforts, this time?"

"Oh, it is all Eham," Benaten says with indulgent sarcasm and a magnetic smile, nodding at the Priestess.

"Yes, yes, perfectly delightful, everything," the First Priest Vardavar interrupts, patting Eham on the shoulder in a fatherly gesture, and then coughs. "Now, be so kind, young man, as to direct me to the refreshments. The heat outside is unusual for this time of night, and our ride was also overheated, so unfortunately it has affected my vocal—"

"But of course, please do come this way, Venerable One," Eham says at once, with a practiced gesture.

Benaten nods at him with an assertive look, but remains standing in place while the Priest of Kassiopei follows the younger brother to the drink fountain.

I see that Benaten periodically glances past the Priestess of Amrevet-Ra at the other arrivals—his father and the two who came with him.

Now that I'm able to look away, I do the same.

Surprisingly, I *recognize* the tall, cold noblewoman with impassive dark eyes, a beautiful oval face, and ruby painted lips that were not made to smile. . . . It's the same First Lady Ximunat who had been at the Service Competition this afternoon, picking and choosing among us. She was the one who ignored Uru, Girsul, me, and numerous worthy others who completed the race across Denderaat Bridge, all in favor of the most handsome and beautiful.

And now, this same Lady Ashura walks next to Lord Muutat Bisfuri, engaging in charming banter and laughing in an exaggerated manner, all while resting her manicured hand on his forearm. Tonight, she is dressed in a spectacular gown of pearl and gold, made of a fine fabric that hugs all her voluptuous curves, leaving nothing to the imagination except the true expression of her glamorously shadowed eyes. . . .

Immediately behind Lady Ximunat comes the young Lord, her son. Enhuvarat Ximunat is a young man of exceptional good looks, tall and elegant in posture, not unlike his mother, and well-aware of his attraction. His long dark hair is gathered in a segmented tail, a slim sculptured circlet of gold hugs his forehead, and his eyes are a vivid dark blue. He sports the same male fashion as most of the younger noblemen, a well fitted upper jacket, deep blue to match his eyes. However, underneath he wears an exotic garment of fine airy silk that emerges from the front of his jacket like a frilly scarf, and also continues beneath the jacket, sweeping over his sleek pants like a cloak of spun gold.

I find myself staring so hard at his fashion choice that my jaw drops. And I force myself to look away and take in the sight of the older Lord of this House.

It must be said that Lord Muutat Bisfuri himself is an impressively handsome man, displaying a fine figure tonight. He might be of a lesser physical stature than his first son Benaten, but he certainly has the effortless confidence of the great Lord of the wealthiest noble House of *Atlantida*. Muutat Bisfuri is perfectly groomed, with the beginnings of a beard, and his dark brown hair is contained with a gold circlet studded with gems.

His jacket is silvery grey trimmed in persimmon bands of silk at the sleeve wrists, with matching pants and pointed shoes.

Lord Bisfuri arrives before his serving staff and graciously receives a flower, putting it in the center of his wide collar of gold and gems. He then makes a welcoming hand gesture to Lady Ximunat, and she takes a lotus blossom also. She brings it up to her nose and then suggestively brushes it against her full lips—before tucking it in the bracelet at her left wrist.

Her son, the handsome Lord Enhuvarat, takes his flower, and twirls it between his elegant manicured fingers, as he walks past us.

Lord Muutat, along with Lady Ashura and her son, then join Benaten and the Priestess, all of them continuing onward toward the grand hall.

All of us in the staff receiving line exhale in relief— prematurely.

In that very moment, the Steward of Ceremonies cries out at the top of his considerable voice, announcing the most terrifying arrivals of all.

The Imperial Kassiopei are here.

CHAPTER
TWENTY-SIX

The servants of Bisfuri start bowing deeply at the waist, gazes cast to the floor, hands outstretched, offering flowers. And the noble guests in the vicinity also pause, gathering themselves for obeisances.

Menahit gives me a sideways look of widened eyes, because I'm staring, having forgotten to bow. I recall myself, and copy her motions, but not before I've seen the three Imperial newcomers arrive and walk toward us past the arch trellis, followed at a short distance by a whole retinue of others. And even then, I persist, stealing quick glances from my bent position because . . . Bastet, I simply must.

"The Imperial Lord Narmeradat Kassiopei, Crown Prince of the Divine Kassiopei Dynasty!" Steward Kidu exclaims, pausing for impact. Then he continues, "The Imperial Lord Oron Kassiopei, Prince of Kassiopei and the Imperial Lady Arlenari Kassiopei, Princess of Kassiopei!"

Prince Narmeradat walks several paces ahead of his younger brother and sister, with the confidence of an ancient god come to life—striking, overbearing, and yes, terrifying. His attire is surprisingly informal: a sleeveless white linen jacket and pants, with only a hair-fine pattern of gold trim around his collar and shoes. The muscles of his arms are nicely defined, and his long golden hair falls in waves around his shoulders. He barely glances at the surroundings with a bored gaze of his lapis lazuli-blue eyes that appear to have a black line "drawn" around the eyelids. That dark outline is a natural trait—the divine *wedjat* inherent in the Kassiopei lineage, together with the *niktos*-black brows and preternatural vigor (something I learned from watching the shows on our media-box).

The Crown Prince pauses to pick a flower from one servant, then continues a step and takes a second one. The expression of his face transforms into a faintly mocking sneer of general disdain. He holds both flowers in his hands and twirls their short stems as if they are fidget toys. He then heads in the direction of the Bisfuri, who in turn retrace their steps to meet him half-way.

"*Wixameret*, Imperial Lord Narmeradat!" says Lord Muutat Bisfuri loudly, in a musical voice, taking a step forward and inclining his head to the minimal degree necessary. "You grace us with your shining presence tonight."

"My Imperial Father and Mother send their regrets to the House Bisfuri. They're unable to attend your feast this time. Instead, they send their entire brood to your door," Narmeradat replies in an equally loud, low voice imbued with traces of dark humor, and power.

The Imperial Kassiopei are known to have divine power voices, I recall, even as my skin prickles at the strange tangible sound of that voice.

Meanwhile, the Imperial twins, brother and sister, approach the line of servants. Oron Kassiopei is slightly taller than his older brother, but has a milder expression and less of a commanding presence—as though he knows his place and has no intention of assuming anything more. His sleeveless jacket and pants are light brown, with no other adornment, except for the gem-studded gold collar which is slightly more formal than his older sibling's.

Oron has similar handsome features as Narmeradat, the same *wedjat* eyelids, blue eyes, and golden hair of the Kassiopei Dynasty, worn loose down his back. But his visage seems to be lit from the inside with an interesting energy and benevolence. He even looks directly at the faces of the servants lined up in rows on both sides, takes the first flower offered to him with a gracious nod and carries it like a gift.

Princess Arlenari Kassiopei walks alongside him, wearing a pale, sky-blue dress of several layers of fine gauze fabric, and a short delicate veil floating in a cloud over her upswept golden hair sculpted in a twist shape on top of her head. Droplets of pearls are threaded throughout her hair, and slim gold bracelets encase her slender wrists. Every step she takes with her gem-encrusted shoes is silent and light. Her lovely oval face appears to be serene and unfocused, and she looks mostly ahead of her, with occasional odd glances to the side and up, as if to admire the lofty ceiling . . . or avoid meeting other people's eyes.

At some point, it is inevitable that she must turn in our direction, as we servants stand with our floral offerings. She happens to be on the side closer to me and Menahit, while Prince Oron is closer to the opposite row of servants.

Menahit, I, and the woman directly to my right, bow deeply, offering blossoms, never knowing if ours would be the one chosen. In sudden panic, I force my gaze toward the floor, seeing only with the edges of my sight the light blue shimmering fabric of the Imperial dress.

Mustn't look . . . dare not look . . . she's the weird one . . . strange princess, possibly touched by the gods; probably has the Evil Eye.

Don't look!

And then, just like that, like some kind of ignorant *hoohvak*, I can't help but glance up, right as she's about to pass me.

Our gazes meet; we're almost the same height.

I see startled blue eyes, darkness-outlined *wedjat* eyelids, underneath raven brows. Up close, her oval face is delicate but less doll-like, with thin, hollowed cheeks. Her glossy lip color is slightly lighter than the dark red that is my own *noohd*. . . .

For some foolish reason, the notion that she's Imperial but also wears glossy *noohd* on her mouth like ordinary people, enters my head. *Bastet, guard me from thinking nonsense!*

The moment is a mere heartbeat, but I do the unthinkable. I thrust the flower I hold at her, and barely whisper, "My Imperial Lady—for you!"

Sacred Hathor and Bastet and all the benevolent gods, what have I done? And more importantly, why?

I hear the rush of blood in my temples, and the world possibly stops in terror at my affront to one of the divine Imperials in whose presence I'm unworthy to be.

But in that instant, Princess Arlenari Kassiopei slows her pace and pauses before me. A slender hand (with delicately manicured nails and fragile wrists) rises and meets my own. She takes the great lotus flower from *my fingers*, momentarily brushing them with her undoubtedly divine ones.

"Thank you . . ." she says very quietly, looking at me with sincere, clear eyes. And then, clutching the flower I'd just given her, she nods almost shyly and turns away, resuming her walk.

Strange, but her divine touch doesn't feel any different than anyone else's. . . . Oh, but Bast, forgive my blasphemous thoughts!

I exhale and once again forcibly lower my gaze. But first, I manage to notice Arlenari's brother, Prince Oron, turn his head and glance at me with curiosity and a complete lack of reproach. There is indeed a twin resemblance between them—a similarity of features, but also a kind of benign demeanor. It occurs to me, now that I've seen her and looked directly in her face, it's unlikely the princess has the Evil Eye.

Speaking of eyes—for just one brief instant, from further up ahead in the small grouping of nobles, I see Benaten Bisfuri's intense grey eyes fixed upon me.

Oh, no. . . .

Somehow, I'm still standing. How is it that I've not been stricken dead by the gods for my weird insolence?

Crap of a goat . . . it could still happen.

At the very least, I'm probably getting fired.

Or am I?

The Imperials walk beyond us, and Lord Muutat Bisfuri himself again steps forth to welcome them with another gracious sweep of his hand and a courteous but shallow bow. Unlike the rest of us, Bisfuri is apparently lofty enough to be held to a minimal expression of obeisance. I can no longer hear what they're saying as they move away toward the interior and the grand hall.

Next to me, Menahit widens her eyes and gives me an open-mouthed, silent glare which is amazingly eloquent: I really screwed up.

And yet, so far there are no consequences. Instead, there are more guests coming—namely, members of the Imperial retinue. The Steward of Ceremonies resumes calling out more noble names and ranks and Houses.

"*Ter* Stryr Giparu of the Great House Giparu and *Ter* Arguam Giparu!"

Now that we no longer have to bow so low, I can keep my head up and freely observe the two very handsome young men with long, reddish-brown hair, warm tan skin, and a family resemblance saunter past us.

Ter Stryr is older than his possible brother, and he only wears what could be a shining collar and a short tunic of spun gold to cover his lower body, leaving his remarkable torso and shoulders bare, as well as his muscular legs, and feet encased in light sandals. His provocative, dark-eyed gaze is sensual and disturbing as it sweeps over us, and he takes a flower from the young woman just ahead of Menahit in line.

But I immediately forget about his sculpted abdomen when I see the strange reality of the impossible, *rippling* collar of iridescent, living rainbow *light* wrapped around his manly neck.

Could that be . . . ?

Strolling right next to him, Arguam, the younger *Ter* Giparu, with pale blue eyes and a complex, amused expression, wears a similar tunic and little else. His lighter reddish hair falls to his shoulders, just above an identical radiant collar. He takes a flower and, with slow deliberation, picks off the petals, dropping them one by one, so that eventually his blossom falls apart in shreds, leaving nothing but the core.

I stare at both young men as they walk away. Slowly, I comprehend.

The two nobles of the House Giparu are wearing *pegasei*, like jewelry around their necks.

IN THE NEXT FEW DAYDREAMS, more elite nobles pass by us, and then the stream of arrivals slows down. That's when I see that the servants in our rows who happen to be dressed as entertainers, step out of line, and start leaving, until only the uniformed servants remain.

"Semmi! You too, go!" Menahit whispers, nudging me with her elbow. "Time to head to the entertainer dressing room and prepare for your act."

My heart starts beating faster. I do as she says and break away from the reception line. Stepping awkwardly in my new golden sandals, I follow the others, keeping out of the way of any guests, and return to the grandeur of the feast hall.

All this time, while we've been receiving the fine guests in the antechamber, the last-moment decorations in the main hall have been completed, exquisite braided garlands hung, vases and tables positioned, sound system components hidden, miniature orb-lights set sailing in the air. And now the immense chamber is packed with so many noble elites in such finery that together they could fill up a busy marketplace. I have no other frame of reference to describe so many people all being in one place, hence I think of the big open-air market nearest our home in Denwen's Pit. . . .

Probably not the best comparison to make.

Sounds of festive music, loud conversation, laughter, hit me from all directions, and I'm momentarily lost in a sea of sparkling humanity.

Clusters of noble guests form various groups, reclining on the pillow-strewn divans and settees along the walls, or striking artful poses while standing to better show off their outfits and jewelry. Servants bow before them, carrying trays laden with delicacies. Courtesans circulate among the crowds, some seated alongside nobles, others strolling gracefully, with elegant smiles for all. I don't see where the Imperial guests have gone, and I definitely see no sign of the Bisfuri hosts.

In fact, I recognize no one I know, not even the serving staff.

I pause several times, utterly lost, feeling completely out of place, despite my own sparkling outfit.

Somehow, I make my way toward the back corner of the hall to the musicians' area, where the drums, harps, and pipes are loudest. Erevi's band is playing a popular dance tune, while just behind them, I see my destination, the niche with the dressing room. Multiple people are coming and going there, carrying props such as feathers and ribbons.

As I approach, a sudden rush of performers erupts from the room. Acrobats! These entertainers immediately get into the act, spinning and jumping to amazing heights, running out into the center of the hall, even as the music changes in urgency to pure drums to accompany their arrival.

The guests make sounds of delight and clap in rhythm as the famous Acrobats of Imperial Poseidon move out among them, holding bright lengths of fabric. They use it to spin colorful optical illusion figures in the air. Meanwhile other acrobats converge in the center of the hall, while a stage on a hovering platform arrives out of nowhere, lowered from the ceiling. It is accompanied by a rain of golden sparkle from on high.

The acrobats dance and fly to the beat of the drums. They begin forming intricate figures on the stage floor and engage in body contortions that are both amazing and disturbing. . . .

Guests clap with various degrees of enthusiasm. These elites are not as easily impressed as I am.

I permit myself to gawk for a few moments, then enter the crowded dressing room.

THE SUPERVISOR in charge of scheduling is a small man with a loud voice. He stands with a digital tablet and taps the screen and points fingers at people as they surround him.

"Name? What kind of act?" he asks everyone. "You? And you?" And then he gives out the starting times and order of appearance.

I shove my way toward him eventually, past others—just as I hear a gorgeous chorus of voices rise outside in the hall, as singers begin a different performance.

"I am Semmi—I mean, Semirameos," I say. "I'm a Storyteller."

The little man gives me one quick, evaluating look, checks his schedule, then says, "Storyteller, you're next after Hoitura and Belora do their dance in half an hour. Which means, watch them, and be ready to go up on stage immediately after they're done."

"Which . . . stage?" I ask with trepidation.

"Tonight, there's only one," he says curtly. "You'll need a voice amplifier. You!" and he points to a uniformed staff member. "Attach the voice amp button on her collar, before we forget."

And then, before dismissing me, he narrows his eyes and squints at the tablet screen. "You'll be announced as—what is it again, Semmi? Too casual. Semirameos? Ah, no, that's too complicated. You're *Semiram*."

I DON'T BOTHER to protest my new "name" and merely stand aside to wait my turn. I take deep breaths to calm my thundering pulse and the blood pounding in my temples as though I've run here on foot all the way from Circle Ten.

The terror of my impending storytelling act hits me once more, and suddenly I feel my breath collapse in my lungs.

This, while the *hoohvak* plot of my ridiculous story spins in a drunken circle through my mind. Over and over. . . .

To center myself, I try to keep my attention on the two dancers who have been identified to me as Hoitura and Belora. The two young women stretch and warm up on the floor nearby, powerful bodies twisted in complex contortions. Only a few daydreams more, and they are up next.

And then, it's going to be my turn.

MY TEMPLES POUND like a flock of caged birds stuck in my skull as I follow the impossibly limber Hoitura and Belora outside, cursing my own name and whatever stupidity possessed me to pretend to be a Storyteller before *Ter* Bisfuri.

The dancers run up the stage and begin a fast-paced sensual dance, rolling their bellies and shaking their breasts. They are barely covered in wisps of shimmering fabric and an infinite number of metallic bracelets and anklets, while their arms have magically transformed into slithering snakes. . . .

I pay their artistry no heed, but instead, slowly edge my way closer to the stage past the crowds of guests and servant onlookers. I take frequent shallow breaths, while knives of anxiety start ripping through my gut.

My flittering gaze finds the Bisfuri group at last, along with the Imperial Princes. They are reclining on nearby cushioned chairs, paying no attention to the dancers whatsoever. Lady Ximunat is on the other side of Lord Bisfuri who sits next to the First Priest of Kassiopei, their heads leaned close together, while the First Priestess of Amrevet-Ra is conversing seriously with Benaten, with his aunt Lady Ishtaz on the other side.

Meanwhile, Prince Narmeradat lounges with his feet propped up on a settee, and next to him are Lord Enhuvarat Ximunat and Behamenut Bisfuri, with chairs pulled up, while Stryr and Arguam Giparu stand before them, showing off their living *pegasei* collars. A few steps back, Prince Oron sits talking with someone whose back is turned, and I don't see Princess Arlenari, though she could be on the other side of them. . . .

I look away, returning my poorly focused attention to the dancers who continue to gyrate with amazing skill. Crazy thoughts pass through my mind.

Maybe I should just run away and disappear. Mangy goats take these people!

I walk a few more steps closer to the stage, nervously touching the voice amplifier button on my collar. *What did they say to activate it? Tap twice? Three times?* Holy Bastet, I suddenly can't remember!

No, it's definitely twice. . . . Tap twice, then introduce myself and begin speaking.

Just as I'm fidgeting in place, I feel a gentle touch on my shoulder.

I almost lash out in reflex, turning around quickly, but stop myself from kicking, just in time. Good thing too, because I see a familiar face.

The glamorous *chimeratene* Ixenoel stands before me.

"Well, well, Semmi. You're a lovely sight, my dear," Ixenoel says with a playful smile.

"Oh, *nefero niktos!* Nice to see you here!" I reply breathlessly. "Ixenoel! Sorry, I almost kicked you—"

"So good that you didn't." Ixenoel chuckles in a voice of honey. "You do remember me."

"Of course! How could I forget?"

One perfect brow goes up on the androgynous face of rare beauty. "You couldn't, of course. To forget Ixenoel is unthinkable."

I smile, then laugh, and then quickly glance around again at the stage and the dancers who are finishing up their performance, judging by the crescendo of music and their rapid movements.

"Oh no. I'm supposed to go up there next . . ." I whisper.

"Is that so?" Ixenoel looks closely at me, seeing my anxious state. "And you're worried?"

"No, I'm *terrified.*"

"What? Such a bright bird you are, so how can it be?"

I feel a rush of cold, and a growing numbness in all my extremities at the reminder. "I've never spoken before such a great crowd before. And—and never told a story to so many people. It's a silly story. And I'm not really a Storyteller—"

"Oh, hush now," Ixenoel interrupts me, placing a warm hand over my own, then gives it a squeeze. "There's nothing to be afraid of. Just tell them your wonderful story!"

"But—" I look up at the tall *chimeratene* with panic filling my lungs.

"Let me teach you a little secret trick of the entertainer trade. It's proven very useful under many circumstances." Ixenoel leans in close to my ear and speaks in a very quiet but eloquent whisper. "Imagine that your audience—all the noble lords and ladies with their lofty manners and finery—are passing gas."

"What?"

But Ixenoel smiles very wickedly. "*Farting*, my dear. They are all farting. Grossly and loudly. Just keep imagining that, and then go up there and tell your story to all these malodorous fools! Toot! Toot!"

My mouth falls open. And then I start to laugh.

"There you go. No more nerves."

And, Bast knows, Ixenoel is right. . . . A warm feeling returns to me, and it's precisely on time, because just then the wild music ends. The two dancers descend from the hovering platform stage, hopping the last steps to the floor.

There is applause, followed by a lull in the crowd, and the noise of conversation returns.

My performance is next.

WITH A BURST OF ENERGY, I walk to the platform, climb the steps, and find myself alone in the center of the dais that is the stage. I glance down below, and the nearest guests have already noticed me, turned to look. . . .

To them, I'm just another performer.

My job is to entertain them.

Quickly, I glance about, and see the tall and stately Ixenoel nearby, waving and winking at me. The *chimeratene* silently mouths the words: "Toot, toot!"

I hold back a smile, and take a deep breath. Then I tap my sound amplifier, twice.

Before my courage fails me, I open my mouth and say, "My Lords and Ladies! *Ter-i-taq!* I am Semiram, the Storyteller! Let me tell you an amazing, magical tale that you will never forget!"

My amplified voice reverberates though the hall, surprising

even me. I sound loud, garish, at the same time high-pitched, slightly whiny, and strange—even to myself.

Is that really my voice?

But none of it matters.

I begin my story.

JUST A FEW SENTENCES IN, and a weird, subdued silence comes to the grand hall. Guests move in my direction, more and more heads turn, conversations grow quiet and fade away entirely. Even the servants pause in their endless motions around the chamber.

Don't think about the Imperials and every noble in the room looking at you. . . .

But I force myself to ignore all this weirdness, and continue telling the story of the *sha* king. My voice modulates from a near whisper to a loud commanding level, and it *rings* across the feast hall. Heartbeats pass and I forget to be afraid altogether, as I'm pulled in deeper into the reciting of the tale.

It's gotten so quiet now that it's uncanny. But I don't really care, because the enthusiastic *spirit* of the story has taken over entirely. And then, as I continue talking, I notice another wonderful thing happening—the audience responds to certain parts exactly as intended.

Bast merciful, they're laughing!

These lofty nobles are laughing at the funny parts of the story, in precisely the right moments. It's as though they're swept along, like the chunky contents inside a boiling pot of soup, by the motion of the stirring spoon—which happens to be me! When my voice expresses humor, they recognize it and laugh, and when I give them tension or suspense, they grow still with anticipation. . . .

I get to the part where the *sha* king asks the *sha* women who are potential brides lined up at his palace, "What is the one thing you can do for me better than anyone else?"

And since it's her turn to answer, my female heroine Sharzaad says: "I will tell you the best story in the world. But only if you promise not to choose me as your queen."

And the *sha* king immediately makes his decision.

I smile with energy born of mischief, as I pause dramatically. And then I say:

"The *sha* king decided that he's been without a wife all these years, doing just fine, and there was no reason to change things. Whatever *hoohvak* nonsense possessed him to look for a queen anyway? He had plenty of beautiful, clever, attentive concubines in his harem, and his life was perfectly uncomplicated. No need to bring in some beautiful but clever and wicked *sha* woman and give her authority over him. A good storyteller on the other hand—now that was worth something more than a monkey's ass!"

There is audience laughter. . . .

"And so," I continue, "the *sha* king told Sharzaad that he had no intention of making her his queen. In fact, he swore that if some madness ever possessed him to make her his queen—or make anyone his queen, for that matter, be it a *sha* woman, a cow, or a baboon—then Sharzaad was permitted to give him *one* hard slap upside his head and knock some sense back into him. 'You,' he said with a wicked gleam in his eyes, 'As of this moment, you are hired to serve as my official Palace Storyteller —but with one caveat. If the story you tell me does not live up to my expectations as *the best story in the world*, then I will have you executed on the spot.'"

In the great hall around me, the audience stops laughing and grows silent. I resume speaking after a sufficiently long, dramatic pause.

"Poor Sharzaad! She was terribly frightened, but her face did not show it. She regretted having said all the things she did that got her in this predicament. But, too late now, she had to please the *sha* king with her story . . . or lose her life."

I raise one hand up for emphasis and lean forward, before speaking.

"And so, Sharzaad told the *sha* king she was profoundly honored, and was going to tell him the best story, as promised, over a nice meal tonight. 'I like turnips and stew, with all kinds of mushrooms,' she added.

"The *sha* king agreed, and immediately dismissed all the remaining *sha* women still waiting in line, telling them to get the crap out of there, which effectively cleared out his palace grounds. And then, later that night, Sharzaad was given a bath, nice clothes, and a new comb to get her frizzy hair under control, then taken to the *sha* king's personal quarters.

"The meal was amazing, and Sharzaad ate like a goat who's gotten in a neighbor's back yard. The *sha* king sat waiting for her to start telling the story, but she kept eating, one dish after another, cooked with every different variety of mushroom they could find. . . . There were the tiny round mushrooms in bunches on long stems, the big ones that are formed in clusters of five or seven, the little button ones, the ugly misshapen blobs that cost a fortune, and many, many more—all *delicious*. Finally, after she ate everything on the table, and started on the *sha* king's own plate, he lost his patience and told her to begin the storytelling, or else.

"'Very well,' Sharzaad replied, and put one more delectable mushroom in her mouth, then burped loudly. 'O great *sha* king, the story I'm about to tell you is the most important, mysterious, joyful, and dangerous story in the world. When I am done telling it, you will know exactly why it is the best story possible, in this world and all others.'

"'Well then, go on,' said the *sha* king, intrigued like never before. And Sharzaad proceeded. 'This story is the story of *you*,' she said. 'The story of you and your kingdom and your reign.'

And then, in the next three hours, she told him a miraculously detailed chronicle of his own life, from birth to this very moment, concluding, 'And thus, my king, here we sit, you listening while I speak, and now we have come to the end—that is, the end of all the available material in this story—as of this moment. I'm unable to continue, since your story is still telling itself. We must wait and see how it resolves.'

"'Wait, you say? *Wait?*' the *sha* king exclaimed. 'You tricked me! What kind of strange story is this, without a proper end?' But Sharzaad smiled and said, 'My king, do you not concede that there can be no more important or better story than the story of you and your kingdom and your reign? Because if you say otherwise, you admit that *something* or *someone* out there, in this world or others, is more important or better than you. If you concede this, then I'm happy to be executed on the spot.'"

I pause for emphasis yet again, and watch the audience in the grand hall around me fixed in absolute silence.

"And so," I finish, "the *sha* king had no choice but to agree that the story Sharzaad just told him was the best story in the world. He grudgingly rewarded her with the official Storyteller position in his palace, and all the mushroom dishes she could eat. In exchange, Sharzaad promised the *sha* king that she would faithfully keep track of the rest of his story unrolling, for as long as it takes, meanwhile telling him many entertaining others, to while the nights away. And if at any point he decided he needed a queen—any queen, including herself—she would slap the *sha* crap out of him."

A wave of laughter hits, just as I stop talking. I pause, then bow deeply before them all.

There's a thunder of applause. It is followed by the resumption of conversation, and the party.

I straighten, smiling in relief, now that my performance is over, and apparently has been well received. . . .

That's when the explosion comes.

A bright flash of rainbow light erupts from the general direction of the Imperial group and their entourage, becoming a sparkling, iridescent cloud of quickly shifting colors. It rises overhead, a growing *entity* of light, then streaks outward and in every direction, bouncing, racing, amid screams and yells of the guests. . . .

One of the Giparu brothers—or cousins—or whatever they are—one of them, the younger one called Arguam, has just lost his shining *pegasus* collar.

TWENTY-SEVEN

A mid the chaos, *Ter* Stryr Giparu curses loudly and yells at his brother Arguam, forgetting himself to the point that everyone in the vicinity and far across the hall can hear him.

"*Varqood, hoohvak!* What did you do? How did it break out of its quantum containment field? Do you know how much each of those things cost? That was a rare specimen twin *pegasus*! *Varqood!* Now we'll have a mismatched pair when I get a replacement! You'll be the one explaining this to Uncle Zulumaat! *Varqood!*"

From what I can see at my distance, Arguam Giparu doesn't react much to his agitated relative, and there's hardly any expression on his blandly attractive face. For several long moments he keeps silent, as though humoring the other and letting him have his say. Eventually he shrugs, seemingly without a care, and speaks something in a quiet voice that I can't make out.

"Ah, *varqood!*" Stryr replies loudly to whatever was just said, and makes a gesture of slapping Arguam on his forehead without actually making physical contact with him.

Imperial Crown Prince Narmeradat chuckles, shaking his

head in amusement. As for the others, I only see Lord Muutat Bisfuri looking around with some minor concern, glancing up at the colorful residue of the *pegasus* still drifting in the air, but especially at the most bothered guests. The priests and the rest of their lofty group mostly observe impassively, holding goblets of drink.

Meanwhile, the rainbow cloud that was the *pegasus* has spread all over the grand hall in a fine mist and has mostly dissipated. The noble guests nearby are still looking up and shrinking away, some in a state of confusion. Several ladies try to bat away at the sparkling embers in the air around them, reminding me of children or cats. At once, servants with oversized papyrus fans step in to assist them, inadvertently scattering exquisite decorations from elaborate wigs with each fanning. Soon, the air reeks of expensive perfumes and scented oils from all directions.

Holding back an unexpected giggle, I take the opportunity to get down from the platform, hoping to sneak away.

Just as I land on the floor and look up, I notice that Benaten Bisfuri is looking in my direction and talking to a servant. He also gestures at me to approach.

Oh, no . . . is he calling me? Crap of a goat.

I feel a sudden pang of nerves, and start making my way toward the elite group, while the servant sent by Bisfuri hurries to intercept me.

"Entertainer, *Ter* Aten wants to speak with you now—come!" the servant tells me, and we both return to where the high-born nobles are seated.

I approach the seated Bisfuri and their Imperial guests, and immediately bow as low as I can. The manner and arrangement in which all of them are seated comprises a vaguely circular grouping, so it is not too difficult to encompass them all. Unsure to whom I should be bowing primarily, I make an awkward sweep with my body, before aligning myself in the direction of my actual employer, Benaten.

"Im Ter . . ." I say quietly, looking up after a sufficiently long pause. I keep my gaze only on *Ter* Bisfuri, trying not to look at the Imperials or any of the other nobles present. But I can feel their curious gazes on me. . . . *They're all examining me.*

"Semmi," he replies. "You and Girsul handle my *pegasei*. Do you remember what must be done to retrieve them if they escape the containment?"

"Oh . . ." I say in surprise, not expecting this question. "Um, no. I don't think anything can be done if they break out—"

Crap of a goat . . . why is he asking me? I should be asking him! And what about my performance? What did he think?

Benaten Bisfuri looks at me with a serious, focused gaze. "Are you sure? Think hard. Better yet, go and find Girsul and bring him here."

"Yes, *im Ter*," I respond, bowing again, and start to go.

"She's right," someone else in their group speaks up. I venture a quick glance and it's none other than the First Priest of Kassiopei. "There's no known way to recapture a *pegasus*. I would say that *Ter* Giparu has lost his permanently."

"Well then, I defer to your knowledge, Venerable Vardavar," Benaten says and lifts a finger at me to indicate I should wait.

"What a talented creature you have here, Aten. She tells a clever story and also handles your *pegasei*? Interesting range of skills."

I glance in the direction of the speaker, and see Prince Narmeradat examining me with an amused, lazy gaze. At once, a pang of anxiety stabs my gut, and I freeze like a *hoohvak* for just one moment, frighteningly unsure how to react, then bow silently.

"My staff is very well versed in multiple disciplines," *Ter* Bisfuri replies. Then he again addresses me. "No need to get Girsul, for now, Semmi. Oh, and yes—well done on the storytelling. You made my aunt, the Lady Ishtaz, laugh, keeping your promise."

"Thank you, *im Ter*." I bow again, lowering my eyes, and feel a sudden, quick flush rising in my neck and cheeks.

What about you? a curious, persistent thought nags at me. *Did I make you laugh?*

Seated next to Benaten, Lady Ishtaz—dressed in a glittering pale rose gown of several layers—starts somewhat at being singled out, and mutters something defensively about amusing nonsense. She then glances at her brother, Lord Muutat, a few seats away, to gauge his reaction. Lord Bisfuri, however, is once again engrossed in an intimate conversation with Lady Ximunat who has her hand stroking his upper arm.

"I also laughed," says a pleasant voice. I quickly glance at Prince Oron, who looks back at me with open curiosity and a smile reaching his eyes. "A rather wise story, in addition to being funny," he continues. "Thank you for telling it so well, Semiram the Storyteller."

I bow again. "Thank you, My Imperial Lord. . . ."

"Indeed. An interesting use of voice," First Priest Vardavar remarks suddenly. I look up with anxiety to see his very intent, serious gaze boring through me.

Bastet, he sees right through me. Probably knows I'm not a real storyteller, that I know close to nothing about pegasei, *that I just lied to get a job . . . and . . . what is he alluding to? Did he like my performance?*

My first impression of this Priest of Kassiopei, when I first saw him enter the antechamber, was different. He came across to me as mild, even scattered. But now—now, I'm suddenly on my guard because in his complex gaze there are layers of depth and *power*.

Out of nowhere, I get a disturbing, creeping sensation, as though insects are crawling under my skin. . . . *Why is he looking at me like that?*

In that moment, *Ter* Stryr Giparu, standing next to his younger brother (or cousin—I still don't know), steps away from Arguam and nears us, then points at me. "You—Entertainer," he says loudly. "So, you're a handler. Tell me if my remaining *pegasus* is in danger of escaping from this containment." And he points at his shining iridescent collar.

I pause, glance anxiously at Benaten, then at the others, but *Ter* Bisfuri nods encouragingly at me.

And so, I lean forward to examine the bright collar on the handsome nobleman's very naked chest . . . trying not to die of fright . . . trying not to touch any part of his lightly bronzed skin, and especially not that infernal *pegasus*, right before my nose—at least not just yet.

"I've never seen anything like this," I admit stupidly, after a few heartbeats of staring at the swirling colors barely moving underneath the rainbow surface. "But it seems to be well contained, and it is very bright, which means it's been properly fed."

"Yes, I had it fed right before we came here, just before my handler shaped it into the wearable collar containment form," Stryr tells me impatiently. "What I want to know is if this shape contains any inherent vulnerabilities. Both the *pegasei* were fed and contained in the exact same manner."

"I'm very sorry, but I'm not sure. I—I don't know, *im Ter*," I reply, looking down. "I haven't been working with the *pegasei* all that long."

Stryr makes a noise of frustration. "Then someone else, tell me what it could be! Because, how did my fool brother lose his?" And he throws one withering glance in the direction of Arguam.

So, they are indeed brothers, I think.

Arguam looks back at him, unblinking, and then just shrugs. "It just fell apart," he says quietly.

"How? *How?*" Stryr exclaims, his voice rising once more.

"What *exactly* were you doing, huh?"

"Nothing, *chazuf.*" Arguam's angelically calm face starts to frown. I stare at his own glistening, perfectly tanned bare chest lacking any other adornment, now that his collar is gone.

"My guess—your handler didn't key it properly," Prince Narmeradat says in a placating tone which reflects his own beginning annoyance. "Don't be concerned any longer, Stryr. It was an unlucky accident. The pretty, shiny thing managed to escape somehow."

"Yes, and now it's gone," Behamenut puts in carefully, leaning forward in his chair. "These creatures are unpredictable. Heed the Imperial Lord and relax, Stryr."

"Indeed. Forget about it and enjoy the party," Lord Enhuvarat Ximunat calls out from his spot several seats away, next to his mother.

"What happened to the Princess Arlenari?" suddenly says the First Priestess of Amrevet-Ra, speaking up for the first time and handing her goblet to the nearest servant. "Was she not seated with you, My Imperial Lord Oron?"

Prince Oron raises one brow, and looks around him. "Oh, she was, earlier. I thought she might've gone to speak with Lady Nanivel, over there—" And he points to another group of nobles nearby.

"What?" Narmeradat says. "Did Arlenari disappear again?"

"I don't see the lovely child anywhere," First Priestess Tuataan says sternly.

"Isn't she next to Lady Hiraeth Vamsu?" Lady Ishtaz squints in that direction. "Oh, no, never mind, it is only Bilan Qurvamsur, with her newly gilded hair—that Lady is far too daring, that color on her, why—of course, it could never match in shade the original splendor of the Kassiopei, forgive me—"

"Back to the Princess Arlenari, Aunt," Behamenut says, widening his eyes slightly and giving Benaten a quick glance.

"I believe I saw her . . . picking flowers," Arguam says with a strange expression.

Narmeradat laughs sharply. "Hah! That explains it. Recently, our Imperial sister decided that she must wander off at every opportunity. She especially tends to disappear at the bigger parties. She must've gone after a shiny object, such as a tray of crystal glasses, and lost her way when distracted by the sight of a pretty flower—"

"Nar, stop mocking her. She'll turn up," Oron says with a mischievous chuckle. "Usually somewhere unexpected."

"I'll have the servants look around for her," Benaten says, glancing at Behamenut and then at his father, the Lord Bisfuri, who appears ready to stand up, for whatever reason.

"Ah, don't bother." Narmeradat pops a sweet pastry in his mouth, taken from a tray offered by an attentive servant. He then sits up also, saying, "I need to stretch my legs and take a closer look at that quite elegant Lady in green next to—"

"Just one moment, My Imperial Lord," Lord Muutat Bisfuri interrupts him gently, quickly rising from his seat first. "Before you take your stroll, I must do something—I've an announcement that you will find of interest."

Narmeradat pauses. "Is that so?"

"My dear—" Lord Muutat turns to the Lady Ximunat. "Come, please, Ashura, this must be done properly—up there on the stage."

"Ah yes, of course, my dearest Muutat," she replies with an overly bright smile, standing up with the help of his solicitous hand.

Benaten Bisfuri once again exchanges a glance with his brother, and now fixes his rather intense gaze upon his father. For the first time tonight, I notice that he is frowning.

Meanwhile, Lord Muutat and Lady Ashura walk together to the levitating platform, her arm resting on his. They climb up to the stage—but not before Lord Bisfuri takes a small amplifier pin from a staff worker nearby, attaching it to his impeccably elegant jacket collar.

Lord Muutat stands next to Lady Ashura on the platform, and the guests in the vicinity grow silent, recognizing that their noble host himself is about to speak.

Lord Bisfuri taps the amplifier on his collar. He then takes the Lady's hand.

"I request your attention, My Imperial Princes of Kassiopei and all of you esteemed guests! My sons and I have welcomed you to our humble feast, and we are honored by your gracious presence tonight. But I must interrupt the festivities briefly to present to you the happy news pertaining to Bisfuri, this ancient Great House—and to the equally noble Great House Ximunat!"

Immediately, excited whispers fill the hall.

"It is with my utmost joy," Lord Bisfuri continues, "that I must inform this Court of the betrothal and upcoming nuptials of the most noble, beautiful, and virtuous First Lady Ashura Ximunat and myself! As our two Great Houses unite through matrimony, the gods and all of you bear witness to our pledge of undying loyalty to each other. We might be widow and widower, both of us eternally grieving for the passing of our first spouses, the loss of our domestic bliss, but the gods will have it that we don't persist in despair. Instead, they grant us this earthly reprieve and another chance to love—"

The hall around me erupts in exultation and applause. Lady Ximunat beams at Lord Bisfuri, barely inclines her head loftily in all directions and smiles widely, showing her pearl-white teeth.

Lord Muutat raises Lady Ashura's pale, bejeweled hand in an elegant gesture. Suddenly he turns it over and brings his mouth to her wrist for a brief but sensual pulse kiss. . . . Then, as the multitude of guests murmur and utter mockingly scandalized exclamations at such a public display of intimacy—as is customary—the Lord and Lady lift their clasped hands high over their heads and stand united for several heartbeats, looking out at the guests with bright smiles.

"I gratefully accept your proposal to unite our two glorious ancient lineages," Lady Ashura says in a ringing voice, then lowers her head in a brief, classic bow to Lord Muutat.

"As of this moment, my betrothed agrees to cede the designation of 'First Lady Ximunat' in favor of another," Lord Muutat proclaims in a pleased tone. "She now accepts the designation of 'First Lady Bisfuri'—a role and rank that will go into effect as soon as we are formally wed. She becomes my Wife and Mother to my sons, while I become the Father to hers! And now—all of you, our gracious guests, please continue to enjoy the feast! Bring out the celebratory wine of Amrevet-Ra!"

There is more general applause and well-wishes coming from all directions. Lord Muutat Bisfuri and his future First Lady descend from the platform, still holding hands. At the same time, servants run to fetch numerous trays with clear goblets full of sparkling rose-amber drink.

At least some of the staff must've been warned this announcement was coming, it occurs to me. *Otherwise, however did they manage to pour those drinks?*

While all this is happening, I observe the reactions of the elite nobles seated around me. Yes, I did not miss the short, quickly stifled gasp uttered by Lady Ishtaz, just as her brother Muutat brought up "First Lady Bisfuri." And now, I glance at Benaten and see the grim, serious expression fixed on his face.

No, he is not pleased by this turn of events. And neither is his younger brother, Behamenut.

Both the sons of Lord Bisfuri stand transfixed—indeed, they appear struck dumb by the happy news their father just revealed. I see their gazes connect, and an intense look passes between them, which I don't think I understand or can even begin to interpret.

Meanwhile, Lord Bisfuri and his new Bride return here to

reclaim their seats. But first, they stand smiling, receiving the flood of personal congratulations being heaped upon them.

Lord Bisfuri turns to his sons, Benaten then Behamenut, and opens his arms in a kind of half-embrace, gesturing them to approach.

"Come!" he says, looking first at his eldest son.

Benaten hesitates for a fraction of an instant, then approaches his father, and the two men embrace formally. "My congratulations to you, Father, and to your Bride," he says in a slightly cool voice, followed by a faint inclination of his head.

He then steps backward, and is faced by the Lady Ximunat, who looks at him closely with a fine smile on her sensuous lips. "Come, my new son," she says, lifting one hand gracefully, which Benaten may not ignore.

And so, he takes her hand and leans down to embrace her as her hands come around him, and they linger momentarily. "Welcome, My Lady," he says in a formal tone, and his rich, low voice expresses very little in the way of emotion.

"Not 'Your Lady.' You may call me Mother," Lady Ashura replies, looking up into his eyes and examining him with her unblinking gaze.

But Benaten smiles coldly. "Not quite yet," he says, stepping back. "Maybe after my Father and you are properly wed."

"Ah . . . very well," the Lady retorts. "But—soon." And then she turns to embrace Behamenut, who has just finished his turn formally embracing and greeting Lord Bisfuri.

Lady Ashura then calls her own son. "Enhuvarat, come! Greet your new Father, *im amrevu* boy."

Enhuvarat rises from his seat languidly and nears them. This time, Lord Bisfuri reaches out to embrace Ashura's offspring. "I'm glad to welcome you, young Lord Ximunat, my new son."

"I am honored by your welcome," Enhuvarat replies politely. He is then embraced by his own mother, who apparently has shed tears, because her eyes appear to glisten.

For some reason, I doubt the tears are real. . . .

Enhuvarat then approaches Benaten and Behamenut, and they formally embrace also, with one hand placed on the other's shoulder.

"You are all brothers, now." Lord Muutat smiles, watching them with a pleased expression.

"We are brothers," Benaten repeats formally, echoed by Behamenut and Enhuvarat.

Next, Lord Bisfuri and Lady Ximunat approach the two Imperial Princes, and give them formal obeisance by inclining their heads. Narmeradat stands up—he did, after all, plan to take a stroll around the hall earlier—and offers his hand, palm up, to the betrothed couple.

Lord Muutat and Lady Ashura place their joined fingers on top of Narmeradat's open palm in a brief touch, a traditional gesture indicating they are at the mercy of the Imperial Dynasty.

"I assume, my Imperial Father is aware of this arrangement?" Narmeradat asks with a mocking smile.

Lord Bisfuri inclines his head again. "Indeed, the Imperial Sovereign has given his blessing to this union."

"In that case, congratulations on the joyful news," Narmeradat says casually, with a tiny smirk. And then he just walks off in the direction of a nearby group of young, elegant noblewomen.

Prince Oron rises in turn and greets the betrothed couple. As he stands, I can't help but gauge his greater height and sense his *presence*, more so than that of the Crown Prince.

In that moment, servants arrive at our location with large trays of the sparkling wine, and Lord Bisfuri and his new Lady, reclaim their seats next to the priests. The Venerable Vardavar and the Venerable Tuataan immediately offer their congratulations and blessings. Lady Ishtaz does the same in a highly agitated voice.

"I'm going to take a small walk myself and see the wonders

of this party, and hopefully find my sister Arlenari," Oron announces to the group casually.

"I'll join you," Benaten says at once, and then, for some reason, glances at me.

"Semmi," he says. "Walk with us and look for the Imperial Lady. In fact, run ahead and check each of the smaller niches and the adjacent rooms around the hall."

"Of course, *im Ter*."

I bow and take off, making my way through the crowded room, at the same time as Benaten starts to move away with Prince Oron, putting on a charming smile and nodding at courtesans and guests in their vicinity.

As I glance back moments later, I see Oron and Benaten strolling together, no longer paying heed to the guests, engrossed in a serious conversation.

I run around the grand hall, politely inserting myself into elegant groupings to see who's there, and follow servants laden with trays who clear the path ahead. All the while, I keep my eyes open and all my attention on finding the Imperial Princess in her pale-blue dress. Every time I see a woman with a little veil over bright gold hair, I pause, hoping it might be she, but, no such luck.

After crisscrossing the hall at least twice, and losing sight of *Ter* Bisfuri and Prince Oron, I start the tedious examination of every nook around the perimeter, entering every side room. . . .

Bast help me . . . oh, the things I see. . . .

I stick my head inside rooms and there are people in various states of undress, noblewomen with lifted skirts and couples going at it like monkeys, or multiple partners wallowing on divans among pillows, with courtesans interspersed among them. People are pouring wine and other drink over each other and onto the pristine marble floor in disgusting sticky puddles, tossing goblets and smearing globs of creamy food over naked bodies and licking it away. These drunken, whoring *hoohvaks* are laughing and arguing over intimate positions.

Whenever anyone bothers to notice me looking in (which happens rarely, thank the gods), I'm either invited to join in or shooed away. Fortunately, I ignore these *shar-ta-haak* fools and disappear before anyone can restrain me.

In other rooms, I see elderly ladies or noblemen simply sleeping on the fine couches, probably having found the party too much. I don't blame them; I wouldn't mind lying down on those soft pillows too, after the long day I've had. My feet in these hard golden sandals are chafing. . . .

"Have you seen the Imperial Princess Arlenari?" I ask the occasional servants I run into who are cleaning up messes in empty rooms. But always they shake their heads. Some even point me to check behind drapery, until I roll my eyes.

A quarter of an hour later, frustrated, I indeed start shoving curtains and heavy drapery aside in various corners—finding several drunk nobles pissing on the walls, but no Imperial Princess—then make my way toward the front of the hall.

It's getting late, I'm guessing at least tenth hour of Khe, but there is no end to the noise level, music, and festivities. *Crap of a goat*, I curse silently. *Do these rich* chazufs *ever sleep? Some of us have to be back at work the next day. . . .*

Over on the entertainment platform hovering in the center, the Dancers of Dust and Water, a famous national dance troupe that even I've heard about, are forming an incredible human sculpture of many levels. Beautiful dancers wrapped in red veils stand on each other's shoulders, and keep climbing up to form new tiers, their human tower reaching for the ceiling.

I pause to gape at the dancers briefly, then continue to meander past groups of bejeweled elites, and can't help overhearing snatches of conversation. In addition to mindless chatter about fashions and society gossip, there's also more serious talk, especially among the older nobles. Many of them mention "the Sky Rock," while others whisper about their fears and concerns that "the space-flying ark-ships" will not be built in time, or that there won't be room for all their precious belongings.

Others yet ramble about the slow and tedious process of holding Service Competitions and how hard it is to find good servants these days.

I find myself boiling with fury at such comments, and get as far away from them as I can, so as not to lose my temper.

At some point I exit the grand hall into the antechamber which is now considerably emptied, and littered with flowers. A few bored servants remain stationed near the flower arch trellis, to greet any latecomer guests, and several drunks linger near the circulating wine fountain.

I wipe sweat from my forehead with the back of one arm, wishing for a drink of water for my parched mouth. Maybe I could take one of those half-full goblets abandoned all along the rim of the fountain and drink the dregs . . . I probably shouldn't, or they might fire me.

As I consider what might happen, I notice a faint movement of shimmering blue fabric in the shadows cast by the grand staircase, on the side opposite to the entrance leading into the feast hall. Something makes me go in that direction, and I find myself in the nook that contains the open doorway to a long corridor leading into a different area of this immense building. I've been here before at some point over these past few days, and recall that it leads outside and toward the other buildings of the estate, and the stables.

There's nothing here in this nook, when I get there. No furniture, no person in light blue. Just the entrance to an empty darkened corridor.

Bast, protect me from this sha *foolery.*

I sigh in weary annoyance. Then I turn around to head back.

That's when a lotus blossom falls on the marble floor at my feet.

Princess Arlenari stands before me, clutching a linen cloth before her like an apron, overflowing with flowers.

I JUMP BACKWARD and make a little sound, but can't help what follows from my *hoohvak* mouth. "Ah, crap of a goat!"

Immediately, I slam a hand over my orifice.

The Princess stares at me with widened eyes, and appears to be equally startled by my presence.

"My Imperial Lady! So sorry! Please, forgive my impertinent words!" I exclaim, bowing profusely. "But oh, I'm so glad to find you! Everyone's looking for you—"

But the moment I start talking, she shakes her head violently, and switches her flower bundle to one hand, clutching it against her abdomen. The other hand she raises to her face, putting the index finger against her lips to indicate silence.

I freeze and go quiet, and we stare at each other, breathing fast.

"Please . . ." she whispers, after a few tense heartbeats. "Please don't tell them where I am."

"Oh." My eyes widen again. "I—I was sent to find you by *Ter* Bisfuri. He and the Imperial Prince Oron were worried—"

"They always say that," Princess Arlenari interrupts, and her delicate face goes slack with a kind of sad weariness. "But it's never true. They don't really care where I am, so this is just as well."

"Um . . . all right," I say, not sure what to think. "But—what are you doing here?"

Arlenari glances at the bundle she is holding. "I'm collecting these . . . and taking them outside where they can fade in peace," she says in an odd voice with several wistful pauses. "So many . . . discarded like trash on the floor, after a meaningless moment . . . abandoned to wither and be trampled. Such a sad fate for these beautiful living things. Grown with loving care, under precise conditions of humidity and sunlight . . . only to be cut down on a whim and presented to people who don't want them."

"Oh yes! Such a waste, I agree completely," I reply with enthusiasm. "I was just saying this earlier to this girl I work with —" I pause momentarily wondering if I'm overstepping myself, but the Princess just listens curiously, without judgement.

And so, I continue, "I was just telling Menahit how we should just reuse the flowers as people drop them. I mean it makes sense, right? These fancy *chazufs* throw them away, so we just pick them right back up and give the same flowers to the next person in line! No waste, no one would notice! Good economy too! But Menahit was saying *noooo*, we can't do that—"

I shut up and bite my lip, realizing that I may have gone a bit too far. *She's the Imperial Princess, and I just called her kind of people* chazufs! *Oh, Bast, I'm dead, for certain. . . .*

But Princess Arlenari continues staring at me. Suddenly her lips tremble, and she starts to laugh, shaking silently.

My mouth opens at first, and then I grin back at her.

"You . . . you're the one who gave me my flower at the door," she says, smiling with a kind of innocent joy.

"I did." I laugh a little. "But—don't worry, it wasn't from the floor, it was a completely fresh flower from that big bowl behind me, perfectly clean, I swear—"

"Thank you again." Princess Arlenari glances at the colorful bundle cradled in her one arm, then reaches inside a small pocket in the folds of her glittering dress. She takes out a large lotus blossom. I realize it's the same one I gave her.

"I kept mine." She tells me softly. "I am going to take it home and put it in a bowl of water, to give it a few extra moments of life."

"Oh, okay," I say. "Well, that's good . . . I guess."

Princess Arlenari examines that flower, growing serious again, and appears to be lost in thought. Then she carefully puts it back inside her hidden pocket. "Now, I must get back to my sad task. And I appreciate you for not telling anyone where I am."

"Don't worry, I won't tell." I stare at her, feeling an unexpected stab of pity. And then I gather the courage to continue. "May I ask, My Imperial Lady, why do *you* need to do this yourself? I promise, the servants of Bisfuri will remove all the flowers from the floor after the party and take them outside, so you don't need to exert yourself—"

"I know they will," she says. "But will they *thank each one* before returning it back to the earth from which it came?"

"Probably not," I say, biting my lip. Honestly, I have no idea what else to do, so I open my big mouth again. "Would you like me to help you?"

Argh! What sha-*induced madness just prompted me to volunteer for this nonsense?*

Imperial Princess Arlenari smiles tentatively at me. "Would you?"

I nod, and roll my eyes a little, which she notices, and her smile widens. So, she's not entirely a half-wit. Though, I still wonder if she's been dropped on her head a little when she was a baby.

"All right," I say quickly, glancing behind us into the antechamber. "You stay here, and I'll go run around and pick up these things. I won't be able to get all of them, but just the ones right underfoot near the entrance, otherwise people will ask me too many questions. I'm probably not supposed to be doing this anyway, but—"

"Did the *sha* king eventually come to love Sharzaad?" Princess Arlenari interrupts my ramble with a question that takes me by surprise.

"What?" I stop talking and my eyebrows rise. "Oh . . . in the story?"

"I liked hearing it very much," she says, looking steadily at me. "But now I need to know what happens to them . . . after all those years."

"Um . . ." I freeze in a sudden instant of panic.

I have no idea. . . .

And then, something weird flows out of me—*more story*. It's as if, the moment I *think* of the story, it *continues itself*, exactly where I left off.

"I—I would need to ask the *sha* king himself—I think," I reply with a little smile, regaining my confidence.

"Would you ask him, please?" Arlenari nods slowly, for some insane reason not finding my answer strange at all.

"All right." I pause, scrunching my forehead with exaggerated effort and craning my neck, as though I'm communicating with someone sitting inside my head.

After a sufficiently long pause I straighten and continue. "He says—he says he cannot tell me right now, because not enough time has passed yet for him and her, since they're both just stuck inside the story, you know. And it's all still happening . . . in here."

I point a finger at my temple.

"I know." Arlenari watches me with a mixture of soft curiosity and calm understanding that I've never seen anyone direct toward me. "I'd like to revisit this story again—however much there is of it. Do you mind writing it down for me?"

"I—" My lips part. "I—I don't know how to write," I admit like a *hoohvak*, and feel a rush of heat in my cheeks.

"Oh. . . ." she says.

"But—I can record it for you!" I exclaim. "I'll just need to find Girsul—he works with me and does tech stuff—and see if he can set it up for me. I can tell the story to a device, such as a tablet, and then you can just listen to it any time. And maybe the machine can translate it into writing—"

"That would be lovely," Arlenari says softly, blinking, with the shadow of a smile at the corners of her lips. "Bring it to me at the Palace."

"Of course, My Imperial Lady!"

The Princess simply looks at me.

And in that moment, I am awakened to another realization— this one, quite horrible, something I've never felt before— personal *inadequacy.*

She is pitying me because I cannot write.

From where I come, most people don't know how to write, but we also don't *mind* it that much. It's a kind of luxury, a special higher skill that the noble elites possess—and occasionally, a few specially trained commoners who work as scribes, teachers, or other such educated jobs.

But for the most part, we all get by just fine with memorizing spoken or recorded words, recognizing big, colorful picture-logos on buildings, flashing lights, and a few basic numbers. We get clever at noticing the patterns of light control buttons on buses and public spaces, working warehouse machinery, not to mention the controls on the media-box. And a few of us figure out a handful of basic written letters, thanks to the habit of a lifetime.

It never occurred to me that the upper-class skill of writing and reading is something I might *need.*

And now, suddenly, I do.

I desperately need to write, so that I can give the Imperial Princess *my story.* Writing words down preserves them when human memory fails, fixes them in time, allows them to be gifted.

As I stand, newly paralyzed with my inadequacy, a burst of noise comes from the opposite side of the staircase, the entrance to the grand hall. There's ringing female laughter and brash male exclamations, and people are coming.

I turn around to see who it is, then glance back at the

Imperial Princess standing behind me near the darkened hallway entrance.

But she's *gone*.

Crap of a goat.

She must've run back outside with all those *hoohvak* flowers. Poor thing. . . .

I shake my head, thinking that at least now I probably don't need to worry about my offer to help her collect the flowers from the floor. Fine with me.

And then I get vivid and persistent images in my head of what this girl's life must be like. I picture fancy rooms—the kind I've seen in popular dramas about rich people, on the media-box. And then I imagine the Palace—which I've seen only from the outside during news shows about the Imperials, again on the media-box. Inside that Palace, it's probably as big or larger than this amazing Bisfuri estate, and even more magnificent.

She is surrounded by servants and luxury, yet she's all alone.

Why am I thinking these *shar-ta-haak* things? It's none of my business.

Frowning at myself and this intrusive thought nonsense, I step out from the shadowed alcove into the antechamber, and see Imperial Prince Narmeradat standing right near the drink fountain, with several beautiful women surrounding him. Some of them wear the blood-red teardrop gem on their forehead to indicate *amretene* status.

". . . this will make you laugh, My Imperial Lord, I promise! Let me show you—" a young woman speaks, smiling wickedly and reaching for the Prince's thigh.

"If you make me laugh, right now, I just *might* select you to serve me personally when the time comes to fly away," he replies, ogling her scantily-clad body, but not returning her touch, and instead refilling his goblet in the fountain.

"Oh, take me!" another female moans, delicately pushing herself up against him from the other side.

"No, me! I can make your *varqooi* cry and you laugh, all at the same time! As you fly to the stars, I'll please you best of all—I'll do anything, *anything*, whatever you like!" a third courtesan exclaims, and then lifts her arms overhead and starts to sway and dance before him.

"Show me how you dance, yes . . . move your pretty *puzuk* for me," the Prince says languidly, but then looks away with distraction at yet another courtesan who begins to sway and shake her even more impressive attributes to the beat of the music coming from the main hall.

I stand frozen, for some reason unwilling to go out there and risk being noticed. Because, to be honest, this very handsome Imperial Crown Prince evokes a disturbing, dark anxiety in my gut. Unlike his younger sister and brother, I realize I do *not* like this man. It might be treason to think this way about my future Imperator, but he gives off a creeping sense of unease. And I always trust my gut about such things.

Fortunately, I don't have to be stuck in the shadows too long, because a servant arrives from the hall to inform the Imperial Prince that Lord Bisfuri is looking for him to discuss some important business.

"Business at this hour? How tedious, ladies—my very, very pretty ones. But, mustn't disappoint our fine Host," Narmeradat says in a sarcastic tone to the women, and then heads back inside the hall, with his retinue scrambling after him.

I take a deep breath and come out. At this point, I would really love to go home but, when are we even permitted to leave? I could go ask someone in the serving staff area, or find Girsul or Menahit. Probably, best to go find *Ter* Bisfuri, tell him I couldn't find Princess Arlenari, and see if he needs me for anything else tonight.

I head back inside the great hall, to get this endless day over with.

But the gods have different plans for me.

CHAPTER
TWENTY-NINE

I enter the hall just as the latest music stops and Behamenut, Lord Bisfuri's youngest son (and so-called formal host of this event), gets up on the floating platform. He appears slightly flustered, but then taps his sound amplifier and calls everyone's attention.

"We're going to play a game!" he says loudly. "You know Hunt the Hidden, right? That's what we'll play right now. And let me tell you, the trinket you'll hunt today, hidden somewhere around this great hall, is an object of priceless value! It's a jewel-encrusted gold scarab, the size of my palm, with a great ruby set in place of its head, and an emerald between its wings!"

At once, exclamations of awe come rolling through the hall in waves.

"Upon my signal, everyone can start searching, and you get half an hour. Whoever finds this priceless scarab within thirty daydreams, gets to keep it! Remember, it is definitely concealed inside this hall, including all the adjacent rooms, and it could be anywhere. And if no one finds it when time is called, then one of the Bisfuri will name anyone they like to be the winner!"

Even more excitement sounds from all around. A few of the noblemen and ladies get up from their seats eagerly.

Up on the platform, Behamenut chuckles and rubs his hands. He then pulls out a device which appears to be a fancy hovering clock (the expensive kind shown frequently in media-box commercials). He taps it, calling up an enormous hologram of glowing dashes and lines which I recognize to be numbers floating high above his head. "Are you ready, *im ter-i-taq*? Begin!"

He tosses the clock up in the air, the device levitates, and the projected numbers start blinking and racing in what I assume is a countdown.

The hall erupts in squeals, giggles, and the thunder of running people.

Bast, help me, what is happening?

I stand in place, stunned, while courtiers rush all around me. Meanwhile, the other serving staff are also fixed in their spots, trying to keep out of the way of the crazed guests.

Several objects immediately get knocked to the gleaming marble floor. There are clattering dishes and breaking crystal. . . .

I scan the room, locating the Imperials, the First Priests, and Lord Bisfuri's personal group. They are the only ones who remain seated in their casual semi-circle, watching the mayhem around them with disdainful amusement (and in the case of the priests, with stern disapproval).

Unlike the others in the group, Lord Muutat Bisfuri wears a serious expression, and is deeply engaged in a conversation with Prince Narmeradat. Likely, he's discussing business, as I recall from the antechamber earlier, when the Prince was summoned by a Bisfuri servant. Leaning forward, Lord Muutat speaks something in Narmeradat's ear and gesticulates with one bejeweled hand, while the Prince appears to frown.

Benaten Bisfuri is here also, next to Prince Oron, both having returned from their stroll around the room. I watch his raven-black head turned sideways, the elegant, chiseled line of his profile, as he listens closely to something the younger prince is saying.

In that instant I happen to notice, of all things, Lady Ashura. Fleetingly, she turns her cold, beautiful face, and I see her *eyes*. And then, for some strange reason, her intense gaze fixes on Benaten. She stares in that general direction—in *his* direction—then turns back to laugh at whatever Lord Enhuvarat is telling her and Lady Ishtaz.

I carefully maneuver past the jostling guests toward my employer, just as Behamenut approaches also, after making his announcement on the platform.

"Well done, Eham," Benaten says with a smirk, then notices me, standing behind his brother. "No luck finding the Imperial Princess?" he asks me.

I meet the steady gaze of his grey eyes and feel a sudden flush overtaking me. "No, *im Ter*," I reply quietly, feeling bad about having to lie to him, of all people. But I did promise the Princess I would say nothing, so. . . .

Bast help me, my head is burning up from this unnecessary, unexpected lie!

"Everything okay?" he asks, and I feel that he can see right through my little *hoohvak* deception.

"Oh . . . yes, *im Ter*. I looked all over, even checked behind curtains. . . ."

"You did? Very thorough of you," *Ter* Bisfuri says, and one corner of his mouth twitches.

"Is there anything else you need me to do tonight, *im Ter*?" I ask politely, hoping he would just dismiss me for the night already.

"Well, since there is no Imperial Princess to be found," he says, with a brief glance at Prince Oron, "You are free to—"

"Arlenari might have slipped out to return home," Oron says

just then. "She often ends up back at the Palace whenever we can't find her at different functions."

"So, you're saying this has happened before?" Benaten glances at him again.

Oron exhales and runs his fingers through the ends of his long, golden hair, twirling a strand. "Yes, it's something she seems to enjoy doing. Or maybe she is just not happy to be out instead of staying in her quarters—reading scrolls of fanciful stories or playing with her musical instruments."

"The Imperial Princess prefers reading to Court?" Behamenut asks incredulously.

Prince Oron smiles at the younger Bisfuri. "To be honest, I, too, often prefer reading, or walking the gardens, to most Court functions. Not counting this splendid affair, of course, Eham. Your party is flawless."

"Thank you, my Imperial Lord." Behamenut appears pleased. He then looks up to check the hovering clock overhead, with its big hologram numbers flickering in the air high above, continuing to move rapidly in the throes of the countdown. . . .

In that moment, sounds of a minor commotion come from one of the wall niches, including a few alarmed female cries, followed by an actual angry scream.

Heads turn to stare, a few of the guests pause their hunting game, and several servants in the vicinity rush toward the excessive noise.

As this is happening, Lord Muutat shakes his head in annoyance and turns away from Prince Narmeradat to look at the First Priest of Kassiopei apologetically, as though to excuse the commotion.

Loud waves of talk move through the hall. "Did they find it? Did someone find the scarab?"

Just then, two Bisfuri servants hurry in our direction. I see it's Girsul and Vakrem, the big security guard.

They arrive and immediately bow before the elite nobles.

Vakrem speaks first. "My apologies, but Lady Hatshepsut Hekufati has been hurt. The Lady Satiah Ideva got in front of her as they were scrambling for the golden scarab—"

"Lady Hatshepsut then pushed Lady Satiah with her elbow," Girsul interrupts, moving his own elbow to demonstrate. "I was there, I saw it. At which point Lady Satiah struck her cheek and the side of her hand—"

Benaten makes an exasperated sound and rubs his temple with one hand, while Lord Muutat Bisfuri's concerned expression deepens into a frown.

Prince Narmeradat leans forward with interest. "Is there blood?"

Vakrem inclines his head again. "My Imperial Lord, yes, unfortunately. Lady Hatshepsut's cheek appears scratched deeply where Lady Satiah's gold ring cut her skin."

"How bad is it?" Benaten asks, rising—after a hard glance and nod from his father, and the curious stares of Lady Ishtaz and the others.

"Bad enough that the Lady Hatshepsut is demanding Imperial Justice." Vakrem keeps his expression neutral but again bows in the direction of Narmeradat and Oron.

"Ah, very well." Narmeradat stands up, without bothering to hide his enthusiasm, after a quick glance at his younger brother. "Let's go see the blood and handle it accordingly."

Oron hesitates for a moment, then rises also.

"Go look for the medic, bring him here quickly," Benaten commands Girsul who rushes off to do his bidding.

And then *Ter* Bisfuri glances at me. "You, come along."

PRINCE NARMERADAT, Prince Oron, and Benaten move quickly, weaving through the party crowds, past curious guests, in the wake of Vakrem. I follow them, keeping back politely.

We arrive at the area of the great hall near the wall where the commotion happened. Loud, agitated female voices can be heard from within the room beyond the recessed niche. Vakrem bows once more, and indicates to the Imperials to step ahead of him. Everyone then enters the small room through the niche.

I enter last, after all of them, and see the chamber is furnished with two short couches on both sides of an elevated mantel shelf. The top of the mantel is occupied by several flower-filled crystal vases, and between them, the unmistakable glint of gold in the shape of a scarab. This is indeed where the precious jewel trinket has been hidden. The height of the mantel makes it just slightly out of reach.

Just below it, two noble ladies stand, glaring at each other and exchanging insults. The one holding a linen cloth against her cheek is taller and slimmer, with delicately tan skin and very beautiful features. She wears a tall, gilded wig with intricate metallic spikes and several short veils that cascade down her back, and connect to her cream-white dress by tiny golden chains.

The second lady is more voluptuous and has darker skin. Her natural hair is swept up in a pearl-studded hairdo, while her curvy figure is wrapped in a diaphanous red dress with slits on both sides of her shapely legs.

The moment they see the Imperial Princes, the two ladies fall silent for a few heartbeats and bow their heads in courtly obeisance. Then they begin talking, one louder than the other.

"My Imperial Lords, she pushed me first!" cries the lady in the red dress. "She got in my way as I was reaching for it—"

"Liar!" cries the other with the cloth held against her cheek. "You scratched me on purpose, devious *sha*!"

"I did no such thing! I was defending myself from your odious elbow—"

"Ladies! Enough!" Prince Narmeradat says, putting one

hand up. He takes a step forward and reaches out to pull the cloth away from the hurt lady's cheek. "*Im nefíra* . . . Lady Hatshepsut, is it? Allow me to see."

"Yes, My Imperial Lord," Hatshepsut says, turning her face closer toward him. Her cheek is indeed bleeding, but it's just a tiny trickle, and a little spot of red on the cloth.

Narmeradat moves even closer to her and looks down from his height to stare. "Does it hurt?" he asks.

"Yes, very much." Lady Hatshepsut lowers her eyes and puts on the expression of a martyr, then looks up at him through her long dark lashes.

"I promise, the physician will be here soon," Benaten says, also stepping closer to examine her. "Fortunately, it doesn't appear to be that serious—"

"Not serious?" Lady Hatshepsut's beautiful hazel-brown eyes flash at him with outrage.

"What of me, *me*? My body?" the other young woman, Lady Satiah, exclaims with a pout and a frown. "My chest hurts and there will likely be a horrible ugly bruise tomorrow, right here—" And she points to her breast.

At once Prince Narmeradat hands the cloth back to Lady Hatshepsut and turns toward Lady Satiah. "Show me immediately, *amrevet*," he says with a lascivious stare at her plunging neckline.

Satiah takes a deep breath to inflate her already sizeable chest and steps forward with a tragic expression on her pretty face, then slowly pulls down the top of her dress to reveal even more of her body.

"I am *bleeding*, my Imperial Lord! And I deserve to have the scarab for my suffering!" Hatshepsut attempts to regain Prince Narmeradat's attention. Then she turns to Prince Oron with a minor wail, but the younger Prince does not react, merely watches with an expression of mild discomfort.

"No! I'm the one who should be given the scarab—"

"Both of you need to be *punished*," Narmeradat interrupts suddenly, with a sarcastic smile. He then pushes past the two women and easily reaches the mantel shelf to take the sparkling jeweled scarab in his own fingers. "A pretty piece, Aten." He glances at *Ter* Bisfuri, then resumes examining the scarab, which sparkles with fire as the light hits the great emerald and ruby.

"Feel free to keep it, My Imperial Lord," Benaten says after a tiny pause. "That should be punishment enough for these lovely ladies."

"Punishment enough? Not so fast." Narmeradat looks up from his perusal of the golden trinket and watches Hatshepsut and Satiah with a very cold glare that somehow also exudes a kind of fierce, sadistic energy.

"Please, My Imperial Lord . . . whatever do you mean?" Hatshepsut turns her head sideways at him and her expression loses all of its petulance.

"You—and you—" Narmeradat glances at her then at Satiah, "will now be punished for your unseemly behavior."

"What, My Imperial Lord?" Satiah's glossy red mouth parts. "But she—"

"*Silence.*" The Crown Prince's deep, serpentine voice modulates and suddenly acquires a weird, added layer of *power* for which I have no proper description (except that it makes my skin crawl with fear). "You asked for Imperial Justice, and you shall have it."

"Please forgive me, My Imperial Lord," Hatshepsut says in a much different tone of voice than before, bowing her head with its widened eyes.

"Even though you bleed, and you are beautiful, I find *you* to be more at fault," Narmeradat replies. "Call your personal servant."

He then glances at Satiah. "And *your* punishment is that you shall administer *her* punishment."

"What?" Satiah appears confused. "How, My Imperial Lord?"

"Call your servant, *now*," Prince Narmeradat repeats to Hatshepsut, training his serpentine gaze upon her.

"My servant?" Lady Hatshepsut echoes. "But—my servant—she's waiting outside, with the car. . . ."

Benaten turns to me unexpectedly. "Semmi, find Lady Hekufati's maidservant and bring her here. Go!"

Instantly, my heart pounds with anxiety. I have no idea what's happening here, but I nod to my employer, then start running.

I HURRY through the immense hall, moving past the crowds of guests and servants, then slip out of the antechamber and through the grand front entrance which I've never used before, into the thick, warm night outside.

Down a steep flight of marble steps I go, toward the driveway where endless rows of expensive hover cars line the way, levitating a foot above ground, with drivers and servants of the party guests loitering everywhere. Torches flicker on top of ancient posts, and orb-lights float like golden moons to break up the darkness.

"Ei!" I call out. "Looking for Lady Hekufati's car! Where is Lady Hekufati's car and staff? Her maidservant is needed inside!"

Several drivers look up at me lazily, saying nothing. A few of them point down the row.

I run along the driveway, periodically calling out, "Are you Lady Hekufati's staff? No?"

Finally, a uniformed young man leaning against a mirror-polished black car looks up and waves back at me. "Over here!"

I notice, next to him is a young woman, wearing the same style of household uniform, sitting on the elevated portion of the walkway curb, and nodding off, with her dark-haired head leaned forward. She starts with alarm at my voice and the mention of Lady Hekufati, and scrambles up. "Yes?" she asks.

I note the rose-colored domestic service tassel on her collar.

"Are you Lady Hekufati's personal servant?" I ask, breathing fast.

"Yes, I'm Naamat. . . ."

"Come with me, quickly, you are needed inside," I rattle off, and begin heading the way I came from, toward the front entrance.

"Why, what's wrong?" Naamat asks me, as she hurries at my side, matching my pace. "Is the Lady Hatshepsut all right?"

I glance at her soft, earnest expression, her widened brown eyes set in a pleasant, ordinary face, the sand-brown skin and the dark hair pulled back tightly and pinned up. "I think your Lady is all right—I mean, she *looks* to be all right—but she got in a fight with another Lady," I say. "So, she's got a bloodied cheek—"

"Oh, no!" The servant girl opens her mouth in anxious worry.

"Yes," I continue, as we run up the flight of stairs at the front entrance. "And the Imperial Prince told them both they are to be punished, and he ordered her to call you, her servant. . . ."

The more I speak, the more I start to get an unpleasant feeling of what's to come.

Lady Hatshepsut's poor maid just listens with resignation and follows me silently into the building, through the antechamber and into the grand hall.

WE ARRIVE, breathless, at the location of the incident, and enter the small chamber through the wall niche. All eyes turn toward us.

"There you are, Naamat!" Lady Hatshepsut exclaims with a

strained expression on her lovely face. She then turns with uncertainty toward Prince Narmeradat.

The maidservant casts fearful glances at the Imperials and the others present, then bows deeply, muttering quietly, "My Lady, how may I serve you?"

Narmeradat barely looks at the servant girl and instead turns to Vakrem, who happens to be standing off to the side, out of the way. "Guard, give me your *hedah*."

Vakrem hesitates only for a moment, to glance at our employer. Benaten barely nods at him, with an otherwise expressionless face, indicating for him to proceed.

My heart starts to pound just then, as I watch *Ter* Bisfuri . . . because for the first time, something about him truly terrifies.

He appears, in that moment, cold as ice.

And so Vakrem reaches at his belt and removes a short, tri-folded punishment stick from its holster. He snaps it open, unfolding it to its full length of a long man's arm, while Lady Hatshepsut watches his practiced movements with growing fear.

And then Vakrem hands it politely, handle first, to the Crown Prince.

Narmeradat takes the *hedah* and examines it, weighs it in one hand thoughtfully. Next, he takes a few steps away and with a sharp flick, makes the *hedah* cut the air with a hard hiss.

Lady Hatshepsut lets out a tiny fearful gasp.

Everyone in the small chamber watches, almost stunned.

Abruptly, Narmeradat looks up, his gaze imbued with energy. "Come, Ladies. Approach and stand here, before me. Let us begin!"

Lady Hatshepsut and Lady Satiah move hesitantly toward him with widened eyes.

"Now," the Crown Prince says, almost comfortably, almost with warm overtones of humor. "You will accept your well-deserved punishment."

He glances at Lady Satiah. "Take the *hedah, amrevet*. I assume you know how to use it?"

"Oh no, please, My Imperial Lord—" Lady Satiah protests, but takes the stick in her slightly trembling fingers.

"Oh, My Imperial Lord, *no!*" Lady Hatshepsut shakes her head, pleading with her eyes.

But Narmeradat stares down at her with a slow, sadistic smile curving his lips. "Come, *im nefira*, accept your punishment. Five cutting strokes of this very nice *hedah*. Or maybe even a few more."

Lady Hatshepsut gasps again, and her expression loses all composure.

At the same time, Prince Oron's expression darkens and he frowns at his older brother, while his lips part.

Narmeradat's smile deepens. "Ah, but don't be so afraid, lovely one. *You* of course will not be touched, as the noble daughter of the Great House Hekufati. Your personal servant is here for a reason. She will receive the strokes in your stead and on your behalf."

"Oh! My Imperial Lord!" At once, Lady Hatshepsut's face recovers, and she exhales in relief. But then she glances guiltily at her maidservant Naamat.

Poor Naamat! She and I both finally come to understand what is happening, but only now. *Just now.* A look of disbelief comes to the girl's face, but she remains motionless and only starts blinking rapidly and darting her eyes, as she stands before her mistress.

"Come on, Narmer, no, don't . . ." Prince Oron says in that moment.

But Narmeradat ignores him. "Tell your servant to step forward, right here, and put out her hands," he says to Hatshepsut.

"Well. . . . Go on!" the Lady echoes him, speaking to Naamat in a bare whisper. "Do as the Imperial Lord commands!"

Naamat moves forward stiffly, keeping her eyes lowered, and ends up before Lady Satiah who's holding the *hedah* stick. The servant girl slowly raises both her hands, slender and thin, and stretches them out at chest level.

"Turn your hands, palms up!" Narmeradat tells the maidservant in a hard voice. And then he glances at Lady Satiah. "Begin the punishment—yours and hers, my sweet Lady. Strike her, *now!*"

In that instant, Satiah raises the *hedah* and barely taps Naamat's upturned palm.

Naamat flinches (probably more from the expectation of pain than actual harm), but stays fixed in place.

"Again! Harder! Do not hesitate!" Narmeradat watches with a fierce energy in his eyes.

Lady Satiah glances at him with momentary uncertainty, then lifts the *hedah* and swings with somewhat more power, striking again.

This time Naamat must really feel it, and she blinks.

"What's this? Nothing! You must hit harder!" Narmeradat commands. "Is that the best you can do? Surely, you've punished your own servants before, you know how to do it! *Strike!*"

Satiah nods silently, then swings again, and strikes. . . . Again, and again, and again.

Naamat stands unmoving, quiet, receiving the blows. She keeps her thin hands held out before her, only flinching silently. Her palms show red welts, and one of them is seeping blood.

"That was five strokes," Benaten says coldly. "It is done, My Imperial Lord. Let us return to the festivities in the hall—"

"It is done when I say it's done!" Narmeradat snarls suddenly. He grabs the *hedah* out of Lady Satiah's hands and motions her to step aside (which she does gladly).

"Your servant is not very repentant, Lady Hatshepsut," he says, without looking at her, and staring at Naamat with cold fury. "Why does she not cry? For your own sake, she must beg for mercy and cry—"

And suddenly Narmeradat swings the *hedah* very hard and hits Naamat's hands with such force that she lowers them from the impact and staggers in place.

"That's enough!" Prince Oron exclaims. "Narmer, stop, *please!* Nar!"

"Don't interrupt your future Imperator when he is conducting business, my brother," Narmeradat retorts through his teeth, without looking away. "Why doesn't she cry?"

"What kind of unfortunate business is this?" Oron speaks again. "She's but an innocent—"

"She is guilty by proxy!"

Lady Hatshepsut, puts her hands over her mouth in genuine fear. "Cry, Naamat! Beg and cry . . . at once," she mutters. "Beg forgiveness and mercy from His Imperial Lord!"

Narmeradat swings again.

"I beg . . . forgiveness. . . ." Naamat's voice comes faint and agonized.

"My Imperial Lord, if this servant's hands become any more damaged, she will be unable to serve the Lady Hekufati properly for the rest of the evening," Benaten speaks loudly, in a rational, cold tone.

Narmeradat swings the *hedah* and strikes.

"Mercy . . ." Naamat whispers, sinking on her knees, hands dripping blood.

I watch this in horror. It occurs to me that the poor girl is so confused from what is being done to her that, up till now, she's been too frightened to react in a way that might appease the Crown Prince.

I desperately try to think of something to do. My eyes dart around the room, noting the persons present, hoping that someone might step in and do something, anything—but what?

This horrible man is the Crown Prince and he has the ultimate authority over all those present.

And then my gaze falls upon the curtains hanging near one corner, where I see the faintest motion in the folds of fabric. Through a sliver between two sections of curtains, comes the glint of one terrified blue eye.

Somehow, impossibly, Princess Arlenari is here, watching.

CHAPTER
THIRTY

Desperate to make the punishment stop, I get an insane idea: I'm going to fall to my knees right now, alongside Naamat and beg and cry for mercy. . . . That should be a good interruption (not to mention, a distraction from the fact that the misfortunate Princess is here, hiding behind the curtains).

Most Compassionate Bast, help me . . . protect me from what I'm about to do!

I take a deep breath—

But before I manage to do something I'll regret, my gaze falls upon Benaten's face.

My employer is staring hard at me.

In that instant (just as I invoked Bast) he appears to have sensed my intent to do *something* dangerous. Not sure how he knows—maybe he can tell that I'm trembling and fidgeting like a *hoohvak*, or appear severely agitated—but his commanding grey eyes *fix me in place* with an immobilizing glare. At the same time, for a single heartbeat, he barely shakes his head at me.

No.

I freeze.

Just then, a loud pealing noise of ringing chimes resounds from the main hall.

"My Imperial Lord," Benaten Bisfuri says at once, in his rich, persuasive voice. "The game is over, and you have the gold scarab. The countdown has ended, and the guests await all of us now, especially you."

"Ah, *shaitunaat* . . . very well," Narmeradat says, stopping the *hedah* stick in mid-stroke.

Everyone in the room shifts with relief, and I hear several exhaled breaths.

Prince Narmeradat steps away from Naamat (who remains in a shaking heap on the floor with her bloody hands still outstretched) and carelessly returns the *hedah* to Vakrem. "Imperial Justice has been served."

He then adds, "Someone make sure Lady Hekufati's lovely face gets examined by a medic. We don't want her to have a scar." The Crown Prince speaks this without even glancing at her, and simply walks out of the room.

At once, everyone comes alive.

I carefully glance at the curtains near the corner where supposedly Arlenari is hiding. No movement there. . . . Now that I look again, I begin to wonder if I hallucinated her presence.

Bast, help me, I'm so tired, I'm starting to lose my mind.

"Go see what's holding up the physician," Benaten Bisfuri says to Vakrem, who immediately nods and rushes out of the room.

Lady Hatshepsut makes a sound of distress and approaches her maidservant, then leans down and puts her hand on the girl's shoulders tentatively, "Come, Naamat, it is over, please rise. You did well—"

"She doesn't look well at all," Lady Satiah remarks from behind, frowning.

Hatshepsut looks up at her with a furious glare and whispers, "Get out!"

Lady Satiah makes an angry sound and hurries out of the chamber.

I decide that it's probably all right for me to move also, so I hurry toward Naamat, and put my arms around her to help her stand up—with the nominal assistance of Lady Hatshepsut who uselessly fusses and touches her servant awkwardly on the back, while I do all the heavy lifting.

Naamat stands with shaking, outstretched hands covered in blood, and I straighten from helping her.

"Poor girl. How is she?"

Glancing behind me I see both Benaten and Prince Oron, who is still here, watching with concern. The Prince is the one who asked the question, which surprises me.

Just then, the Bisfuri physician arrives, a serious, middle-aged man, with Girsul and Vakrem behind him. The medic sets down his equipment bag and advances toward Naamat.

"May I treat the Lady Hekufati?" he asks politely.

Lady Hatshepsut suddenly remembers she has a scratch on her cheek. "I am she," the lady announces, turning her face to the medic. "I've been wounded with a sharp object—"

"Ah . . . of course, my apologies, My Lady," the physician says after an uncomfortable moment, and dutifully turns away from the bleeding servant girl.

"After you attend the Lady, be sure to take care of the servant also," Benaten says. "Her hands are severely hurt."

"Yes, yes . . . of course," Lady Hatshepsut says guiltily, sitting down on the nearest divan while the physician takes out jars with potions and salves and starts applying something to her cheek. "Will there be a scar? Please make sure I do *not* have a scar!"

"No scar, my Lady, I promise," the medic reassures.

While this is happening, I hold Naamat's shoulder and look at her closely. "I'm so sorry," I whisper near her ear.

The girl blinks and takes deep juddering breaths, then gradually breathes evenly without shaking. Her eyes are reddened and her cheeks are streaked with tears, but she doesn't lift her damaged hands to wipe her face.

I take a small linen cloth from the physician's bag, while he's otherwise occupied with Lady Hatshepsut, and wipe Naamat's face. She nods at me with gratitude.

Suddenly, Prince Oron is at our side. "Here—let's help her sit down on the other sofa," he says softly, leaning down from his great height to take petite Naamat by her upper arms, just below her shoulders, but above any wounded areas. With utmost care and gentleness—which surprises me yet again—he guides her to the second divan.

"Let me see your hands," he says then, as the astonished servant girl sits down, glancing somewhat fearfully up at him.

She complies, turning up her palms and thin wrists, covered with red, open welts. Many of the welts reach her elbows.

Oron winces and shakes his head at the pitiful sight. "I am— truly sorry that you suffered this, girl. On behalf of my Imperial brother, I—*apologize*."

"Oh! No need! Oh, My Imperial Lord!" Naamat says anxiously, starting to shake again. "It's all right, I am happy to serve the Lady Hatshepsut, always. . . ."

"It's far from all right." Oron touches her shoulder lightly. "Your hands need to be treated immediately." He glances back at Benaten. "I'm happy to cover any expenses, Aten—" he says in a serious voice. "Please have her healed as well as possible— also *without* scars."

"Of course," Benaten nods at him, his expression grim. "I was going to have her cared for here anyway, at least overnight —with Lady Hatshepsut's permission, of course."

"Yes, yes, I give my permission, naturally," Hatshepsut

exclaims, standing up at that point. "She is a good, loyal servant, and I will not have her come to harm. Please take care of her. The night has been too long, in any case. I should be going now. . . ."

"You will be provided a replacement servant for tonight, from my own staff, if you so choose," *Ter* Bisfuri continues.

"No need," Lady Hatshepsut says, moving toward the exit, "I thank you for the lovely party, and do keep me apprised tomorrow of her condition—"

And she hurries away.

The medic finally turns toward the servant girl.

Prince Oron, still at her side, leans down once more and speaks in a soft voice, "What is your name?"

"My—name? Oh, my Imperial Lord, I am Naamat."

"Naamat. . . . May you recover well and quickly, and forget the pain . . . and this unfortunate incident," the Prince says with a kind smile directed entirely at her, then straightens. "Now, I must head out also, Aten. Let's continue our conversation soon—"

"Yes," Benaten replies. "Tomorrow."

"Very well." And Prince Oron walks quickly out of the chamber.

THE PHYSICIAN BEGINS CLEANING Naamat's wounds, then applies salve, followed by strips of cloth bandages. "It is done. However, someone must apply steady pressure here, for at least ten daydreams," he says, motioning to me. "Will you?"

"Of course," I say, and come closer to observe what needs to be done.

Benaten, conversing with Vakrem and Girsul, looks at me. "Semmi," he says, "I know you need to return home, and it's long past your work time. So, after you stay to finish this—just ten more daydreams—you are dismissed for the night. Stop by

Steward Hekadut's office to receive your pay, including overtime for these long hours."

"Thank you, *im Ter*!" I say with a note of excitement.

Bisfuri turns back to Vakrem and Girsul. "Same for you two —dismissed for the night. The party is winding down already, and we're done here. Pick up your pay at the office."

"Thank you, *Ter* Aten." Vakrem nods curtly and turns to leave.

"What of cleanup?" Girsul asks, pausing.

Benaten rubs his forehead with one hand tiredly, pushing back his raven mane of hair. "Local staff will stay to clean up a bit longer, but both of you who live far, can go. And all three of you can sleep in tonight, an additional two hours. Come back after ninth hour of Ra tomorrow morning. Oh—at the office, have a house servant come up here to assist this poor girl and arrange for a bed for her to sleep tonight in the servants' quarters."

Girsul and Vakrem bow and head out.

The physician packs the last of his things in the bag and nods at me as I sit holding Naamat's bandaged hands. He then bows to Benaten in a businesslike manner, and promises to return and examine the patient in the morning.

"Very well," *Ter* Bisfuri says to us, the only ones left. "Now I'm going back out there, while you sit for a few more daydreams until the house servant comes—"

"Benaten! What in the world is going on here?" A sultry female voice sounds from the entrance, and we all stare to see Lady Ashura Ximunat. She approaches quickly, and stops directly before him.

"Where have you been all this time? Your dearest Father is terribly concerned and sent me to look for you—"

Ter Bisfuri looks down at his future stepmother, and one of his brows rises. "My Lady," he says. "Apologies to my Father, but we've had an incident that needed to be handled."

"Yes, yes, awful," Lady Ximunat says, resting one bejeweled hand over Benaten's upper arm and squeezing it. "Both the Princes have just now rejoined our cozy little group, and I've heard all about the terrible behavior of two young Ladies who should know better."

"Indeed," Benaten replies. His gaze briefly moves to her hand with its elegant fingers covered with glittering rings, as it continues to hold onto his arm, lingering longer than normal. "We're almost done here, and—"

"Imperial Justice has apparently been served." Lady Ashura glances around the room briefly, seeing Naamat and me off in the far corner, perched on the edge of the divan, then promptly ignores us. "The servants are handling the rest of this nonsense, good. Now, before we go back, let me see if you yourself are well, my handsome boy—what's this? Blood?"

Lady Ashura edges even closer to him, and places her other hand over his jaw, where apparently a droplet of blood has splattered and landed from the *hedah* that the Crown Prince was swinging all over the place (I'm guessing).

Benaten almost takes a step back at her touch, and his eyes grow cool. "What?" he says in some surprise as Ashura strokes his jaw lightly with the tips of her fingers.

She then lets go and examines her fingertip, then appears to inspect his face again, and speaks in a low, purring voice. "There's definitely blood . . ."

"Well, it's not mine," Benaten retorts, his expression growing more and more reserved.

"Ah, then one of the servants," Ashura says carelessly. "Good . . . for it would be such a shame to mar such beautiful skin as yours. . . ."

Benaten says nothing in response to this, but his face is fixed like a mask.

Over in our corner, Naamat and I exchange quick glances.

In that instant, Lady Ashura suddenly makes a small sound,

and then appears to sway on her feet. "Oh . . ." she sighs, and then grabs hold of Benaten's muscular upper arm again and, with her other hand resting against his chest, starts to collapse *onto* him.

Ter Bisfuri has no choice but to catch her as she falls, ending up holding her in his arms.

"It's the blood—the sight of it makes me ill sometimes, dearest boy," the lady says in a breathy voice, glancing up at him craftily sideways from underneath her long, luxurious lashes. "Please . . . I must sit, briefly . . . help me sit down."

"Of course." Benaten's low voice has lost all its natural charm and inflection, all the rich, dark, velvet-deep undertones (that are so seductive and prominent when he plays the Man in the Niktos Cloak). He half-leads half-carries Lady Ashura to the unoccupied divan on the other side of the mantel. Here, she collapses, resting deeply against the pillows.

"Do you need water, My Lady?" he asks, standing over her. His vocal tone has become remote and inflexible. "Should I call our medic back?"

"Ah, no . . . let me recover here, I just need a few moments." Ashura throws her head back, flickers her eyes closed, then opens them again and pats the seat next to her. "Come, sit down with me and keep your new Mother company for a little while."

"Very well. But—not for long, since we're expected back." Benaten sits down next to her, with room to spare between them. He remains silent.

Naamat and I try not to look, but can't help seeing this peculiar scene play out. . . .

Silent heartbeats pass, and Lady Ashura simply watches Benaten with her beautiful dark eyes fixed upon him, hardly blinking. Her gaze roves all over his body, up and down. . . .

If I weren't so tired right now, I might be convinced that she is staring at him with *hunger*.

No, that's just *garooi*, that can't be right.

But the more I look, the more I notice that a kind of lustful smile has come to her glossy lips, which she parts . . . and her tongue slowly appears to lick them.

"Feeling better?" my employer says to his stepmother after several more silent beats.

"Much," Lady Ashura replies, with the same lascivious smile. "But not entirely. . . . Come, now, sit closer to me, dear boy. . . . Such a beautiful young man you are, did you know? But, of course you know. Men such as you always do."

Benaten looks at her steadily, but doesn't move.

Instead, a moment later, Lady Ashura herself scoots over, closer to him, so that their legs are almost touching.

Holy Bast! My anxious gaze darts at Naamat. I can tell she, too, looks disturbed.

"I feel so much better now," Lady Ashura says softly. "But you know what would make me feel even better?"

"No, I don't." Benaten's face is a mask.

"This . . ." Ashura suddenly reaches forward and places her hand on his thigh.

At once, Benaten starts slightly. He then places his own larger hand over hers and *lifts* her hand away. "My Lady," he says through his teeth, and his grey eyes fill with fierce energy. "Not sure whatever *this* is, but it is not right. You are about to be married to my Father, and this is inappropriate."

And Benaten Bisfuri stands up. "I'm going to pretend this didn't happen. I will return to our party, and as soon as you're sufficiently recovered, you may follow."

And he turns his back on her, his long, glossy mane of *niktos*-black hair swinging angrily.

"Benaten! Wait!" Lady Ashura exclaims, her own expression darkening with petulant outrage. "You may not refuse me, not like this! How dare you?"

But Benaten has left the room.

Moments later, apparently feeling perfectly healthy now,

Lady Ashura stands up and storms out on her own, completely ignoring the fact that two servants have just borne witness to this ugly scene.

Naamat and I exhale and look at each other.

"Crap of a goat . . ." I whisper. "These *hoohvak* rich and powerful nobles are crazy *chazufs*!"

Just then the curtain not too far from us sways, and Princess Arlenari Kassiopei steps out from behind the heavy folds. She appears wide-eyed and very, very sad.

"We are insane, yes, and we are often evil," she says to me. "We're hardly worthy of your service."

Meanwhile Naamat stares at the Princess as if she's a *sha* spirit come forth from the walls themselves. "Imperial Princess!"

"I knew you were hiding there—My Imperial Lady," I say, feeling a sudden flood of ease that she seems to inspire in me. Indeed, I barely recall myself enough to call her by her title.

"Thank you once again for not giving me away, Semiram the Storyteller," Arlenari replies with a tiny smile at me.

"Oh, yeah, just Semmi, that's my name." I say, continuing to feel the lightness.

Princess Arlenari comes closer to both of us, and stares at Naamat's bound hands. "So much pain . . ." she whispers. "Please, forgive us."

She glances at me then, and speaks quickly, "I must go. But I'll see you very soon, when you come to the Palace and bring your recorded story. Don't forget! *Nefero niktos*, dear Semiram and . . . Naamat."

Saying this, Princess Arlenari silently exits the room, moving catlike—like the great goddess Bast herself—and leaving us open-mouthed.

CHAPTER
THIRTY-ONE

The house servant arrives soon after, sent by Vakrem, as instructed by *Ter* Bisfuri. She is older than both of us, with pale, pinkish skin and wheat-colored hair gathered in a neat, tight bun, and says her name is Zarai. She immediately bends to examine Naamat's bandages and tells me it's okay to release the pressure hold I've been applying.

"See, no new blood has seeped through the wrapping, so it has stopped," she tells us with practiced movements as she checks the condition of the wrapping cloth.

Then, Zarai tells Naamat to follow her. "And you are free to go home," she says to me. "What a long night, eh?"

We rise, and get out of this infernal room, back into the greater hall. The noble guests are mostly leaving, though quite a few linger to chat and some are wandering drunk. The main entertainment platform is empty and the musicians have stopped playing, which is a courtly hint that the festivities are over. Already, Bisfuri servants can be seen picking up the abandoned drinkware and dishes left all over, and cleaning up the floor.

I take a huge breath of relief, and rush in the general

direction that Zarai and Naamat are heading, toward the antechamber that contains the hallway leading to the now-familiar service areas, including kitchens, and offices.

I'm about to get paid!

I note in passing that the elite group with the Imperials and the Bisfuri has broken up, and there is no sign of the Kassiopei who must have departed already. Lord Muutat is speaking with the priests and all of them appear to be headed to the exit.

I catch a glimpse of Lady Ashura, back at her betrothed's side. She's absolutely unabashed, talking confidently with Lady Ishtaz and a few other nobles whose identities I have no way of knowing. Behamenut and Enhuvarat, in the company of several courtesans, are laughing at something that *Ter* Stryr Giparu is saying (and I can't help staring again at Stryr's shining *pegasus* collar reposing against his naked chest) while his brother Arguam is quietly drinking straight from a large chalice-shaped refill pitcher lifted from a servant's tray. . . .

Ter Benaten Bisfuri is nowhere to be seen. I assume he left the party early (probably in disgust), and I'm not at all surprised, given what just happened.

Just as we exit the grand hall into the antechamber, we are greeted by a loud swell of noise. A small crowd of remaining guests are all rushing to the drink fountain. They jostle each other, ladies squeal, and more heads are turning as the departing elites who have gone toward the exit start to turn around and return to the fountain.

"Hathor the Graceful . . . what now? Why are they stopping?" Zarai mutters with weary annoyance.

We pause, our path blocked because there is such a clamor of people at the fountain.

"What? What's happening?" we ask the nearest servants stationed at the exits.

"Apparently, on his way out, the Imperial Crown Prince threw the golden scarab into the fountain! Just now, as he left," a servant informs us with a grim look. "The Imperial Lord laughed and said that whoever wants it can go swim in the wine!"

"Bastet and Hathor. . . ." Zarai opens her mouth but holds herself back from saying something more. She sighs and shakes her head.

We all pause again, and watch helplessly as lords and ladies plunge into the fountain up to their elbows, sloshing the dark liquid with their hands, and several of them climb the stone rim and step over the ledge, wading and splashing with their feet.

"Can you see it? Can you see the scarab?" many of them exclaim, pushing to get closer. "Is it deep? Move! Is that it? No? Where is it?"

Naamat, Zarai, and I finally find an opening in the crowd and push past these crazed, greedy *chazufs* who already have so much (but apparently not enough). Carefully stepping on the wine-soaked, slippery marble floor, we get out of there, escaping into the service hallway.

"We go this way," Zarai tells Naamat, pointing at a smaller passage just up ahead. Naamat nods and then turns to me quietly with a little smile. "Thank you for all your help, Semmi. *Nefero niktos.*"

And so, we part, since my way continues down the main hallway to the offices.

I arrive breathlessly at the Steward's office, wondering what time it is. Fortunately, the door is wide open as several other servants stand in a short line before Steward Hekadut at his desk. He has his digital tablet out, and next to him is a large safe box full of shiny, pristine coins. He checks each of the staff in his list, then counts and allocates their money.

Holy Mother Bast, so many coins! I can't help but stare, since this box is three times the size of the cashier's box at the Chiprahat warehouse—up to now, the biggest previous employer I've had.

When it's my turn, Hekadut checks his tablet, then glances at my outfit. "Change into your regular clothes, please," he tells me, "Put this dress on its original hanger and bring it here. The shoes, too. You'll receive your payment as soon as I receive and inspect the dress."

"Oh—yes, okay," I say with a sudden pang of trepidation.

And so, I rush to the long wardrobe area, beyond the front office portion, and locate the storage shelves with my bag of clothing and old shoes (and my new staff uniform that will be adjusted by a seamstress in the morning). Here, I undress in the darkest niche behind a privacy screen.

My hands shake as I attempt to carefully undo the clasp on the lavender dress, and very carefully pull it up and off me. It seems to be okay. . . . Then I undo the gold sandals and liberate my sore feet.

I put on my plain, poor clothing, well-worn, comfortable shoes, leave my new uniform in its bag on the storage shelf, and return to the front of the room with the precious dress and gold sandals.

The Steward beckons me with one finger, so at least I don't have to stand in line again.

I hand him the expensive clothing, including the purple entertainer tassel, and he looks over everything with meticulous attention to detail.

"Very well," he says at last. "The dress is in suitable condition, so no deduction in pay."

I let out a deep breath of relief.

And then he counts out and hands me . . . *ten* metal coins. "This includes your overtime pay. *Nefero niktos.* Next!"

And I'm done.

Ten coins! Ten amazing coins, all at once!

I step out of the way, holding the hefty metal pieces in both hands and starting to shake with nerves and a kind of wild exultation. The most I've ever been paid at one time, for a week of work, was three coins. . . .

Mother of Mothers, greatest goddess Bast, thank you!

And, thank you, *Ter* Bisfuri.

I stuff the coins in my pockets and run outside into the night.

AT THE LONELY BUS STOP—SITUATED on the exterior bank of the Circle Two canal, surrounded by the estate greenery which now appears menacing black, discolored by the night—I see a few other remote Bisfuri workers. They tell me that the best thing to do at this ungodly hour is to catch the express hover bus which comes once every half hour around the clock. Whenever there are late parties at the Bisfuri estate, they tell me, it's the only option to get to distant Circles at this time of the night.

Speaking of time, it's well after midnight. The express bus arrives, we get on, and then spend nearly an hour stopping at various Circles and letting off people. By the time I get to the last bus stop on the way to Denwen's Pit, I'm nodding in my seat, periodically jolted awake with giddy excitement at the awareness of all those coins jingling in my pocket.

Once off the bus, I run along the bridge from Circle Nine then finally arrive at our dark street. I open the door, and tiptoe carefully in the darkness of our room past my Father snoring on the couch.

Just as I head outside to the toilet, I see Amurabia sitting on a little chair near the firepit with her eyes closed. The fire is still going, the tea kettle is warming on the grate, and the faint orange glow illuminates her wrinkled face.

"Mei-Ma!" I start, and put my hand over my mouth to stifle a little scream.

"Ah, blessed Gods, Semmi, you're home." Grandmother starts also, then whispers, looking up at me. "I was so worried—

so worried about you at that fancy party with those rich people. It's really late. . . ."

"I know! So sorry that you stayed up and couldn't sleep. . . ."

And then she examines me closer and stretches one hand to touch my cheek. "Oh, my child . . . your face. And your hair. . . . You look beautiful, like a great lady. Come, let me see you—"

I'd forgotten all about the Face Art paints covering my face, and the fancy hairdo. "Hah, yes! I was a Storyteller, *Mei-Ma!* I did it, I told my story and they liked it," I whisper with excitement, trying to keep my voice down as much as possible so as not to wake up the rest of the house and the neighbors. "It was unbelievable, and oh—we're *rich!* I got paid ten coins for working late!"

I dig into my pockets and pull out the coins, dropping them in Grandmother's lap. Amurabia's almost entirely toothless mouth parts in wonder, and then she smiles at me.

And then, with the firepit crackling and sending forth golden embers, I pour myself a mug of tea and tell Grandmother what happened that day and night—all of it, including the morning with the Service Competitions, and the evening party with the elites and Imperials.

When I'm done, Amurabia sits in thoughtful silence, shaking her head. She then squeezes my hands with her gnarled ones and sighs. "What a world," she says. "What a strange, terrible world. At least your employer, *Ter* Bisfuri, is a good man. . . . But now, off to bed! You have work tomorrow. We'll talk much more about it later."

I SLEEP like the dead for the remainder of that night, not even bothering to scrub the Face Art paints from my skin. And when I come awake, it's true morning, past dawn. Uru and Father are both awake, finishing up eating and about to head out.

Grandmother is probably still asleep, since she stayed up so late to keep me company.

Glad to have had the two extra hours to sleep in, I still go into a frenzy of rushing to get ready.

When I show up in the living room, Uru sees me and starts to laugh, spitting chunks of flatbread from his mouth. "Your face, Semmi! You look funny, like a *kadakum*! And your hair is all sticking up!"

"Shut up, little *chazuf*," I tell him tiredly, glad of the reminder to scrub my face. It turns out to be more difficult than I expected, and requires a lot more soap than usual.

Somehow, I manage, getting almost all the accursed Face Paint off my cheeks, lips, and eyelids. Only a few weird stains and smudges remain, mostly around my eyes, making me look a bit like someone landed blows on both sides of my head and I have two bruised, blackened *hoohvak* eyes.

When I return inside, Uru looks at me again, giggling. "Oooh, monkey face!" he says.

"Enough," I retort, and try to catch the boy's ear, but he evades me.

Father just mops up the last bits of lentil and carrot stew from his bowl and eats the flatbread thoughtfully.

"Are you going out today, *Papai*?" I ask him.

He nods.

"What kind of job?"

"The same. Digging more trenches, deeper ones this time. They told us to come back and said there will be a lot more work of this kind in the coming days."

"Sounds like at least a three-coin day again, right?" I grab a clean bowl from the shelf near the wall and head to the big kettle to ladle myself some of yesterday's leftovers that I never had a chance to eat last night. "Wonder why the digging?"

Guzum shrugs. "Who knows? I don't ask. But—definitely, three coins, maybe more tonight."

"We're gonna be rich!" Uru proclaims, heading for the door where his hoverboard is propped up. "All right, *eos*!"

"*Eos*," we respond as my little brother opens the door.

He grabs his board, sings the tones to make it levitate, hops on, and disappears down the street.

"Wait!" I swallow in haste then call out in Uru's wake. "Ah, Bast. . . . I forgot to ask the boy if he's working today or doing Service Competitions stuff."

And then I glance at my Father again. "What about you? Service Competitions? I don't remember you saying anything—"

He gets up just then and goes for his sun hat. "Don't know," he mumbles from the door. "Maybe later. Got to work first."

And he, too, is gone.

I CATCH the express hover bus, the kind that has the fewest stops, and get to Circle Two in the morning sunshine. It's only a few daydreams after ninth hour of Ra, so I am mostly good.

When I run past the guards at the front gates of the estate, they seem to recognize my face, treating me as one of the regular Bisfuri staff, and don't even bother stopping me.

I get a tiny jolt of satisfaction from that, and continue toward the service entrance. But first, there's the registration table and the large billboard with today's Competition information posted. A few of the servants linger here, even at this later hour.

"What?" I ask, pausing briefly.

"Imperial Pilot Competition," the closest person tells me, pointing at the smart board display. "Registration opens today."

"Ah, okay," I reply. "Not for the likes of me."

"Yeah, me neither." The servant makes an annoyed sound.

And I continue on my way.

. . .

ONCE IN THE SERVANT HALLWAYS, I rush to Steward Hekadut's office, and pick up my uniform from the wardrobe storage shelves, together with a red messenger tassel. Then I head directly down the hall to find a seamstress called Vilras. Her work office is behind the door with the orange tassel on it.

I knock, and hear a female voice saying "come in."

Inside, the office is a medium sized room with several tables and stacks of shelving. Bright daylight comes in through the windows and several staff servants are seated around the tables and weaving looms lining the walls, doing small detail work. There are seamstresses, embroiderers, weavers, and other artisans working on fixing broken tools, pottery, and other household items. Everyone is chatting casually as they work, mostly about the Service Competitions, last night's Bisfuri party, and all the cleanup that's still happening in the great hall, and especially around the wine fountain.

"*Nefero eos*, I'm looking for Vilras," I ask. "I need my uniform fitted."

"Over here, girl," says a light-haired, pale-skinned woman with a kind smile. She reminds me a little of the house servant Zarai from last night, almost a family resemblance.

Vilras takes my uniform from me, and then we walk over to a little privacy screen in the far corner, where I quickly put it on. Then Vilras makes me turn this and that way, as she pulls at the fabric and marks folds and sticks pins in various places around the hem and waist of the skirt and the arms of the shirt.

Next, I change back into my regular street clothes, and Vilras takes the uniform from me. "I'll have it ready for you by the end of the day. Come back after fourth hour of Khe," she says.

And I head out the door.

THE FIRST THING I decide to do is look for Girsul. But just as I consider heading to the stables and checking the *pegasei* cage, my Bisfuri employee badge starts to vibrate and ring in my pocket. I pull it out and see the amber blinking light in the center, indicating an incoming message.

Now that I actually know how to use it, I admit I still feel a stab of anxiety as I tap the comm badge to hear the message.

At once, I hear the deep, velvet-rich voice of my employer. "This is Benaten Bisfuri. Semmi, where are you? You're late. Please come to my Quarters at once."

I let out a small squeak of terror and begin to run.

Breathless, I arrive upstairs at Benaten's work Quarters in the main building, and knock on the door. Moments later, Girsul opens it, and I rush inside.

There is no brilliant illumination and bustling staff here today. Instead, no one else is in the front room, only Girsul, myself, and our employer.

In stark contrast to the fashionable glamor of yesterday, Benaten Bisfuri is wearing a plain cotton shirt with long sleeves that can be easily rolled up, dark menial work pants (the same kind he wore to greet Grandmother and me on that first day, coming indoors after doing unknown labor outside), and his usual boots. His mane of *niktos* hair is negligently tied back in a segmented tail, and he sprawls with casual indifference in a chair, with his feet up on the short serving table before him.

I admit, even now, despite his basic attire, he still manages to exude fascinating, effortless elegance. . . . However, his normally benevolent, faintly amused expression is *gone*. His face is serious and intense in a manner I've not seen in him before, not even during some of the worst moments of last night—such as when Naamat was getting punished.

And then . . . those bizarre, unbearable moments with Lady Ashura. She made her lewd advances, and he withdrew in every sense, shut down.

Indeed, the last time I saw him was during those disturbing moments when he left that room, leaving her and all the festivities, last night.

At once, I'm overwhelmed with foreboding, as if someone dumped a pail of cold water over my head.

Holy Bast, help us all.

"My apologies, *im Ter*," I say hurriedly, not quite meeting his cold eyes. "I was picking up my uniform then took it to the seamstress to get adjusted—"

"That's fine, you're here now." Bisfuri straightens in his chair, puts his feet down on the floor in one smooth motion, and leans forward. He beckons me and Girsul to approach closer.

"Do you know why you're here, both of you?"

My stomach is wrenched by even more anxiety.

"Um, new assignment?" Girsul says, as we both take a few steps forward. I merely open my mouth then close it, unsure how to respond.

Benaten looks at Girsul. Then he looks at me.

With a sudden stab of terror, I force myself to gaze into his grey eyes. And there I find a curiously unreadable expression.

We suffer a pause that's almost too long, too strange to bear. I hear my heartbeat echoing in my temples.

And then Bisfuri speaks.

"Yes. More than just a new assignment. A new *responsibility*. But first—you're about to hear some things that must never leave this room."

Benaten leans forward even closer toward us, and his rich, deep voice modulates with a kind of cutting intensity that raises the fine hairs on my skin. "Swear to me now, that you will speak of it to no one, not even your family or loved ones."

"I—" Girsul begins, with a quick, darting glance at me. "I swear. Of course, *im Ter*."

I open my mouth, and then I echo him. "*Im Ter* . . . I swear to be silent!"

"Good. And you'll never speak of it to my brother," Benaten continues. "Eham knows many things about me, and he's in quite deep. But—he must remain uninformed about *this* particular subject."

"All right," Girsul says.

"Of course," I mumble.

What in all the underworld shaitunaat *is going on?*

Benaten Bisfuri pauses once again, and this time focuses strictly on me. "Semmi, before I continue—two things. You were the only one outside my trusted circle to ever recognize the Man in the Niktos Cloak and connect him to my real identity, thus demonstrating rare observation skills. And two—you've kept this information well to yourself (and confined within your family), which shows me that you are trustworthy enough for what I'm about to divulge to you."

"Yes, *im Ter*."

"And Girsul—" Bisfuri looks at the young man. "You've been keeping secrets for me successfully for some time now. You've also been keeping some things *from* me, rather successfully until just recently."

Girsul's eyes widen. "*Im Ter*—?"

But Benaten interrupts, raising one hand. "I know where and *how* you live, and all about your little sister."

"Oh, *im Ter!*"

"Did you think I wouldn't eventually find out why my trusted servant is always late and leaves his job in the middle of the day?"

"I'm so sorry, *Ter* Aten!"

"Enough, I don't care about any of it. What I *do* care is that you thought so poorly of me for all these months, to believe that your unfortunate circumstances would diminish your worth in my eyes and require hiding the truth."

"*Im Ter* . . . sorry! So sorry!"

I've never seen such an agonized look on Girsul's usually mild and calm face. His posture has changed, and he stands cringing, head hung, blinking rapidly.

Benaten grows silent for several long heartbeats, letting the other man stew.

And then he resumes: "You've served me well, Girsul, and discreetly, and for that I will overlook your insulting mistrust of my judgement."

Girsul looks up with amazement. "Oh, *im Ter!* Then—then you'll still put your faith in me?"

"Admittedly, my faith has taken a blow. I'm annoyed and personally somewhat disappointed in you. But I do understand —the root of your fear is desperation on behalf of your sister, not some other nefarious reason. So yes, you are still to remain in my employ."

"Thank you!"

"I expect, from here on, you will demonstrate appropriate honesty alongside your loyalty." Bisfuri watches Girsul gravely. "No more lies and *hoohvak* excuses. The thing you're about to learn is far too serious for any irregularities. Nothing must interfere with your ability to perform the new job with *integrity.*"

"I understand." Girsul nods vigorously.

"I do too," I say carefully. "And I promise I didn't lie to you about anything, *im Ter*, I do live in Denwen's Pit with Grandmother, my brother Uru, and my Father—"

"Yes, shush." Benaten puts up his hand again. "Now, with all of that out of the way, let me tell you what you'll be doing for me from now on."

Girsul and I stare at our employer with trepidation.

Benaten Bisfuri takes a deep breath and exhales. At last, he speaks.

"You know me as the Man in the Niktos Cloak—a fictional vigilante character who puts on a *hoohvak* weekly show on the entertainment feeds. And only a tiny few, yourselves included, know me as an actual vigilante who, upon occasion, flies around at night on his hoverboard, doing dangerous and questionably good deeds on behalf of the common people of Poseidon. That second part is half-legend and entirely unconfirmed, mostly propagated by rumor and gossip on the Windnet—precisely how I like it to be, since it serves to obscure what's actually happening."

Girsul grows still, paying intense attention.

"There is another thing I do." Benaten looks at both of us. "I work in secret on behalf of the Imperial Prince Oron Kassiopei. Most recently, on something very particular. You've seen me talking with him. And you might even have some suspicions, ideas of your own as to what it's about—maybe something related to the infernal Sky Rock and the grand escape plans of the elites?"

Images of Benaten strolling through the feast hall with Prince Oron last night, deep in conversation, come to mind, and I start to nod.

"Whatever you imagine or think you know, is mostly wrong. Yes, it has something to do with the coming doom. But—unlike the other Imperial Kassiopei and the noble Houses, Prince Oron is not concerned with preserving himself. Instead, he has a plan to *save* the general population."

I almost stop breathing and freeze.

"What?" Girsul makes a startled sound. "Is that kind of thing even possible?"

"I thought there was nothing to be done?" I burst out. "And that's why the Service Competitions? Because everyone in Atlantis and the whole world is supposed to die in the coming flood and fire? Unless they win a place on the fancy ships to the stars?"

"There is—another, third option," Bisfuri replies. "Prince Oron is building a special place—a *sanctuary* here on earth that will be able to survive the flood and other dire conditions."

Sudden, wild hope surges through me. . . .

"Oh!" I exclaim. "Then we'll all be saved! Oh, holy Bast!"

But Benaten shakes his head sadly. "No. Unfortunately, as of yet, no one is guaranteed safety in this sanctuary."

"Why not, *im Ter*?" I stare with wide eyes, full of desperate unspoken questions.

"And where is it?" Girsul asks. "Where is this safe place?"

"It is still being built, and may never be completed in time. Remember, the Sky Rock will be here in a matter of weeks." Benaten speaks in a lowered voice, pausing to put a finger over his lips to indicate quiet. "As for where this place is, you'll find out very soon."

"So then—" Girsul starts to speak.

"Let me continue. Prince Oron, in the process of building this sanctuary, requires certain resources. Resources that only Bisfuri can provide. Unfortunately, these same resources are also required in the building of the great ark-ships that will take us to the stars. Can you guess, what are those resources? Show me how smart you are."

"Is it—orichalcum?" Girsul ventures. "Since House Bisfuri is rich with this metal."

"Yes." Benaten's expression shows energy. "It is indeed. An endless, unfathomable amount of orichalcum—most of it being mined on Bisfuri land, in various locations around Atlantis and beyond. These priceless accumulations—formally placed at the disposal of the Imperial Dynasty by House Bisfuri—are already going toward the building of the ships. Indeed, *all* of it will ultimately end up being used. Anything left will be taken by the Kassiopei and the nobles to our new destination outside this world. Even as we speak, all over Atlantis and on the wild continents across the ocean, the earth is being *stripped* of orichalcum."

"Oh. . . ." Girsul stares with dawning comprehension. "So that's why Lord Bisfuri was gone on that trip recently?"

"Correct. My Father was inspecting various sites, observing the mining and delivery process of raw orichalcum and orichalcum-treated technology and machinery parts, making sure it is expedited for the Imperial needs. The process is being managed in utmost secrecy, details and locations withheld from the public, to assure that nothing interferes with the shipbuilding plan."

Benaten pauses, and looks at us. "Nothing and no one. That is, except for *me*. It's my own secret-within-a-secret that I divert some of these already clandestine shipments headed to the main Imperial building project to Prince Oron and his secret work crew, so that he can equip his sanctuary with whatever I can give him. No one can know what we're doing. . . . The other Imperial Kassiopei and the noble Houses would put an immediate stop to it. They are far too selfish and greedy to spare even a small amount of this precious resource to save commoner lives. Might as well let all these dirty, Ra-forsaken *bakris* in the outer Circles and provinces burn and drown."

There's a profound bitterness to his words, underneath the sarcasm, I note, as I continue listening and watching his serious face.

"We do share one thing with the other Kassiopei—an urgency regarding the construction timeline. Even as the ark-ships are being built, the sanctuary is being built simultaneously —in as much haste as possible with what little resources we can skim off the top and pass on to Oron's workers. Until it is safely completed and ready to receive the population, it must be guarded—not only from the public but from the Imperial Family and every blessed member of the elite. That's why this third option is unknown. If and when it is ready, only *then* will Prince Oron reveal this daring truth to the world."

"No false hope," Girsul remarks.

And no angry, terrifying, divine relatives getting in the way, I think.

Benaten runs one hand over his forehead, smoothing his brow. "And now," he says, "now you will learn your own small but important role in this. For that, we'll need to head to a different location here on the estate. And—we'll need the *pegasei*."

"Oh. What must we do?" I ask.

Benaten stands up. "First, go, feed them in the sunshine for at least half an hour. Then bring all three *goats* to the grotto beyond the last waterfall. You know the one I speak of, Girsul. Near the top of the hill tiered with all the ponds."

"Yes, *im Ter*," Girsul.

"Be discreet, but not overly so. If anyone asks, act casual. Meet me there promptly within the hour."

Bisfuri heads for the door, and we follow.

GIRSUL and I hurry to the stables, collect our special goat charges, and bring them outside to the little courtyard where they bask in the sun, away from prying eyes.

As we work—or better to say, mill around, holding the orichalcum leashes, while the *pegasei* goats recharge—we cast meaningful glances at each other. Not daring to discuss what we've learned, we're both impatient to get going to our meeting spot and *learn more*.

"Where is it again, the grotto?" I ask.

"Just beyond the airfield, not too far," Girsul replies, motioning with his head. I notice he has a kind of new confidence about him.

"You must be relieved that he knows about your home

situation now," I say after a few more daydreams of silence. "See, *Ter* Bisfuri is very reasonable."

"He is, isn't he?" Girsul lets out a long breath. "I still can't believe it."

"How do you think he found out?"

The young man shakes his head, allowing a little smile. "Probably had me followed by little flying cameras."

"What? Really?"

"Yeah, the same kind we use during episode filming. To get better angles and close-ups."

"They can fly that far? I thought they can only hover around the room."

Girsul chuckles. "No, they can do whatever *shar-ta-haak* thing the techs tell them to do. And since they're so small, most people wouldn't notice. Excellent gadgets for spying."

"Oh. . . ." I open my mouth in amazement.

WHEN THE *PEGASEI* goats are sufficiently radiant and a little bloated from their sun-feeding, as usual, we cover them up with the black fabric. Then, we carefully walk them out of the exercise yard, tugging the leads a little to keep them moving.

The three goats walk in a stiff, mechanical gait and, good thing very few people are around to witness this uncanny sight. We pass the second large building and continue toward the back of the estate—moving along the gravel road next to the wide-open space of the airfield with its metallic hover-parked cars gleaming in the sun, casting short shadows on the mauve pavement.

Then, the ground starts rising toward a hillside, and the parkland greenery is interrupted by a large pond, paved with delicate mosaic stones, into which small waterfalls empty, creating a gentle rush of water. The waterfalls in turn originate from other smaller ponds, arranged in stepped rising tiers along the hillside.

Here, dappled sunlight filters past tree crowns, landing between delicate leaves and swaying branches to dance in the water and along the ground. Everywhere, bright colorful wildflowers peek among the grass, and occasional bees and *sesemet* flies rush by on the breeze.

We climb steadily, meandering past ponds, and follow the path leading uphill, until we reach a section of the hillside near the top, where a large waterfall cascades between rocks, emerging from the very ground.

I end up having to pull the goats hard behind me whenever the *hoohvaks* wander into random obstacles and shrubbery, apparently unable to discern curvature in the path, basically following straight lines. "Ah! Crap of a stinking *pegasus* goat . . . no, no, this way," I mutter at them.

"The grotto is right there." Blinking in the sun, Girsul points up ahead, holding on to one goat harness, while I grasp the other two by their leads.

And as we get closer, I see it—a tall hedge wall of bushes and creeping vines hiding a dark opening in the hillside. Just beyond the waterfall, a small creek becomes visible. It is pouring from the rocks, which is the source of the water.

"Do we just walk in there?" I ask, holding on tight to my infernal *pegasei* goats.

Girsul casts quick glances around us to verify if anyone else is nearby, but our immediate vicinity and the hillside itself is empty.

"Yeah, let's go." Pulling his one goat after him with one hand, Girsul steps forward, and uses his other hand to move aside hanging bunches of green vines.

He disappears into the dark opening, and I follow.

. . .

TWO STEPS INTO DARKNESS, and we're inside a small cave. I watch the stony ground underfoot, worn and slippery with water spray. Right behind me, the feet of the *pegasei* goats illuminate the floor brightly, which is oddly convenient. Meanwhile, the cave echoes with running water—picking up the acoustics of the waterfall outside and the nearby creek as it gurgles against the stone, moving here in the interior near one of the walls and cutting an ancient channel.

Now that I'm out of the bright sunlight, my eyes adjust to the low illumination. The grotto is not entirely dark but plunged in grey twilight, with sufficient daylight seeping in through multiple cracks in the rocks overhead. Looking up, the stone ceiling appears low enough for me to touch if I jump up and stretch my hand. The cave chamber itself is maybe the size of our living room back in Denwen's Pit.

I have to stop, because Girsul has stopped two paces ahead of me.

And of course we have our shining goats bumping into our legs like automated fools.

"Nice work. Now take off their coverings and let's see them."

The deep, honey-smooth voice of my employer causes me to start, since I didn't see him as we came in. But now, Benaten Bisfuri steps away from the shadows of the rear wall and draws closer to us. His grey eyes have darkened and taken on a sharp glitter.

"Of course, *im Ter*," Girsul says at once, and we both pull off the black fabric covers to reveal our *pegasei*.

Three shining rainbow forms immediately raise the illumination level in the grotto, making it almost cheerful.

Benaten makes a little amused sound, then leans down to stare at one of the goats closely. The creature doesn't react, but the proximity to it casts an iridescent glow over Benaten's lean face and jawline.

"What curious beings they are . . ." he muses. "Truly otherworldly. But—they'll do very well."

"Yes, they make fine goats. Now what?" I stand, suddenly feeling impatient, continuing to grasp the two leads in my tired hands, after having dragged these *hoohvak* goats all the way up the long hill.

Then I realize how impolite that sounds, as if I'm plainly talking to Uru. And I quickly amend, "What must we do now, *im Ter*?"

In reply, *Ter* Bisfuri steps backward, and then returns to the rear wall. He places one palm against a small darker stone at chest level, and suddenly there is a grinding sound of stone shifting. . . .

Holy Bast. . . .

I stare in amazement as the entire wall behind him starts to slide to one side, revealing a wide passage.

"Whoa! I didn't know there was something else beyond there." Girsul turns sharply at the grinding sound.

"Come," our employer says casually. "I'll explain everything. Watch your step, and watch your head. There are occasional irregularities in the stone floor and sections with a low ceiling, and we'll be going down. There's no other light along the way, but the *pegasei* will suffice."

W e enter the passage, which is sufficiently wide for at least three people to walk side by side. Our *pegasei* illuminate the rough stone all around us.

At once, the ambient temperature falls, and the air turns cold and slightly musty, compared to the warm day outside.

"What is this place?" Girsul remarks, gaping upward and reaching out with one hand to touch the jagged stone walls around us with curiosity while guiding the goat to move directly ahead of him to better light the way.

"This is part of an ancient cave and tunnel system," Bisfuri says, walking in front of us. "And we're entering it from one of the *many* access points around the City."

"Oh. . . ." I look up and around at the crudely rounded ceiling and walls of stone encroaching on both sides, then glance underfoot, to avoid tripping over rough spots on the floor.

"Just how big is it?" Girsul asks.

Benaten makes a laughing sound. "You cannot begin to imagine. . . . It's underneath the entire City of Poseidon."

"What?" Girsul is so amazed that he stops and almost trips on the goat he is now dragging behind him—only a moment ago, the stupid thing was in front of his feet but ended up wandering off at a diagonal, bumping against the cave wall, and then got turned around.

"We're inside an immense underground network." Bisfuri makes another amused sound. "Soon you will see more. Keep moving."

"But—how come I never heard of any such underground tunnels?" Girsul resumes walking, shaking his head in disbelief.

"Not many people have. In fact, this remarkable network is a well-hidden secret, as far as the general City population is concerned. The few who know about it are members of the noble elite and select priesthoods." As Bisfuri speaks, we continue moving, and the floor indeed begins to slope downward, while our passage gradually widens.

The *pegasei* goats effectively light our way, and in a few daydreams of following the slightly meandering tunnel, suddenly the passage opens into a large cave. It is easily the size of the grand antechamber in the Bisfuri main building.

"Whoa!" Girsul exclaims again, as he and I both stop at the opening, rooted in place at the terrifying sight of the lofty ceiling of the cavern, shadowed in darkness. The glow of the *pegasei* is barely sufficient to illuminate the lower recesses of this place.

I suck in my breath and try to comprehend our present location—where are we exactly at this point, underneath the hill? Just how big is this cave? Everywhere I look, there are nooks and curving hollows in the walls, deeply sunken spherical depressions—like giant stone bubbles—and what appear to be dark gaping holes in the stone around us, which might be other passages. . . .

"This is so big!" Girsul mumbles. "I can't believe it's here, and no one knows!"

His voice echoes in the greater open space of the cave.

"If you think this place is large, you need to prepare yourself," *Ter* Bisfuri says, walking several paces into the cavern, his voice and his footfalls echoing also. "There's a kind of hub—a grand cavern carved in the rock, many, many times larger than this one. It is located directly below the Center Circle of Poseidon, almost exactly underneath the Imperial Palace and the *Kassiopeion*. Tunnels and passages such as this one converge there from every direction. And if you follow the passages outward, they, in turn, go off into endless, unfathomable regions, for immeasurable distances inside the earth—across this continent and beyond, underneath the ocean."

Sacred Bast. . . .

Grasping the two leads, I pull at the goats bumping against my knees and take a few steps inside the cavern, moving slowly as I gawk around me.

And then I almost let out a shriek. . . . Because two people wearing dark hooded cloaks step forth from the shadowed portions of the rock wall nearby, emerging out of nowhere, and stand before us.

"You kept us waiting, Aten," the man says with sarcasm in his somehow familiar voice.

"I almost didn't think you would come today," the woman speaks in a soft, melodious voice, also remarkably familiar.

They throw back the hoods of their cloaks, and I realize, I *do* know them.

The young woman is one of the noble ladies from yesterday's party. I don't recall her name, only the lively expression of her blue eyes. Last night she was in a long silver dress, and her light brown hair was sculpted in an intricate knot. Having received a flower from me at the arched trellis reception line, the lady had responded with "how lovely," then thoughtfully attached it to her dress instead of simply tossing it.

Today, this same noblewoman is wrapped in a plain black cloak, wears no Face Art whatsoever, and her hair is pulled back in a simple *sesemet* tail. Indeed, she can easily pass for a servant.

As for the young man—very handsome, with long, reddish-brown hair and a pragmatic, dark-eyed gaze—he is none other than Stryr Giparu.

Last night, he had nothing on but a lower-body tunic, was bare-chested and sleek, daringly wearing a shining *pegasus* collar. . . . Now, however, his loud and brashly provocative manner is replaced by somber control. All court flippancy is gone; he is cool and businesslike as he steps forward to approach Bisfuri.

"I had to get two of my trusted servants involved and brought up to speed," Benaten replies, closing the distance and taking something small from Stryr's black-gloved hand. The object briefly sparkles like a metal coin, and it occurs to me, that's a Thoth-pin, a gadget for storing data. And then he glances back at Girsul and me.

"They'll be handling the *pegasei*," Bisfuri elaborates, turning back to the newcomers. "But I had to make sure they could manage. This is Girsul, my sound tech and messenger, among other things. And this one—she is Semmi. You might remember her from last night as the Storyteller."

"Yes, I recall," the lady says, turning to me. "Very entertaining tale. You also gave me a pretty flower at the entrance."

"Oh!" I attempt to bow, lowering my head while holding the two goats. "Yes, my Lady, I remember . . . you kept it and did not throw it away like the others."

The young woman smiles. "I prefer not to create waste."

"True, she doesn't waste anything, not even words," Benaten speaks to me and Girsul. *Is there the tiniest trace of amusement in his tone?* "Meet the Lady Nanivel Egemavda. You might've had the pleasure of learning her name during the formal court introduction announcements, but now you will behold the real Lady Nanivel. Don't be fooled by her placid demeanor, she is precise and terrifying."

Neither Girsul nor I know how to respond to that.

The lady herself quietly laughs.

Benaten continues, "As for this man—you very likely recall *Ter* Stryr Giparu, because he made a spectacular scene at the party, blaming his brother thoroughly for the escaped *pegasus*."

"I had to uphold my witless *chazuf* reputation. Besides, Arguam had it coming, mishandling his prize like a *hoohvak*," Stryr says, adjusting the heavy fabric of his cloak around his throat and loosening the ties . . . until a rainbow iridescent glow appears, illuminating his face in eerie contrast from below, and revealing the now-familiar *living collar*. "As you can see, I still have mine. The one my brother lost so carelessly was intended for Lady Nanivel. Now, we're one creature short."

"Not to worry," Benaten says. "Today, I'll use my hoverboard —this time. But we'll need that additional *pegasus* eventually. Girsul, can you procure more from the same source?"

Girsul frowns with effort. "Um, no, not the same source, that one's gone, *im Ter*. But I'll see what I can do. I know another guy—"

"Very well. Take care of it later today." And Bisfuri sings a series of tones. At once, the grey shape of a hoverboard separates from one of the cavern walls, and flies toward us, stopping in a horizontal hover position before him.

I look in that direction and see that several more upright hoverboards remain there, lined up vertically against the stone. Must be a storage area of some sort.

What else is there?

"Semmi," my employer tells me. "Give Lady Nanivel one of your goats. She'll be using it from here on."

I immediately hand the lead of one of the *pegasei* goats I hold to Lady Nanivel.

She takes it carefully, but without showing any fear or hesitation. In fact, she exudes confidence as she steps away, pulling the lead lightly, so that the *pegasus* must follow her.

Benaten turns again to me, and also looks at Girsul.

"And now, time for your assignments," he says. "First, you will be training the *pegasei* to take on specific animal shapes. And then you will learn to *ride* them inside this network of tunnels, in order to carry out certain duties . . . and assist us."

"Ride them . . . *here?*" Girsul's face appears confounded.

"Yes, in the tunnels."

"But . . . isn't it narrow in places?"

"Yes, it is," Stryr says, as he removes the *pegasus* collar from his neck and holds it carefully with both hands. "The passages are variable in size and sometimes they get so small you can barely move or crawl through them."

"Those are not the ones we'll be using," Nanivel corrects him. "We'll be flying through sufficiently wide passages. But yes, it is still awkward to maneuver through them, even on hoverboards."

"Flying?" I ask. "My Lady, I thought we would be riding?"

Nanivel and Stryr exchange glances with Benaten. And then Nanivel answers me gently enough that she indeed sounds terrifying. "It is best that you fly through the tunnels without touching the ground. There are—*things* there. Very old, ancient things that *crawl*."

I feel my breath slowing with a cold, preternatural fear. Girsul's expression looks equally uncertain.

"There are also pits and random deep holes, cave-ins in the stone floor. Not to mention, various inconvenient serrations and sharp gauges in the rock underneath and all around the tunnel sides," Stryr adds. "Trust me, you wouldn't like to walk or ride over any of it. In many instances, it's an impossibility, the deeper you go."

Crap of a goat. . . .

I feel myself starting to shiver.

"And that's why we—*you*—will need to choose very particular flying animal shapes," *Ter* Bisfuri says.

"Such as the horse with wings?" Girsul switches the lead of his *pegasus* from one hand to the other nervously.

"No, not that one, unfortunately," Benaten says. "Too big a wingspan. In most cases, that creature will be unable to flap its wings properly in these narrow tubes and get enough air lift to rise off the ground."

"What about a very little horse?" I ask. "Or a donkey with wings? Maybe even goats?"

"Such as these?" Stryr chuckles. "Whose idea was it to turn these particular *pegasei* into goats?"

"Hers," Benaten replies with a faint smile. "A very good idea, actually. Much easier to keep them discreet than in the original winged *sesemet* shape."

"I don't dispute, merely find it amusing." Stryr strokes the iridescent surface of his *pegasei* collar with his fingertips, as though testing its nature.

"The problem with riding miniaturized versions of large animals is that the aerodynamics don't translate correctly. Your little flying goats and *sesemet* would have to flap their proportionately little wings faster than a bee to rise off the ground and carry your weight," Lady Nanivel says in a tone of authority. "Believe me, it's been tried. However, the reverse works fine. Take a small creature shape and enlarge it, and in many cases, though, not all, it is more aerodynamic."

Right now, I'm not entirely sure what the word "aerodynamic" means, since I've never heard it before. . . . But I'm beginning to guess some of the meaning by the rest of what Nanivel is saying.

"My Lady, does it even matter if it's a real or proportionally real animal, since the *pegasus* creates its solid form out of nothing, regardless of size?" Girsul asks carefully, so as not to insult.

"Not out of nothing," Benaten responds. "These creatures consume sunlight and then pull real quantum energy from *elsewhere*, some other unknown dimensions, converting it to physical matter. And that's definitely not nothing. As long as they're sufficiently fed, the amount of energy they are capable of bringing into our reality is nearly unlimited. But yes, a single *pegasus* is not confined by properties such as size or volume in our physical world."

"But its physical shape *is*." Stryr adds. "Confined by physical laws. Such as little wings needing to flap faster, or in a different pattern entirely, to create lift."

"Understood, *im Ter*," Girsul says. "So then, what? We try smaller animals, but scale them up?"

"Yes, creatures such as birds," Nanivel says. "Make them as big as necessary, and in most cases their wings-and-body balance will be adequate. But fine-tune the overall body shape so that you can sit and ride without falling off. Take into consideration the placement of the wings on their bodies."

I listen to all of this with curiosity, then have to ask, "But if we must fly, why not just use hoverboards? Why do you need the *pegasei* creature forms?"

Benaten nods at me. "A valid question. Here's why. The places where we will be flying have orichalcum *sensors*. We will be detected during approach, and all will be ruined. So, no hoverboards, and indeed, nothing with any orichalcum content. I can't even bring my Niktos Cloak."

My mouth falls open.

Bisfuri continues, "Another reason is, we must be very quiet on approach—silent, in fact. So, no sound commands, no singing of tone sequences. Once we transform the *pegasei* into a chosen shape and sing that initial tone, they will follow the non-verbal cues and commands we give with our *minds*."

"And on that note," Stryr says, "it's time to practice transforming them. I'll start with mine. Let's see—an avian form that not only flaps wings but can soar and glide to conserve motion—"

"What form? Think well before you act." Nanivel looks sharply at him. "Remember, plan ahead before you break quantum confinement. Especially since you're releasing your *pegasus* from this weird, little, *non-standard* inanimate shape. Otherwise, you're going to lose it also."

"Don't worry, I'm not Arguam." Stryr raises the collar at chest level before him, laying it flat on the palms of his hands. "As for the form? I've been thinking of this particular shape while we were on our way here, and decided on a falcon. Now, stand back and give me room."

And Stryr sings the voice command sequence.

S tryr Giparu has a powerful singing voice, a low tenor or
high baritone—something I'm not surprised about, having
heard him yelling so much last night at the Bisfuri Party. And
now, echoing all over the cavern, he sings the keying notes at the
iridescent collar reposing in his hands.

I notice, he's carefully holding on to the collar's chain
portion. Apparently, it's the orichalcum quantum containment
harness, cleverly disguised as an extension of the jewelry piece.

As soon as he initiates the keying sequence, the *living object*
in his palms begins shimmering wildly and loses its cohesive
shape. And then it starts to expand, swelling into a colorful
rainbow mist cloud. No longer dormant in his hands, it hangs in
the air before him, pulsing, and tugging wildly at the ends of its
harness.

We all stare as *Ter* Giparu grapples with his *pegasus* creature,
and then it starts to form into an enormous bird the size of a
donkey. Seriously, that's what it looks like to me, at first glance,
strange and awkward, until its shape becomes more defined.

A pair of large pointed wings sprouts on both sides of the
giant falcon, and its tail sharpens into a point, feathers folded.

Two powerful avian legs, like sapling tree trunks, reach for the ground.

The creature is grey and tan in plumage, like a true bird, but there are traces of barely suppressed iridescence in the hue of its feathers. For whatever reason—maybe because of its recent transformation into a new shape, which might expend energy—it's no longer glowing as brightly, the way it did when it was just a *thing*, a wearable collar. And now, it hops once, then settles in place, turning its avian head this and that way, eventually training its beady eyes on Stryr.

They must be communicating. . . .

In other words, the man is visualizing his intentions, and the *pegasus* reads his mind and learns to obey.

Stryr's expression is intense with focus, while he continues to sing the command until the *pegasus* falcon stands before him, completely still and ready. It is so big that its back rises nearly to the level of Stryr's waist.

And then it slowly unfurls its wings. . . .

My mouth falls open, and so does Girsul's, as we observe this impossible creature. Admittedly, its wingspan is smaller than the classic winged *sesemet* shape that Girsul originally created back in the stables—but not by much.

How in the world will it fit inside a narrow passage? And how do you ride it?

Stryr Giparu stops singing and advances forward, placing one hand on the back of the falcon's neck. He sweeps his long cloak aside to give himself room for motion, then steps over the tail and straddles its back, leaning forward, lying between the wings. One hand grips the harness that's now around the bird's neck, while the other digs into the thick feathers just below.

"Can you fit there?" Benaten asks. "You seem to be positioned too low on its back. Once it starts flapping—"

"We're good," Stryr replies curtly.

"Adjust your cloak, or take it off altogether," Nanivel remarks. "It's in the way of the wings."

"No, it's not." Stryr gives her one intense, aggravated glance.

"Yes, it is." Nanivel is implacable.

"Hathor's buttocks! I'm bringing the cloak. It's too cold in those tunnels without it." Stryr turns behind him and twists the bottom portion of his cloak into a thick rope, then folds it into a ridiculous knot, shortening it considerably as it still hangs down his back.

Nanivel sighs. "Ah, you're such a child."

At which point Stryr glares at her once, then pointedly ignores her, focusing on his falcon.

Benaten observes the two of them and shakes his head in amusement.

I momentarily wonder how well these three nobles know each other, and how far back their association might go. . . .

But in that instant the great falcon hops forward, flaps its wings mightily, flares its tail. Stryr leans close against its back as they suddenly rise into the air of the cavern, flying toward the dark and distant ceiling.

We look up at their unified flying shape, and hear the flapping of the powerful wings, like wind farm blades, from on high.

And then Stryr lets out a whoop, followed by peals of laughter. "So much better than a hoverboard!" he exclaims loudly. The wild sound of his mirth echoes insanely against the stone walls.

"Crazy *chazuf*!" Nanivel says with minor reproach. "Shut your mouth before anyone else can hear you—someone deep inside this tunnel network, or on the surface. And please don't fall on our heads."

"He looks steady enough," Benaten says, watching the falcon and its rider slowly circle above.

"Fine, my turn." Nanivel looks down at her shiny goat, then glances at the rest of us. "Please stand back."

And the young woman sings a keying command in a beautiful soprano voice, focusing on the creature before her.

The *pegasus* goat immediately responds, its shape dissolving into a rainbow cloud of light.

And then the tug of war with the harness begins. Lady Nanivel holds on tight with both hands, singing the steady tones relentlessly, until the sparks and embers of light coalesce into a shape of another great bird, very similar to the one Stryr created.

However, this particular bird is not a falcon. Judging by its black plumage, it looks like an oversized crow or raven.

"Nicely done," Benaten says, observing the lady hold the harness, which is now attached around the raven's neck. The *pegasus* bird unfolds its *niktos*-black wings, smaller than the falcon's.

"Notice the placement of the wings," Nanivel says. "Yes, they are intentionally deformed—narrower than normal at the base, and attached lower on the sides. Now, there's more space to sit without having to lie flat against its back all the time."

And she steps around and gracefully raises one leg to climb on the back of the raven. I note that she is wearing masculine pants underneath her cloak.

Once she is securely seated, with her booted feet barely toeing the ground, Nanivel undoes the ties of her cloak and removes it. She folds the fabric neatly lengthwise, rolls it several times until it's a narrow tube, then ties it around her waist. "Much better," she says, then pats the neck of her raven and smiles lightly at us.

"Ready to go up?" Benaten asks.

Lady Nanivel takes a deep breath. "I've imagined this so many times, ran through the *pegasei* flight scenario in my mind, over and over, while exercising my *sesemet*. The riding technique is not much different. Yes, I'm quite ready."

And the next moment, she flies.

The raven beats its smaller wings efficiently, and Nanivel sits astride, not needing to lean forward as much as Stryr because of the way her bird's body is shaped. They rise up to the cavern ceiling, narrowly avoiding Stryr and his falcon who swoop past with reckless speed.

Only the three of us remain on the ground—Benaten, Girsul, and I.

Ter Bisfuri watches the two nobles overhead then looks at us and points to our goats.

"Now, you. Transform your *pegasei* into something with wings, then practice riding them. Keep low to the ground for now, until you feel confident enough to rise higher."

"Yes, *im Ter*," Girsul says. I notice his expression is very tense.

Benaten then glances at me. "Are you ready, Semmi? Don't be afraid, it's not much different than riding a hoverboard. Decide on a creature, then sing the command. Feel free to pick an easy bird shape and imagine all the wing details—"

Bast help me!

I don't want to admit to my employer that I've ridden my brother Uru's hoverboard only a few times and nearly fell off every time. . . .

And so, I nod silently and take a deep breath, staring at my goat—while next to me Girsul is getting ready to do the same thing with his.

Sacred Bast, please help me choose a proper flying bird, not a hoohvak *chicken*, I think. And now that I've thought of it, of course, all I can see in my mind's eye are chickens. A whole flock of red-and-brown speckled hens running through the yard of one of our neighbors, and among them their two big black-and-brown roosters with flopping combs—back in the days before the golden gods came and everyone got rid of their yard animals. . . .

No, just no. Not chickens!

I think and think desperately, trying to visualize another bird, any useful flying bird—even as I hear Girsul already singing the keying command to transform his *pegasus* goat into something else. . . .

I turn away, trying not to look or listen to his specific keying notes. Now I'll have to pick some other note to sing, since I don't want to mess up his voice keying. But first, I must choose the bird shape.

Maybe, I could try for a duck. . . . I can remember regular neighborhood ducks waddling around on the road in front of our house, loose and free. I'm reasonably sure I can imagine all the details of their wings and beaks and bellies.

So be it.

I step away so that I can see my goat better. Glowing with rainbow light, it stands rooted in place and appears to be staring into cavernous space before it, ignoring all the activity around it. I take a deep breath, focus on the goat *and* the mental image of a fat duck. . . .

The duck in my memory is sunning itself, its little beady eyes closed. It's sitting in front of Babi's hovel next door, the midday sun shining bright on its dark brown wing feathers with a spackle of rusty red on its back, and a lighter underbelly. . . .

I pick a single note—a herding call—and start to sing the keying command, and get an annoying urge to sneeze. I stop, sniffle and scrunch up my nose, then resume singing. Again, wanting to sneeze, such bad timing.

Furthermore, now there's a weird buzzing in my nose and forehead. I try to ignore it, and continue singing the note until my forehead genuinely aches.

What in all *shaitunaat* is going on? My nose is not dripping, so I don't have any sudden onset sickness, unless there's a *sha* curse growing inside there, up in my nostrils. . . .

I frown, tighten my brows, blink rapidly to stop myself from sneezing, and sing a slightly different note, to see if it's more comfortable, and if that might make the tickle of vibrations go away.

But that makes it actually worse.

And now, I swear on my own *hoohvak* head, the spot in the middle of my forehead, just above the bridge of my nose, really, really *hurts*. The pressure is sudden and more intense than a splitting headache, and it seems to resonate with the note that I'm singing, in a strange way.

At the same time, my goat suddenly seems to come *awake*—if such a thing is possible. Its stiff posture loosens, and it barely turns its neck toward me, while its nearest eye focuses on me in the most disturbing way imaginable. Just as I meet its creepy gaze, a strange swirl of color suddenly races down its back, like a trail of stars. . . .

What is happening?

Red and orange and purple and green . . . the lights pulse brightly then fade to the ordinary brown and black of the goat's coat along its back, while its lower extremities continue to glow with iridescent light.

Holy Bast! Why isn't it transforming? Where's the rainbow blob of mist?

Am I doing something wrong?

The itching headache intensifies, and now it seems I'm about to die. . . . Suddenly I feel a burst of *power* inside my mind.

A blinding flash.

Sharp pain explodes, rips through my forehead.

Its location is deep under the skin in the middle spot above the bridge of my nose. My Grandmother calls that spot the Sacred Eye of Thoth. The *third eye*.

Mother Bastet!

And then, like an old wound, a forgotten hole in my head, something *opens*.

The *hole* is now a tunnel, then an immense cavern—greater

than the one we're in now—and then I am violently pulled out of my body and snapped back in.

Oh no, my ka!

Am I being attacked by evil *sha* in this accursed cavern, despite it being the middle of day? Have we gone too deep into the ground and somehow approached the underworld and awakened them?

Everything is spinning. . . .

Rooted in place, I stand upright, yet I can barely feel myself, my body, my breath.

Even the sounds of the world around me have receded—the voice of Girsul singing nearby, the whoosh of flapping wings above, Bisfuri speaking something. . . .

I am floating. Possibly, for one heartbeat, I briefly lose consciousness.

There's a rush of noise in my head, and terrible dizziness.

The noise is now a roaring flood. . . .

And I have become the tunnel through which it travels.

An infinity of things passes through me, in the blink of an eye—images, colors, shapes, textures, noises, tastes, smells, agony, exultation . . . I see the boundless *niktos* sky full of immense stars and tiny motes of dust. I see moments of my past spinning backward like a yarn, people, events, my family, neighbors, strangers, endless piles of chopped mushrooms. . . .

Again, I snap back into the present moment. . . . Oh, my poor embattled *ka*!

Inhabiting my body once more, I blink. And then I realize I'm still *singing* the accursed note, the keying command, *no time has passed*, and all my visual focus is on the little goat before me, its eye watching me back with intensity.

That's when I find a strange other *presence* within my mind.

A voice, deep as an ocean, piercing as the screech of a *bakris* bird, soothing as olive oil in Grandmother's old salve jar . . . it floods my conscious mind and speaks inside me in a language that is not *Atlanteo*, and yet I somehow understand it.

Sentient one. You are aware. You are sentient, the voice tells me. *Don't be afraid. Continue resonating at this frequency. On this frequency we can communicate.*

I stop singing.

I gasp for air and get ready to scream.

No. Don't make a sound, the voice in my head tells me.

I freeze in terror. And just like that, I feel a wave of peace settle over me. It has to be some kind of sorcery, because it makes no sense for me to be suddenly so calm in this dire moment.

At the same time, the *pegasus* goat before me dissolves into a rainbow cloud of light—even as I continue to hold its quantum containment harness.

I mean you no harm. But you must tell nothing to the others of your kind. The voice inside my mind modulates in strange ways so that I'm unsure of anything about it.

I open my mouth and take a deep breath, then whisper, "Are you one of the *sha*?"

No, the otherworldly voice replies.

At the same time, *Ter* Bisfuri must hear my muttering, because he glances in my direction.

I turn my head away slightly, so that Bisfuri cannot see my lips flapping. "Are you one of the gods?"

No . . . not a god. Not the kind you imagine.

Despite the wave of enforced calm pressing down on me, I feel a tingle of fear run down my back. "So, then you *are* some other, unknown kind of god?" I persist, with a breath of anger. "You can't take away my *ka*! I won't let you! I still need it for this life, I'm not ready to die!"

Don't move your mouth to speak with me. Use your mind, and I will hear you. I do not require your ka.

But I can't help myself. Again, with the mouth flapping. "I

don't believe you!" Fiercely, I whisper out loud, hissing with violence, "Whoever, whatever you are—how did you get inside my head?"

"Ei, Semmi, what? Did you say something?" Girsul asks behind me. "Having trouble with your *pegasus* transformation?"

I turn around, and the young man is standing directly behind me, holding on to a very large bird that could be a hawk or another falcon.

Don't tell. Say nothing. Pretend you are still choosing my shape. The voice fills my head, echoing with a mixture of perverse calm and utter force.

Well, stinking crap of a chazuf goat, I "think-speak" back at the alien voice inside me. *How am I supposed to pretend? You're this hoohvak pegasus, aren't you?*

I force my expression to be as neutral as possible, for Girsul's sake. I even force a little smile, as I shake my head casually. "Sorry, was talking to myself."

And in that moment, the voice in my head changes in its underlying nature, from threatening to benign. I swear, I can sense amusement, like a warm, rich flow of honey spreading in my mind.

I am, it says.

And then it speaks an incomprehensible, unintelligible, alien word.

A *aah-eeeh-iiih-oooh-uuuh-gjkfkhhh*, says the voice inside my head. Or at least that's what I think it utters, hissing, singing, echoing in my mind. Somehow, I know that it's not real, not what is actually being conveyed. . . .

My conscious mind receives the real *word* and converts it to nonsense sounds and syllables. The real word—it is like the wind blowing in the open spaces.

Truly, I have no means in my own language to explain.

It is the name of my species, the voice of the being inside me says. *I will not utter it again, since you cannot perceive it. Instead, continue to call us* pegasei, *the imaginary name your species gave us as soon as we entered your world . . . when you fixed us in your equally imaginary chosen shape of space-time-matter.*

"Space-time-matter . . . what?" I mind-speak. "I don't understand. What shape?"

The creature of your world that you call sesemet, *a horse. With the addition of wings.*

"Right, the *pegasus*," I think at it. "The *hoohvak* flying horse. Which doesn't exist."

I repeat. We did not choose the shape. The first of your species to communicate with us offered us that particular construct from the contents of their mind, forcing us to coalesce into this unnatural form.

"Whoever it was, had to be drinking entire wine sacks," I mind-speak, working very hard on keeping my mouth from moving. "So why didn't you just switch shape to an actual horse or something else that's real, eventually?"

By the time we learned more of your universe and your world, it was too late. The pegasus form became firmly associated in your consciousness with our species. And, being guests in this inflexible reality, we complied.

"Huh?"

Unlike us, your species is made of seemingly fixed matter, solid in your ways. In the greater scheme of things, it is an illusion. Matter is entirely temporary. But you prefer to perceive your environment this way—to fix in place all the things in your world—including your notions of sentient identities.

I open my eyes wide.

In this space-time, you held the advantage, the being continues. You molded us into what you wanted us to be. And thus, it was simpler for us to conform to your original choice. Indeed, it was inevitable.

"Inevitable? Bastet help me. . . . What are you really made of?" I ask inside my mind.

Energy. Order. Sentience, the being replies, after the tiniest pause. But in your lesser universe, we are what you perceive as light. We consume and process light to retain our own quantum cohesiveness.

"Yes, I've fed you in the sunlight, I get that. But—if you're light, how exactly do you shapeshift? The last time I've seen sunshine, it didn't just spontaneously turn into chickens or eos pies!"

Theoretically, it could. But it would need a catalyst to begin the complex process.

I can almost hear laughter in the being's voice, as it

elaborates. *Photon energy in your universe can change its state and degrade into matter, which can then assume various intermediate phases (solid, liquid, gas . . . chicken, eos pie). So can we.*

Inside my mind, I literally hold back an imaginary snort.

A high-speed, precise collision of two light particles results in positrons and electrons—fundamental particles of physical matter. We require no such collision. We provide the catalyst—our own selves, our sentience. Our focused will initiates the same reaction. Simply put, we break apart and reform into anything in your physical world.

I wrinkle my forehead, trying to grasp this impossible nonsense. As heartbeats pass, I stand, somewhat stupefied, still outwardly staring at the cloud of rainbow light which now hangs motionless before me, with only the quantum harness loosely hovering in a loop around it.

It occurs to me: I'm no longer afraid of this thing in my head. It's just too . . . ridiculous.

"So, okay," I think-speak. "You—I mean, you, light blob . . . *pegasus.* You're telling me that light knocks about with itself and breaks up into little, smaller pieces which then combine to become solid stuff? Like, if I snap open a pea pod, the peas fall out, and then we can mash them together to make stew? Is that—"

Yes. An acceptable analogy. We are like your pods degrading into your peas. Except we can reform back to being pea pods, then break apart, again and again. And each time we can become other things of your world, not merely peas. What we become depends on what forms we are presented with—within your minds.

"Wait—why do you need our minds?"

And then the being tells me something that I find stunning.

We need the sentience of your minds to interpret your universe to us. On our own, we understand nothing of this physical plane. Matter, in all its permutations—in all its discrete or continuous states of being—is all meaningless noise.

However, once we are shown the world as you see it, we remember, learn, and retain the ordered patterns of physical information you give us. We become capable of navigating your world via the sentient map you provide.

"Semmi?" Girsul's voice again cuts through my momentary stupor.

"Huh? Yes, just a moment!" I mutter in a rising tone of irritation. "I'm still thinking about bird wings!"

"Don't overthink," Girsul continues. "Just go with a basic easy bird, like this one, see mine—"

"Yeah, okay, all right!" I snarl back, so that Girsul goes quiet at my tone. Quickly, I glance at him and see his expression of confused surprise at my harsh reaction.

Oh, Mother of gods, if only he knew what's happening inside my head.

Even as I think it, I sense another surge of amusement coming from the *pegasus*. The weird sensation I can only describe as a warm pool of honey pouring from one spot of my mind and encroaching upon the rest of me. All this strangeness and more is originating from the middle of my forehead. It sounds like a high wind is tearing through an open window during a storm. . . .

I force myself to focus.

"All right—what are we going to do now?" I mind-speak with frustration, this time snarling silently inside my own head. "No more nonsense! Right now, I need you to transform into some kind of useful flying bird for me. And then I need to somehow ride your light-blob-turned-solid shape—what should I call you? What's your actual name?"

The being in my head, like a bubbling fountain, begins to "overflow" with even more amusement.

How easily your kind assumes dominance over another. . . . Very well. I will let you ride this form, it says.

As for my name—just as the name of my species makes no sense to you, I cannot properly translate my individual "designation" into a sound frequency-shape of this universe. My species has no entity names in the sense that yours does. Our identities are fluid and intertwined. We flow together in a bright river—

"Ah, crap of a goat, enough!" I exclaim in my mind. "I can't handle your crazy yammer. No time! Unless you want the others to notice that I've lost my mind, stop saying things that make no sense. You have no name? Fine, I'll just keep calling you 'light blob.' Do you really want to be 'fixed' like that? No? Then give me a *hoohvak* name! Or, blessed Hekatri help me, I'm going to make it even worse and call you a stinking—"

Hekatri, the being echoes me. *Hekatri . . . He-e-eka-a-atri-i-i.*

"No!" I mind-cry. "Not Hekatri. She's the bright goddess of clarity, you can't use such a lofty name! I merely called upon her to grant me strength right now, in this very *hoohvak* situation."

Hekat . . . Hekut . . . Heket, the being says. *He-e-eke-e-et. Will a variation be acceptable?*

"Hmm," I think-mumble. "I suppose, that's all right. As long as you don't disrespect the goddess and bring wrath on my soul. Heket it is. Heket, Heket."

Yes, the presence in my head responds. *I will answer to the name Heket.*

"Good." I form the thought with a silent huff of satisfaction. "Now—Heket, you will transform into a bird that can fly around in this horrible cave and fit inside the narrow tunnels. A bird that I can ride. We'll discuss your residence inside my head later."

I cannot transform unless you give me an image of the creature you require. Also, what should I call your own self? Should I give you a name also?

I'm briefly taken aback. Considering that this *pegasus* is stuck inside my mind (for however long, Bastet help me), I've assumed it somehow knows my name already.

No, I do not, the being replies. *I only know the information you provide spontaneously by thinking about it, or information that you specifically direct to my attention.*

"Good to know," I mumble-think. "My name is Semmi, short for Semirameos. Call me either, but Semmi is best."

I will call you Semmi.

The being who named itself Heket goes blessedly silent for a few heartbeats—something that I deeply appreciate. And then it asks: *Show me, sentient one called Semmi, what kind of living creatures usually live inside your caves?*

"What do you mean?"

Show me everything that dwells inside caves in your universe. Think of it, visualize it in your mind, and I will see it also.

The moment Heket asks me this, I immediately think of scary crawly bugs that might live in the cracks between the stones. . . . Spiders in webs. . . . Ugh.

I see them, Heket responds immediately. *However, according to your images, they do not fly.*

"No, they don't!" I think-exclaim, with an inner shudder. "Ignore that."

What else lives in caves?

And then, out of nowhere, I remember a squeaking colony of flying night creatures that I once disturbed by accident as a little child, when I climbed a big pile of rocks serving as a sad excuse for a hill in my neighborhood.

Bats. . . .

"Ah, sacred gods, please, no . . ." I think immediately, with another shudder, this time in real space. "Those are vermin! Flying mice, not birds. They have nasty webbed wings, and little beady eyes, and these weird claws on their wings. . . . They hang upside down, and some of them drink the blood of the living—"

But they are native to caves. And they fly, Heket replies calmly.

And in the next instant, the cloud of rainbow light before me starts to coalesce and darken, pulse and contort. . . . And it takes on the form of the biggest, most terrifying bat I've ever imagined in my life.

I slap one hand over my mouth to hold back a squeal, as I watch in horror this horrendous mouse-thing forming.

The giant bat grows to the height of my waist, with a dark-brown furry coat, little wings, an elongated snout. . . .

At first, it balances awkwardly on its hind legs, tottering for a mere heartbeat. Then it collapses forward onto its expanding webbed wings, using the single long hook in each wing like a thumb to stand up partially, dragging the rest of its wing-joints on the stone ground.

"Whoa!" I hear the surprised voice of Girsul behind me, as he sits mounted on the back of his bird of prey. "What did you do? That's not a bird—"

"I know it's not a bird," I say with a quick glance behind me, all while trying not to run. Desperately, I hold onto the harness that is now in a ring around the mousy creature's giant neck. "It's a stinking bat, I know! But—it flies and lives in caves—"

It meets all your requirements, the *pegasus* inside my head remarks.

"Shut up!" I hurl a thought-yell at it. "I can't believe you turned into this filthy thing!"

Then I feign courage and confidence, for Girsul's sake, and carefully speak out loud, "It's exactly right for flying through these tunnels."

And, to demonstrate my confidence further, I take a step forward, and then another. With a deep breath, I climb from behind on the mouse-monster-bat's furry back . . . settling awkwardly between those webbed wings and lying forward to clutch its fur, without letting go of the harness.

Why do you say this elegant creature is filthy? Heket asks.

And in that moment, I receive a vision-thought that's definitely not my own.

An alien thought.

I suddenly see the huge, dark vermin as a gracefully aligned *living construct* of geometry.

How did I not see this before? The bat is formed perfectly, with divine precision, and it is beautiful. . . .

The creature's body upon which I rest is supple and suddenly warm. Its back is wide and strong. Even the brown fur in my fingers is silken-smooth and soft to the touch.

In that moment, the bat turns its mouse-head to look back at me with one, no-longer beady but intelligent eye of pure *sentience.*

And then it winks at me.

"Girsul! Semmi!" I hear the voice of *Ter* Bisfuri, coming from overhead. "What's taking so long? Come up here!"

Next, I hear the beating of wings as Girsul's bird springs upward . . . and they rise, flapping and pushing against the air powerfully.

Are you ready for me to fly, sentient Semmi? the *pegasus* bat asks me, with an unexpected tone of gentleness in its thought-voice.

I take a shuddering breath, clutch the fur and the harness. "I'm ready," I think at it.

The immense bat wings on both sides of me come alive. Suddenly, I feel the powerful air currents churning as we take off, rising effortlessly into the air of the cavern.

NOT UNLIKE AN ACTUAL BAT, I utter a frightened squeak, dizzy and helpless, in those first moments of flight. Then I clamp my mouth shut, and continue grasping the bat fur around its neck, lying forward as close to it as possible.

The floor of the cavern recedes, suddenly cast in shadow, because our *pegasei* are the only sources of light, and now all the light has risen toward the ceiling. We have magically inversed the illumination in this great space, and now the stones of the upper reaches come into view.

Stryr Giparu and his falcon soar chaotically around us—
unlike Nanivel Egemavda who makes very careful aerial passes
in a straight line, casting light upon the upper stones.

Benaten Bisfuri is on his hoverboard, levitating in place near
the ceiling, one booted foot in the bottom stirrup, so that his
hoverboard stands up at an incline while he stays on with
confident elegance. He watches the others circling, and watches
Girsul and me approach from below.

Girsul is as careful and tight-lipped as Lady Nanivel as his
bird swoops upward in a controlled manner.

My bat and I, on the other hand . . . Bastet and Hekatri and
Hathor help me, but in those first few instants the bat flies with
a slight up-and-down jerking motion, as though it is learning
the mechanics of its physical shape. And then, as it continues to
beat its wings, it improves, smoothing its flight.

When I rise closer to *Ter* Bisfuri and his hoverboard, I hear
his deep, amused voice.

"Interesting choice of flying animal, Semmi," my employer
says to me as my *pegasus* bat flaps its huge wings to remain at
eye level with Bisfuri.

"Sorry, hope you don't mind, *im Ter*. It seemed the best
choice, since we're in a dark cave," I reply, tying to justify this
bat creature I'm saddled with, literally.

"I think it's smart," Nanivel says, approaching from behind
atop her black raven. "Next time, I might make mine a bat also."

Bisfuri merely nods. "As long as it works out for you."

"So, what now?" Stryr calls out, coming at our grouping in a
rush of wings. "Should we head out into the tunnels?"

"Whoa, slow down," Nanivel says, engulfed by the churn of
incoming air created by Stryr's falcon. The tendrils of her
pulled-back hair fly up and tangle around her face.

My bat and I remain stationary in the air, waiting for Benaten
to issue our next instructions.

Don't be afraid, I will not allow you to fall, Heket speaks in my thoughts, sending a wave of now familiar calm at me.

"I'm not afraid," I grumble-think at him. "Why would you think I'm afraid?"

You are holding on too tightly. Loosen your hold on the harness, or you will tire quickly.

"Oh yeah?" I think at it. "You're just trying to make me lose my grip so that you can escape!"

There is a silent heartbeat.

And then the *pegasus* in my head replies, *I promise I will not escape. You have my word.*

I frown, and my fingers dig deeper into the bat fur. "And why should I believe you? I still know nothing about you, really."

Because we do not lie.

The thought strikes me suddenly—except, it comes from all sides. It's not just Heket that speaks inside me, but a *chorus*.

Other *pegasei* voices echo from behind, below, and above.

My eyes widen, as I look around, up, and down, and see Stryr's great falcon fix its golden eyes on me . . . while just below, Girsul's indeterminate bird of prey has turned its sharp-beaked head to stare directly at me with piercing black eyes . . . and right behind me, Nanivel's raven swivels its neck, and suddenly it is looking into my very soul.

CHAPTER
THIRTY-SIX

"What in all *shaitunaat* is happening now?" I exclaim in my mind. "You're *all* inside my head now? All you stinking *pegasei* light blobs? No!"

We are all connected, Heket replies, his unique voice standing out above the clamor. *When you speak to one of us, you speak to all.*

"Holy Mother Bast! What have I done to deserve this foul plague upon me?" I mind-yell, gripping the bat's fur and trying not to fall off, because now my head is truly spinning.

You issued the sound frequency at which the data flows.

You opened the barrier.

You resonated correctly. . . .

They all speak at me simultaneously, and I feel as though my mind has turned to boiling porridge—popping with turnips, carrots, and barley—and is about to burst.

Breathe, sentient Semmi. Heket's voice once again separates from the others and slithers gently next to my *ka*, sending concentric waves of tangible calm in my direction.

I take a deep breath, and the dizziness recedes somewhat. . . .

No, it is not all gone. It's an aspect of fear, and fear sits there like a wild creature, in the back of my mind—along with this—this unspeakable *herd* of light blobs.

I focus in that direction, cast my inner gaze upon them, and they are all there, strange, swirling, alien sound "shapes." I'm beginning to recognize them enough to separate them, more or less.

I take another shuddering breath, regaining a small portion of control.

"All right," I mind-speak. "So, now there's three of you. Are there more out there? If I call out, will more of your *pegasei* kind reply, from a distance?"

Yes, Heket says. *All* pegasei *will reply, always. . . . But most of our voices will be faint and distant. So many of us are currently bound and imprisoned by your species in specific locations in this space-time that we cannot come to you.*

It is up to you to issue the universal frequency each time to initiate contact. However, it requires a great deal of concentration to command the required energy at a distance. Unless you can focus with sufficient force to reach out to us, you will find the communication link to be minimal.

"Well, that's a relief." Mentally, I give off annoyance and sarcasm, like a puff of hot air. "Can't have an army of you banging around inside my mind. That would make me expire in madness."

Fear not, Semmi. We do not intrude upon your mind space unless you address us directly.

"That's great. Now, please shut up for a few moments so that I can listen with my real ears to what *Ter* Bisfuri is saying."

At once, my awareness of the *pegasei* entities inside my head recedes—as if they've indeed retreated inward and voluntarily shrunk away, if such a thing is possible—and the outside world comes into brighter focus.

"Before we enter the tunnels," Benaten is saying, "I need to prepare my two employees who have never been inside with a proper explanation of what's expected."

He pauses meaningfully and glances at Girsul and me, then continues. "As I mentioned on the way here, the tunnels are part of an immense network. They're also specially marked with color light beacons for the cardinal directions of travel."

"Oh yeah? So as not to get lost?" Girsul asks.

"Yes. You'll find that there's always a small light fixture at the base of each tunnel entrance, each different junction, and branch. Most of them are one solid color—one of four possibilities, to represent directions. Blue is north, Green is west, Yellow is east, Red is south. For example, if you see a yellow beacon ahead of you, that means this specific portion of the tunnel network is aligned east-to-west, and you are facing east."

"Ah, I understand," Girsul responds.

"Yes, very sensible," Nanivel speaks up. "Those are the local City tunnels."

"But that's not all," Benaten says. "Sometimes, you will run into the occasional bigger, wider tunnels that bear a multi-beacon light grid with *all* four colors. Those are the tunnels you want to *avoid* at any cost, because they are not local—they lead outside the City and into the bowels of the earth. Some of these are trans-continental, running underneath the ocean to the rest of the lands on the other side. Enter them, and you might never come out unless you have a very good notion of where you are headed."

"Oh, holy Bast . . ." I utter with a fresh wave of fear.

"Indeed, praying to the gods might help under such circumstances," Stryr says.

"But, best to avoid altogether," *Ter* Bisfuri concludes. "If you see four-color beacons, you turn around and go back, then look for another local passage."

"Understood," Girsul replies quickly.

"Good." Benaten nods, then again continues. "The next thing

you must know is that these tunnels are primarily how the shipments of orichalcum are transported from their sources in the various mines on Atlantis and continents beyond the ocean to the biggest Bisfuri warehouse facility here in Poseidon—which happens to be located on Circle Eight. Semmi, you know the area."

"I do? Oh . . . I mean, yes, when I worked at the Chiprahat Exquisite Foods warehouse, that was on Eight."

"Correct. And the Bisfuri warehouse is not too far from there. It's the largest multi-block industrial complex."

Suddenly, comprehension strikes me. "Is that why you were there, *Ter* Bisfuri? That first morning when I saw you?"

Benaten's face reveals a secret smile. "I was on my way from the Bisfuri facility, about to enter the tunnel network. The closest entrance there is not too far from the street where you were walking. It's hidden inside a building, via alley access."

"That alley!" I exclaim. "You were fighting some street *chazufs* who were hurting some innocent people."

"Yes, it turned out to be a worthy cause, but not intentionally. I had no choice but to clear out that alley of possible witnesses so that I could get inside the building and enter the tunnels. And then I had to double back and pretend I was headed in a different direction outside the alley, after you saw me. Because, yes, I could see you watching from that corner. I could not let you or anyone know my true course."

Seeing my stunned expression, Bisfuri smirks. "Sorry to disappoint you, Semmi. The Man in the Niktos Cloak is not quite the hero you imagined."

Is there the tiniest raw edge to his tone? I think.

Maybe it's that vulnerable something that makes me confess out loud, "The Man in the Niktos Cloak will always be a hero, *im Ter*. Sometimes he just finds the injustice without looking for it, because the gods choose to send him there."

"I appreciate your faith in the vigilante," Bisfuri says with amusement. "But now, enough talk. We are about to cross half of the City underground, and this first time you will simply observe the direction and the way to the warehouse. Once you know the way, then you can begin the work."

". . . Which is?" Stryr interrupts. "You haven't actually told them what they'll be doing in the tunnels."

Bisfuri throws him a quick, almost mischievous glance. "That's because they will be doing a variety of work within the tunnels. Some of it will be simple distraction of the Bisfuri guards. Some of it will involve marking the orichalcum cargo with special tracking sensors while I myself distract the guards accompanying the shipments."

Noticing Girsul and me both staring at him with growing alarm, Benaten smiles. "Fear not. You will not be in any serious danger at any given point. But you will need to learn to lie if questioned or stopped—which you will not be. The brunt of this will fall upon me and these two." And he motions toward Stryr and Nanivel.

"Yes, *im Ter*," I say quietly.

"Understood, *im Ter*," Girsul echoes me.

"Besides," my employer adds, "I am Bisfuri. And all these shipments are technically under my purview. It's just the small deviations from the official routes that will have to be disguised and explained away—all of which I will handle. Now, enough, let's go. Follow me!"

And Benaten Bisfuri directs his hoverboard downward, plunging toward the large tunnel opening on the opposite side of the cavern from where we arrived.

At once, Nanivel swoops down after him, followed by Stryr.

Girsul and I glance at each other quickly, hesitate only a moment, then follow them.

. . .

WE ENTER the large tunnel one at a time. My *pegasus* bat plummets almost before I instruct it to move, which I find disorienting but, never mind it now. . . . I hold on for dear life and fly inside last, after Girsul, feeling the wind from the powerful churn of wings of everyone's *pegasus* ahead of me.

In the brief instant, just as I pass through the entrance, I notice that there's indeed a small, single-color light glowing from a beacon lodged in the rock near the floor of the threshold. It is red, which means we are heading in the southern direction.

"We'll just follow them along this tunnel, all right?" I speak inside my mind, directing my voice at Heket. "So, fly onward please. And don't bump around or slam into the rock walls! You hear?"

Yes, I hear, Heket's amused voice responds. I mentally bristle with irritation, because he—or she, or whatever it is—should not be amused now, but should be seriously concentrating on not getting us splattered against the sharp stones of the passage.

You are safe, Semmi. Do not fear. We will not scrape the walls.

"Harumph!" I mutter out loud, which fortunately no one hears due to the flapping of wings.

Fortunately, this tunnel is large enough that there is no danger of any of our *pegasei's* wings striking the sides. The light that issues from their bodies is rather faint at this point, just enough to create twilight. There's barely enough visibility to show us where we're going.

Bisfuri's voice sounds from somewhere ahead, "Watch the upcoming curve."

And indeed, the tunnel starts to circle around, so that I grit my teeth in anxiety. My fingers dig into the bat's fur, and my legs and knees press against its back tightly. But my bat and the other birds ahead all handle the curve effortlessly.

"About five more daydreams in this direction, then we switch to a different tunnel," Bisfuri calls out. "Watch for a yellow light. How are you doing in the back?"

"All good," Nanivel's voice sounds.

"Fine here," we respond, one after another.

Girsul speaks, then coughs.

"Keep your faces down, as much as you can, to avoid the wind in your eyes," Bisfuri continues. "It becomes annoying at first, then dries you out. Eyes, nose, throat. You'll get used to it eventually, but for now, be aware—"

He grows silent, cutting off mid-sentence, because there's a distinct new sound up ahead.

Strange voices, interspersed with knocking thuds.

Or rather, distant echoes of human voices and knocks, coming from somewhere in the bowels of this tunnel system.

STRYR CURSES SOFTLY. Meanwhile, Benaten slows down. I can't exactly see him do it, since my line of sight is blocked, but I *know*, because Girsul's bird slows down ahead of me and comes to a stop, which causes my own bat to stop flapping.

"What is it?" I whisper.

"Quiet," Bisfuri responds so softly that I can barely hear him, even with the heightened stone acoustics of the passage around us. "Everyone, stop."

Several long heartbeats pass, while we hover silently on our *pegasei*.

The distant voices and knocks sound haphazardly, but then seem to be retreating.

"You think it's the Neph-Tiari again?" Stryr whispers after the sounds fade sufficiently.

"Yes." This time, it's Nanivel responding. "I recognize at least one of the voices. Same crew."

"In the adjacent tunnel or in ours?"

"Adjacent," Bisfuri says. "But the connection between the two tunnels is coming up. We'll have to wait them out."

"Judging by the knocks, they re-diverted another one of your pre-marked orichalcum shipments, Aten," Nanivel says. "That's a hovering platform knocking against walls due to disrupted route programming. Still think they came upon that first one by accident?"

"What is Neph-Tiari?" Girsul asks just then.

"Someone you don't want to meet. Not down here, and not up there on the surface," Bisfuri replies. "Neph-Tiari is a dangerous street gang with vast criminal ties in Poseidon's underworld."

"Huh. Never heard of them," Girsul mumbles, almost guiltily.

"Few have. The Neph-Tiari organization works in the shadows, manages to be very inconspicuous and not very well known to the public."

"Their boss, or leader, or whatever head *chazuf*, is like a ghost," Stryr says. "Goes by the designation Ba-Pef."

"Not that much of a ghost," Nanivel says. "I've seen him."

"You can't be sure." Stryr makes a small sound. "Whoever it was that you thought you saw—"

"One of the henchmen addressed him as Ba-Pef," Nanivel retorts.

There's a pause.

Then, Benaten's voice comes, sounding almost amused, "If Ba-Pef is regularly stealing Bisfuri orichalcum, I can use it to my advantage."

Nanivel clears her throat lightly. "How so?"

"Any shipment losses can be conveniently blamed on gang activity," Styr answers.

"Exactly. As I continue to divert these small amounts of my Father's orichalcum—a platform here and there—if anyone notices, we now have a perfect scapegoat." Benaten pauses again, and there's general silence, for several heartbeats. He must be listening to make sure the voices are completely gone.

"All right, I believe our road is clear," he continues. "The *chazufs* have gone deeper into the adjacent tunnel, and we will pass their location and keep going toward Circle Eight. We keep to this tunnel, then switch over to yellow, as planned. Anyone moving in the adjacent tunnel will have no access to that particular yellow junction."

"Are you certain?" Stryr's voice sounds somewhat doubtful.

"Yes, entirely," Bisfuri reassures him. "I've no desire to have to fight a gang while attired as I am now, without my vigilante disguise. Trust me, I've been inside and memorized all these nearest passages that are pertinent to my work, in order to verify the map."

"Oh! There's a map?" Girsul asks.

"A very ancient, very thorough one, of the complete tunnel network of Poseidon," Benaten replies. "You will see it soon. For now, let's keep moving."

We resume flying forward in the tunnel, as quietly as possible. This time, Benaten keeps us at a slower speed to minimize the sound created by the motion of the *pegasei* wings.

"Yellow junction coming up, on your right," he whispers at us from up ahead, and the powerful acoustics of the passage carry his voice sufficiently. "Verify that the beacon is yellow before entering. Always, verify first, for your own safety, even after you've grown familiar with the layout and the tunnel map."

"Legends say, if you get lost, you'll still be wandering until you die and turn to bones, or reach the underworld." Nanivel's whisper echoes upon the stones around us, sending chills down my spine. "The dead are sometimes found in the passages. . . . Nothing but skeletal remains."

"Some of those skeletons are cursed by the gods to never rest. They must wander in the darkness for their transgression of attempting to enter the underworld." Stryr's voice sounds in turn. "Their souls become ghosts and wander separately, while their bodies are doomed to attack the living. They come out of the darkest tunnels and wrap their fingerbones around your throat and close off your windpipe—"

"Crap of a goat . . . *no!*" I exclaim, hearing such abysmal horrors; I simply can't help myself.

Desperately clutching the fur of my *pegasus* bat, I find myself trembling. Suddenly, it seems as if the walls of the passage are closing in around me—indeed, around all of us—and my lungs are constricting. . . .

"That's enough," Benaten's low voice cuts in. "Stop frightening my staff with nonsense."

Stryr snorts, and Nanivel barely stifles a giggle.

Holy Bastet, are these chazuf *nobles joking? They are! May a thousand pus-filled boils strike them!*

"Who says it's nonsense?" Nanivel persists in a loud whisper. "There are some dreadful old stories found in priestly records of this tunnel network. In addition to the roaming dead and the ghosts, there's mention of the Ogdoa, the first gods—"

"Ah, yes. The ones from *zep tepi*, the sacred dawn of time," Stryr interrupts. "Not the golden gods from the sky who visited us just a few years ago."

"Yes, the original gods are different," Nanivel's voice continues. "And in those stories *they* are still here, roaming these passages inside the earth."

"If they are, I don't want to know," Girsul mutters, just ahead of me.

I stifle another fearful whimper.

Suddenly, a wave of warm, soothing calm starts to pool inside my consciousness, flowing from some inner point outward, to fill my head. . . . There's an illusion of something inside me expanding, or maybe rapidly approaching from a distance. Then, I hear the mind-voice of Heket.

Breathe, Semmi. There are no gods and no ghosts here.

And just like that, I feel the ridiculousness of my fears, and the stone tunnel around me regains its vastly uninteresting normalcy.

"What about the *sha?*" I ask with my thoughts.

There are also no sha *here. Only rock . . . and several living entities of your own human species. . . . Up ahead.*

"What?"

But in that moment, the sound of *Ter* Bisfuri's low whisper interrupts my mental conversation. "Tunnel junction! Everyone, take the one on the right! The left eventually connects with the adjacent tunnel, and we don't want to be there and meet the Neph-Tiari."

I see it, a looming split in the wall, as the main tunnel we're in suddenly separates in half and goes off in two directions. The riders ahead of me start veering off to the right into a dark, slightly smaller passage.

Heket! Turn right! I cry out in my mind, but find that my *pegasus* bat is already following the others.

We plunge to the right, and I note the light flash of the yellow beacon lodged in the floor, as we pass.

We move onward briefly along this tunnel, for a span of maybe five daydreams, making our surroundings bright with the *pegasei* glow because of the narrow diameter of the passage, and the walls closer around us, and then. . . .

"Everyone, halt!" Bisfuri calls out in a hard whisper. And then he adds, harshly, "We are not alone."

"What in all *shaitunaat*—" Stryr stifles a string of curses as he almost runs into Nanivel, while the rest of us start piling up behind him. There's a rush of beating *pegasei* wings as our mounts switch to a hovering equilibrium pattern.

"Quiet!" Bisfuri's whisper cuts like a knife. "Our way is blocked. Freight platforms. And possibly, more Neph-Tiari."

"What, in this passage too?" Nanivel's inflection reveals surprise. "Are we turning around, then?

Benaten Bisfuri pauses for a moment before answering. "No, we keep going. I have no time for this crap."

"What, then?"

"First, get off your *pegasei*, all of you. Transform them into something small—objects or creatures. Something inconspicuous you can carry in your hands. Sing the commands quietly. We're going forward. Around the platforms, if we must. Let's hope they're abandoned. And if not—"

At once I see everyone ahead of me getting off their birds, and singing voice commands as softly as possible.

You don't need to sing, Heket tells me just then, as I awkwardly slide off the giant bat's furry back. *Simply show me what shape to take. Visualize it.*

I pause to think. The first thing that comes to mind is a turnip. One big purple turnip growing in a pot back home, which Grandmother keeps on the roof garden.

So, I "show" my thought to Heket, with a little guilty pause. "You can turn into that, can't you?"

I feel a wave of amusement from Heket. *You want me to transform into what you call a root vegetable?*

"Well, if it's not too much trouble," I mind-speak. "I'll just carry you in my hands. I even have a big pocket—"

Next thing I know, the bat at my side stops hovering and touches down awkwardly on the stone floor with its hind legs. It swivels its head around, giving me an odd look of one dark eye, drags its enormous webbed wings on the ground, and takes a step backward. Then it dissolves into a cloud of rainbow light, coalescing before my face.

I put my hands up, cupped together, and the glowing, shapeless mass of light solidifies into a large turnip, and settles in my palms. It is warm to the touch, purple on top, white on the underside, and glows slightly with residual light. And yes, the *turnip* is somehow still wearing the quantum harness around its diameter.

I have no time to appreciate the ridiculousness before me *(a quantum-harnessed turnip!)* because I see the others perform similar transformations.

Stryr's falcon is back to being a shining collar necklace. Nanivel has a small silvery rat in her hands. And Girsul's great bird is now a bracelet of some kind of reddish metal that looks like bronze.

Only *Ter* Bisfuri remains on his hoverboard, hovering upright at an almost vertical angle, barely off the ground, with one booted foot in the board's stirrup—his usual flying stance.

"Well done, everyone," he speaks in a whisper. "The *pegasei* must not fall into Ba-Pef's possession. Regardless of what he might already own, we shall not give him additional ones."

"Understood, Aten." Stryr quickly undoes the coarse knot holding his twisted cloak behind him. He tucks the bright collar inside his shirt, then unfurls the cloak and pulls it around him to deepen the disguise. As soon as his collar necklace is out of sight, the level of illumination in the tunnel is reduced.

Similarly, Nanivel removes the rolled fabric belted around her waist, snapping it open, and attaches her own cloak over her shoulders. She places the little silvery rat inside an interior pocket.

Before it disappears, I note that the *pegasus* rat also remains harnessed—not that it needs it, since it's frozen in place like an inanimate toy. And meanwhile, the tunnel dims further.

In this growing darkness, Girsul slides the *pegasus* bracelet higher up his arm and covers it with his sleeve.

My ridiculous turnip is now the only source of light remaining.

I suck in a deep breath and drop the turnip inside my skirt pocket.

We're plunged into darkness.

But only for a few terrifying heartbeats.

Suddenly, three small light orbs bloom forth in faint yellowish light.

Able to see again, I blink in relief, and perceive that the three nobles are holding them in their hands, like apples.

"I really dislike using these in the tunnels," Benaten says softly. "Even at the lowest setting, the orbs are too bright."

"Agreed," Stryr replies, spinning his orb in his fingers and then setting it loose to hover in the air before him. "But we have little choice. Either this or the *pegasei*."

"No *pegasei*," *Ter* Bisfuri and Lady Nanivel whisper in unison.

"Fine, let's go." And Stryr whistles a short tone, commanding his orb to float forward, casting shadows against the narrow tunnel walls, while he goes after it, with his cloak swinging behind him.

Continuing to maintain easy balance on his hoverboard, Benaten exchanges glances with Nanivel. He then looks at Girsul and me with a reassuring nod. "Go, all of you. Carefully. I'll be right behind you."

And even as we hesitate, I see him reaching inside a roomy pocket of his dark, basic work pants. He brings out a golden oval thing, slightly rounded, with two eye holes, nose and mouth holes, and a strap.

A golden mask.

"Glad you listened and brought my present," Nanivel says, seeing the mask. "Now, put it on, no matter how much you hate using it, since you don't have your cloak and the rest of your usual disguise."

"I know." Bisfuri raises the oval mask over his face and attaches it behind him with a smooth motion of one hand, pulling the strap closed.

"I see you practiced," the lady says with an amused sound.

The golden mask regards her silently, framed by the raven-black hair visible at his forehead, with the rest of it gathered behind him in a segmented tail.

Seeing *Ter* Bisfuri transformed like that, I feel a sudden chill. If the Man in the Niktos Cloak is sleek and elegant, the Man in the Golden Mask is anonymous and terrifying.

And then my sense of foreboding explodes. A new sound comes from *behind* us, from the direction of the larger passage which we just exited. . . . The sound of many feet.

Quick approaching footfalls scrape softly, echoing around the stone walls.

"Go!" The rich, low voice issues from the Golden Mask, as my employer commands us forward. At the same time, he moves like quicksilver, unfolding his three-tiered short metal staff that's been hidden inside his shirt.

I stifle a shriek and start running, with Girsul and Nanivel doing the same.

CHAPTER
THIRTY-EIGHT

I run in a wild panic, not daring to look behind me, hearing the start of a skirmish. All at once, there's the clangor of hard objects striking . . . the clash of fighting sticks . . . ragged breaths and numerous male cries.

My chest constricts with terror, and I force myself to turn around, once.

In the low light of a single orb barely illuminating the scene, I note at least ten threatening figures in dark clothing, and they're attacking Bisfuri simultaneously from all directions.

Bastet, help him!

He's taking them on *alone*, moving with the same fluid grace that I've seen on that first night in the alley on Circle Eight. Without dismounting from his hoverboard, he spins his staff weapon before and behind him, in impossibly fast, blurring motion, and easily evades the attackers. His Golden Mask gleams with blank menace, while all their combined shadows dance wildly on the walls of stone.

Lady Nanivel is running close after me. I see she has taken out her own short stick weapon, a tri-folded *hedah*. With a practiced warrior move she snaps it fully open into an extended rod, and grips it in one hand. "Move! Go!" she hisses at me, even as I stare at her precise movements in disbelief.

"But what of *Ter* Bisfuri—?" I hesitate, glancing back yet again at the raging battle behind us.

"He can take care of himself! *Go!*"

The lady's expression is fierce and determined, her features implacable in the faint glow of her light orb that she's sent racing through the air before her. Right now, it's the only thing illuminating our way.

I don't need to be told a third time. My quick feet pound the rough stones of the tunnel as it curves slightly up ahead, blocking the line of sight of whatever's up there. No sign of Stryr who's gone ahead of us—or his light orb.

Meanwhile, Girsul is bringing up the rear, a few paces behind. From what I can glimpse, he also has some kind of weapon out, possibly a short knife.

I'm the only one completely unarmed.

A few more steps of running, following the curvature of walls, and the tunnel before us brightens suddenly.

I stop and freeze.

No more than twenty paces ahead, there's a large hovering freight platform, well illuminated by a row of light fixtures embedded along its perimeter. It appears to be literally *stuck* within the tunnel. And it's surrounded by rough looking men.

Crap of a goat!

The platform is a long rectangle of orichalcum-treated metal, about the thickness of a fist, loaded with containers and crates. Its width along the short sides must equal the width of this section of the passage, because it hovers two feet off the ground, tightly lodged against both walls, and vibrating with a barely audible buzz.

At least ten shabby-looking workers are trying to get it unstuck, hammering and chipping away at the ragged stone sides of the tunnel with urgency.

And another six are fighting with Stryr Giparu.

The moment they see us coming, there's a brief pause. "Keep working!" someone yells. However, several of the men leave Stryr or their masonry tasks, and come at us, with intimidating cries and raised hammers. The others remain, striking away at the walls.

Stryr swings a *hedah* in one hand and a short whip in the other, and appears to be well in control, because several men lie on the ground around him, contorting with pain. "There you are!" he calls out to Nanivel. "Come join the dance!"

Nanivel says nothing, but rushes forward past me to strike with her staff at the nearest man who brandishes a long knife in one hand in addition to a hammer in the other. Their weapons clash twice, and they go into a feinting stance.

I make a stifled noise, just as Girsul reaches my side and stops, waving his own short blade at two more approaching hostiles.

"Stay close, Semmi," Girsul blurts. "I can cut them, don't worry—"

"*Shaitunaat!* I don't have anything to fight with!" I exclaim, looking around frantically for something I can use as a weapon, including stones on the ground—but there's nothing even remotely suitable.

I can fling my shoes at them, I think, as a man approaches Girsul . . . and right behind him a second man comes in my direction, not in any rush, strolling arrogantly.

Or you can fling me.

The sound of Heket's voice in my mind jolts me out of a moment of despair.

"You?" I mind-cry, starting to back away from the man closing in on me. "But I'm not supposed to reveal that I have you! *Ter* Bisfuri warned us—"

You must never reveal our communication to the others of your own kind. But nothing prevents you from letting me transform again, to help you.

"But I need to hold on to your harness!"

You do not. I already promised I will not escape. And the harness binds me regardless of physical contact. Only your voice command can set me free.

Meanwhile, the man—tall and muscular, with short-cropped dark hair, dead black eyes and an ugly scar along his jaw and throat—moves at me, almost as an afterthought.

I must look skinny and inconsequential to him, because suddenly he pauses, as though changing his mind. He raises one powerful, light brown-skinned arm wrapped in leather bands up to his elbows, to gesture to another man behind him, and merely points at me.

"Should I take her?" the third man asks, seeming to defer to the scarred man.

The scarred man barely nods, and turns his attention negligently from me to Girsul, Nanivel, and Stryr.

That's when I reach into my pocket and find the *pegasus* turnip. Taking a step back, so that I'm almost touching the passage wall, I hurl the turnip at the scarred man with all my strength.

"Turn, Heket!"

The scarred man has amazing reflexes because, without looking, he catches the turnip aimed at his head, with one hand . . . then slowly swivels his head at me. However, seeing what is enclosed in his fist, his lips curl into a sneer.

His dark, hollow, rasping voice issues for the first time. "Little bitch."

"Heket, now!"

Show me. Heket's thought touches me in that exact same heartbeat.

"Snake!" I mind-cry, visualizing a cobra uncoiling to strike.

And the next moment the scarred man's fist is filled with

shimmering, rainbow light which solidifies into a long snake body. The snake undulates, coiling once then twice around his arm, and the man lets out a harsh exclamation. He immediately releases his grip and tosses the snake away from him in a startled reaction, backing away a step.

He's visibly shaken. . . . I see a moment of genuine fear in his eyes. Then his expression hardens and he returns his attention to me. "You!" he says in a darkest voice of the *sha*. He is terrifying.

The *pegasus* cobra coils on the ground several feet away from us, where it was thrown. It starts rising and swaying, unfurls its neck-flaps into a threatening hood, but doesn't advance.

Tell me what else to do with this creature's body, Heket's voice inquires inside my head.

My mind locks up in anguished indecision. "Maybe, strike him? No, wait—just hiss and make some noise first, and move closer to me—"

Immediately the *pegasus* cobra utters a long, deadly hiss that sounds both unnatural and menacing. And then it begins slithering and undulating in my direction, effectively putting itself between me and the two men.

The scarred man and his subordinate who had spoken up earlier, both keep some distance from the snake, observing it sway with mesmerizing motion. . . .

"That's good, Heket, continue hissing!" I whisper in my mind.

Out of the corner of my eye I see Girsul feinting and circling his attacker, Nanivel exchanging staff blows with another, and Stryr fighting several men from the top of the platform which he just climbed. . . .

"Take her," the scarred man says abruptly. Tearing his attention away from the cobra, he casts a swift, killing stare at me.

"But—she used sorcery, Ba-Pef!"

"*Not* real . . . a marketplace trick," the scarred man retorts in a sarcastic, merciless voice, narrowing his black eyes.

Bast help me—this man is Ba-Pef! He's the terrifying leader of all these criminal chazufs!

My heart jolts with new alarm.

The subordinate man takes a step toward me.

"Get away! I'll curse you!" I snarl, taking another step back and finding myself against the wall. "Don't you come near me, either of you!"

"What will you do, little bitch?" Ba-Pef's deceptively quiet words scrape at me with ghastly scorn. "Throw another vermin? How many have you there, hidden in your skirt?"

"My skirt? What?" I exclaim, suddenly finding my loud, strong, righteous fury-voice, and at the same time forgetting fear. "Why in Bastet's sacred name would I have more snakes in my skirt? Why would anyone? What kind of *hoohvak* would carry around *more than one snake*, and in their skirt, of all places, in these godforsaken tunnels? You think I've a basket in there?"

I take a step forward as I rant. The scarred man for some reason lets his jaw go slack, and opens his eyes fully as he listens to me, almost in surprise. His subordinate meanwhile, remains motionless in confusion.

But I'm not done. "No more snakes! But there are gods and the dead in this place!" I say with such anger that I almost end up breathless. "And *they* are not in my *skirt*! Don't make me call them from the underworld!"

Ba-Pef regains his implacable, terrifying expression, and his hard line of lips begins to curl as he sneers at me again. "Go ahead, then. Let me see your sorcery, little bitch. . . ."

"Heket!" I flood my mind with all my inner rage, visualizing a hellish scene from my wildest mushroom-armies-doing-battle region of my imagination. "When I raise my hand, you transform again, and this time make it big!"

And just as I'm about to swing my arm in a dramatic gesture, there is activity in the tunnel, coming from the direction behind us. Suddenly another light orb streaks toward us, followed by a gust of air, fleeing shadows . . . and Benaten Bisfuri arrives, flying on his hoverboard. There is no one else behind him.

He whistles softly, and his board comes to a hard stop, turning upward and levitating at an upright angle. Abandoning it, he springs from it with effortless ease, his boots striking the ground without a sound.

And then Bisfuri walks toward us, holding his staff loosely, and still wearing the Golden Mask. I notice his light shirt is splattered with blood. . . .

"What did I miss?" he asks in his rich, low voice, almost flippantly. With quick turns of his head, still anonymously hidden by the mask, he takes in the scene, including me and the slightly glowing, undulating cobra on the ground near my feet.

Now that he's here, I experience a sudden flood of relief.

Ba-Pef turns his full attention toward my employer. At the same time, I hear Stryr exclaim, "Finally!"

There's a three-heartbeat pause in the fighting.

Without taking his gaze off Bisfuri, Ba-Pef raises one hand, gesturing to his crew, and both the fighters and workers take heed. They abandon hammering at the walls, and the ones fighting Nanivel, Girsul, and Stryr fall back, circling closer to their leader. It's as though they suddenly understand that a *serious new adversary* has arrived.

"You fought my men back there," Ba-Pef says in a menacing voice to Benaten. "They drove you right to me. You should be afraid now."

"You no longer have any men back there," Bisfuri replies calmly, taking a step closer.

Ba-Pef's expression turns even more deadly. For a long moment he says nothing, only examines Benaten's figure, now just a few steps away from him. He does not yet reach for a weapon.

They are evenly matched, it occurs to me—even though Ba-Pef is somewhat larger and bulkier with muscles, while Bisfuri is more sleek.

It also occurs to me, Ba-Pef is not that old, possibly Bisfuri's age. But he seems older because of the scarring and a weathered, leathery cast to his slightly darker skin . . . and those dead eyes.

Oh, holy Bast . . . if they were to fight now, which one of them would win?

I glance beyond them, up the tunnel, to see Nanivel carefully edging closer. Stryr is no longer on the platform, also moving in this direction. Girsul has been backed near a wall by two men, but he continues to wave his knife before him and miraculously avoids their jabbing motions.

Ba-Pef speaks at last.

"Mask . . . show me your face."

"Show me your *varqooi.*"

At Bisfuri's taunting response, Ba-Pef slowly bares his teeth in a grin. He then unexpectedly makes a show of fumbling at the front of his pants. "We could enjoy this. Right now. . . ."

"Some other time," the Golden Mask replies. "Right now, you're in my way."

There is another pause.

"Ah . . ." Ba-Pef drawls. "That voice. . . . How do I know your voice?"

And then his stone expression registers a moment of insight. "You! On that stupid show—Niktos Cloak! You are—"

"I am."

Ba-Pef begins to chuckle. His *sha* laughter makes my skin crawl. "You forgot your costume? Is that why the Mask, today?"

"Laundry day," Bisfuri replies, with a chuckle of his own from beyond the Golden Mask.

"So, what brings you here, Man Without the Niktos Cloak?" Ba-Pef takes a step forward, reaching inside his shirt with one powerful arm, and takes out a thin metal weapon that looks like a dagger with two sharp ends and a ring grip in the center. He spins it slowly in his fingers then gestures at the surroundings. "You know . . . all of this, *here* below ground, this part of the City belongs to me."

"And now it's mine." Bisfuri begins to rotate his staff casually, matching the deceptively lazy movements of the scarred man. "That orichalcum freight that your Neph-Tiari *hoohvaks* managed to lodge into the walls, is my property."

My heart starts pounding in my chest. I feel a sudden swell of terror on behalf of Bisfuri.

"I'm going to rip that Mask from your face," Ba-Pef says, circling his opponent slowly. "I will have my pleasure finding out who you are, before I gut you."

At this point, everyone else has ceased fighting. Ba-Pef's henchmen and those of us with Benaten have generally fallen into semi-circles around the two men, giving them space in the center of the tunnel.

I throw despairing glances at the two nobles and Girsul, and see their fixed, grim expressions. Judging by everyone's faces, this isn't going to go well. . . .

I take a deep, shaking breath, my palms flattened against the rough stone of the wall behind me. And in my thoughts, I address the *pegasus* cobra near my feet.

"Heket," I think-say. "I'm going to show you a very old, frightful vision that I've seen in my nightmares. Before *Ter* Bisfuri and that evil *chazuf* start to fight, you must transform into it—do it right now!"

I focus all my imagination into showing Heket the precise *thing* that must be done.

I see it, the *pegasus* replies inside my mind.

Just as *Ter* Bisfuri and Ba-Pef close the distance between them, weapons extended, the hissing, swaying cobra near my feet shimmers, becoming a soft rainbow cloud of light. It initially appears to sink unto the stone floor, fading away with tiny embers and sparks. And then, from the same spot on the ground, darkness rises. . . .

It rises slowly, accompanied by a deep, grinding, otherworldly clamor—the sound of many rustling things combined into a *whispering chorus* . . . or maybe a *hiss*, growing in volume.

Scales rubbing against stone.

It's the same horrific sound I've heard in my most terror-filled dreams. And the sound accompanies the corresponding nightmarish image which I've seen depicted on dilapidated, ancient temple walls found in the overgrown ruins of my earliest childhood.

As a girl of maybe six or seven, I discovered the abandoned

temple in passing, while exploring my Circle Ten neighborhood. Foolishly venturing north, to the opposite side of the Circle from the Armpit which included my home, I made it into the area known by the locals as the Crotch. The temple ruins in the Crotch—basically, walls and a few thick columns jutting amid broken stones—were said to belong to the oldest, genuinely primeval god whose name I learned only much later.

He who harnesses the *ka*, the dark collector of souls. His faintly etched depiction on the cracked remnants of walls evoked a wordless horror in me. Neither serpent nor man, a thing of coils and strange, alien appendages, with evil *sha* eyes that somehow followed me from a distance. The first time I saw them as a child, I ran. . . . But then, gathering courage, I returned to look at the etched image and tried to understand what it represented.

A god so old, he must have come from before *zep tepi*, the dawn of time, before the Ogdoa themselves.

So old that he created himself.

Incomprehensible.

And from there on, this god haunted my imagination and my nightmares. Until someone, most likely my Mother, taught me that god's name and function, while my Grandmother later consoled me.

Nehebkau.

The snake god.

"Don't be afraid," Amurabia told me a long time ago, seeing how Eigeti did not elaborate, (being late to her job) and I was still terrified. "Nehebkau will not harm you if he sees inside your heart and finds it light as a feather of Maat. And I promise you, child, your heart is sufficiently weightless."

That's when my nightmares of the incomprehensible being stopped in frequency. Up to this day, I still see him occasionally in my most disturbed dreams, but he is there as a lingering shadow bystander, a reminder more than an actual threat.

But not so in the here and now. . . .

"Heket! You must be dire and terrifying, the worst threat imaginable!" I cry-think, continuing to feed the *pegasus* my amplified vision of Nehebkau.

The darkness scraping the stone floor of the tunnel before me solidifies, and its clamor is now loud enough to make the fighters pause, and everyone else stare.

Benaten and Ba-Pef continue to exchange a rapid volley of hand blows, blocking each other's powerful strikes with their weapons and bare arms. Bisfuri has a short gash on his forearm and sleeve where Ba-Pef's wicked dagger managed to slice him. And Ba-Pef has been bruised hard by the Golden Mask's staff crashing into his shoulder.

Again and again, they circle and strike . . . but now they must pause frequently to glance in my direction, and the gathering *thing* on the floor.

The thing grows, roiling with appendages, exactly as in my nightmare. The appendages have become seven distinct cobras coiling upwards from the ground and hissing, seeming to spring from the same root. Each one of them is unnaturally large and thick in diameter, resembling full-sized pythons.

And their thickness continues inflating. . . .

The Neph-Tiari onlookers exchange exclamations, and many of them curse, starting to back away. One man retreats toward the orichalcum platform, trips and falls backward, then scrambles back up, squeezing past the freight, and simply flees up the tunnel.

Meanwhile, Bisfuri's noble colleagues appear to be plunged in uncertainty, though not to the extent of the Neph-Tiari. Several paces away, Girsul casts huge-eyed stares at me and raises his eyebrows interrogatively, as if expecting me to somehow confirm. . . .

Seeing the evolving mass of snakes, Ba-Pef growls. Pausing

his double-edged dagger mid-strike, he takes a step backward from Bisfuri. *"Shaitunaat!* Not possible! No!"

Even Benaten spares a quick turn in my direction, his Golden Mask facing me briefly, as if to verify that the thing of darkness poses no real threat. He must know that it's just a *pegasus*, I think. At least I hope he realizes it.

The seven cobras roil and hiss, reaching the ceiling, and they expand in all directions before me, filling the tunnel with undulating coils of pitch darkness.

The Neph-Tiari start running.

And then comes the grand moment of the "show."

The snakes converge suddenly, their tail portions blending together to form *something else*. In their place, a dark shape of a man forms, a true giant who stands up with his head touching the ceiling.

The god is now fully formed, seemingly carved out of obsidian—no longer semi-corporeal smoke but with a hard, polished sheen and an impossible glow around the edges of his silhouette. And his head is not human, but that of an immense cobra.

Even I feel a moment of stabbing fear at the sight of him standing right before me, his colossal scaled shape blocking my view of the scene, his wide, monstrous back to me, facing the others.

And in the next heartbeat, Nehebkau raises his right hand, opening a great shadow-fist into a hand with long claws. And he points it at Ba-Pef.

No voice issues out of the god, only a scraping clamor, echoing harshly on the passage walls. The relentless din multiplies, reverberating and turning into a dull *roar*.

Ba-Pef freezes in place, for one instant. His eyes grow wide, and then he spits on the ground before him in disgust—spits at the *sha*.

Spittle has power. Gods decreed, it is the most urgent

protection from the Evil Eye, especially the evil *sha* eye. But apparently, today it's not enough.

"*Not* real . . ." Ba-Pef repeats harshly. He glances behind him to see that all his men have gone. Almost stumbling, he takes another step back, then another. "Mask, we are not done. . . ."

"Oh, we're done," Bisfuri says in a remarkably calm voice.

"Next time we meet, we finish this. You're dead." Ba-Pef spits on the ground again savagely, wipes his mouth with his leather-bound arm. "You and your bitch sorceress. Whatever *this* is—"

Just then, the dark snake god takes a single step forward, toward him, claws outstretched, and bellows.

Ba-Pef runs. He scales the platform with one effortless leap, then continues past it, disappearing up the tunnel.

"Who's the bitch now?" I call out in his wake.

It might be *garooi* of me to further provoke that evil and dangerous piece of *ehoo*, but right now I can't help basking in a combination of relief and triumph. "Keep going, *chazuf*, and take your filthy, stinking *oruhu* with you!"

I really, really hope he hears me.

"Well done, Heket," I think-say in my moment of pride. "That was beautiful, thank you. Now, transform again, please. I can't see anything; your giant scaly back is blocking my view—"

I extend my right hand, and in the next breath the snake god dissolves into a cloud of rainbow light. The cloud flows toward me and coalesces on my open palm into the familiar shape of a barely glowing, ordinary turnip.

"Hathor's udders! Be careful, Semmi. You almost made me believe," says *Ter* Bisfuri, turning to me.

He approaches, pulling off his mask. Underneath, his lean face is dusty, splattered with a sheen of sweat and a fine spray of someone's blood. But his grey eyes are animated with humor and something else, a kind of close scrutiny directed at me. . . .

"That was quite something." Lady Nanivel walks toward us,

snapping her *hedah* stick shut. "I too, almost doubted reality for a moment. Thought—*what if* we genuinely awakened ancient gods? Remarkable control of transformation, Semmi. Such attention to detail, down to the horrific sounds it made! You have a very skilled *pegasei* handler in her, Aten."

"Oh, I do," my employer replies, quickly looking away from me and folding his own staff into thirds before hiding it in his shirt. "Exceeding all expectations."

"Thank you, *im Ter*," I say, keeping the line of my mouth very tight, so as not to burst with inappropriate excitement.

"Very well timed, too," Stryr Giparu says, approaching also. "I especially appreciate that I couldn't even hear her sing the voice commands to control the *pegasus*. Quite discreet. Well done, Semmi!"

"Thank you, *Ter* Giparu, Lady Egemavda," I say, really wanting to break into a smile at this point, but not quite sure it would be acceptable for someone like me to smile openly at these nobles, despite their flattering compliments.

"This Ba-Pef appears to be a very dangerous adversary," Nanivel says, watching Girsul bend down to pick up something from the ground in the spot where Bisfuri and Ba-Pef had been fighting. "It's fortunate that so few are aware of the *pegasei's* full range of shapeshifting capability, including inanimate objects. Else, we might've had a different outcome, had he recognized that it was only a *pegasus* being used to taunt him."

"This is precisely why I keep all *pegasei* business very discreet." Benaten rubs his arm lightly, where a fine line of blood has seeped through the torn place in his sleeve. "The less is known of these creatures' capabilities, the more of a general advantage we continue to hold."

"You're hurt, *im Ter* . . ." I say, staring at his sleeve with sudden concern.

"Yes, he managed to cut you, Aten," Stryr says. "How bad is it?"

"Negligible. Very light scratch," Bisfuri retorts casually. "I'll clean it when we get back."

"Let's hope there was no poison on that dagger. Some of these street gangs, from what I know of them, are rumored to use that foul method during combat."

Bisfuri shrugs. "I feel fine so far. Blade edge poisons are usually fast-acting. But, if I collapse, just load my carcass on the hoverboard."

Stryr chuckles. "Understood."

"So, what now?" Nanivel looks around, taking stock of our situation, including the abandoned freight platform. "We can't exactly proceed forward, knowing they have all gone that way. Could be many more of them up ahead."

"Can we go back?" Stryr asks. "I assume you knocked the crap out of those Neph-Tiari henchmen back there. Any dead?"

"Not sure," Benaten says, glancing at the passage behind us with a frown. "There might be a couple of bodies, but most of them ran eventually and, I'm assuming, took the other tunnel at the junction from where we came in."

"That's likely where they came from in the first place." Nanivel says. "This does not bode well for what work we must do in these tunnels. If the Neph-Tiari are spreading so far underneath the City, and taking control of these marked orichalcum platforms, not sure how we can navigate the network unimpeded—"

"Pardon, *im Ter*, you need to see this," Girsul says just then, coming up to us. In his hand is a small, coin-shaped object that he offers up to Bisfuri.

"A Thoth-pin?" Bisfuri glances at it. "Where did you get this?"

"On the ground, where you fought the *chazuf*."

"Interesting." Bisfuri takes the data storage device. "Could he have dropped it?"

"Very likely, *im Ter*. Either Ba-Pef himself or one of his men."

"Nice work. I'll take a look at it when we get back." Bisfuri deposits the Thoth-pin in his pants pocket.

"So, what are we doing, Aten?"

Instead of answering, Benaten walks toward the freight platform. "Idiots," he says, shaking his head in disgust. He then sings a short tone sequence, and the platform lurches, making a creaking sound against the rock walls where it's stuck. Then, the sides of it start retracting inward, approximately the distance of my hand.

In the span of two breaths, the platform is dislodged from the tunnel and now hovers freely, a few feet off the ground. Its freight containers are undisturbed.

"All they had to do was resize it," *Ter* Bisfuri says, throwing an annoyed glance back at us. "Instead, they almost damaged expensive transport equipment. *My* property."

"Be glad they don't know," Stryr says. "It means they're just discovering how to grab these platforms. We have time to move most of our own freight around before they get a transport expert who knows your proprietary tech. Eventually, they'll figure out how to work these things, taking into consideration tunnel width in advance."

"I don't like it," Nanivel says, her expression serious. "Things are already difficult, and this makes it nearly impossible."

"None of it matters for much longer," *Ter* Bisfuri says, pressing a small recessed section on the side of the platform to reveal a control panel. His fingers tap in some kind of sequence, then he conceals the panel again.

Immediately, the platform begins moving forward, gaining considerable speed, following the perimeter of tunnel walls without striking them—probably because of something called smart sensors which are part of basic navigation (I know this because I've seen too many commercials on the media-box advertising hover vehicle features).

"Wait—if the Neph-Tiari are up there, why are you sending them the platform like a blessed gift of the gods?" Stryr asks.

Benaten turns to him with a smirk. "I'm not. At its present velocity, the platform is going to plow through anyone and *anything* in its way. I don't envy any *hoohvak* foolish enough to try to stop its current programming. It's one thing trying to steal one of the stationary ones which I've marked and left behind to be picked up by Noi. It's quite another to try and catch this!"

"You really are a cruel *chazuf*, Aten." Nanivel raises one brow at Bisfuri, smiling. "Does this mean we continue forward?"

"It does, indeed. Get out your *pegasei* and make them fly." And Benaten Bisfuri whistles to call his hoverboard.

"Heket, if I don't sing the voice command this time at least, they will get suspicious," I announce in my thoughts, even as I sing the note sequence to pretend-transform my *pegasus* once more. "Sorry to have to ask again, but can you please turn into that same big, furry bat as before? It seemed to work out fine."

I understand, Heket's voice replies inside my mind. *I will oblige you again, sentient human. But, be aware: it requires increasingly more energy from us every time we change shape in an environment without a source of light. The more we transform, the sooner we will need to feed. And the larger shapes require even more energy. . . .*

And in the next moment the turnip disappears, replaced by the rainbow cloud of sparks, and then the now-familiar giant bat, dragging its clawed wing appendages on the ground and giving me its beady-eyed look.

Except, this time I somehow recognize there's awareness and humor in those alien eyes as they follow me.

Around me, the others have turned their *pegasei* into their preferred avian shapes—falcon, raven, and some kind of hawk (Girsul's bird is a little ambiguous, or maybe I just don't know what manner of creature it's supposed to be)—and are mounting them in haste.

I follow their example and climb on my bat's furry back, making sure I'm not in the way of the webbed wings, for optimum flapping.

Bisfuri is already back on his hoverboard, and he motions with his hand for us to follow. "Stay as quiet as possible, and be ready for several tunnel changes and junctions ahead."

With a powerful beating of wings, we head along the tunnel network.

THIS TIME, our way forward is unimpeded by anyone, and the trip is uneventful. We switch tunnel passages several times, carefully paying attention to the light beacons, from yellow to red, then green, then red again, as we move generally south underneath the City.

"Where are we now?" Stryr asks softly at some point. "Any idea which Circle we're currently under?"

"Almost there," Benaten replies. "We're somewhere underneath Seven. I know it feels longer than necessary, but we're limited by what tunnels are available in this area."

"Right," Nanivel says. "On the surface it would've taken us half the time flying in a straight line. Here, we have to follow the tunnel layout."

Honestly, it feels to me like an hour has passed, but I can't be sure because of the monotony of this underground network, with only the occasional bursts of panic about taking the correct junction. How in the world does Bisfuri remember where we're going and not get lost? Then I recall he has gadgets and a map, and he somehow memorized it.

And yet, this permanent, oppressive darkness is steadily becoming unbearable. Already I'm feeling stifled, overwhelmed with a sense of the earth pressing down on us, the tunnel walls closing in. . . . If not for the *pegasei* glow and the occasional tunnel beacons, there would be no light.

Bast help us . . . I need air . . . the underworld is squeezing my spirit, pulling at my ka.

That's when Heket's mind-whisper sends waves of calm at me.

Breathe, Semmi, all is well.

Now and then, as we continue to fly, Benaten points out particularly small junctions without any beacons at all at the entrance. "Those are exits to the surface," he says. "If you enter, you'll eventually be inside a narrow rising tube leading to a manhole, a grotto, or other surface outlet. Some are located inside old buildings or other pre-existing structures. A few are dead-ends because the openings have caved in or were manually covered up."

"Good to know," Girsul mumbles with his face down in his bird's feathers. "In case we have to run."

Another quarter of an hour later, we pass yet another junction and enter a green-beacon tunnel.

"Everyone, halt," *Ter* Bisfuri says. "We're here. Get off your *pegasei*, quietly."

The tunnel around us is one of the wider ones. However, it doesn't look much different from all the others we've traversed.

While the rest of us dismount from our *pegasei*, I watch my employer abandon his hoverboard, leaving it propped against the tunnel wall. He takes out several small items and weapons from his pockets, removes a wrist band, and sets them all on the ground next to the board.

Benaten turns to us, glancing at Girsul and me, in particular. "We'll walk the rest of the way. Today, we're only walking as far as the entrance, because I need my staff to properly observe the facility ahead of us. But next time, you'll enter and be prepared to fly around quickly, as needed, then get out of there. That part is somewhat tricky, and I'm about to explain why."

And then he adds, "Notice, I am leaving behind the hoverboard. From this point forward, the Bisfuri warehouse proximity sensors are active, and they will register my hoverboard and any other orichalcum as an intrusion. Everyone, if you have any orichalcum objects on you, leave them here, next to my board. Semmi, Girsul—your employee badges."

"Oh," I say, pausing next to my *pegasus* bat, and fumbling in my pocket. I set my precious badge down on the ground next to Girsul's.

Meanwhile, I see Nanivel and Stryr emptying their hidden pockets of various small gadgets and a truly endless number of weapons that must contain orichalcum.

"Even trace amounts of orichalcum will set off the sensors." Nanivel glances at me as she drops a handful of daggers, throwing discs shaped like *astroctadras*, and numerous gadgets on the ground but retains her *hedah* stick, which must contain some other metal. Then she removes her earrings and a bracelet, setting them on top of the pile. "Smart jewelry. Forgot to leave it at home. Next time."

"Anything else?" *Ter* Bisfuri asks sternly. "Stryr, check your back pockets."

"Yes, sweet mother of mine." Stryr chuckles, then searches his pants from the back. "You know this is not our first time. We've been here before without tripping your precious Bisfuri sensors."

Benaten nods. "It's been a long day. Humor me."

Stryr finds a couple of coin-shaped Thoth-pins, and rolls his eyes before dropping the storage devices in the gadget pile.

"And now, for the long and convoluted explanation." *Ter* Bisfuri turns primarily to Girsul and me. "We need the ability to fly once inside the depot. Why? I'll explain in a moment. But for that we need either hoverboards or other sufficiently large orichalcum-treated objects that can be levitated to carry our weight. Or, we need the *pegasei*. The problem with hoverboards is that they will set off the depot sensors. The problem with the *pegasei* is that their orichalcum-based *quantum harnesses* will also set off the sensors."

"What?" Girsul curses. "So, what do we do?"

"Then why are we even using *pegasei* for this job, *im Ter*?" I ask.

In answer, our employer turns to Nanivel. "Did you bring the shielded pouches?"

"Yes, of course," the lady replies, taking out a folded square of fine fabric out of her pocket. She unfolds it into four pouches. "Each of you who has a *pegasus*, take one," she says, offering them to Girsul, Stryr, and me, and keeps one for herself.

We comply.

"This extremely expensive material is specially made to shield and isolate anything containing orichalcum." Benaten resumes speaking. "As you know, *pegasei* must be harnessed at all times, else they escape. You can't just take off their harness and leave it behind. So, we transform the *pegasei* themselves into small objects, and then put them inside these bags along with their harnesses. Not something you can do with a hoverboard!"

"O-o-oh . . ." Girsul mutters.

"Safely shielded by the bags, you'll carry the *pegasei* with you into the shipping area of the depot, undetected," Nanivel says. "Remember, use the bags to hold only the *pegasei*; leave all your other stuff behind in the tunnel, to avoid things clanking inside the pouch and creating noise. Then, once inside the sensor perimeter, you can take the *pegasei* out and transform them back into creature shapes that you can ride around the place."

"The depot sensors don't care about any orichalcum that's already present inside the depot, since everything there is orichalcum," adds Stryr. "It's only when you approach or depart the facility with unregistered orichalcum that the sensors trigger alarms. It's an anti-theft security system."

"Correct," Benaten says. "Therefore, when you exit the depot, you must once again transform the *pegasei* into objects, pack them into the pouches, and walk past the perimeter boundary on foot. Once out of range, you can ride again."

"The whole thing is rather mad," Nanivel says, shaking her head. "Aten's insane idea. But it's a good solution to an impossible problem."

AND SO, we transform our *pegasei* mounts into small items, place them inside the shielded pouches, and begin walking along the passage.

"Step softly," Bisfuri tells us, his rich voice dipping to a faint whisper. "Keep the shielded bags wrapped tight. And watch the way before you. We're about to enter the depot."

About a hundred paces ahead, we see a brightness in the tunnel. And as we draw closer, it resolves into strong artificial illumination. Benaten puts a hand out to halt us yet again. Then he turns and mouths the word "watch," pointing two fingers at his eyes.

We approach the entrance, keeping to the tunnel sides, and pause, freezing against the walls.

Beyond the entrance is an unexpected wide-open space, a huge cavern with a distant ceiling, illuminated by endless light orb fixtures overhead and along the stone perimeter. From our present location, we would need to go down a short rocky incline before reaching the main level floor.

Multiple tunnels similar to our own lead inside the cavern from all directions. The place is filled with freight platforms and warehouse workers in Bisfuri uniforms, unloading the arriving cargo in boxes and containers. Others are loading empty platforms with departing cargo that is carried down from upper levels where the manufacturing sections are located. Armed guards stroll among them, circling the depot.

I have no idea what any of this stuff is, inside those huge boxes, except that it must be made of orichalcum.

Benaten turns to us again and finger-signals to his eyes, then points to various landmarks inside the depot. He points to specific tunnel entrances around the perimeter, mouthing the words "in" and "out" and using additional gestures, points to the upper-level stairwells and elevator platforms. Then he points out the staff areas and what looks to be offices behind clear glass.

I stare, trying to comprehend and memorize everything I see. Girsul does the same. Finally, Benaten signals for us to return.

Walking on tiptoe, I fall behind the others as we disappear back into the safe darkness of the tunnel from which we arrived.

Only after we make it back to the spot where the hoverboard and our gadgets wait for us, does *Ter* Bisfuri speak as normal.

"That is the place where we will be doing our work. The depot is located directly underneath the Bisfuri warehouse complex. Raw orichalcum ore arrives from various remote mines. Manufactured technology departs, heading underneath the City and beyond to the area where the sky ships are being built," he tells us. "Note the entrances I indicated. Outgoing and incoming cargo is marked differently. We will mostly be diverting the incoming raw ore from the mines. The finished materials and parts are primarily *hull plates*. From these plates the ships are being assembled. Some of it we'll need to divert also."

Bisfuri pauses. "You might be thinking, why not intercept the shipments before they arrive here? Trust me, this is the easiest way. The containers already here are cleared and registered, while those still in transit are heavily guarded."

"Nearly impossible to approach, much less capture," Stryr says. "And yes, we've tried. Not worth the risk."

"Tell them about the staff shifts and worker schedule," Nanivel adds, moving to pick up her orichalcum items from the ground.

"Yes." Benaten nods. "I will provide the schedules when we get back. You'll need to know when the shifts begin and end, when the depot workers take breaks."

"Most of *our* work happens between shifts." Stryr bends down and gathers up his personal items from the ground, stuffing them back in his pockets. "That's when the depot is nearly empty, except for a few guards. You'll learn their schedule also, in order to avoid them."

"*Ter* Aten, what exactly must we do with the cargo?" Girsul asks.

"You will be marking containers and platforms, primarily," Benaten replies, as he too retrieves his small weapons and items from the ground. "Setting small trackers and rerouters which I'll provide."

"What kind of trackers?" I ask. "What do they look like?"

"Tiny clear stickers, smaller than your fingernail, almost undetectable," Nanivel says. "And in case you wonder, they aren't made of orichalcum, that's why you can carry them past the sensors. They don't need a shielded pouch."

"You'll be sticking them on the sides of boxes and on the platforms themselves," Benaten says. "And once you feel more confident, you will also program the platform panels. Don't worry, I'll show you exactly what to do, later. As for rerouters, those are to be used only if the panels cannot be accessed. They're somewhat bulky and noticeable, hence a last-resort option."

"The most difficult part of the job is just getting to the cargo and platforms," Stryr says. "That's why you must fly. You swoop in when no one is looking, set the trackers or punch in the controls on the platform panel, and then you fly away.

Automated programs and remote control will take care of the rest."

"Oh, did Aten mention? The floor of the depot has some sensors too," Nanivel says with a roguish smile. "If you step on it without authorized footwear, the alarms go off. So, you'll be doing all of this while you hover above ground."

"Bast, Sacred Mother . . ." I whisper.

Stryr and Nanivel chuckle.

"Enough." *Ter* Bisfuri gives warning glances to his two noble friends. He then hops back on his hoverboard. "And now we head home."

IT TAKES us another uneventful hour at least to backtrack along the same passages, flying as swiftly as possible on our *pegasei*. When we get as far as the tunnel where we've dealt with the Neph-Tiari and Ba-Pef, then slightly further (that first yellow junction), we find two dead men sprawled on the ground, dressed in black clothing.

"If they don't disappear in the next few days, I'll have my people come in and clear away the bodies," *Ter* Bisfuri says in passing.

"Neph-Tiari don't like to leave a mess." Nanivel looks away from the corpses with distaste, and leans into the wind. "I'm certain they will handle them overnight."

We continue flying, and soon we're back in the now-familiar cavern on the grounds of the Bisfuri estate on Circle Two, underneath that hillside. Remarkable how much smaller this cavern seems now, after I've seen the one housing the Bisfuri warehouse depot. . . .

Here, Stryr Giparu and Nanivel Egemavda indicate they must part ways with us.

"If you don't mind, Aten, I'm keeping this *pegasus*," Lady Nanivel nods at her raven mount. "I'll leave my hoverboard here with you for safekeeping. And she points at one of the several boards leaning against the cavern wall; I've noticed them earlier.

"Fair enough," Bisfuri says. "It was intended for you anyway. The *pegasus* is yours. Or, if you prefer, you can leave it here and my staff will continue to care for it."

"No, I'm definitely taking it with me." Nanivel pats the feathers of her raven.

"Please be sure to feed it in the sun, my Lady," I blurt out. "It needs to be fed soon. . . ."

Thank you, sentient Semmi human, a voice says in my head. *I am indeed depleted of energy. We are all depleted and will require sustenance very soon, after such prolonged activity in darkness.*

I realize the speaker is not Heket, but Nanivel's raven, addressing me.

"Of course," Nanivel replies meanwhile. "I plan to feed it thoroughly once I get home. Tell me, Semmi, since you're so good with these things—do you think it will last another hour trip, or should I bring it up now into the light?"

"What should I say to her?" I ask the *pegasus* with my mind.

Feed us, now! At once, all the *pegasei* voices raise a horrible din inside my head.

So, I pretend to think, examine the raven, examine my own bat, then proclaim with as much authority as I can manage: "I strongly believe they all need to be fed immediately. They were in the dark far too long. Also, they had to shapeshift so many times, which expends additional energy and drains them faster—"

At that part Bisfuri raises his brows, curiously watching me.

Oh, no. . . . Did I just say too much by admitting to know about *pegasei* transformation expending extra energy? Wait— how do I know that anyway? Did the *pegasei* themselves tell me this, or did *Ter* Bisfuri, or Girsul, at some point?

Bastet . . . I am definitely losing my mind!

I was the one who told you, Heket whispers in my thoughts. *Inhale, Semmi.*

I feel a flood of relief, then firmly say out loud: "At the risk of losing them, they need to feed now."

"That settles it," Stryr Giparu says, "I need to be fed likewise. Let's all go up, sun-bathe these splendid creatures, and then have a nice meal ourselves, over in your Quarters, Aten."

With the *pegasei* transformed one final time into small objects for easy carrying, we hike back through the small joining tunnel to the entrance grotto with the running water nearby, then emerge near the top of the hill next to the waterfall.

The bright afternoon sunlight hits us with a blinding radiance, after so many hours spent in near darkness. Suddenly, we're under a brilliant blue sky, washed by a warm breeze fragrant with honeysuckle and other wildflowers. What a nice contrast to the eternally cold and dank tunnels.

Source of light! Feed us!

I try to ignore the eager voices inside my head, and lift the turnip in my fingers up toward the light, rotating it this and that way for generous exposure. Immediately, I sense the relief and satisfaction in Heket's mental presence.

Nanivel squints, putting one hand over her eyes, holding her little *pegasus* rat in the palm of her hand and letting it bask in the sun.

Stryr winces at the sunlight, then takes out his pectoral

necklace and twirls it in his fingers making it sparkle even brighter.

And Girsul holds up his *pegasus* bracelet, until it gleams more brilliant than gold.

Ter Bisfuri watches us silently for a few moments, then says in a tired voice, "I'm filthy and need a shower, so I'm going ahead. When you're done here, come to my personal Quarters. The afternoon meal will be waiting for you."

"We're all somewhat dusty ourselves." Nanivel wipes the light sheen of sweat and dirt from her forehead with the back of her hand and glances down at her own clothing. Now that we're in the light of day, the outfit underneath her cloak is revealed to be a plain linen shirt and pants, worthy of a laborer, not a noble lady.

"But you definitely bear the worst of it, Aten," she adds. "Go, clean yourself. And for the love of Hathor, please take care of that bloody gash on your arm before a nasty pestilence sets in. We'll see you soon."

"*Ter* Aten, should we stable the *pegasei* as goats when done feeding them?" Girsul asks.

Benaten considers for a few heartbeats. "No," he says. "Bring them both to my Quarters. I've decided—I prefer having them close at hand, confined in these simple object shapes."

"Very well, *im Ter*. Also—" and Girsul clears his throat, glancing thoughtfully at our employer's sweaty face and bloodied, grimy shirt, pants, and boots. "Do you require any other manner of assistance from me today?"

"No, you're free to go," Benaten replies after the tiniest pause. "Give Semmi your *pegasus* after the feeding, and stop by the kitchens to get your own meal. Take some food home with you, for your sister."

"Thank you, *im Ter*!" Girsul says, his expression coming alive.

"I'll see you tomorrow. Dismissed."

And then Benaten turns to me. "Semmi—you too, visit the kitchens for your well-earned meal, when done here. Then come to my Quarters with both the *pegasei*. I still have a task for you today."

I nod, and Bisfuri proceeds down the hill ahead of us.

HALF AN HOUR LATER, the *pegasei* are bloated with light (as they tell me with joyful clamor inside my mind) then properly concealed on our persons. Carrying them discreetly, we descend the verdant hillside and enter the estate courtyards.

The nobles head for the older building which houses *Ter* Bisfuri's personal suite, while Girsul and I walk to the main building and the kitchens where the staff eats. The two *pegasei* now in my charge are safely hidden inside my deep skirt pocket.

When we enter the corridors near the service kitchens and pantries, a wonderful savory aroma of cooking food, herbs and spices, wafts in the air, making my mouth water.

Girsul gives me a meaningful smile and exhales in relief. "What a day, eh? I'm ready to eat a whole pot of whatever they're making today."

"Oh yes . . . me too." I find myself seriously salivating, while my stomach rumbles, as if on cue.

The kitchen is crowded, and the afternoon work shift is here, which includes us. The kitchen workers are filling the Bisfuri staff's plates from a long table with serving trays. Fragrant steam is rising, and so is loud conversation.

We get in line, and soon receive large plates piled with dollops of various colorful dishes—definitely more than I've ever seen together at one meal.

"Are those mushrooms?" I ask one server, seeing a rich brown stew with herbs, and what looks like pieces of cut fungi and delicate filaments of mycelium floating in a creamy sauce along with onion, carrot, and walnut pieces and grains of barley.

The server nods and ladles a huge portion onto my plate, then adds some steamed greens and sprinkles more fresh herbs on top.

I open my mouth in anticipation and try to not choke on my drool.

We move down the line, and finally reach the section with large baskets filled with freshly baked flatbreads encrusted with thyme, chives, and dill. Girsul grabs a flatbread, and I do the same.

Then we head to one of the long tables and benches that still has seating room, and sit down.

A serving woman comes around the table carrying jugs of honey-saffron beer and hot tea, along with empty mugs.

I dip my bread in the mushroom stew and fall upon it ravenously, ignoring all conversation around me for those first few moments.

"Semmi!" someone says. "That's your name, right, girl?"

I look up and see a vaguely familiar female servant seated across from me. I think I've seen her, along with other seamstresses, in the sewing work room this morning. "Yes?"

"Vilras has your uniform ready early," the seamstress tells me. "You can pick it up now after you eat."

"Oh, thank you," I reply awkwardly with my mouth full. "I'll be sure to go there."

"No rush." The seamstress nods at my plate. "Eat first. You'll be glad to have this uniform in time for the Bisfuri Domestic Service Competition, which is going to be held the day after tomorrow. I hear they expect us to wear staff uniforms for it, and those of us already in the service of Bisfuri will get priority consideration."

"What?" Girsul stops chewing and pays attention.

"Oh, when can we sign up for this Domestic Competition?" I ask.

"Starting today." A man sitting on the other side of me pops an olive in his mouth. "They just posted it a few hours ago."

"Cutting it close, are they?" Girsul wraps his flatbread around some succulent vegetable chunks and takes a big bite. "Announcing it late, then holding it within two days, with so little notice."

"I believe that was intentional," another woman down the table says, picking up her mug of beer. "I imagine, House Bisfuri wants to hire as many of its existing employees as possible—for which I'm grateful—so we get to hear about it first. By the time others learn about it, they may not bother to register."

"That makes no sense. Everyone can still check the smart boards all around Poseidon and see it posted, by law, for all the public to see," the man next to me responds. "Remember, the Houses were all ordered to comply, and preferential treatment is supposed to be illegal. So, there isn't going to be any advantage if you're in Bisfuri uniform."

"Yeah, that's right," Girsul says. "The Competitions have to be impartial to all entrants, according to Imperial decree."

"Whatever." The woman shakes her head. "And if any of you really believe there's no preferential treatment going on with these infernal Competitions, you're all gullible *hoohvaks*."

Another man nods. "Agreed, the whole thing is rigged. They're just making us go through these impossible tasks and then picking and choosing whomever they please, not actual winners."

We all fall into subdued silence at that and resume eating. The ugly thought did cross my mind yesterday, especially after taking part in the House Ximunat competition on the Denderaat Bridge, which I still think Uru and I both won and were passed over unfairly by Lady Ashura.

I can only hope that House Bisfuri will handle things more honestly and impartially. I just need to let my little brother know so he and I can both register tomorrow.

. . .

WE FINISH EATING, and Girsul heads home, while I go to see Vilras to pick up my uniform which looks pristine in its protective sheath.

"Put it on starting tomorrow," she tells me with a critical look. "You appear rather unclean, girl—your face all dusty, and your skirt covered with dirt, unlike this morning. What kind of filthy work have you been doing anyway? Take better care to look presentable."

I think of the dark tunnels in which I've been for the past several hours and say nothing. "Yes, I will, thank you," I mumble to Vilras, taking my uniform and getting out of her office in a hurry.

I arrive in Ter Bisfuri's Quarters, knocking on the door softly, and hear his familiar rich voice answering from a distance, "Come in."

I open the door into the living room area, and there's no one there. Half-empty dishes and sparkling crystal decanters and goblets are scattered on a low serving table in the center, containing leftovers of an elegant meal. The surrounding chairs and divans are empty.

Ter Stryr Giparu and Lady Nanivel Egemavda must've eaten and left, it occurs to me, in the time that Girsul and I had our own meal and I dealt with the seamstress.

"*Ter* Bisfuri?" I say a little awkwardly, taking a few steps inside the room, and then peek down the short hallway into the next room and the continuation of his suite. I stand with my uniform in its pristine package draped over my arm and the two *pegasei* in my pocket. I don't dare go any further.

"One moment, I'll be there," Benaten's voice sounds again.

From where I stand, I can see him moving about the inner chamber that appears to be a dressing room. He is wearing nothing but a towel wrapped around his middle, and a clean pair of polished black boots. In the bright daylight coming from a window, his tanned upper body gleams, every lean curve of muscle sculpted with sun, and his mane of *niktos* black hair falls down his back in curling tendrils, still wet from his bath.

I watch, holding my breath for some reason. And then, out of nowhere, I feel my cheeks growing warm with somewhat inexplicable embarrassment.

Nothing I haven't seen before, I tell myself, recalling my employer's many costume changes during the filming of his show, not to mention his semi-nude scenes on screen. But for some reason this time feels different somehow, more intimate. . . .

Maybe it's because he is alone, engrossed in a personal moment, and not trying to show himself off for anyone. In fact, now I see what he's actually doing—he's applying a series of ointments to his forearm, carefully rubbing the area where he was injured by Ba-Pef.

Immediately my *hoohvak* shame evaporates. Just as I'm about to offer my help, there's a loud knocking at the doors to his Quarters.

"Benaten! Are you inside?" The voice belongs to none other than Lord Muutat Bisfuri.

Benaten stops what he's doing to his arm and looks up. I can see his suddenly closed-off expression as he turns, and our gazes meet. "Yes" he replies loudly. "Come in!"

My heart starts racing with anxiety, and I also turn around awkwardly and stare at the door as it opens and Lord Bisfuri enters the living room. He wears an elegant dark shirt over perfectly tailored pants, pearl-encrusted bracelets on both wrists and shoes trimmed in gold.

Muutat Bisfuri sees me first. I bow at once, and take several steps backward, still clutching my uniform. "My Lord," I mumble quietly.

But he ignores me, and casts a quick look around the room,

his countenance settling into disdain as he sees the leftovers of the meal.

"I see you've been entertaining," he says loudly without bothering to look in the direction of the inner quarters. "Who was it this time?"

"I'm in here, one moment," Benaten says, still hastily rubbing his arm. I begin to wonder if he's attempting to use some kind of cosmetic concealer to cover up his injury and hide it from his father. "It was some friends of mine, no one you would consider of particular consequence."

"If you mean whores—"

"No. It was *Ter* Stryr Giparu and Lady Nanivel Egemavda."

"Ah . . . Giparu and Egemavda? Then, yes, of no consequence indeed. May I approach?" Muutat Bisfuri asks. "Are you decent?"

"One moment. Yes."

"Including the boots?"

"Yes . . . always." Benaten's voice comes coldly, somewhat strange in its lifeless manner of reply.

"Very well." Lord Muutat Bisfuri begins to walk toward his son, then pauses momentarily and gives me a brief glare. "There's someone here. Dismiss your staff before we talk."

"No need." Benaten himself comes out of his interior chamber and walks toward his father. He is still bare-chested, clad only in the long towel around his lower middle. However, I see that his forearm shows only a faint healing line in place of an actual recent injury scar. It must definitely be cosmetic, because only gods heal this fast and, despite his heroic vigilante persona, *Ter* Bisfuri is only mortal.

"I need my servant here because she still has work for me," Benaten says in a casual tone, not glancing at me. "If I dismiss her early, she will still need to be paid. I would then need to call in another servant to do her work. I assume you would rather not have me squander our coins unnecessarily, especially now?"

Lord Bisfuri frowns and gives me a quick, thin-lipped look. "Yes, fine, she can stay. I assume your staff is used to being discreet in the matter of all your unsavory procurements and . . . evening entertainment *activities*. Make sure she keeps her mouth shut even more than usual."

At this, I quickly lower my head, only allowing my gaze to rise after a few beats.

But from that point onward, I am blessedly ignored.

As I stand there, relegated to the background, it occurs to me to wonder, *What exactly does Lord Bisfuri think his son does? He has no idea what really goes on, but he must have some offensive assumptions, judging by his overall manner. . . .*

"So, Father, how may I be of service?" Benaten assumes a subtly flippant tone as he points his sire to the various seats.

Muutat Bisfuri walks around the low table covered with leftovers, giving the dishes another distasteful glance, and sits back in a deep chair with cushions. He crosses his elegant legs, then says softly. "We have a problem."

Ter Bisfuri steps over the low table in one sleek motion, and takes the seat on the sofa directly across from his father. He adjusts the towel over his middle almost insolently, then leans forward with confidence to face the Lord, lacing his fingers together while resting his elbows on his knees. "What kind of problem?"

Lord Bisfuri observes his son for a few silent moments. He then nods at the faint scar-line on Benaten's arm. "What happened there?"

Benaten raises one brow and glances at his forearm negligently. "You mean this? I was tending my garden this afternoon and one of my favorite rose bushes has extraordinary thorns. Fear not, the scratch will be healed in a few days."

"Next time, wear sleeves." Muutat Bisfuri's frown deepens. "It's bad enough you must play in the dirt like a callow boy, but

I'll not have you *mar* yourself any further. At least Behamenut keeps himself *clean*—"

"Understood, Father." Benaten stares hard at Lord Bisfuri without blinking. "Now, you were saying something about a problem?"

"Yes." Lord Bisfuri exhales, then sits back deeper in his chair. "Recall the incident during my recent transcontinental trip to the Huang River mines."

"You mean the *shamshir* vessel flight malfunction? Plasma cloak failure at low altitude, early during takeoff. The primitive locals saw it from the ground and panicked, assuming the ship was some kind of great flying lizard or serpent from their legend, coming to destroy them?"

"Yes, that incident. The savages looked up at us and cried *draguos*, which is a myth they have of a flying creature of destruction that also breathes, or eats, fire. It didn't help when the plasma cloak finally engaged—which made the *shamshir* look like it was briefly engulfed in flames—before the quantum shield finally went in effect, and the ship disappeared, as far as they were concerned."

"It made you quite upset," Benaten says, examining his fingernails. "We spoke about it at length. What else is there to talk about? Malfunctions happen, usually at the worst possible times. The fact that it was witnessed is unfortunate, but ruled a no-fault accident. I read the official report—"

"That's not all of it," Lord Bisfuri interrupts. "There's more. A new development, today."

"What?"

"I just received word from the Far Eastern continent. From the head overseer of mining operations in the entire Middle Territory. That's thirty-seven of our richest orichalcum mines. They are rioting, as of this morning."

Benaten frowns. "Who is rioting?"

"The mine workers. All of them. Indentured serfs, free

laborers from Atlantis, and the shackled primitives local to the sites. *Everyone*. All because the ignorant *hoohvaks* spread the rumors of the *draguos* in the sky. It started with the one sighting, and news spread for *mag-heitars* in all directions along the Huang River primitive population."

Benaten listens with a grave expression.

Lord Bisfuri continues, "And because there's a grain of truth to it—the fact that there's the impending Sky Rock, which *we* know about—our own civilized Atlantean free laborers concluded that the Sky Rock is already visible in the skies and is about to strike the world early. So, they put down their tools. And then the serfs stopped working, and the shackled savages attacked machinery and attacked overseers—"

"That *is* a problem."

"We *need* that orichalcum." Lord Bisfuri exhales in frustration. "They may not stop production for even a moment, much less this!"

"How bad is it?"

"Very bad. The overseers barely have control for now, but . . . there aren't enough guards or stationed military troops to lend support to all the mine locations. And if the shackled ones escape, there will not be enough manpower to finish mining in time—"

In that moment there's a knock on the door. A familiar woman's voice sounds loudly. "Muutat, *im amrevu*, are you in there? Benaten, dear boy, is your Father with you?"

Lord Bisfuri stops talking at once. He lifts one finger and shakes his head at his son in silent warning. And then he replies in a loud, suddenly charming voice, "We are here, my dearest Ashura, come in!"

I glance quickly and catch Benaten's startled eyes before his expression turns frigid.

CHAPTER
FORTY-TWO

L ady Ashura Ximunat enters the living room like a sparkling cloud of pale rose gossamer veils.

Delicate layers of dragonfly-wing fabric flutter from the long skirt of her dress—full on the bottom and skin-tight around her hips, waist, and upper body. Her sleeveless arms are bound in gold bracelets and armbands, and a heavy, wide collar of gold, studded with colorful gems covers her elegant neck, leaving her chest cleavage peeking underneath. Her dark hair is pinned up, and her eyes and sensual lips are outlined in mauve and kohl.

As always, she is both beautiful and imposing. Actually—no, she is terrifying.

Because now there's an immediate sense of *darkness* that I get when I see her, despite so much pristine pale skin and sparkle.

"There you are, my dearest," Lady Ashura says pausing at the entrance for effect, then walks directly toward Lord Muutat Bisfuri, with a beaming smile. "I see two of my four favorite men in Poseidon are present here. Hope I'm not imposing on a private conversation with your fine son?" And Ashura glances briefly at Benaten before returning her full attention to Lord Bisfuri. As usual, she completely ignores my presence.

Benaten remains seated, his face composed, and only gives the lady a brief nod.

"Not at all, Ashura, you are now family," Muutat replies, standing up. He takes his future wife by the hands, squeezing them gently. "We were just finishing up. When did you get here?"

"Oh, I just arrived. We were going to dine early tonight, if you recall. Enhuvarat is at the Palace again, so you and I have this blessed evening to ourselves."

"Ah, yes! Forgive me, I lost track of time."

"Nothing unpleasant has happened? You do look so serious —and the dear boy, too." Ashura remarks, freeing one hand and placing it against the Lord's cheek then stroking it in slow circles. "So serious. . . ."

"Of course not, *im nefira*." Muutat puts his own larger hand over hers, and pulls it back down, this time to kiss it lingeringly on the wrist.

I try not to stare at their revoltingly romantic display.

That's when Benaten stands up. "Pardon me, Father, my Lady—I must finish dressing."

And he quickly walks past them toward his inner rooms, holding his towel around his middle with one hand, and disappears down the hallway.

"Keep your arms in sleeves tonight, young *hoohvak*," Lord Bisfuri says in his wake. "It will heal faster."

"What will heal faster?" Lady Ashura's expression fills with sudden intense concern, and she glances back and forth, from Muutat to the hallway.

"Oh, nothing serious. My son likes to pretend he is a gardener, and today his roses attacked him. An unsightly gash on his arm."

Lady Ashura makes a little exclamation. "May the gods protect him! Even a seemingly harmless cut on the skin can become inflamed if not treated properly. Muutat, you know I have some considerable skills in healing, making injuries go away and blemishes disappear entirely. . . . Let me take a look at his poor arm, and I promise I will make it heal without even the slightest shadow of a scar. I know how much you dislike flaws. It would be a shame if something happened to such perfect skin as his. It runs in the family, you know; you and he both have such a wonderful complexion—"

"Oh, my dear, I would absolutely hate to trouble you with this hassle," Lord Bisfuri says, but there's a slight hesitation in his tone. "I'm sure I ought to send our house physician to look at him, now that you mention in. . . . He *should* be looked at, to avoid scarring."

"Why, it's no trouble at all." Lady Ashura places her fingers gently on Muutat's shoulder and squeezes. "It will be the least I can do to help your lovely boy—*our* lovely boy, my new son—ah, what joy it gives me to say it. It shouldn't take long. I will examine the area of the injury then call my servants to deliver the proper unguents from my villa, in haste."

"Very well, then."

Lady Ashura smiles then pulls Lord Bisfuri's head down for a swift kiss on his cheek. "It's settled. Why don't you go on to your chambers and wait for me, and we can begin our meal as intended. Go on!"

"I can never say no to you, *im amrevu*. I beg you, do not take too long." And with one glance in the direction of Benaten's inner suite, Lord Muutat Bisfuri exits his son's Quarters.

"Benaten!" Lady Ximunat calls out loudly, pitching her voice higher than normal, and heads for his inner residence. "You heard your Father, I must look at your injury at once!"

"No need. All is under control, my Lady . . ." *Ter* Bisfuri replies from within. There's a slight harshness to his normally resonant voice. "I'm not in my clothes at present, please don't bother to come in."

"Nonsense, sweet boy! You can be sure I've seen it all before, no need to hide yourself from me." At that point, Ashura enters his dressing room. "Now, let's see your arm!"

From the angle where I stand, I can barely see the interior room and Lady Ashura's back as she saunters forward, approaching Benaten in, what I assume, must be an excruciating, vulnerable moment for him.

A wild thought comes to me. Quickly, I lay down my uniform on the nearest chair. Then I put one hand in my skirt pocket and grasp the quantum turnip. I squeeze it, for good measure.

"Ei, Heket?" I think-speak in my mind, searching for the being inside my head.

I am here, the *pegasus* replies at once, his presence unfurling as though out of nowhere. In sympathy, the turnip in my fingers starts to pulse and feels warm to the touch.

"You know that cobra transformation in the tunnels? Not the big monstrous one, but the little ordinary snake?" I continue, taking the turnip out of my pocket. "Please, transform into the same snake, and go inside that room right now! Hiss and make a horrible noise at that awful noblewoman!"

Do you need me to strike her?

"Oh no, no!" I mentally cry out, putting my free hand over my mouth in alarm at such a notion. "Just frighten her until she leaves!"

Very well. Throw me.

And I do.

The turnip explodes mid-air into a cloud of rainbow light, then coalesces on the floor into the cobra form. The snake casts me a strangely wise look from its lidless eyes, then undulates and slithers rapidly, springlike, as it flows down the hallway and into the suite.

Exactly two heartbeats later, I hear a shrill female scream.

I bite my lower lip and hold my breath in order not to cackle with a wicked flood of unexpected, wild emotion.

. . .

"*SNAKE!* VENOMOUS SNAKE!" Lady Ashura cries, moving backward so quickly that she nearly trips on her own long skirt and veils. I can see her flailing silhouette all the way from the living room. "Do something, Benaten! Oh, holy Ra!"

"I will take care of it," Benaten replies after the slightest pause. "It must've crawled in from the open balcony. No need to raise your voice."

"How can you take care of it? No! No! Look how it rises! Don't get any closer to it, or it will strike you—"

"Right now, it's best you should leave, my Lady. For your own safety."

"Indeed, I cannot bear to watch—Benaten! Please call the guards! Oh. . . ."

And the next instant Lady Ashura flees back into the living room, clutching the skirt of her dress. She pauses only for a heartbeat, seeing me, then her eyes narrow.

Oh no! She must've seen my face, my shaking mouth, as I barely hold back my chuckles and try to avert my gaze toward the floor, even now.

"Are you laughing? How *dare* you?" She takes a step toward me, then slaps me resoundingly on the cheek.

I stagger backward and put one hand up to my face, reeling from her unexpected blow, my cheek and jaw stinging.

"Oh, no . . . I'm sorry, my Lady . . ." I mumble, but Lady Ashura Ximunat storms past me and exits the Quarters, slamming the door behind her.

Holy Bastet help me . . . what have I done? I think.

But the next moment, I hear footsteps, and Benaten Bisfuri comes out of the interior chambers.

This time, he's fully dressed—casual long pants and white linen shirt with long sleeves, similar to his outfit of this morning. And he's still adjusting the laces at the front of his shirt with one hand. For whatever *garooi* reason, I can't help noticing the sun-gilded skin of his chest underneath, before he pulls the fabric together.

Since when am I noticing such things? Ugh . . . that's ridiculous.

But I have no time to dwell on that thought because in his other hand my employer is carrying the *pegasus* snake.

"Clever move, Semmi. *Very* well done!" he says softly in his rich, low voice.

I listen to his manner of speech, his subtle tone, and realize that his confident, honey-smooth balance has been restored.

Ter Bisfuri approaches me. He stops close, looking down at me with a faint smile. And oh, the excited relief, the joyful *energy* in his eyes. . . .

"This," he says, holding up the cobra that has gone completely limp, silent, and unthreatening in his hand. "This was a truly inspired choice. Thank you for rescuing me yet again. You truly served me well today, more times and in more ways than I could imagine."

"Oh, *im Ter* . . ." I begin to say something.

This is when he glances at the side of my face with a frown. "What's this? You have blood on your cheek."

"Oh." I put my hand up to my face that's still tingling from the slap. When I bring it away, my fingers are stained red. "Lady Ximunat . . . was offended. She thought I was laughing. I—she didn't like me looking at her. She has sharp nails—"

"She hit you?" His frown deepens.

"It was nothing, *im Ter*. I shouldn't have laughed. Should've kept my eyes down. My fault!"

He shakes his head, and his grey eyes are now cold and intense. His mood has changed once again, just like that, from positive energy to grim reserve.

"Come with me," he tells me in a cool voice. "It needs to be cleaned."

I am about to protest, but his expression is adamant enough

for me to keep my mouth shut. Still carrying the *pegasus* snake, he heads back to his dressing chamber and I follow.

TER BISFURI'S private dressing room is larger than our entire hovel in Denwen's Pit. There's a spacious seating area, and wardrobes full of expensive clothing stretch across two of the walls. Mirrors and cosmetics clutter the surface of a long vanity table, and huge windows leading onto a balcony cover one wall, floor to ceiling. There's a doorway leading even deeper into what must be his private bedroom and bath.

"Sit," Benaten tells me, pointing to a luxury divan strewn with pillows. Meanwhile, he places the snake on the nearest cushion where it remains motionless like a toy, watching us.

"I'm sorry, my skirt is so dirty, *im Ter*," I mumble. "I don't want to stain your—"

But he interrupts me in a commanding tone. "Sit down."

I obey, perching on the edge of the fine fabric upholstery.

He walks to the table and rummages through several jars and bottles, then selects an ointment jar.

"I was just using this salve on myself," he explains, taking out a pristine folded towel from a drawer, then sits down right next to me with the towel and ointment. "Turn your head this way."

I do. And suddenly I feel his fingers on my cheek.

A shock runs through me.

His touch, it is electric. I don't know what it is, but it feels like I've been pricked with a sharp needle, or maybe scalded with a little flame from a wick . . . and then my entire cheek and face is suddenly on fire. . . .

Bastet, what is happening?

He holds my jaw lightly with his strong, warm fingers, then pats my cheek in gentle motion with the towel. I jerk away slightly because the towel is apparently moistened with some kind of spirit which makes the cut on my cheek genuinely sting with sharp pain.

But he says, "Hold still." And then he opens the jar, dips a finger, and runs it across my cut.

The pain goes away immediately, replaced by a soothing cool sensation. But this sensation is actively at war with the strange searing *awareness* I continue to feel in every place where his fingers touch my face.

He strokes my cut a few more times while I sit perfectly still, barely able to breathe, enthralled like a complete *hoohvak*. It doesn't help that, at this proximity, I can smell a pleasant musky scent coming from him—either his damp, newly-washed hair, or possibly his skin. . . .

"That should take care of it," he says finally, releasing my jaw and sitting back. He looks at me for several long heartbeats without blinking, then says. "Try not to get it wet when you get home, at least until morning."

"All right," I mumble.

"There should be no scar," he adds. "The cut was shallow enough it will be gone in a few days."

"Yes, *im Ter*. You know best."

At that, he chuckles and stands up to put the ointment away and drops the used towel in a wash basket nearby. "Indeed, I do. I've learned to take care of this kind of thing myself, since it happens so frequently. The vigilante gets a lot of cuts and bruises regularly, and I prefer not to have my personal servants involved. Particularly since only a few know about my true activities. Which means, I myself must know how to clean up wounds, heal them, and disguise them from prying eyes."

"Such as Lord Bisfuri, your Father?"

Benaten pauses, then turns around to look at me. "Yes, especially him. Hence, all that stuff." And he points to the bottles and jars on the table. "Though, I must admit, I do enjoy enhancing my beauty and natural attributes with Face Art as much as any man of court."

Is there repressed laughter in his words?

Now I'm unsure how to respond.

Fortunately, my employer changes the awkward subject. "Where is the other *pegasus*, Semmi? I assume, you have it with you?"

"Oh yes!" I dig in my skirt pocket for Girsul's *pegasus* in the form of a bracelet, then hand it over to him.

Benaten takes the bracelet, shimmering faintly with rainbow colors. He turns it over in his fingers before setting it down casually on the divan cushion next to the snake. Thoughtful, he stands looking at them both.

"I find it remarkable how well you are able to handle these creatures," he says suddenly, turning to me. "You've developed a rare skill in such a brief amount of time. What's your secret?"

A storm surge of panic strikes me. My eyes widen, and my lips part, then I clamp them shut again. *What do I do?* I can't tell *Ter* Bisfuri about the *pegasei*. And yet, I promised never to lie to him.

Furthermore, I can't always tell if he's speaking flippantly, in jest, or expects a real answer.

And so, I decide to tell him a partial truth.

"I only observe and listen to them," I reply. "The more I listen, the more they speak to me. They are—they are like stories."

"A-h-h-h," Benaten says with a smile. "Observation is a powerful tool indeed." And then he actually laughs. "Indeed, why did I even bother to ask you, a Storyteller, this *hoohvak* question? The answer should've been obvious. I hired you for your observation skills, after all. You observed me and discovered my secret. And now you do the same with these quantum beings. You, Semirameos, Semiram, Semmi, are merely being *you*. And they, these beautiful ones from another place, are showing themselves to you. Wonderful curiosities to be studied. In addition to all their practical uses for us, they can supply you with new material for your clever tales."

"Yes, *im Ter*." And then, with a different twinge of worry on behalf of both the *pegasei*, I add, "They will need to be fed again in the morning, *im Ter*."

"Of course. I'll do it myself, out on the balcony, once the sun is bright, or have Girsul handle it."

"Oh, but I would be happy to do it—" I exclaim, feeling another pang of alarm.

Wait, was that my own thought, or did Heket and the other nameless *pegasus* insert this nagging reminder inside me?

It is all you, sentient Semmi, Heket tells me, just then.

All you, not us, the other *pegasus* adds. *Your own sense of responsibility.*

We thank you for remembering, both of them utter in unison, sending uncanny, plural echoes rebounding. And just maybe, from some unfathomable distance, I can hear the group echoes of even more *pegasei* voices inside my mind.

Seriously, feels like a stable in there.

Meanwhile, *Ter* Bisfuri is replying to me, saying something. And so, I tear my attention away from the *pegasei* in my head to listen to him.

"You will not be working here tomorrow, Semmi," Benaten tells me, which causes my heart to nearly leap out of my chest with anxiety. But then he clarifies, "That's because I have another task for you. It will require you to go to the Imperial Palace in Circle One."

I recover my ability to breathe. "I see."

Benaten walks to a tall cabinet near the wall, expensive polished mahogany, and he presses what could be a random spot along its surface. A small secret drawer pops open.

He reaches inside and takes out a round coin-shaped object.

By now I'm familiar enough with these things to recognize a Thoth-pin.

He returns to the divan and sits down again, next to me. "Take this. Tomorrow morning, no later than eighth hour of Ra, arrive at the Palace. Wear your Bisfuri uniform in order to be allowed past the gates."

"Okay. . . ."

"Then, once on the Palace grounds, you will find Prince Oron Kassiopei—*discreetly*. Do not ask anyone, go straight to the interior Palace Gardens. He should be there, waiting. Hand him this Thoth-pin. If anyone stops you on the way, make up something. Do *not* mention Oron. Give any excuse, any—"

"*Im Ter*," I interrupt, because something else occurs to me. "Last night—I'm very sorry that I had to withhold it from you until now, but I must tell you something. I—found the Imperial Princess. You ordered me to look for Princess Arlenari—and I did. She was picking up flowers from the floor near the entrance and taking them outside. I promised her I wouldn't say anything to anyone. We talked a little and—and she told me she didn't want to be found, and that's why—"

Benaten watches me curiously, and raises one of his brows. "So, you obeyed the will of the Imperial Princess instead of me, Semmi?"

"Yes! And I am so very *sorry!*"

"You lied to me."

"And I feel awful about it, *im Ter*! But what could I do?" I continue to chatter. "I'm so terribly sorry I couldn't say anything earlier, but the poor Princess was so unhappy, and I felt so bad for her that I just couldn't say no. But then we talked about my story—"

"What story?"

"The story I told, last evening, about the *sha* king. The Princess said she liked it and wanted me to *write* it down for her and bring it to the Palace. But—I don't know how to write, *im*

Ter. So I told her I could record it for her, and maybe Girsul could show me how, since he knows how to work all that tech equipment, and he could put it on a Thoth button—or pin—"

"Enough! Slow down." Ter Bisfuri shakes his head slightly. But then I see that his lips are curving into a smile.

Strange. He is not angry with me?

I grow silent and gulp, staring at him anxiously. I'm also somewhat confused.

"You obviously don't know," he says after a long pause. "That our entire party, as all other Bisfuri major events and entertainments, has been recorded?"

"Oh . . . really?" I ask.

"Yes. Including your fine Storyteller performance."

My mouth falls open.

Ter Bisfuri leans forward, moving even closer to me, so that I can see the interesting odd-colored flecks in his very interesting grey eyes.

And he says, "This is very fortunate, Semmi. You withheld the truth from me, but for a charitable reason, so all is forgiven. We're going to take full advantage of this situation. You're going to visit Princess Arlenari Kassiopei tomorrow, with a copy of your recorded performance—which I will provide shortly."

I nod.

"Once there, you will of course get slightly lost in the Gardens, until you find Prince Oron and hand him this Thoth-pin. Then, and only then will you continue on your official visit with the Princess, and give her the promised recording, with my personal compliments. Understood?"

"Yes, *im Ter*! And, thank you!"

"Don't thank me, little liar—or should I say, Storyteller. Thank the gods and the lucky circumstances."

I wait while *Ter* Bisfuri goes to another room to procure the recording which must be cut and copied from a digital tablet then transferred to the Thoth-pin. When he returns, he is carrying a tiny, red silk pouch and a red messenger tassel.

"Inside is your Storytelling performance for Princess Arlenari," he says. "Not to be confused with the other very important Thoth-pin intended for Prince Oron. Hence the color pouch so you don't mix them up."

"Oh, I won't!" I promise.

"Good," he says. "Because a mix-up would be a very bad thing. Now, you're free to go home for today. Run this errand tomorrow for me, and take all day if necessary. Wear the red tassel on your uniform. I'll see you back here the following day."

"*Im Ter*," I dare to mention, "the day after tomorrow, the twenty-second day of Setaet, will be the Bisfuri Domestic Service Competition. Am I permitted to participate?"

"Ah, that's right. . . ." Benaten pauses to think, raising one of his brows. "Very well, yes. Sign up for it, by all means. It shouldn't take more than an hour, so plan to work afterwards. There's much to do."

"Of course, *im Ter*," I mumble quickly, then leave his dressing room, casting one mildly concerned farewell glance at the two *pegasei* abandoned on the divan cushions.

On the way out, I pick up my uniform, exit the Quarters, then run into the late afternoon sunshine and head straight to the smart board and registration area in the courtyard outside.

Here, a considerable crowd of Bisfuri employees has gathered, since many people's shifts are over for the day. We all push our way to the registration table to get our spots reserved in the Domestic Service Competition.

When it's my turn to register and I finish the process, I ask, "May I register my little brother? He's not here, but I am."

"Normally we would need his thumbprint," the woman official handling the digital tablet tells me. "But since you work here and can vouch for him, then yes. We'll just use your thumbprint on his behalf."

And that's how I get Uru registered.

SMOKE STACKS of cooking fires rise into the air all around the neighborhood of Denwen's Pit by the time I get home. I'm just in time to help cook our meal tonight, which makes me feel less guilty for once.

On the other hand, there's new guilt because now I have to withhold so much of my day from my family. However, Father looks sickly and exhausted after a long day of endless digging labor, this time in Circle Nine, so he has even fewer questions than usual for any of us.

Meanwhile, Grandmother is too busy to ask me anything. First, she's dealing with the stubborn kindling twigs in the firepit then pouring water into the pot, and refusing my help with the heavy bucket (which drives me insane, as always).

I inform Uru that I put him down for the Bisfuri

Competition, and he gives me a bland look without any enthusiasm.

"What?" I say with tired annoyance as I scrape the dirt off a carrot with a small, blunt cooking knife. "Just because the other Competitions didn't work out, doesn't mean anything. You can run faster than any of their messengers!"

"Whatever. Those *chazuf* Houses—they're all the same, they won't hire me. No matter how fast I run. Everyone says those contests are rigged." And Uru gives me a sad shrug.

"What kind of talk is that? Don't give up, child." Grandmother turns away from the pot she's stirring to glance at my little brother. "The gods whisper in my ear, as they do with all of us old ones. And they tell me you have a long life and a good destiny before you. That means you must continue to believe in your ability to win."

"Even if it's rigged?" Uru asks.

"Yes, even so. *You* are not rigged, child. Do what you do best, and that's how you'll win." And Grandmother turns back to tend the pot.

TOO NERVOUS TO RISK BEING LATE TO the Palace, I wake up the next day at a *sha*-filled, godless hour of darkness, long before dawn. My Bisfuri uniform is lying on top of the old storage box next to my cot, and before putting it on I must wash myself properly.

Carrying the uniform with me, I tiptoe in the dark past sleeping Uru, then past Father in the living room, trying not to trip on goodness-knows-what, then go outside in the chilly pre-dawn.

Quick, quick! Check the latrine seat for bugs before using it. Climb up the ladder to our roof, then set the precious uniform down while I get in the shower stall, pump-fill the shower tank in haste and open the water nozzle. I squeeze my eyes shut and brace myself for the first strike of icy well water—*Bast help me!*

Then I fiercely scrub my curling hair with all its tight kinks, and the rest of me, glancing up at the sky often to check for first light of dawn. Normally I don't wash my hair any more frequently than every Ra-Day, but this is, yet again, one of those times that I must.

Must . . . rinse . . . the filth . . . out.

Can't face the Imperials looking and smelling any less than my best.

When I'm done, I grab the olive oil bottle and work as much as I can through my curls, and towel off.

Next, it's time to put on the fancy uniform. The expensive fabric slides around me, and this time the length and fit of the skirt is perfect. Vilras did a fine job of it.

I rummage through the skirt pocket of my dirty clothes from yesterday and find the two Thoth-pins, one in a red pouch, plus the messenger tassel. My new uniform has two deep pockets on either side, so I put one Thoth-pin in each, and add my Bisfuri comm badge. Last of all, I attach my new red tassel to the collar.

Taking great care, I climb back down the ladder without snagging my precious uniform on anything, and go back indoors to find my better pair of shoes and grab a few bites of last night's supper.

Finally, it's time to run to the bus stop on Circle Nine.

THE FIRST PALLOR of dawn seeps along the eastern horizon when I take the hover bus to Circle Eight, then transfer to the fancy express transport that goes to the interior and the very heart of the City.

I sit in my seat proudly, clean and dressed in my fine uniform, with the messenger tassel prominent on my collar and, for once, feel like I belong here. The other businessmen and high-end passengers are no longer giving me suspicious looks.

The bus flies directly over the City, with a minimal number of stops. I stare down at the twinkling artificial lights on the ground below interspersed with the curvature of the canals full of ink-black water that still reflects the night sky.

When we get to the private stop on Circle Two, with its verdant park surroundings on the Bisfuri estate grounds, for the first time, I don't get off.

My destination is the next and final stop.

The hover bus rises into the air once more, and I clench the arm rests of my seat with anxiety.

We fly over Bisfuri land, and in the growing light of morning I stare with curiosity at the tree tops and the endless greenery, and see the gilded roofs of fine antique buildings which are now quite familiar to me.

A casual thought comes to me: *Ter* Bisfuri is somewhere down there right now, possibly still asleep in his bed. Or, more likely, he's also out early, doing some secret vigilante business as the Man in the Niktos Cloak. . . .

I continue to look out the window at the land below, observe the ponds, water features, and hillsides covered in shrubbery and bursts of wildflowers, including the tallest slope with the waterfall where we entered the grotto yesterday.

We continue onward, and in moments, we reach the final canal that separates Circles Two and One. Unlike the others, this innermost canal has a name, the Khemenu Canal. Its waters are the most transparent and pure, lapping gently at the Imperial shore of Circle One, most commonly referred to as the Center Circle.

Beyond the shore I can see cultivated green lawns, groves of trees with leaves like garlands of pale silk, various shrines and temples of the gods scattered among them, and gravel walkways leading inward. They culminate in grand walls of mauve and white-veined granite inlaid with ebony, beyond which are the tall gilded roofs, spires, and domes of the Imperial Palace.

My breath catches in my throat. . . .

And then I notice strange activity along the curving border of Circle One, clearly visible on approach from overhead. It appears that holes are being dug at infrequent regular intervals at the very edge of the shoreline.

Approximately every five hundred paces, green sod is lying in mounds, displaced. The grass is uprooted and piled up in previously pristine spots of lawn to reveal dirt underneath in unsightly patches. Even now, a few laborers dig with shovels and hoes. They are mostly ignored by the visitors and passersby.

Could they be planting trees?

As I ponder the mystery of such disruptive gardening, we arrive at our destination.

The hover transport lands at a graceful bus stop with a sculpted arch trellis covered in climbing roses, marble benches, and a curious stone staircase leading directly into the water.

Here I get off, along with a handful of other passengers. Some wear noble House uniforms such as myself, others are clad in understated finery.

I may have been to Circle One as a tiny child, once or twice in my life with my Mother and Grandmother, to visit Bastet's largest temple situated here, to touch the sacred cats and receive festival blessings. But none of us have ever set foot past the great walls, beyond which access is restricted to the public.

And now, I am about to enter the Palace.

I gather courage and walk along the largest gravel path in the wake of several other people who seem to know what they're doing and where to go. As I near the main gates, I look up at the considerable height of the walls, and then I see something even more unexpected than random holes in the lawn.

High up in the air, far above the Palace, hangs a large disk. I try to understand what it is that I'm seeing and it finally occurs to me, it's a stationary hovering platform. Its silvery underside is illuminated by the light of morning, turning the slate grey surface to golden sparkle, the kind found in orichalcum.

As I widen my perusal of the sky, not too far from the first hovering disk, hangs another similar one. In fact, there are several such objects visible from the ground, obscured only by the looming walls. All of them are motionless, parked very high in the air overhead. Strange how I missed noticing them when my hover bus was still in flight.

"What are those?" I ask the nearest passerby just ahead of me, a young woman also wearing a staff uniform from a Great House.

She glances up to where I point. Then she shakes her head. "Don't know. Maybe something to do with the upcoming Pilot Competition."

"Ah," I say.

And we continue onward and enter the gates.

BEFORE ADMITTING me onto the Imperial Palace grounds, the imposing Palace guards scan my Bisfuri employee badge then don't give me a second glance. The fact that they ask no other questions, don't bother to search me (something for which I was bracing myself) merely observe my Bisfuri uniform and messenger tassel and nod at me as I walk past them, fills me with a strange, almost delirious sense of satisfaction.

Holy Bast! I could be a criminal or an assassin, and they just let me inside! My imagination goes into a dizzying spin of possibilities and exciting action yarns. Though, having an employee badge is very likely a sufficient indicator of benign intent.

But then I see the rows of full-body sensors on the gates

themselves, and additional sensors on upright posts on either sides, as I walk through.

I recognize them because I've seen sensors at the Chiprahat warehouse. Except, these are installed in continuous strips, so that every part of my body got scanned, probably including the contents of my stomach.

Yeah, I'm a hoohvak *to think there wouldn't be high security here.*

On the other side of the gates, is a garden paradise. If I thought the public outer portion of Imperial Circle One was lovely, this is beautiful beyond anything in my experience.

Gravel paths are replaced with exquisite paving stones forming subtle color mosaics in different shades of mauve, rose, brick, and cream. Accent stones of veined marble vie for attention with slivers of obsidian, slabs of granite, and hairline rivulets of gold. And that's just the ground!

The mosaic paths are edged by manicured shrubs and flowerbeds, and perfume wafts on the breeze. Statuary rises from among the flowers—brightly painted and gilded forms, both human and divine, the latter distinguished by various sacred animal heads. Peacocks roam everywhere, and fountains pump sparkling water. Trees here are all exotic, delicate, shaped by skilled gardeners into harmonious shapes not always found in nature.

I stop and stare, my mouth falling open so much that I can probably trap flies. But even the flying insects here are elegant—dragonflies with translucent wings, huge butterflies with royal markings. And rare birds flitter among the branches.

Further toward the interior, I see the walls of the actual Palace rising in the distance. From what little I know of the Imperial Palace, mostly by watching media-box news, it consists of eight separate buildings shaped like blunt pie wedges lined up in a circle to form a common round structure which is hollow in the center. The Palace structure is called the *Ogdoadum*. And at the very center of it stands the *Kassiopeion* temple.

I pause to check the clock function on my Bisfuri badge, and the tiny hologram tells me it's just past seventh hour of Ra. I'm an hour early.

I suppose my next step would be to wander the gardens for the next hour and see if I can locate Prince Oron.

And this is what I end up doing. As daydreams flow by, I familiarize myself with the park layout of the gardens, the various open spaces and groves, the hidden waterfalls and ponds. I make my first round, quickly walking the inner perimeter of the walls, then circling closer and closer to the Palace buildings. This garden is immense!

I run into other people occasionally, most of them service staff hurrying somewhere, and a few noble elites on a rare morning stroll. There are also several gardeners working among the flowerbeds, but no Imperial Prince among them.

Finally, I find my anxiety flowing away, replaced by the natural peace and quiet of the gardens. I slow down my nearly running pace and stop at a small grouping of benches, where I see some gardener paused to rest, his straw hat off on the bench next to him.

I almost walk past him but for the gleam of golden Kassiopei hair.

It's Prince Oron.

I am amazed to see him dressed in such plain laborer clothing, not unlike what *Ter* Bisfuri wears. A white linen shirt and dark pants, open sandals. His long shining mane is gathered behind him in a segmented tail, and the breeze stirs a few loose strands of hair around his forehead.

Prince Oron sits on the bench, leaning forward slightly, perusing an antique looking book-scroll.

I freeze in my tracks. Then, taking a deep breath, I approach and bow my head while I curtsey. "My Imperial Lord," I say.

Prince Oron looks up from his reading.

I see his calm blue eyes, pale lapis lazuli in shade. His expression is kind and completely non-threatening.

"Yes?" he says. And then, seeing my Bisfuri uniform, he adds, "Do you have something for me?"

I reach in my pocket, and take out the Thoth-pin—the one which is *not* inside a red pouch. Mentally I force myself to pause before acting, to think, to question, *is that the right one?*

But yes, it is. I *know* it is. And so, I offer it to the Prince. "This," I say in a whisper.

"From Aten?" he matches my whisper.

I nod.

"Very well. Please convey to him: immense gratitude from Noi." Prince Oron Kassiopei takes the Thoth-pin and puts it in his pocket. "A beautiful morning, isn't it?" he asks with a light smile. And then he narrows his eyes from the sun and looks closely at me. "I know you—Semiram, the Storyteller!"

"Yes, My Imperial Lord," I incline my head again. "I'm actually here to see the Imperial Princess Arlenari."

"Of course. That is indeed why you're here. My sister continues to speak about you." Prince Oron watches me in amusement. "She really enjoyed your story, and so did I."

I feel a rush of heat in my cheeks. "Thank you so much, My Imperial Lord."

"Wonderful. She'll be quite pleased to see you. Go on, then, since we're done here."

I take a step, then pause again and open my mouth once more. "If you don't mind me asking, My Imperial Lord, where might she be found? I'm truly sorry, but I don't know where her Quarters are in the Palace—"

"Arlenari is often outside at this time of day, not in her Quarters. She and I share a love of the gardens. I prefer these lovely grounded ones, while she—she likes the hovering ones in the sky."

And Prince Oron points upward.

I glance overhead, and see a marvelous sight. About two hundred paces away, near the Palace buildings, small rectangular platforms overflowing with greenery hover in gradual steps, reaching for the sky.

They are nowhere near the height of those curious orichalcum disks that are currently parked all over the Palace airspace, far, far above. Instead, the highest of these verdant platforms hovers at about the level of the Palace building roof.

Suddenly I recall exactly what these green platforms are, from seeing them a long time ago in some Palace news coverage.

They are called the Hovering Gardens of Atlantis.

H aving done my errand for Prince Oron, I now hurry through the ground gardens toward the spot where the hovering ones begin. The lowest rung of the Hovering Gardens is a platform that's barely two or three feet above the ground, accessible via a small movable staircase.

I take the staircase two stairs at a time, and find myself standing on the floor of this platform which is all sod and green grass, with borders of colorful flowers and a potted tree. The whole thing is a rectangle the size of a large room.

I cast my gaze around and see the next staircase, also movable. Remarkably, it is hooked onto the current platform and the next platform above, via its bottom and top ends, for stability. A very clever contraption, to keep the floating tiers from simply drifting apart in the air.

I leap up that staircase and find myself on the next hovering platform, again only about three feet higher than the previous one. But now, as I look down, I can see it's six feet above ground.

This platform has a central stone mosaic on the floor consisting of paving stones, and a border of flowerbeds. There's a little marble bench in the center.

I pause for a moment and look up to observe the pattern of hovering rectangles above me, laid out in seeming randomness, but somehow also forming interesting geometric shapes in the sky. Lines and angles, and endless short staircases lead from one level to the next above.

In some places there are no staircases, only curving bridges or simple horizontal planks connecting multiple platforms on the same level. And the higher up ones are larger platforms, from which I can hear the sounds of splashing water, indicating aerial fountains.

How did they get the water up there? How and where is it circulating?

And then I see it. There are several waterfalls very high above, and the water cascades down from those higher platforms onto the ones below, running along chiseled planks and gulleys, and even a few enclosed pipes which spiral down to the lower levels, all while forming their own sculptured symmetry.

I would love to stop and just enjoy the amazing structure, but I have a job to do. Princess Arlenari is on one of these levels, and I must find her.

I continue climbing up the hovering platforms, but they are all empty. No other park visitors have found their way up here. Momentarily, I wonder if these gardens are specially reserved for only the most elite or royal visitors.

And then, somewhere on the upper middle levels of this artfully chaotic structure, I think I see a human form. Someone else is walking up there.

I increase my pace, fearlessly climbing the levels, until I am at the platform right below where I thought I've seen someone, and just three tiers below the level of the Palace roof.

"My Imperial Lady!" I call out. "*Nefero eos!* It's Semmi! I mean, I am Semiram, the Storyteller, here to see you. *Ei!* Hello! My Imperial Lady! I have a gift for you, as promised—"

"Hello."

I hear a female voice directly behind me and nearly jump out of my skin.

Princess Arlenari Kassiopei is standing only a few steps away, looking at me with her blue eyes wide in excitement and with a happy smile. She wears a simple linen dress and sandals, and her golden hair is tied in an ordinary *sesemet* tail that falls down her back. The breeze blows strong up here, sending the tendrils of her hair into a wild nimbus around her head.

"Ah! Mother of *Shibet!*" I exclaim, placing one hand over my heart. "Hathor and Bast, you scared me! How did you—did you just get down here? I thought that was you up on that level right there." I amend my outburst quickly. "I mean, my apologies, My Imperial Lady—"

"*Nefero eos*, Semmi or Semiram. I am so glad you came." The Princess just smiles at me, and stands there, with her hands crossed at the wrists. She almost appears shy.

I regain a modicum of courtesy, and bow before her, then reach into my pocket and take out the little red pouch. "Imperial Lady Arlenari, as you requested, this is a recording of my Storytelling performance at the Bisfuri party. *Ter* Benaten Bisfuri himself gave it to me to give you."

"Oh, it is?" The Princess takes the pouch and opens it, to find the Thoth-pin. "Please tell *Ter* Bisfuri I am very grateful. I promise, I'll listen to it many, many times!"

I curtsey. "Yes, My Imperial Lady, I will tell him."

"And thank *you*, Semiram, Semmi. You, of course, most of all."

"It is my pleasure to serve you, My Imperial Lady."

There is a somewhat awkward moment of silence between us.

I bite my lip and swallow. "I suppose, I need to be going. . . ."

But Princess Arlenari's expression immediately turns

anxious. "Why?" she asks. "Why do you need to go? You just arrived!"

"Oh," I mumble and hide my hands in my new roomy uniform pockets. "Yes, well . . . I just wasn't sure if you needed anything else from me, My Imperial Lady. Your brother, Imperial Lord Oron, said you would be here, and I don't want to impose—"

"But you are not imposing!" the Princess interrupts me in a voice that's still full of anxiety. "Please don't go just yet, Semmi or Semiram. Please, stay!"

Forgetting to feel nervous about myself, I grow a little uncomfortable on her behalf.

"It's actually just Semmi," I say yet again (I've mentioned this to her at least once at the Bisfuri party, but I don't think it registered with her). "Semiram is for Storytelling."

"I see, thank you for explaining," she says quickly, finally acknowledging my name preference. Stepping back, she begins rocking on her heels, then shifting from foot to foot. "So, I will then call you Semmi unless you are telling a story, in which case I will stop calling you Semmi and call you Semiram. Until you begin another story, in which case I will again call you Semiram. I think that makes sense, doesn't it?"

I stand patiently, watching the Princess fidget. At this point, the poor thing is simply babbling.

"Sure," I say, when at last she grows blessedly silent. "Makes good sense to me, My Imperial Lady. I can stay. *Ter* Bisfuri is not expecting me any time soon, at least not today."

"Oh, good!" Princess Arlenari exclaims. "Then you can keep me company. And we can have some tea!"

AND SO, we climb a few more platforms up, while Princess Arlenari points out her favorite flowers, or bugs, or paving stones, or goodness-knows-what in the Hovering Gardens. She certainly has many favorites, all of them very minor details and small parts of the landscaping features.

It occurs to me, you have to spend a great deal of time in these gardens to know every rock and flower to such an extent. She must practically live here.

". . . And this water spout makes a different musical note than the first one," she tells me.

Arlenari sings two bright notes in a beautiful soprano voice while pointing to a row of tiny fountain spouts, as we sit on a marble bench on one of the larger upper tier platforms high above ground. "This is the sound it makes. And the second sound is coming from this one."

We're now just below the level of the roof, almost the highest tier, and from where we sit, we can observe a wide panorama of the park grounds and see small figures of people working or strolling below.

I admit, she's right about that water spout. If I pay attention and lean forward with my ear turned toward it, there is a slight tonal difference in the tinkling sound the water makes cascading into the small reservoir below.

"Yes, I can hear it," I say, sitting up and wiping my nose and forehead with the back of my hand because my face is now covered with the fine spray from the fountain. "And the third one makes a different tone too. The waters are all coming from pipes of different lengths, progressively longer, that's why. I've seen a neighbor play music on a reed pipe which has short and long reeds to make different notes like that."

"Yes!" Princess Arlenari exclaims. "I am so glad you can hear it, Semmi, you are the first one who does! I've shown this fountain to other people and made them listen, and no one believes me."

"It's not a matter of believing," I say. "Just a matter of listening closely. Whoever built that pretty fountain made the waters play a pretty tune too."

In reply, Princess Arlenari smiles at me, and her eyes are radiant.

OUR TEA ARRIVES SOON, on large hovering trays, carefully maneuvered toward us by two servants who march up the stairs behind them, all the way from ground level. I watch in some amazement as the hovering service levitates nearer, never having seen such a presentation of food. But it does make sense, here on these Hovering Gardens, to have hovering tea.

The tea itself is in tall glass pitchers, while the trays also contain covered dishes of little *eos* pies, dumplings, and other delicate finger foods, finer than anything I've ever seen at the best market stalls. In addition, there are plates of fresh fruit and berries, candied fruit and dates, and sweet honey syrup.

The servants pour tea into glass goblets, and offer them to the Princess and then to me, her "visitor." No one seems to question my presence here or express any surprise that I, a mere servant, am keeping Princess Arlenari Kassiopei company.

I carefully accept the goblet full of fragrant amber liquid, and don't dare sip it until Arlenari herself does—just in case there is some kind of Protocol or rule for that.

"You may go now," she tells the servants, and they curtsey and leave, moving down endless staircases and platforms toward the ground. *At least they didn't have to carry the trays up here*, I think.

"Why aren't you drinking the tea?" Arlenari asks, as I stare in the wake of the departing servants. "You don't like it?"

"Oh no, My Imperial Lady, my apologies, but am I permitted to drink before you do?"

The Princess gives me an odd, focused look. "When you're in my company, you may drink and eat whenever and whatever you like."

"Thank you, My Imperial Lady." I take a sip of the delicious hot tea.

Just then, I look up briefly at the hovering level directly above, and see a quick blur of motion.

For a brief moment, a cloaked figure steps forward, silhouetted against the sunlit morning sky, seemingly watching us. There's a flapping of brown fabric in the strong breeze, and then the cloak pulls back, retreating from the platform edge, and is gone.

"Somebody is there," I tell the Princess, pointing up. "There's someone up there in a brown cloak."

However, by the time Arlenari turns in that direction, there is no one.

"Spies everywhere, always spies," she whispers suddenly. And she doesn't bother to look up again.

WE SPEND some more time in the gardens, and Princess Arlenari is genuinely unwilling to let me go.

Not that I even care to leave at this point. It's rather nice to relax and not have to do anything, just listen to her talk in a dreamy voice about somewhat outlandish but generally pleasant things. Not to mention, I get to eat delicious food and rest my feet more than I've ever done during any given morning.

Curiously, not once does the Princess bring up the events of the Bisfuri party. The unpleasant and downright horrible things she witnessed together with me and several others are either forgotten or repressed, and the only thing she chooses to recall is my Storytelling.

Eventually the morning heat becomes a little too much, as the hot sun burns down on us, and it's close to noon. So much brilliant sunshine, even here in the elevated gardens with their random spots of overhead shade.

Suddenly I get an intrusive thought, prompted by all that fierce sunlight. Are the two *pegasei*, Heket and the other nameless one, being properly fed this morning?

And immediately, from all the way across the distance of Circle Two and the Bisfuri estate, Heket's alien presence stirs in my mind.

Holy Bast! It can hear me!

My eyes widen with effort as I strain to listen.

"Heket, is that you?" I mind-ask.

Yes, I am here Semmi, the voice replies. *I am feeding at this exact moment. And so is the other of my kind.*

"Wait! I'm all the way across the canal in Circle One!" I mind-yell. "How come I can hear you and you can hear me? What kind of impossible *shar-ta-haak* thing is this?"

Sentient human, we are still connected.

"But how?"

There is no spatial distance between us.

"Huh?"

I can almost hear the amusement in Heket's voice.

Space does not exist.

My eyes widen even more.

"Come with me, indoors," Princess Arlenari says to me in that moment.

I blink, trying to shut away the voice in my head, and focus on the here and now.

"Semmi?" the Princess asks me with an immediately serious expression. "Are you well?"

"Oh, yes, of course, My Imperial Lady," I reply, clearing my throat and pretending to choke a little on whatever it is I am still chewing.

"My apologies," I add, pointing at my throat, then take a quick gulp of tea. Not sure what cup I am on right now, and my belly is so blissfully full, but it's time to stop stuffing myself.

Arlenari seems to accept my vague response, and stands up, abandoning her empty tea goblet.

"To the Palace. This way," she says, and heads for the nearest staircase leading up.

"We're not going down to the ground?" I set down my own empty plate and drink.

"No." Arlenari turns back to me with a light smile. "We're going to cross over to the roof."

I FOLLOW the Princess up to the highest tier of the Hovering Gardens, and from there, take the attached walkway directly onto the Imperial Palace roof. This part of the roof is a small, stone-paved courtyard and observation area, beyond which the actual roof slopes upward, cresting with sharp angles and peaks upon which you should not attempt to walk.

Arlenari crosses the courtyard and keeps going, hopping lightly down a short flight of stone stairs, and I follow. She opens a door in the walls and we head inside a twisting corridor. It appears ancient, the stones here rough and crumbling, until just a few paces ahead, everything transforms into polished luxury.

I have no words for the things I see here, only endless corridors that open into ornate halls, elegant wall hangings with legendary images from antiquity, columns, statuary, polished wood, and marble trimmed with gold.

So much gold everywhere. . . .

And I thought the Bisfuri estate was magnificent. The Imperial Palace is just unbelievable.

Occasional servants pass us, and all of them immediately bow before Princess Arlenari, something she hardly notices.

Finally, we arrive inside a suite of Quarters that belong to the Princess herself.

"Come, Semmi," she beckons me through the grand doors into a living room that sets fear into my soul.

I take one step, and pause, gaping in awe. The chamber is flooded with sunlight from grand balcony windows, and the mad sparkle of gold and faceted jewels encrusted into *everything*, simply overwhelms me.

The furnishings here are formal, with intricately embroidered fabrics, threaded with gold and gems. Carved heavy furniture, grand porcelain vases on stands, pearl borders on graceful curtains and upholstery.

And then I notice one wall rising all the way to the ceiling, filled with endless cubbyholes containing tubes that appear to be book scrolls. It must be an entire library—from what I understand libraries to be, even though I've never seen one.

And so, I take a few steps inside the room, and point at the scrolls in their little wall nooks. "Is that a library, My Imperial Lady?"

Arlenari glances to where I'm pointing, makes a little sound that could almost be annoyance, and shakes her head. "No, that's just a single bookshelf. Want to see my library?"

"Yes, My Imperial Lady, if it's not too much trouble," I say in amazement.

The Princess leads me out of that front room and into a corridor, and then a few steps later, opens a door to a different chamber.

She flips a wall switch and an artificial light orb ignites at the entrance. It is followed by a row of similar orbs fixed along the walls, revealing a dark hall almost the size of the Bisfuri antechamber, with a vaulted ceiling and overhead chandelier illumination.

There are no windows in this room, only walls with built-in shelves of mahogany wood, stacked to the ceiling with scrolls. A single long table with benches stretches down the middle of the chamber. There is a peculiar dry smell, of ancient wood and something else I have no words for.

"This is my library." Princess Arlenari pauses to turn around with her hands spread out and takes a deep breath, to inhale the peculiar dry air.

I put my hand over my heart.

"Would you like to look around?" Arlenari asks me. "Feel free to touch the book scrolls, but don't unroll any of them without asking. Some are very ancient and very fragile, and may never be handled again, only scanned with optical technology that can read the insides without unrolling it."

"Thank you, My Imperial Lady," I say in a breathless voice. "I've never touched a scroll before."

And then I approach the walls and start walking the room perimeter. Awe, the greatest terrifying awe overcomes me. . . . It is followed by a profound sense of wonder, filling me to such an extent that the top of my head tingles with raw energy and exultation.

At some point I stop at random, and gently touch a scroll, then pull it out from its storage niche.

"Bring it here," Arlenari tells me, and climbs up on a bench with her knees, placing her elbows carelessly on the table. I get the sense that she does this often, crawling over the wooden bench and table like a small child, ignoring the flattened pillows stacked nearby, while utterly consumed with the scrolls.

I do as I'm told, and carry the scroll with both hands, holding it light as a feather. I set it down on the table before the Princess.

"Is this one okay to unroll?" I whisper.

Arlenari takes a look at the faded round stoppers on both ends that hold the scroll in place. There are barely visible makings etched on the old wood and they mean something.

"No, take this one back." Arlenari shakes her head. "And be very careful when you replace it in its spot. Get another one."

I replace the precious scroll and select another one, again at random. This time, Arlenari nods and opens the scroll herself, unrolling it to show me exactly how it's done.

A beautiful interior on faded papyrus reveals itself. There are markings and images in reddish-brown ink. None of it makes any sense to me of course, and even the pictures are almost incomprehensible.

"I cannot read, My Imperial Lady," I say with regret and shame.

"No matter," she replies. "I will read it to you."

I have no idea how much time passes, because there are no windows in this room. Princess Arlenari Kassiopei reads to me in a soft, expressive voice, a story out of legend. It seems to be the middle of some larger epic, so I'm not entirely sure who the characters are, because they are already in the middle of their adventures.

However, I settle in quickly, mesmerized by her cadence, and listen to her speak about ancient gods and heroes and demons and wondrous creatures. There are battles and weddings, betrayals and redemptions, deaths and mysteries. There are immense powers of sorcery and little ordinary things of no consequence. There are beings and objects and holy relics and memories of a past so far off that it must be the dawn of time.

"What kind of beast is that?" I interrupt occasionally, with questions such as this one, and without any concern for offending her with my blunt manner.

"The Void Bakriku is a great *bakris* scavenger that eats what is left of the dead," the Princess explains. "It is as big as a *sesemet*."

"Oh, really?" I ask. "Where does it live? I've never seen a *bakriku* that big!"

Arlenari looks up at me from the scroll, and there is mischievous energy in her eyes. "It lives in stories."

"Oh, so an imaginary beast?" My eyes widen with curiosity and intense attention.

She nods.

"What about this other one, the Lightning Uum?"

Arlenari smiles. "I've never seen an owl cast forth lightning, have you?"

"So, the *uum* is just magical in this story and doesn't exist also?"

"It exists. In the *story*."

"I think I understand now," I say. "Someone made up the creature, the same way I made up my story about the *sha* king."

"Someone, yes. A long time ago."

"And they wrote it down?" A gentle wave of sorrow passes over me again.

Arlenari looks at me thoughtfully, then replies, "Not necessarily. Not all stories or books are always written. The original storyteller might have told the story out loud, same way as you, and someone else recorded it in writing, in book format, putting the final version onto the scroll."

"But that other someone . . . they at least knew how to write the words."

Arlenari continues to watch me. "Scribes are taught. No one is born knowing how to write, you know."

I nod. "Yes, My Imperial Lady. I can only dream to have that kind of skill that the scribe has. Then I would be able to write down my own stories."

"You can learn to be a scribe."

"I—I'm afraid, I don't have that . . . privilege." I speak very carefully, so as not to offend.

There is a moment of silence. And then Arlenari frowns and

looks away from me. "You could learn," she repeats again, softly.

I look at her with a kind of informed pity that comes from being reconciled with hard reality.

"Even if I could," I say in a very quiet voice, "there is no time. The Sky Rock will be here soon, and the world will end for all of us. Not for *you*, My Imperial Lady, obviously. But, most likely, for me."

Princess Arlenari's frown deepens. "No," she says suddenly, with fierceness. "I do *not* accept it."

WE RETURN to the epic story recorded in the scroll. Arlenari continues to read, but something has changed in her manner. It is no longer entirely lighthearted. Periodically, she pauses, looks up at me with an intense, thoughtful glance, then continues yet again.

Eventually I find myself getting rather drowsy. Not used to so much passive inactivity during the afternoon, not to mention such a full stomach, I begin to doze off. I jolt awake, terribly embarrassed. Then, to keep myself alert, I make the effort to ask her more questions. Admittedly, the story itself is quite interesting, and she tells it very well, so the fault lies only with me.

"What is the difference between a Uraeus and a Draguos?" I ask. "Why is the warrior more afraid of fighting the Draguos?"

"It's mostly a matter of the elements they control," Arlenari explains. "The Gravity Uraeus can cause the earth to buckle and collapse unto itself, forming great sinkholes. It can cause earthquakes and change the landscape. But the Uraeus is merely a giant worm, a snake."

I nod.

"On the other hand, the Magmatic Draguos can call up fiery magma from the bowels of the earth, causing it to erupt and rise to the surface as lava. The lava burns and annihilates anyone and anything in its way except the Draguos itself, which can eat it safely. Then it can belch and breathe flames. The Draguos can also use the lava flows to carve out monstrous tunnels in the earth's crust."

Immediately, I'm reminded of the incredible and very real tunnel network underneath the City of Poseidon and supposedly, the entire world. . . .

"The tunnels formed by lava can be used by the Draguos to travel anywhere in the underworld," Arlenari continues. "Even the Uraeus can use those tunnels to crawl. But the Draguos is not a snake, but something more. It has a long serpent body but also appendages on which it can walk, and feelers in its head with which to sense. The Draguos can also fly, with or without wings!"

"So then, is the Draguos a kind of *shar-ta-haak* lizard?" I ask.

"Indeed, maybe," the Princess answers with a faraway look. "Who knows? The origin of this legend is lost in the deepest past. Maybe the Draguos came from the sky, hence the possibility of wings. Maybe it needed no wings to fly, and can swim through the air like a sky fish."

And now I recall the recent conversations I overheard at the Bisfuri estate, mentioning the word *draguos*. The wild people living on a distant continent mistook Lord Bisfuri's flying ship for a fiery *draguos*, and now there are worker riots. . . .

I shake my head, putting all these strange, unrelated pieces together. Furthermore, I'm no longer sleepy because my bladder is terribly full, and I need to answer the call of nature.

"My Imperial Lady," I interrupt as politely as I may, with some embarrassment. "Would it be possible for me to briefly visit the service and staff area?"

Arlenari pauses. "Why?"

I bite my lip. "Well, um, my apologies, but I need to—well, I drank so much tea and now I need to go and find the latrine."

"Just use my toilet. It's down the hall." Arlenari pushes the scroll aside and gets up. "Come, I'll show you."

"Oh, but I couldn't!" I say with haste, feeling heat rise in my cheeks. "That would be wrong and inappropriate. I'll just go find the staff quarters—"

"Nonsense, come!" Arlenari walks toward the door of the library.

I cannot help but follow.

THE IMPERIAL BATHROOM and toilet area is again beyond my imagination. Everything is marble and gold trim, and there are amazing towels, bottles of lotions, perfume, and artfully formed pieces of soap. There is a huge sunken pond in the floor, filled with running water, stalls with endless shower fixtures, and an elimination toilet seat like a throne.

Princess Arlenari points me to the chamber, then exits, leaving me to myself. Out of habit, I check the sparkling-clean seat for bugs, then want to slap myself for being such a *hoohvak*.

When I'm done, I return down the hall to find Arlenari at the doors of the library, waiting for me.

"Shall we continue?" she says.

For a moment I consider, but then catch the bright orange light of sunset coming from the front room where we arrived.

"My Imperial Lady, please forgive me." I cringe on the inside, because this kind of thing is very difficult to say to an Imperial Princess, even one as kind and understanding as she is. "Your story is the most wondrous story I've ever heard, and I enjoyed hearing it with all my heart. But it is late, and even the express bus takes a long time. . . . I do need to return home and help my Grandmother with supper, then I have to work tomorrow—"

"Oh, I see." Princess Arlenari's eyes lose their joyful energy.

"I am so sorry," I repeat. "I really should be going—"

And then out of nowhere, the Princess makes a little excited sound. "I know! I'll have my driver take us, and then it will be no time at all. I'm coming with you!"

For several heartbeats I am speechless. "What? My Imperial Lady—"

But Arlenari heads to the brightly lit front chamber and taps some kind of wall gadget near the door. She speaks into it. "I need a driver immediately. Have him meet me and my guest on the balcony."

"Oh—but—what—" I follow her stupidly, uttering unintelligible words.

"Come, Semmi!" the Princess interrupts me and crosses the room toward the ceiling-high windows burning with persimmon sunset, which I realize are also doors leading to the outside.

We step outside, into a warm evening breeze, and I find myself on a grand terrace balcony that stretches far in both directions along the Palace walls on this high level.

"The driver will be here within a daydream or two," Princess Arlenari says comfortably, squinting into the bright light. She walks toward the ornate balcony railing, then presses some hidden lever in the metal and stone. At once, a portion of the railing separates and descends outward, while a wide section of the floor extends forward, creating a platform big enough for a hover car.

I finally find my courage. "My Imperial Lady, please, no, I beg you. . . . You can't come! Trust me, you don't *want* to come where I live! I live in Denwen's Pit!"

Arlenari turns to look at me, her Kassiopei gold hair ruffled by the wind. "So what?"

"But that's all the way in Circle Ten!" I exclaim. "It's a hovel town, very poor, with some rough people, not safe at all for someone like you!"

"So, are you saying I will not be safe with you and your family?"

"Of course not, I don't mean that at all, My Imperial Lady, but—"

"But what? My driver and the guard will make sure of my safety. Incidentally, you really don't need to say 'My Imperial Lady' every few words. It's rather tiresome to hear."

My mouth goes slack. "What should I call you then, My Imperial—"

Arlenari puts up her hand in a gesture to silence me, but there's a funny smile on her lips, almost as if she's about to share a secret with me. "You have my name."

"No! But I cannot speak it in such a manner!"

She thinks for a moment. "I suppose, yes, you cannot simply call me Arlenari in public because of Imperial Protocol. That is unfortunate. However—" and her smile returns, even more crafty. "I have a second name."

"You do?"

She nods. "Yes . . . I gave it to myself. My name is also *Arleana*. Ar-leh-ah-nah. No one else knows it. But now you do. Why? Because, why not? And since you now have my secret name, you're obligated to use it. But, only when we're alone."

"I—I am honored, My Imperial—" I cut myself off, and finish, "Arleana."

The Princess smiles widely at me. She then points at a dark speck in the sky approaching very quickly. "There's my driver."

The speck resolves into a black luxury hover car, painted with a sleek metallic finish. It lands soundlessly on the terrace platform before us. A door sails open, and a uniformed Imperial guard emerges.

He's a huge, muscular man with very pale skin and a bald head. He bows silently before Princess Arlenari. "Where to, my Imperial Princess?"

"Circle Ten, Denwen's Pit," she replies happily, then gets in the back seat of the car and beckons me to follow.

I pause momentarily to gauge the guard's reaction, but he is impeccably trained not to show emotion.

And so, I get in the car, and find myself sitting on the luxurious cushioned seat *right next* to the Kassiopei Princess of Imperial *Atlantida.*

THE GUARD GETS in behind us in the third-row seat, while I see the back of the driver's head ahead of us.

Unlike the guard, the driver reacts by turning around to glance at the Princess, and says, "Are you certain, My Imperial Lady? Did you say Denwen's Pit? That's all the way in Circle Ten—"

"Yes, very certain," she replies, then looks at me with a gleam of excitement.

"And where exactly in Denwen's Pit are we going?" the driver asks politely.

"Pit Row Twenty-Three," I say in a quiet voice. "House number five . . . on the left side of the street."

The driver nods, and we take off.

IT'S hard to describe the combination of perfect quiet of the hover car cabin interior and the wind-swept vehicle exterior, the wild speed of flying non-stop over the City during the final moments of glorious, waning sunset.

Our direction is generally southwest, and the Circles of land interspersed with mirror-bright canals flash by in the slightly tinted window through which I stare down at the landscape below.

It takes us about half an hour to arrive in Circle Ten, a trip that normally takes me anywhere from one-and-a-half to three hours. I watch the dark smokestacks of my neighborhood rise in columns all around, as the familiar cooking fires burn and artificial street illumination turns on in some places.

The sky is turning dark twilight blue overhead, and the last peach colors of sunset fade at the horizon beyond the end of our Circle. Coming down from such a high altitude right into Denwen's Pit instead of the usual bus stop at Circle Nine, for once I can see the outer City walls. Beyond the walls, the last canal encircles Poseidon like a grand moat, before some of it continues further out into the ocean. . . .

"There," I say, paying close attention to the familiar landmarks from such an unfamiliar vantage point above. "That's my street, I think!"

I recall the only other time I'd landed in a hover car so close to home. That was when *Ter* Bisfuri sent my Grandmother and me back home with a staff driver in a private household car, on that first day when he hired me. I wasn't paying much attention to anything that time, especially with the glare of daylight and the cloud of anxiety overwhelming me.

But now is somewhat different. The light is soft, near dusk. Maybe I've grown far too accustomed to the fine luxuries of the nobles, but I'm actually enjoying this ride.

The Imperial hover car descends quietly on my street, sails right up to our hovel, and maybe because of the dusk and time of evening, none of our immediate neighbors seem to notice.

It hovers in perfect silence about a foot off the ground, only sending up dust from the initial wind created on approach. The guard gets out first, casting a watchful eye over the empty street. He listens to the voices coming from some of the nearest yards where families cook their supper. Thankfully they are too preoccupied to hear us arrive.

I take a deep breath and emerge into the evening air. That's when the worry and anxiety and shame strike me hard. What will the Princess think once she sees everything? And I mean, *everything*.

Oh, holiest goddess Bastet, have mercy. . . .

Arlenari gets out of the car and stands next to me, looking around curiously. Her gaze is calm and fearless.

"My Imperial Lady, it might be best if I went ahead and checked the interior," the guard says.

But the Princess shakes her head. "No, wait here. Outside the door is sufficient. No need to frighten my hosts with your imposing appearance, Emzar."

"As you wish." But the guard's otherwise controlled face shows a flicker of concern, which I manage to catch, since I'm also bursting with stress.

Arlenari turns to me with a faint smile. "Shall we go inside?"

WITH A SLIGHTLY SHAKING HAND, I open the door to my home. *"Mei-Ma?"* I call out, and my voice cracks somewhat.

Bast! Suddenly, I have the pitiful voice of a coward.

My family are all out in the back yard, probably still cooking. Our tiny living room has no other light except for an occasional single candle which today is lit, because the media-box is still off.

"Mei-Ma! Papai! Uru!" I call out again, in a voice not quite my own, stepping inside, as my heart pounds. "Are you there?"

I turn around, and see that Princess Arlenari has come in right behind me. Her expression is full of repressed excitement.

"Yes, come, Semmi! Good that you're finally here," my Grandmother's voice sounds. "We have onion and lentil soup today. Come help me carry the pot—"

"We have a visitor, *Mei-Ma*," I say loudly again. "Would you please come out here?"

"A visitor? Already?" Grandmother hollers. "The media-box

is not on, they're too early. All right, bring them right in, we have plenty of soup, fortunately."

I cast a look of despair at the Princess, take a big breath and start to holler back. "This is an *important* visitor! Please, for the love of Bast, *Mei-Ma*, just come out here! Right now!"

"It's quite all right," Princess Arlenari tells me. "I will go to meet them."

And without waiting for me, the Imperial Princess of *Atlantida* walks through my pitiful living room and steps outside into our smoke-filled, onion-stinking back yard.

CHAPTER
FORTY-SIX

"Oh good," Grandmother says, as soon as she sees Princess Arlenari, followed closely by me, enter our yard.

Standing over our fire pit, Grandmother is getting ready to move the large kettle and not paying too much attention to the newly arrived. A few steps away, my brother Urumer is crouched over a bucket of water where he's rinsing out bowls. And my Father is sitting on the ground on top of a sack, waiting for the food and looking dazed, as usual.

"*Nefero niktos*—girl, you and Semmi can both help me carry the pot indoors. Your Father is too tired after digging all day, and claims his back is out, though I'm not convinced. Uru! Out of the way, little *sha*!"

Uru springs up and moves several steps back from the water bucket, clearing the path for the kettle's journey—first, onto the cooling stone for a few daydreams, and then onto the table in the living room where the pot will remain all night to avoid the insects and who knows what else that lurks outside in the dark. We'll be eating the leftovers in the morning.

"No, *Mei-Ma!*" I say loudly in despair, "This is—"

But the Princess puts up a hand to silence me, and says, "I am Arleana. It is nice to meet you."

Holy Bast! She just gave her secret name to Grandmother and Uru and Father. . . .

Grandmother glances in our direction with a sharp look, for the first time paying attention to the "visitor," then nods. "Arleana, you say? Very well, child. Now, come and help me here. You and Semmi can hold up the pot together."

"But—" I open my mouth.

Meanwhile, the Princess simply walks up to Grandmother, and stares at the kettle with its four handle knobs sticking out in opposite directions around the rim. "What must I do?" she asks. "Do I just take this handle—"

"No! Stop!" Both Grandmother and I yell. And by the grace of all the gods, the insane Imperial Princess halts before putting her bare hand on the scalding-hot metal.

"Merciful gods, girl! Haven't you ever picked up a boiling pot of soup before?" Amurabia scolds Arlenari loudly. "You need to use a thick cloth to protect your hands! Here!" And Grandmother points to a stack of clean rags lying in a little basket near the cooling stone.

"Oh," Arlenari says, pausing. "All right."

I rush toward her, grabbing three of the sack-cloth rags on my way, and stand on the other side of the fire pit.

"Here, My Imper—*Arleana*," I correct myself quickly. "Take this cloth, and put it over that knob, while I grab this one. See, like this. *Mei-Ma*, here's yours."

"The pot is full of soup, so heavier than usual, with all that water," Grandmother adds, looking closely at Arlenari's pristine hands, and possibly noting her very light brown skin which is that famous Imperial Kassiopei shade of pale, sunlit bronze and definitely lighter than mine.

It occurs to me, it's fortunate for her that the Princess is wearing an extremely plain linen dress and sandals. Even so, the sandals are very good quality, and the dress is of a superior fabric; at the least, an outfit worthy of an upper servant. My Grandmother, whose work is sewing and embroidering fabric, is likely to recognize the fine and expensive nature of this high-caliber linen material. . . .

There's also Arlenari's golden hair. It might be gathered in an ordinary tail behind her, but its exact color is somewhat unmistakable. Although, under these odd circumstances, it's easier to assume it's the result of an unusual gold dye. Because the alternative is unimaginable.

"Use the cloths now, girls. The three of us will all lift at the same time." Grandmother wraps the rag cloth I gave her around the bulky, long knob handle closest to her, winding the rag multiple times over the hot metal.

I do the same thing to the handle closest to me, slowly, demonstrating how it's done, and hoping that the Imperial Princess will understand and do the same.

Arlenari watches both me and Grandmother, then winds the rag the same way.

"Ready?" Grandmother asks, glancing from me to Arlenari.

"We carry it over there, and set it on that stone," I add quickly, just in case it's unclear.

"Good, now lift! Carefully!"

And we all take hold of the safely wrapped handles, and strain to raise the heavy kettle. Judging by her serious expression, Arlenari appears genuinely surprised by the weight. Meanwhile, I grunt and try to take up the bulk of the load to make it easier for her and Grandmother.

Grandmother and Arlenari are positioned together on one side, while I'm on the other side of the firepit, so I carefully edge my way around, still holding on to my handle.

With quick but careful steps, we carry the heavy, sloshing kettle several paces, and set it on the cooling stone with a deep clank.

Relief! Oh, gods, what relief!

I glance at Arlenari, and she seems somewhat . . . *amazed.* Indeed, she looks ridiculously satisfied.

It's as if she has never lifted a heavy object before, never in her life performed a menial labor task.

She hasn't, I remind myself.

"Well done, everyone," Grandmother says, wiping her hands together. "Uru, bring the dishes and the ladle. We'll pour the fresh soup here and take our bowls inside while the pot cools down even more. Filling our bowls now will lighten the pot, too, by the time we carry it indoors. And the bread should be ready soon; it's baking in the clay pot over there, in the coals."

After resting the ladle on top of the kettle rim, my little brother approaches us with a stack of our old wooden bowls. There are only four, since no one planned for company tonight, and our regular neighborhood guests usually don't come here to eat but to watch the media-box.

He pauses, coming to the realization after handing one bowl to Grandmother, one to Father, and keeping one for himself. There's only one dish left, so he appears unsure of what to do.

"Uru, give this to the guest," I say sternly. "Then go find *Mamai's* old bowl and I'll use it. Go on!"

Uru turns to Arlenari. "Here, take it, Arle—what's your name?"

"Arleana," the Princess repeats, looking at Uru with curiosity, as she accepts his proffered bowl.

"Yeah, okay." My brother makes a little grimace at her, then sticks his tongue out. "I'm Urumer, and you have a *garooi* shiny head."

"Uru!" I exclaim in sudden panic. "Watch your mouth! You don't speak like that to guests, *hoohvak!*"

"Yes, I do!" Uru snickers and runs off to get Mother's bowl.

"So sorry about that," I mumble, turning to Arlenari. "My little brother is a yappy fool with a filthy *sha* mouth."

Instead of being offended, Arlenari's eyes are brimming with excitement.

Grandmother watches the exchange closely and says nothing.

Meanwhile, my Father stands up with a tired grunt and comes up to us, bowl in hand. He stands before the kettle, unusually hunched over (which makes me think his claim to having a back injury is real) and looks at what's inside the pot.

"This is Guzum, my Father," I say to Princess Arlenari, trying to sound casual. I haven't exactly introduced anyone to her, at least not in a formal manner befitting her station, which makes me anxious.

Arlenari's expression remains open and curious as she glances at my Father and his stooping back covered by a worn, dirty work shirt with dried sweat stains on it.

He, meanwhile, stirs the soup with the ladle, picking out chunks, and fills his bowl without any reaction. Not even a grunt. When done, he wordlessly nods to the Princess, the way he might greet any girl from our neighborhood, and simply walks past her, heading indoors with his food.

Grandmother watches him go, and takes up the soup ladle.

"And this is Amurabia, my Grandmother," I continue my belated, awkward introductions.

"Come closer, girl. Hold your bowl with both hands, and I'll pour your soup, since you're a guest," Grandmother says all at once, dipping the ladle into the pot. At the same time, she taps Arlenari on her elbow.

"Oh," Arlenari says and offers up her bowl, as told.

"Hold it in place, don't slosh it." And Grandmother empties the full ladle into Arlenari's bowl, then dips again to fill the bowl all the way. "Now go on inside, child. Find yourself a seat on the bench next to Guzum. Careful, soup's hot. We'll bring in the bread shortly."

"Yes, please go in. . . ." I echo my Grandmother and widen my eyes meaningfully at the Princess.

Thankfully, Arlenari does as she's told. Holding her bowl before her, she makes her way inside the house. I have a crazy urge to follow her and make sure everything is all right, just in case she somehow spills the soup and scalds herself. But I also don't want to make Amurabia suspicious by my weird behavior. So, I stay back, holding in my anxiety, and let my Grandmother fill her own bowl—which she hands to me instead.

"Take it, Semmi." Grandmother nods at me. "I'll just use Eige's bowl once Uru finds it."

"Are you sure?"

"Yes. Now, go in and keep your new friend company. I'll bring in the bread."

As I head indoors, I hear Grandmother holler in my wake, "Go ahead and turn on the media-box!"

WE SETTLE in on the long bench in front of the media-box. Father sits in his frequent spot at the far end, with Arlenari on his right and me next to her. Uru finds our Mother's bowl and runs out into our back yard so that he and Grandmother can finally get their soup.

Meanwhile, I sing the tone sequence to call up the media-box programming.

The media-box turns on, illuminating the room properly. Father lifts the bowl to his mouth impatiently and begins to slurp and blow at his steaming-hot soup, not even waiting for the bread.

I glance at the Princess at my side to see if she's bothered by my Father's abysmal lack of manners, something of which I'm painfully aware, especially now that I'm employed by the elites.

Apparently, not. She stiffly holds the bowl in her lap, and simply waits, looking uncertain. With a sudden pang of new anxiety, I worry that this simple food of ours is not appropriate for her. . . .

Moments later, Grandmother and Uru enter, carrying their soup bowls. Amurabia also brings the clay pot with the flatbreads.

I spring up quickly to help, leaving my soup bowl on my seat and take the pot from her, letting Grandmother sit down at my other side. I lift the steaming lid and the freshly baked aroma of wheat bread fills the room. To be honest, I'm still full from eating amazing Palace food all afternoon, but that fresh bread smell makes me salivate.

I pass around the small, round pieces of flatbread to everyone, starting with Grandmother herself, then Father and Uru. So as not to act too eager and quell any suspicions my family might have about her, I turn to Arlenari last.

The Princess receives her bread and sets it on her lap next to her soup bowl.

I pick up my own soup bowl in haste and sit back down next to her. "Try to eat," I tell her softly.

Princess Arlenari looks down at her bowl then looks up at me. "Is there a utensil? A spoon?"

I gulp. Not sure how to tell her, but we own only a couple of eating spoons, and we take turns with them. Right now, I think Uru is using one, and the other is somewhere in the dirty dishwater bucket. Normally we just drink soup, and dip the bread to sop up the chunks.

"You don't need a spoon for this," I whisper to her. "Drink it and use your bread to pick up the pieces."

"Interesting. Is that how soup is eaten in Denwen's Pit?" she whispers back.

"For the most part, yes." And I demonstrate by lifting the bowl to my lips and sipping.

Then I almost spit out the liquid in my mouth, and start

coughing, because in that same moment, the media-box main screen shows a feed from the Imperial Palace. . . .

It's a recorded Court function, with Crown Prince Narmeradat and the Imperatris Merneit seated on lesser thrones in a garden setting, talking to some officials. And right behind them, there's Princess Arlenari, standing near a flower bush in the sunlight and playing with a little spinning wind-toy that gently flutters in the breeze.

Holy Bastet!

I overcome my choking and freeze, glancing quickly at my family members, then at Arlenari herself, who seems entirely unaffected—except for a barely perceptible sound of annoyance she makes at the sight of herself on screen. Neither Guzum nor Amurabia notice or show any signs of recognizing our royal guest, and simply continue drinking their soup.

I quietly exhale in relief. At least the Imperial Princess is better dressed in that recording than she is now, so the resemblance is not as noticeable. And once again, there's the matter of her being out of context.

That's when Uru, seated on the other end next to Grandmother, turns around and leans in our direction.

"*Ei*, Arleana!" he says, pointing at the screen with a teasing boy laugh. "There's your shiny hair! And you look just like that weird, crazy princess!"

This time, everyone in the room stops eating and turns to stare at our guest.

Except for the voices on the media-box, there is absolute silence.

Arlenari takes one delicate sip from her soup bowl, lowers it in her lap, then looks at Uru.

"Actually, I was trying very hard to be as normal as possible that day," she says. "But it was windy outside, and I really wanted to try out the spinner. Much more interesting than listening to my Imperial Mother and Narmeradat discuss the upcoming Heru arrival."

And the Princess picks up her soup again and takes another polite sip.

My Father, seated on the other side of her, drops his bowl, splattering what little soup is left on the front of his shirt and pants, while the bowl strikes the dull earthen floor and rolls away.

Uru's mouth falls open.

As for my unshakeable Grandmother, Amurabia merely nods. "I had a feeling we had a very fine guest with us tonight. Not sure how or why we deserve such honor, but . . . welcome to our home, Imperial Princess. I hope the soup is to your liking."

"Are you really the Princess? What are you doing here? No, I don't believe—" Uru chatters wildly, having gotten up from his seat and abandoned his soup dish precariously on the floor at his feet.

"Sit down, boy!" my Father says out of nowhere, in a loud voice which is not at all typical of him. I notice, his hands are shaking, and he's moved back along the bench, as far away as possible from Princess Arlenari, short of falling off the end.

But Uru is not to be contained. "Who are you? Why did you come here? Did you get lost? You said your name is Arleana! Did you fly from the Palace?"

"Uru, if you don't shut your mouth, I will beat you for real!" I exclaim, while my heartbeat races with panic.

"Enough, Uru!" Grandmother takes Uru firmly by his skinny arm and pulls him back down to the bench next to her. The boy struggles for a moment then stills in place with an impatient frown.

Princess Arlenari watches all our reactions, and then, in the first moment of silence, says, "I am not lost. I came here with Semmi because I wanted to see how it is. And yes, we took a car from the Palace. My driver is presently waiting outside, along with the guard."

"Oh, blessed Hathor," Grandmother sighs. "You mean there are men waiting outside all this time?"

"Yes, it is their job." Arlenari looks at my Grandmother with an almost surprised expression.

"Job or not, I expect they're tired and hungry." Amurabia shakes her head. She then pats Uru on his back and tells him, "Uru, go out there right now and bring those poor men inside. Tell them we have lentil and onion soup."

"Wait, *Mei-Ma*," I speak up. "Not sure that's such a good idea. They really do have staff jobs, and it's their duty to make sure the Imperial Princess is safe—"

"Nonsense. They can guard her from here—"

"What about the fancy hover car?" I insist. "Who's going to guard it?"

"Ooh, I gotta see the car!" Uru is up from his seat and rushes to the door.

Princess Arlenari watches my little brother with a mixture of curiosity, amusement, and confusion.

In that moment, my Father apparently decides he has to stand up also and do *something*. And so Guzum rises from the bench and backs away, swaying on his feet. Then he bows at the waist and with some difficulty gets down on his knees before the Princess. He lowers his head all the way, touching his forehead to the floor, muttering, "Begging mercy . . . Imperial Princess, mercy on us!"

Arlenari parts her lips in surprise.

Amurabia meanwhile says, "Guzum, what are you doing? Stand up, fool, now you're embarrassing the household and our royal guest."

"Yes, please do stand up," Arlenari says. "This is entirely unnecessary."

But my Father whimpers pitifully and shakes his head, still not daring to lift his head to look up.

"Bastet!" I exclaim and leap up from my seat yet again, almost dropping my own soup bowl. "Apologies, My Imperial Princess, but he's likely drunk and more confused than usual."

In haste I move toward the pathetic man, grab him around the waist and elbows, and attempt to pull him up. *"Papai!* Get up! Up, now!" I hiss loudly near his ear.

"No, no . . ." he mumbles, but finally, with my help, staggers upright. His expression is dazed and fearful as he merely stands in place, keeping his gaze lowered, and doesn't attempt to glance in Arlenari's direction.

I give up, and swiftly return to my seat next to Arlenari.

In that moment the outside door opens, and Uru returns, alone.

"They won't come," Uru complains. "The guard said thank you but he must stay outside. And the driver won't leave the car."

Grandmother shakes her head again. "Oh well, not much we can do then."

There's an uncomfortable pause.

Princess Arlenari watches all of us. "I'm very sorry," she says with a touch of sadness. "I can see it was probably wrong of me to come here and cause a disruption in your family. I did not think. I am . . . sorry, Semmi."

She stands up. "I'll go now. Thank you for the delicious soup."

"Oh, no, not at all!" I rush to speak. "Please forgive all of us, My Imperial Princess! You honor us by being here. Please forgive my family. They were just surprised, that's all!"

"Surprised, yes," my Grandmother adds softly. "Now, it doesn't mean we want you to leave. Indeed, we're happy to have you here, Imperial Princess. Please, stay as long as you like, especially now that the surprise is over."

Arlenari stops in uncertainty.

"Come, sit, sit," Grandmother nods and motions with her hand toward the bench. "Had I known you were coming, I would've baked my *eos* pies. Ask anyone in Denwen's Pit, I make the best *eos* pies in all of Poseidon. . . ."

Arlenari sits back down.

"Guzum, in the name of all the gods, don't just stand there," Grandmother says in a firmer voice. "Either go lie down in my room, or sit back down and be a grown man."

My Father makes a move toward the bench, but hesitates, appearing genuinely fearful of sitting next to Princess Arlenari.

"Uru," my smart Grandmother adds. "You go sit over on that end, between your Father and the Imperial Princess. Help him along. Right now, go!"

And Uru, who's been tarrying near the door, quickly moves to our Father's side and leads him back to the bench, sitting down strategically between him and the Princess. Then the silly boy grins widely and turns his face to stare at Arlenari, up-close.

The Princess ostensibly ignores him and instead glances at me with an unreadable expression.

In the meantime, I can see my brother slowly inching closer to her. . . . And then his sneaky little hand moves around from behind, in an outrageous attempt to touch the back of her golden hair gathered in a *sesemet* tail.

"Uru, *behave!*" I exclaim, horrified.

In that same instant, Arlenari suddenly reacts by snatching Uru's hand with her own and swatting it away, then in lightning reflex slaps him on the forehead lightly with the palm of her hand.

"Oww!" Uri yelps and moves away, stunned.

He's not the only one. I stare at them in disbelief, expecting Imperial outrage. Instead, Arlenari turns to look at me again, and she is laughing.

"What?" she says, chortling. "You don't think I know how to deal with little *sha* brothers when we were growing up?"

I can hear everyone around me letting out held breaths. Even my Father stops shaking and looks up in dazed curiosity.

Grandmother makes a little sound of amusement, then says, "Well. Seems that all brothers are the same, even Imperial ones."

Arlenari nods, smiling at all of us. "Oron always pulled my ribbons. And Narmeradat was even worse. He liked to snap my long hair from the back. So, I would hit him, sometimes on the nose."

"I think it's time to boil the tea kettle," Amurabia says, and I see the corners of her mouth curving upward with uncommon humor.

AND SO, we spend the next hour having tea in our family's mismatched drinkware—worn clay mugs and wooden grails—and watching the media-box casually. Fortunately, no one else from the neighborhood knocks on our door tonight, so we don't have to worry about explaining the presence of our Imperial guest.

Having accepted the best drinking vessel in the house from my Grandmother, Princess Arlenari sips her tea delicately, with understated elegance, the same way she handled her soup. This is probably the result of her Imperial fine manners.

It occurs to me, Arlenari has relaxed completely. She makes occasional, lighthearted commentary about what's on the screen, including a few unexpected tidbits of private knowledge and revelations about specific members of the nobility. Lord so-and-so wheezes loudly when he eats. And Lady so-and-so wears so many thick layers of Face Art that pieces of paint chip off and fall on her clothes. . . .

We listen to her pleasant vocal cadence with fascination. It is said that members of the Imperial Kassiopei Dynasty have remarkable voices, imbued by the gods with power and the ability to affect and command . . . and I can hear it now, in hers, no matter how subtle.

Indeed, I observe the faces of my family, and can see the peculiar effect on all of them, a kind of soft growing wonder. They have relaxed also, forgetting the impossibility of our company.

Eventually Uru yawns deeply, and my Father starts nodding off.

Arlenari gets up, and thanks us for the evening. Turning to my Grandmother in particular, she inclines her head. "I will not forget your hospitality, *Taq* Amurabia," she says formally. "Your family and everything in this house brought me an evening of joy. Again, thank you. *Nefero niktos* to this gracious house and its hosts."

"Oh, please, I'm no *Taq*, just an ordinary woman. You honor me far too much," my Grandmother protests with a smile, standing up from her seat to bow lightly. "Remember, you are welcome to visit any time. Just be sure to warn us ahead, so I can make the *eos* pies."

I follow Arlenari outside, with Uru tagging along.

Our little street is quite dark, but there's enough *niktos* radiance from remote artificial illumination and starlight that the stern face of the guard comes into view. His alert eyes glitter as he immediately opens the car door for the Princess.

"Semmi, I must thank you in particular." She pauses near the entrance to our hovel, looking at me closely. "You've given me a wonderful day I'll never forget. Please, return to the Palace again and see me."

"Of course, My Imperial Princess," I say, starting to curtsey.

But she puts her hand up to interrupt me. "No . . . it's *Arleana*, remember," she whispers with a secret smile in her eyes.

Then, Arlenari turns to Uru. "*Nefero niktos*, Urumer. But if you ever attempt to touch my hair again, you will suffer my *insane* wrath."

Uru's expression fills with fear. "Oh . . . I'm sorry! Imperial Princess, you're not insane, I didn't mean—" He sticks his knuckles in his mouth.

At which Arlenari chuckles again, shaking with laughter.

She throws us one final mischievous glance, then gets in the hover car. Moments later, the vehicle rises into the night sky.

Uru and I stand at the door of our hovel, in the silent darkness, stunned by the enormity of what we've just experienced.

Then we return indoors, and the family babble begins. Grandmother, Father, Uru, myself, we chatter and analyze, question every detail, and wonder. . . . At some point, my family even notices my fine new Bisfuri uniform. So, I end up telling them about my visit to the Palace, but without revealing the nature of my secret tasks on behalf of *Ter* Bisfuri.

I don't know how any of us manage to sleep at all that night.

MORNING COMES MUCH TOO SOON. And it's not just any morning, but the day of the Bisfuri Domestic Service Competition.

Despite the sleepless excitement of the night before, Uru and I both wake up before dawn, and get ready in haste, since we must be there by eighth hour of Ra when the Competition is scheduled to begin.

Our Grandmother and Father are still sleeping in exhaustion from the excitement of the previous night when we close the door behind us and head outside into the blue twilight of early dawn. I'm wearing my Bisfuri uniform, still in near-pristine condition after an easy day at the Palace yesterday, and my employee badge is safely in my pocket.

Uru has his cleanest shirt and pants on, and he even lets me pat down his hair and unkink some of it with a proper comb.

"Now remember, best behavior, all right, *chazuf*?" I warn him as we board the hover bus at Circle Nine. "Don't embarrass me at my place of work."

"I won't," he whines, plopping down in the seat next to me. And then he looks at me with a sneaky smile. "Will Princess Arleana be there?"

"What? No!" I widen my eyes at him. "Why in Bastet's sacred name would the Princess be at the Bisfuri Competition? And don't call her Arleana, that's her secret name."

But my brother giggles, looking around at the few other passengers who are with us at this early stage of the bus ride. And he mumbles under his breath. "I know a Princess, I know a Princess. . . ."

"Shush!" I tap Uru on the side of his *hoohvak* forehead.

BY THE TIME we arrive at the verdant shores of Circle Two, the sun is up, and our bus is overcrowded with people we've picked up along the way. Looks like everyone is here for the Bisfuri Competition. When we get out, the usually empty bus stop and the tree-lined gravel path of the estate is already filled with crowds from all Circles of Poseidon.

Everyone is headed in the direction of the main buildings, as we've been instructed. Most people around us are not wearing Bisfuri uniforms. I feel a moment of pride and belonging as I walk the familiar path with my head held high, attired in my fine uniform, and with my little brother at my side.

When we arrive at the gates, the crowds are immense, and the black-clad guards stand before them, blocking our passage and not letting anyone inside.

Those of us in Bisfuri uniforms however, get singled out.

"You, and you, step closer." A guard motions to me and

several other employees, and we squeeze our way forward, near the front. I pull Uru along by the hand, not letting him from my side. Until we know what comes next, I want him to have every advantage possible in this Competition.

It's almost eighth hour of Ra, according to the time on my employee badge. We stare past the gates at the buildings, where only a few staff members are visible in the distance, and few others are hurrying about. However, additional guards are lined up inside the gates, and registration tables have been moved right up to the gate entrance, forming a long row, so that you have to walk past them to enter the grounds.

The giant smartboard with all the Houses and lists of active Competitions has also been relocated from its spot near the wall of the rear building and now hovers freely in the center of the courtyard, visible from every direction.

Then I see the familiar figure of Benaten Bisfuri walking from the main building toward us. He is wearing a fine jacket and pants (as opposed to the simple workman clothing which he usually prefers), and is attended by two staff officials carrying a large chest.

Moments later, Lord Muutat Bisfuri himself arrives, accompanied, unfortunately, by Lady Ashura Ximunat. They stop not far from the gates in an observation spot, and are immediately flanked by security guards.

Both are finely dressed as befitting their rank, and the Lady wears a pale rose dress of iridescent fabric with a tight-fitting bodice. Her dark hair is artfully arranged in an elegant hairdo, and her bared arms and wrists are covered in gold bracelets that blindingly catch the sunlight.

Benaten walks up to the gates and directs the guards to prepare to open them.

He then taps a voice amplifier on the front of his jacket and addresses the crowd. His rich, low voice fills the courtyard, and for a moment I feel its tangible, soothing presence, like a warm embrace, all the way to my bones. . . .

"On behalf of the Great House Bisfuri, welcome to the Bisfuri Domestic Service Competition," he says. "As soon as we open the gates, you will proceed in orderly fashion to the registration tables and confirm your attendance with the staff. But first, here are your instructions for the Competition itself."

As Lord Bisfuri and Lady Ximunat stand watching, *Ter* Bisfuri motions to the two staff who open the chest. Inside are short wooden sticks, about the length of a man's forearm, brightly painted in various domestic service tassel colors such as messenger-red, kitchen-yellow, general servant-pink, and more.

The two staff members take out the various sticks, one at a time, and lift each one high above their heads to demonstrate to the onlookers.

"Wooden tokens such as these have been hidden all around the estate grounds," Benaten continues. "There are five hundred of them, in total. However, only three hundred fortunate souls can be selected for Bisfuri Domestic Service under various roles.

"Your task is to search the interior grounds, on this side of this fence, and bring a token here to the registration area as soon as you find one. Don't go inside any of the buildings; they are off limits. The first three hundred of you will be allowed to proceed to the second task.

"However, not everyone will succeed at the second task. Therefore, the rest of you with a token may wait here to be picked as alternates. You will be given a chance to compete in the second task, in place of those disqualified, until all three hundred spots are filled.

"And now, you have exactly one hour to find a token. Proceed to be verified, and begin!"

The gates open, and the crowd surges forward all around us.

My heart starts pounding with anxiety as I pull Uru by the hand and we are among the first to rush past the gates.

U ru and I run to the registration table, and I quickly give the Bisfuri official my name and thumb print. Then I shove Uru ahead of me and give his name and our family relationship.

The official casts a long glance upon my brother, but then observes my staff uniform and nods. "Thumb print, boy," he says mildly. "Next time, please register in person."

And we continue to the estate grounds.

As we move beyond the tables and the line of guards, we pass *Ter* Bisfuri who stands watching the incoming crowd. Our gazes meet, and his impassive, unreadable face momentarily comes alive with energy. His lips curve in a faint smile, and he almost imperceptibly nods at me.

A sudden rush of heat strikes my cheeks, and I bow my head in haste as I move past him. And then Uru and I are free to begin our task.

As we step beyond the line of guards, along with everyone else, we stare in passing at the container filled with the painted wooden tokens. It's our one chance to study up-close the items we must seek.

"Listen, Uru," I say, as we begin walking. "We have an advantage."

"How?" my brother asks.

"I work here!" I hiss in a loud whisper. "I know some of the layout, the buildings."

"We're not supposed to go inside the buildings."

"I know that. But I'm familiar with the land, the yards, the hillsides, and more. . . ." I pause, watching dozens of people already running past us. "Those of us who are employees all have that advantage. So, we have a better idea where things might be hidden."

"Okay, so what do we do?" Uru looks at me with impatience.

"You're going to follow me, and stay at my side!" I give him a stern look. "Don't go off on your own. First, we'll circle the entire area inside the fence so that you'll get an idea of the layout of this place. I'll show you everything. Then we'll split up to cover more ground. Understand?"

"Yeah, let's go."

And we start running.

IT TAKES us about a quarter of an hour to trace the fence perimeter and then crisscross the major landmarks. As the sun rises in the sky, and the morning heats up, we hurry along walkways between buildings, venture into small private gardens, terraces, courtyards, the stables and animal exercise yard (which makes me think of the *pegasei* and wonder if they need to be fed, but there's no time for that kind of worry; I need to focus on the task at hand). Then we race past the tiered fountains and ponds toward the hillside.

There are people everywhere, doing the same thing we are. So far, no one seems to have located any of the colorful tokens. Occasionally, I see other Bisfuri uniformed staff, and everyone is looking closely at the ground, squeezing through bushes and shrubbery, and some are even overturning stones. A few people start climbing trees and looking among the branches.

And then, come the excited cries. One by one, competitors are finding the tokens. One man not a few steps ahead of us, turns a flower vase and finds a bright pink token stuck in the soil between the roses.

Uru curses loudly, expressing his frustration. "That *chazuf* just found one! It was right there!"

"It's okay, you'll find the next one." I try to reassure him, feeling the exasperation on his behalf. "Soon! Keep looking. . . ."

"Time to split up?" Uru says sullenly. "I already know the layout. I can do it faster on my own."

I nod. "All right. But, be careful! And try not to damage any property. As soon as you find one, return to registration, don't wait for me—"

"See you!" my brother exclaims, and sets off running like the wind.

I take a deep breath and detour in a different direction.

I WANDER AIMLESSLY for another quarter of an hour, this time focusing not on the ground but at waist-level objects and above, looking at garden benches and statuary, at small nooks and tops of staircases with railings, and places between buildings. Any burst of color catches my eye, while rising anxiety fills me with a sickening, gnawing sensation in the pit of my stomach.

The hour is almost at the halfway point, and I've found nothing. . . . So little time!

This deceptively simple Competition is turning out to be more difficult and frustrating than I imagined.

As I walk quickly, I notice that we, the competitors, are not alone here. A few guards patrol, probably to make sure that everything is in order, and no strangers enter the private buildings.

I also observe several well-dressed nobles strolling along the gravel paths. Unlike us, they walk at a leisurely pace, laughing and chatting among themselves. I hear their talk, in snatches, about some gathering at the pavilion, with refreshments for the guests.

It appears that Lord Bisfuri has incorporated an entertainment event for the elites into the Domestic Service Competition.

So . . . they're here to gawk at us, while we run around like desperate fools, overturning rocks.

My thoughts take a dark turn, and I kick at a small pile of freshly cut grass and weeds that the gardeners have not had time to remove. Contrary to my hope, there's nothing underneath.

That's when I see Girsul jogging in my direction. He waves at me and matches my stride.

"Any luck?" he asks me.

"No, nothing." I frown. "My brother Uru is also out there somewhere, searching."

"Nothing here either. Wherever they hid those things, they did a fine job."

"I wonder who was put in charge of hiding them?" I muse out loud. "I'd like to wring that *chazuf's* neck."

"Yeah." Girsul looks distracted. "I just came back from registration, and there are maybe fifty people who have found any tokens so far. I also talked to *Ter* Aten, and he said that at this rate they might have to give us more time."

"That would be nice." I wipe sweat from my forehead, feeling the heat of the sun bake my skin despite the fresh breeze. "I thought, as employees we might have an advantage."

Girsul bends down to examine the ground near a dense row of shrubs, without any success. "Nah. Doesn't seem to make a difference. Anyway, *Ter* Aten's headed this way; said he was going to walk the grounds to see how everyone's doing. Lord Bisfuri instructed him to check on things. As if he could do anything to speed things along. . . ."

"I overheard there's something happening in the long pavilion," I say. "Saw some nobles heading there. Maybe that's where these accursed tokens are hidden!"

Girsul makes a sound of disgust. "Yeah, they're having a garden party, today of all days. I think *Ter* Eham is there, dealing with it."

We wade into some raised flowerbeds, watching the ground underfoot and taking care not to crush too many plants, then make our way into a private stretch of park behind one of the older buildings.

There's a small courtyard here, with stone benches, sculpted flower vases, and dappled shade from trees filtering out most of the sun. As we approach from beyond the trees, I see Benaten Bisfuri enter the courtyard from another direction. He is walking slowly, looking down at a digital tablet in his hands and not paying much attention to his surroundings.

Just as Girsul and I begin to draw near our employer, we see a woman in an iridescent pale rose dress hastening toward him.

It is Lady Ashura Ximunat.

I curse softly at the sight of her.

"Sh-h-h. . . ." Girsul puts up his hand, motioning for me to be quiet.

I shut up, and we both stop, hidden by the thick, aged tree trunks and shrubbery.

"That woman is awful!" I mouth the words silently.

"I know," Girsul whispers back. "Just wait. Let her finish her business, and we'll see *Ter* Aten after she leaves. They say she punishes and dismisses servants for nothing, so I don't want her attention on me, if I can help it."

I nod, thinking, Girsul doesn't know the half of it. He wasn't present when Lady Ashura made lewd advances to Benaten, tried to touch him, and worse. *Ugh!*

My blood starts to boil at the very thought. . . .

I decide to tell this to Girsul later. For now, we must stand and wait until it's over, whatever it is.

"Benaten!" Lady Ximunat calls out softly.

Ter Bisfuri lifts his head and freezes in place. Even from this distance I can see the sudden guarded coldness in his eyes.

She comes close and stops before him.

"Lady Ashura, what is it?" he asks, lowering his tablet.

But the lady looks up at him, saying nothing, and begins to smile.

At least three heartbeats pass in silence, with only the breeze moving the leaves in the trees and the distant voices of various people elsewhere on the estate grounds.

"Such a beautiful day, and you are working so very hard, my . . . even more beautiful boy," she says at last, placing her hand firmly on his arm and rubbing it up and down lightly over the jacket sleeve.

"How may I help you, My Lady?" Benaten says in a dead voice, with a long glance at her hand presently *touching* him.

"You can accompany me to the pavilion. Your dearest Father is to meet us there, eventually. He has some business to attend to before enjoying the company of our fine guests."

"My Father instructed me to watch the Competition and keep track of the numbers," he replies, taking a measured step back, so that the lady must either step closer to keep her hand where it is, or release him.

Ashura chooses to not let go. She steps along with him, this time running her hand up to his shoulder and squeezing it with her elegant, clawed fingers.

"The Competition is not going anywhere," she says in a purring voice. "However, I do need to get to the pavilion. And with so many strangers on the property, it isn't safe, not without a strong young man such as yourself to protect me."

"We have guards for that." *Ter* Bisfuri replies, like ice. "What happened to the guards accompanying you, My Lady?"

"I appear to have lost them somehow." Lady Ashura glances once behind her, carelessly. "Indeed, they are incompetent, and should be dismissed."

Girsul makes a tiny, sympathetic sound and turns to me, his eyes widening, as if to say, *I told you so.*

"The guards hired by this House are some of the best professionals, and are not to be disparaged," Benaten says, and his low voice dips in a manner I've not heard from him before, not ever. It is pure *anger.*

"Well then, I'm sure they are, if you say so," Lady Ashura continues in a flippant manner. "But regardless, I will have you at my side. Stop whatever it is you are doing, and come with me."

"I can't do that. I am otherwise preoccupied." Benaten looks down at her with a steady, unblinking gaze. He is undaunted. "However, I will call the guards here to take you safely to your destination. Be so kind as to sit down here and wait, while I make the call." And he points to the nearest bench and takes out his comm badge.

"Oh, come now," Lady Ashura suddenly exclaims in a tone of annoyance. "You cannot be this naïve, boy! I thought you were more worldly, considering how much time, rumor has it, you spend with *amretene* whores. You want this as much as I do—"

And suddenly she wraps both hands around his neck and pulls him toward her, pressing herself against him, and lowering his head forcibly to her mouth for a fierce, hungry kiss.

The kiss lasts only a moment, because Benaten Bisfuri makes a deep sound and pushes Lady Ashura away from him. She staggers backward, barely recovering her balance, with a surprised exclamation of fury.

In the next heartbeat, Lady Ashura strikes Benaten across his cheek with the palm of her hand. We can hear the resounding *slap* from where we stand.

But he catches her wrist and then wrings it roughly, pulling it downward before she can slap him again . . . or take another breath, or comprehend what is happening.

His vigilante training taking over.

"Don't *ever* do that again," he says in a killing voice, still grasping her by the wrist. "You betray and shame my Father, and I will not stand for it."

"How *dare* you!" the lady cries, wrenching her hand away. "How dare you reject me!"

"I reject you before all the gods! If you ever touch me in such a way again, I will inform my Father directly." Benaten is looking at her with a blazing expression, and his anger is palpable. "The first time it happened, I let it slide, hoping for a misunderstanding. Hoping you were confused, drunk—*anything*. But never again."

And without another word, Benaten Bisfuri turns his back on Lady Ximunat and strides away quickly, even as she calls in his wake, "No, you *cannot*! Think what you're throwing away! *Benaten!*"

Lady Ashura stands there, breathing fast. Then she adds calmly, "Very well. Go back to your pitiful whores."

She looks around, and there is still no one in the vicinity. No one, except us to witness, but she doesn't know it.

Suddenly, Lady Ashura stands up straight, then reaches for the back of her artfully coiffed hair and pulls it out of its orderly shape, so that it hangs strange and tousled around her shoulders. Next, she smears her Face Art, in particular her *noohd*, making a mess of her mouth and letting her lip color streak across her cheeks and nose. She rubs her hands over her eyes to smudge the kohl eyeliner. Then, she grabs the fabric at the front of her dress until the tight bodice tears, further exposing the tops of her breasts.

Girsul and I stare in stunned disbelief.

Finally, contorting her face into a terrible rictus of pain, Lady Ashura Ximunat begins to keen and wail, punctuated by shuddering weeping. She screams at the top of her voice, "Help! Help me, someone! Gods, oh merciful gods! Please, help me!"

IN MOMENTS, people come running from all directions—contenders, guards, Bisfuri staff, everyone.

"What happened, My Lady?" they ask, surrounding her.

Lady Ximunat wails even louder and starts to beat her breast with her fists, clutching the ripped fabric of her bodice.

"He—he forced me! I've been—I've been violated! Please—find my beloved Lord Muutat Bisfuri! Please, take me to the pavilion! Right now! I must have my Lord Bisfuri!"

"Who did this, My Lady? Who? Was it one of the competitors?"

"No! So terrible! Take me away from here! Bring My Lord who shall be my Husband to me, at once!" she cries. "I will only speak to him!"

Still hidden in our spot, Girsul and I exchange horrified looks.

"Wait, what is she doing?" Girsul whispers. "Is she actually pretending—"

"It's what she does!" I hiss back.

Girsul's expression is a mixture of grim doubt and confusion. "But she's the future wife of Lord Muutat! How can she? What does she think, going behind his back, and with his son?"

"I've seen her try it before, that night at the Bisfuri party! That's why *Ter* Bisfuri left early!"

"No. . . . Crap . . . oh, gods. . . ." Girsul shakes his head, leaning with his back against a tree trunk. "We need to warn *Ter* Aten!"

"Agreed," I say, as my heart begins to pound. "And then we need to go and tell Lord Bisfuri what we saw, before she makes her false accusations—"

But Girsul looks at me with an even more terrified expression. "Semmi, no. . . . We can't do that."

I frown. "What do you mean?"

"Think—it's our word against hers! No one will believe us over a Lady of a Great House! We'll be dismissed immediately! Or worse, they'll punish or imprison us for false testimony!"

"Oh crap, oh, crap . . ." I whisper, putting one hand over my mouth.

Just then I look down and see one of the stupid wooden tokens we've been looking for. This one is painted messenger-red and stuck in the ground, right at my feet. Yes, I genuinely forgot what we're supposed to be doing right now.

"Take it," Girsul says immediately. "Then let's hurry to find *Ter* Aten!"

I hesitate only for a moment, then grab the token.

"This way," Girsul whispers, pointing behind, in the direction where we came from. "Don't let them see us."

And so, we back away from the general area of this misfortunate courtyard.

Then we start running as fast as we can, in search of Benaten Bisfuri.

Word still has not spread about the incident, so Girsul and I are well ahead of anyone, as we race though the estate grounds.

"She's going to be taken to the pavilion," I say, gasping for breath. "We can probably catch *Ter* Bisfuri before anyone comes for him."

"Yeah, let's hope they didn't get to him yet, or to the Lord himself," Girsul replies.

Just as we pass the stables, I see my little brother, wandering aimlessly among the crowds. Uru sees me and waves, then comes running alongside us.

"Hey, I can't find anything, Semmi," he complains. "Did you find—"

"Yeah," I interrupt, slowing my pace a little, and thrust the red wooden token in his hands. "Here you go, Uru."

"What? But that's yours," Uru says. "I can't take yours!"

"Yes, you can, *chazuf*, it's yours. Now take it and go to registration and wait there along with the others."

"But what about you?"

"Don't argue, Uru, just do as you're told for once." I raise my voice at him. "Now I must do something else work related, so Girsul and I have to be there. See you very soon! Now, scram!"

And without looking back at my little brother, I catch up with Girsul.

DESPITE OUR BEST efforts we can't seem to locate *Ter* Bisfuri. It's as if he's disappeared.

"Let's just go to the pavilion," Girsul says. "Since *she* will be there, and probably Lord Muutat. Best chance to find him."

"Maybe we can catch *Ter* Bisfuri on the way there," I say. "Intercept him if needed. That is, if he's been ordered to go there."

I try not to imagine what it would mean if Benaten is ordered to appear by his Father. It means the lie has been told. . . .

We finally make our way toward the shaded pavilion structure in the heart of the park, a long rectangle without walls, installed on top of a slightly elevated dais, with marble stairs running around the perimeter on all four sides. The structure has four corner posts and a tent roof of light fabric with an overhang, to protect against the sun. Inside is an outdoors relaxation area with pillow-strewn divans, low tables, and refreshments.

Apparently, we are too late to apprehend and warn our employer, because a minor crowd has gathered. Amid a babble of voices there are noble guests, endless Bisfuri staff, and guards in black uniforms. Lady Ashura Ximunat is at the center, reposing on a settee, pillows all around her. A man in a medic uniform is leaning over her and examining her face while several noblewomen hover nearby, exclaiming and clutching their veils.

Just as we draw near, we see Lord Muutat Bisfuri himself hurrying up the stairs, accompanied by several guards. Trailing him is his matronly sister, Benaten's aunt, Lady Ishtaz.

"Crap . . . we're too late," Girsul says, as we slow down our pace to a walk and approach carefully.

"I don't see *Ter* Bisfuri," I mutter under my breath.

Girsul scans the crowd anxiously.

"What happened to you, my love?" Lord Muutat exclaims, coming toward Lady Ashura, who sits up and then throws herself in Lord Bisfuri's arms with renewed artful weeping. She shakes with sobs, hiding her smeared face against his chest, and moans, then looks up and begins her tirade of deception.

"He forced me! My dearest, beloved, he—he attempted to violate me! But I fought him, I fought hard, with all my meager womanly strength . . . but oh, he was so strong, so much bigger than me—"

"Who? Who was it, Ashura?" Lord Bisfuri's voice grows with depth and menace. Tell me at once and I will kill him with my own hands!"

But the lady continues to play coy. "He overpowered me, and—and tried to take me against my will! He touched my body, yes, ripped my dress, see here—he kissed me like a lecherous madman—look at the violence done to my face—and I could only struggle like a poor helpless butterfly in his evil web!"

"Who, in the name of all the gods?"

"Oh, Muutat, I'm terrified, so terrified to tell you! Promise me, please you will be—merciful, for you must, for it is—"

"*Who?*"

"—your own flesh and blood!"

Stunned exclamations are heard all around.

"What?" Lord Bisfuri's face is like a thundercloud. "What do you mean?"

Lady Ashura lifts her tear-streaked face and looks into his eyes with an expression of martyrdom. "It was your *son* . . . Benaten. Oh, I'm so sorry to even utter such a thing, but he—surely, he must not have been himself!"

Guests react with shock. But there are quite a few voices of protest from the Bisfuri staff.

"What?" Lord Bisfuri roars. "My son did this to you?"

"Yes, my love . . . but I beg you to have mercy, for he must be ill, so very ill . . . or not himself, surely not himself, to have attempted such evil. Physical excesses—carnal excesses such as his—they can lead to unhealthy obsessions. . . ." Lady Ashura clutches Lord Bisfuri's hands with her own, and lifts them toward her chest to press against her heart. She resumes shaking and keening softly.

Muutat Bisfuri straightens, moving backward from his future Wife. He stands in horrible silence, looking down at her for an interminable moment of incomprehension that feels like dismal eternity.

And then Lord Bisfuri cries loudly, "Bring him to me! Guards! Bring Benaten here! Bind and drag him if you must!"

"No need, My Lord Father, I am here."

The familiar voice of my employer sounds loudly from behind us. It is deep and rich and resonant with confidence, but also very solemn and dark.

Benaten Bisfuri approaches quickly, walking with a straight back, head held high. The digital tablet is still in his hand. He climbs up the stairs and enters the pavilion, stopping before his father and Lady Ashura. The crowd parts before him.

At once, guards step in to surround *Ter* Bisfuri.

In that instant I catch sight of the younger brother, Behamenut, and his bewildered, terrified expression, as he stands nearby watching his older sibling.

"No! Not my Aten!" Lady Ishtaz suddenly breaks the silence. "That's impossible! My fine, kindhearted boy—your son— would never do such a thing, it is not like him—"

"Silence!" Lord Muutat cuts her off. He turns to his eldest son, speaking in a menacing voice, terrible like the serpent god

Nehebkau. "You have been accused of a vile act of horror. What do *you* have to say for yourself?"

"It's a lie, all of it. None of it is true," Benaten replies, meeting his father's stare with unblinking eyes.

Lady Ashura gasps, whimpering, and puts one trembling hand to her mouth.

Lord Bisfuri parts his lips. His frown intensifies, contorting his normally smooth forehead, so that now there's a pulsing vein there. "Are you saying the Lady Ximunat is *lying*?"

"Yes, she is."

Lady Ashura gasps again, and this time shakes her head, covering her eyes with her clawed fingers and delicately weeping.

"You have not touched her, then?"

"I have not and never will. I do not dishonor my Father."

"Then who did? Are you are suggesting My Lady has gone mad? That she somehow got herself hurt in the most unspeakable way and is blaming you? How do you explain *this*?" And Lord Bisfuri stretches his hand to point at the seated Lady Ximunat. His arm is shaking with anger.

"I don't know," Benaten says with a sharp glance at Lady Ashura with her smeared face and torn bodice. "This is not how she looked when I last saw her."

"Then you admit to seeing her!" Lord Muutat roars.

Ter Bisfuri's complex expression is impossible to describe. He pauses, gathering himself, then explains in a dead voice, "I was keeping track of the Competition, walking the grounds as you instructed me. She caught up with me in the lesser courtyard, back in the park. We spoke briefly. She tried to . . . touch me. Attempted to kiss me—"

At this, there are muffled exclamations in the crowd. Lady Ximunat cries out and covers her face with renewed weeping.

"I did not let her. I put her off and left immediately. But first, I told her I will not stand for that kind of thing. That's all. That is all I *know*. Nothing else happened between us. As for why she is in this condition—I *don't* know!"

Benaten pauses, and suddenly his unreadable mask cracks. For a moment, his face is agonized as he looks directly at his Father. "I thought hard about telling you any of this. . . . That your future Wife could behave in such a manner, with such dishonor. I didn't want to say anything at all. Especially not anything that might ruin your happiness. I wasn't going to. But now, because of these abysmal, false accusations, I must speak out and tell the ugly truth. I am so sorry, Father. I did not think it would come to this. . . . I understand none of it and . . . I'm so sorry."

Lord Muutat Bisfuri appears stricken, eyes liquid with emotion. "I want to believe you, boy," he begins, but just then Lady Ashura interrupts.

"How could you?" she exclaims, lifting her tear-smudged face toward Benaten and displaying her most righteous expression. "How could you continue to lie to your loving Father even now after what you *did*, even after the whole world sees me harmed most wickedly?"

"I did nothing! I want nothing to do with you!" Benaten says, turning for the first time to look at her directly, and his eyes are fierce and desperate. "I don't know what kind of game you're playing, Lady, or to what end, but it is not—"

"A game? How dare you? After I've accepted you as my own son, had every intention of loving you, being a true Mother to you? From the start you latched onto me with your sickening lust and followed me everywhere I went, and tried to put your lascivious hands on me, again and again! Yes! Today, my dearest Muutat, my kind friends, was not the first time!" Lady Ashura sweeps her gaze at everyone gathered around her, then returns to glare at Benaten. "For you've attempted to have your way with me before, indeed, the very night of the blessed engagement between your noble, gentle, most kind Father and myself—"

"What?" Lord Bisfuri cries.

Benaten shakes his head, his eyes filled with darkness. "My Lady," he says through his teeth. "It was *you* who tried to approach me that night also, another ugly lie—"

"Enough!" Lord Bisfuri roars again, his voice cracking. "I've heard enough! You are my spawn but you are not my son!"

There is general tumult in the crowd.

At my side, Girsul's face is terrifying. As for me, I'm shaking with outrage, my hands balled into fists.

And then one of the Bisfuri guards speaks up. I recognize the familiar, large, muscular figure of Vakrem, who works for Benaten but is also apparently chief of household security overall.

He speaks in a loud but careful voice. "My Lord Bisfuri, we have enhanced surveillance enabled today, because of the Competition. We can check the recordings of the courtyard and any other areas of the estate. It might help to verify what happened—"

Muutat Bisfuri turns in his direction, momentarily pausing, a dulled expression replacing his fury. "What did you say? Surveillance? Oh, yes, *yes*! Let's see it, immediately! Show me the recordings."

"Yes, My Lord. It will take just a few moments. Allow me to bring the equipment here." And Vakrem hurries down the pavilion stairs, then jogs quickly toward the nearest building.

Long, strained daydreams pass as everyone waits.

Lady Ashura meanwhile, resumes whimpering. "I can't believe, Muutat, that you suddenly want to rely on a cold, heartless recording instead of accepting my honest, loving confession."

"Ashura, dearest," Lord Bisfuri says gently. "You must understand the impossible position I'm in right now, torn between you, and this—this unfortunate spawn of mine. I'm aware of his excessive sexual proclivities, and I am inclined to believe you, of course. But having confirmation is important, considering the severity of the accusation and crime."

"Yes, yes, of course, my sweet Muutat," she replies. "Check the recording, and oh, but I cannot bear to think the horror you will witness yourself. My humiliation will be displayed for all to see—"

"My Lord Father," Benaten says with a glimmer of hope. "When you see the recording, you will know I spoke the truth. The proof has to be there. Whatever happened to the Lady—"

"Oh, have you no shame? How can you continue thus, Benaten?" Lady Ashura speaks up again. "Your unholy obsession drives you even now. Just look at yourself! There are scratches on your face, from my own nails as I tried to fight you off! Look at him, everyone!"

Lord Muutat turns to look at Benaten's face, and orders him to approach closer so that he can examine him. Everyone else stares.

Indeed, there are faint lines of nails across Benaten's jaw and cheek.

It's the spot where Lady Ximunat slapped him, I recall.

"I see it!" Lord Bisfuri concludes, his voice rising again with renewed anger.

"She struck me when I pushed her away," *Ter* Bisfuri says coldly.

"No, rather, you held my wrist and squeezed it cruelly!" She raises one hand to show off her slender wrist and arm covered with gold braces. Unfortunately, it looks like there indeed might be a slight red welt there. The Man in the Niktos Cloak has strong fingers.

Crap of a goat. . . . I start to shudder again. *It doesn't bode well for him.*

Benaten blinks, glancing down then back directly at her face.

"I had to hold your wrist so you wouldn't strike me a second time," he admits.

"Sad lies and excuses!" the lady cries. "But even now, this is another admission! He touched me, he put his violent, greedy hands upon my helpless body—"

"No, no," Benaten protests lifelessly, shaking his head again in disbelief. "It's *not* what happened."

In that moment, Vakrem arrives, carrying some kind of large, box-shaped piece of tech with a screen attachment. Setting it on one of the low tables, he snaps it open before Lord Bisfuri, and then enables a visual image display in the form of a small hologram of the estate that pops up over the screen.

Everyone strains to look, as Vakrem turns around, then his gaze lands on Girsul. "You, quickly," he beckons. "You know how to fast-search through the recording safely, right?"

Girsul nods and makes his way up the pavilion steps. In moments he manipulates the image so that tiny figures race around the perimeter, then finally locates and zooms in on the courtyard, thankfully from a different side than the one where we were hiding.

The image is enlarged and everyone sees a hologram of Benaten walking, engrossed in his tablet, then Lady Ashura approaching, by all appearances calling out to him. . . .

And then, the image corrupts and disappears. Girsul frowns and mutters under his breath, and tries to reset and manipulate the visuals again.

It's no use.

The image skips, and the next time we see the hologram courtyard, it's with a small crowd of onlookers gathered to assist Lady Ashura, who appears to be in her present disarray. *Ter* Bisfuri is already gone from the scene.

"What does this mean?" Lord Muutat Bisfuri asks, frowning.

"My Lord, the recording seems to be damaged," Girsul says with a quick, guilty glance at Benaten. "Not sure why—"

"*Hoohvak!* How can that happen?" The intensity in Lord Muutat's eyes is menacing. "Tell me, how? Why, of all things, can't we see the most important moments?"

"This servant is far too loyal to your son, that's why!" Lady Ashura inserts a biting comment, like a snake. "This one, and so many others here work for him, I'm told . . . *im amrevu*, do not trust the staff. Your son must pay them very well. They're all protecting him, my dearest Muutat!"

"With apologies, My Lord," Vakrem speaks up, ignoring the lady's snide remarks. "It is possible that the recording was intentionally manipulated with a cam jammer."

"What?"

"A small device that can transmit interference. Whoever used it had to have it on their person, which blocked all the nearest surveillance cameras from recording. It can be turned on and off at will."

"Sacred Hathor!" Lady Ashura puts her hands to her cheeks. "So, this is what your son did, and how he got away with his abuse! Search him! See if he has that gadget on him—what do you call it, a cam jammer?"

Lord Bisfuri nods at Vakrem and the other guards. "Do it."

And for the next few moments, *Ter* Bisfuri stands motionless as his digital tablet is confiscated and he is subjected to the indignity of many invasive hands on his body, up and down the length of him, followed by sensor sweeps. The guards try to be as respectful as possible, but it is inevitable.

"No, not there," Lord Muutat says suddenly. "Not his boots. Don't touch his boots. . . . Very well, enough."

The guards stand back, while Benaten narrows his eyes at Lord Bisfuri, in a brief, tragic moment of disdain.

"Why stop now?" he almost *taunts* his Father. "Go ahead and search everywhere, including down *there*."

"Silence!" Lord Muutat cries, and again his voice cracks with furious emotion.

"There's nothing, My Lord. There's no cam jammer that we can locate," Vakrem announces in his same careful tone.

"Search him again!" Lady Ximunat clutches her bodice. "Get different servants to do it!"

"We will search the courtyard instead. Most likely it was discarded there," Vakrem says, instructing several guards to head to the site for a search of the grounds.

"Yes, yes," Lord Muutat says in a kind of dull apathy. "Do that next. Search, search everything."

Vakrem nods, then gestures to Girsul to perform additional scan commands via the tech unit. "We can also expand the hologram video search beyond the courtyard. Widen the range to see if anyone else arrived soon after and crossed into this zone during that exact time frame. See if anyone was present at the *edge* of the scene *after* Ter Bisfuri left, as he claims. Some other individual might've committed the crime."

Vakrem pauses, looking over Girsul's shoulder closely. "Hm . . . it doesn't appear there was anyone else, judging from a quick scan of the extended perimeter footage, just now."

Except for us, I think. *Good thing Girsul is handling this!*

Lord Muutat Bisfuri exhales deeply, his breath shuddering. "Very well. And so, it is. What to do? Oh, what to do now? Mother of gods, my worthless son, my beautiful bride. My life, oh, my life. . . ."

"It looks like you have a choice before you, My Lord Father," Benaten Bisfuri says with unexpected sarcasm. "Her . . . or me. Whom do you believe?"

Silence.

And in the silence, Lord Bisfuri glances at Lady Ximunat, then at his son.

"I believe my own eyes," he says softly. "What's obvious is that my gracious future Wife has been violated and harmed, and on top of that, accused of lying. There is no forgiveness for such evil. Not even for flesh and blood."

The light in Benaten's eyes fades. "I see."

"Good, that you see," Lord Muutat Bisfuri continues. "Because now you are no longer a son of mine. In memory of your blessed Mother, I restrain myself from granting you the worst corporal punishment. Instead, I *disown* you. Before all these witnesses gathered here, I formally disown you and banish you, *Benaten*. Your name will never again issue from my lips. You are no longer Bisfuri. I have only one living son now. Behamenut is my new heir—"

A few steps away, a muffled sob issues from Behamenut, and his face fills with terror.

Lord Bisfuri raises one hand and points at Benaten. "Be gone from this house, by dawn, tomorrow. Take only what is yours from your late Mother's side. And yes, take your personal servants with you. As of this moment, all such are dismissed from their service to this House, for I don't want them, nor do I trust them. You on the other hand, may do with them as you will. . . . Now, get out of my sight! *Go!*"

Lady Ishtaz begins to wail softly.

Lady Ashura, on the other hand, has conveniently stopped weeping. Curious, how she watches, with an almost satiated expression, both her future Husband, and even more closely, his disowned eldest son.

Even now, she stares at him with hunger, I think, *even now*.

And in the dawning horror of all these events—including the grim realization that Girsul and I, and so many others, are now unemployed—I watch Benaten nod, acknowledging the command of his Father.

He spares no glance to Lady Ximunat or hardly anyone else, as he walks down the pavilion stairs, his back held so straight, so stiff, that it could be fixed in the rigor of death.

The rest of us have been dismissed also.

We follow him.

M y heart pounds so much it hurts, and I feel breathless with anxiety as I hurry after Benaten, along with Girsul and several other stunned Bisfuri staff, all of us out of a job.

Benaten walks rapidly before us, and reaches the older building where his personal Quarters are located.

"What do we do now?" Servants talk in subdued voices, throwing concerned glances at Benaten as he approaches the small side entrance.

"What about the Domestic Service Competition?" someone asks.

"Hush! How can you think about that now, *garooi*?" another replies. "Do you imagine anyone here has any chances of being selected by House Bisfuri after we were just dismissed?"

"They might even cancel or postpone the whole thing because of what happened. . . ."

Merciful Bastet, no. . . . What will I tell my family?

With a pang of despair, I think about Uru, waiting for me at registration. He has no idea. What will he do? Will they let him advance in the Competition? Being related to me has become a liability.

"*Ter* Bisfuri!" Girsul says loudly, quickening his step to reach Benaten's side. "*Ter* Aten, what should we—"

Benaten stops walking and turns around. "I am no longer a *Ter*," he says in an unreadable voice. "Nor am I Bisfuri. Use my ordinary given name."

Immediate protests issue from everyone.

"You are *Ter* to me, and always will be, *Ter* Aten," many servants rush to say.

He stands before us at the doors of the building, while everyone gathers in a semi-circle around him.

Benaten's grey eyes are somber, with a dangerous liquid glitter that has in it a touch of madness, as he looks at each and every one of us.

"I am truly sorry for what has happened to you," he says. "Lord Bisfuri, whom I may no longer call 'Father,' has misjudged all of you gravely, and has done you an injustice. Your loyalty has always been to the House Bisfuri, and that included me. No more, no less."

He pauses, one hand on the door handle. "Come, all of you, upstairs. Bisfuri dismissed you, but not I. If you choose, you can now work for *me*, directly. I'm a man with no other name, but with a number of resources. What do you say? If you want to leave now, if you don't believe I'm innocent of the accusations, and you despise me, I understand, go. Otherwise, consider yourselves still *employed*. Follow me!"

He opens the door of the building, and in an unexpected tumult we come after.

INSIDE BENATEN'S living Quarters there's a bustle of activity. Quickly, word has spread as to what has happened. Servants arrive from all over, variously dejected, crestfallen, or stunned, having learned that they are now no longer a part of

Bisfuri household staff, and that the benevolent *Ter* Aten has been disowned.

I see many familiar faces including the two decorator designers Menahit and Dunea, Chifuz the mission officer who had accompanied Lord Bisfuri on the trip to the orichalcum mines and secretly reported to Benaten, and even the high-end technician Mihravat who apparently works for Benaten directly and hence must go.

"Vakrem has not been let go, lucky *chazuf*," Menahit remarks while packing Benaten's personal items and removing them from his bedchamber, as instructed. "As chief of household security, he officially reports to Steward Hekadut who in turn reports to Lord Bisfuri, not *Ter* Aten."

Benaten meanwhile, walks slowly through the rooms of his suite, his expression dulled with apathy, and points out select items to be packed.

"I'm so sorry, *Ter* Aten, so sorry," people keep saying. They pause to speak to him with genuine affection. "I know you've done nothing wrong."

"I am grateful that you believe me," he replies solemnly, letting a flicker of a smile touch his lips. And then, as soon as he turns away from each person, the smile fades into lifeless nothing.

"Where will you be going, *Ter* Aten?" Dunea asks with sympathy.

"I have a residence on Circle Five," Benaten replies after the slightest pause. "It's a property belonging to Lady Aymira, my late Mother, bequeathed to me, among other things."

"Oh, is that so?" Dunea nods kindly. "That is good to hear, *im Ter*."

"For now, that is where I will stay. It is also where I will summon you when I require your usual services to me," he adds, before strolling away, moving aimlessly down the corridor to the living room.

. . .

MEANWHILE, I find myself in a continuous bewildered state. And so, I follow along, from room to room, noticing that Girsul is doing the same thing. Again, we exchange glances.

Benaten needs to be told that we witnessed the events with Lady Ashura. We are the only real witnesses to the truth—his truth.

He must be devastated right now. It is clear, he is not quite himself. And yet, he also has moments when a determined look comes to his face, periodically surfacing from the morass of numb despair. Watching him struggle to maintain control breaks my heart.

He *knows* that life must continue, events must go on. In the greater scheme of things, nothing has changed. But also, everything is transient. Everything is only for now.

There are things to be done, vital work. He knows there's no time for extended despair because the Sky Rock is coming and the world is ending for everyone, not just him. Indeed, he is now subject to the same commoner fate.

A strange thought comes to me. Benaten no longer has a place on the great ships. He is now just like the rest of us.

Or is he? Will he have to fend entirely for himself? Maybe Prince Oron Kassiopei or some of his other noble friends will help him? Or would they reject him now that he's disowned?

I don't get the opportunity to ponder this convoluted notion, because I hear my employer's deep, rich voice, uttering my name.

"Semmi, Girsul," Benaten says to the two of us, pausing in the corridor between rooms. "Come with me, both of you, now. We must talk privately, in the back."

We move deeper into the suite, past his dressing room with which I'm now familiar, and into his actual bedchamber. Unlike the other rooms, where servants are moving items and packing, there's no one here. Menahit finished whatever she was doing here, and not much has been moved as far as I can tell after looking in from the hall and listening to her complain.

Benaten's bedchamber, which I'm just now seeing for the first time ever, is occupied by a grand bed in the center, several divans and chairs, and lovely antique tapestries on the walls. The room is decorated in dark, rich colors, and the bedding is such deep *niktos* blue that it appears black.

In the middle of the bed, on top of the coverlet, lie two brightly gleaming objects. A bracelet and a turnip, both swollen with light and pulsing like the rainbow.

A pang of instant guilt strikes me. Oh, how could I forget the *pegasei*?

"Heket!" I exclaim immediately inside my mind, focusing on the turnip. "Are you alive? Did you get enough light?"

I am well fed and alive, sentient Semmi, the voice in my mind replies. *I am glad you are here.*

Meanwhile, Benaten points to the *pegasei*. "They have been fed today. Just now, in fact, right after I dealt with Lady Ximunat in the courtyard, I left to come directly here to feed them on the balcony."

"So that's where you were," Girsul says. "We couldn't find you."

"I want each of you to take one," Benaten continues in a tired voice. "You will hold on to each *pegasus* and care for it on my behalf. Take it home with you. Things are going to be . . . very uncertain now, so I want to make sure they are well cared for. I, myself, might not have the means to do so reliably, where I will be going."

"Um . . . are you quite certain, *im Ter*?" I ask in an awkward voice. "We are to keep them with us now? What if something goes wrong?"

"Nothing will go wrong," he replies, looking steadily into

my eyes, so that I find I must blink self-consciously. "I know you will do well."

"You don't want to just feed them yourself in your new residence?" Girsul persists. I can tell he's also uncomfortable having such a major responsibility thrust upon him. He would be taking a priceless *pegasus* home to his poor tent camp in an abandoned warehouse, full of questionable neighbors and occasional unknowns passing through.

"My new residence is underground. The part that matters, that is." Benaten says, watching our reactions. "There's not enough light there for these creatures. No immediate access to full spectrum illumination. There may not be time to reach sunlight and feed them properly if I had to rush them outside every day in addition to everything else I must do."

"Oh!" I open my mouth in surprise.

Benaten laughs ruefully. "You will see it soon. Assuming you still want to continue working for me directly."

"Of course!" both Girsul and I exclaim.

Benaten nods slowly. "Good. Because there's much work to be done. *Nothing* has changed in that respect. I will continue to pay you the same amount, fairly. You do understand?"

"Yes," I whisper. And then I blurt, "*Ter* Bisfuri—I mean, *Ter* Aten, we saw you today with Lady Ashura. We were there, Girsul and I. We stood behind the trees and saw everything. We *know* you're innocent."

"Yes, we can testify for you, if you need us," Girsul adds.

Benaten's face fills with energy. "Thank you. I am glad someone else witnessed the truth. However, I will not subject either one of you to my Fa—to Lord Bisfuri's ruthless scrutiny. It no longer matters, none of it. We're past that point."

Benaten exhales then sits down on his bed, and picks up the *pegasei* objects. Taking one in each hand, he casually tosses them to us, as if they're apples. As expected, I get my turnip.

"They're in your fine care now," he says again, and allows a smile to travel across his lips. "This is what I wanted to talk to you about, mostly."

Catching Heket with both hands, I feel the warm weight of the little turnip. Gently, I cup it with my fingers.

"The other thing is," Benaten says, lowering his voice so it's barely audible. "As of tomorrow, I'll no longer have access to the underground tunnel network from the waterfall grotto, here on Bisfuri land. Which means, I will have to familiarize you with a different access point, in a different Circle."

Girsul nods. "Understood."

"As I mentioned, my new residence is in Circle Five. It's only a small estate above ground, but underneath the house it is quite expansive. And yes, it connects to the tunnel network."

Benaten is about to tell us more, but in that moment, loud voices are heard coming from the front of the suite near the living room entrance. I recognize the voices of Lady Ishtaz and Behamenut.

"Where is he? Where is my boy?" his aunt cries with emotion. Moments later, the lady herself arrives and rushes through the bedroom toward her nephew. Behamenut comes after, pausing at the bedroom entrance with a thoughtful frown.

Benaten gets up from his seat on the bed and meets his aunt halfway, taking her in his arms.

Lady Ishtaz weeps at his chest. "I tried, Benaten! Hathor and Bastet know, I tried! I defended you, argued with him on your behalf, all this time," she says in between her sobs. "But my brother is both stubborn and broken right now. . . . That horrible Ximunat woman has him entirely under her control, possibly by means of *sha* sorcery. He is stupidly infatuated, and believes himself in love with her."

"I know," Benaten says, holding the older woman in his embrace. "The man, who is no longer my Father, is deceived. And the attraction of a Bisfuri and Ximunat Great House alliance appeals too strongly."

"No longer your Father? Fie! Nonsense! He will come around; this is temporary insanity! I will talk to him again in the morning, after he's had time to calm down and think clearly, and I will keep talking to him until he relents! Muutat is an idiot, but ultimately he knows right from wrong—"

Benaten shakes his head sadly, but says nothing. I notice his eyes are glistening.

"Where will you go?" she asks suddenly. "Your Mother's house?"

"Yes."

"That's good," Behamenut speaks up now. He takes a few steps inside the bedchamber and pauses before his older brother and aunt. "I will come to visit you there, Aten. I'm really sorry."

"I know," his older brother replies, reaching out with one hand. He pulls Behamenut toward him for a common embrace with their aunt.

They stand close, three as one, the two brothers and their aunt. Girsul and I watch them in sympathy and silence.

Eventually Behamenut says, "I want none of it. I don't want to be his heir. You know I can't do anything right. The responsibility alone will kill me. Please, Aten, do something to change his mind. . . ."

"Eham, you'll do fine. I can do nothing, at least for now. Be strong, and stand by him the best you can. It's all anyone can ask."

"*Varqood . . .*" Behamenut mutters.

"Watch your language, child!" Lady Ishtaz says with minor outrage.

And they separate, ending their long embrace.

"Well. . . . You should go now, Aunt Ishtaz," Benaten says softly. "I'm fine, but I need to get ready. There's much to be done before dawn when I have to be gone from this house."

Lady Ishtaz issues another sob, nodding. "Oh, come, let me kiss you," she says, reaching for Benaten again. She pulls him closer and smacks him warmly on the cheek at least three times, for good luck, then wipes the spot with her fingers to clean a bit of her brightly colored *noohd* from his skin.

Benaten stands with a faint smile, tolerating her ministrations.

Lady Ishtaz eventually heads for the exit, with a sorrowful glance behind her. "Come, Eham, let your brother work, he is busy now. Oh, what a dreadful day."

"I'll only be a minute, Aunt," Behamenut mumbles in her wake.

However, as soon as she's gone, he sits down on the bed next to Benaten who returns to his previous position there.

"*Varqood . . . varqood*, what's going to happen now?" Behamenut whispers, with a glance at all of us, and notices the glowing rainbow objects in our hands. "I assume they both know?"

"Yes, they know, speak freely before them."

"You're going to continue working with Noi, right?"

"Correct. Nothing has changed."

"Well, one thing has changed. Father just cancelled the second portion of the Domestic Service Competition for today. Says they will reschedule it for the coming days, but today he cannot think well enough to make final selections because of all that's happened."

I make a tiny sound of distress.

Benaten glances at me, then back at his brother. "What exactly does that mean?"

"Enough people completed the first task of finding the tokens. That's at least three hundred-fifty people, which is enough for the next part. They were told to check the schedule postings daily and come back with their tokens to finish the Competition when it's time."

"Some comfort, I suppose." Benaten rubs his forehead tiredly, then rubs the bridge of his nose and his eyes.

"Why don't you take a short nap," Behamenut suggests. "You need the rest. Still a long day and night ahead. You'll have a clearer head."

But Benaten shakes his head. "A clear head will make no difference. It is my heart that needs relief."

"You can't afford to get sick, not with all the things you must do," Behamenut persists.

"Just go, *hoohvak*. I'm fine."

"No, you're not." Behamenut turns to Girsul and me for support. "You two, tell him."

In answer, Benaten leans forward suddenly and rests his head in his hands.

I notice he is staring at the floor, or more accurately, staring at his own feet.

His feet, in those sleek, black boots.

What is it about those boots? I think, recalling some odd things, some incomprehensible interactions, especially Lord Bisfuri's strange preoccupation with his son's footwear.

At the same time, Behamenut notices the direction of his brother's gaze.

"What?" he asks. "What, Aten?"

Benaten lifts his gaze, and his grey eyes are filled with intensity. "I'm taking them off," he says in a low, harsh voice.

And then he smiles a strange smile.

Girsul glances curiously at me and my confused face. In that moment I realize that Girsul knows something I don't.

"No . . . don't." Behamenut says at once. "He will be so angry now if you do. Even angrier than he is already—"

"Good." Benaten's dark, sarcastic smile gives me a jolt of fear.

He leans down and reaches for his right foot. Pulls up the pant leg and then undoes an intricate clasp on top of that boot, just beneath his knee.

Then he takes the boot off, pulling slowly.

The boot comes off, revealing his leg below the knee, paler than the rest of him, likely from not being exposed to the sun. . . . And then, around the ankle, it culminates in a stump. There is no foot, only a poorly formed portion of heel protruding, covered with flesh and skin.

"A-a-a-ah." Benaten exhales a fierce sigh of angry relief.

And then he glances at his brother, at Girsul, and finally at me.

"Well," he says, his grey-eyed gaze meeting mine with almost a challenge. "Now you know my other secret."

My lips part as I stare at him, feeling a flush of impossible emotion flooding me, setting my head on fire. There is so much, so much, that it's choking me, and my eyes for some reason start to fill with liquid. "Oh," I say. "Oh. . . ."

There is a strange pause.

"How?" I ask, uttering the most stupid thing I can. "How did it happen?"

Benaten chuckles. "I was born this way."

I continue staring, because now my eyes have so much liquid that it's hard to see.

"You were born with a little more than that," Behamenut adds in an uncomfortable, faint voice.

"True." Benaten nods, smiling ruefully. "I used to have a heel. But after three cuts, this is all that's left."

"I didn't know it was three times, *Ter* Aten," Girsul says. "I thought—"

"If you must know the whole story," Benaten looks at me again. "I will tell you. Because now, I *can*. I am disowned, and I'm finally free to be *exactly* as I am. No more hiding and concealing before the other nobles—"

"Does it . . . does it hurt?" I interrupt bluntly. Then I blink and feel a fat *hoohvak* tear slide down my cheek.

"No, Semmi, it does not," Benaten tells me with a strange, vulnerable look in his eyes. "It hurts only if I wear the boot improperly or too long. And it never used to hurt before he forced me to have the cuts."

"You mean . . . Lord Bisfuri?"

"Yes. My *former* Father could not bear it when his firstborn son and heir came out imperfect from the womb. You see, Lord Bisfuri loves perfection. He is an artist and architect at heart, and he must have beauty and perfection in all things surrounding him, in all *people*. Few things and people meet his impeccable standards of taste. . . .

"And thus, my so-called once-Father attempted to fix me. My 'imperfection' was concealed from the public. While I was an infant of only a few months, he had the best medics secretly perform a corrective surgery, then attempt to regrow my foot with the most advanced medical technology available to the noble elites.

"But the foot they grew was imperfect, crooked, wrong. So, when I was three, Lord Bisfuri had them cut my imperfect foot off, this time a little more, and try regrowing it again. The result was better, but still not up to his standards. I remember waddling as a tiny boy and limping on my strange new misshapen foot which hurt for months while it healed until they fitted me with my first boot to disguise it.

"They gave me another two years of natural growth as a child. And when I was five, Lord Bisfuri ordered his son's foot to be cut again, and regrown again. This time, the regrown foot was even worse, more twisted, more ugly. It was concealed by another boot.

"When I was seven, the man who used to be my Father forced me to endure my final cut and regrowth procedure. At this point the foot did not regrow as much as previously, the agony of extended healing was almost intolerable, and the medics admitted that things would only get worse if we continued trying.

"My former Father's anger was such that he would not look

at me for almost a year. Finally, he came to me and told me that I was to be fitted for a new, permanent set of boots, and as I grew, new boots would be made for me, for as long as I lived. Lord Bisfuri ordered me to never speak of my true condition to anyone outside the family, and I had to swear an oath to him, on pain of brutal punishments.

"'Why, Father?' I asked him many times over the years, 'Why does it matter so much to you how I am formed?'

"Angered by my question, my then-Father finally told me: 'I would sooner have my son *varqood* whores in public in front of an audience before allowing him to reveal his ugly imperfections to *Atlantida*.'

"His words impressed upon me, branded my soul and bound my spirit. I believe my *ka* still feels the palpable blows of those words even now, like paternal curses. . . . I hear it always, his voice and his exact intonation, playing in the back of my mind, and sometimes when I sleep."

Benaten pauses speaking, but his gaze stays on me, steady and subtle. And then, out of nowhere, he laughs. "He wanted this of me, and I *obliged* him. As I swore that oath to keep my body's defect a secret, I made hilarious, wicked plans for myself. I would do exactly as he said. I would *varqood* whores in public in front of an audience. I was an obedient son who honored my Father."

I catch my breath.

"And that's how the idiotic story-feed called *The Love Life of the Man in the Niktos Cloak* came to be," he concludes. "Of course, it all turned out much different, more complex, when I come of age. Finding my young man's courage, I hired *amretene* courtesans and acrobat actors, created *shar-ta-haak* plot scenarios, decided upon a story gimmick. To that end, I studied real combat. I learned to hone my movements and agility until I could move better than others who had the full use of both of their feet. I taught myself to fly effortlessly and fight from a hoverboard, all while wearing my polished forever-boots. I also added a touch of mystery and flair—the orichalcum cape, dark like the *niktos* night. It started out frivolous but eventually came to serve me as a defensive weapon."

"So that's why you became the vigilante," I say in wonder.

But Benaten shakes his head. "No. The vigilante took over because a son's malicious rebellion was never going to be enough. The Man in the Niktos Cloak could not exist for long without a purpose. *I* could not exist without a purpose. Semmi, I realized that I could only be *him* for the long term if I believed in something, could do something that gave me meaning."

B enaten watches me with a complex, oddly serene gaze, and then says, "It's all right. There's no need to cry, Semmi— though I appreciate that you care enough to do so. This is old, really old, stale family history. Ugly family secrets; all families have one. I only reveal this now to clarify and prepare you for what's possibly coming next."

"No . . . oh no. . . . I'm not . . . crying." I stumble on my words, dense and awkward. And my face inflames with more heat as I rush to wipe my cheeks and make a *hoohvak* sniffle noise with my nose. "I'm so sorry . . . just, for everything that happened to you."

"Don't feel sorry for me, because I've done quite well for myself since." He smiles gently at me, sympathetic to my reaction. And then he leans forward and takes off his other boot, the one on the left, revealing an ordinary foot, the leg above it muscular and well formed, only pale in color to match the other side. Because of the cruel restriction imposed on him, it's clear that both of his feet have likely never seen the sun.

"Indeed," he adds, "I should thank the man who was my Father, because he set me on this course of rigid physical training. The only frustration remaining is now gone. I *don't* have to wear the boots always, only if and when I choose. Admittedly, they do make some aspects of walking easier. But I no longer need to hide the fact that one of my feet is different from the other."

Benaten switches his gaze from me to Girsul, to his brother. "However," he adds, "the Man in the Niktos Cloak must still maintain his secret. Nothing's changed there. I'll wear the boots when I'm being the vigilante. *He* can't afford to reveal any hint of vulnerability to his enemies."

Girsul nods. "Yeah, that makes good sense."

"As for Benaten, the disowned son of Bisfuri, I can limp on one foot in broad daylight, wear mismatched shoes with just one boot or a mechanical insert, and *varqood* them all. Or I can do this—"

Benaten gets up from the bed, and hops on his left foot lightly, ending up across the room. Balancing on his powerful leg with ease, he pulls open a drawer in one of the wall cabinets, rummages briefly, and takes something out.

Next, he turns to face us, without bothering to support himself in any way against the furniture or walls, and examines whatever's in his hands—all while continuing to stand on his left foot for long moments, without his right stump ever touching the floor. At last, he hops back effortlessly, returns to the bed, and sits down.

"You have no idea how much practice that took," Behamenut remarks, pointing at his older sibling with appreciation. "Years and years of balance training, while locked in secret rooms. Walking canes and support sticks of various sizes are still hidden in the back of his closet. And now my acrobat brother can do even more on that left foot alone."

"With that out of the way," Benaten keeps his fingers closed over whatever he took from the cabinet, and returns his attention to Girsul and me. "The two of you are free to go home for the remainder of the day. Stop by the offices to turn in your employee badges and be sure to get paid for the balance of wages owed to you."

"Oh," I say. "What about my staff uniform?"

I only got to wear my Bisfuri uniform proudly for two days.

Benaten chuckles. "Keep it. Burn it. Or turn it in to Hekadut along with your badge."

"Yes, *Ter* Aten," I say.

"About the badges," Girsul asks. "If we return them, how do we communicate with you, *im Ter*?"

"With these," Benaten says, opening his palm to reveal two replacement comm units that look exactly like the badges but without the Bisfuri House sigil. He tosses one of them to each of us. "Copy your Bisfuri badge configuration over to the blank comm unit," he says. "Girsul, show Semmi how to do it. I'll be contacting you later tonight with directions to my new residence."

I hand over my badge and the new comm to Girsul, and he puts the two devices together then taps some spots on the surface of both. Lights go on then disappear. "Done," he says and returns the two items to me, then does the same things with his own units.

"Are you sure we don't need to stay a bit longer and help you with something, *im Ter*?" I ask carefully.

Benaten smiles at me with amusement, sarcasm, and world-weary sadness. "Yes, I'm certain. I have entirely too many good people at my disposal right now. Now, go, and be ready to come to Circle Five tomorrow morning—let's make it eighth hour of Ra to give me time to settle in. . . . I'm going to close my eyes now and take that nap, and hope to die . . . while the rest of my loyal employees continue to turn this suite upside down. *Varqood* everything."

And with that, we leave Benaten and his brother in the bedroom. The new comm devices, and our *pegasei* are safely hidden in our pockets while we walk past the other former Bisfuri servants working in the suite, on our way outside.

STEWARD HEKADUT'S office is busy with employees. In addition to the usual, a line has formed, consisting of staff who have just been let go. Everyone is turning in their badges and getting their final wages. Complaints and disgruntled mutterings are heard, anxious and angry stares exchanged.

There are more people here than I imagined. Many I've never seen before; all of them apparently reporting to Benaten. It occurs to me, not everyone had gone up to his suite, only those of us most loyal. Some might even believe the foul accusations and lies thrown at him. Not to mention, they're likely furious that because of him they're out of a job, and out of any running for the Bisfuri Service Competitions. . . .

When it's my turn, I inquire about my uniform.

Hekadut examines me and says, "Looks to be in fair condition. No deductions, so you get the full six coins due to you as soon as you turn it in."

"I don't have anything to change into, if I take it off," I say, only now realizing my predicament.

"Bring it by later, same as everyone else," he says casually, nodding at the other uniformed staff in line around me. You get three coins today, and receive the rest once it's turned in."

I thank him, turn in my Bisfuri badge, grab my three coins, and head out.

STRANGE TO THINK, except for one more trip here to return my uniform, I am walking through the Bisfuri estate for the last time. . . . A pang of wistfulness passes through me.

It is still somewhat chaotic on the grounds, especially at the gates. Staff rush about, and there are quite a few additional guards present, but almost no one is left of the crowds of competitors. A few officials are doing something at the registration tables, while the giant smartboard has been returned to its place against the wall of the building.

The grand, ancient buildings, the beautiful park greenery, the scent of roses, the soft diffusion of sunlight filtered through the lacework of trees. . . . I'm going to really miss working for Bisfuri. . . .

I remind myself, that's nonsense, *I'm still working for the best of them,* Ter *Aten himself.*

For some reason it feels strange to call him the casual form of his name, Aten.

Why? I really don't know. Others such as Girsul do it with ease. But I should get used to it. Benaten, or Aten, the *man* is the same.

At the gates, I say goodbye to Girsul, whom I will see tomorrow, of course, at our employer's new location.

"Hope Uru is waiting for me," I mumble. "I wouldn't be surprised if he went home."

"Yeah," Girsul replies without enthusiasm, appearing to be engrossed in his own grim thoughts.

Girsul leaves while I stay back to look around the registration area and the gates, but there's no sign of my little brother.

And so, I give up and head to the bus stop, and home, dreading the long explanation I will have to give to my entire family.

WHEN I GET to Denwen's Pit, it's still early afternoon, unusual for me to be back from work so early. My heart starts to pound with anxiety as I open the door to our hovel, rehearsing my explanation in my head.

Amurabia and Uru sit in the living room, drinking tea. My

brother is chattering wildly while Grandmother listens with a resigned expression.

The moment Uru sees me he jumps up from the bench. "Semmi! You're back! That was so bad, so bad! After you left, I found out so many awful things happened. They had to stop the Competition halfway because the Lord was so angry. And they got rid of so many workers!"

I sigh. "I know, Uru. I'm one of those dismissed workers."

"Semmi, child," Grandmother says gently. "Why don't you get a mug and pour some tea. Then sit. Speak later, after you catch your breath."

And so, with a mug of tea cooling in my hand, I tell them everything. Well, almost everything; I don't divulge the secret work we'll be doing in the underground tunnels, or that I currently have a live *pegasus* in my pocket.

When I'm done, my Grandmother shakes her head slowly and sighs. "Well, that was quite a story," she says softly. "Your *Ter* Aten has suffered far more than he deserves in his young life. He's a good man; I could see it the moment I met him. I'm glad he gave you a chance to work for him directly instead of his Father's misfortunate Great House."

I nod, feeling my face stuck in a permanent frown.

"As for their Service Competitions for which you're no longer eligible, so what?" Grandmother continues. "Another one will come up, with another Great House."

Uru makes a whiny noise and shows me the wooden red token he still has on him.

"When they reschedule the second portion of the Bisfuri Competition, you will try for it," I say to encourage him. "Might as well."

"Yes, you must," Amurabia says. "Don't give up on yourself, my boy. Take every opportunity you can, while you still can. Your story is being written by your deeds, and no one can take that away from you."

That seems to have a soothing effect on Uru, as our Grandmother's words often do. But he's still somewhat restless and has more questions about what happened. Apparently the Windnet gossip he's absorbed in the last few hours of being at the Bisfuri estate is insufficient.

"Why did Lady Ximunat lie like that about Lord Bisfuri's son?" he asks out of nowhere. "He didn't do anything bad to her, right? So why is she being such a *chazuf*?"

"She is powerful, the Lady of a Great House," I respond. "She is used to getting anything she wants, and she wants—" I grow quiet, suddenly uncomfortable with the subject which includes an explanation of grownup *lust*.

Fortunately, Amurabia picks up where I trail off. "It's what happens in the story of life, Uru. Some powerful people live their life by telling lies when they're angry, unhappy, or even frightened. Others do it to gain an advantage, especially when they really want something."

"But why?"

Grandmother sighs. "Well . . . in this mortal life, the gods made it so there are only two kinds of human story. The kind that is about love or the kind that is about power. One is very simple, the other very complicated. Some people want both. But eventually all must decide which one of the two they want *more*, because you can only have one or the other."

"Why can't you have both?" Uru is annoyingly persistent.

"Because they are eternal opposites, like Ra's sun and Khonsu's moon. If you choose power, you lose the best part of you and spend all your time fighting for authority, influence, and clout, then defending your claim to it. Lying, cheating, accusing, are all forms of combat in the name of power."

"And if you choose love?" Uru listens closely.

"Well, child, if you choose love—which I hope you and everyone else does—then you let go of all the other nonsense and become your true self. When you're true, there is no need for lies as weapons, or fighting for things and desires that really don't matter. Things intended for you will come to you of their own free volition. See how simple that is?"

"I don't know," I say. "It might be simple for the one making the choice, but it doesn't stop other people who *didn't* choose love from taking advantage. Seems like *Ter* Aten got an unfair deal while staying true to himself, by being wrongfully accused. Nothing simple about that."

"Wrongful accusations are indeed some of the worst that can happen to a good person." Grandmother nods slowly. "An assault of darkness upon a soul. It can ruin a life."

"So, what can one do?"

"Give it time," Grandmother says. "Maat and the other gods will resolve all and bring healing."

"Usually, for that kind of healing, we'll have to die first," I grumble.

"If a person doesn't want to wait for divine justice and the Depet of Eternity, they can take justice into their own hands," Grandmother says, after a deep swallow of her tea. "That's one possible choice in one's life story. But it is a dark one. It would mean you're no longer on the path of love but retribution, which in turn takes you in a roundabout way to the path of power. Very difficult to come back from that to the way of love. I strongly recommend against it."

"Huh?" Uru says. "Are you saying we should do nothing to fight injustice and just wait for the slow gods to rearrange the world, eventually?"

Grandmother shakes her head, and the lines of her face wrinkle even more with the effort of thinking. "Sometimes I forget I'm old and my mouth starts to ramble in confusion before I can make sense. I'm saying something else altogether. Let me think. . . ."

"What, *Mei-ma*? What are you saying?" Uru persists, then glances at me and rolls his eyes.

"Ah, I have it! Instead of taking justice into your own hands, let your hands become instruments of the gods," Amurabia says carefully. "Shape your life story so that it is indeed the story of love. But there are times when you must act bravely to defend love. Do the best you can. See the difference there? Do not dole out justice as you see fit. Instead, expose injustice as you know to be true."

"Don't dole out justice, expose injustice," Uru repeats in a sing-song way.

"Stop mocking an old woman, little *sha*," Grandmother interrupts with a smile. "You ask too many questions and look what happens to this old head of mine. I end up giving you too many useless answers."

"We were talking about Lady Ximunat," Uru says.

"Please, enough about that woman," I say tiredly. "Can we not talk about her anymore—"

At that point, Guzum, our Father arrives, so Uru immediately launches into the events of the day all over again.

My weary Father sits down on the bench between Grandmother and me and listens with a resigned expression.

"I still have a job, *Papai*," I interrupt Uru. "*Ter* Aten will be paying me the same coins."

In that moment, my new comm badge buzzes, then the sound transforms into gentle bell tones in my pocket. I take it out, being careful not to reveal the *pegasus* turnip right next to it.

There's a recorded message from Benaten. His rich, low voice sounds rather unlike his usual self. Instead of the honey smoothness that makes you warm, there's a hollow distance. He simply tells me the address on Circle Five, then adds, "Come at eighth hour of Ra, and bring your uniform, folded and packed. In other words, don't wear it. *Nefero niktos*, rest well, Semmi."

"See, I have a job," I repeat in the general silence that ensues.

"Good," my Father says in his normal weary voice.

And we start getting the supper ready.

. . .

I WAKE up just before dawn, from a *hoohvak* dream of flying on a *pegasus* bat, completely lost underground, with the tunnel and the earth itself closing in around me.

The recall of yesterday's events strikes me like a flock of evil *sha*. In the bluish twilight, I turn toward the neatly folded Bisfuri uniform lying near my cot, then immediately mind-speak, "Heket, you're still alive?"

I am here. I would like to feed, soon. The answer comes immediately.

The turnip is still hidden in the uniform pocket, exactly where I left it last night—after carefully considering all the places in my home and deciding that there was no good spot to hide the *pegasus* and risk Uru or the others finding it.

Ah, crap of a goat, I think tiredly. Just for a moment I'd hoped the creature wouldn't answer. But no, that's awful, why would I think that? I don't want it to die! In fact, I'm anxious about feeding the *pegasus* well and on time and keeping it alive. And not just because *Ter* Aten commanded it.

The responsibility of caring for another, weighs heavily on you, Semmi. I am glad, Heket's calm presence answers within my mind.

"Shut up!" I grumble silently, ashamed of my own thoughts.

But the sense of amusement in response is palpable.

Trying to ignore the alien *chazuf* in my head, I move around in the dark, find my old clothing and put it on. Uru and the rest of my family remain asleep, so I sneak through the living room, and do the usual things.

Then I pick up the uniform with utmost care, and transfer the turnip into the pocket of my old skirt. Its rainbow glow momentarily fills the room, so I hurry to block it with my own body before concealing it again in the folds of fabric. Good thing my skirt is made of coarse, thick material, else the glow of the *pegasus* would seep through . . . and everyone on the street and on the bus would see it.

Next, I check the badge comm unit, before transferring it to my skirt pocket also. I call up the tiny holo-map and look at the dot that is my destination on Circle Five, and the streets surrounding it.

Then I head outside into the early dawn.

MY BUS RIDE IS SHORTER, since we're only flying to Circle Five, halfway into the City. As I sit and stare through the windows at the twinkling lights of the cityscape below, I'm consumed by worry thoughts about Benaten, about how he must've spent that last sorrowful night.

I imagine how he felt, leaving his Father's house in the darkness, as commanded, never to return. . . . Maybe the last of his servants accompanied him, transporting his personal things in a hover car. In multiple hover cars. Or maybe he left alone, on his hoverboard.

My nonsense thoughts are cut short as the bus clears the adjacent canal and descends at the nearest stop on Circle Five. I get off, shivering slightly in the chill wind as the dawn brightens.

The fixed street lanterns and night orbs are still glowing along the streets full of old trees and well-kept houses. I run along the biggest street, checking my holo-map destination. Occasionally, I pause next to a particularly confusing street sign and tap the button below the writing to hear a recorded mechanical voice confirm the name of the street (for those of us who cannot read the squiggles and must memorize or guess).

At last, I arrive before the dark, wrought-iron fence and gates of what must be Benaten's own residence that once belonged to his Mother. On the other side I see tall trees and a thicket of shrubbery. And beyond, there's the roof of a building, much larger than I expected.

He did say it was a small residence and for some reason I expected a hovel like our own home in Denwen's Pit. Instead, this is an estate.

It may not be the size of Bisfuri land, but it's unmistakably a nobleman's residence.

I try the gates without knocking, and they open, with no guards on the other side. I follow the small gravel road past the overgrown shrubbery toward an elegant old building covered in places with ivy vines, and then see Girsul, just ahead of me. He is standing near the entrance, holding his own folded Bisfuri uniform and talking with two men.

As I get closer, they turn, and I see they are not servants, but Benaten himself, and next to him, Stryr Giparu.

Ter Aten is dressed simply this morning, in his usual kind of working man's clothing, and I notice he's wearing his boots. *Ter* Giparu does not have a cloak today and is also clad like a commoner, in dark pants and white linen shirt with rolled up sleeves.

They watch me approach, and Benaten's expression gives off energy. "Semmi, you made it," he says. "You brought your uniform, good. You'll be needing it."

"*Nefero eos, Ter* Aten," I say. "And *Ter* Giparu."

Feed us now, Semmi. Heket's voice intrudes into my mind.

I blink, startled, then reach inside my skirt pocket and bring out the turnip. "*Im Ter,*" I say hurriedly. "I have a strong feeling we must feed the *pegasei* immediately. Girsul, you brought yours?"

As if I need bother ask.

Before Girsul can say anything, the second, nameless *pegasus* speaks inside my head. *Yes, I am here and need to be fed likewise.*

My eyes widen. *Crap of a stinking rainbow goat. . . .*

Girsul fumbles in his pocket, while Benaten raises one brow and watches me curiously. "Now? It's not even full morning. Let the sun rise somewhat. The two of you can feed them in the courtyard behind the house, not here in the front where passing strangers can see."

Feed us! The two *pegasei* speak loudly in unison, making me wince. I feel the twinge of a genuine headache starting. What in Bastet's sacred name can I say to my employer to convince him?

"I am very sorry, *Ter* Aten, but if we don't feed them now—" I begin.

"Ah, might as well have them do it now," Stryr says. "Since we'll be flying underground, they need to be well charged."

"Fine. Take out the *pegasei* and let's head to the back. I will show you the grounds and we can talk privately." Benaten starts walking away from the front entrance of the house, following a narrow path along the wall of the building.

We follow him through more overgrown bushes and shrubbery on both sides, and emerge in a paved clearing where two expensive hover cars are parked, levitating silently, with doors open. Three servants are unloading boxes, and carrying them into a rear entrance of the building.

I know two of them: pale haired officer Chifuz and Mihravat the technician. The third is an unfamiliar older man with thinning grey hair, a short beard, pale skin, and a muscular build, who gives me a sharp look before heading inside the house with a large box.

"See that guy?" Girsul nudges me with the same hand in which he holds his bracelet-shaped *pegasus*. "That's Xingir Guai, his physical trainer and combat master."

"Oh," I whisper back.

"As you can see, my things are still being unloaded," Benaten says to Girsul and me. "I was going to have you accompany me in the tunnels to Circle Eight. However, Stryr has some interesting news this morning, which changes my plans. While you feed the *pegasei*, let him tell you himself what you'll be doing this morning."

"We're going back to the Bisfuri estate on Circle Two," Stryr says with a roguish expression. "Girsul and Semmi, you two will take your usual City transportation. With the excuse of returning your uniforms, you'll be permitted on Bisfuri grounds. However, you will not leave through the gates. Instead, you'll climb the hill to the waterfall, enter the grotto, then the cave where we met previously. I'll be there, waiting for you with a stack of hoverboards which are stored there."

"I need all my hoverboards back," Benaten says with a rueful smile. "I could only bring the one hoverboard I kept in my work quarters as a prop for the media feed show. There was no way I could visit the grotto last night, especially not unobserved. So, it must be done after the fact, preferably today."

"Why today?" Girsul lifts his *pegasus* bracelet, turning it slowly, letting it bask in the light.

"Because," Stryr Giparu replies with a smile, "I just restored this sad *hoohvak's* will to live. How, you ask? I convinced your employer to enter the Imperial Pilot Competition, and register all of you along with him, as a single Team. And for that you'll need hoverboards."

"What?" Girsul's face is incredulous.

My own mouth falls open.

"As of this morning, there is an interesting rule change," Benaten clarifies. "The Imperial Kassiopei decided that Pilots have to compete both individually and in Teams. And special Team registration is for one day only, today. If I am to compete at all, I must attend in person to register at Circle One and sponsor my employees as Team Leader. And since I deprived all of you of a chance to serve Bisfuri and earn a place on the ships, it is only fair that I provide an alternative."

"But I'm not a Pilot!" I exclaim in amazement. "I know nothing about—"

"Neither am I." Benaten watches the glowing turnip in my hands, shimmering with rainbow light in the sun. "But we all know how to fly. As for the rest, Pilots will be trained. All we must do is win the Competition."

CHAPTER
FIFTY-TWO

I n this astonishing moment of new possibilities, I'm struck by a truly daring notion.

"*Ter* Aten," I blurt out, emboldened by hope. "My little brother Urumer is really good at using the hoverboard. He flies like a bird! Is there any chance that you might accept him on your Pilot Team, please?"

There, I've said it. Bast, help me!

Benaten looks at me with interest.

My heart pounds wildly. "I'm so terribly sorry for my impudence," I continue, because, might as well, "I have no right to ask, but if I am to fly, then he will fly so much better than me! Please, *im Ter!*"

Benaten appears amused by my request. "His name is Urumer?" he asks.

"Yes, Uru."

"And how old is he?"

"Seven, *im Ter*. But he's very sharp! Quick and smart for his years. He works as an excellent messenger in the markets—"

"A little young, but . . . very well." Benaten nods slowly. "Your judgment has been sound so far, Semmi. I'll take your reassurances that he is suitable. I will add him to the registration list."

"Oh, thank you, *im Ter*! Thank you, and may all the gods bless you, infinite numbers of times!" I exclaim, barely holding back a wild grin, while my heart starts beating even faster, swelling with warm energy.

"Bring your brother here tomorrow," *Ter* Aten says. "And now, let's get to work."

WE SPEND the rest of the day retrieving hoverboards. While Benaten takes care of Pilot registration (whatever that entails) on Circle One, the rest of us do our part.

Girsul and I conceal our newly-fed, bloated *pegasei* in our clothing, and head for the bus. At Circle Two, we arrive at the Bisfuri estate and enter the grounds completely unimpeded by the guards at the gates, and turn in our uniforms to Steward Hekadut. We even receive three coins each for our efforts.

And then comes the hard part.

Once back outside the main building, we do our best to avoid being noticed by the current staff and make our way in roundabout fashion past the stables, the airfield, and then climb the hill to the waterfall grotto.

Earlier, *Ter* Aten explained to Girsul how to open the secret tunnel entrance in the cave wall. We manage to press the correct spot on the rock that moves the door, and it lets us into the cool maw of darkness.

With our *pegasei* out in the open to illuminate our way, we arrive at the large cavern. True to his word, *Ter* Stryr Giparu is there, waiting for us, next to numerous boards stacked against the cavern wall.

"How are we going to move all the hoverboards?" Girsul asks.

"Very simple. Stack them on top of each other and use the

bottom one as a freight platform. Moving them is not the problem," Stryr replies. "The biggest issue is guarding their safe passage across the tunnel network. And that's why I'm here, since Aten can't be here today to protect you."

"Should we ride them?" I ask.

Stryr considers for a moment. "Up to you. It might be good practice. Or ride the *pegasei* after setting the voice keying command so that the boards move forward automatically."

"I'm going to try the board," I say, after a moment's hesitation.

Girsul looks at me with interest. "You sure?"

"No, not sure at all," I respond. "I don't even know where to start. Usually, my brother Uru has the board already levitating and ready to go, and I just climb on. . . ."

Stryr makes a sound of amusement.

"You need to key it first," Girsul says. "Then use a few voice commands for moving forward, side to side, and so on."

"Bastet . . . I don't know them," I say.

That's when *Ter* Giparu takes the nearest board leaning against the wall and pushes it down and forward. The hoverboard falls, becoming horizontal. It stops in the air just a few finger-widths away from hitting the ground.

"Lesson one," he says. "A hoverboard is activated by simple forward motion, even before you key it. Hover mode has been enabled. Now, key it, as you would any other orichalcum object."

I clear my throat then sing the basic keying command.

"Good. Now, get on it."

I take an awkward step onto the board, feeling it give slightly underfoot, then its resilient strength pushes back.

"Now, your other foot," Stryr says.

I breathe in deeply, then put my other foot on the board in front of me. For a moment I wobble slightly, keeping my balance.

I usually fall off soon after, I think. *Ugh.*

"You might want to put one foot in the stirrup behind you," Stryr says, watching me wobble. "All these boards have stirrup cutouts, specially designed by Aten to make it easier for him to balance his right foot."

"Oh yeah," Girsul recalls. "I noticed how he puts one foot in the stirrup. That makes good sense."

I nod, sliding the foot near the back into the narrow slot opening until I feel my toe go inside the slot.

I start to wobble even more, then end up hopping off the board altogether.

Just as I expected, I fell off the hoohvak *board.* At least it was levitating close to the ground, so I didn't hurt myself.

"You can practice later," Stryr says. "For now, you can sit on the board. Just straddle it as we fly. No skill necessary."

"Oh!" I say, "I can do that!"

"Of course. Any *hoohvak* can." Stryr winks at me. "The trick is to not fall off once the board starts moving. That's all that matters. Sit, stand, lie on top of it as if it's your *amreve* or a vanquished enemy, whatever."

And then he demonstrates several basic voice commands for hoverboard motion, after dropping another one from the wall. "Go forward. Stop. Go backward. Lean right, lean left. Rise, descend. Those are all the ones you need."

I watch and listen, and even Girsul pays attention.

"Now let's get these boards ready to move," Stryr says, pointing at the whole arsenal.

We stack the hoverboards carefully in two batches, using the bottom one in each batch as the freight platform, then use several cords to bind each stack together.

I keep one board for myself, and Girsul keeps another. "Might as well practice too," he says, stepping on his board with care. "We can save the *pegasei* for another time."

"As you like. I prefer my falcon," Stryr tells us, taking out his *pegasus* collar and transforming it into the giant bird.

Meanwhile, I use the rise command, and my board floats higher up from the ground so that I can sit on it, pulling up my skirt a little, with my feel dangling.

Stryr watches both of us fumble slightly. "You two bring up the rear and try to not fall off. The board platforms fly in the middle. I'll be in the front, looking out for Neph-Tiari. Ready?"

"Yes, *Ter* Giparu," I say.

Stryr shakes his head at us, with a chuckle. "Remember, Aten's doing this because of all of you. So, make the effort!"

"What do you mean, *Ter* Giparu?" Girsul pauses his wobbling and stares at the nobleman. "What do you mean, because of us?"

"I mean exactly what I said. The real reason Aten is even bothering with the Pilot Competition has nothing to do with saving his own skin." Stryr's expression becomes unusually grave. "He wants to save the whole *hoohvak* lot of you. I wasn't joking when I said I had to convince him to compete and not give up on himself. Knowing how Aten is, I had to make it all about the others—his staff, his people. The only way he agreed was after I mentioned the new Teams requirement."

FORTUNATELY, our flight through the tunnels is uneventful. No sign of the Neph-Tiari gang or anyone else in the passages besides us. The fact that we take a different set of tunnels to get to Circle Five, going a much shorter distance, might explain our luck.

I sit or half-lie on my board all the way to our destination, mostly trying to keep my feet from slamming into rock walls and the occasional rough spots on the ground. The process is not half bad. With enough practice, I suppose I can get even better.

"How many days do we have before the Pilot Competition, *im Ter*?" I ask Stryr as he flies ahead of us.

"Good question. If I recall, it's been moved up to the last day of this month, the twenty-eighth day of Setaet."

"Oh man, so soon?" Girsul complains. "Today is what, the twenty-third? If we count today, that's just five days to get ready."

"Five days can be a lifetime."

"*Varqood* me . . ." Girsul mumbles.

Stryr chuckles.

WE DELIVER the hoverboards to Benaten's new residence. The tunnel we're in widens underneath Circle Five and then branches off into two. Not far from the junction, we see another smaller niche in the tunnel wall.

It turns out to be a small offshoot tunnel without any beacon designation, which means it's a dead end or a surface exit point.

"Here we are. We take this exit," Stryr tells us, reining in his falcon.

We slow down and voice command the hoverboards to turn into the tunnel, which is barely large enough to accommodate us and the hard angle necessary to rotate the boards in a perpendicular position. Somehow, we manage to fit both the stacks inside, and proceed.

In moments, the tunnel rises at an incline. We see daylight and a circular opening directly overhead. The passage widens slightly, and turns into a stone chamber, not unlike the grotto at the Bisfuri estate. On one side there are wide stairs carved into the rock wall, leading up.

We get off our boards and take the staircase, then emerge into bright sunlight, amid thick, unkempt shrubbery, with Benaten's estate house visible nearby.

Stryr's falcon transforms once again into a necklace which he puts around his neck. We carefully direct the stacks of hoverboards to rise right after us. The boards float slowly, their orichalcum grey surfaces sparkling with specks of gold in the sun.

I notice that the opening in the ground from which we came has a round stone rim of mauve paving stones.

"Aten told me this used to be an old well," Stryr Giparu says. "Or maybe it was retrofitted and made to look like that from the outside, to divert attention from the fact that this is an entrance to the underground."

"Not bad." Girsul admires the framing stonework.

"You'll get to know this particular exit point really well from now on, since you'll be working with Aten in the tunnels," Stryr says. "This is the main access point from the outside. However, there's another one directly underneath the house. Aten will explain. Let's go see if he's back."

We leave the hoverboards in their stacks near the well opening, deactivating their hover mode with a tone sequence, so that they are piled right on top of the overgrown grass. And we head toward the house.

ACCORDING to the servants still working inside the building, Benaten has not yet returned from his business at Circle One.

I stare with curiosity at the large antechamber in which we stand—beautifully antique, full of dark woodwork reliefs carved into the walls amid marble, but covered with dust that has not been cleaned for some time—and wait for *Ter* Giparu to check his comm unit for messages.

Stryr finally looks up and tells us that Benaten will be delayed. "He conveys to everyone that all of you have been registered successfully for the Pilot Competition, but he has additional business at the Palace."

"You mean, with Noi?" Girsul asks carefully.

"Could be. I don't know." Stryr's handsome features acquire a cynical cast. "Apparently, the news of his disgrace is making the rounds at Court. He will be doing some explaining, and likely getting snubbed by high-ranking *chazufs* who only yesterday considered him their best friend."

I feel a stab of sorrow and anger on my employer's behalf.

"So, should we wait for *Ter* Aten now?" I ask.

Stryr shakes his head. "Don't bother. He might not be back for a while. You can help with the cleaning here, if you like. I do know he'll expect you back here tomorrow, at which point you will get further instructions. As for me, I declare you're done for the day."

AND SO, Girsul and I both head home early once again (after first feeding our *pegasei* in the sunlight, at my suggestion, to make sure they're well charged for the night). But this time, the mood is entirely different. We, and the rest of *Ter* Aten's staff at the residence are invigorated with the amazing news of the Pilot Competition.

Bast and all the great gods be praised, I think. I'm bringing Uru an opportunity we could never dream of. . . .

As I hurry down our little street in Denwen's Pit, my lungs are full to bursting with new energy and hope.

"Where's Uru?" I exclaim the moment I enter our house. "*Mei-Ma!* I have excellent news!"

Amurabia is working on her needlework in her little room, but comes out as soon as she hears the joy in my voice.

"What happened, Semmi?" she asks. "Uru is at the market running around as usual. Should be home soon, I imagine."

I tell her the amazing news.

Grandmother's wrinkled eyes widen. "A Pilot? You and Uru, both? What does that even mean? What kind of Competition is that? What would you have to do?"

I shake my head, but I'm smiling widely. "I don't really know, but it's something to do with flying on the hoverboards."

"Hoverboards? Oh, no, child, that sounds terribly dangerous!" For a moment, Grandmother's expression shows even more alarm. "You know how Uru always crashes into that accursed post on the corner? What if—what will he do? How fast would he be flying? And as for you, you don't know how to use the hoverboard!"

But I laugh. "It doesn't matter! I used one today! In fact—" I shut up, remembering that I can't talk about the nature of our work in the tunnels. So, instead I say, "I tried it, and they told me I can just sit on the hoverboard, and it was easy enough. I can do it, *Mei-Ma*. I know I can!"

Grandmother lets out a long breath, but then starts to smile back at me. "If you really think you can manage," she says gently. "Whatever it is, shouldn't be all that bad. After all, *Ter* Aten would not put any of you in a bad situation. I trust him to take care of you."

Indeed, I think, feeling a twinge of doubt, now that Grandmother appears so confident on our behalf. *Merciful Bastet, help us all.*

URU ARRIVES SOON AFTER. When he learns about the Pilot Competition and the hoverboards, my little brother's mouth falls open in the biggest surprise of his young life.

"Semmi! *Mei-Ma*! We're going to be flying!" he exclaims. "The gods are good, *Mei-Ma*! We're going to ride hoverboards! Where are we flying? How fast? What is a Pilot supposed to do?"

"All I know, Uru," I retort with amusement, "is that *Ter* Aten wants you to be there with me tomorrow, and he will let all of us know what comes next!"

"So, I'm going to Circle Five with you?"

"Yes, you are, little *sha*!"

"So, I bring my hoverboard?" Uru starts to bounce up and down and clap his hands against his knees.

"I believe so!" I can't help but laugh at his monkey enthusiasm. "Though, not sure how we're going to bring it on the bus. Hm-m-m. I think they have storage space?"

"They do, they do!" Uru continues dancing and jumping. "I love *Ter* Aten!"

"Hush, little *chazuf*." I roll my eyes at him. An automatic *hoohvak* reply passes through my mind, a reply which I don't verbalize because it's so ridiculous.

I think I love him too.

Wait, no. I did not just think that.

Crap of a herd of stinking goats, no!

My mind is in turmoil that night. All because of one thought. One idiotic, impossible thought that starts out as Uru's silly blather. And then, like a single airborne spore of a poisonous mushroom, the involuntary and unwanted thought takes root in my head, growing deep, spreading like an entire mycelium organism under the surface of my *hoohvak* consciousness.

I think I love him.

Holy sacred goddess Bastet, what is happening to me? I've lost my mind!

While Uru and the rest of my family celebrate the evening, I brood slightly, trying not to appear too obvious. Amurabia tells Guzum he can have an additional mug of beer, then tells us she will make *eos* pies the next day. She and I start chopping the vegetables while the kettle boils for supper.

As for Uru, he just runs around our back yard and jumps in place, singing nonsense syllables. Now and then, he rushes to the hoverboard propped up near the door, looks it over, wipes it down with a rag, then starts jumping again.

Even Grandmother hums a quiet tune as she works.

When we finally get to bed, I can hardly sleep. Uru is also restless in the other cot, but for a different reason. I hear him chortling and giggling. Finally, close to midnight, exhaustion takes me.

I WAKE UP BEFORE DAWN, with a hard shock of anxiety. I don't know our schedule for the day, and early is better than late.

Immediately, I check the badge comm, and there's a message from *Ter* Aten. We're to report to Circle Five, by seventh hour of Ra. Good thing I did not sleep longer, or we'd be late.

"Wake up, Uru," I whisper, and then add, "Pilot time!"

My brother immediately sits up, sleep replaced with excitement. We get ready, cram our mouths with last night's leftovers, and then head outside into a crisp, windy, bluish dawn.

Uru hops on his hoverboard and flies slowly alongside me, then slightly ahead of me, since he can't help speeding up as usual.

As we proceed to the bus stop, I check the pocket of my skirt to make sure the *pegasus* turnip is there. "Heket! I'll feed you as soon as it's sunny," I mind-speak, walking faster to keep up with Uru. "Try not to perish, okay?"

Thank you, sentient Semmi, the being replies. *I will not die today.*

"That's good," I think at him, and continue running after Uru who naturally has no idea of the conversation taking place inside his *garooi* older sister's head.

Suddenly, it strikes me. Uru is going to find out about the *pegasei*. . . . He'll be there when Girsul and I feed them. And everyone will be talking all kinds of secret things around my little brother.

Or will they? How is this going to work?

Did I just make the biggest mistake of judgment by asking Benaten to include Uru?

Crap of a goat.

WE SUCCESSFULLY UNLOAD Uru's hoverboard from the storage compartment of the hover bus and get off at Circle Five. My brother gets back on his board and again flies while I try to keep up the pace.

We arrive at Benaten's estate just before seventh hour. Uru stares at everything with fresh curiosity, including the overgrown ivy on the walls of the house, and the wild greenery encroaching on the narrow paths.

Some of the staff is already gathered in the back courtyard, including Girsul who waves at me, and even more people arrive in the next few daydreams. I know most of them, but not everyone.

"*Ter* Aten told everyone to wait here," Menahit mentions to me, as Uru and I make our way closer.

"Off the board, Uru," I whisper at my brother, and thankfully he listens, jumps off and then drags the thing behind him.

"Are we really going to be in the Pilot Competition? All of us?" Dunea appears somewhat uncertain, and I don't blame her. She is older, and not someone who would normally ride a hoverboard.

"Let's just hear what he tells us," Chifuz says, standing casually with his arms folded.

"Easy for you to say, you're military," Menahit retorts. "Some of us have never touched those flying things. I know décor, not hoverboards!"

Dunea whispers, "I'm scared."

"It's not so bad," I say. "Did you know, you can sit down on it and just hold on?"

"Oh really?" Menahit's eyes widen with interest.

This is when Benaten arrives, walking down the narrow path into the courtyard.

At the mere sight of him, I feel an immediate painful jolt in my abdomen, a combination of panic and joy. Nothing has changed; it's the same *Ter* Aten as usual, plainly dressed, with his long, raven mane of hair held back in a messy segmented tail behind him, and his boots on.

But the moment I see his grey eyes and lean jawline, the masculine energy in his gaze, my heart starts pounding. . . . It's not him, it's *me*, all me, being an impossible fool.

This needs to stop.

Fortunately, I don't have time for my *hoohvak* thoughts, because everyone comes alive, crowding around him.

"*Ter* Aten!"

"*Nefero eos*," he says, stopping the babble with one hand upraised. "I have hopeful news for all of us. I know you have many questions. As you heard yesterday, I made the decision to participate in the Pilot Competition. The change in my personal circumstances means I no longer have the guaranteed position of a high-ranking nobleman in the coming events. So, now I must earn my place in another way, same as anyone else here. And I'm offering this same opportunity to all of you."

"But why the Pilot Competition, *Ter* Aten?" someone asks.

"Because it is sponsored by the Imperial Dynasty and offers the largest opportunity for success." Benaten turns to the man who asked. "It's the biggest Competition and also the most straightforward—unlike the capricious and petty requirements of the Great Houses in their individual Competitions. There's a solid chance for a great number of people to make it, and the Teams aspect makes it clear. The Pilots are vital to the journey, and many will be needed for the ships."

"What about the skills requirement?" another man asks.

"It might surprise you, but from what I learned, the skills needed are basic and less specialized than most other types of

Service. You must have good reflexes, be able to fly fast, maneuver, and stay on your flight vessel—which for most contenders will be the hoverboard."

"That's interesting," Chifuz says. "The original Kassiopei announcement, as I remember because I noted it down, only mentioned larger air vehicles such as transports, *depets*, buses. It referenced 'other means' almost as an afterthought. So why hoverboards?"

"Maneuverability," Benaten replies. "I did some thorough research yesterday, and according to my excellent sources, the race course will favor smaller vehicles. Hoverboards might not have the speed of a hover car, but they can go with ease where a larger vessel may not."

"At least you won't fall out of a hover car," Dunea says softly.

Benaten glances in her direction. "You can still crash it, badly. Ultimately, there's a tradeoff."

"If you say so," Girsul speaks up. "I trust your decision on this matter, *Ter* Aten."

"Glad to hear," our employer says. "However, I want everyone here to know that I still haven't ruled out the use of other larger vehicles, at least for some of you who absolutely cannot use hoverboards. So, don't despair just yet. Nothing is final until the actual day of the Competition."

Dunea smiles sadly, acknowledging him.

Benaten continues, "In addition to flying skills, you must also be able to work with others as a Team. Everything else will be taught to you if you pass the Competition."

"I'm surprised, *Ter* Aten, that no tech skills are required," Mihravat the technician speaks up.

"Not at this initial stage. However, for those of you who are already well-versed, it will help in the long run."

Mihravat nods.

"And now," Benaten resumes, "here is what all of you will be expected to do. The Pilot Competition is indeed a Race. You'll be flying across all ten City Circles. There will be ten starting points, or Start Gates. They're still being constructed, as of now, I'm told. . . . When completed, they will be located at the outer walls of Poseidon in Circle Ten, spread out at even intervals, encircling the City. On the morning of the event, you may choose to line up at any one of the Start Gates.

"As soon as the Race begins, you will fly from your Start Gate toward the center of the City, Circle One. This is the individual stage of the race. The goal is to fly as quickly as possible without touching the ground."

"Sounds simple enough," Chifuz says. "Did they say how high up in the air we need to be?"

"Excellent question," Benaten replies with a smile. "You may fly as low or as high as you like. In fact, for those of you who are beginners, I recommend you keep closer to the ground. There are no altitude rules saying you must soar like a bird in the sky."

A few chuckles are heard.

"However," *Ter* Aten continues, "here's the hard part. Along the way, you must fly *under* one *bridge* of *every* canal, without touching the water below, before proceeding onward to the next Circle. Bridge sensors will register your passing underneath a bridge. If you fail to do this at every canal, or if you make contact with the canal water, you will be disqualified from the Race."

Grumblings are heard among the staff.

"What if you get sprayed with water?" Uru exclaims with a chortle.

Benaten glances at my idiot brother. "Don't get sprayed."

"But what if some *chazuf* decides to spray you?" Uru persists.

"Hush, Uru!" I hiss. Everyone is likely wondering who's this insolent little *hoohvak*. . . .

I stare at my employer with mortification at my brother's big mouth, but there's a glimmer of amusement in Benaten's expression.

He pauses for a moment, focuses his attention at Uru. "A valid observation. There will be quite a few *chazufs* out there during the Race, and they will be trying all kinds of underhanded techniques to disqualify their competition. Unfortunately, my answer is, I don't know. I don't know if anyone will differentiate between you getting maliciously soaked and actually touching the canal. So, don't let it happen to you. Understood?"

"Yes, *Ter* Aten," Uru says, his face turning serious but somehow managing to register mischief.

Bast help us!

"Very well," Benaten resumes the instructions. "Once you reach the Center Circle, the heart of the City, this is where the Team stage of the Race begins. Ten Finish Gates will be installed at even intervals all around the shore of Circle One. High in the air above each Finish Gate will be a circular hovering platform, one per Gate."

Suddenly I remember visiting the Palace to see Prince Oron and Princess Arlenari and seeing the strange large objects hovering in the sky overhead, right above the walls. . . . *Could they have been those platforms?*

"Each of you must pass through one Finish Gate, at which point the sensors will register your time. This part is very important. Speed counts!" Benaten pauses, observing everyone with intensity. "You'll then immediately fly up toward the nearest hovering platform overhead. Since this is the Team portion, we will be doing this together."

Serious, grim faces look back at him.

"The goal is for the fastest Teams to claim one of each ten platforms. As soon as all the members of one team make contact with the platform, it becomes ours—we key the platform with voice commands and make it move. That's when the second and final portion of the Race begins."

Benaten pauses for emphasis. "Our Team goal is to fly our platform—*drive* it back across the City to the outer walls of Poseidon at Circle Ten, toward any Start Gate—all while keeping any other Team from claiming it. Once we arrive there, we must secure the platform on top of a pole tower associated with that Start Gate.

"As soon as the platform docks in place, the Team will be declared a winner, becoming one of the Top Ten Pilot Teams. Anyone else on the platform but not part of the winning Team, will also be admitted to the Pilot program, but with secondary privileges. So yes, it's important that we get on a platform and *stay there*, no matter what happens. This is how we save our lives."

Growing voices of concern come from the staff. People mumble and shake their heads.

"This *shar-ta-haak* Pilot Competition sounds much too difficult, impossible even, *Ter* Aten," a man says. "Assuming we even get through the first part individually, make it to the Finish Gates at the Center Circle, who determines if a platform is ours?"

"Sensors," Benaten replies. "Everything is determined by sensors inside your identification tokens, which you'll receive before the start of the Race. The ID tokens look very similar to your comm badges. I will be handing them out to you."

"Wait—you're saying that people from other Teams can be on the platform with us?" Chifuz asks.

"Yes. Others can share our platform, as long as we're the dominant Team."

"Okay," Mihravat asks sullenly. "But what do we do if another Team tries to take over our platform?"

Benaten thinks before answering. "We *defend* it. We keep it voice-keyed to our Team. While we're still in flight, it's quite likely that another Team with more members might catch up with us. Expect this to happen, multiple times even. Technically, they can attempt to take the platform from us at any time during the flight, but only before we dock the platform."

"So, there might be fighting? Oh, blessed Hathor . . ." Dunea asks, with fear in her voice.

Benaten turns to her with a sympathetic expression. "Yes, very likely so. But not everyone on the Team will be expected to fight. Leave that to *me* and to those who are able. The rest of you will be needed to drive the platform and maintain the voice commands—the reason for having a Team."

Dunea sighs and shakes her head. "*Im Ter*, I don't think I can do this. I'm no longer young. And this is so far beyond me that. . . ." She doesn't finish and lowers her gaze.

Benaten looks at her with sympathetic eyes (as do many of the staff). "I understand. It is a bitter thing to be doing, all of this. All the Service Competitions are cruel at best. But—so is the destruction that's coming with the Sky Rock. You don't have to make your final decision now. Think about it, and let me know before the day of the Pilot Race. This goes for everyone, all of you here."

Dunea nods silently.

Benaten takes a deep breath, and continues giving us the details.

"Now then. All your names are registered for the event. This means that you have the *choice* to participate, and you are guaranteed a place on my Team. I will also provide all the transportation necessary—in other words, hoverboards, and anything larger. There are enough units for all of you." And he points to the back of the yard where the familiar hoverboards lie in two tall stacks on the grass.

"You will have the rest of today and three more days to practice and prepare. The Pilot Competition is on the twenty-eighth day of Setaet. Yes, I realize it's short notice, but so is the apocalypse. I understand that some of you have doubts about your own capabilities. I repeat, you are *not* being forced to participate."

Benaten glances around at all of us, and his gaze pauses meaningfully on Dunea and Menahit before moving on. Then, his resonant voice rises in strength. "However, I urge you to consider this opportunity seriously, and at least to *try*."

Benaten pauses, and his energy-filled gaze sweeps over us with a sudden fire. "Some of you are already proficient in the use of hoverboards. You will do well to help the rest. Who here can fly?"

"I can!" Before anyone else can speak, my brother's childish voice breaks the silence. He raises and waves one hand fiercely, while holding on to his board with the other.

Ter Aten turns in our direction. "Ah, the boy who's worried about canal water spray."

"*Ter* Aten, this is Uru, my brother," I speak up, while my heart pounds so hard that I feel my lungs constricting. "It's true, he is really good! He brought his own hoverboard."

Benaten observes Uru with a sharp gaze, then nods. "We shall see. Anyone else?"

More voices are heard, including Chifuz, Mihravat, Girsul, and several other men whose names I don't know.

I begin to raise my hand then put it down and stay quiet. My so-called ability to fly is laughable. None of the few other women here speak up at all. Indeed, they appear uncomfortable.

Benaten's trainer, the bearded older man called Xingir Guai steps forward then. "I'll be assisting all of you with this," he says in a quiet, solid voice. "With your permission, *im Ter*—"

"Of course." Benaten motions to him. "Please proceed."

"I am Xingir," the trainer says. "Everyone, move back and clear the area. First, I want those of you who can fly *at all*, no matter how poorly, to get yourself one of the hoverboards, and line up here. Starting with you, boy, who already has his own board."

Uru surges forward with an excited smile, and stands in the middle of the courtyard. Meanwhile, the rest of us back up, clearing a large circle, and make our way to the hoverboards.

Dunea, Menahit, and two other women whose names I don't know, stay back with a few of the remaining men.

In some embarrassment, I follow Girsul and the other men toward the pile of hoverboards, and pick one.

Then I get in the very back of the line.

CHAPTER
FIFTY-FOUR

"I want to see what each one of you can do on a hoverboard," Xingir says. "You will get on a board, fly around this courtyard once, and come back. Let's start with you." And he points at Uru.

My brother jumps forward, drops his hoverboard so it hovers near the ground, then leaps on it with both feet in his usual feather-light stance. He sings the few simple notes to command the board and it lurches quickly, rising high into the air over our heads in a matter of heartbeats.

Uru leans into the wind like an expert, and soars around the courtyard at breakneck speed, with knees slightly bent, balancing perfectly with his skinny, little-boy legs. When he returns and descends, hovering barely off the ground, Uru taps the back end of the board with one foot, so that it swings into a vertical position just as he hops off, demonstrating a sleek dismount. The hoverboard ends up standing next to him, propped against his fingers as he lands.

Everyone makes sounds of appreciation, while Xingir nods comfortably. "Well done. I can see you've been flying a lot."

Uru's face beams with a smile, as he steps back, with his upright board in his hands, making room for the next person.

Chifuz steps forward and drops his board. Voice keys it, then stands up on it, sings the go command, and is airborne. He flies with ease around the courtyard, showing his military training in the clean, perfect stance and effortless balance. He returns, without any flair, but demonstrating that he is highly proficient.

Girsul is next. I already know Girsul can fly decently, but unlike the previous demonstrators, he is not particularly comfortable. And so Girsul takes his time, steps on the board with an initial wobble, then rises into the air somewhat slowly and flies lower than either Chifuz or Uru.

When he returns and steps off the board, he exhales in relief. "I need more practice."

Xingir watches Girsul without judgment. "You'll get the practice. Not too bad. Next!"

Three more men follow. One of them flies confidently, like Uru, but almost falls off when descending, so definitely overconfident. The other two can barely stand up, and balance wildly, flying very low to the ground.

"No problem. Keep practicing. You will get better before we're done here," Xingir tells all of them.

And now it's my turn.

My stomach fills with anxiety, as I step forward. Feeling self-conscious in front of everyone, as if I'm a Storyteller going up on stage to tell a story, I cast down the board before me.

Breathe, Semmi, a familiar alien voice speaks in my head. Heket must feel my sudden turmoil.

"Thanks, Heket . . ." I think-mumble in reply.

But I can't pay attention to the *pegasus* at the same time as I deal with the hoverboard. So, I try to ignore the waves of comfort that issue from him, flooding me.

I sing the voice command to raise the levitating board higher off the ground before I get on—because not even Bastet and the other great gods can convince me to *stand* on it. I hitch up my skirt just enough so that I can straddle the board, and I sit down. "Sorry," I mumble out loud. "This is how I ride."

And then, feet dangling, I rise into the air. . . .

It's a different sensation, flying in the open, compared to being inside the dark tunnels with a relatively low ceiling. Suddenly I feel a terror of heights as I find myself high over everyone's heads, staring down at the distant courtyard below, bordered by unkempt shrubbery. Even the sun seems brighter here, now that I'm slightly closer to holy Ra. . . .

Reaching the level of tall tree branches, I lean forward, face bathed in the crisp morning wind, and put both hands down on the board, holding onto either side with my fingers.

An unexpected memory comes to me, of flying on a *pegasus* bat, comfortably seated, clutching its silky fur. . . . Now that I've ridden both, I can confirm that it's far less frightening to ride a *pegasus* than a hoverboard. Too bad that's not really an option for the Race.

I circle the area and voice command the board to descend. It comes to a stop before Xingir. I swing one leg over and get off.

He gives me an amused look and says, "That'll work."

I feel an overwhelming sense of relief, and happen to glance in the direction of *Ter* Aten.

Benaten watches me intensely with a faint smile.

At once, heat engulfs my neck, rises to consume my face. . . . I blink and look away quickly, then take a step back, pulling my board with me.

Bast help me . . . what accursed, hoohvak *feelings. . . .* This is becoming ridiculous.

NOW THAT WE'VE shown what we can do, Xingir turns to the rest of the staff who supposedly don't know how to use a hoverboard at all.

"You can see, as she just demonstrated, that you don't need special skills or abilities to fly on a hoverboard," the trainer says, pointing at me. "What is your name, girl?"

"Semmi," I reply.

Xingir nods. "Feel free to do what Semmi did there. Sit on the board, lie on it. No one cares. As long as you stay on and don't fall off, you can ride in the Competition."

The remaining women and men appear to be much relieved, judging by their expressions.

"Indeed," Xingir continues, "the most difficult part will be teaching you the basic voice commands. But as you know, that part is not that difficult at all. You'll have the tone sequences memorized in a couple of days. Just in time for the Pilot Competition."

He rubs his hands together. "Now, who wants to try first?"

FOR THE REST of the morning and afternoon, we practice flying in the courtyard and around the estate. Xingir Guai himself is highly skilled on the hoverboard, and he is a good instructor. He walks around and demonstrates various stances and positions, useful hand grips for those of us who ride sitting down. He sings voice commands, and encourages beginners, with a solid, easy smile that never condescends but inspires confidence.

Meanwhile, the more experienced hoverboard users such as Chifuz and Uru, practice advanced moves and share useful bits of advice with the rest of us. Uru also indulges in a bit of showing off, as he constantly executes absolutely pointless little jumps and other antics while on his board.

After a few hours, even the most reticent among the staff, such as Dunea, make the attempt to fly. Dunea sits down on the hoverboard, lies forward on her stomach, and hugs the board for dear life, as she rises just slightly above waist level, flying slowly.

"Hathor and Bast . . ." she mumbles, over and over, as she circles the courtyard.

"This is actually not bad at all," Menahit states, after having had her own turn sitting on a hoverboard.

"I told you," I say with satisfaction. "We can all do it!"

Nearby, Chifuz overhears us, and pauses with a wink. "I'm starting to think we have a full Team."

AT SOME POINT during our training, Girsul comes up to me and says discreetly, "Sun basking time?"

He and I walk beyond the courtyard to a small but sunny nook near the estate walls, where we take out the *pegasei* and give them a thorough feeding.

"Everyone here knows about them, right?" I ask carefully. "We don't really have to hide."

Girsul chuckles. "I suppose, but just in case someone doesn't, we don't want *Ter* Aten to be concerned about it."

"To be honest, I'm more concerned about my little brother seeing me handle these *pegasei*," I say, putting the shining rainbow turnip away in my pocket because Heket just told me it has fed sufficiently. "Uru doesn't know I have it, and neither does anyone else in my family. And I plan to keep it that way."

"Same here. No one in our home camp knows." Girsul continues to turn the *pegasus* bracelet with his palm, so that it catches the light. Unlike me, he doesn't have a *pegasus* in his head telling him when it's time to stop.

WHEN WE GET BACK, Benaten is speaking again, and everyone has paused their hoverboard riding to listen.

"Tomorrow, we'll continue to practice the basics, and then discuss strategy," he tells the gathered staff. "There are things you'll need to pay attention to, in order to keep up with the others during the Race. We need to consider what special tricks and techniques might give all of you an advantage. As Leader of this Team, I'm going out right now to investigate and examine some of the general areas of our Race route. I also have additional business to handle."

He pauses, searching the staff with his gaze. "Chifuz, you'll come with me. . . . The rest of you, continue training with Xingir for at least one more hour before resuming your regular duties. Next time I see you, we're going to have a Team plan. Good effort, everyone. See you all back here in the morning at seventh hour."

And our employer leaves us, along with Chifuz, both heading back inside the house.

"Where are they going now?" Uru asks, tugging my skirt. "Aren't they going out?"

"They are," Menahit replies. "They're probably going down to the tunnels *underneath* the house, and leaving that way."

Uru looks amazed. "There are tunnels underneath the house? What tunnels?"

I bite my lip. "Uru, I think it's best that *Ter* Aten tells you himself, and only if you need to know. Yes, there are tunnels and he uses them for some secret work he does."

"Oh, you mean when he's being the Man in the Nik—"

"Shut your *hoohvak* mouth, Uru!" I rush to interrupt. "Don't ever speak about that in public, not even here! Got that? Or I'll pull your ear!"

Menahit shakes her head in mild amusement. "Let the boy find out now. He will eventually, now that he's working here."

"Well, he isn't exactly *working* here," I say awkwardly. "He is flying with us, yes, but—"

"Probably should ask *Ter* Aten to hire him on." And Menahit gets back on her hoverboard.

. . .

AFTER SEVERAL MORE HOURS OF hoverboard training, Xingir dismisses those of us who don't have other specific tasks for the day, and Uru and I return home.

"That went well," I tell my brother in relief as we ride the late afternoon bus. "I think I'm going to ask *Ter* Aten if he might indeed hire you."

"Yes! I can be a messenger for him!" Uru chortles with excitement.

"You certainly can, *chazuf*. But first, we need to continue to practice for the Pilot Race."

And we do.

For the next three days.

Sacred Bastet and all the great gods of *Atlantida*, there are so many things, a whirlwind of things taking place over those three days. Exciting, but also repetitive and arduous, all at the same time.

Every morning, we go to the estate courtyard to train, and those of us such as Girsul, Uru, and I, stay there until late afternoon.

Ter Aten informs us that, until the Pilot Race is over, our training takes precedence over any work in the underground tunnels, because he needs a solid, functional Team. Meanwhile, he himself disappears for most of the three days, doing his clandestine business, and occasionally taking Chifuz or select others with him.

Every time Benaten leaves, Uru stares in his wake with admiration. He then pokes me in the ribs or whispers near my ear, "The Man in the Niktos Cloak . . . hehehe!" And when I tell him to hush, he adds, "I want to go with him. . . ."

"I know you do." I sigh in amusement, shaking my head at the little *sha*. "Maybe later. But now, we all need to practice, as he ordered."

Our continued training on the hoverboards consists of flying while sitting, lying down, occasionally attempting to stand up on it, and endless other stance variations.

Xingir Guai insists that we practice flying through very narrow vertical spaces, to mimic possible limitations of flying under a bridge. To that end, a rope is strung across two trees, and lowered further down, for each flying pass, until it's very close to the ground.

"Learn to fall down flat on your stomach and hold on, at a moment's notice. Learn to squat and crouch on the board. Learn to stand up from a low or seated position."

We attempt to do what he says.

"When you get up, keep your hands firmly on the sides of the board, so that you are always gripping something," he adds. "Maintain a strong grip!"

Easier said than done. By day two, my fingers ache from squeezing the *hoohvak* board so hard.

Dunea, Menahit, and the other two women do a lot of groaning, and continue to fly sitting down for all of it. Only a few of them attempt to get up and crouch or kneel.

I learn the two women's names: Emzarabi, a tiny, very pale-skinned young woman with bony arms and brown hair, and Nemadoris, close to my height and somewhat on the heavy side, with a round, warm face, curly hair and light brown skin like Uru and me.

Emzarabi is generally terrified of the hoverboard, and makes high pitched sounds whenever her board makes any hard turns. Nemadoris is calm and resigned, wrapping her arms around the board, but has a bad habit of closing her eyes when flying.

"You do that and you will crash," Xingir reminds her. "Yes, the sun is bright, and there's wind and dust in your face. But you must look where you're going. So, open your eyes, squint, look down, but always look! Also, lift your feet more, keep them back, closer to the board, don't just dangle them."

His stream of minor criticisms and advice for all of us is endless. Fortunately, it is all useful.

At some point, Xingir passes out rope and various cords to everyone on staff. "As a last resort, tie yourself to the board."

And he demonstrates, looping the cord around the waist and then underneath the board, and ties specific knots that are easy to unravel in one pull. So, for several hours we also practice tying and unraveling knots. Menahit and Dunea enjoy this part, since they are nimble-fingered and dexterous.

I learn the names of the three other men on staff who choose to stay on the Team (while three others regretfully tell Benaten they cannot do it, because of their personal circumstances or physical shortcomings). They are Aramazd, Yereg, and Tehom. Black-bearded, muscular Aramazd, with a shaved head and skin reddened by the sun, is the overconfident one, who flies fearlessly, but not that well. Brown-haired Yereg and pale-skinned, red-haired Tehom are both very careful, both somewhat older, and they tend to sit on the board.

In the long run, all that matters is that we all don't fall off.

There's one other thing we discuss.

"We don't have any information on the nature of the hovering platforms," Xingir tells us. "All we know is, they appear disk-shaped from the ground, but they're strictly guarded, and there's absolutely no access to them. No one is permitted to fly up there to see them before the actual Race."

Many staff members shake their heads. Unhappy, frightened whispers are heard.

Xingir watches our reactions with sympathy. "We can only guess as to what's on the top layer, what kind of surface we'll be dealing with. Assuming the worst—that it's a slippery, smooth, or featureless, orichalcum surface—we need to be prepared to stand up on it without any guardrails, as it moves."

"Wear sturdy shoes," Menahit says with a sigh.

"Correct. Also, as a last resort, each of you will be given

hand grips. Like this—" Xingir reaches inside his pocket and takes out an odd-looking fabric glove. All around the outside of the glove there are bumps and little suction cups. It's the kind of grip glove I've seen delivery carriers wear when they work hauling in the markets.

"Use this to hold on to the platform, if needed."

Finally, by the end of the third day, on the eve of the Pilot Race, Benaten gathers us and passes out small, *astroctadra*-shaped metallic pins, each the size of a thumbnail.

"Tomorrow, you will attach this to your clothing, preferably on the inside of a pocket or some other safe spot, so it doesn't easily fall off. This ID token is your only identifying object, and it's critical that you have it with you for the duration of the Race. It is programmed with your name, Team number, and Team name. We are Team 43. Team Niktos."

We are also given updated maps with the exact locations of all ten Start Gates on Circle Ten, and all ten Finish Gates on Circle One. Mihravat the technician personally loads the data update onto each one of our badge comm units. This is when I learn that Mihravat is responsible for all the various tech programs that Benaten uses in his secret work in the underground.

"Pick any Start Gate that's convenient to you," Benaten tells us. "Be there, with your boards, at least an hour early, around seventh hour of Ra, so that you can line up and be scanned, and listen to the official Imperial instructions. The Race itself starts at eighth hour of Ra. During the Race, make your individual way to any of the Finish Gates, and then find me there so that we can all claim a platform."

"How will we find you, *im Ter*, among the crowds of contenders?" Yereg asks with an anxious expression.

"I will transmit the number of the platform that looks most promising—in other words, least occupied. So, watch your messages. In addition, the new map data shows all of you on the map of the City, based on the location of your ID token. Check the map to see other members of your Team, including myself. As long as you are not disqualified, you appear as a moving dot."

"Should we come armed, *im Ter*? And what weapons are permitted?" Aramazd asks.

"Yes, you may bring whatever weapon you can use well. But it is not obligatory."

Ter Aten pauses, looks at all of us with solemn intensity. I feel the gaze of his grey eyes briefly upon me and shiver with inexplicable emotions.

"May all the gods watch over you," he says at last. "Fly fast and smart, and be careful. Stay away from others who might try to distract you. It is better to be a little slower than reckless, especially under the bridges. And most important of all, once you get on the platform, *stay on*, regardless of which Team takes control."

Benaten turns to look meaningfully at Dunea, Menahit, and a few others. "This is the moment to make your final decision. Yes, I have decided to provide those of you who need it, a proper hover transport. So, you won't have to struggle with the hoverboards. However, you'll still have to face the platform yourselves during the second stage."

He pauses. "We were just informed that, to avoid having an early advantage, Teams are not permitted to have all their members using the same Start Gate, so avoid Gate 7 where we will have our large transport. Mihravat will be driving you, since his technical flight skills are superior. Those taking the transport, which can fit six people, must meet him at Start Gate 7. The rest of you, use any other Start Gate, and I will see you at the Finish Gates!"

CHAPTER
FIFTY-FIVE

Month of Setaet, 28th Day.
84 days until Impact.

Today is the day of the Pilot Competition.

I wake up in the dark, long before dawn, because I can hardly sleep. The anxiety had gripped me the night before and would not let up, until I fell into a restless, hallucination-filled slumber. I'm sure that Uru was similarly affected, because I could hear him turning in the cot all through the night.

And now, it's time.

I sit up, and whisper, "Uru! Wake up, we have to get ready."

"I know," he replies at once, groggily, which tells me he is not sleeping.

We fumble with our clothes in the darkness, and put on our best shoes. As always, I reach inside the pocket of my skirt to confirm that the turnip is safely there. Not sure how or when I'll have time to feed Heket during the Race, but the *pegasus* is my responsibility and has to come with me.

In the living room, our Father also seems to be awake, as he mumbles something to us from his bench.

"We'll be fine, *Papai*, go back to sleep," I reply, moving past him to the inner door to the back yard. Uru is already there, running for the toilet seat.

The sky is barely turning grey with dawn. After taking my own turn on the toilet and washing up, I head for the kettle with our leftovers. The spicy lentil stew tastes like sand for some reason, and I have no appetite, but I swallow it down anyway. Standing at my side, Uru shovels it in his mouth, but appears equally disinterested.

Back indoors, our two hoverboards are propped upright against the wall near the front door.

Yesterday, it was very strange having to bring my borrowed hoverboard home with me for the first time. I rode it, sitting down, all the way from *Ter* Aten's estate to the bus stop on Circle Five, with Uru riding his standing up, as he normally does. We loaded the boards into the hover bus storage bins, unloaded them when we finally got off at Circle Nine, and again rode the boards directly home. . . .

"We need to check the map to find out where we must go, Uru," I say, as we attach our ID tokens to the inside of our clothes. "You too, so that you know how it's done."

I stick my token pin into the fabric of a secret little interior pocket of my shirt, right over my heart. It's the same place I keep my personal Evil Eye amulet blessed at the Temple of Bastet. Uru has a similar pocket, sewn with care by our Grandmother, with his own amulet, and I help him pin his token securely.

And now, the maps. . . .

Uru was given his own temporary comm badge for the Pilot Competition, but he has no idea how to use it. I demonstrate how to call up the hologram map on mine, and he quickly copies my actions. At once, our living room becomes visible, thanks to the hologram glow.

We stare closely at the tiny maps of Poseidon projected over the palms of our hands, and see a scattering of dots in different colors all throughout the concentric circles. I pinch and separate my fingers to expand the holo-map, enlarging the view.

There are ten prominent dots, shining bright amber-orange, positioned at regular intervals around the outer perimeter of Circle Ten. Another ten incandescent white dots shine around the much smaller perimeter of Circle One. These must be the Gates—orange ones for Start, white ones for Finish.

I notice one super bright blue dot on the map, and it is right over our house in Denwen's Pit. Next to it is a smaller red dot. And there are other similar red dots spread all over the City map. I count them with some difficulty in my head, with the assistance of my ten fingers, and apparently there are twelve red dots in total.

"Uru, look," I say, "This blue dot? That's me. And the red dot next to it is you!"

"How do you know that's you?" my brother asks.

"There are twelve other red dots on the map, I just counted. That's the rest of our Team, since we have a total of fourteen people on our Team," I say. "Now look at your own map. You also have a blue dot, and it represents you. But if we compare our two maps, the blue and red dots are reversed. We're standing right next to each other. If you step away from me, your blue dot should move, and my red dot should move. Makes sense?"

Uru immediately tests this by walking to the door, and indeed the dot that represents him starts to move away from mine.

Meanwhile, I notice that one of the red dots on the map is larger and brighter than the others, and it appears to be moving rapidly away from Circle Five, and heading outward, in our general direction.

"Look, this one's bigger than the other red dots." I call my brother back over and show him. "It has to be the Team Leader, *Ter* Aten."

"O-o-oh!" Uru is impressed. "He must be flying very fast."

Now that we have our maps figured out, we pick the Start Gate closest to us on Circle Ten.

"We're going right here, Uru. That's Start Gate 6, directly southwest of our home." I point it out on the map. "Got that?"

He nods.

"One last thing," I say. "Did you remember to put the cord and rope and hand grips in your big pocket?"

Uru reaches in his bulky pants pocket, then nods again.

"And you have your little knife?"

"I always have it," my brother says, starting to hop in place with excitement.

"Good," I say, and pat my own small knife in my pocket next to the turnip and my folded loops of rope and hand grips. "Be careful, if you must use it, little *sha*. If you have to knife somebody—Bastet help us—make it count. Understood?"

"Understood."

"Then, let's go!"

ONCE OUTSIDE, we get on our hoverboards, and fly down the street, in the opposite direction from where we usually go each morning. Today, we're heading deeper into Denwen's Pit, towards the southwest outer walls of Poseidon.

The first thing we see is that numerous other people are out and about already, and it's still barely light. The *niktos* sky is turning a lighter shade of indigo and grey, and it is dotted with dark specks of airborne vehicles. Many of them are hoverboards.

I have never seen so many flying vehicles in the skies over Circle Ten, especially not in this direction. Indeed, all this additional traffic is headed *away* from the center of the City.

Are they all going to the Pilot Competition?

Uru and I also continue to move outward, toward the City walls, flying low over the streets of our impoverished neighborhood. With each passing block, the hovels all around us get even poorer and more dilapidated, revealing crumbling walls of limestone and broken fences. A few local dogs bark at us as we go by.

In the distance, the City walls loom. Grey metal and once-liquefied concrete stone, without any trace of orichalcum. They are ancient, and their height is immense.

Twice taller than the Imperial Palace walls, the City walls of Poseidon stand just beyond the wide, open space where the last of the squat houses and sparse trees end altogether. That area is no man's land, consisting of a desolate dirt roadway that encircles the City just before the sterile walls begin.

And that's where we see Start Gate 6, our destination.

The first thing that greets us from the distance is the pole tower—an upright obelisk structure formed of scaffolding, built from the ground up, newly erected, and attached directly to the wall.

The pole tower rises, silhouetted against the dawn sky, far above the walls, narrowing into a platform dock on top. Its highest point is likely three times the height of the Imperial Palace walls, in comparison.

Start Gate 6 is aligned with (and positioned directly in front of) its specific pole tower. It consists of an arch, also formed of sparse scaffolding, no more than two stories high, and the width of a small building. The space between the two legs of the arch is wide enough to accommodate five hover cars side-by-side. Directly above the arch floats a glowing holographic symbol of six notches, indicating the Gate number.

From its place in the middle of the desolate roadway, this structure faces the City. Numerous contender vehicles are already lined up in both directions along the wall, in a chaotic hovering multitude, ready to pass through the Gate.

The air overhead is a beehive of hover cars, hoverboards, and a few bus-sized larger transports. And the arriving crowds are only growing.

Two immense smartboards are installed high on the City walls of Poseidon, one on either side of the pole tower. And on the ground, at the left leg of the Gate and at the right leg, uniformed Imperial officials stand behind information tables.

"So many people!" Uru says, as we fly up to the Gate, and then attempt to find a spot in the so-called line on either side of it.

"Yeah, I had no idea there would be so many entrants in the Pilot Competition," I say in surprise. "There are more contenders here than at any of the other Service Competitions. And this is just one of *ten* Start Gates."

We pick the left leg of the arch and get in the back of the line there, since it seems slightly shorter than the other side. Even so, we find ourselves many feet away from the Gate. And as soon as we arrive in our spot, more vehicles and people get in line behind us.

Soon, we're surrounded by other contenders. Hover cars levitate silently, sending up dust as they land. People stand next to their hoverboards, arms folded, or sit on them, waiting. Men, women, and even children—so Uru's young age is not unique.

Grim, intense expressions everywhere, wary eyes. . . . Most of them don't appear to be together as a Team either. The line will not begin to move until the officials make the start announcement, and we have at least half an hour before that.

"Check your map, Uru," I say, as my brother squats in one sleek move, then sits down on his board cross-legged, with his feet tucked underneath him. "I want to make sure you remember how to use it."

Uru complies, and the little hologram pops up over his hands.

"Can you see the other red dots?" I ask. "I'm curious which Start Gates our Team members chose."

Uru pinches the map and stares for a few moments. "They are all over the place, at different Gates. I see five red dots bunched together at Start Gate 7."

"That would be the people from our Team taking the special transport, with Mihravat driving them. One of them must be Dunea. The others could be Emzarabi, Yereg, or Tehom."

Uru nods.

"Can you see any other red dots at our own Gate?" I ask. "Or is it just us?"

"Don't see anyone else."

"All right." I take a deep breath, dangling my legs underneath the hoverboard. "Now see if you can locate *Ter Aten*—"

Suddenly, a grand amplified voice issues from the smartboards overhead, drowning out every other sound.

"Attention, Contenders! On this twenty-eighth day of Setaet, *wixameret* and make ready for the Pilot Competition sponsored by the Imperial Kassiopei of *Atlantida*."

Everyone looks up. The smartboards have come alive with an Imperial feed. The face of Blessed Churu himself fills the screens, clad in his formal regalia, looking over us benevolently.

"My people!" the Imperator says. "I am proud of your courage and skill, and your loyalty to this Dynasty, City, and Nation. This day will show us the best of you. Those who achieve the objectives of this Competition will be admitted to the Imperial Pilot Corps. And now, listen to the instructions for the Pilot Race, and prepare yourselves. I wish you all success, and may the gods of wind and speed watch over each and every one of you."

The face of Churu disappears. It is then replaced by an aerial view of Poseidon, while a mechanical voice reads the formal instructions. There is otherwise perfect silence, as we all listen intently.

"Contenders! At eighth hour of Ra, the Start Bell will toll. From that point on, you and your vehicle may *not* touch the ground until you complete the Race. You must be riding your vehicle to enter the Start Gate. Board your vehicles now."

At once, everyone who is standing on the ground, rushes to mount their hoverboards, while those in hover cars and larger transports are ready to go.

"Uru, your long cord, now!" I say in haste, fumbling with my own ropes. "Remember, we must be tied to the board at all times, even when standing on it."

Uru stands up on the board in his flying stance, then takes out his long cord. He winds it around the rear portion of the hoverboard several times, ties a special anchor knot as we've been taught, then ties the other end around his waist, with enough give so that he can maneuver properly.

Since I'm sitting down, I use the shorter rope to wrap around myself and the board multiple times, and tie a single knot at my waist.

Both of us sing the command to raise our hoverboards off the ground to a sufficient height. Everyone around us is doing the same.

Meanwhile, the mechanized voice continues.

"Contenders, you are all registered and have received the information necessary from your Team Leaders. Your identification tokens must be worn for the duration of the Race. Make sure you have yours, or you will be disqualified.

"The ID tokens will light up red when you pass the Start Gate and remain lit for the duration of the Race for as long as you are active. In addition, a tone will sound, indicating your official start time. If you are disqualified, your ID token light will go out.

"As soon as you hear the Start Bell, you may enter the Start Gate and proceed to the Center Circle of Poseidon. Once there, you must pass through any Finish Gate, as quickly as possible. Your flight time will determine your individual score. The less time you take, the better your score.

"Along the way, you must pass under one bridge of every Circle canal, in order. If you skip a bridge at any Circle and attempt to backtrack, you will be disqualified. If you make contact with the water in any canal, you will be disqualified.

"After you pass the Finish Gate, you must immediately gather your Team. There must be at least ten members still active, in order to be eligible for the Team portion of the Race. Together with the Team Leader each Team will fly toward any one of ten platforms parked in the sky above every Finish Gate.

"Once on the platform, Team members must abandon all their other flying vehicles. Use the platform itself as your new vehicle.

"The Team with the best Team Score will claim the platform. Team Score is based on a combination of two criteria—smallest ratio of disqualified members and the average score of all active member individual scores. All of this is calculated in real time, and is subject to change at any moment until the end of the Race.

"The objective of each Team is to claim one of the platforms and drive it back across the City to any of the Start Gates, then dock it on top of the pole tower corresponding to the Gate. In this portion of the Race, your course is direct, and you are *not* required to pass underneath bridges.

"Every active, non-disqualified member of a given Team must be present on the platform in order to claim it. The edge of the platform will light up green to indicate it is claimed. In addition, your ID tokens will change color to green and sound a tone. If more than one assembled Team occupies the platform, the Team with the highest Score will be granted the claim.

"You must do everything within your means to keep your platform under your control, including combat with other Teams. All methods are allowed, including lethal force.

"If a Team Leader is eliminated or disqualified at any point, the ID tokens of the remaining members of that Team will immediately light up yellow. Members may continue to occupy a platform and hold on to their place, but they will no longer be eligible to become Prime Pilots, only backup Pilots.

"The Team that has control of the platform when it is docked will be declared a Top Ten winner. Members of the Top Ten Teams will become the Prime Pilots accepted into the Imperial Pilot Corps program, and their Team Leaders will earn additional privileges.

"Any other individual members of losing Teams that manage to remain on the platforms up to the moment they are docked, will also be accepted as backup Pilots. Their ID tokens will light up yellow. Anyone who is *not* on a platform or physically in contact with a platform at the time of docking, will be disqualified."

The mechanical voice grows silent. A long pause, during which we hear the wind blow.

"Contenders! It is now eighth hour of Ra. Wait for the countdown of five heartbeats and begin the Race!"

People all around us start shifting, leaning forward and adjusting their stance on their hoverboards. . . .

Suddenly, my heart is pounding.

"*Five. . . .*" booms the mechanical countdown.

"Uru!" I whisper urgently. "Fly fast but be careful, always!"

"*Four. . . .*"

"Don't wait for me!" I continue. "Got that?"

"*Three. . . .*"

Uru glances at me fiercely, then nods.

"*Two. . . .*"

"See you at the Finish Gate!" I stare at him, willing all the gods' blessings upon him, my emotion spilling over in my eyes. *I love you, little* sha.

"*Start!*"

A great booming bell tone sounds, and with it, the crowd starts moving. Everyone is vocalizing the initial commands to surge forward. Uru and I do the same.

As we approach our turn at the Start Gate, we can see people and vehicles at the front of the line already streaking through the arch of the Gate, like a swarm of hornets. Audibly loud tones sound each time a contender gets scanned in passing.

Ding! Ding! Ding! A cacophony of tones fills the air. Wherever they might be hidden on their persons, their ID tokens are lighting up.

In a few heartbeats, we're there too, moving through the wide space underneath the arch.

The ground is still barely away from my hanging feet, and I can see the rocks and loose gravel.

Uru is just ahead of me, and I follow him.

Ding! Uru's token rings as he enters.

Ding! My token resounds, with a mild vibration at my chest.

We're through the Start Gate and officially in the Race.

This is it . . . there's no going back now.

Bastet, help us!

"Go, Uru, go!" I yell at him, leaning forward on my belly and grasping my board, as other people fly past me and over me, fixed in smooth, upright stances, gaining altitude quickly. Great hover cars whoosh by.

Keep above the ground . . . mustn't touch the ground.

"See you, Semmi!" Uru cries, with a wild smile and a single glance back at me. Then he too maneuvers, rising higher into the air.

Suddenly, I hear desperate cries and piercing screams begin all around, as already some contenders collide, barely out of the Gate, and people start falling.

A woman not too far ahead and above me is struck by the nose section of a hover car, and dislodged from her board. Her rope harness doesn't help her; shrieking wildly, she tumbles from the height of almost two stories, falling on the hard ground . . . and goes silent.

Crap of a goat!

I stare before me, my gaze straining to find Uru, but he has disappeared into a tiny speck in the rapidly brightening sky, and I can no longer see him. So, I lean even closer to my hoverboard, keeping my body streamlined, hugging it with my arms and wanting to shrink involuntarily, so as not to get hit.

Right now, I am still flying slowly. I'm also low to the ground, barely over the height of one-story roofs. The outlying hovel rooftops of Denwen's Pit are rushing at me from below, dangerously close to my dangling feet.

I need to go higher, but doing that, I risk collision with more skilled flyers.

I probably need to keep low for a little longer. Let them all scatter wide into the City, until there is less traffic.

Just keep away from the hoohvak *rooftops.*

It occurs to me, as I am flying toward the interior of Poseidon, I'm also flying back in the direction of our home, which happens to be closer to the inner edge of Circle Ten. Soon, I see a few neighborhood streets, and then there's our street.

I glance fleetingly to my right, to see our house with its familiar rooftop. In two heartbeats I pass it, and keep going.

Soon, the Circle will end, and I will face my first bridge.

THE BRIDGE COMES SOONER than I imagine. Ironically, it's the same bridge I use every morning to run to the bus stop on Circle Nine.

How well I know its top side—worn paving stones and the metal railing posts anchored in small stone pylons. Now I get to see what's underneath.

Words from our training come to me: "Slow down on approach. Watch for any passing traffic including boats on the water or other flying contenders."

I glance around warily, then angle my hoverboard to descend . . . but not too far.

Don't touch the water.

Don't hit the underside of the bridge either.

The musty stink of the canal hits me as the light of the sky disappears. Briefly, I am in a dank and dark tunnel reminiscent of the underground network, as I fly carefully, keeping closer to the ceiling. The stones nearest the water are slimy green, with waves lapping over them. The water itself is brownish-black with filth. . . .

Fortunately for me, no one else is flying through here right now. I've been moving slower than most other contenders, so they're likely far ahead of me already.

Or maybe, Bast has granted me this one small mercy.

As soon as I emerge from under the bridge, my ID token dings.

I've been scanned. Now, on to Circle Nine.

• • •

AS I ENTER the air space over Circle Nine, I observe the grand panorama of the City around me, specifically looking out for other flying contenders. I see them everywhere, dark specks against the blue sky.

Everyone is keeping to themselves at this point, intent on their speed.

It's time for me to attempt to fly higher, since the rooftops here are starting to rise, with buildings of multiple levels predominating.

I wonder how Uru is doing? *Holy Bast, watch over him, please!*

Singing the command to rise, I hold on tight, and suddenly feel a wild surge of dizziness. Gods help me, I am so high above the ground! For the first time, I'm flying higher than I've ever been, almost at the height of a hover bus. . . . Occasional birds soar past me. The nearest contender is a barely visible silhouette far ahead, crouching on their board.

I squeeze my eyes shut with a surge of terror, and then think of Nemadoris and force myself to open my eyes and breathe. Meanwhile, my fingers grow stiff from clutching the board so hard and pressing my legs to the underside.

In a few heartbeats, my vertigo subsides. It's still there, but I am more in control.

At this point, I convince myself to increase speed.

If I don't go faster, I will have no chance in this Race. Not to mention, I will let down my little brother Uru, *Ter* Aten, and the rest of my Team.

Lowering my face, squinting against the wind and brightness of the sky, I surge forward, feeling the powerful air resistance.

And, because I'm such a *hoohvak*, only now it occurs to me—this Race is *grueling*, and it's going to be very, very *long*. I need to unclench my fingers before they go numb, because there are still many hours to go, things will only get worse, and I need to conserve my strength and stamina.

What was I thinking, entering this *shar-ta-haak* Pilot Competition?

THE WIDE CANAL and the nearest bridge between Circle Nine and Circle Eight looms before me. Suddenly, the air traffic has increased. Out of nowhere, other contenders are amassing, and I hear cries up ahead.

Merciful Bast, what is going on?

I slow down, preparing to dip and go under the bridge, but I can see there is something happening there.

Contenders approach, and then pull up sharply and halt, levitating in place. One or two people keep going, and they are suddenly bounced back sharply and tossed off their hoverboards.

A man screams as he falls down into the canal with a loud splash. His board is still airborne and spins wildly in place, still attached to its rider via rope, while the contender surfaces, cursing wildly, then pulls at the board as if it's an escaped bird. He is soaking wet and disqualified. . . .

"What's down there?" a woman asks, not too far from me.

"A wall of nets!" another replies, hovering below us, near the water. "The entire space under the bridge that's above water is blocked."

People curse. Several contenders fly over the bridge, circling it, and one of them goes too far, ending up just barely past the bridge on the side of Circle Eight.

"That *chazuf* just got disqualified and probably doesn't even know it," the woman next to me says, shaking her head. She stands on her board with easy skill, her skirts flattened against her legs by the wind. "They told us not to backtrack."

"That's right," a man confirms. "Once you're at the next Circle, you can't go back to the previous Circle and pass the bridge. You're done."

"So, what about this *hoohvak* bridge?"

"We fly to the next bridge!" a young girl calls out. "Follow the canal and stay over the water without going into the next Circle."

And that's what we do. The next closest bridge is within sight. I follow everyone, taking care to stay on the Circle Nine side of the canal.

When we get to the bridge, and people start descending, the vanguard arrivals again pull up sharply and hover in the air before the underside of the bridge.

"Same thing!" one of them cries with anger. "Nets blocking the way."

"Hathor and Bast! Why would someone do that?"

Contenders grumble and curse even more. As for me, I'm starting to feel a churning anxiety in my gut. "What if every bridge is like that?" I ask.

People turn to look at me from every direction.

"*Varqood!* Could be . . ." a man retorts grimly. "What if they set it up that way on purpose, as part of the Race?"

"No one told us!" someone yells. "They didn't tell us there would be obstacles."

Another man laughs grimly. "Why should they? It makes sense. Real Pilots get no warning if there's trouble ahead. The Imperials probably want to see how well we handle this kind of thing, as part of the trial."

In that moment, a hover car descends next to us, hovering low above the canal water. The driver must see the netting in place, and is considering what to do. Moments later, the same car rises—while we scramble to get out of its way in the air— and flies away, in the direction of the next bridge.

There's little else we can do but head after it.

· · ·

WE FOLLOW the curve of Circle Nine along its canal, moving slowly north and charting a circular path, bridge by bridge.

After five consecutive bridges it becomes apparent that they are all rigged with netting underneath. Hover cars and larger transports are gathering, and the traffic has grown to an impossible density in the air. They must be coming from all the other Start Gates on this side of the City.

So far, it appears that no one can get through to the next Circle.

A few contenders attempt to cut through the netting with their knives, but are immediately disqualified, judging by the loud dings issuing from their clothing and their loud cries of anger. Apparently, netting is considered part of the bridge, which in turn is part of the *ground*, and you cannot make contact with the ground. . . .

So now everyone just waits, hanging in the air, stalled for a solution.

I hug my board and squint in relentless terror of colliding with anyone and anything around me. A few people on hoverboards pass by so closely that I feel a breeze from them.

All the while, my gaze desperately searches for Uru in this crowd. No sign of my little brother.

I wonder how the rest of my Team are doing, wherever they are.

Then, inevitably, the collisions start happening around me. . . . Some lose their footing and fall. Many others recover themselves well and climb back on the boards before hitting the ground.

At least a quarter of an hour passes.

Suddenly, a large black transport makes its way down to the canal, lines up before the bridge, then keeps going.

Its front end begins to discharge fiery plasma bursts at the netting barrier. . . .

In a heartbeat, the netting is disintegrated, clearing the way.

Cries and cheers go up all around, as the transport moves through the opening under the bridge. It emerges on the other side, hovering low, then rises slowly. Two doors slide open, while still in the air, and a big man emerges, hanging insolently off the transport to wave at us, then makes rude gestures with his thumb.

From where I am levitating in the air, I can see his grinning face as he turns his short-cropped dark head. That's when I recognize the prominent scar along his jaw and throat.

He is Ba-Pef, the leader of the Neph-Tiari.

Crap of a goat! He's in the Race too? He, and probably the rest of the Neph-Tiari gang.

A pang of fear stabs my gut. . . .

Meanwhile, Ba-Pef gets back inside, his transport rises in the air, and continues onward to Circle Eight.

Now that the way under this particular bridge has been cleared, we all surge down, flying underneath the bridge past a few scorched remains of netting. Contenders are entering from both directions, it doesn't matter which, as long as we get scanned.

I suppose we owe Ba-Pef that much. *Ugh.* . . .

Waiting for a clear path, I carefully swoop under the bridge and hear the ding from my ID token as I emerge. Finally, I'm free to advance to Circle Eight.

AS I FLY over the industrial parts of Circle Eight, I think how most of this is familiar territory for me.

Somewhere nearby is the Chiprahat Exquisite Foods warehouse, where I used to work only a few days ago, but it feels like a lifetime now. . . . And further along are the many sprawling Bisfuri warehouses, with the immense, secret, restricted area underground.

I glance at the streets below and keep going, moving deeper

toward the interior of Poseidon. Everywhere around me, other air traffic fills the sky.

Soon, I cross the entire Circle Eight and reach the canal before Circle Seven.

The nearest bridge is in sight.

I sing the voice command to descend, and watch the nearest contenders in front of me to see what happens as they approach the space underneath.

Now that we know there could be bridge obstacles, what can we expect from this one?

Soon, we find out.

Even as I fly nearer, pausing at the midway point above the bridge so that I can observe both directions in the canal below, I can hear periodic screams coming from underneath the bridge. I also hear strange sounding blasts going off.

One man approaches the space under the bridge with caution, his hoverboard coasting slowly. He pauses, balancing loosely on his feet for several heartbeats, looking before him. Then, apparently satisfied that it's safe to proceed, he flies under the bridge.

A few moments later, there is a blast and a male scream. . . .

Then, on the other side, an empty hoverboard emerges, dragging a charred body through the water.

I freeze in terror, hovering in place. Then I force myself to go down to the canal level so that I can see for myself, from the best vantage point, what exactly is happening.

Another two people have seen what happened to the man earlier. They appear confounded and also remain motionless, suspended in the air. Eventually, they join me down below near the canal water to look.

"Did you see what happened?" a man asks.

I shake my head.

And so, we wait. In moments, another contender arrives. He gives us one cool glance, then glances at the deceptively clear area under the bridge. Then, before any of us have the chance to warn him, he flies quickly past us into the space underneath.

"Wait!" I exclaim, but too late.

As the man passes the middle point of the short tunnel, sudden blasts of flame issue out of a vertical row of pipes on both sides of the tunnel, heading all the way down to water level. . . . The man screams, becomes a fiery torch, and is incinerated.

His board spins out, strikes one side of the bridge but continues moving, while his burnt remains sink into the murky water of the canal.

The flames disappear, and the pipes in the stone are empty and harmless once more.

My mouth falls open, and I exchange horrified glances with the two people next to me. As more contenders arrive, we inform the others of the danger under the bridge.

"How do we get through?" everyone asks.

While we ponder, hover cars approach. One car keeps going, and the moment it passes that same midpoint underneath the bridge, it gets blasted on both sides by fire.

However, the car emerges on the other side with only a few embers clinging to its highly polished metallic surface, and keeps going, as if nothing happened.

Those of us on hoverboards curse, because obviously the larger transports now have an advantage over unprotected people.

Same thing happens with the next large transport. This one is even a bigger hover car, and it coasts through without any mishap, despite being licked by flames.

Meanwhile, the rest of us gather around the bridge, levitating in an anxious hive.

Moments pass.

Once again, we're stuck between Circles, faced by an impossible obstacle.

"What if we fly very fast?" a young woman asks.

"You want to try it? Bast help you," a man retorts.

"What if we sit down like her," a man says, pointing at me. "And then we lie flat as we fly very fast? Less area for fire to hit."

"Sure, you first," another man replies with dark sarcasm.

"What about flying in a rapid spin?"

"What if two of us fly sideways next to each other, with our boards facing the walls so that both bodies are protected—"

"And that way get only our feet and hands slightly burned? Why not? Go ahead, *chazuf*."

"Maybe we wait for two hover cars to fly next to each other, acting like barriers, and we fly between them?"

As people offer more *shar-ta-haak* suggestions, a young, very skinny boy of Uru's age plops down flat on his board. He turns around and flies away, low over the canal, far enough to get a running start.

He sings a voice command in a high-pitched little voice. Lowers his head down, stretches his hands before him so that his arms protect his ears, and flattens himself as much as possible. And then he streaks forward like a projectile.

I put one hand over my mouth in horror . . . even now, I'm thinking of Uru.

The boy hurtles under the bridge. There's a blast of fire, but he emerges on the other side, with only mildly scorched hair and sides.

He yelps, patting down his clothing, but immediately whoops in triumph, because his ID token had issued a satisfying ding.

"Unbelievable, *chazuf* made it!" people say, watching the little boy fly away toward Circle Seven.

And contenders began copying him, going *very* fast.

Many get through the obstacle with minor scorching or no problem at all. A few get serious burns and emerge on the other side unable to continue in the Competition. Several end up jumping into the canal intentionally, to quench the flames on their person.

Meanwhile, I'm incapacitated by overwhelming fear and remain fixed in my hover spot, watching the others.

What is wrong with you, Semmi, girl? I scream at myself inside my own head. *What kind of* hoohvak *coward are you? You can do this! You must go!*

Transports and hovercars go by, passing me and a few others too intimidated by the flames to move.

You're just sitting there, leaning forward on the accursed board, like a useless sack of sour wine, I tell myself.

How hard can it be, to continue doing what you're already doing? Just lie forward all the way, keep your head down, then go fast! . . . If it helps, imagine all of shaitunaat *is after you!*

The turmoil inside me gets so bad that I'm ready to burst. My heart is pounding so hard that even the *pegasus* inside my mind can tell I am going insane. Sudden waves of calm surge my way, and I know it's not my own calm—it has to be coming from Heket.

Deep breath, Semmi.

Fill yourself with peace.

Find a way.

"All right . . . yes, I know," I mind-speak at the alien being, hoping that Heket does not sense the extent of my shame.

Shame is meaningless, Heket replies, continuing to project calm. *What matters is your next action.*

"Easy for you to say, light blob!" I mumble-think. "You're already some kind of fire being. And I—"

And you are human, understandably afraid of fire and not very proficient in using your flying device.

Crap of a goat! A surge of living anger surfaces inside me. I voice command my board to reverse course and move away from the bridge along the canal, so that I can take a running start.

Enough cowardice. I'm doing this.

Levitating just above the water, at a sufficient distance from the bridge, I take a series of fast breaths, then grip the board. I lower my head until my chin touches the orichalcum surface, clench my legs against the hoverboard, and prepare to take a run at it. . . .

Just then, another contender before me, lying flat against her board, attempts to fly under the bridge. She flies quickly, but apparently not quickly enough. The next moment she screams, is burning, splashes down . . . and her ruined body floats away in the canal.

I squeeze my eyes shut, open them.

Varqood everything, I'm going.

Grandmother, help me. . . .

I glance one last time around me, at the stone walls of the canal, the lapping ochre-brown water. Then I narrow my eyes and look up at the azure vastness of the morning sky.

And that's when I see *him*.

He arrives as a speck of darkness, silhouetted against the brightness of day. In three heartbeats, he resolves into the elegant shape of a man clad in black—so dark that it eats all light. Suddenly, his shimmering cloak unfurls around him like the *niktos* wings of a night bird. The impossible fabric reflects unexpected, iridescent radiance amid the black.

The rider slows down, sinking from the sky toward me on his board, his black boots in a confident stance.

"Semmi, stop!" he calls out in his deep, rich voice, smooth like honey.

I stare up at him in disbelief.

Face hidden in darkness, concealed underneath a hood, the Man in the Niktos Cloak levitates over me. I can see the underside of his board, as he casts a shadow upon me from above, obscuring the daylight.

"Ben—I mean, *Ter* Aten!" I exclaim, feeling a swell of confusing warmth rising at my slip of the tongue. "What are you doing here?"

"I am here to help you," he replies in a matter-of-fact tone, then crouches down and offers me his large, elegant, black-gloved hand. "Come. Before you manage to kill yourself. I will take you across."

"But—" I say like a *hoohvak*, "how did you know I would be here?"

He chuckles. "You forgot about the map? My map is even better than yours. I know where all of you are and which unique map marker you are. As Team Leader, I'm responsible for you—all of you."

I nod, stupefied.

"Now, untie your cord."

I loosen the knot to undo the ropes around my waist. Then I sing a voice command to make my board rise toward him. As soon as we are level, he grabs my hand in his strong grip and pulls me even closer.

I make a small sound because he is lifting me from my board and onto his. In moments, my feet feel the non-slip surface, and I gasp again, because one of his arms closes around me, pulling me against his chest.

With his other hand, suddenly he snaps open his long whip.

Cutting the air with a hiss, the end coils with terrible, skilled precision around my board, coupling it to his. He pulls it powerfully, testing the hold, tightening it.

"Oh! What? How?" Ridiculous sounds and words fall from my mouth.

"Do you trust me?"

I lift my face to look at him. . . . Up close, I see his lean jaw, beautiful, angular cheekbones and chiseled lips and nose.

But the rest of his face is not merely hooded. Pitch-black Face Paint outlines his eyes, continuing to the upper portion of his face and forehead, in the shape of a mask. This way, if he drops back the hood, he is still difficult to recognize.

"I—" I mumble.

"Semirameos, do you trust me?" he repeats. His grey eyes watch me seriously from their frame of utter black, appearing luminous by contrast.

I blink, for some *hoohvak* reason starting to tremble. "Yes . . . *im Ter*. Of course, I—"

"Good. Put your arms around me, and hold on tight."

"Oh—"

Awkwardly, I reach forward and wrap my hands around his waist, while my pulse starts pounding wildly in my temples.

"Closer," he says. "Rest your head. Cover yourself."

I exhale silently and then press my face against his chest, feeling his hard muscles through the ebony silk fabric.

As he sings a short series of voice commands, I feel the rumble of his deep voice vibrating in his chest against my cheek. Suddenly, the fabric of the Niktos Cloak *floats* and closes around us, wrapping us in a cocoon of orichalcum, so I cannot see the outside world.

It's a good thing, because this is when the world lurches, spinning suddenly around us. Everything turns in a whirlwind as we hurtle forward at an impossible speed.

It takes ten heartbeats, maybe twelve, for us to pass underneath the bridge. Around the sixth heartbeat, I hear the projectile roar and feel the blast against the cloak as the flames strike us from both directions. . . .

But the Niktos Cloak holds, serves as a safety barrier, and the next instant we are beyond the point of danger, and emerge on the other side.

I know, because my ID token makes a familiar ding sound. So does his—indicating to me that this is the first time he has flown under the bridge between these particular Circles. Which means, I'm the first member of our Team he has assisted. . . .

For some reason, it's a strangely comforting thought.

Benaten pushes back the cloak, and daylight returns. I stop squeezing my eyes shut and lift my head to look, then carefully draw a little back from him, though my arms are still wrapped around his waist. Glancing down, I see that we're hovering well above the water of the canal.

"Are you all right?" he asks with a smile. "I don't see any fire damage."

"Yes." I smile back, and suddenly feel my neck and cheeks burning in a different manner. "And you too, *im Ter?*"

"All good," he retorts cheerfully, even as he uncoils the whip, and my board is set free. "Back on your board," he tells me, and I extricate myself from the terribly embarrassing but weirdly pleasant proximity of his lean and muscular body.

Crap of a sha-*possessed goat. . . . My weak mind . . . this is so wrong.*

Meanwhile, he holds his gloved hand out to me, helping me step over to my own board and carefully sit back down.

As I'm hastening to wrap my own ropes around my board, I see that my employer flicks his hand. A hologram map pops up from a band on his wrist, and he observes it closely, then glances at me.

"Go on to the next Circle. Looks like I still need to help Menahit, Nemadoris, and Girsul to get across this one."

"Uru!" I think immediately of my little brother. "What about Uru?"

Benaten checks his map again. "Your brother has managed just fine, all by himself. I see Uru currently traveling on Circle Five, well ahead of us."

"Ah, thank all the sacred gods!"

"Indeed. Now, go. Be careful. See you at the Finish Gate."

Before I have the chance to respond, the Man in the Niktos Cloak rises in the air, leaning into the wind, and speeds away along the canal toward some other bridge location.

I continue into Circle Seven.

THIS PART of the City is middle-class residential, with several large cultural venues and entertainment pavilions.

My way through the Circle is unimpeded, and the air traffic has become less dense. I wonder how many contenders have dropped out of the Race or have been disqualified at this point?

Feeling more accustomed to being high up in the air, I increase my speed and altitude. Soon enough, I pass over several large arenas, including Tiamat Pavilion. Its rooftop is intricately sculpted with a thousand divine figures, in mauve, ebony, and gold. In this dazzling venue music festivals are often held. Not that I've ever been to any, but I know all about it from watching feeds on the media-box.

Circle Seven ends eventually, and I squint at the sky to check the position of the morning sun. It is crawling higher toward zenith, which probably means it's around tenth or even eleventh hour of Ra.

The bridge between Circle Seven and Six is ahead.

I start my descent slowly, watching the others before me, as usual, for any indication of possible danger in store for us.

Here I find many hover cars and large transports gathered in the air. And once I get to the canal level, I can see the problem. A scaffolding barrier has extended the walls of the bridge from both sides, so that a much narrower opening is available for everyone to pass.

Apparently, it's sufficient for hoverboard riders, but not for most transports.

It occurs to me: this is a reversal of the intended consequences posed by the obstacle in the *previous* Circle. While that other one eliminated hoverboard riders, this one eliminates larger vessels.

Just as I consider my approach, two transports collide not too far in front of me.

Hoverboard riders scatter out of the way as dented and ripped metal pieces of one damaged vehicle fall . . . and so do the occupants of the interior, choosing in haste to jump into the water along with the flotsam. Their ID tokens go off with sorrowful dings.

Meanwhile, one of the transports tries to fit into the opening under the bridge, and gets jammed and stuck in place, effectively blocking everyone's way across.

People curse loudly at the mess.

Time to abandon this bridge altogether and try the next.

WE FLY to the next bridge, finding the same type of scaffolding erected underneath, which narrows the passage.

"Go, go!" people yell. "Go, before the big cars arrive!"

I take a deep breath and command my board to move carefully along the narrow passage between the scaffolding. I make it all the way across without touching any of the walls, and hear a ding from my ID token, indicating a positive outcome.

Rising over the canal, I glance back to see a hover car cleverly turned on its side, flying *sideways* under the bridge, so that it barely manages to squeeze horizontally through the passage. . . .

It's quite a test of Piloting skills and proof that there is indeed a solution—the designers of the Pilot Race obstacles would not have created impossible ones.

Then I hear yells of outrage, because another large transport has come up with a different, cruel solution.

The transport hovers over the canal with its doors open, and the occupants have commandeered some unfortunate contender's hoverboard. The sad *chazuf* has been pushed into the canal while they use his board, one after another, to pass under the bridge, then fly back around and return to their vehicle. This way, they have all been scanned properly and can just fly on to the next Circle.

Apparently, nothing in the rules prevents them from using this loophole.

"Run! Get out of here!" other contenders cry, warning each

other about this malicious technique. "Go, before the other cars figure it out and take our boards!"

My heart starts to pound again, and I hurtle toward Circle Six, to get as far away as possible from this treacherous situation.

I FLY over Circle Six with confidence, and without any mishap, going quite fast at this point. The high-rise buildings and the technology complexes strain like obelisks and needles toward the sky, and I avoid them as much as possible, since flying over all *that* would mean flying so much higher than a bird. . . .

When I get to the bridge between Six and Five, there is nothing out of the ordinary. I observe the space under the bridge, and see contenders on hoverboards passing freely. And same, as far as transports.

It is almost suspicious, and I hesitate a little, but then decide to just go. . . .

Nothing happens to me, and I get scanned.

So, onward to Circle Five.

THIS ELEGANT, tree-lined area filled with wealthy estates, is rather familiar territory. I've grown to know quite a few of these streets on my way to *Ter* Aten's estate. As I fly, I watch my shadow racing over the wind-stirred ocean of leaves of the treetops below my feet, and through them, a lacework of sunlight on the gilded rooftops, gardens, and the distant ground.

Circle Five ends, and the bridge between it and Circle Four proves to be equally unimpeded by obstacles.

Sacred Bastet, thank you.

At this point, as I pass underneath and get scanned, I start to hope that the worst bridge obstacles are behind us.

· · ·

CIRCLE FOUR CONTAINS exquisite greenery-filled neighborhoods on par with and surpassing Circle Five. This is the beginning of the residential area of the third tier of the wealthiest of the noble elites, known as Low Court. Even more sprawling estates can be found here than in the previous Circle. Most Great Houses have their main court residences here.

I fly over the whole thing swiftly, determined to make up some time that I've lost at the earlier bridge obstacles.

Briefly I wonder if I should take out my badge comm unit and check the map for locations of the others on my Team. But no, I'm far too afraid of accidentally dropping it from this great height. I'll wait until the Finish Gate. . . .

And then I happen to glance to the side, and see something I was afraid of seeing for quite some time now. In the distance—even higher above me and moving in the *opposite* direction from all the rest of the tiny flying figures who are my fellow contenders—is the first platform.

I recognize it because I've seen these disks over the Imperial Palace walls, and my heart lurches with anxiety. It means that other contenders are so *far* ahead of me in the Competition that they have reached the Finish Gates, grabbed a platform, and are already on their way back, flying over Circle Four. . . .

In moments, the platform approaches, filled with people. It's an immense, flat disk, silhouetted with darkness against the sky. I can see it's packed with many human figures on its top side. They are balancing to stay on, and some are struggling violently with each other. . . .

Another two heartbeats, and the platform passes overhead, far to the left of me, but close enough that I can hear their shouts and angry voices carried on the wind. And it keeps going back to the outskirts of the City.

Crap of a goat! I have to pick up my pace, or by the time I get to a Finish Gate there won't be any platforms left.

THE NEXT TWO Circles and bridges go by in a whirlwind of speed.

Circle Three has many public open-air venues and arenas for grand sports spectacles. In addition, its spectacular residential areas are home to the second-highest tier of nobility, known as Middle Court.

Circle Two is residential High Court, the loftiest tier of the noble elites. I see a scattering of majestic estates on the side I've never visited, and then mostly Bisfuri land, verdant and full of elevated topology in the form of hills. That part is bittersweet in its familiarity.

The bridges connecting all of them are unimpeded by obstacles. I pass, get scanned, move onward—all with a rising sense of drudgery evoked by tension and fatigue.

At this point, I am genuinely exhausted, cursing myself in my *hoohvak* mind, and calling upon the gods to give me strength to not fall off the infernal hoverboard and meet my death far below.

My fingers have lost nearly all feeling, numb from gripping the board. The skin of my face is windblown, and my eyes are dry.

The objective of the Race has become a matter of endurance, more than anything. The Race designers probably knew it—no need for additional obstacles when our bodies will start to give out. At least those riding in large transports are not burdened the same way.

Periodically, I think about how *Ter* Aten stayed behind to help the rest of our Team to get past the obstacles. I know how fast he can fly on his own, but still . . . he has taken so much extra time and added detours to his route.

He must go impossibly fast now, to make up for it at the Finish Gate.

And then of course I think of Uru, and how he probably made it to the Finish Gate already, and is waiting for the rest of us. I wouldn't be surprised if the little *sha* is the first one there.

Please, o Sacred Blessed Bast . . . please let there be a platform left for us to use. . . .

Now and then, my anxious thoughts remind me that there's a *pegasus* turnip in my pocket, and it needs to be fed soon. Eventually. *Ugh* . . . something else to worry about. Poor *hoohvak* creature, I really don't want it to die.

At last, I scale the familiar hillside of Bisfuri land, with its distant ponds and waterfalls, and the slope on the other side ends more abruptly in a minor cliff over the canal.

The final bridge looms before me.

Beyond the glittering, clear-water Khemenu Canal, lies the Imperial Center Circle.

The Finish Gates are in sight.

I SWOOP DOWN, with a now-familiar confidence, to pass underneath my last bridge, hear the ID token ding, and then race onward to the closest Finish Gate. It has a glowing holographic symbol of three notches over the arch, so it's Gate 3. Numerous hoverboards and transports are doing the same.

The Finish Gates consist of arches made of scaffolding, similar to the Start Gates, but on a much smaller scale. They are only tall and wide enough to accommodate two hover cars side-by-side or a single large transport. And they are positioned on the very shore of the Circle, in the grassy lawn area.

A sudden memory comes to me. I recall the trenches and holes being dug recently in the green turf in those exact same spots. So that's what that was for. . . .

Now, as I approach, I take care to keep away from the

ground, and sing the voice command to pass in the very middle of the arch.

My ID token dings, scanning me and registering my final time for this first portion of the Pilot Race. Now the Team portion begins.

As soon as I emerge on the other side of Finish Gate 3, I see two members of my Team: the light-skinned, bearded Xingir hovering nearby on top of his hoverboard, and next to him, Girsul.

"Hathor be praised, Semmi!" Girsul calls out, waving at me. "You made it! I just got here."

"You made it too!" I reply with a huge surge of relief as I pull up to them. "What about Uru? Have you seen him?"

"The boy's up on the platform over Finish Gate 10," Xingir replies with a serious glance at me, even as he continues to scan the vicinity for others. "That's where all of us will be going. Both of you, head up there right now. I'll be down here a little longer to guide a few more of our Team stragglers."

"What about *Ter* Aten?" I ask. "Is he—"

"Don't worry about *Ter* Aten, he will be on the platform. Now, go, both of you. I'll see you up on Platform 10. Understood? Hurry!" Xingir turns from us and begins flying toward Finish Gate 4.

Girsul and I immediately redirect our boards, and we fly past a hive of other contenders along the curving shore of the Circle. As we rise, I look around and notice that there are indeed no platforms visible over Finish Gate 3, or the next Gate 2, or even Gate 1, which we can barely see in the distance.

"Yeah, they're all gone," Girsul yells out from his board, flying just ahead of me. "Xingir says only four platforms are left. The rest have been claimed by other Teams and are on their way. We're going to have to fight for Platform 10."

"How do you know where the platforms are?" I ask.

"Check your map. You can see six of them moving away

toward the outer walls of Poseidon. Last I looked, there were only four white dots left in their original place on the map."

I mumble a curse.

Since the Center Circle is relatively small in diameter, we arrive at Finish Gate 10 in a few daydreams. It happens to be the very next Gate after Gate 1. And there it is, its corresponding platform parked high overhead.

"Let's go!" Girsul leans into the wind and his board speeds up, rushing toward the platform.

I follow, immediately after.

Unfortunately, we're not the only ones. Dozens of other contenders on hoverboards, and several transports are converging on Platform 10 from all directions.

The edge of the platform disk remains unlit, meaning that no Team has yet claimed it.

When we arrive at the platform, there are seven other people on it already. One of them is my little brother.

"Uru!" I exclaim.

"Over here!" Uru waves enthusiastically at me and Girsul. He appears fine, just covered with dust, and his hoverboard is gone.

I recall that all hoverboards and other vessels have to be abandoned, once we step on a platform.

I approach, sailing barely over the edge of the platform, and feel a sudden stab of vertigo and anxiety as I fumble to untie the safety ropes anchoring me to the board. Then I step off my hoverboard and look at it wistfully.

Girsul easily hops off his board onto the platform, and stands right next to me. "Let it go," he says with a nod, noticing the direction of my gaze. And then he kicks his own board so that it moves away and continues floating aimlessly in the air, slowly receding from us.

I take a deep breath then gently kick my board so that it moves away also.

I am now marooned on this platform.

No other way off.

The surface of the platform under my feet feels oddly precarious as I stand, surrounded by nothing but air at this great height. There is no safety railing, nothing around the edge. It is quite a large disk, with room enough for at least fifty people. But if any of us fall from this height, we die. . . .

The other six people stare at us newcomers with blank gazes, each one standing aloof. Four men, two women. None of them are together or seem to know each other, which means they are all on different Teams, waiting for the rest of their Team members to get here.

Same as we are.

However, now there are three of us on Team Niktos, therefore we have a small advantage.

Even as I think all this, more contenders arrive. A transport approaches, unloading four more people, all on the same Team. One of the women already on the platform signals to them. And just like that, they have the number advantage. Meanwhile, their abandoned transport is programmed to auto-drive back to its place of origin, unlike our hoverboards that have been set adrift and will likely never be recovered by anyone on our Team.

Poor Uru, he just lost his hoverboard, his sole means of messenger work.

Uru tugs my skirt. "Semmi, where do we go from here?"

"I think we'll find out once *Ter* Aten gets here." I take Uru's arm and pull him closer to me and away from the edge. Right now, I really just want to hug the boy, but I'm afraid he won't let me. . . .

"They better hurry up," Girsul grumbles quietly. "Soon this platform will have no more room for anyone else. At least there's no green light around the edge, so it's still unclaimed."

I feel my pulse pounding louder in my temples. Reaching in

my deep pocket, I take out the badge comm and call up the map to see where the rest of our Team is.

While I try to decipher the various color dots, more hoverboarders arrive, one by one.

Then, another transport pulls up quickly. I look up with growing despair, expecting more strangers coming out.

Instead, the door opens, and Mihravat emerges, followed by Dunea, Emzarabi, Yereg, and Tehom.

More of our Team are here!

We hail each other with relief, and they crowd onto the platform next to us. Most of our new arrivals stare with fear past the edge at the distant ground below.

Meanwhile, Mihravat closes the transport door, taps something on his wrist unit, and the empty vehicle moves away with purpose.

"So, who's missing?" Mihravat says in a matter-of-fact tone, standing fearlessly with his back to the edge of the platform.

"Six people," Girsul replies. "*Ter* Aten, Chifuz, Menahit, Aramazd, Nemadoris. And Xingir is near the Finish Gates waiting for some of them."

At this point, another transport arrives, this one carrying three more contenders from another Team. Muscular and menacing, they step onto the platform and give everyone threatening looks.

The atmosphere on the platform changes. I sense immediately that, unlike everyone else here with us, these are not good people.

Bastet, help us. . . .

The blessed goddess seems to hear my plea, because in that moment I see the familiar black rider approaching, silhouetted against the daylight, and surrounded by the shimmer of his cloak.

My heart skips a beat.

The Man in the Niktos Cloak arrives from the direction of

Gate 9. Flying behind him are two more people, both seated on their hoverboards in the same manner as me, and clinging to them for dear life. I see Nemadoris, hugging her board with both arms, and then Menahit, keeping her head down as she flies.

The three members of our team approach, and *Ter* Aten pulls up on his board but does not get off. He balances easily, locked in his elegant stance, waiting for the two women to carefully drive their boards forward past the edge of the platform, then pretty much collapse into the ready hands of the rest of our Team.

Only then does he leap off his board onto the surface of the platform.

As he does so, the reaction of the others on the platform is priceless.

The dozen or so unknown contenders who share the space with us stare at him with faces full of wonder, amazement, even shock.

"I know you . . . Niktos Cloak!" a man says, breaking the silence. He points at Benaten and glances around at the others, as though seeking confirmation. "That's the Man in the Niktos Cloak!" he repeats. "Right?"

People all around the platform nod. Three of the menacing strangers remain unmoved, watching coldly.

"I am," Benaten replies loudly. While his upper face remains concealed by the hood, his lips curve into a quick, brilliant smile.

Immediately everyone starts talking.

But *Ter* Aten ignores them and instead focuses on us, his Team. "Ready to go?" he asks, looking around at all of us and taking inventory. When he turns to me, I notice a brief pause. A flicker of another smile comes to his lips, before he moves on to others.

"We're still three people short," Mihravat remarks.

"I know. They're coming." And *Ter* Aten points behind him

where several hoverboard riders approach, including Chifuz, Aramazd, and finally, Xingir.

They are followed by three other contenders we don't know, but at this point it really doesn't matter. The moment Xingir, the last of our Team, steps onto the surface of the platform, a loud tone issues from the disk under our feet. Then, the edge of the platform lights up a bright green.

"Team 43 controls Platform 10," the Man in the Niktos Cloak announces in his rich, smooth, resonant voice, which causes everyone to look at him again. "And I am in charge."

While Benaten speaks, Xingir uses a length of rope to bind everyone's remaining hoverboards into one big stack, then sings a special command that executes programming to send them back home—or wherever, I have no idea. The stack of boards sails off into the distance. And with that, we are now completely platform-bound.

"We need to get going. What's the platform status around the City?" Benaten asks the technician, Mihravat.

"Three are already docked at Start Gates 5, 8, and 9. Two are almost at Circle Ten, at their present trajectory heading for Gates 7 and 3. One platform is halfway across the City, on a trajectory toward Gate 6." Mihravat responds immediately, examining his hologram map. "Our available options are Gate 10, 1, 2, or 4, all unoccupied."

"Very well." Benaten considers just as quickly. "Three of these are adjacent. Let's head north, aiming for Gate 1, for now. Keep me apprised of the other moving platforms."

And then our Team Leader sings a voice command sequence, keying the platform to him, and giving himself navigation control.

In the next heartbeat, the platform lurches underneath our feet then starts *moving*.

. . .

MANY OF US CRY OUT, trying to keep balance, and everyone crowds inward, away from the edge. The two most vulnerable women on our team, Dunea and Emzarabi, hold each other, and the two most vulnerable men, Tehom and Yereg press inward, next to them.

"Everyone, hold on!" Xingir says in a calming voice. "Regardless of your Team, we must all help each other now, to stay on."

"Hold hands if you must, no one will think less of you," Mihravat remarks with sarcasm.

Our platform sails slowly, giving us a grand view of the Center Circle and the gilded rooftops of the Imperial Palace, then starts gently rising. It passes the canal between Circles One and Two, and continues into Bisfuri air space.

And still, it ascends higher.

In moments, we're so far above the ground that the landmarks become too small to see. We are completely alone, above other City traffic, surrounded by nothing but brilliant blue sky and the blazing sun overhead.

The wind is strong here—strong and terrifying. . . . An ocean of air currents sweeps over the platform, ruffling our hair and clothing, as we cling to each other, and try to keep away from the edge.

Benaten stands facing the direction in which we are moving, head slightly lowered to keep the hood over his face, with no way to judge the expression of its obscured upper part. Only his composed mouth is visible.

"Is there a reason why we are so high up, *im Ter*?" Chifuz asks.

"Yes," *Ter* Aten replies. "Fewer chances that others will find us here unintentionally, catch up to us, and challenge our Team for this platform. We're remote enough here that we can fly more slowly than we would otherwise, down in the traffic below. It's a tradeoff between speed and a safer pace."

Chifuz nods. "The faster we fly, the more people we might lose. Understood."

THE PLATFORM MOVES STEADILY NORTH, now

flying over Circle Three.

Periodically we check the map status, and it informs us we are the last of three platforms still enroute to the finish.

"One platform ahead of us, moving over Circle Four, trajectory still uncertain," Mihravat says. "Another one is behind us, closing in, and also headed north."

"Not good," Xingir says. "We don't want to have a conflict over docking Gates."

"We won't, if we continue to stay ahead," Benaten responds, as we now enter the air territory over Circle Four.

"Let's hope they don't see us," Nemadoris speaks up.

"It's not a matter of being seen, but of being tracked," Mihravat says with annoyance. "If they want to specifically find us, all they need to do is check the map."

Nemadoris sighs, and shuts her eyes from the onslaught of wind.

Meanwhile, the other contenders on our platform appear to be resigned that their Teams are not here to challenge us. At least it seems that way.

Turns out, I am terribly wrong.

J ust as we pass the next canal and enter Circle Five, still flying alone and unimpeded, someone calls out to say we are being followed.

"Over there!" a man not on our Team yells, pointing behind us at two dark specks traveling very fast, at an altitude slightly lower than ours.

We strain to look, and the moving objects quickly resolve into the shapes of a large black transport and a disk, which is unmistakably another platform.

"*Varqood!*" Aramazd exclaims.

"That's the platform following us," Mihravat remarks, stating the obvious.

"Ignore it," Benaten says through his teeth. "If that Team wants one of the adjacent Gates ahead of us, it can have it."

"Yes, *im Ter.*"

We watch the platform below and the accompanying transport cautiously. But instead of going past us, they match our slower speed and start rising to our level. And from what we can see, there are only a handful of people occupying that platform, which is both suspicious and disturbing. Compared to them, our platform is packed.

People on our platform curse. Partial Teams huddle together, not quite trusting anyone else, and the loners look frightened. I think everyone understands that something bad is coming.

"What? What's happening?" Uru asks, since he is shorter than the grownups and blocked from seeing past the edge by me (on purpose) and is near the middle of our crowd.

I don't say anything, only put both hands on my little brother's shoulders and hold him, attempting to block the view, but not succeeding. Uru is a slippery little *sha* and squeezes forward past me to stare.

In moments, the other platform is at our level. It closes the distance until it is about the length of two hoverboards from us, sufficient for a long jumper to cross.

The ten people on the platform, grim and muscular men, watch us in silence, while the black transport flying alongside it suddenly advances forward, and its doors slide open.

And now, I recognize that transport. . . .

Ba-Pef.

The leader of the Neph-Tiari, stands in the doorway. He then steps outside, hanging insolently out of the vehicle, holding on with one powerful hand.

He scans our packed platform with narrowed eyes, then focuses on Benaten. "*Ei,* Niktos Cloak!" he calls out harshly. "I told you I wasn't done with you. I'm here to take your platform."

Benaten reacts swiftly, moving through our crowd to stand on the side closest to the transport. "Looks like you and your Team already have one," he says in a composed voice. "How many platforms do you need?"

Ba-Pef barks a laugh, then glances behind him. "I only want the one that's *yours.* You see, I have more than one Team. This one—"

he points to the one behind him. "This is just one of several. All loyal to me, to Neph-Tiari. I assigned their Team Leader just so they could drive this platform for me. And get rid of the competition."

A dark realization comes to me. This minimal ten-man Team of Neph-Tiari claimed their platform by means of violence. That's why there are no other contenders on board.

"I've been watching you, Niktos Cloak—or Mask, whatever you are, *bakris*," Ba-Pef continues. "I suspected you'd be in the Pilot Race. I haven't forgotten our little meeting in the tunnels. . . ."

"And I haven't given you a second thought." Benaten's lips barely tighten with scorn.

Ba-Pef's scarred face turns deadly. "Did you know, there are Neph-Tiari on every single platform in this Race? Including yours. They reported your position to me."

On cue, the three big, menacing men on *our* platform grab the closest people to them—a woman and two men—and suddenly shove them hard, off the edge of the disk.

There are desperate screams as the misfortunates fall into the abyss below.

No . . . Holy Bast!

The rest of the crowd on our platform comes alive with furious yells. Members of our Team crowd together, while those who are professional fighters, Chifuz, and Xingir, take combat stances and draw weapons against the three Neph-Tiari, covering the rest of us from them.

Benaten lifts one gloved hand and slowly beckons Ba-Pef with one finger. "Come, you want me, not these others," he says like a serpent, stepping forward. "Dance with me on this platform—or are you afraid? Word will spread of your cowardice. I'll make sure of it, even if I have to return from the dead to haunt you. . . ."

Ba-Pef leans forward, grinning widely, and suddenly leaps across the chasm, onto our platform.

More terrified screams erupt. We make what little room we can, shifting our positions on the surface of the disk. Except for Ba-Pef and Benaten, everyone has drawn weapons at this point.

Even I pull out my small knife, and force Uru behind me.

More Neph-Tiari watch from the doors of the transport, as everyone circles each other, feinting occasionally but not yet engaging. They, and the ten gang members on the other platform, appear ready to join the fight and board us from two directions.

Though, would the ten men abandon their platform? Someone has to stay behind to drive it. Such feverish *hoohvak* thoughts pass through me uselessly.

Holy Bast, you who are merciful, please hold us and protect us. . . .

During that tense moment of silence, I can hear Dunea and several other women and men whispering similar prayers as they huddle in the center.

Ba-Pef and Benaten continue to circle each other.

"Come, Niktos, take off your hood and let's see your pretty face." Ba-Pef bares his teeth and reaches for the two knives holstered at his belt.

"Only for a kiss," Benaten replies, taking out his own segmented short staff.

Ba-Pef lunges at him.

The Man in the Niktos Cloak deflects with this staff, and they resume circling once more.

As the leader of the Neph-Tiari steps around, brandishing his two knives, his three imposing men on our platform choose to attack also. They clash with Xingir and Chifuz, with fierce yells. This causes the rest of us to move carefully as we shift positions, just to maintain our footwork balance on top of the platform disk.

I grasp Uru, keeping the boy next to me, while Girsul tries to help Yereg and Dunea as they almost lose their footing.

At one point, as I step around and past someone, I suddenly catch the eye of Ba-Pef.

"Ah. . . . Your little bitch sorceress is here too," he taunts with one hard glance at me, as he strikes Benaten with his knives. "I'm going to enjoy throwing her off this platform."

In reply, *Ter* Aten swings the three segments of his staff quicker than lighting, and one of Ba-Pef's knives goes flying on the floor, then slides near the edge. And remains there.

Ba-Pef curses.

Just then, one of the other contenders not affiliated with our Team grabs the knife, and moves to the side of our Team to join our lineup against the Neph-Tiari.

He's not the only one. The rest of the non-affiliated decide they prefer being on the platform controlled by benevolent Team Niktos as opposed to being thrown to their deaths by these deadly newcomers. Suddenly the balance of power has evened out.

"I think you should get off my platform, Neph-Tiari," Benaten says loudly. "Or you're going to be the one I'll throw off."

In answer, Ba-Pef takes a sudden step to the side, toward me, and grabs my arm. He wrenches me with his considerable strength, and I feel myself being tossed forward, stumbling, sliding, about to go off the ledge. . . .

Just then my brave little brother Uru grabs me with both hands, clinging to my arms and keeping me from flying off the platform. I gasp, still teetering, while he pulls me back, yelling, "Semmi!"

In the next heartbeat, Ba-Pef swings again, and this time his beefy fist slams against Uru.

Uru's skinny little body is no match. He immediately goes sliding and falls, disappearing over the edge of the platform.

"Uru!"

I shriek.

The world falls from under me. . . .

I barely notice how Benaten drops his staff and grabs his whip. Reacting with impossible speed, he throws himself bodily to the floor and at the same time cracks his whip over the end of the platform.

The long black whip of the Man in the Niktos Cloak cuts the air, and then, miraculously, it catches on something down below. On *someone.*

"Hold on!" Benaten calls down, looking over the platform, holding the now-taut whip with one powerful hand, and keeping himself anchored with the other.

Meanwhile, several members of our Team, including Girsul, dive on the floor to keep him grounded, to keep him from also falling off. Several more of us, including Menahit and Nemadoris, face off against Ba-Pef and his three men.

"Don't let go, Uru! I've got you!" Benaten yells down at him, and then begins to carefully pull up the whip. In three breaths, I see my little brother's hands and tousled head appear, and Benaten and the others pull him up and over onto the disk surface.

"Uru! Uru!" I cry, my face contorted, as I drop down and crawl on my knees toward them, and then cover my little brother with my body. Uru looks badly shaken, and wraps his arms around me in atypical fashion.

"Thank you, oh, thank you, *im Ter*!" I exclaim, looking up with emotion, but the Man in the Niktos Cloak has already risen and is now once again facing Ba-Pef.

"*Get off, now,*" he tells Ba-Pef in a voice like thunder, advancing at him.

There must be something particularly terrifying in his tone, because the leader of the Neph-Tiari actually steps backward, pausing momentarily.

That's when one of his three terrible men, circling a few steps away, takes the opportunity to grab another one of our Team.

Girsul turns his back for one instant, and that's when the Neph-Tiari wrestles him from behind.

Chifuz immediately comes to his defense, but the platform is crowded, and just slippery enough to cause difficulty. Girsul strikes back but loses his footing, and suddenly he ends up falling backward . . . and off the ledge.

Girsul, no!

I am still feeling mentally bludgeoned from the nightmare of almost losing Uru, but a strange moment of sharp clarity washes over me.

Pegasei.

I open my mouth and yell with all the fullness of my voice, hoping he can hear me from down there, as he plummets to his death, "Make a bird! Girsul! Make a rainbow bird and fly!"

He has the other *pegasus* in his pocket; he can save himself! Unlike anyone else here, if he falls, he has a chance! And for that matter, so do I.

If anyone else falls, *I* can save them.

Bolstered by this sudden wave of confidence, I slide forward on the floor of the platform, and fearlessly reach for the edge to look down. . . .

Did Girsul hear me in time? Did he come to the realization himself that his fate is in his own hands? Or do I need to jump down after him?

I strain my vision, looking at the dizzying vastness of air below and the distant ground (we're somewhere over Circle Six now, because we just passed another canal), and I search for a bit of bright motion, a speck, a dust mote of rainbow light. . . . Anything.

I am granted no time to wonder.

Because in that exact same moment, the platform we're on suffers a great lurch, followed by an upward *impact* that causes the floor of the disk to dip on an incline and drop from under us.

Since I'm at the ledge already, I grab and try to hold on—just long enough to look back and see that, in the process of more Neph-Tiari attempting to board us, the black transport has collided with our platform.

Whether by accident or intentionally, the front of the transport struck us from below, causing the perfectly level, horizontal disk of the platform to flip upward rapidly, ending up almost vertical.

There are wild shrieks, yells, horrible screams of despair, as the entire platform turns and its occupants shift, fall, collapse on the floor, then begin to *slide*, grasping the surface of the disk desperately, just to stay on.

I watch in impossible, slow motion as everyone around me starts falling.

Uru, my little brother who has fallen once already, is one of the first to fall *again*, with a high-pitched scream, as he slides to the bottom and *off*.

Then, Chifuz, followed by Nemadoris, Menahit, Aramazd . . . there go Dunea, Tehom, and Emzarabi, shrieking and holding each other.

I blink, and the Man in the Niktos Cloak plummets, ending up on the bottom. He looks up at me for the last time, and I catch the luminous fire of his grey eyes. . . .

He cries out a strange shortened form of my name, "Eos!" before he slips away like a black shadow of night, and his iridescent cloak unfurls around him.

My name, as he speaks it, echoes in my mind.

Eos!

Xingir, Mihravat, sliding down and grabbing Yereg's foot.

Ba-Pef goes next, along with the remaining other contenders not on our Team. The three Neph-Tiari plummet last.

And my own hold on the uppermost edge of the platform gives out, grip loosening.

I slide down, and *off*.

Then I am in freefall.

· · ·

VERTIGO. . . .

My breath is momentarily knocked out of me as I fall in the arms of the wind, tossed by an ocean of air, tumbling to my death.

And then clarity kicks in, the same clarity that had me in its rational grip earlier. I reach into the pocket of my wildly flapping skirt, and my fingers close around the slightly warm, pulsing, turnip-shaped object that is the *pegasus*.

"Heket!" I call loudly, fiercely with my mind. "Help me!"

At once, I feel and hear the alien presence inside my head.

You need me to transform.

"Yes!"

Give me a shape. Show me.

I briefly think of the great bat with its silvery fur and veined leathery wings. And then I see the others falling in the sky below me—tiny specks, dozens of people, members of my Team, other contenders who shared our platform, and even the evil Neph-Tiari, all of them about to die.

Uru is among them.

And so is the Man in the Niktos Cloak.

No.

A great bat is not enough. Neither is a hawk.

Suddenly a flash of memory comes to me, a conversation I had days ago, almost in another life, in the dimly illuminated library of the Imperial Palace. Princess Arlenari reading, telling me insane and wise stories of impossible creatures from myth and legend.

In another flash, the memory is conflated with an earlier one, in which I hear about a Bisfuri ship malfunctioning on a mission to the distant continent, and being misconstrued by primitives from the ground. *Shamshir* vessel plasma cloak failure.

What I need is a snake. A really long and big one.

An immense serpent that pierces the earth like a great worm, and consumes magma. But not exactly a serpent, for it *flies*. And it has four legs and slim insect wings. And it exhales a breath of lava and fire from its maw, past its long filaments of whiskers, like a great flying carp fish.

This creature, it has a name out of legend.

Draguos.

I visualize it in my mind, sharp and immense, and I offer it up to the *pegasus*.

"Make me a *draguos*, Heket. Let its body and tail be thick and covered with scales, and let it stretch for a quarter of a mag-heitar in the sky!"

Throw me, Semmi. Let me feed in the sun so that I can grow big enough.

I take the turnip out of my pocket—even as the ground spins closer and closer—and I throw it upward and away from myself.

"Hurry!" I mind-cry. "Feed and grow! And then use your tail to sweep like a broom across the sky. We have people to pick up!"

The turnip explodes into a rainbow cloud of light, at first barely indistinguishable from the bright sky and sunlight. And then it deepens in color and *expands*.

The *draguos pegasus* grows with explosive speed in the sun. An elongated, reptile head forms—with eerie *wedjat* eyes the color of sunset, narrow pupils of a cat, wide nostrils of a crocodile, but strange flowing whiskers. The trunk of its serpent body undulates, and suddenly my fall is cut short.

I find myself lifted up by an immense scale-covered object, the color of persimmon, of late sunset, and of coals in a hearth fire. . . .

"Bigger!" I cry, straddling the curvature of its trunk, covered in smooth, warm, slightly iridescent scales. I wrap my hands and arms around it as much as I am able, for it is far beyond anything I could have anticipated. "The tail—use your tail to sweep along far below, and pick up everyone who is falling."

Everyone? Even those who sought to harm you?

"Yes. Even the accursed Neph-Tiari," I reply after a brief moment.

And the *draguos* does as I ask.

The serpent tail is so long, I cannot see its proper end in the distance. But it flickers and sweeps through the air currents, as though it has an intelligence of its own.

It curves and rebounds with impossible flexibility, and it encircles the tiny human beings who are falling. Moving alongside them with remarkable speed and precision, the tail flicks and snaps, dives down, soars up, down again, snagging and lifting them up, one by one, so that they are positioned in various places along its length.

"Did you get Uru?" I ask with fearful anticipation, after a few heartbeats.

Yes, sentient Semmi. Your young sibling is firmly seated and grasping my tail.

"What about Benaten? Did you get *Ter* Aten?"

I have him. Look behind you, he is not too far down my tail.

I look backward, and suddenly see the opalescent and translucent great wings on both sides of me. Apricot at the roots and faintly rose-colored at the tips, the wings flap powerfully, with delicate silvery veins branching out throughout the wing fabric. However, they act more as rudders than a bird's uplift wings, because the *draguos* flies in impossible fashion.

I tear my surprised gaze away from the wings and look straight behind me, further down the *draguos* back. That's when I see the dark shape of the Man in the Niktos Cloak, crouching low on the scaled surface.

He sees me looking, and he inclines his raven head, unobscured by the hood that has fallen down his back. And then, balancing carefully, Benaten makes his way closer to me.

When he is directly behind me, I see his lean, exquisitely handsome face, with its painted-on black mask, his raven hair pulled back, escaped tendrils tangling in the wind. And his grey eyes—they are filled with wonder.

He leans forward, reaches for me, and places his gloved hand on my shoulder with unexpected gentleness. "Semmi," he says in his rich, honey-sweet timbre of voice. "Semirameos . . . Eos. What miracle have you conjured? What have you done?"

I stare back at this man—this good, kind, honorable man. Warmth floods me like sunlight. And I smile, with all my *ka*, my *ba*, my *akh*, all sacred parts of my triumvirate spirit rejoicing at the sight of him.

"Ben," I say simply, forgetting all distinctions of nobility, social class, or servitude.

And then I exclaim, "We need to get back our platform!"

HEKET INFORMS me that every falling being of my species has been intercepted before hitting the ground. Even Girsul— who had indeed saved himself by transforming his own *pegasus* into a falcon, and then wisely landed onto the greater *draguos*, somewhere along its roomy tail.

However, I look around and all I can see are immense *draguos* tail coils in constant undulating motion—fiery, ruddy orange, covered in polished scales sparkling in the sun, silhouetted against the blue sky and the landscape of the City below.

Ah, crap of a goat! The entire City . . . and everyone on the ground. What must they think?

Right now, ordinary people going about their day must look up and see this *shar-ta-haak* spectacle in the sky. . . .

The *draguos* is so complex and immense that I can't envision what, in Bastet's holy name, anyone on the streets of Poseidon might be seeing. At this point I'm not even sure of our actual altitude in the sky, or if we're merely undulating in waves that span wide distances.

As the *draguos* coils approach and recede in perpetual rhythmic motion, I finally begin to see the various members of our Team, and others, clinging to and sitting on the different sections of the tail.

"I never knew a single *pegasus* could do all this," Benaten marvels. "The energy consumption alone must be incredible."

The Man in the Niktos Cloak stands up slowly, booted feet planted wide to balance on the scales. He stares overhead, and points in the distance. "There's the platform. I only see one."

"Heket," I say in my mind. "I thank you with all my soul. Thank you! Now, please, can you put us all back on that platform, somehow?"

I will do as you ask.

The head of the *draguos* turns, so that I see a great *wedjat* eye blink at me. At once, the *draguos* coils its body upward and we rise.

Soon, we are at the level of the platform disk, which has righted itself since the accident, and floats in a horizontal position as originally programmed.

Benaten goes first, leaping down on its surface. He turns and offers his gloved hand to me, catching me as I slide down awkwardly from the scaly creature's back.

"Thank you . . . *im Ter*," I say, as if suddenly recalling my place. But Benaten gives me a mischievous look, then slowly releases the fingers of my hand that he still holds.

"Now let's get the rest of our Team," he says.

One by one, the coiled segments of the tail deposit people back on the platform. Everyone appears dazed and in awe, some are fearful, and several people such as Aramazd, Dunea, and Tehom, are in tears.

I see Girsul among them, and the moment he notices me, his eyes brighten with relief. "Well done, Semmi!" he says, coming up to me, then mumbles near my ear. "Mine's in my pocket. . . . It saved me."

"What? What is this *thing*?" a contender not on our Team asks. "I thought I died, and then, this terrifying beast caught me!"

"Don't worry about it," Benaten replies. "What matters is that you are safe."

"Don't *worry* about it? Are you joking—?"

In that moment, I see my little brother.

"Uru! Oh, Uru!" I cry, while the boy slides down the scales like a monkey and jumps into my arms.

Uru's eyes are wide with impossible excitement, and he starts to chatter at me about this magical beast and how it grabbed him from the air, and where did it come from. . . .

You almost died.

I squeeze the child with my arms, pressing him close to my chest. Even now, he had already forgotten, he doesn't understand. . . . Bastet be praised that he does not.

Xingir steps onto the platform, appearing genuinely shaken. He nods his head and looks at Benaten. "A *pegasus*? Remarkable. Whatever you did, *im Ter*—"

Benaten turns to him swiftly. "I've done nothing," he says in his deep, resonant voice so that everyone can hear. He then points at me. "It's all her doing, she's the handler. Her name is Semirameos, so you know whom to thank."

In that moment, the coils deposit the Neph-Tiari leader. Ba-Pef leaps onto the platform, eyes narrowed, and then widens them, seeing me. For the first time his menacing black eyes carry a complex, strange expression as he stares.

But my employer steps between us. "You," Benaten says to the Neph-Tiari. "If you so much as breathe in her direction, I will kill you. If you want to live, you will do nothing until we finish the Pilot Race."

"What . . . is she?" the Neph-Tiari leader asks bluntly.

I peek around Benaten's wide back. "What am I, *chazuf?*" I say furiously. "I'm the one who will rip out your *oruhu* and feed them to my *draguos* if you ever try to hurt these people!"

Then I show Ba-Pef a crude finger gesture and spit on the platform floor for good measure.

THE REST of the contenders are now back on the platform. We force Ba-Pef and his three Neph-Tiari to stand at one end of the disk and not move, upon force of immediate removal.

At this point the platform lights up green again, and Benaten voice-commands it to continue forward, as though nothing has happened.

And yet, everything is different now. The *draguos* flies alongside us, undulating through the air, an impossible guard and companion accompanying us to the end.

Everyone on the platform stares at it, points and wonders incessantly. They also keep looking at me. Even among *Ter* Aten's loyal employees, not everyone is aware of our *pegasei* or what my connection is to this creature.

Currently, we are somewhere over Circle Seven, about to pass the canal and enter Circle Eight.

Meanwhile, there's no sign of the black transport, or the other remaining platform. They could have gone ahead, or possibly the transport crashed. Mihravat checks the map and tells us that indeed the other platform is over Circle Ten, on its way to docking at Gate 2.

In fact, we're the last platform in the Race that still remains undocked. And the only Gate that's left unoccupied is Gate 1, directly north of the City.

"So," I say to Uru. "We're going to Denwen's Crotch."

. . .

WE ARRIVE on the northern outermost side of Circle Ten within the hour. The City walls loom before us, and so does the pole tower of scaffolding, directly behind Gate 1.

A minor crowd has gathered on the ground, waiting for our arrival. Looks like the whole neighborhood is here, because Crotch residents don't get much spectacle otherwise. Not that we get any more of it down south in the Pit, but at least our streets are cleaner, I think.

Benaten sings the command sequence on final approach, as we start to descend toward the pole tower.

But the crowd below screams and points at the *draguos* more than at us.

"Um, time to handle the creature, Semmi," Girsul says to me discreetly.

I nod, then turn away, pretending to sing a voice command, when in reality I am communicating with Heket in my mind.

The *draguos* responds by starting to shrink suddenly. In a span of a few heartbeats it disappears into a truly huge cloud of rainbow light—much larger than normal because of the amount of mass it has to convert.

The crowd on the ground screams and points in amazement as the flying beast transforms and fades before their eyes.

Meanwhile, the cloud of light floats toward me. Trying my best to conceal this from the people on the platform and not really succeeding, I put out my hand. The *pegasus* lands and becomes a small rainbow turnip, which I somehow manage to cover up with my fingers before dropping it into my pocket.

Next to me, Uru stares, his eyes grown huge and his mouth open.

Just then, our platform starts to dock.

The ground rushes toward us . . . and then we feel a lurch as the platform makes contact with the top of the pole tower of Start Gate 1.

A loud bell tone sounds from the Gate. It is followed by cheers in the crowd.

In the same instant, all our ID tokens go off: Ding! Ding! Ding!

We made it.

A loud mechanical voice issues from the smart wall. "Congratulations, Team 43 and the remaining contenders," it says. "You have successfully completed the Pilot Race. You are officially accepted into the Imperial Pilot Corps. You may check your tokens for your Pilot status. Green indicates Primary, yellow indicates Backup."

Our platform erupts into cheers, cries of relief, and for most of us, incredulous laughter.

We all reach for our tokens to make sure. Uru and I pull out ours from the hidden pockets, and we are *green*. Wait till Grandmother and Father hear this!

"We made it, Uru! You're going to be a Pilot!" I grab my brother in a crushing hug, and he chortles and yells, then begins to jump up and down like a baby goat.

"Hathor and Bast!" Dunea cries, as she stares at her own tiny green token in disbelief, while tears stream down her wrinkle-worn face. Menahit raises her green token high over her head and keeps her hand over her mouth. Nemadoris looks at her green token, appearing stunned. Yereg and Emzarabi wipe their eyes and shake their heads.

"Thank the *Ter*!" Girsul reminds everyone. "Thank our Team Leader!"

I gaze around the platform to see the rest of the contenders not on our Team with yellow tokens. Most appear generally pleased. They might be Backup Pilots, but they are still accepted into the program. Which means, when the Sky Rock comes, they also get to fly to the stars with the elites, and they too get to live.

We get to live.

I continue to glance around at the rest of Team Niktos and the others. My lips tremble at the corners at the sight of their joy.

Then, I see the Neph-Tiari, looking grim with their yellow tokens. I catch the eyes of Ba-Pef who holds his yellow token disdainfully between two fingers, and now stares at me with an unblinking, piercing gaze.

Hah! The *chazuf* could've had his own winning Team and platform, I think, but no. It's his own infernal fault that he is only Backup.

I refuse to be intimidated by his relentless glare. So, I lift my fingers again, forming the rude, obscene gesture from the streets of Denwen's Pit, and I point them in his direction.

The resulting expression on his scarred face is priceless.

In that moment, there's a grinding sound in the center of the platform. Some people stumble to get out of the way, because a small circular portion, the size of a manhole cover, suddenly separates from the rest of the platform disk and begins to sink below the floor. It reveals an opening and stairs formed of scaffolding.

"So that's how we get down," someone says, and the rest of us chuckle.

And so, we climb down from the platform, and approach the officials on the ground below. They scan our tokens one last time, and formally register us as IPC Pilots.

"You and your Team Leaders will be hearing from us in the near future," we are told. "Keep your ID tokens. Your detailed instructions will follow."

As soon as they are scanned, the Neph-Tiari and their leader disappear in the crowd.

The rest of us remain, looking at each other with exhausted smiles.

Benaten speaks then, in his rich, low voice, with only a hint of weariness.

"Congratulations, Team Niktos. I am proud of you, and I am

grateful for you," the Man in the Niktos Cloak tells us, looking each of us in the eyes. "Now the real work begins. Go home, rest, get drunk to celebrate tonight. But I will see you in the morning—late morning."

"*Very* late morning," Xingir adds with amusement.

Everyone laughs.

As we begin to disperse, Benaten turns to me with a curious expression in his grey eyes. "Wait," he says quietly, leaning slightly over me, stopping me with a light touch of his gloved hand on my upper arm—which sends a fierce current of sensation and strange energy through me. "I want to thank you in particular, for all you've done—not just today, but many times over, before that, and yet again, now . . . Eos."

"You're welcome . . . Ben," I reply in a *hoohvak* giddy voice. "I mean, *Ter* Aten."

But his eyes are serious. He says nothing else, not another word, merely continues to look at me in the strangest manner of all, full of vulnerable, *raw* intensity, as though fixing me in his mind permanently.

And then he barely inclines his head, pulls the hood of his cloak low over his forehead, so that his upper face is in shadow.

His shimmering cloak swirls behind him as the Man in the Niktos Cloak disappears into the crowd.

The End of EOS:
Dawn of the Atlantis Grail, Book One

The story continues in . . .
DEA: Dawn of the Atlantis Grail, Book Two
Coming Soon!

Don't miss another book by Vera Nazarian!
Subscribe to the mailing list to be notified when the next books by Vera Nazarian are available.
We promise no spam, only book release and special news announcements.

Want to talk about it with other fans? Join the fun at . . .
The Atlantis Grail Fan Discussion Forum and
The Atlantis Grail Discord

*Have you read **The Atlantis Grail**? Start with **Qualify**!*

ATLANTEO GLOSSARY

The following *Atlanteo* language words appear in the novel *Eos*.

Amretene – elite rank of courtesan.
Amreve – lover
Amrevet – love
Amrevu – beloved
Astroctadra – A four-point star shape, in both two and three dimensions.
Atlanteo – the language of Atlantis, with Classical *Atlanteo* spoken in Ancient Atlantis, and modern *Atlanteo* in the original series *The Atlantis Grail*.
Atlantida – the Atlantean term for Atlantis the continent, and for Imperial *Atlantida*, the nation.
Bakris – carrion, insult.
Bakriku – vulture
Bau-ehl – elephant
Camral – camel
Chazuf – jerk, a-hole, generic crude term for guy, can be an insult or affectionate.

Chimeratene – elite rank of *amretene* courtesan of ambiguous gender, androgyny or intersex.

Chubrui – wild, unbridled, crazy.

Chuvu – thanks, short for "*chuvuat*" which is thank you.

Dea – day, afternoon.

Depet – boat, ship.

Depet of Eternity – euphemism for death.

Draguos – dragon, serpent style.

Ehoo – poop, *ehoo*-pot, chamberpot.

Eos – morning

Eos **pie** – a kind of hand pie, usually fruit-filled.

Garooi – stupid, fool.

Hedah – punishment stick, a short rod for striking; can be tri-folded.

Hoohvak – idiot, fool.

Im amrevu – my beloved.

Im nefira – my beauty.

Imperator – monarch sovereign ruler of Imperial *Atlantida*, similar to emperor. Full title: Archaeon Imperator.

Imperatris – female monarch Sovereign ruler of Imperial *Atlantida* or consort, spouse of the reigning Imperator. Full title: Archaeona Imperatris.

Im Ter – My Sir, slightly below the designation My Lord.

Ka, ba, akh – soul triumvirate, religious and spiritual terms for the three parts of the soul. The *ka* is the immortal life force, the aspect that is divine. The *ba* is the individuality—the specific person, colored, tainted, and shaped by the life experiences in the physical world. The *akh* is thus complete being reunited with all its soul parts in the afterlife.

Kadakum – clown, jester.

Kassiopeion – temple of the Kassiopei cult of divinity. The temple building is located in the Imperial Palace complex in the exact center of Poseidon.

Mag-heitar – measure of distance similar to ten kilometers.

Mamai – mother

Mam-ra – matriarch, head of household.

Mei-Ma – grandmother, literally grandma, short for "*Mei-Mamai*."

Mei-saai – grandchildren

Nefero dea – good day, good afternoon.

Nefero eos – good morning.

Nefero niktos – good night.

Nefi – giants, Nephilim.

Niktos – night

Noohd – lip color, lip gloss.

Oruhu – balls, gonads.

Papai – father

Pegasei – quantum trans-dimensional aliens introduced in the main series *The Atlantis Grail*.

Pegasus – singular form of *pegasei*. The original concept of the Ancient Greek flying horse, the Pegasus, evolved from the composite images of ordinary horses and birds that the *pegasei* gleaned from the human minds and compiled into the imaginary animal shape that later became mythic.

Puzuk – butt, behind, rear end.

Puzukaat – buttocks

Ra-Day – the seventh day of the week, similar to Sunday, used for spiritual devotion, otherwise a regular work day.

Sesemet – horse

Sha – demon

Shaitunaat – the demons of the underworld (collective term).

Shamshir – ancient fighter vessel or mid-range transport vessel.

Shar-ta – casual, short form of "*shar-ta-haak*" which is buffoon, fool, stupid, idiot.

Shebet – crap, junk.

Steleon – text enclosed and framed by the oval cartouche of the Kassiopei Dynasty.

Taq – honorific designation, usually noble, similar to Mistress or Madam, but less than Lady.

Ter – honorific designation, usually noble, similar to Sir or Master, but less than Lord.

Ter-i-taq – gentlemen and ladies, a general respectful group address.

Turufili – mushrooms, equivalent to truffles.

Uraeus – legendary great serpent from the underworld; Headdress and gold insignia band in the form of a serpent ready to strike worn by the Imperator. Greater and lesser forms exist. Lesser form is a coiled serpent at rest worn by the Imperial Crown Prince.

Uum – owl

Varqood – very strong expletive, an obscenity similar to F word; the procreative act.

Varqooi – the male member, phallus.

Wedjat – the Kassiopei eye, genetic, with a fine dark outline around the eyelids, a kind of natural eyeliner, similar to the Eye of Horus.

Wixameret – welcome

Zaurhi – stringed musical instrument.

OTHER BOOKS BY VERA NAZARIAN

Lords of Rainbow
Dreams of the Compass Rose
Salt of the Air
The Perpetual Calendar of Inspiration
The Clock King and the Queen of the Hourglass
Mayhem at Grant-Williams High (YA)
The Duke in His Castle
After the Sundial
Mansfield Park and Mummies
Northanger Abbey and Angels and Dragons
Pride and Platypus: Mr. Darcy's Dreadful Secret
Vampires are from Venus, Werewolves are from Mars

Cobweb Bride Trilogy:
Cobweb Bride
Cobweb Empire
Cobweb Forest

The Atlantis Grail:
Qualify (Book One)
Compete (Book Two)
Win (Book Three)
Survive (Book Four)

The Atlantis Grail Novella Series
Aeson: Blue
Aeson: Black

The Atlantis Grail Superfan Extras
The Atlantis Grail Companion
People of The Atlantis Grail

Dawn of the Atlantis Grail (TAG Prequel Series)
Eos (Book One)

Amrevet Days (Adult 18+ Series)

Amrevet Days One

(Forthcoming)

Dawn of the Atlantis Grail (TAG Prequel Series)
Dea (Book Two)
Niktos (Book Three)
Ghost (Book Four)
Starlight (Book Five)

The Atlantis Grail:
The Book of Everything (Book Five)

The Atlantis Grail Novella Series
Xelio: Red
Brie: Red

The Atlantis Grail Superfan Extras
The Atlantis Grail Zodiac

Amrevet Days (Adult 18+ Series)
Amrevet Days Two
Amrevet Days Three

Thank you for your support!

ABOUT THE AUTHOR

Vera Nazarian is a two-time Nebula Award® Finalist, a Dragon Award 2018 Finalist, and a member of Science Fiction and Fantasy Writers Association.

As a double refugee, after immigrating from the USSR during the Cold War, and then escaping from the Civil War in Lebanon (by way of Greece), she spent 35 years in Los Angeles, California. She now lives with many wacky cats in a small town in Vermont, and uses her Armenian sense of humor and her Russian sense of suffering to bake conflicted pirozhki and make art.

Vera sold her first story at 17, and has been published in numerous anthologies and magazines, honorably mentioned in Year's Best volumes, and translated into at least eight languages.

She made her novelist debut with the critically acclaimed *Dreams of the Compass Rose* (2002), followed by *Lords of Rainbow* (2003). Her novella *The Clock King and the Queen of the Hourglass* made the 2005 Locus Recommended Reading List. Her debut collection *Salt of the Air* contains the 2007 Nebula Award-nominated "The Story of Love." Other work includes the 2008 Nebula Finalist novella *The Duke in His Castle*, science fiction collection *After the Sundial* (2010), *The Perpetual Calendar of Inspiration* (2010), three Jane Austen parodies, *Mansfield Park and Mummies* (2009), *Northanger Abbey and Angels and Dragons* (2010), and *Pride and Platypus: Mr. Darcy's Dreadful Secret* (2012), all part of her *Supernatural Jane Austen Series*, a parody of self-help and supernatural relationships advice, *Vampires are from Venus, Werewolves are from Mars: A Comprehensive Guide to Attracting Supernatural Love* (2012), *Cobweb Bride Trilogy* (2013), bestselling series *The Atlantis Grail,* now optioned for film, which includes *Qualify* (2014), *Compete* (2015), *Win* (2017), and *Survive* (2020), novellas *Aeson: Blue* (2021), *Aeson: Black* (2022), fan guides *The Atlantis Grail Companion* (2021), *People of the Atlantis Grail* (2023), and the *Amrevet Days* series for grownups.

In addition to being a writer, philosopher, and award-winning artist, she is also the publisher of Norilana Books.

Official website: https://www.veranazarian.com

Get on my Mailing List! https://www.veranazarian.com/signup.html

Author Direct Store: https://www.veranazarianbooks.com

The Atlantis Grail Discord: https://discord.gg/8zPBzumqsM

TAG Fan Discussion Forum: https://atlantisgrail.proboards.com/

Astra Daimon and Shoelace Girls (Facebook fan group):

https://www.facebook.com/groups/adasg/

The Atlantis Grail – SPOILERS (Facebook fan group):

https://www.facebook.com/groups/tag2spoilers

TAG official website: https://www.theatlantisgrail.com/

TAG Fandom website: https://www.tag.fan

Patreon (Adult 18+): https://patreon.com/VeraNazarian

Ream (Adult, 18+): https://reamstories.com/veranazarian

Norilana Books: https://www.norilana.com

BlueSky: https://bsky.app/profile/veranazarian.bsky.social

X: https://x.com/Norilana

Facebook: https://www.facebook.com/VeraNazarian

TikTok: https://www.tiktok.com/@veranazarian

Instagram: https://www.instagram.com/vera_nazarian/

YouTube Channel: https://www.youtube.com/veranazarian-tag

ACKNOWLEDGMENTS

There are so many of you whose unwavering, loving support helped me bring this book to life. My gratitude is boundless, and I thank you with all my heart!

To my absolutely brilliant first readers, advisors, topic experts, editors, proofreaders, fandom moderators, TAG Con Committee members and friends, Elizabeth Logotheti, Ellen Jauregui Contard, Harriet Bennett, Heather Dryer, Kerry Vosswinkel, Mary C. Sellar, Nancy Huett, Nydia Fernandez Burdick, Ricki Bristow, Roby James, Shelley Bruce, Susan Franzblau, Teri N. Sears, and West Yarbrough McDonough.

A special profound thanks to the wonderful Chris Marble for immense and timely support, going above and beyond, during complicated times.

To my wonderful producer Richard Joel of 405 Productions who is working hard to make the film project a reality.

To all the amazing and hardworking ConCom volunteers of our annual TAG Con convention.

To the lovely and wonderful group of Vermont writers and friends, Anne Stuart, Ellen Jareckie, Jeanne Miller, Lina Gimble, and Valerie Gillen, and to my dear friends in more distant places, Jeffry Dwight, Lisa Silverthorne, and Patricia Duffy Novak.

To all the wonderful and enthusiastic members of the "Astra Daimon and Shoelace Girls" Facebook group, "The Atlantis

Grail - SPOILERS" Facebook group, and the official TAG Discussion Forum on ProBoards.

To my Patreon and Ream supporters, thank you, one and all, from the bottom of my heart, you are the absolute best! Special shoutout to Joanne Utrera for Imperial Kassiopei Tier Support.

To my awesome and fabulous Wattpad friends and fans who keep re-reading each TAG preview chapter and making me smile, laugh, and otherwise delight in your hilarious, stunning, amazing, and insightful responses to the story! Thank you immensely!

If I've forgotten or missed anyone, the fault is mine; please know that I love and appreciate you all.

Finally, I would like to thank all of you dear reader friends, who decided to take my hand and step into my world of *The Atlantis Grail*.

My deepest thanks to all for your support!

Before you go, you are kindly invited to leave a
review of this book!

Reviews are a wonderful way to help the author! They are also an exciting opportunity to share your honest thoughts with other readers, so **please post yours**, in as many places as possible, including TikTok and Instagram!

Scan Code for Linktree.

www.ingramcontent.com/pod-product-compliance
Lightning Source LLC
Chambersburg PA
CBHW022016050726
47499CB00004BA/953